THE ROOT OF ALL EVIL

Also by Roberto Costantini

The Deliverance of Evil

ROBERTO COSTANTINI

THE ROOT OF ALL EVIL

Translated from the Italian by N. S. Thompson

Quercus

First published in the Italian language as *Alle radici del male*
by Marsilio Editori in Venice in 2012

First published in Great Britain in 2014 by

Quercus Editions Ltd
55 Baker Street
7th Floor, South Block
London
W1U 8EW

A CIP catalogue record for this book is available
from the British Library

ISBN 978 0 85738 933 6 (HB)
ISBN 978 0 85738 934 3 (TPB)
ISBN 978 0 85738 935 0 (EBOOK)

10 9 8 7 6 5 4 3 2

Typeset by Jouve (UK), Milton Keynes
Printed and bound in Great Britain by Clays Ltd, St Ives plc

This is a work of fiction, not a study in history. I make no claim to reconstructing the truth, but simply imagining the possible.

As a result, the references to real persons, living or dead, and to actual events, as well as the description of several locations, particularly in Tripoli, have been modelled to serve the needs of that fiction. All other characters and situations connected with these references are entirely the product of literary invention.

For Wilma and Ulderico

and the free people of Libya

TRIPOLI – طرابلس

PORT

WHEELUS FIELD AIR BASE

TO SIDI EL MASRI

GARDEN CITY

ROYAL PALACE

SHARA BENASCIUR

CATHEDRAL

SEA FRONT ADRIAN PELT
SEA FRONT CONTE
VOLPI DI MISURATA

WADDAN HOTEL

CORSO VITTORIO – SHARA ISTIKLAL

VIA ROMA – SHARA 24 DICEMBRE

VIA LAZIO – SHARA MIZRAN

RED CASTLE

MARKET

ARAB CEMETERY

PIAZZA ITALIA –
MAYDAN AS SUHADA

VIA PIEMONTE –
SHARA IBN ILAS

VIA SICILIA – SHARA OMAR AL MUKHTAR

ARCH OF
MARCUS AURELIUS

OLD COAST ROAD
TO SABRATHA

INTERNATIONAL
FAIRGROUND

BEACH

JEWISH
CEMETERY

LIDO
CLUB

SULPHUR
BATHS

BEACH
CLUB

LA
MONETA

UNDERWATER
CLUB

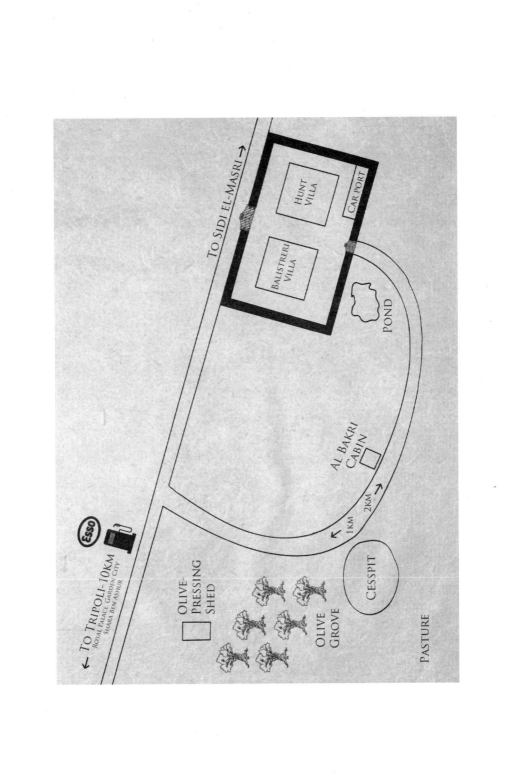

LA MONETA

VILLA

JETTY

PATH

BEACH

ROCKS

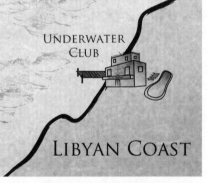

UNDERWATER
CLUB

LIBYAN COAST

Prologue
Saturday, 1 February 1958

The fly-screen door between the villa's living room and the veranda overlooking the large garden stands wide open. Although the air is warm, there are no mosquitoes in Tripoli in February.

From outside, the croaking of frogs breaks the silence of the African night.

All of us are in the living room for the finale of the Sanremo Song Festival. All three families: the Libyan, the American and the Italian.

The Al Bakri family has six members: the father, Mohammed; his four sons Farid, Salim, Ahmed and Karim; and their little sister, Nadia. Mohammed's two wives are, as usual, kept to the wooden shack they all live in.

The Hunt family consists of William; his wife, Marlene; and young Laura.

Then there are the five of us, the Bruseghin-Balistreri family: my grandfather, Giuseppe; my father, Salvatore; my mother, Italia; my brother, Alberto; and myself, Michele.

On the Marelli television set's black and white screen, Domenico Modugno's singing the festival's winning song, '*Volare (nel blu dipinto del blu)*'. I'm sitting on the three-seat sofa between the two most important women in my life. The one who gave birth to me and the one with whom I'll live. Life is very good, with everything before me. Along with the song, I'm flying up in the blue, singing:

'*Volare, oh, oh! Cantare, oh, oh, oh, oh!*'

PART I

I'm on my feet, my tunic sticking to me because I'm sweating with fear. The soles of my naked feet are on a wooden surface, a table placed next to a cement wall. A metre below I can see the earth and mud floor. A beetle's climbing towards the table. My feet are free, my right arm as well, but my left wrist's held by one bracelet of a pair of handcuffs; the other bracelet is locked round a metal tube that runs vertically up the wall. The beetle's climbing up the tube again. There's a rope round my neck; I can feel the huge knot pressing against my throat. It's tight round me, but not enough to stop me breathing. If I remain upright, that is. But if I try to kneel or sit down, the noose will strangle me.

Friday, 25 May 1962

Two cowboys are facing each other on the dusty square beneath the hot eye of the sun in a sky of blue. Hands are ready to draw pistols from their holsters. Among the crowd watching this gunfight is a girl who first loved the cowboy played by Kirk Douglas, then the one played by Rock Hudson, and now who she loves is anybody's guess.

In the darkness of the Alhambra Cinema only the projector's hum can be heard. I look at my grandfather Giuseppe's impassive face as Rock Hudson and Kirk Douglas exchange a last glance or two.

'Who's going to win, Grandad? The one who's quickest on the draw?'

My grandfather's Giuseppe Bruseghin, born in 1899: a peasant from the Veneto and loyal to the ruling House of Savoy. After the rout at Caporetto, then the Austrian collapse during the First World War, he was one of the few not to jettison arms and uniform and hide himself away on some farm. He doesn't like guns or gunfights and only puts up with Westerns because of me, the grandson he dotes on.

'Michelino, in real life it's not always the first to shoot who wins.'

He tries to clip me playfully round the head, but I dodge his hand. I don't like his answer.

Kirk's quicker on the draw; Rock fires straight after. A long, silent pause. Rock and Kirk exchange glances one last time. Then Kirk looks at the girl and keels over. She runs over to him as he lies on the ground, not to Rock Hudson, the winner.

'But Grandad, doesn't the girl always fall in love with the winner?'

My words are silenced by protests from the neighbouring seats.

Every so often Grandad pretends not to hear. But I'm well aware of this: he does it when he doesn't want to answer. In 1940, his son, Toni, had joined the *GIL*, the *Gioventù italiana del littorio*, as the Italian Fascist Youth Movement was known, and had gone off to fight in the wretched war. He was killed on the last day of fighting, still wearing his Fascist uniform, while everyone else was getting out. So when King Victor Emmanuel III; his son, Umberto; the politicians; and the Fascists took to their heels, escaping northwards and leaving the Italian troops at the mercy of the partisans on one side and Germans on the other, Toni went out to meet the enemy.

My grandmother died of typhus and a broken heart straight after Toni's death. My grandfather had to bring up his daughter, Italia, on his own: an adolescent girl who read Nietzsche and made an idol of both Mussolini and her brother, Toni.

It's when I sound too much like Toni that Grandad doesn't answer me.

In the end we learn that Kirk's character went into the gunfight with his pistol unloaded on purpose. I read the credits, bewildered. If Kirk knew he'd loaded his gun with blanks, there must have been something in his look before shooting that I'd missed. The Alhambra's sliding roof opens up on Tripoli's clear blue sky, letting in the smells of eucalyptus and horse droppings, the sounds of carriages and carts and the muezzin's cry calling for afternoon prayers.

It's two in the afternoon, and the first show's over.

The usherette comes round with drinks and ice cream. Grandad buys me another packet of nuts and gets up to leave.

'Please, Grandad, can we see it again?'

He's used to these requests, as this isn't the first time. He knows I'm bored at home. Friday's the Moslem holy day and my best friends, Ahmed and Karim, are with their father at the mosque. I wouldn't be studying anyway, given there was no school on Saturday or Sunday.

'All right, Michelino, but only once more, not twice, like the other day!'

We live in Sidi El Masri, just outside Tripoli, ten kilometres from Piazza Castello at the city centre. The Sidi El Masri road's a long boulevard flanked by eucalyptus, with no houses until the twin villas owned by our family.

The two villas built by my grandfather stand on one side of the boulevard, surrounded by a wall two metres high and accessed through a large wrought-iron gate leading on to the metalled road. The gate is ornamented with the linked initials of my father and mother's names, Salvatore and Italia, creating a symbol that looks strangely like the American dollar sign. My mother hates it, but my father likes it. It was his idea, and it's a reminder that a real family is always *united*.

Behind the villas there's a wicket gate in the surrounding wall that leads out into the countryside and to Grandad's olive grove. Just outside the gate there's a small pond with frogs and then a dirt path that runs for two kilometres through the bare fields to the Al Bakris' wooden shack, where Ahmed and Karim live, right next to a horrendous cesspit.

After their shack the dirt road runs on for a kilometre along the Bruseghin olive grove. A car can barely get down it. Herdsmen use it for their goats and have their huts beside it. It curves round and joins the boulevard after our two villas, just before the Esso petrol station on the way back into Tripoli.

Although the two villas are a couple of kilometres from the olive grove and the herdsmen, the smell's just the same – especially from the cesspit that serves as a latrine ditch for all Tripoli's wooden shanties, and as fertilizer for the olives.

I love the smell of earth, eucalyptus and olives and am very proud of Grandad's olive grove. He got married at the end of the First World War and studied for his building surveyor's certificate. He arrived in Libya in 1932, six years before the mass colonization of the country that Mussolini called the Fourth Shore, bringing his wife and two children, the twelve-year-old Toni and Italia, who was only two. Thanks to his qualification, he was able to help with the construction of the new agricultural villages founded by Libya's Italian governor, Italo Balbo: Castel Benito, D'Annunzio, Mameli, Bianchi, Garibaldi, Crispi and Breviglieri. In exchange, the INFPS – the National Fascist Institute for Social Security – together with the King's legal representative, awarded him an estate a few kilometres outside Tripoli, plus a thousand olive trees ready for planting.

But the land was covered in sand. Grandad employed six Libyans to work with him; they cleared the sand away and erected barriers to keep the dunes at bay, thus putting a brake on the infamous *ghibli*, the hot wind that blows in from the desert.

Then they dug the well down to the water table and created irrigation channels, and Grandad was eventually able to plant the olives. He knew it would take years for them to produce anything, so in the meantime he kept his job as building surveyor, helping to construct housing for the colonists. Thanks to those years of sacrifice, today Grandad owns Libya's largest olive grove.

My father, on the other hand, can't stand the smell of olives. It reminds him of his childhood in Palermo, two parents and five sons in a single room, the lavatory shared with three other families.

For him, it was the smell of poverty.

★　　★　　★

We see the entire film again. As Kirk Douglas goes to the gunfight with an unloaded pistol, I study his face very closely.

Now I get it.

Grandad takes me back to the villas in the Fiat 600 and at six I have a snack of buttered bread and jam, nuts and dates. I then get astride the veranda railing, about a metre and a half from the ground. The *mabrouka*, the Arab housekeeper, has been told not to let me, but she's supervising the cook, who's preparing the evening's couscous. The gardener pretends not to notice, and my father's away at the office in Piazza Italia, next to the castle in the city centre. Jet, the boxer dog, looks at me with big soft eyes in his flat muzzle. He looks at me like that so as to seem less ugly: that way maybe he can scrounge a date. I always give him one, even though my brother, Alberto, says they're bad for him.

This railing's my horse and I'm Kirk Douglas. I've my guns, hat and boots with spurs that I got for Christmas. I know it was Papa and Mamma who gave them to me, not Father Christmas. Grandad likes to think I still believe and that it was Father Christmas, not him, who gave me a Zorro outfit.

I'm galloping along furiously, perhaps too fast. Papa doesn't like to see the marks of the spurs in the railing's white paint. For him, they're the mark of my idiotic dreams. He's telling me more than ever to think of reality and my homework, like my elder brother does.

Fortunately, as usual, Papa's in town working. He's with a disagreeable young man called Emilio Busi, who's just come over from Italy and dined with us a few days ago.

It's very hot. My neck's dripping with sweat, an ant's running along my arm and the sparrows are making a heck of a racket. I squash the ant. The sparrows'll pay for it later with my Diana 50 air rifle.

Having come back from prayers in the mosque, Ahmed's waiting for me for our gunfight. He's in the middle of the stretch of dust and sand, dressed up as a cowboy with the costume they gave me years ago that I don't wear any more.

As always in our gunfights, Ahmed's prepared to die. He takes the role seriously, as he does everything in life. He's tall, dark, with slightly wavy black hair and a sullen but intense look, just like his younger brother, Karim, and his little sister, Nadia. They all take after their beautiful mother, Jamila, Mohammed's second wife. Handsome Arab kids.

Ahmed's a little *pezzente*, which is what the native Libyans call Italians like me, 'a little grabber'. I'm the son of one of Tripoli's richest and most influential families and yet I've chosen him as my closest friend. 'Friend' isn't a word we use, and neither of us likes speaking of friendship, like a pair of girls. But it's obvious I prefer to spend every afternoon playing out with him rather than being taken to the exclusive clubs along the coast to play with the Italian, English and American boys there.

The plan for our games is always the same: he loses and I win. It's a pact that's taken for granted and, usually, there's no exception. But today there's a change.

Laura's standing in the shade of the eucalyptus tree, chatting with Karim, who's her age. He doesn't want to be in the film. He's very religious and says that Westerns are for unbelievers. Laura's always telling Karim how handsome he is.

Laura offers to act in the film, just to please me, but she never shows any great enthusiasm. She's nearly two years younger than Ahmed and me, and it's obvious she likes me, but she never does what I say.

I should put Nadia in, in her place, just to spite her. Nadia's always hanging around wanting to play with us and would love to act in our film. But I know Laura couldn't care less if I cast Nadia in her place or not. And then Arab women don't act in films, even pretend ones. Ahmed and Karim wouldn't take it kindly.

'Stop chattering, Laura. You have to watch the gunfight.'

Karim's protective. 'My fault, sorry.'

He's always taking her side.

I get off the horse-railing and go up to Ahmed. Jet's with him, licking his hand. In the afternoon, when he wants to go and run like crazy through the fields, it's the two of us who take him. But Ahmed's the one who runs around after him.

'I'm keeping an eye on him. Too many females with rabies out there,' he says.

I walk up to him, hands in my gun belt.

'You win today,' I whisper in his ear, and enjoy his look of amazement.

Ahmed shakes his head and stares at me. He doesn't like surprises; he prefers everything to go along as planned.

'Mikey, I'd rather lose, like I always do.'

'Don't worry, Ahmed, you can lose. But this time I'm going to die, you stay on your feet. Now, take ten steps back.'

With our backs to each other, we start to measure the paces, while Karim counts them out. That's the part I have him play. Then we turn round and look each other in the eye.

Laura isn't paying attention – her mind's on a butterfly. Or occupied with her own thoughts, which are always a little strange. She once said that she didn't like either the sun or the dark, and that she wanted *time to pass quickly but still*. Ahmed thinks she's mad, but Karim says she's a genius.

Then we each fire a shot. A few seconds of suspense. Kirk Douglas falls to his knees. Now I'm on the ground, a hand on my chest, my eyes half closed. I see Ahmed's Rock Hudson standing still, dumbfounded, almost scared by this unexpected outcome.

Finally, Laura and Karim pay attention. Surprised. This is the first time I've been beaten in a gunfight. Ahmed's looking pale and says nothing. They all come up to me as I play the part of Kirk Douglas's dead body. Now Laura should go to Ahmed's Rock Hudson, my rival, the winner. But she doesn't. She stands there, looking down at my corpse, deep in thought.

And at this point Jet comes up and licks my cheek, probably attracted by some jam left on it. I hear Karim sniggering, and I open my eyes, furious.

'I'm sorry,' says Karim, 'but we don't get it – you're always the one who wins.'

I explain the new twist to the plot. As Kirk Douglas, I unload the gun before the gunfight so as not to kill my very best friend, Rock Hudson.

Laura smiles at me, nodding in approval.

'*Bravo*, Mikey. The winner always turns out to be hateful.'

Ahmed's still confused.

'I want to be the one who dies.'

Laura darts a look at him.

'You wouldn't let yourself be killed because your gun wasn't loaded. Not even by Mikey.'

Ahmed looks askance at her. He seems upset. There's no love lost between them. He's afraid that one day I'll show more regard for her than for him.

Karim steps in. 'I wouldn't let myself be killed for either one of you. But I would for Laura.'

He's the spitting image of Ahmed. They look so alike, but their characters are opposite. Karim's the idealist, Ahmed the realist.

Ahmed strokes the dog. He looks at me.

'Should we take Jet for a run, Mikey?'

I'm trapped in here. There's nothing I can do, absolutely nothing. Except resist, not let myself bend at the knees and have the noose strangle me. I'm in his hands, and the life of others means nothing to him.

The noose is at the end of a rope. I can touch the rope with my free hand, the right one, and follow it up with my fingers. I touch my head. It's bare, completely shaven. My hair, my beautiful black hair, has all gone. I follow the rope with my eyes in the semi-darkness. It goes up to the ceiling, passes over another metal tube, a large one that would easily take my weight. The rope goes over the tube and drops back down again. The single small window lets in only a little light. I can't see where it leads. But I can manage to see the beetle that's reached the ceiling above me.

Saturday, 26 May 1962

Every Saturday evening, people are invited round and the space in front of the two villas fills up with all the important people among the Italians, Americans and Libyans: owners of estates, entrepreneurs, directors of the *AGIP* oil company or the Banco di Roma, diplomats, American officers from the Wheelus Field Air Base, dignitaries and ministers of Libya's King Idriss.

On these evenings, we take turns with Arab, Italian and American cuisine. Tonight's an American night: a barbecue of hamburgers and sausages prepared by William Hunt, followed by Coca-Cola and popcorn bought by his wife, Marlene. Laura's mother doesn't like to cook.

With a bag full of popcorn, and bottles of Coca-Cola, Laura and I sneak off behind the villas, where her father William's built a car port to keep the sun off the cars. We sit down underneath it to chat. It's only childish gossip. She's ten, I'm twelve.

'Your mother doesn't cook either, does she, Mikey?'

'Never. My grandad says she should never have married.'

'But then . . .'

'When she was eighteen, she met Papa. He was already qualified as an engineer.'

'And as handsome as Clark Gable.'

I look at her, amazed. Sometimes this little kid *is* crazy, just like Ahmed says.

'What?'

She laughs.

'Marlene says it, but she's just joking. Your papa's Sicilian, isn't he?'

'Yes. He's the fifth son of a cobbler and a chambermaid, with four older brothers. He grew up in Palermo's poorest district and was the only one of the brothers to go to university.'

'How come he went, and not the other brothers?'

'He was born in 1925, so was too young to fight in the war. But his four brothers did, and so stopped their education. Then they helped the American forces to land in Sicily.'

I pull a face, and she sees it.

'Don't you like us Americans?'

'I don't like Italians. They always betray you.'

She looks at me a little confused, then changes the subject.

'How did your father get the money for his education?'

'He worked as an assistant to a barber and studied English at night.'

'Then he met your mother?'

'He finished university in 1948 and came to Tripoli for a Sicilian firm. He met my mother and they married straightaway. A year later, Alberto was born, and the year after that, I was born.'

'Your mother's very rich, isn't she?'

She has this way of coming out with things. Just as they are. Anyone else would find a different way to say it.

'My grandad has the money. The villas and the olive grove are his. Mamma seems unfriendly, but she's only very shy. She doesn't speak much, but she reads plenty of books. History, philosophy, that sort of thing.'

'And she's a Fascist, isn't she?'

Again, she has that way of coming out with it. Papa would be against her being my girlfriend.

I look at her.

'Did your mother tell you that as well?'

'No, my dad said it. He says it's a shame, because your mother's like a queen.'

'A queen?'

'Yes, Dad says that if your mother had been born in the sixteenth century she would have been a queen.'

I don't want to talk about my parents any more.

'Tell me about your mother and father. How did they meet?'

'Oh, it's a wonderful story, Mikey. The opposite of your parents'. The poor but beautiful one was my mom. Dad comes from a very wealthy family of Texas oilmen.'

'Isn't he a war hero? My mother told me he was.'

Laura doesn't seem proud of it. Not like I'd have been.

'They gave him a medal when he was with the Marines in Korea. Now he's like an ambassador, but he's not really. Although he works at the Wheelus Air Base, he's always travelling about on *missions*, as he calls them. And then he leaves me and Marlene on our own.'

'Your mamma's very beautiful.'

I say this with genuine enthusiasm, and she smiles.

'Mom's twenty-seven, fifteen less than my dad. She was born in California and she was such a beautiful baby that her parents called her Marlene because they hoped she'd become famous, like Marlene Dietrich.'

'My father says she's more like that American actress he likes so much, Ava Gardner. And how did they meet?'

'Marlene wasn't even sixteen when she left home to take acting lessons in Hollywood. She worked in a diner to support herself.'

'A little like Papa!'

'Yes. She served my dad a steak in 1951. He was there in Hollywood for a weekend, but was actually living in Virginia on a course at Langley Air Base.'

'And then you were born?'

'Kids don't get born straightaway, you know, after just a kiss. Dad finished his course at Langley and married her. And I was born at the end of April in 1952.'

'You really take after your mother. But your complexion and eyes come from your father.'

'My parents say that I take after him as well in my character.'

'So you could kill an enemy?'

She looks at me a little sullenly.

'I hope my dad has never killed anyone. Or if he did, it was only to defend other people.'

'Were you in America before coming here?'

'No, we've been in London, Paris and Rome. Dad was always travelling about, and Mom went to the film festivals. After three years in Rome, here we are.'

'Is your mother happy about being in Libya?'

'Not at all – she says it's a sandpit. But Dad's given her a special present to help change her mind. It's a new sports car, and it's coming tomorrow. It's a Ferrari.'

Hours must have passed. Outside is the silence of the night; in the room, strange noises that I can't understand. I'm terrified. I think about the beetles and feel ill. My stomach and bladder want to burst. I can't hold out any longer — I have to go where I stand. When he comes back, he'll just laugh at me. Now I can hear some familiar sounds outside. A rooster crowing, a goat bleating. Dawn's pale light enters through the tiny window. I've been here on my feet, locked up, for twelve hours at least. I can't move. No food, no water, no sleep. My thighs are rigid. On the floor, my excrement, surrounded by beetles. The glimmer of dawn makes the outlines a little clearer. On the floor, at the foot of the table, the bastard has left a bottle of water. Temptation. Bend down, sweetheart, if you're thirsty. And hang yourself.

Sunday, 27 May 1962

A flame-red Ferrari 250 GT Spider California is a coupé convertible. I see it next morning outside the Hunts' villa.

On Sundays, Alberto and I are regular guests there for an American breakfast: pancakes, cornflakes, toast, eggs and bacon. That's how I see the red Ferrari.

My parents never have breakfast with us boys on a Sunday. Papa goes to Mass at seven and then on to the Hotel Waddan to read his paper, *Il Giornale di Tripoli*. Later he drops in on Don Eugenio at his parish church, St Anselm's, where all the Italians who count for anything in the city meet up. Mamma always keeps to herself. I think she's no time for Mrs Hunt. I've no idea why.

Alberto only takes little bites of what's on offer. Instead, he asks Mr Hunt how they build the skyscrapers in the United States, that vast country so far away. He also asks him about the new young President, John Fitzgerald Kennedy. William Hunt isn't very keen on him.

I listen in and grab whatever I like most without bothering too much to ask. Cornflakes, French toast, pancakes and syrup. Laura's mother likes me and calls me *Michelino-the-Hoover*, because I swallow everything in sight.

After a grapefruit juice and a slice of flatbread toast, Marlene Hunt's already been out jogging, which she never misses. She always takes her run along the path that starts behind the villas: two kilometres through the arid countryside as far as Ahmed's wooden shack and the cesspit. She does it twice, there and back again. Eight kilometres every day, and in less than an hour.

'When I start taking longer than an hour, then I'll know I'm getting old,' she says.

She comes back, glowing and panting, covered in the sweat that makes her running vest stick to her and puts a shine to those long legs below her shorts. My father's right: she looks like Ava Gardner, but even more beautiful.

Marlene aims a clip at the back of Alberto's head, offers a kiss to Laura and a smile to me. Nothing to her husband. Then she goes off to take a shower. When she comes back, she's wearing a pink T-shirt with not much underneath and a pair of cut-off jeans.

'Hey, kids, would you like to go the seaside in the Ferrari?' she asks.

I rush off home to get my trunks and sandals.

'We're going to the beach. Let my grandad know,' I tell the *mabrouka*.

We jump into the Ferrari. Marlene and Laura sit up front, Albert and myself behind. We fly down the Sidi El Masri road towards Tripoli, overtaking a few old Fiats, Hillmans and Morrises. The wind slaps into our faces; we don't even see the eucalyptus trees whizzing by at the side of the road.

'Too fast for you?' Marlene yells out.

No, I want her to go even faster.

It takes us only a couple of minutes to get from Sidi El Masri to the Tripoli outskirts. Marlene stops for petrol at the Esso station.

The guy at the pump is Vito Gerace. He is a Sicilian of about fifty from the same poor district in Palermo as my father, and is one of my father's minions. He's a rough sort, with a great bush of hair and heavy eyebrows that meet over the bridge of his nose. People say that he gets drunk in the brothel every Saturday night.

The Gerace family came to Libya from Palermo along with my father, Ingegnere Salvatore Balistreri. Vito's wife is Santuzza, ten years his junior, and a distant cousin of my father. She's a good-looking woman, humble and cheerful, and works as a seamstress for the wealthy Italians and Americans.

Vito has a son, Nico, who's my age, and we share a desk in the same class at school. His regular features come from his mother, but his curly hair, bushy eyebrows and hairy arms and calves come from his father. Along with the hair, a noticeable speech impediment has given him an inferiority complex and no self-confidence.

Vito Gerace raises his black eyebrows and stares first at the Ferrari 250 GT Spider and then at Marlene Hunt, his eyes coming out on stalks. He takes an awfully long time to clean the windscreen so he can ogle her suntanned legs.

Nico looks her over admiringly, too. He knows she's acted in Hollywood and he has a fixation on all actresses of cinema and television. He's got pictures of all the stars stuck on the underside of his desk: Rita Hayworth, Ava Gardner, Marilyn Monroe, Brigitte Bardot, Sophia Loren. All of them together, available for him in his imagination.

As we come into Tripoli through the Garden City district, Marlene's forced to slow down. We drive past the Royal Palace, with its copper domes, and come to the cathedral square, with its ugly box of a post office built by the Fascist regime. There aren't many cars, but the place is full of carriages, carts drawn by camels, bicycles and pedestrians in the middle of the road.

We take Corso Vittorio Emanuele, otherwise known as Shara Istiklal. Shops run by Italians are closed on Sundays, while those belonging to Jews and Arabs are open, including our favourite ice-cream parlour, Girus.

Marlene parks the Ferrari between a donkey and a Fiat 600, and out we get. Everyone's looking at us, and I mean everyone. Not at us boys, but the Ferrari and Marlene Hunt, who looks as beautiful as a goddess.

After an ice cream we go down Corso Vittorio to Piazza Italia with its Fascist-era arcades. We turn round by the fountain and take Corso Sicilia, the Italian name which even Libyans prefer to Shara Omar Al Mukhtar. Coming out of the centre, we set off again at speed towards the beach. We pass on the popular ones, the Lido and Bagni Sulfurei, with its smell of Wadi Megenin, and head towards the more exclusive beaches attached to private clubs with English names like 'The Beach' and 'The Underwater Club'.

Another ten minutes and we're at the Underwater Club. We're already in our trunks and get into the seawater pool. William Hunt arrives later in his Land Rover, but stays resolutely in his clothes, smoking a cigar in the shade of the terrace.

Tall and blond, with steel-blue eyes, he's a Texan who appreciates Libya's desert more than its sea. Also its petroleum, which we hear so much about. Meanwhile, Marlene does her usual fifty lengths of the pool, then gets out, spreads out a towel and lies down in the sun.

She really is a goddess; you only have to look at her. Although only twelve years old, I can see that myself, with her eyes that go right inside you, her shiny raven hair running in waves halfway down her back, her slender, tapering legs, her bikini top undone at the back for the perfect tan and the bottoms pulled down just within the limits of decency.

Laura tells me her parents are complete opposites. Marlene's easily bored. She'd like to go to the swish parties held at the embassies, grand hotels and out on terraces overlooking the sea, but William says they're nothing but places for *airing other people's dirty linen in public.*

I can see all men's eyes continually turning to look at Marlene. I should think William Hunt knows; he must do. Laura, as well. But I don't know if they're happy about it.

Our morning at the beach over, we go back to the villas. Ahmed and Karim come over after lunch. They go to the Libyan school on Shara Ben Ashur and have lessons on Sunday morning.

We play football on the spare ground in front of the two villas. Two against two, Ahmed and me against Alberto and Karim. We kick the ball about among the beetles and lizards, and there'd be no problem, except that Laura's the referee and she stops play with an old whistle just whenever she feels like it. She knows nothing at all about the game. So we take our cues from the Italian radio Sunday-soccer broadcast. When the Juventus game's over, then so's ours.

Laura knows there's only a minute to go. Karim trips over the ball and she blows the whistle for a penalty. Ahmed looks furious.

'Laura, you're crazy!'

Jet's slumped in a corner by his kennel, panting with the heat and drooling a great deal. Ahmed and I've spent a whole hour with the tweezers this afternoon, pulling out the damned ticks that nest in his ears.

'Shall we go for a run, Jet?'

His two large eyes simply stare back at us. Normally, he's up and running as soon as we say the words. But this time there's no reaction. He lies there, gasping for breath and drooling.

'He's too hot,' says Karim.

Ahmed shakes his head, unconvinced. 'Jet would go for a run even in the *ghibli*.'

He's my dog, but Ahmed considers him under his protection. Woe betide anyone who touches him.

'Perhaps we can take him after sunset, Ahmed.'

We exit by the back gate. The pond's almost dry, the frogs making a melancholy croaking noise. We run along the path behind the villas up to the wooden shack where Ahmed and Karim live with their extended family.

From there we pass through the Bruseghin olive grove and by the huts of the men who herd their goats there. We never pick olives up from the ground; it's hard to tell them from the goat droppings.

Sunset's the right time for our big-game hunting. I shoot the doves in the eucalyptus trees with my Diana 50 air rifle, while Ahmed concentrates on the scorpions with his throwing knife. Out of fairness, it's never from a distance of less than two metres away.

Karim never takes part. He reads the Koran, Arabic poetry and the history of Libyan heroes such as Omar Al Mukhtar, who was hanged by the Italian colonial powers. Karim never kills anything, but he collects the bloody booty for us.

When we come back for Jet, Grandad's standing by the kennel. Next to him is the young local vet, wearing a rubber glove as he caresses the dog's head. Jet looks at us with his sad eyes, his nose on the ground. Grandad shakes his head. The vet turns towards him.

'I'm sorry. Jet has rabies.'

Grandad, my parents, Alberto and the vet go inside, into the living room.

Ahmed, Karim and myself stay outside, next to the dog. Ahmed talks to him in Arabic.

After a while the Hunts come over from the villa next door, my parents perhaps having called them. William and Marlene go straight into the house; Laura comes over to join us.

'He's got a bite mark on his side,' she says, pointing to a dark-brown patch of skin.

'It'll be one of those mongrel bitches out there,' Ahmed replies, pointing to the outside wall at the back. In fact, they've been gathering there every evening at sunset for a couple of weeks now, yelping and whining. You can hear them right now.

'They're in heat,' Laura had told me a few days earlier. Seeing I'd no idea what she was on about, she had explained the fact in that direct and easy-going way she had, as if the matter-of-fact meaning of words was enough to carry their own weight.

Then out comes the vet, followed by my grandfather. They have such a sad look that the vet's words are almost unnecessary.

'It'll take Jet two or three days to die from rabies. We're going to put him down, so he won't suffer.'

Ahmed gets up and leaves without a word.

'Unfortunately,' the vet's saying, 'Jet's saliva's infectious. If he's licked you, it only takes a slight cut . . .'

'We all have to be vaccinated,' says Grandad, cutting him short.

Forty injections. But they're nothing compared with the pain of getting the infection. I still have the Diana 50 in my hand. I leave Laura and Karim stroking Jet and run behind the villas to the small back gate.

As I dash out, I hear the whining turn to snarls. Ahmed's standing next to three of the dogs with a large locust in his hand. The dogs love them. He hurls it against the outside wall. The largest and bravest of the dogs ventures near. She sniffs at it suspiciously, then bends down towards the dead locust.

Ahmed's ready with his Swiss knife in his hand, open at the longest blade. He leaps astride the dog and plants the blade deep in her neck. The dog lets out a tremendous howl and tries to shake him off, but Ahmed traps her between his legs and, because he's left-handed, puts his right arm round to pull the blade out.

He must have struck an artery, because the blood gushes out. The dog bucks and pushes Ahmed off, then tries to bite him.

But Ahmed's pretty quick. He sticks the knife in the animal's right eye and cuts it out with a circular twist. At this point, the other two dogs make a move to attack him. I aim the rifle at the nose of the more aggressive one, where I know it really hurts.

And from fifty metres the pellet of a Diana 50 hurts like the devil. The dog howls and runs away. I quickly reload, but there's no need. The second dog's already running off.

The first dog's now howling desperately. She's bleeding heavily from the stab wound and her eye socket and makes no reaction when Ahmed gets astride her again and inserts the blade in her throat.

I watch him as he tugs with great strength until the throat's slit and the animal falls to the ground.

Ahmed extracts the knife, cleans it on some blades of grass, clasps it shut and puts it in the pocket of his shorts.

'Thanks, Mikey,' he says.

Then he turns away and makes off down the path to his wooden shack.

More hours pass. Every so often, that bastard shows his face, a scornful grin on it. In the sky, the sun must be rising. Or perhaps setting. I've no idea any more. Now there's a yellowish dust hanging in the air. The light from the tiny, dirty window streams through it. It reminds me of everything I want to have, which is my life. I can now feel the length of rope that rises from my neck, crosses over the large tube set into the ceiling, then drops down again. I follow it until it comes to another very small shaven head and ends in a noose tight round another neck.

This neck belongs to a baby girl nearly ten months old. She weighs about nine kilos. I weigh sixty, and she weighs nine. If I try to bend down or sit on the table, the rope will stretch, the nooses tighten and we'll both be strangled. The little mite's sound asleep; perhaps he put a sleeping pill in her bottle. The sounds I heard last night were those of my daughter.

Monday, 28 May 1962

We buried Jet yesterday evening, and it's school today. Happily, we're nearly at the end of the dreadful school year. Fortunately, the school building's large and cool, with long corridors and high ceilings that help against the *ghibli*'s choking heat.

Next to school there's the concrete football pitch, and the eucalyptus trees down one side to mark the touchline, so whoever's playing on that side finds themselves dribbling past the trees as well as the opposing side.

At one end of it stands the pitch where the old guys play *bocce*; at the other, the bar with table football and bar billiards, which the adults play with a cue, while the kids launch the ball from their hands.

My brother, Alberto, is the school's star pupil, but he's leaving secondary school now. He comes top in all subjects, but always runs the risk of being caught up with because he passes on his answers to the others in class and then gives private lessons for free to help the biggest of the dunces.

I'm pretty weak in all subjects. I just don't like studying. Or my classmates. I prefer Ahmed. We take courses in the martial arts together and are both pretty good at them.

The only friend I have in school is my classmate Nico Gerace, the kid who drools over film stars and singers. He's the son of the petrol-pump attendant and the seamstress, the only poor Italians in Tripoli. If my father didn't help them, they'd starve to death.

Our religious instruction is taken by Don Eugenio, the parish priest at St Anselm's, which is close to the school.

Don Eugenio's a young man under thirty, with a smooth, chubby face like a child. His light-blue eyes look kindly in his well-cared-for face; his wide, good-natured smile is framed by a head of blond hair. His manners are humble and he only ever wears a cassock and sandals.

Although he graduated in theology, Don Eugenio's excellent at maths and gives private lessons to various kids, myself and Nico included. Only the richer parents have to pay, so Nico's lessons are free.

Papa says Don Eugenio's the most intelligent priest he knows and the most generous to the poor. He says he's also excellent at managing the money he collects for charity, investing it for a good dividend. That's the way he's able to help the poor in Sudan, Niger and Chad.

But there's another thing about him that's important. Along the Corso Vittorio arcades and in the Italian Club, the talk is that Don Eugenio could be the grandson of Alcide De Gasperi, the man who headed the Christian Democrats and the government after the war. Nobody knows if this is true or not, but they say Don Eugenio goes off to Rome every month as private confessor to the President, one of the most important men in Italian politics.

Perhaps this is why all the Italians who count in Tripoli – from the landowners to managing directors of the big firms – go to him for confession. All except my grandfather. Then they gather at St Anselm's on Sunday afternoons, drinking coffee, playing cards and discussing business.

I'm happy to share my desk in class with Nico, but the rest of the class treats him like a pariah. In fact, I'm the only one who ever speaks to him, the only one not to rib him and the one who protects him from the others' sneaky tricks. They make fun of him for the thick black eyebrows that meet over his nose, the curly hair he vainly tries to straighten, his hairy arms and calves and his ridiculous lisp. On top of everything, he always stinks of petrol, the smell his father brings home every day.

I've no idea why I look out for him, really. Perhaps only to do the opposite of what the majority does. I really hate that word, 'majority'. It makes me feel less free, obliged to say: Yes, things are fine the way they are.

Today, Don Eugenio decides to have everyone read a passage out loud from the textbook. One sentence each, around the desks in order. And every single one of the pupils makes a silent calculation about which sentence Nico'll have to read, hoping that it'll be a complicated one full of 's' sounds. Today's subject's the Crusades, and Nico's sentence is: 'The word "assassin" comes from the word "hash-shashin", which was used in the Christian West for the followers of Imam Hasan Al Sabbah and comes either from his name or from the word "hashish".'

Nico's also already seen which is his sentence. This is going to be a real scenario. He gives me a look like a lamb going to the slaughter. Meanwhile, as each pupil reads his passage out, excited sniggers spread around the class in anticipation of the spectacle.

Don Eugenio isn't even listening. He's reading a book entitled *Balance Sheets and Profit and Loss Accounts*.

When it's my turn, I rattle off the sentence and carry on as if nothing were wrong: 'The word "assassin" comes from the word "hashshashin", which was used in the Christian West . . .'

'Don Eugenio!'

Walter's top of the class and class monitor, the one with the highest marks in every subject.

The priest lifts his head enquiringly. 'Yes, Walter, what is it?'

Walter gets to his feet. In contrast to mine, his black school smock's always buttoned right to the top and the white bow doesn't look twisted and as if a rat had been chewing at it.

'This is Nico's sentence that Michele's reading; he's already read his.'

He makes a face, playing to the gallery of his classmates but not daring to look me in the eye. He gets smiles and sniggers all around.

Then, as if by itself, I hear my voice saying, 'Walter, you're a complete prick.'

Don Eugenio abandons his book, which falls to the floor with a thud. There's no change in his rosy-coloured complexion, but his light-blue eyes are a single sheet of flame. In the silence, you can hear a fly buzzing around the classroom.

He then gets up and comes over to me silently in his black cassock. With a wide sweep of his arm, so that everyone can see and remember, he grasps a tip of ear between his thumb and forefinger.

But the ear that he slowly begins to twist is not mine. It's Nico's. A gradual movement showing no effort, which makes the ear become redder and redder, and Nico has to struggle to keep the tears of pain and humiliation from his eyes. All I get's a look of disapproval.

You're Ingegner Balistreri's son, and I can't lay a finger on you.

After it's been released, Nico's ear remains flaming red for at least ten minutes. And in the eternity of those ten minutes, while Don Eugenio stops the reading and takes up his explanation again, I take in the class's glances at Nico. Some are scornful; others condescending. Not a single look shows any solidarity. I start to compile a list of the sneaks and idiots among my classmates. The ones who're a waste of space and that I could cheerfully kill.

After class, Don Eugenio keeps the two of us back. He gives me a note that my parents have to read and sign. But that's not enough for him. He beckons us to come over to his desk. I do as he says, my instincts telling me it's better to get this over in silence. But Nico's trembling like a jelly beside me. The priest smiles at us with those blue eyes in his baby face.

'You have committed a very serious breach, Michelino, at the very moment you're about to become one of Our Lord's servants. Swear words are used only by the uneducated.'

He looks at Nico, who studies more than I do but whose parents are indeed uneducated.

The thing is, although no one asked me, in about ten days I have to start serving as an altar boy at Mass. The choice was Don Eugenio's, thinking to please my father, a large donor to the cost of rebuilding his church. And Papa wants me to serve at Mass, as my brother, Alberto, has done, in order to show all those who matter in Tripoli, and also those in Rome, that the Balistreri family's based on sound Catholic values.

'I won't say them any more, Don Eugenio.'

I make this promise with no show of enthusiasm. I don't like being shut up in there with him and simply want to get out to break-time. A few days before, lisping through his tears, Nico told me that, for making too many errors in his private maths lesson with him, Don Eugenio had made him take his shorts down and spanked him as punishment.

'I'm sure you won't say any more swear words, Michelino, that goes without saying.'

Don Eugenio waves away a fly that's buzzing around Nico's face, then strokes his prickly mass of curls. Nico looks at me forlornly from under those two grotesque bushy eyebrows. I contain my anger by biting the white bow of the hateful black smock, chewing on the corner that's bitten and worn away by my anxieties. I'm frightened, but have no idea what to do. After all, he's the teacher.

'In order to be an altar boy, you must be pure, Michelino. Remember that God sees everything and that in the end we have to face the Last Judgement.'

I say nothing. He hesitates, his hand still on Nico's hair. He stares at me with those light-blue eyes. Who knows what he'd like to do to me? He hasn't noticed my clenched fists, that my knees are braced and I'm grinding my teeth.

He smiles at me.

'You can go off and play football now, Michelino.'

'And Nico?'

His light-blue eyes come to rest on my friend.

'Nico must learn not to be a nuisance in class and to read when it's his turn. I'll make this clear to him now, and tomorrow he'll come to the presbytery and make confession.'

As I leave, I can feel Nico's desperate eyes drilling into my back.

I should be there in his place.

'Where did you hear a word like that, Michelino?'

My father pulls a grim face as he reads Don Eugenio's note. Alberto's in the room, but keeping silent. Italia's reading a book and smoking. Grandad's in town, playing *bocce*.

I say nothing. After a while, he repeats the question.

'Where did you hear that word?'

I look him straight in the eyes.

'From you, Papa.'

Alberto gives me a smile. My brother's always on my side. Sometimes openly; sometimes in a more subtle way.

Papa gives a slight start. He studies me for a long time, wondering if I'm lying. He could rest on his authority and deny it. But I know him too well. My father always gives himself a way out. And he never loses his temper. If he does, you never see it.

'And when did I say this word, Michelino?'

'When you and Mamma were listening to the radio in your bedroom a few weeks ago. The door was open.'

'And you were eavesdropping, Michelino?'

Alberto steps in.

'I was there with Mikey, Papa. The radio said that Italy'd elected a new President. You were saying to Mamma that this Antonio Segni had won because the Fascists had voted for him and those lunatic monarchists that wanted the King back.'

Unbelievably, I saw a gleam of consideration for me in my father's eyes, such as when I shot my first dove with a Diana 22 before moving on to the 50.

Now that Alberto's on my side, I feel calmer. So I tell him more.

'Then you added, "This Segni's only a prick that won't last long, anyway."'

Papa smiles at us. He's a little embarrassed, but in the end happy that there's a bond of understanding between his two sons, who're so different but so united. And, for him, a family must be united. Always, and no matter what happens. He says it over and over again. They'd drilled it into him since he was a little boy in Sicily. His parents, his four elder brothers, his parents' friends, the people who lent his father money when his work as a cobbler didn't bring in enough to feed the family.

The family must be united, always.

Papa smiles. 'Did I really say that? Well, I shouldn't have, because there are certain words you shouldn't say, and also because President Segni's a good Catholic who was elected by Parliament. Thank God we now have a free democracy in Italy.'

He often mentions this word 'democracy' and always links it to another word, 'free', as if he wants to justify something unpleasant – like offering an excuse when none's needed.

He now adopts a calm and indulgent manner and puts on a smile that makes him look like Clark Gable.

'Michelino, your mother's also certainly not pleased that you've been talking like a street urchin.'

Like a street urchin. Spoken with the scorn of a man who grew up in the worst gutters of Palermo.

My mother lays her book down, puts her cigarette out and darts a quick glance at my father.

'Michelino, leave swear words to ignorant people. Now, are you having any problems with Don Eugenio?'

She understands everything without having to say it, just like me.

Papa's not happy with this question.

'What problems could Michelino possibly have with Don Eugenio? He's a pillar of our community and a great help to the poor.'

My mother doesn't reply. She picks up her book again, lights another cigarette and pours out a little more of the pungent golden liquid that my father calls her poison.

In the end, Papa tells me to apologize for the swear word, make confession with Don Eugenio and study my catechism so that I can serve at Mass.

In exchange for this, I can sign up for the martial arts course at the gym in the Arts and Crafts School and take Ahmed with me. My father'll pay for him. He doesn't see what use it'll be, but always finds a way of keeping everyone happy. He can't imagine that we'll get to be black belts and that Taekwondo will help us get on.

Our way of getting on.

This evening, the large garden's lit only by the small lights mounted on the wall surrounding the two villas. The south wind's bringing the Sahara's sands into the city. The *ghibli*'s started.

Nico, Ahmed, Karim and myself take shelter in the darkest corner, next to the back gate behind the Hunts' villa. The car port that William Hunt built to give shade for the Ferrari and the Land Rover gives only partial shelter from the gusts of wind and sand.

Alberto's studying, so he's not with us. Laura's gone to Wheelus Field with her parents to watch a baseball match. So we can talk a bit more freely.

Nico says that Don Eugenio made him take his shorts down and spanked him again as soon as I'd gone away. And that tomorrow after school he has to go to confession with him in the presbytery.

I'm beside myself with rage. I look at Ahmed. I can see him again as he carves that dog's eye out, then slits its throat.

'We have to get him to stop it, the pig. I've got a plan of action.'

While the sand starts getting everywhere in our clothes, they all listen closely to me. Karim stares in admiration, Ahmed nods silently, but Nico has a problem with it.

'I can't do it, Mikey. I'm too scared.'

I try to bolster him up.

'Nico, if you don't do this, you'll always be scared of him and he'll be able to carry on doing those things to you. If you go along with me, you won't be frightened of him any more, nor of anyone else.'

'Can't you do it instead of me, Mikey?'

In his fear he's now lisping his 's' sounds.

No, Nico. I'm Ingegnere Salvatore Balistreri's son. Don Eugenio wouldn't dare. You're the one who's the pariah.

'We're Libyans, Mikey,' Karim cuts in. 'What if Don Eugenio has us arrested?'

'I'll protect you. If he reports you, he'll have to report me as well, and he'll never do that.'

Ahmed takes out the knife he used to kill the dog. I gave it to him as a present on his last birthday.

'If it doesn't work, I'll take care of that priest.'

I look at my three friends. The *ghibli*'s blowing more sand under the canopy roof, and it's now getting in our eyes.

'Let's make a pact, the four of us,' I say. I get Ahmed to give me his knife.

We squeeze in between the Ferrari and the Land Rover, but the sand even gets in there.

I quietly make a cut on my left wrist. Drops of blood well up from it.

Then it's Nico's turn. He's now smiling happily. He makes a cut on his wrist and looks with satisfaction at the blood. For him, it's an honour to do as I do.

Karim's less keen. He's not happy about mixing his blood with two Christians and makes only a small cut. He looks at the tiny drops of blood uncertainly.

Then he hands the knife to Ahmed, who looks us straight in the eyes, as serious as ever. He likes the idea and shows no fear. He grips the knife in his left hand. In silence, he makes a much longer and deeper cut than ours and the blood flows copiously from his right wrist.

The single bulb hanging under the Hunts' car port is now caked with sand and emits only a flickering, grainy light. We can smell oil and petrol. We can hear the *ghibli* whistling, the palm leaves shaking and the eucalyptus rustling.

The four wrists come together and our blood mingles with the sand.

A brotherhood of sand and blood. For ever.

More hours pass. He's brought in a straw-bottomed chair and sits there opposite us, sharpening a stick with his knife. Every so often he gives my daughter and me a look of boredom. If I collapse on to the table, we'll die, my daughter and I. In his own wretched language, I ask him why. He doesn't even look at me. Now, I really feel the terror: my legs start trembling, the sweat turns cold as it runs down my spine, my urine trickles down my legs, my tears are falling and there's no stopping them. I simply have to keep awake. I stare at the strip of light under the roller-shutter door, the few millimetres that mark the difference between life and death. I mustn't give in. I only have to keep my eyes open. That's simple enough.

Tuesday, 29 May 1962

We're well prepared. Everyone has their part to play. Nico's the victim, Karim the photographer, Ahmed the enforcer, and I'm the one who can't be reported for it.

Four little bastards against one great big one. We should be enough.

At the end of the lesson, Nico tells Don Eugenio that he's ready to make confession.

We know that the priest'll take him off to a room on the first floor of St Anselm's presbytery nearby. It's the one he uses for his private maths lessons. There's a small confessional in it.

We're already well hidden when they arrive. Don Eugenio ushers him in and locks the door. Then he slips into the confessional. Nico gets on his knees outside.

Immediately, he begins his recitation, lisping as he goes.

'We touched ourselves. Myself, Mikey, Ahmed and Karim.'

'In what way, Nico? I have to know everything in order to decide on the penance.'

'All four of us pulled down our underpants. Then we measured our peckers.'

His 's' sounds are exaggerated. Hidden under the desk, Ahmed, Karim and myself have to wait there without bursting into laughter.

'Can you show me how, Nico? Please stand up.'

The priest comes out of the confessional. His light-blue eyes fix on Nico. Don Eugenio's good-natured smile seems like an obscene grimace.

'How far down did you pull your underpants? Let me see.'

Nico's shaking. He knows we're hidden there. Why don't we make a move?

Because it wouldn't be enough to get, Nico. We have to go further. You have to go further.

Closing his eyes, Nico does as he's told. His shorts and underpants drop down to his knees. He looks ridiculous. He's only twelve, and yet his thighs are as hairy as his calves.

Then Karim pops out from underneath the desk behind the priest. Don Eugenio jumps at the clicks of the old Kodak. He turns round and looks, dumbfounded, at Karim and Nico.

'Nico, how dare you? I'll have you and your whole family ex-communicated! As for you, you miserable little . . .'

I come out from under the desk as well. Don Eugenio clams up. I'm the real problem for him. What would my father say?

But this isn't enough, and we know it. Ahmed comes out and plants himself between Nico and the priest. In his hand, he has the Swiss knife, the one from the blood brotherhood, the one with which he kills scorpions and cuts the throats of rabid dogs.

Don Eugenio turns pale, unsure whether to give us all a slapping or to give in.

Ahmed removes any last doubt, pressing the knifepoint at the priest's Adam's apple, drawing a few drops of blood.

The first drops of so much blood.

Who knows why that thought comes into my mind.

'We won't say a word. But we have the photographs,' I tell Don Eugenio.

But this isn't enough of a threat for Ahmed.

'If you touch my friend again, I'll slit your throat, you *gawad.**
Understand?'

And now I know why the thought came to me.

Because Ahmed would really do it.

Marlene's been teaching Laura how to photograph for several months
now. There's a broom cupboard in the villa they use as a dark room
and Laura already knows how to develop the rolls of negative. We
have no other choice but to go to her. We tell her about the photos
of Don Eugenio, but leave out the knife to the throat.

As I imagined, she doesn't agree with what we're doing.

'You as well, Karim?'

As if we three were hardened criminals and Karim some kind of saint.

Karim looks away.

I cut things short. 'We have to develop them now.'

She pulls an amused face.

'Really? And just where are you thinking of developing them?
The photographer's opposite the Cathedral?'

'We have to protect Nico,' Karim says.

She thinks for a moment. Karim's the most believable one among
us. We may be right.

'Did you hit Don Eugenio?' she asks.

'No, no,' Karim quickly replies.

'No, absolutely not, I swear it,' Nico adds in confirmation, keeping his fingers crossed behind his back. Then he makes the sign of
the cross.

The lisping of the 's' sound makes Laura smile. It makes her soften,
and she is now more open to persuasion.

She looks at me. 'If you hang around with Ahmed, Mikey, you'll
end up just like him.'

---

* 'Queer' (author's note)

She says it with sadness in her voice, showing her concern for me. I know what she means.

An outlaw. A gangster.

Ahmed looks at her coldly and says nothing. Then she makes her decision. I know she'll do it for Nico.

'OK, I'll help you out. Give me the film, Mikey. I'll develop the negatives.'

Ahmed shakes his head.

'Don't trust her, Mikey. She's only a kid. And she's crazy.'

Laura makes to go off. I grab her arm and stop her. She brushes my hand away sharply. A lock of hair falls over her clear eyes: her father's eyes. She's furious.

'You're an idiot, Michele Balistreri. Listen to your dear Ahmed and you'll turn into an outlaw just like the ones in your films.'

I hand over the roll of film. No one says a word, and off she goes.

I keep my eyes fixed on the light below the roller-shutter door, the few milli-metres between life and death. How many hours have passed? I no longer know; I can't tell what time it is any more. It's over, my legs are about to give in, my eyes are about to close in sleep. But it's only now that his damnable calculation becomes clear. Only now that I see why my right hand is free. So that I can stretch it out towards the water on the table. If I make an effort, I can reach it; sixty kilos against nine, I can do that. It's what the bastard's waiting for. That I'll sacrifice my daughter's life just to wet my lips. For him, it's entertainment. But I'll not give in.

Wednesday, 30 May 1962

I'm alone in the garden when Laura comes over with an envelope she's sealed down with sticky tape.

'Have you seen them?' I ask, avoiding her look.

She pulls a face to disguise the smile.

'Of course I have. You have to do that to develop them. But I looked at them as little as possible.'

'We're not faggots, I swear it.'

Her beautiful mouth, the same as Marlene's, curls into a snigger.

'Maybe, who knows? We'll see.'

Then she breaks out into laughter and runs away to the safety of the Hunt villa.

Ahmed's right. Laura is half-crazy.

In the evening I'm alone again in the garden. Ahmed's back in his shack after the martial arts lesson, and Laura's at home in the villa.

Papa's voice can be heard through the French window. He's clearly upset.

'The ambassador and his wife will be offended, Italia, if you don't come yet again.'

'Tell them I've a headache.'

'I've already used that excuse.'

'Then find another. You're pretty good at inventing things.'

'Listen, Italia, this idea that you're not going to any more receptions is ridiculous. A social life is essential for business. I've just bought the Moneta island – I'm going to build a villa there to entertain people and—'

'I'll go there so that I can read in peace and quiet, Salvo, not to be mistress of the house and take care of your social life.'

'You've never even invited our neighbours for dinner again!'

'Quite. William Hunt may be a useful friend for you, but I don't like being around failed Hollywood actresses.'

'That's unfair, Italia. People only gossip about Marlene because she's good-looking and has an extremely important husband.'

'Really, Salvatore, is that so? And you know so much about her?'

'But, Italia, how can you not talk to our neighbours?'

'I'll talk to them when necessary. I'll talk to him, the few times he's here, because he's a serious man. And to Laura, who's a delightful girl, as beautiful as her mother, but much more respectable, like her father. So you can do the talking to Marlene Hunt, if she matters so much to you.'

Everything is spoken in hushed tones. But it's this that scares me most and stabs me in the heart. Even if he wishes I were different from what I am, my father's still my main role model. He's a handsome man, well liked by everyone. He had to study in the face of great sacrifice and is now a great success in business. I care for him a great deal.

But if he makes my mother suffer, that changes everything, because I love her more than anything in the world. She's the purest thing for me. She's like my grandad and my Uncle Toni, who went off to face the enemy single-handed while the routed Fascists were taking to their heels. For me, my mother's the Kirk Douglas character who goes off to the decisive gunfight with his pistol unloaded.

And Mamma, I'm just like you are.

It's night, but I can't get to sleep. Some of it's down to the nervous excitement from what we did to Don Eugenio, but the conversation between my father and mother's also unsettled me. I look over to the empty bed where my brother sleeps, but he's in London, studying English and making some useful friendships.

And learning how to steal legally, as Mamma says to Papa.

I turn over on my other side, towards the open window. I've no trouble with mosquitoes biting me; my blood's not the kind they like. But the heat's suffocating, there's too much light from the full moon and too much noise from the frogs croaking in the garden fountain. The eucalyptus are motionless; there's not even a breath of wind to waft their scent to me.

The clock on the wall says it's eleven thirty.

I've finished my bottle of water, so get up to take another from the kitchen, when I spot the glow of a cigarette out in the garden. When the figure inhales, I see Italia's face light up. She's walking about aimlessly, lost in thought. Papa must still be at the British Embassy reception.

Out of the blue, I see a shadowy figure approaching her.

'*Ciao*, Italia. Too hot to sleep?'

William Hunt's Italian's far from perfect, but it's acceptable, like Laura's. They learned it during their years in Rome.

The two adults speak in whispers in the dark. I'm confused, not knowing if I'm party to an everyday conversation between two neighbours, or something else. It goes on for several minutes. I watch, hypnotized, as the glowing end of my mother's cigarette criss-crosses William's cigar. She does most of the talking, given he's the strong, silent type and in any case prefers to listen.

Mamma seems calm. Tall, holding herself erect, her light hair cut short to her neck, her elegant features are a little too pale and serious to be seen as beautiful in the way Marlene Hunt is. But Mamma's a real queen, while Marlene's only a film star.

The conversation ends. They say goodbye to each other without shaking hands and my mother comes back into the house.

I'm nearly twelve and certainly not a mamma's boy, but I need her presence right now, just a couple of reassuring words for a minute in order to get calmly back to sleep.

I knock at the living-room door before entering. She's sitting on the sofa. 'Can't you sleep, Michelino?'

As usual, she's got a cigarette in one hand and in the other a glass of that dark-golden liquid Papa calls her poison.

'I'm hot, Mamma. I was thirsty, I went into the kitchen and . . .'

She doesn't ask me if I saw her with William Hunt. She smiles, happy for me to be with her.

'I think those martial arts lessons excite you too much. Come and sit yourself down here with me until you feel sleepy.'

I sit next to her on the sofa, as I used to when I was little boy. Something I haven't done for three years, given it's only something little kids do. Physical contact with my parents is now only a fleeting touch or an affectionate clip.

The African night's hot air enters through the two open French windows, along with the croaking of the frogs. And swarms of mosquitoes, attracted by the light.

'Don't the mosquitoes bite you, Mamma?'

'No, Michelino, only Alberto and Papa. They have sweeter blood.'

'And the two of us?'

She smiles. 'Ours is sour – it's like poison to them.'

'Like what you drink?'

She looks at me with a frown.

'You don't have to parrot everything you hear from grown-ups, not even if it comes from your father.'

'But is it bad for you or not?'

'It's called whisky. And it can damage your health if you drink too much of it.'

I had a sudden and infinite need for contact with her. To feel reassured that everything in the Balistreri family was fine.

'I did something very serious today, Mamma. A mortal sin.'

'Michelino, I just told you not to parrot things you haven't properly understood.'

'But there are the Commandments, Mamma. They were written by God.'

She looks at me indulgently. She knows I haven't believed in Father Christmas for some time.

'And how do you know who really wrote them, Michelino?'

I'm left speechless. If they'd heard her in Tripoli, they would have reported her to the Pope in Rome. They would have excommunicated her. If Papa had heard her, it would have been worse still.

I tell her about Don Eugenio, all in one go. Everything, from beginning to end. About Ahmed and his knife as well. She hears me out in silence. I go to my room and get the photographs of Nico with his pants down in front of Don Eugenio and hand them over to her. I notice the faint lines in her face becoming deeper. I suddenly see her as an old woman.

I wait, but she says nothing. She seems to be trying to catch a thought, a memory of something that Grandad told her.

'Toni was just like you at this age.'

I know this is both a compliment and a concern. I also know that Papa's forbidden her to tell me about Uncle Toni. And Grandad Giuseppe never tells me about him either.

'Can you tell me about him, Mamma?'

'No, Michelino, I promised Grandad Giuseppe I wouldn't.'

'But in what way am I like him?'

She thinks for a minute, then she gets up and goes over to the bookshelves on the wall, full of all the books she never stops reading. She takes one, quite a short book, and comes back to the sofa. She holds it out to me. Friedrich Nietzsche, *Ecce Homo*.

'This is one of Grandad Giuseppe's books. Toni started to read it when he was twelve. He couldn't understand a word, but he liked it. Then, at secondary school, he went on with it. He gave me all his books before going off to the war.'

'Would he kill Don Eugenio?'

She inhales the smoke of her cigarette, takes a sip of her poison.

'Listen to me now, Michelino, we're not going to tell your father about Don Eugenio or about the photographs. It wouldn't do any good. But you'll see that you won't have to be an altar boy and he won't give you any more trouble.'

I look at her doubtfully. She gives me a smile.

'Tomorrow, Don Eugenio's going to tell your father that, because of that swear word in front of your classmates, he couldn't possibly have you serving at Mass.'

My tongue's so swollen I can't breathe. If I stretch out my arm, I can reach it. I could drink that water. The urge is irresistible. I look at my daughter a last time, because after this I'll never be able to see her again. As my right arm stretches out towards that wonderful bottle, I know I'm already dead. I can feel the rope beginning to tighten round my neck. I daren't turn to look at my little one, tied to the other end. I daren't think of her neck. My right hand is flat on the ground, crawling through the mud and the beetles towards the bottle. He gets up, having finished whittling a point at the end of the stick. A single thrust; the pain's excruciating. The point passes through my hand and pins it to the mud. As the knot tightens round my throat, he forces me to turn my head round. My little daughter's been raised thirty centimetres off the ground, the noose tight round her neck. She's wide awake now, her swollen tongue hanging out, her eyes looking at me in terror, her mouth formulating the word 'Mamma' for the first time. And also for the last.

Saturday, 30 June 1962

You had to know how to get along with Italians, and it was better that you did get along with them. Mohammed Al Bakri came to understand this one day in September 1931, when he was only six years old and living in the Jaghbub oasis in Cyrenaica. His father and two elder brothers had just been seized by Marshal Graziani's soldiers, accused of being members of the Libyan resistance. In less than a week they were put on trial and hanged. Italian troops surrounded the oasis with barbed wire and poisoned the wells used for drinking water. The surviving women and children escaped across the desert and, after two exhausting months, a few of them reached Tripoli. Mohammed and his mother were the only survivors in the Al Bakri family.

In Tripoli, his mother found work as a scullery maid in the house of a real gentleman, a man named Giuseppe Bruseghin, a good man who treated the mother and son very kindly. Then came the disasters in Giuseppe's life: the deaths of his son, Toni, and his wife, Margherita. Bruseghin was left on his own with that difficult daughter. Mohammed thought that Signorina Italia would never find a husband. But after the war she met and married Ingegner Salvatore Balistreri. Mohammed Al Bakri had understood this man from the beginning, thanks to his

Bedouin intuition, the same one that lets them cross the desert by following only the stars. And this Ingegner Balistreri was a genius in business and a man who was generous to those who were his faithful and devoted followers. He taught Mohammed how to write, how to do arithmetic and much else. So Mohammed became his right-hand man, feared and admired by all his employees, Libyan and Italian.

Mohammed was certain that he would work for Ingegnere Balistreri all his life. The engineer was the shrewdest businessman in North Africa; everything he touched turned to gold. If he served him well, Mohammed knew that one day he would be able to buy a horse, then a carriage, then a Fiat 600 and, eventually, some land and perhaps a house like the Italians had. And, perhaps, if they both enjoyed good health and good fortune, a good deal more as well. *Inshallah*.

But, for the moment, what he had was a Libyan's pay, which was little. A wooden shack instead of a house and a large family. One man, two wives, four sons between the ages of ten and sixteen, and little Nadia, his eight-year-old daughter and his treasure. Ahmed, Karim and young Nadia were the children of Jamila, Mohammed's second wife, and were tall and slim for their age, good-looking and bright. Sixteen-year-old Farid and fourteen-year-old Salim were the sons of his first wife, Fatima, and were less fortunate. Farid had taken after Fatima. He was robust and stocky, with frizzy hair, a large nose and thick lips. Salim, on the other hand, had taken all his features from Mohammed; he was short and angular with a hollow face, an aquiline nose and wore his straight hair in a pudding-basin cut.

Of the two, Farid was the brains, while Salim was the muscle. Farid cut a deal, where Salim tyrannized; Farid was cold as ice, Salim was boiling hot.

Mohammed had asked the Ingegnere if he could build a brick house on the piece of land two kilometres from the villa, where they had the shack. It was uncultivated ground in the middle of the countryside, bordering on the cesspit used by those houses not connected to the sewers and by Bruseghin's agricultural workers for manure. The Ingegner had agreed.

Saturday was a good day because Mohammed did not have to be in Ingegnere Balistreri's office and his two younger sons were not at school. The elder ones had not been to school for two years, having been expelled for hitting their classmates.

For Mohammed and his four sons, Saturday began at dawn with ritual ablutions, followed by *salat al fajr*, the dawn daily prayers recited looking east towards Mecca and the rising sun. They ended this first of the five daily prayers with two genuflexions, the *rukus*.

Then, immediately, they set to work. Mohammed had calculated the number of bricks, the amount of lime and the implements needed. With the money he had put aside over the years while working for Ingegnere Balistreri, he could afford to buy the materials, but not the labour.

This Saturday was possibly the last one possible for any physical labour before the great heat of July and August. The flies were already sucking up the sweat that soon welled up on you. Thousands of flies, what with all that manure, and thirsty more than hungry for food.

With the jeep borrowed from the Ingegnere, they had brought the sacks of lime from Tripoli. Along the metalled road to Sidi El Masri, they had stopped at the Esso station and loaded up jerry cans with water. A kilometre later, they had taken the dirt track that ran through the herdsmen's goats, past the Bruseghin olive grove and up to the wretched cesspit.

The work was proceeding slowly. While Mohammed mixed the lime where the house was to stand, the boys emptied the sacks near the ditch. Karim, the youngest, was dragging a sack of quicklime with his two hands over the dusty ground to be mixed. He was not complaining, only moving slowly.

'Come on, Karim,' Farid shouted at him, a cigarette hanging from the corner of his huge lips.

'*Jalla, gawad!*'★ Salim shouted at him. His mouth was a thin, cruel line. For him, the best thing about fishing was taking the fish alive out of the water and holding it firmly in his hand until it could no longer breathe.

'Leave off. Can't you see he can't manage?' Ahmed protested.

He was only twelve, but he was as tall as his elder brothers.

'Oh, Professor Ahmed is coming to the defence of the little poof, is he?' said Salim mockingly.

Ahmed made no reply. He went up to his younger brother to help him.

'Leave it, Karim. Let me take the bucket.'

'No, Ahmed,' ordered Farid. He puffed smoke out of his wide nostrils as he had seen the real tough guys do in American movies.

'Why?' Ahmed asked.

'If Karim doesn't get used to the work, then we'll have one less builder, and we can't have that.'

'I'm trying, Farid,' said Karim.

Karim was standing firm, not wishing to complain. He was panting and trying to shift the heavy weight, but could not move the bucket.

Salim gave him a kick up the backside that had him rolling over in the dust. Karim doubled up with the pain, but did not cry out, complain or cry. Salim picked up a frog and threw it at him. Then he went up to him.

'Get up, you little poof, right now.'

Ahmed stepped between the two of them. Salim gave him a cruel look. He could not wait to get his hands on him.

★ 'Get a move on, you queer!' (author's note)

'If you don't get out of the way right now, I'll kick you all the way back to the shack.'

Ahmed was calm. In fact, he was happy. He was learning something about himself: how not to be frightened. He was managing to keep a clear head, like he did with Mikey at the martial arts lessons.

Farid had come up as well. His frizzy hair was full of flies and, with the cigarette hanging from his full lips, he was playing the part of the tough guy with brains. Not the animal, like Salim.

'Karim has to work like us. Now get out of the way.'

Ahmed looked at his father, who was mixing the lime and had no idea of the fight breaking out among his sons.

'I'll count to three, Ahmed, and if you don't get out of the way I'll make mincemeat of you,' Salim threatened.

But Ahmed already had his moves planned. He had only to provoke them.

'*An-din-gahba . . .*'* he hissed at his elder brother.

He then took advantage of the moment of incredulity and bewilderment. He bent down to grab a handful of lime from the bucket and, when Salim lunged at him, he was ready. The lime hit the eyes of Farid and Salim, blinding them. They screamed and cursed, blindly trying to hit out at him, but he moved about so that they could only hear him hissing '*An-din-gahba . . . An-din-gahba . . .*'

He was able to lead them where he wanted. When they were on the edge of the cesspit, he gave them a warning.

'Hey, brothers, have you done it in your pants? I'm picking up the smell of shit!'

Farid and Salim caught on and stopped themselves dead, paralysed with fear. Their eyes, noses and lips were covered in flies, which rose from the ditchful of semi-liquid shit and were buzzing loudly, as if to push them in.

---

* 'Son of a bitch' (author's note)

Ahmed thought a moment. He could easily throw them into the ditch, but afterwards they would take it out on Karim.

'Keep calm, brothers, you won't end up in the shit, but you're very close. Stay nice and steady now.'

At that moment, Mohammed gave an angry shout.

'Hey, you boys, will one of you bring me that damned lime to mix? Right now!'

'Yes, Papa, I'll see to it,' Ahmed replied. Then he turned to his brothers.

'I'll take the lime to him and come back and help you. Make sure you stay where you are.'

He went off, walked the hundred metres and placed the bucket down for Mohammed.

'Here's the lime, Papa.'

'Thanks, Ahmed. What are those two idle brothers of yours doing?'

Ahmed turned round. What he saw made his blood run cold.

Karim was running up in silence, knowing he needed every bit of his strength. He chose Salim, because he was the lighter of the two, and gave him a hard push.

Salim cried out and took a step backwards, waving his arms as if trying grab on to something, then fell almost in slow motion into the soft, slimy pit.

He floundered about, shouting and terrified, spitting out the shit that had got into his mouth.

Ahmed lowered himself into the manure up to his waist. He took two steps towards his brother, trying not to slip. He grasped him by the arm and dragged him to the side of the pit.

Salim's foot met a hand blocking his path. His screams reached all the way to the heavens, mingling with those of the muezzin calling to prayer.

Saturday Night and Sunday, 30 June to 1 July 1962

I catch the confidential bit of news during the usual Saturday-night gathering at the villa. General Jalloun, Tripoli's chief of police, is talking about it with Papa and Don Eugenio. Two corpses have been pulled out of the cesspit. A young woman and her young baby daughter. What little skin there was left on the skeletons was dark, so they were not Libyans from the coast, but possibly from Fezzan, or even the Sudan.

'People from the Sahara,' says Don Eugenio.

'Poor things, coming in from the desert at night, they must have fallen in,' says my father.

'They've been there some time, although it's impossible to say how long. No one's been asking after them and the police have no time to make any inquiries about people like that,' the general concludes.

I get the message. This is the world I have to grow up in. The lives of some human beings are worth no more than a pair of monkeys'.

Friday, 26 May 1967

In the five years that followed, I went on with my education, but dedicated much more time to martial arts, hunting and fishing than to my textbooks. I only went to school because my mother wanted me to and because no one dared fail the son of Ingegnere Balistreri. He'd become more wealthy and more important in these five years, although I didn't quite understand the nature of the import–export business he had.

Apart from his right-hand man in operations, Mohammed, the two people Papa spent most of his time with were Don Eugenio and Emilio Busi.

There'd been no more problems with Don Eugenio after the episode five years earlier. Not for me, nor for Nico, nor with anyone else, as far as I knew. Only once did I ask my mother if she'd spoken with him about the photographs. She responded evasively, but clearly.

'Don Eugenio's a highly intelligent man and is conscious of his mistake. He won't ever repeat what he did.'

I met Emilio Busi for the first time in our house in the spring of 1962, and then more frequently over the past two years.

Busi was born in 1935 and was now thirty-two. Tall and lean, with thick, dishevelled hair, he wore horrendous square black glasses that gave him the look of a bookworm. He chain-smoked the nauseous plain-tipped Nazionali cigarettes while his shrewd eyes behind the thick lenses studied you through the smoke. His dress sense was completely ridiculous: short-sleeved checked shirts, high-waisted trousers that were too short in the leg, then white socks and moccasins.

My father and grandfather had told me more about him.

Busi came from the mountains between Tuscany and Emilia, where I'd read everyone was a partisan during the war. His father was one of the Resistance leaders against the Fascists.

A partisan with the Catholics' white armband. A sort of Christian Communist.

Papa was always talking about him as if he were a good example to follow. Fighting the Fascists and the Nazis in the mountains, Busi's father had formed many friendships, especially with the right men, who wore white non-Communist armbands like himself and became important people after the war.

One of these men, Enrico Mattei, had taken control of the old AGIP oil company and created ENI, a state oil company, to fight back against the 'Seven Sisters' – as he called the Western cartel – formed in 1951 after Iran had nationalized its petroleum production, which had denied ENI membership. Before dying of cancer, Busi's father brought his son, then training to be a Carabiniere, to Mattei's attention.

At the beginning of 1960, Emilio Busi graduated from the Carabinieri's Officer Training School in Rome. But then ENI offered him a job. So he left the Carabinieri force and promptly joined the Italian Communist Party. ENI posted him to Syracuse in Sicily, where he worked on realizing one of Enrico Mattei's dreams: the refinery and petrochemical plants between Gela, Augusta and Syracuse set up to exploit the deposits found in the Ragusa basin. Thanks to his excellent relations both with his ex-colleagues in the Carabinieri and with the trade unions who looked on him favourably as a Communist, his work went well. But the ENI project in Sicily was the first step towards expansion in North Africa and the Middle East, and the 'Seven Sisters' weren't happy about this at all.

One of the firms that worked on the preparation and construction of the site was the one formed by my father's four elder brothers. It was they who told Busi about their brother in Tripoli, who could possibly lend a hand in dealing with Libya and the Americans.

Busi's first visit to my father was in that spring of 1962 when he spoke to him about ENI's projects in Sicily and North Africa and about Mattei's problems with the American oil companies. So Papa introduced him to William Hunt, who had the right kind of connections in Washington.

Then, on 27 October 1962, Mattei was killed. His private jet, a Morane-Saulnier MS.760 Paris, accidentally exploded while returning from a trip to Sicily.

From this point on, my father's version of events differs from my mother's. My father says it was *an accident*, whereas my mother maintains it was nothing of the sort. According to her, the instigators were the Americans and their Italian friends and the perpetrators were *the Sicilian friends of the Italian friends*. Papa would listen patiently, smiling and shaking his head.

In any case, Mamma maintained, ENI's industrial project in Syracuse had gone ahead anyway, but with modifications that made it more acceptable to everyone. According to her, the Balistreri brothers' firm had worked actively to secure these changes.

My father strongly objected to my mother's version of events. There wasn't a scrap of evidence for any attempt on Mattei's life. ENI's new board of directors was leading the company in the direction Mattei had wanted, although perhaps in a less visionary manner, but with a more realistic approach in terms of the interests of Italy and its people. As for his brothers, their company had regularly won public tenders; it was one of Sicily's largest firms and enjoyed an excellent reputation.

Two years ago, however, after working in Sicily for five years, Emilio Busi had left ENI and moved permanently to Tripoli, giving out that he was now a business consultant for various Italian companies that wanted to set up in Libya. But he never mentioned any names. *Professional secret*, he used to say, in a serious tone of voice.

At seventeen, I'd no real idea what a *business consultant* was and what exactly Busi did. Here, too, the explanations given by Papa and Mamma were similar in part, but also very different.

My father said a consultant is a businessman who gives advice to his clients on how to make money in Libya and is paid for it.

My mother said he's a man who's only interested in his own ideals and, in order to pursue those, he transforms his clients' unspoken dreams into reality.

Busi's money and the money of others came into Papa's explanation; in Mamma's, it was Busi's ideals and the money of others. There was a mixture of respect and contempt in her explanation. And a touch of fear.

And it was because of my mother's touch of fear that I disliked Emilio Busi.

The Underwater Club's restaurant was crowded, as usual. There were Italians, Americans, and a few Libyans, who were almost all members of King Idriss's government. The band was playing 'Ruby Tuesday'. Several couples were dancing, almost all the ladies in evening gowns and the men wearing dinner jackets and bow ties. On the horizon, you could see the lights of the fishing fleet sailing out for a night on the calm, dark sea.

Papa and Mamma didn't dance. She didn't like to. Papa had managed to get a secluded table out on the terrace, overlooking the sea. Sitting around it were my parents, my grandfather, Emilio Busi, Alberto and myself.

Papa loosened the knot of his bow tie and brushed a hand through his raven hair.

Mamma was forever telling him to get it cut, as long hair wasn't becoming for a businessman now nearly forty-two. But Papa thought he looked very handsome with it, and he was. For him, long hair was a sign of virility.

He turned to Grandad Giuseppe.

'It may be that our family and some of Signor Busi's clients will become future business partners.'

'And what business would that be?' my mother asked.

She posed the question in her usual manner. Cool but polite. For a moment, my father looked at her as if she were a stranger. Then he recovered his natural charming manner: the great salesman who could sell ice to the Eskimos. He turned to Grandad again, speaking to him in the hope of convincing her.

'The future of any business links between Italy and Libya will be based on two things, petroleum and cars. Enrico Mattei always said so. If a country wants to produce cars, it also has to have the petrol.'

In the general silence, Busi was watching us through the smoke of what must have been his fiftieth plain-tipped Nazionale. He looked directly at my mother, knowing he had to tackle her suspicions in some way or another.

'Signora Italia, the AGIP oil company was created by Count Giuseppe Volpi di Misurata when he was Mussolini's finance minister, after having been Governor of Tripolitana. It was the count who began the search for petroleum here in Libya. And he was a friend of your family, I believe.'

Grandad interrupted him. His manner was more polite than my mother's, but equally firm.

'The count was a guest for dinner, which didn't make him a friend. After 25 July 1943, we neither heard nor saw anything of him.'

I knew that date. It was the day the Grand Council of Fascism expelled Mussolini. I knew very well what Italia and my grandfather thought of those men.

They had betrayed Italy.

Emilio Busi turned to my grandfather. He was more tractable than my mother.

'Anyway, as you know, it was thanks to the research funded by AGIP and Fiat that Ardito Desio discovered petroleum deposits in the Libyan Desert in 1938. Then, unfortunately, the war broke out and Anglo-American interests were able to take over from the Italians.'

My mother gave no time for Grandad to reply.

'Signor Busi, the Anglo-Americans were able to win thanks to an Italy teeming with traitors and turncoats. Like Volpi di Misurata and the Mafiosi who helped the Americans enter Sicily.'

It was very clear she included Busi and his partisan father among the list of those who had betrayed Italy.

My father was visibly embarrassed and upset. Things weren't going at all as he'd hoped. I could see it in his eyes: the charming smile on his dark, handsome face, the smile he put on for church each Sunday, was looking a little tarnished. He tried to find a way to soothe my mother.

'Italia, Libya's oil now runs the risk of ending up totally in the hands of Esso and Mobil. And the car market in those of Ford and General Motors. Isn't it about time we Italians started to claw something back? Don't you think Enrico Mattei was right in his parable of the little cat?'

He'd already told the story a thousand times. The little cat goes timidly up to an enormous bowl of broth, and a large hound attacks it and breaks its back. The broth is petroleum; the dog is the 'Seven Sisters'; and Italy the little cat.

By now, I'd come to recognize my father's tactics. He was now appealing to my mother's anti-American feelings. But my mother was no fool.

'And what does our family have to do with all this?' she asked.

The question was addressed directly to Emilio Busi. He looked at her coldly from behind those bookworm's glasses, through the stink of his tobacco smoke and locks of dishevelled hair.

'Olives are excellent, but the future lies under the sand, not above it. If you can understand that, your family can become a minority partner and become truly wealthy.'

'And you as well, I take it, Signor Busi,' said my mother.

Busi shook his head.

'Forgive me for being brutally frank, but it's simply so we can be clear among ourselves. I have the good fortune to come from a family that has land and a house. I earn quite enough from my work. Luxury doesn't interest me. I don't need the money. But our country's only now coming out of the ruin and poverty that Fascism caused. The people of Italy need low-cost petrol, and they need work.'

'And where do we come in?' my mother asked.

Busi shrugged, puffing out a cloud of smoke.

'You can help speed what will only be an inevitable process. Italy will go ahead, no matter what.'

For some reason, that last, whispered sentence produced the effect of an earthquake or a declaration of war. It was clear that the Bruseghin–Balistreri family was the most important Italian family in Tripoli, and counted for something. But it wasn't irreplaceable. Italy was conferring an honour on it in choosing it. She could always pick someone else. Especially since my grandfather and mother still had Fascist sympathies.

It was Alberto who, completely unexpectedly, intervened.

'Signor Busi, in order to become partners in big business, you need to have a great deal of money, which we don't have.'

In that moment, I became certain of several things. Firstly, I could never be like Alberto. Secondly, not only was he more intelligent than I was, but he was also different from my father. Thirdly, my father wasn't pleased with what Alberto said.

I saw my father struggling between an angry gesture and admiration for his son. An eighteen-year-old with the maturity of an adult. Then he laughed, that habitual good-natured laugh of his, and turned to Busi.

'As always, my son Alberto's right. He's going to university in Rome to study engineering. One day, he'll lead an industrial empire.'

Papa said nothing about me. For the first time, Busi shot me a glance. It was a mixture of condescension and sympathy, bordering on pity.

I'm the less able son. The one who only knows how to land a punch and shoot wild animals.

Monday, 29 May 1967

Nico Gerace's father had died three years earlier, flattened by a truck that was reversing in front of the pumps of his Esso petrol station. Nico had witnessed the whole scene.

And Papa, the ever more powerful Ingegner Salvatore Balistreri, had come to the aid of his widowed cousin, Santuzza, and her son, Nico. He bought the petrol station, and Nico received a fixed wage for working there in the afternoons and at weekends. But Papa insisted that he continue his education at secondary school, and he paid for his books and fees. And Santuzza cut and tailored all Papa's made-to-measure clothes and those of his friends.

My father's explanation for such generosity was very simple.

'Santuzza's one of my second cousins. The Gerace family comes from the same district in Palermo as I do, and it was I who persuaded them to come to Tripoli. That's how we Sicilians do things. If you can help somebody out, then you do so.'

Perhaps Papa was thinking that Nico's presence at school would help his surly dunce of a son, who was a self-confessed Fascist. And having a Fascist son wasn't good for Ingegner Balistreri's business dealings with Arabs, Jews, Catholic priests and Italian Communists.

Outside Italy, Italian secondary school lasted for four years rather than five. The first two years quickly passed, but the third year had its dramatic moments. Partly because my brother, Alberto, had graduated with the highest possible marks and gone on to university in Rome and, without his help, mathematics was a real trial for Nico and myself.

Nico's lisping 's' sounds, his bushy eyebrows, his unstoppable growth of hair and his whiff of petrol made him the school's laughing stock. The girls in class greeted all the boys with the traditional kisses, with myself always first in line. But they never embraced Nico. And the older boys gave him a hard time. The most aggressive were five wealthy little shits who were regular members of the class's first basketball team. Five tall, gangly guys, all brawn, and arrogant with it.

They always called him 'Whiffy', because of the smell of the Esso station, or 'Eyebrows', because, like his hair, they were so bushy.

Nico cheered himself up by filling notepads and exercise books with newspaper cuttings of photos of actresses and singers. And by buying stylish clothes. That's how he spent all the money he earned at the Esso station: flowered shirts, elasticized pants, frizzy hippy hair-dos.

He depended economically on my father and psychologically on me. Without help, he couldn't have resisted for long against the daily taunts inflicted on him by the five basketball players.

'*Hey, Eyebrows, give us a lisp, will you?*'

'*Hey, Whiffy, how do you toss yourself off with those smelly hands?*'

Our blood brotherhood decided it was time to make them stop. Once and for all. It was a unanimous decision that took all of two minutes.

Nico, Ahmed, Karim and myself went into the changing rooms after a match. They were standing naked in the showers and looked contemptuously at us right away.

'Hey, Mikey, we don't want Whiffy and those Arabs in here,' said the team's centre.

I gave him a *tae* kick in the testicles that made him double up and then Nico fetched him a *kwon* punch that laid him out flat under the shower. The other four were about to react, but Ahmed already had the knife in his hand.

We had no plan for a brawl in mind. Too many bruises, perhaps even a broken bone. There would have been no trouble for me, but plenty for Ahmed, Karim and Nico. No, the method of attack had to be something else.

An invisible bruise, something that couldn't be reported. The use of terror.

Ahmed went up to the centre, who was trying to get up, and put the tip of the knife to his throat, as he had done years before with Don Eugenio. Now, the basketball players were paralysed with fear. They looked at me, the only one on their social level, the only civilized one. So I immediately made things plain to them.

'If you say a word of this to your parents or take the piss out of Nico again, we'll kill you. All of you.'

To make the idea clearer, Ahmed made a cut in the centre's throat, from which a little blood began to flow.

'Mikey didn't say we'd beat you up. He said we'd kill you. Is that clear?'

They nodded, almost theatrically. From that day on, no one dared ridicule Nico ever again. And, later, word must have filtered down, because, in the school and on the Tripoli streets, everyone gave us a wide berth. And I was the untouchable son of Ingegner Salvatore Balistreri, and no parent could say a thing.

Nico Gerace slowly began to lose his lisp. He carried on dressing ever more stylishly and went on to sticking up photos of Playmate nudes under his desk. And for the whole of that academic year, no one called him 'Whiffy' or 'Eyebrows' again.

Tuesday, 30 May 1967

It was the last week of school. A young history teacher fresh from Rome with his parka and long beard was spelling out the damage done by Fascism.

'Take the colonization of Libya, for example.'

He stared at us, as if expecting some objection. Then he carried on.

'It was planned and carried out by a bunch of criminals.'

I raised my hand, but he ignored me and sent us out into the court-yard for break-time.

While the others were chattering away, I stood in a corner with Nico. I was thinking about my grandad and about the hellish work he put in over many years to establish his olive grove. I felt my anger welling up.

Then the words of that Communist, Emilio Busi, came to mind.

Wealth lies under the soil now, not above it. There was no longer a place for Grandad's olive grove.

The teacher was having a cigarette in another corner, something that was absolutely forbidden to us pupils.

I went up to him, Nico a couple of steps behind me.

'My grandad was one of the colonials, *Professore*. Would you say he was a criminal?'

He barely looked at me.

'We'll talk about it in class next time, Balistreri.'

'No. Tell me now.'

A knot of students gathered around us. I could feel the tension mounting, but all I wanted was an answer.

'If your grandad was a Fascist, then he was a criminal, Balistreri. Perhaps he hanged some Libyans, perhaps not. But he should have stayed where he belonged – at home.'

My anger, that old enemy of mine I'd always feared and tried to check, suddenly exploded in me. I didn't use any of my martial arts, simply pushed him to the ground with a mere shove. Then Nico and I took him by the arms and legs and flung him into the goldfish pond.

'You shit!' Nico shouted at him, lisping the 's' a little. Then he spat on him.

The headmaster tried his best not to throw me out, but the teacher immediately called the Ministry of Education in Rome. A telegram arrived the following day.

Nico and I were expelled once and for all. Except that, with Papa's money, I could always go to a cushy private school in Rome. But it was the end for Nico. He would be a petrol-pump attendant for the rest of his life.

At home that afternoon was when my father first came out with the word 'loser' for me.

'Your brother Alberto's now studying engineering in Rome. You, on the other hand, only know how to shoot things and lash out with your fists. You'll end up a pump attendant, like that Nico Gerace. You're a loser, that's what you are.'

My mother looked at him coldly.

'Losers, as you call them, Salvatore, can be better men than the victors. You'll see what kind of a world we'll be in fifty years from now, thanks to your victors.'

But the toughest on both of us – my father and me – was Grandad.

'From next week, Mikey, you'll be working in my olive grove. And you, Salvatore, must show more patience with him. I don't want to hear any more talk of victors and losers under my roof. Those are things that only have to do with war.'

My father turned white with rage. Giuseppe Bruseghin had reminded him that it was still his house and it didn't belong to Ingegner Balistreri. And that he had had to fight in a real war, whereas Ingegner Balistreri had only had to combat poverty.

But my father was a man able to control himself and wait for the right moment. And this wasn't it. So he simply bowed politely to Grandad.

I went out to the deserted patch in front of the villas, then went round behind the Hunt villa. The sun was huge ball of fire setting on that dreadful day and on that part of my life.

Laura was wandering around with her new Rolleiflex in front of the car port. Instead of strolling up and down the main street in town with her friends and winking at the boys, she was a fifteen-year-old who preferred to be there by herself, taking photographs of the ants that were coming and going out of the nest in a long, disciplined line.

I was expecting a telling-off from her as well, everyone knowing about my stupid act of bravado. But she said nothing. She pointed to the ants.

'They know they can only survive by helping each other. We should do as they do.'

Ahmed's right. She's crazy.

She lifted the Rolleiflex and pointed it at me. I had the sun in my eyes and instinctively raised an arm to shade them. But she took a picture just the same. Then she gave me a serious look with those clear eyes of hers, as if she were thinking of something truly important.

'Sorry, Mikey. But this snapshot will be a help to you one day.'

Thursday, 1 June 1967

The presidential office in Rome was on the upper floor of a very beautiful seventeenth-century palace that had been restored in the early twentieth century. It stood at the end of Via del Corso, with a view of Piazza Venezia. June promised to be very hot, but at seven in the morning it was still possible to breathe.

The large windows were open on the white façade of the Altar of the Fatherland, the national monument built by Mussolini which Italians now scornfully nickname 'The Typewriter'.

The President had been to Mass at six, as he had done every morning since the end of the Second World War. He always went to church alone and found there only the priest and several old ladies who had known him for years and had no personal favours to demand of him. Along with lunch and supper with his wife, this was the most precious time of his day. It was the moment in which he could talk to God and share his concerns about *what would be good and just* and *what was necessary*. Not for himself, obviously, but for his voters, the millions of Italians who had placed their hopes for the future in him and his Christian Democrat Party. There was a fine line between the ethics of duty and political pragmatism. It was a line he had increasingly been forced to cross.

Lord, I know that sometimes I sin out of presumption and sometimes power demands actions a long way from your teachings. But without that power I could do nothing for others.

It was a healthy driving force, not that of a man who engaged in politics looking for personal financial gain. It was the power to lead, to realize the dream of a democratic and Christian Italy where no one would go hungry and everyone would have work. It was a power that was impossible to acquire and maintain without the ferocity of a man who knows he is right.

At seven precisely, the President arrived back on foot from the nearby church of St Ignatius Loyola, his bodyguard following him discreetly at a distance. Discretion was the hallmark of this indefatigable and highly intelligent man.

Don Eugenio and Emilio Busi were waiting for him in his private office under the vigilant eye of his ancient secretary.

The priest was wearing his usual frayed black cassock and sandals, Busi a large, shapeless suit that made him look as if he were wearing pyjamas.

The President lost no time in preambles or opening chit-chat. He could have well done without Don Eugenio Pizza and Emilio Busi, but they were useful to him.

They were intelligent, unscrupulous and ambitious. Each of them in his own way was even an idealist: Don Eugenio was fixated on helping the world's poor, Busi on driving poverty from Italy. Their idealism rendered them both fairly easy to manipulate, the kind of men that allowed him to lead without appearing to have a heavy hand in doing so.

He had chosen Don Eugenio as his private confessor in order to keep up to date on that patch of sand which was now proving to be full of petroleum. And he had to have a confessor, at least in formal terms. Better to have a young man who had need of him and would never dare ask him difficult questions.

As for Emilio Busi, he really was a necessary evil. He was a contradiction in terms, a hybrid, a dangerous genetic experiment: son of a Catholic partisan, trained as an officer in the Carabiniere and now a member of the Communist Party.

An eye had to be kept on Busi. Thanks to his military training, he had the right connections with the Secret Services, and, thanks to the Communist Party, he also had the right connections with the trade unions. And he had been there in Catania next to the aeroplane when Enrico Mattei left on his last flight. A detail that could indeed be a simple coincidence, but disconcerting nevertheless, given the outcome of the flight.

And what about Enrico Mattei? May he rest in peace. A truly exceptional man. A man with vision. Honest and intelligent. But so stubborn, *so little inclined to compromise*, and so ambitious he could not understand that no single man alone could decide Italy's future. The country had already had one man like that, and he had led it into a disastrous war and economic ruin.

For all these reasons, the President listened attentively to Busi.

'This is a dangerous plan, gentlemen,' he said in the end. 'It isn't easy to manipulate a war. Things can easily get out of hand.'

Busi was ready for this objection.

'The plan is safe, Mr President. The Arabs want this war. Through my channels of communication with the Russians, we've managed to sell arms and MiG jet fighters to the Egyptians.'

The President raised a hand.

'I know nothing of this, and don't want to know anything. And what about America's ally Israel? What are we going to do with her?'

Busi calmed him down.

'We're going to warn Mossad beforehand. The Egyptian air force'll be destroyed on the ground, not a single MiG fighter will take off. The Israelis will inflict a few losses, the absolute minimum necessary.'

The President sighed. He had no liking for the idea of losses. But perhaps Busi was right. This way, there would be fewer deaths.

'And where's Nasser going to find the money for this war?' the President asked.

Don Eugenio smiled reassuringly.

'Humanitarian organizations favourable to the Palestinians and charitable donations. The IOR, the Vatican Bank, finances some of them indirectly. I'm taking care of this aspect.'

The President closed his eyes for a moment. Hearing the Vatican Bank mentioned reminded him of the promise he had made to Don Eugenio.

One day I'll recommend your name to the IOR, the Institute for Religious Works.

The President hoped he would never have to make such a recommendation to the Institute, the Vatican Bank's official name, and expressed a final concern.

'Nasser won't attack unless he thinks he can win.'

Busi's thick lenses hid the smile in his eyes.

'But he'll be certain of winning. It's what his generals will tell him. There are those among them that want to see him defeated, Mr President.'

The President knew that the channel of communication with Nasser's traitorous advisers had been opened by Mohammed Al Bakri on the orders of Ingegner Salvatore Balistreri. This man was the part he liked least. The price to be paid for such collaboration would be very high. Balistreri was a minor but indispensable partner in the future affairs of Libya and Egypt. A very inconvenient minor partner: politically useful, morally dubious and even dangerous, perhaps.

'Be careful with this Balistreri, gentlemen. His brothers—'

'All vote for our party, Mr President!' said Don Eugenio, interrupting him.

'They're excellent men, work hard and are devout Catholics,' said Busi, wrapping it up with a faint trace of sarcasm.

The President closed his eyes so that his visitors could not see his contempt for them. He thought again about his morning conversation with the Lord.

The fine line between what is right and what is indispensable for Italy.

He rose up and looked out of the window at the balcony overlooking Piazza Venezia, where Mussolini had declared war on Britain and France.

A naïve and presumptuous man. He thought he could fight a war and win it, instead of letting others fight it.

Monday, 5 June 1967

It was the first day I was to work in Grandad's olive grove after being expelled from secondary school, and I was up early. The traffic along the Sidi El Masri road in front of the villas was unusually chaotic.

Trucks, vans, carriages, carts, pedestrians, all flying the Libyan and Egyptian flags. A huge crowd of vehicles and people was heading into Tripoli, transistors blazing.

Ahmed and Karim came running up.

'Mikey, a war's broken out!'

We dashed into Tripoli on our bicycles and stopped at the Esso petrol station before we entered the city proper. Nico was standing in his overalls in the middle of the empty forecourt around his two pumps, looking in amazement at the crowds travelling past.

'What's happening, guys?'

Karim looked at him in exasperation.

'Don't you even know there's a war on? We've invaded Israel!'

Nico broke into laughter.

'Look, this isn't *Lawrence of Arabia* and you aren't Omar Sharif. The Israelis'll kick the shit out of you.'

Karim was about to get off his bicycle, but I stopped him.

'Leave it, Karim. Nico, shut up shop and let's go.'

We entered Tripoli through the Garden City and came into the Cathedral Square and Corso Vittorio, where all the Jewish shops already had their shutters down.

Piazza Italia, or Maydan as-Suhada, was overflowing with crowds which extended as far as the castle and the Adrian Pelt promenade. Loudspeakers were broadcasting Radio Cairo. People were shouting with joy and coming in throngs from the twin columns on the promenade, Corso Vittorio, Via Roma, Via Lazio, Via Piemonte and Corso Sicilia.

Swarms of kids had climbed up over the archway of the Souk el Mushir. Ahmed, Karim, Nico and I were tossed about by the thousands of people. The square was full of police and military, many of them extremely young and carrying pistols in their hands. Some of them were shooting up in the air in celebration.

The speech of the Egyptian President, Gamal Abdel Nasser, was broadcast live from all the Arab stations, inciting the crowds.

O most merciful Lord and my brothers, we have been attacked by the Zionist empire. All the Arab armies are marching to the front, where the Zionists will be destroyed. Israel will be wiped off the map and Palestine restored to our Arab brothers.

'We have to go, right now,' said Karim, while the crowd was pushing us in all directions.

Nico burst out laughing. 'You're only fifteen, Karim, where do you think they'll let you go?'

But Karim ignored him and turned to his elder brother.

'Didn't you hear the President, Ahmed? Even boys can fight against the Zionists. We really must go to fight. Allah wishes it, not only Nasser.'

They were so alike in appearance, but so different in character. One an idealist, the other a pragmatist. And Ahmed was the elder brother.

'Our father won't let us go, Karim.'

'Our father can't stand against the wishes of Allah. Didn't you hear? The Libyan army's setting off tomorrow for the front. They're enrolling all volunteers from the age of fifteen up. I'm going, brother, with or without you. I'll be smoking a *shisha* in Jerusalem by the end of the week.'

Ahmed looked at the poorly armed young soldiers around us. They'd never trained for war. He shot a glance at me.

Nico's right. The Israelis will massacre us.

Ahmed was my greatest friend and the one who was most like me. He was my companion in games, martial arts, fishing and hunting. We were united in everything, divided in nothing.

Apart from his hate for Laura Hunt.

'Libya's our homeland, Ahmed,' Karim insisted. 'I'm going to go.'

I looked at the faint white scar on my left wrist. Our blood brotherhood of five years ago.

I turned to Ahmed and Nico.

'Five years ago, we made a pact. And Libya's my homeland, too.'

Ahmed had too much respect or respectful fear of me to reply.

Don't be stupid, Mikey, this isn't your homeland. Your home is way across the sea.

I heard Nico mouthing curses under his breath.

In the end, Ahmed gave in.

'All right, Karim. Let's go and talk to Father.'

During the bicycle journey back we passed lorries, pick-up trucks, carts and motorbikes with sidecars, all full of young men singing out in praise of the war. As I was pedalling, I read the word 'Jew' already daubed over the rolling shutters of the Jewish shops. The Italians were pulling their shutters down as well.

The blood was churning around my stomach, pounding in my temples and boiling in my veins. I was torn by two opposing thoughts.

What I should be, and what I felt like being.

Ahmed and Karim carried on home, while Nico and I went to mine. My mother was in the living room with Grandad. Laura and her father were with them. William Hunt was in the middle of speaking as we came in.

'Israel made a surprise air attack at dawn, just like the Japanese at Pearl Harbor. They destroyed the Egyptian air force on the ground before a single aircraft could take off. It was a preventative strike, as if they'd been warned.'

'But, put together, the Arabs outnumber them ten to one,' objected Grandad.

William Hunt looked at him.

'This isn't the First or Second World War. In military terms, the number of troops doesn't count for anything. Sinai's open country; it's not remotely like Vietnam, with its jungles and tunnels. Out there in the desert, it's the air force that's in control. The Arabs have already lost; they'll be butchered.'

It was that word, 'butchered'. The inescapability of it. The certainty.

No, I wasn't going to leave my friends to die in that shit-hole of Sinai.

I took Nico out of the living room.

'I'm going with them, Nico. Are you coming?'

He smiled. He looked at the scar on his wrist.

'Without you guys, I'm nothing, Mikey. I'll go home, tell my mother, then be back here in half an hour.'

As I was going to my room, Laura came after me. We went in. She closed the door and stood in front of it.

'Aren't you scared, Mikey?'

It was a stupid question. I was about to give her a surly reply, when she rephrased it.

'I mean, scared for your friends, Mikey.'

Yes, she understands everything about me, even things I don't understand about myself.

There was a tenderness in her eyes that I'd never seen before. She moved away from the door.

'Don't get yourselves killed, Mikey. And don't kill anyone either. And the best of luck.'

She came up close, while I stood as still as a post. I felt the light touch of her lips on mine.

Have faith, Mikey. Have faith in those who know you and care about you.

In some way, our painful feelings met like the electric arc the physics teacher once tried to explain to us. Those lips that brushed against mine signified the contact between two souls, not two bodies. Laura Hunt had won me with the lightness of a wordless understanding.

I took less than ten minutes to prepare a rucksack with four things. I wrote a note to my mother and Grandad. They would be eaten up with worry but would understand what I was doing. I wrote nothing to my father.

I crept out of the house and waited for Nico, Ahmed and Karim by the side of the Hunts' car port. As we dashed into Tripoli on our bikes, I saw young Libyans painting signs on the Jewish shops and houses.

We crossed the overexcited city and went down Corso Sicilia, Shara Omar Al Mukhtar and came to the crossroads for Bab Azizia, the recruitment post.

We paused, but only for a moment. We wanted that crossroads in our lives to be clearly printed in our memory.

Our blood brotherhood would take us away to meet with our destiny.

Thursday, 8 June 1967

Three days of a hellish journey in the back of a tumbledown truck full of young Libyans with no real weapons and no uniforms. Some were wearing gym shoes, others babouches. Three days with only brief stops for bodily functions, and no space but that for our backsides on a bench. We travelled along the coast road through Marsa Matruh, El Hamam, El Alamein, Alexandria, and from there another two hundred kilometres to Cairo. The closer we came, the greater the journey seemed to become in both reality and absurdity.

We're going to a place where bombs rain from the sky, bullets fly in your face and mines explode under your feet. We're going off to get ourselves killed. Or perhaps William Hunt'll be right and it'll all be over when we get there and this trip'll turn out to be merely a long and useless excursion.

The heat was suffocating when we arrived at Cairo's outskirts. Most of the Libyans had gone to pieces, dehydrated and suffering from dysentery from drinking water in the wells of Bedouin camps. The stink and the heat were unbearable.

Karim was asleep, slumped against his brother. Nico was snoring, propped up against me. It was sunset by the time we entered the city proper. Everything said this wasn't in the least like a festive city celebrating a great victory.

Ahmed whispered to me in Italian, so as not to be overheard or understood.

It's over, Mikey. The war's over.

William Hunt's prediction had proved to be all too true. The war had been lost before we ever arrived. The further we got into Cairo, the greater the scale of the tragedy became apparent, from the slowly growing crowd of refugees fleeing from the Israeli airforce bombs in Sinai, even leaving their shoes behind so as to run more quickly over the desert sand. We woke Nico and Karim up from their heavy sleep as we drove through the hellish sight of destitute people.

Whole families were out in the Cairo streets to help the refugees, offering them whatever they had in the house: from bread, flour and rice to vegetables and meat. And yet the radios turned up full blast in the bars continued broadcasting the now scarcely credible hymns of Arab glory, which the Egyptian people were finding out were pitiful lies. Old people were crowding the windows and balconies, looking in fear towards the horizon in the east, in fear of seeing the Star of David on the oncoming armoured cars.

Evil-smelling rubbish littered the streets: plastic sacks, broken washing machines, piles of rotting fruit and vegetables picked over by beggars and ravaged by huge rats. Barefoot children kicked balls of rags about among the dung of horses and asses. The muezzin's plaintive cry calling for evening prayers was the only sound in a city which in three days had plummeted from euphoria to desperation.

We arrived at the barracks in an ugly square on the edge of the Christian quarter of Muqattam. The head of the Libyans, whose rank I could never make out, got down and went up to an Egyptian soldier, who had every intention of keeping the entrance barrier firmly lowered. He told the Libyan in no uncertain terms that we should get back to Tripoli. The Sinai front had been routed, the Golan Heights and Gaza Strip already lost.

When our officer asked for food and lodging for us before undertaking the long return trip, the Egyptian sentry simply laughed in his face.

'You've not got it, brother. There's no food or place to sleep in Cairo. Refugees are arriving in tens of thousands from everywhere, fleeing from the Israelis. Go back to Libya right now.'

There seemed nothing else to do. But Ahmed and Karim had relatives in Cairo, cousins of their father, Mohammed.

'Let's go to them,' Karim suggested. 'There's so much help needed here!'

'If they can let us sleep on the floor and give us a bowl of soup, we can all go back tomorrow,' said Nico.

'And how can we go back?' Ahmed asked.

He was right: how could we get back? And go back where?

We became lost in the unbelievable labyrinthine confusion of the old part of the city. Only after a mass of signs did we get to the square behind the Al Azhar Mosque where the Islamic University stood.

By now it was dark. The square was full of young and poorly clad Egyptian soldiers, many barefoot after losing their boots in Sinai during the retreat. There was rage in the Muslim quarter, the refugees shouting at the fruit- and vegetable sellers to give them something to eat for free.

'Our uncle's house must be on the other side of the square,' Ahmed said.

It would be an inconvenience if I suddenly appeared in a Muslim household where there were women and little girls who would have to cover themselves on my arrival.

'You and Karim go; Nico and I'll wait for you here. Then you can give us a shout.'

'Okay, Mikey,' said Ahmed as they set off. 'We'll be back soon.'

Even in the middle of that hubbub Nico was drawn to the cinema posters, which were more numerous than in Tripoli. He went wandering about the square, gazing up around him, just like a tourist would. Meanwhile, I was starving hungry. My stomach finally relaxed at the thought of not having to go and fight at the front, but it was still empty. I went up to a stall and bought a kilo of apples. Then I walked slowly over to the other side of the square to where Nico was wandering about among the piles of filth in front of a billboard for *Lawrence of Arabia*.

All of a sudden, three Egyptian soldiers surrounded me. One of them, the only one armed with an old Russian pistol, stuck the barrel in my ribs and pushed me into a dark alley. The most they could have been was two or three years older than I was. The only one with boots was the one with the pistol. The second was wearing flip-flops, and the third leather babouches of two different colours.

They pushed me down to the back of the alley, which ended in a two-metre-high wall. The feeble light from the few houses and shops gave barely any illumination.

They took away my bag of apples. Then the one with the pistol barked out, '*Filuss, dollars!*'[*] while the other two each held me by an arm.

I knew they intended to take my money and then kill me. It was the simplest way for them. There were no witnesses and, in Cairo at that time, no one would have gone looking for my killers.

I slowly began to close up the distance from the one with the gun, but I was too far away to kick it away with a *tae*. Then, at the other end of the alley, where it met the square, I saw the familiar outline of Ahmed. He was coming towards us alone, shuffling along like a dishevelled and unshaven Omar Sharif.

One of the two holding my arms let go and went up to him.

'*Dhahab, walad!*'[†] he ordered.

---

[*] 'Money, dollars!' (author's note)

[†] 'Get lost, kid!' (author's note)

Ahmed put on a seventeen-year-old's innocuous air and idiotic grin. He took a couple more steps forward, then said in Italian, 'Take the one with the gun!' As he let go a *tae* kick to the chin of the soldier who had gone up to meet him, I simultaneously launched a *tae* kick at the chest of the soldier with the weapon.

There was a sound of breaking teeth, jaw and ribs, accompanied by cries of pain. While the other two were moaning on the ground, clutching broken bones, the third terrified Egyptian tried to move towards the square.

But he found Nico and Karim blocking his path. It was Nico who landed him among the refuse with a *kwon* to the temple.

Karim looked on, appalled at a sight he never wanted to witness. As a fervent supporter of Egypt's troops, he now saw them lying in front of him, laid out flat by the others in the blood brotherhood.

Ahmed went up to the soldier on the ground and pulled the knife out of his pocket. It was no longer the Swiss army knife he had used to scare Don Eugenio but a beautiful one with a saw blade about ten centimetres long used for filleting fish.

'No, brother!' Karim blurted out.

'Quiet,' Ahmed ordered. Then he looked me in the eye. He needed my approval.

'If we let them go, they'll only report us, Mikey. And here, they'll shoot us as soon as look at us.'

Perhaps this had always been written in our destinies, in our genes, in our endless solitary afternoons skewering scorpions, shooting doves, spearing grouper and learning martial arts.

I won't become an engineer like Alberto and my father, not even a petrol-pump attendant like Nico. Laura was right: I'll end up a gangster with Ahmed.

I had no wish to kick the bucket because of those three desperadoes in that filthy back alley in a city that was not ours.

Ahmed grabbed the soldier from behind by his hair, just as he had held the dog that had bitten Jet.

I tried to say no, but the word wouldn't come out. It stayed locked in my brain while Ahmed calmly slit the man's carotid artery.

One of the others was trying to recover the gun. Nico picked it up and pointed it at him.

'No, Nico,' said Ahmed. 'It'll make too much noise.'

So Nico gave him another fearful *kwon* on the point of his chin, and the Egyptian fell like a sack of potatoes.

Ahmed went up to the two now on the ground.

No witnesses.

This time I didn't even look while he slit their throats. First one, then the other, without a moment's hesitation.

We quickly left the alley. But now we knew where our brotherhood of blood and sand was leading us.

Friday, 9 June 1967

Next morning, Ahmed and Karim's aunt prepared a breakfast for us of dry bread, tea and nuts. Then we went out into the teeming square. It was full of all kinds of traffic: men, soldiers, women wrapped in their barracans, donkey carts, goats. Many carts were full of trunks, battered suitcases, furniture and piles of clothes, as refugees were coming into Cairo in their thousands from the Israeli-occupied territories.

But, despite the Arabs' defeat, Karim was optimistic.

'We had to try. Nasser's still a hero. We'll get to Tel Aviv next time.'

I turned to Ahmed. He was looking affectionately at his younger brother, who was so like him physically and yet so different in his ideas.

Karim was his brother related by blood, while I was his blood brother by pact and the one with the same ideas and rage inside.

'We have to go back to Tripoli, Karim. Our mother'll be worried,' Ahmed said to him.

Karim looked at me, unhappy at the thought of asking me a favour.

'Mikey, can you tell my father?'

'Tell him what, Karim?'

'I want to stay here and help these poor people. I want to go to the Muslim Brotherhood's Islamic school.'

'Don't even think about it,' Ahmed cut in. 'You're coming back to Tripoli with us today.'

Karim looked at his brother.

'I'm not going back, Ahmed. You can kill me if you want and take my dead body back home instead.'

Ahmed remained calm.

'Go and take a walk with Nico, Karim. I'm going to have a word with Mikey. Come back in half an hour.'

Nico put a muscular arm round Karim and led him away.

Ahmed and I set off on a tour through the back alleys. The defeated city was swarming about us with an indescribable human chaos of life, a flotsam and jetsam of carts, donkeys, goats, bicycles, filth and noise.

Neither of us spoke. Between the two of us there was no need. We knew we had killed three people and had done it solely to protect ourselves. Or was there anything more to it than that?

'Do you want my parents to persuade your father?' I asked him.

I already knew what Ahmed's reply would be.

'I'll never leave Karim here by himself.'

I smiled at him. I showed him the scar on my left wrist. It was whiter and less deep than the one on his right. But it was from these marks that the blood had flowed and mingled together.

I remembered Laura Hunt's light kiss when she was saying good-bye to me.

That was only a promise; if she really wants me she'll wait for me. We have a pact here that can't be broken.

Monday, 26 June 1967

I phoned my grandfather. He spoke to Mohammed and my parents. They all came to Egypt as soon as the authorities opened the borders and the airport: my mother, my grandfather, Mohammed and Nico's mother, Santuzza. Even my brother, Alberto, came over from Rome. Everyone but Ingegnere Balistreri. It appeared Papa had no wish to speak to his crazy younger son.

As it was practically impossible to find a bed for the night in Cairo, they came on the first morning flight from Tripoli, intending to return that same evening. A cousin of Mohammed's – a close relative whom Ahmed and Karim referred to as their uncle – had an old bus, and we went to pick them up because there were no taxis. During the trip from the airport to his house we drove through a city as alive as it ever was, but devastated by poverty.

Drawing near to the Egyptian uncle's house, we saw that the Al Azhar park, the Islamic University and its mosque were one entire encampment teeming with refugees: ragged barefoot people with rickety handcarts full of household goods and furnishings.

My mother touched the Egyptian uncle's shoulder.

'I'd like to do the last bit on foot, by myself with Mikey.'

He was worried. 'Signora, it's dangerous. It's full of desperate, destitute people . . .'

My mother had never been afraid of destitute people.

If anything, the people she feared were the rich.

'With Mikey for protection, nothing will happen to me.'

After taking out all the money she had, she left her bag on the bus and we stepped off into the crowd. Before even a minute had passed we were surrounded by people begging.

'*Baksheesh, filuss!*'★

Italia handed out coins to the children and banknotes to the women. When the money was all gone, she went into a goldsmith's and, speaking in Arabic, made a deal for the necklace and bracelet she was wearing, everything except her wedding ring. She gave out that money as well, besieged and followed by an ever-growing swarm of people begging.

Only when it became clear that the money really was finished did they all disperse.

I watched the scene in the way, as a child, I had imagined Jesus performed the miracle of feeding the five thousand. When it was over, this elegant woman – her features prematurely aged, a kaftan covering her painfully white skin, her eyes hidden by large sunglasses – broke into tears.

'There's nothing you can do, Mamma. There's too many of them.'

She pretended not to hear me. She had made her decision.

'You can stay here, Mikey, but I want you to continue your education. There's an Italian state school and, here, your expulsion has no validity. If you work, you can finish your education in two years.'

So it had already been decided. We could stay in Cairo, but on certain conditions.

★ 'Alms, money!' (author's note)

We gave each other a hug.

'I promise, Mamma. I'll finish secondary school here, and the other three will as well.'

Italia smiled.

'You'll become inseparable, the four of you!'

We already are, Mamma. We've made a brotherhood of sand and blood. It can't be dissolved now.

INTERMEZZO

July 1967–July 1969

Thanks to the money my mother regularly sent, Nico and I were able to find a small room to rent in Al Azhar. Ahmed and Karim were living with their uncle and went to the Islamic school, while Nico and I went to the Italian one. We had promised our parents that we would study, and we did it seriously, going to school every morning.

But for the rest of the time Cairo was all ours: twenty times larger than Tripoli, teeming with life, drama. And opportunities for recreational activities – and there were plenty to cater for all tastes.

Karim devoted himself body and soul to Muslim Brotherhood meetings for helping the refugees. The cemetery became a residential quarter, with families occupying the funeral chapels. Gradually, the gas rings and cylinders arrived and electric cables hung down from the lamp posts and the chapels with do-it-yourself connections.

Every afternoon, Nico went to the cinema, a different film each day. Then he went to the barber to have his wretched curls straightened and his black bristly beard shaved, and then he was off to visit Cairo's many bordellos. He went there to look, and no more, because he had no money to purchase the goods.

One day, Mikey, I'll buy them all.

Ahmed and I stayed together all the time. Each afternoon, we went to a gym for three hours of martial arts and then we explored the defeated city's endless districts. It was a special time and place, a world to reconstruct, full of opportunity – particularly for the likes of us, who had never worked in an office or a shop.

'We can't just keep on being schoolkids and looking after Karim and Nico,' we said.

It was my idea to start a business, but it was Ahmed who was able to develop it. We began with what we knew best. Ahmed was the organizer, Nico was an excellent driver and Karim had the right contacts in the Alexandria fish market, through the Muslim Brotherhood. Ahmed and myself were aces at underwater fishing, either free diving or scuba, and, among the things my mother had sent us, were our underwater spear guns.

We left for Alexandria on a Friday night in the coach borrowed from the Egyptian uncle, fished all Saturday, sold the catch at the Sunday-morning fish market and were back in Cairo on Sunday evening.

And the money began coming. It was only a little, but enough for our needs. I didn't need it at all, really, but I wanted to show my father that I could do without him.

Then a second idea arose from Karim's complaints.

'These refugees need a job, some future prospects,' he was always declaring.

'You're right,' we said to him, 'but Egypt's on its knees and there's no work here. All they can do is go begging or die of starvation.'

Then, one day, I came up with a different answer.

'We'll take them to where there's work. Only those who can work, mind. We can help their families to stay and survive here by taking the young men off to work.'

'But where?' asked Nico.

'In Libya, where there *is* work and we know the ground,' I answered.

Karim protested.

'But that's illegal, Mikey. And it's immoral to exploit those poor guys.'

I looked at Ahmed and, after a moment, he smiled.

Illegal? Immoral? We've killed three people. We've gone well beyond those words.

'We won't ask the refugees to pay us, but the employers in Libya can,' said Ahmed.

His mind set to work. He would take on the task of finding the first work for the refugees in Tobruk, just over the border with Egypt.

And the project went extremely well. In those two years after the Egyptian defeat of June 1967, the four of us set about work seriously and without the need of setting up a business with invoices and book-keeping. It was all strictly cash, which we kept in the Egyptian uncle's house.

With the first cash we bought a red Fiat 850T: a seven-seater camper van nearly four metres long with sliding doors and a tailgate at the back. Nico adapted it for our purposes. He brought forward the second row of seats and, immediately behind it, inserted a partition wall, leaving only the first of the three side windows with glass and covering the other windows and rear doors with metal sheeting. We could fit five passengers in the seats, and up to six clandestine workers crammed in the rear.

On one side of the van he painted the letters 'MANK', the name of our organization, formed from our four initials, and put up a Barbra Streisand poster in the back.

'When I'm older, I'll manage a star like her and then marry her.'

We laughed at such an idiotic idea, but it was then that Nico began to spend his money on the girls in the bordellos. The opportunities for girls had grown in Cairo, but he'd decided that paying for it was best way of avoiding having to speak to them. So his lisp was kept a secret, and no whore would dare laugh at his eyebrows and hair. I took him to task over it and said that women were to be won over, not bought, and that he could win them over. His body hair was a sign of virility and his lisp had almost disappeared. But Nico had formed his own idea of women, and it would never change.

'They're all alike, Mikey. They're all whores. You buy them a cinema ticket and a Coca-Cola; I buy their services up front.'

My sex life in those two years was very occasional and unsatisfying. The girls were boring and all the same. I found them small-minded, but I knew this was not the case with all of them. The problem was that Laura Hunt was the centre of my poetic attention, while, for some time, her mother had begun to feed a very different kind of fantasy. I had this feeling every time I saw them when I went back to Tripoli for a few days.

During that time we also bought motorbikes at knock-down prices owing to their dubious provenances and thanks to Karim's contacts.

Mine was a 1950 Triumph Thunderbird 6T, the one Marlon Brando rode in *The Wild One*; Nico's was a 1965 Moto Guzzi Stornello Sport, not a powerful engine, but very slick with its white petrol tank and red tubular frame; and Ahmed bought a 1966 Ducati Scrambler, a bike you could cross the desert with. These were our alternative transport to the comings and goings in the MANK van.

Karim evidently did not immediately share our fascination for motorbikes and used part of his money to help the Egyptian refugees.

And, in those two years, Mohammed, my parents and Nico's mother made occasional visits to Cairo. Everyone came except my father, whom I saw only when I went back to Tripoli for Easter and Christmas, and even then I only spoke to him about my studies and never about our MANK organization. It was better to be cautious with him.

In May 1969, a new business opportunity came up. Karim suggested buying a small restaurant on the Nile. The price was excellent, thanks to the good offices of his friends, the Muslim Brotherhood. We thought it over for a while, then the unanimous decision was taken in favour and we stopped with the refugees and the fishing.

So, by June 1969, after two years spent in Cairo, MANK became a legal enterprise. We were four young entrepreneurs in the restaurant business. Nothing that important, but enough to get by on.

Enough not to have to depend on Salvatore Balistreri for money.

PART II

Sunday, 20 July 1969

It came as a complete surprise when all four of us passed our final-year exams, Nico and I even getting our national *maturità* diploma from Cairo's Italian high school without Papa having to do any behind-the-scenes manipulation.

Everyone came over from Tripoli to celebrate: Mamma, Grandad, Alberto, Santuzza, Mohammed and even my father.

Ingegner Balistreri was actually taking some trouble on my behalf.

Perhaps his son isn't a failure. Perhaps he can still make up for lost time.

That evening, we went to our restaurant on the Nile, the Balistreri and Al Bakri families, together with Nico and his mother. We had a meal of fish fresh from Alexandria and the typical dish of greens, *molokhiyyah,* followed by dates. The atmosphere was so upbeat and happy I thought everything would finally be settled for the future.

Mamma would stop her excessive drinking and smoking. Laura and I would start courting seriously. Papa would be proud when I told him that I had not only passed my exams but also started up in business.

'So,' my father asked, 'what exactly is this MANK organization?'

Of course, he'd seen the letters Nico painted on the van. Or did he know already?

Everyone turned to look at me.

'We'll tell you after supper,' I replied.

Papa changed tactics and direction. He turned to Nico.

'Now that you've finished high school and are coming back to Tripoli, I'm going to give you the Esso station and help you build a large workshop that will be all yours.'

I was not happy with this. What he was offering Nico was simply bait to draw us away from Cairo.

Papa hasn't given up. He wants me back in Tripoli. And then at university in Rome.

When it came time to pay the bill, my father took out his wallet.

I placed my hand over his. 'You don't need to, Papa. This restaurant belongs to us.'

As ever, I had underestimated Ingegner Salvatore Balistreri.

'I'm well aware of it, Mikey. It's owned by this MANK organization. That's why I want to pay.'

All the others – with the exception of Mohammed – were taken aback. Of course, Mohammed was my father's Egyptian antenna, getting his information through the cousin in Cairo that had put us up. Everyone was now looking at us with different eyes, a mixture of amazement and admiration. Everyone except Papa and Mohammed, that is.

They know about everything, including the less legitimate side of MANK's activities.

'Aren't you happy, Papa?' I asked him as we left the restaurant.

He took me by the arm.

'Of course, Mikey. Happy and proud. Now that you've graduated from high school, you can go to university in Rome, just like Alberto.'

I felt my feet beginning to sink in quicksand. I was almost nineteen, and my father cared not a damn about what I really wanted to do.

'Papa, business is going well here in Cairo. I like the city and I want to carry on living in Africa.'

And I detest Italy. A country governed by the priesthood, with the workers always taking to the streets and students daubing their university walls with the hammer and sickle. That's not for me at all.

Ingegner Balistreri brushed it all away with a gesture and a few words. All of it. MANK's small business operation, my dreams, everything I really was.

He pointed to Ahmed, Karim and Nico, who were sharing a joke near the camper van.

'Leave that kind of thing to them, Mikey. You and Alberto are destined for much more important things.'

And, looking at the van, I realized how pathetic we must have seemed to him. Two years of work to open a little eating-house on the Nile, in a city still recovering from disaster.

But there were things about me that Papa did not know. Like the murder of three Egyptian soldiers.

I had done everything in order to find myself, get a life and create a space for myself. And a point of contact with my father. But it was hopeless. I could have – and should have – told him to go to hell. But then there was my mother, Grandad, Alberto. And there was Laura Hunt. The way her lips had brushed mine on the day I left.

End of July, 1969

When our families had gone back to Tripoli, the four members of the MANK organization talked things over at length as we smoked a *shisha*. Karim would not hear of going back. He had the war refugees to help – in particular those living in the cemetery, that city of both the living and the dead. Nico did not want to give up his cinema and his whores, and he had found a hairdresser in Cairo he could trust to straighten out his bushy head of curls.

We came up with a compromise solution. As far as our restaurant was concerned, August was a dead month, so we might as well spend it with our families in Tripoli. We could then come back to Egypt in September. In a week, we arranged for the trustworthiest of our employees to carry on the business in our absence and also to ship our bikes out to us.

We left for Tripoli in the red camper van, taking turns driving, one at the wheel, one keeping him company, the other two stretched out to sleep on the back seat and on the camping mat behind the partition – the place where Nico screwed the whores he picked up off the street.

Not that we could sleep, bouncing over the road's many potholes.

Boiling-hot gusts of wind blew into the open windows while we alternately played Arab music and Leonard Cohen on the tape deck.

It was a magical trip, though; even Nico and Karim got along, with interminable discussions that ranged from refugees to whores, Nasser and Moshe Dayan to Elizabeth Taylor and Sophia Loren.

We stopped at El Alamein for a brief half an hour to walk in silence among the tombs there, and saw the epitaphs of the Folgore Division, the young men of the parachute division my mother had told me about:

They fell for an ideal with no regrets, honoured in memory by their enemy, and mark a pathway of honour and glory for the Italian people in both good and adverse fortune.

I wondered what my father thought about these young men.

Friday, 1 August 1969

We were now back in Tripoli. The Hunt family was due to arrive from the United States, where they had spent the whole of July. I had taken a few days to adapt to Tripoli's tranquil rhythms and also to reflect.

That Friday, with the air conditioning on maximum, I was having breakfast alone in the living room. A wind from the desert was bringing in the first signs of sand that heralded the *ghibli* forecast for the weekend. In the forecourt before the two villas, the frogs, grasshoppers and scorpions had taken refuge under the shade of the eucalyptus and palms.

Nadia was pouring caffè latte into my cup. Now that she was fifteen, we employed her as a maid. Each morning, she walked the two kilometres of dirt path through the bare countryside from Mohammed's wooden shack to the Balistreri villa and arrived at exactly half past eight. She first made coffee for my mother, then breakfast for everyone else.

She was always hovering around me, as she had done since she was little. She was obliged by her religion and her father to wear a costume that covered her entire body and wear a veil on her head that left only one eye uncovered. But you could feel that underneath the veil was a beautiful face and under the costume was a body as slim and graceful as those of her brothers.

'Would you like more nuts, Signor Mikey?'

Even when she was little and came over to play, hoping for a role in one of my films, she used to call me 'Signor'. Mohammed must have instructed her to do so. She served me the best toasted peanuts, knowing how much I loved them.

'No thanks, Nadia. Do you like this job?'

'Of course, Signor Mikey. The only thing I don't like is walking along the path by the cesspit.'

'Are you still frightened because they found that young black woman and her baby there all those years ago?'

She was taken aback for a moment. Something had struck her in what I said.

'Were they black, Signor Mikey?'

It had slipped out like that, without my thinking. So many years had passed. Classified or not, the information was old and pretty useless. I told her to prove that we were friends, even if we did employ her as a servant.

'It's supposed to be a secret, Nadia. Can you keep a secret?'

'Yes, Signor Mikey. So they were black?'

'They were. They weren't sure if the baby was a girl or boy, the bodies were too decayed. But they were black.'

'I think the little one was a baby girl.'

Saturday, 2 August 1969

At nine o'clock on its second day, the *ghibli* was blowing strongly. I headed for the Hunt's house, attracted by the smells of French toast and bacon. I was hoping to see Laura, but there was only William Hunt, sitting alone in the large kitchen.

He had come back from the United States with Laura and Marlene the day before, but I had not seen him since I left for Cairo.

'Hi, Mikey, come on in. Marlene's out for a run, despite the *ghibli*. Laura has an upset tummy. One of those girl things. So it's just me here, all on my own.'

'OK, I'll go back home, Mr Hunt. Sorry to bother you.'

'Won't you have breakfast with me? I'm having it in the kitchen because there's too much damned sand outside, but we have corn-flakes, French toast, bacon, pancakes.'

The invitation took me by surprise. I had never been alone with Mr Hunt, and he had never shown any particular liking for me. His preference was obviously for Alberto. But it was difficult to refuse.

'Oh, well, thank you, Mr Hunt. I'd like that.'

We began eating in silence. It seemed impossible to think of any subject we had in common that we could chat about, as he and

Alberto did about international politics and the Vietnam War. But William Hunt had something on his mind.

'You like Laura, don't you?' he suddenly asked me.

Now I knew where Laura's habit of asking direct questions came from. But it was difficult to know how to reply.

'Laura takes beautiful pictures. She'll become a real professional one day.'

'Isn't there anything else you like about her?'

Again, I was lost for words. I stared at the bowl of cornflakes.

Here was a man who'd never stand for any 'bullshit', as the Americans said.

'She's very beautiful, Mr Hunt.'

He laughed.

'Of course, she takes after Marlene, who's also a beautiful woman. Don't you think?'

This was too much for me. In fact, I was reeling from the shock of it.

'Laura's very serious, as well.'

William Hunt abandoned his implications about Marlene and took up the compliment about Laura.

'She's taken that from me, Mikey. She has the qualities of both her parents.'

'And the defects?'

I had given it some thought, I believed. But the question just slipped out.

He did not bat an eyelid. Rather, for the first time since I had known him, William Hunt deigned to look at me with real interest. He thought about it for some time, as if the question needed a well-considered reply. Then he said something surprising.

'Marlene hasn't defects at all. As for mine, I really do hope Laura hasn't inherited those.'

Not to see any defect in Marlene meant either being blind or deluded. But William Hunt seemed neither the one nor the other. As to his defects, I had no idea what he meant.

'Your Uncle Toni died in the war, didn't he, Mikey?'

Now I could follow him.

His defects. The pointless sacrifice of heroes like Toni, like those in the Folgore Division, like his friends who'd died in Korea and Vietnam.

'Yes, sir. And you fought against the Communists in Korea, didn't you?'

I knew what I had been told: a little from my mother, a little from Laura. A desperate battle against 300,000 Chinese, a human avalanche that swept down upon the South Koreans and the Americans, including the X Corps of Marines. The Yalu River was frozen, there was a single wretched bridge, dead bodies everywhere and endless prisoners and civilians. At Ch'osan Reservoir, the Marines were surrounded. A few men parachuted in to help, William Hunt among them.

Heroes. Men ready to die for their principles.

William Hunt nodded. He was tracing memories that could not have been pleasant.

'War's ugly, Mikey. It leads you to do things you'd never, ever want to do. It changes you, for ever.'

At that moment, Marlene came back from jogging, dripping with sweat. She popped her head into the kitchen, waved a hand at us and went upstairs, while I avoided following that exceptional body with my eyes.

William Hunt got up. His orderly had arrived in a jeep to take him to Wheelus.

'I know you read Nietzsche, Mikey. So you'll know that there are no essentially *moral* things, only moral *interpretations* of things.'

He went out and climbed into the jeep, leaving me alone in the kitchen, half speechless in front of my French toast and eggs and bacon.

Ten minutes later, I was still eating in the Hunt's kitchen when Marlene came in. She had changed out of her shorts and running vest and was now in a bikini, ready to go and sunbathe on the veranda. I tried not to look at her. I had already had enough dealing with her husband's bout of dialectics.

'Thank goodness you're here, Mikey. Laura's asleep. I could do with a hand.'

She handed me the sunblock and I stared at it in the middle of a bite of French toast. She turned away, went out of the kitchen and stopped in front of a mirror. With one hand, she lifted her hair off the nape of her neck and held it there. With the other she lit a cigarette, her green eyes watching me in the mirror.

'Come on, Mikey, let's be quick.'

I tried to protest.

'But on the veranda there's the *ghibli*. You'll be covered in sand.'

She laughed, with that extraordinary mouth and those eyes that made you feel as if you were the only man in the world.

'So I'll become a beautiful breaded cutlet, won't I? Do you like cutlets, Mikey?'

I felt my forehead in flames and my legs turn to jelly. I spread a little cream around her neck, then stopped. She looked at me in the mirror, the cigarette hanging from the corner of those fulsome lips.

'And the rest? Do you want me to get sunburn all down my back?'

I spread cream on her shoulders, avoiding her gaze in the mirror. When I reached the strap of the bikini top I stopped again.

'You'll have to undo it, otherwise it'll leave a stripe.'

She said it just like that, absolutely casually. Naturally, the two damned hook and eye closures were impossible to undo with my nervous hands. She stared at me in the mirror.

'You're almost nineteen, Mikey. You must have undone a bra or two. Is it me who's making you feel uncomfortable?'

You don't make me feel uncomfortable. You shake me to the very roots, day and night, when I wake up in a sweat imagining you naked on the veranda.

She put out the cigarette, threw her long hair forwards over her shoulder, brought her arms behind her back, and her hands guided mine to the hooks and eyes. I felt my hands trembling as I undid them. She took her hands away so that she could hold the top of the bikini over her magnificent breasts.

I closed my eyes, praying that she would not turn round and see the large bulge in my jeans. I began spreading the cream with both hands, up and then down, getting ever closer to the elastic of the bikini bottom.

An uncrossable border, the entrance to a forbidden paradise.

Perhaps it was my imagination, but she let out a tiny groan of pleasure.

Pleased to have me in her power. Completely.

'It should be my husband doing this, but he's always at work or travelling. And here am I alone, in the middle of all this sand.'

Her voice wavered between joking and bitterness, as if she were walking along a narrow plank, not knowing on which side she might fall.

'I'm sorry,' I said stupidly.

'What are you sorry about, Michelino?' Now there was a scornful tone to her voice.

I had arrived at the edge of the bikini bottom. I felt the elastic under my fingertips. I tried to lower it in my mind, but failed.

'I'm sorry, but I have to go now.'

I had no idea what I was saying. In horror, I heard my adolescent voice turn raucous and guttural, wavering in pitch in my excitement.

She fastened the bikini top and suddenly turned round, facing me. I was one metre eighty and taller than she was by several centimetres, and yet I felt like a child caught in flagrante, red-faced and dumbstruck. I was terrified by the thought of the erection pressing against my jeans and prayed she would not notice it.

Marlene stared straight into me for a moment with those eyes that made you feel as if you were the only man in the world. And the most stupid.

'You have beautiful hands, Mikey. You use them well. Perhaps we can do this again.'

She gave me a little pat on the chest with two fingers and, as I felt the electric shock waves running through my body, she turned away and went off up the stairs.

I stopped at the edge of that bikini bottom as if on the edge of an abyss.

When I came out, despite the *ghibli*, my father was chatting in the garden with Don Eugenio, Emilio Busi and Mohammed. Four pairs of eyes followed me with curiosity while I waved a hand at them and – pretending there was nothing wrong – went off in the opposite direction.

That Saturday evening, we celebrated our return from Cairo and the Hunts' from the United States. At dinner, the fish had been caught by Salim the night before and cooked by Farid, who extolled its freshness as if he were selling it on the market.

Inside the villa, the windows were firmly shut and the air conditioners on maximum. Outside, the *ghibli* was slowing in intensity before its climax on the third and final day.

It was a notable gathering. The entire Bruseghin–Balistreri, Hunt and Al Bakri families; Nico and his mother, Santuzza; Emilio Busi and Don Eugenio. Twenty happy people.

Everyone, that is, except my mother. She had aged a great deal in the two years I had spent in Cairo. It was as if an illness were slowly eating away at her. Thin lines had appeared in her pale complexion and also many white strands in her short blonde hair. She was now as thin as Marlene Hunt, except that Marlene was all tone and curve while Italia was only skin and bone.

At the end of dinner my father asked for a moment of silence. He had an announcement to make.

'Tomorrow, boys, we're going fishing. There's a bank of shallows around La Moneta that's good for both underwater fishing and inshore trolling. It was Salim who suggested the place.'

Even Alberto was concerned.

'Papa, there'll be a hell of a heat. The *ghibli*'s blowing at twenty knots.'

'Precisely. It'll be an inferno in these villas with all this sand about. It'll be a little better in Tripoli, but it'll be a lot less hot out at sea on that stretch of water.'

It was clear my father was keen on it. That island was the new jewel in his crown. But Nico pointed out a problem as well.

'Tomorrow they're going to close the Sidi El Masri road into Shara Ben Ashur and the Garden City from ten till one, and you won't be able to get into Tripoli. There's a folklore festival with a camel parade from the Cathedral to Piazza Italia. Italian television will be there.'

Nico was always well informed about these things, but my father was not to be discouraged.

'Then we'll have to get into the city before ten. I'll go with Alberto and Grandad to Don Eugenio's for Mass tomorrow instead of to the cathedral, then I'll go to the barber next to the market in Shara Mizran. You'll remember my paper, won't you, Nico?'

Among the new duties my father had Nico perform was bringing him the *Giornale di Tripoli* hot off the press to the barber's at eight o'clock every Sunday morning. That was his usual opening time, but for Ingegner Balistreri he opened fifteen minutes earlier in order to trim his beard and moustache straight after Mass. Then Papa went to sit on the terrace of the Waddan Hotel with his newspaper to have breakfast and chat with the important Italians for a couple of hours.

'Of course, Ingegnere, not to worry.'

'On the dot, Nico, if you please.'

'We'll have to refill the cylinders, though,' said Salim. 'You can fish really well on the bottom of the shallows there.'

I was not enthusiastic, either about going fishing during the *ghibli* or getting up at an ungodly hour for the cylinders.

'It's already half past midnight. I'm not getting up before nine. We can do without the cylinders.'

As usual, my father thought me a slacker. He turned to Ahmed as if I had not said a word.

'Will you see to them, Ahmed?'

'All right. If Nico leaves them at the petrol station, I'll pick them up tomorrow morning.'

'OK,' said Nico. 'I'll put them in the van tonight and drop by the station towards eight fifteen. You can take over, then I can come to the villa to collect Alberto and Mikey.'

All this activity was getting on my nerves.

'Not too soon, Nico. I said I wanted to sleep.'

My father gave me a dirty look, but Alberto came to my defence.

'There's no hurry. Nico and I'll have breakfast together and, as soon as Mikey's ready, we'll set off for Tripoli before they close the road.'

Now my father was happy. He turned to Busi. 'We'll see each other at the barber's?'

'No, this time I'm with Mikey, I want some sleep. I'll meet you at the Waddan at ten.'

Papa looked at the Americans.

'William?'

Hunt shook his head.

'Thanks, but we can't. Tomorrow at Wheelus there's the final of the baseball championship, together with a brunch. Laura, Marlene and I never miss it. We'll be back in the afternoon after the brunch.'

Papa was a little disappointed.

He wants to show off his new island to her.

'You'll see to the office, won't you, Mohammed?'

Sunday was a work day for the Arabs.

'Of course, Ingegnere. I'll be in the office as usual at eight thirty.'

'And you boys?' Papa asked Farid and Salim.

Farid brushed a hand through his frizzy hair and shook his head.

'Thanks, but we're going out fishing tonight and if Salim's on form I hope to be selling a good catch at the market tomorrow.'

Papa did not even ask my mother and Grandad. He knew that neither of them liked fishing. The Bruseghin were people of the earth and olives. She would stay at home in the villa with the air conditioning. After Mass, my grandfather would stroll around the market as usual and then go to the Italian Club for a game of *bocce*.

So that endless night finally came to an end, while the *ghibli* was gearing up for its third and final day.

Sunday, 3 August 1969

Morning

Born in the Sirtica coastal desert, Mohammed Al Bakri was fond of telling everyone about the wind. *The* ghibli *starts in the Sahara, from the dunes of the Calanshio Sand Sea. It blows softly at first, then more strongly. The third day is usually the worst.*

The four Al Bakri sons had done their best to seal the shack with thirty square metres of metal sheeting and some plasticine, an old gift from the Balistreri sons. Their shack had one advantage over true houses. Their floor was already made of sand, covered with mats. All the *ghibli* did was add a good deal more.

It was the sense of smell that confirmed Mohammed's prediction. By the middle of the night, the south wind had risen even earlier than usual and was picking up the smell from the cesspit that lay a few hundred metres from the shack.

Under normal conditions, Cuckoo the cockerel waited for dawn's first light to announce to his four hens and the world in general that he was up and about. And that this was his territory. On this morning, however, he crowed his cock-a-doodle-doo while the stars could still be seen in the sky and dawn was a milky glow on the horizon.

Nadia turned over on her bed base, covered in sweat. She had not slept a wink, what with the fetid smell and the whine of the *nnamus*, the large mosquitoes that came in with the *ghibli*. She was also thinking a lot about Michele Balistreri.

We share a secret together. We're friends.

She was careful not to disturb Ahmed and Karim, who were sleeping next to her on the other side of the old sheet that served as a curtain. Her two other brothers, Farid and Salim, were out night fishing and at that hour were bringing their boat into port. They could then exchange places with Ahmed and Karim on the traditional wooden beds.

The bed base Nadia slept on was placed directly on the floor matting. It was old, but the springs were still in good shape. Papa Mohammed had been given it by his employer.

There were no clocks in the house, only her father's wristwatch, an old Omega given to him by Ingegner Balistreri to be sure that he would get to work on time. Nadia wondered when it would be dawn. It was usually half past six at this time of year. Being the daughter, she was the first to rise, at seven sharp. She had to milk the goat and make tea for the men. Then she had to get ready herself and wake her father's two wives.

Nadia placed a hand on the shack's metal sheeting. It was hot. She guessed it was forty degrees. It would be fifty by midday. She got up and took a peep at the time on the Omega her father placed by the bed at night. Cuckoo had started crowing early. It was not yet six thirty. But in any case she would not be able to get back to sleep.

It had been a hell of a sleepless night, what with the *ghibli* whistling, the heat that came in even through the walls and dreams of Marlene Hunt and the elastic of her bikini bottoms.

I touched it with these fingers. The edge of the abyss.

I had survived the two years in Cairo on a poetic memory of my lips brushed by Laura Hunt's. But, underneath that, deep in my gut, it was Marlene's sensuality that set me on fire and kept me awake at night.

I was feeling groggy when the sound of my father's jeep woke me up completely. I looked out of the window towards the sandy forecourt whipped up by the wind. Papa was in the driving seat, Grandad next to him, Alberto in the rear. I looked at the time. It was six thirty.

The good side of the family was off to church.

At seven sharp Nadia dragged herself off the bed base and found she was covered in *feshfesh*, the very fine dust the *ghibli* carried in, so fine it obscured your vision and choked your breathing.

First thing she did was roll her nightgown right down to her ankles. On this point, Papa Mohammed was unbending. Since the time she had reached puberty, she had to keep her arms and legs covered, even in the home, out of respect for her father, brothers and half-brothers. Outside, she had to wear the barracan that covered her body down to the wrists and ankles. And now, at fifteen, she also had to wear the veil, with only one eye uncovered. How she would have liked to show Mikey her long hair dyed with henna. But she could not. Only the eye.

But she was very happy that he had come back to Tripoli. And that he had spoken to her, even confided a secret in her.

The young woman and the baby girl were black.

Of course, she had to be very careful not to appear a flirt. But Mikey would certainly show her respect, not like all the other Italian boys. Today, she would serve him breakfast before they went off fishing. She had some special toasted peanuts for him.

She had to hurry with the tea and the goat. She had to leave at eight in order to arrive on time for eight thirty at the Balistreri villa. In the shack, it was like being in a hot oven. She went barefoot across the single living space, divided by the sheet hanging from clothes pegs. On one side were the three women; on the other, three wooden beds for the men. There was no space for more beds.

When she went outside, a sliver of pale-yellow sun was beginning to show in the washed-out sky to the east. The *ghibli* caught her with its hot breath, the sand immediately hit her face and the flies, excited by the smell of dung, were buzzing around her.

Nadia slipped quickly into the wooden closet her father had built for the needs of his wives and daughter. It was an old toilet bowl from the Balistreri home but, without a soil pipe, the urine ran along a descending channel that ended up under the nearest olive tree. There was the chamber pot for faeces, which had to be taken immediately to the cesspit, otherwise the hungry flies arrived in their hundreds. Nevertheless, the women of the Al Bakri household were privileged in having an outside toilet, whereas the men had to see to their needs out in the open.

She urinated, then went over to the large, rusty tank. It was a metre square and held the water everyone washed in, protected by a tarpaulin. They changed the water every ten days, and only five days had elapsed since the last time, so it was still sufficiently clean. She rinsed her face and filled an enamel cup to wash her hands after milking the goat.

Barbetta was ready and waiting. She was the only goat they had and the chief source of sustenance, along with the wages Papa Mohammed received from Ingegnere Balistreri. Nadia milked the goat twice a day, at dawn and dusk. She placed herself behind it, and Barbetta gave her an affectionate bleat when she thought she had delivered enough milk. Nadia would then stroke her. Afterwards, she would rinse her hands in the enamel cup and see the goat was watered. She never wasted a drop of water. Conserving water was a real concern for Papa Mohammed, who almost died of thirst as a child when crossing the Sirtica desert to get to Tripoli.

The fresh milk had to be drunk straightaway. In that heat, and with no refrigerator, it would not even last until the afternoon. From one milking came five portions for the five men. Nadia and the two wives had to make do with tea.

Nadia went to the old two-ring gas stove under the little canopy, another generous cast-off from the Balistreri household. She turned on the gas cylinder and used the lighter Papa Mohammed lit his *shisha* with in the evening. She took a pan of water from a second, smaller tank, which held the drinking water. She put the pan on to boil and went back inside.

Making no noise, she took off her nightgown and placed it on the bed. They had no mirrors, so she always brushed her hands quickly over chest and hips to check them, careful that no one should see her. She had a slim and graceful body, and wondered if Michele Balistreri imagined how it was under the barracan. Then she became embarrassed at the thought and asked Allah's forgiveness. She decided to wear the midnight-blue one her father had given her for her fifteenth birthday, which suited her better, she thought.

The family had an old metal chest of drawers from the Ingegnere's offices. Seven drawers on either side; one side for the men and one for the women. She took out the summer barracan and a pair of large linen knickers, along with the band that went round her chest. When she heard the water boiling for the tea she went and shook her mother awake.

She would then wake the others according to the strict order laid down by Papa Mohammed, so that the women could have all their things done and be dressed by the time the men got up.

I had tried to put away the thought of Marlene Hunt's naked back and had fallen into a troubled half-sleep. In my half-sleep, Laura's and Marlene's faces had become superimposed, one blending into the other. But the half of me that was awake was desperately trying to tell me something.

That's not how it is, Mikey. You have to choose, or you'll lose both.

The noise of a car woke me. I looked out of the window and glimpsed William, Marlene and Laura getting into the jeep driven by Mr Hunt's orderly. They set off towards Tripoli. The last thing I saw in the whirlwind of sand was Marlene's glossy black hair, which fell down that glorious back of hers.

Nico Gerace said goodbye to his mother, giving her a kiss and a hug. He did this every morning and, as ever, asked her if she needed anything before he left the apartment in Via Lazio, Shara Mizran, near the market, which they had courtesy of Ingegner Balistreri.

Santuzza straightened her son's shirt collar and smelled the expensive cologne he splashed on his cheeks. She was proud of him. He was so elegant and clean when he could get out of his pump attendant's overalls and get rid of the smell of petrol.

He was still too hairy, but now he no longer lisped his 's' sounds and was much more self-confident. Those two years in Cairo had built up his self-esteem, perhaps even too much. But Santuzza liked her son like that, even if he was too cocky.

Nico left the flat around seven thirty. Down on the street, it was a boiling inferno. But, despite the *ghibli*, there was sufficient visibility.

There was also a lot of traffic, both pedestrian and vehicles, because of the Bedouin camel parade. Nico looked enthusiastically at the outside-broadcast van with the letters 'RAI', *Radio televisione italiana*, Italy's national television, which was on its way towards Piazza Italia, threading a route through the carriages, bicycles and carts.

He drove the MANK van and in less than five minutes parked it on Shara Mizran, opposite the market that had just opened for business. He went in and found Farid and Salim's stall among the general confusion. There was a huge crowd of people, everyone speaking at the top of their voices in Arabic or Italian.

Salim was telling Giuseppe Bruseghin and Alberto Balistreri about the enormous greater amberjack he had caught that night. Small and slender as he was, he had hooked it, let it tire itself out, then pulled it on board. As usual, Farid was busy selling and haggling prices with the customers and other fishermen. He was smoking a cigarette that hung between his fleshy lips, blowing the smoke out through his nostrils.

'I'm going to take the newspaper to your father,' Nico said to Alberto.

'I'll come with you,' said Alberto.

They said goodbye to Giuseppe, Farid and Salim and went out into the baking, sand-filled heat. Nico thought that Italian television would be happy with all this sand to have around the Bedouin and their camels. There was barely enough visibility, but this sand gave a taste of the real Africa.

Don Eugenio scrutinized the sky with distaste. In church, it was fine: you were cool and there was no sand. But the *ghibli* was blowing outside, and he had to drive to Sidi El Masri. He was wearing his usual worn cassock.

He had to go. He had made a commitment and a promise, both important. And Don Eugenio always kept his promises.

Despite his intentions of the night before, Emilio Busi woke up early and in an ugly mood because of the heat, the noise of the *ghibli* and the thoughts that would not leave him alone. He left his house behind the cathedral and went on foot towards the market, trying to protect his eyes and mouth from the sand. His long hair flapped around in the wind and his large horn-rimmed glasses acted as a screen.

He was dressed in his usual get-up of checked shirt, striped trousers, white socks, battered brown moccasins. He cared nothing for fishing – he was a mountain peasant – but he had to humour that show-off Balistreri and remove any last obstacles to their plans.

Alberto and Nico walked to the newsagent's, then to the barber's next door. They delivered the newspaper to Ingegnere Balistreri at eight on the dot, and then went back to the market without exchanging a single word along Shara Mizran. If you opened your mouth, it would be full of sand. They saw one of the RAI's outside-broadcast vans turning round towards the cathedral in Corso Italia.

At eight, Nadia and Mohammed were ready to go out. Ahmed and Karim were up and almost ready as well. They had to meet Nico at the Esso station at eight fifteen to fill the gas cylinders for the scuba diving.

Nadia saw Karim talking earnestly with Ahmed, but could not gather what it was about and went out with Mohammed. The sun was very pale in the chalk-white sky, the temperature forty-five degrees and visibility in the sand cloud down to five metres. In order to conserve energy, no one wasted any words. They said goodbye with a wave of the hand.

Mohammed got into his pick-up truck and left via the dirt track that ran along the olive grove and through the goat pastures to the metalled road for Shara Ben Ashur and Tripoli.

Nadia set off in the opposite direction through the two kilometres of bush and bare earth that led to the Balistreri villa. The two kilometres that she walked down sedately in half an hour and Marlene Hunt ran up and down four times in less than an hour.

At five past eight Alberto and Nico were back in the market. Giuseppe Bruseghin was still chatting away to Salim, while Farid was in loud and earnest conversation with a bunch of customers. The two brothers really did complement each other and were indefatigable workers: Salim fished by night and Farid sold by day. They both worked with a violent passion, as if success would somehow redeem them in the eyes of the world from being poor.

Alberto went up to his grandfather.

'Grandad, Nico and I are going back to Sidi El Masri. Do you want a lift?'

His grandfather said goodbye to Farid and Salim and left the market with them. The traffic on Shara Mizran was still passable.

'Don't you want to stay here?' Nico asked Giuseppe. 'It'll be much worse out in the countryside.'

'Aren't you boys going fishing?' Giuseppe asked.

'Yes, Grandad. Papa's set his heart on it.'

'Salvatore's right. It'll be much better out at sea. I'll get a coffee at the Italian Club and then perhaps watch the camel parade. I'll get someone to give me a lift. You go and wake up Mikey.'

Alberto and Nico got into the MANK van, and set off along Shara Ben Ashur, towards Sidi El Masri, in order to avoid Corso Vittorio and the cathedral square, into which the crowds were pouring for the camel parade.

Away from the sea, visibility became worse. The two golden domes of the royal palace could barely be seen and, as they were travelling through the Garden City, the downpour of red-hot sand struck the windscreen and sides of the van like tiny hailstones.

It took them ten minutes to get to Shara Mizran, twice the normal time, but, at the Esso petrol station at the start of the Sidi El Masri road, there was still no sign of the younger Al Bakri brothers.

'I'll leave the cylinders here. No one's going to steal them,' Nico decided. He got out, took the cylinders out of the back of the van, placed them by the two petrol pumps, and off they went to the villas.

When they entered the gate off the avenue, the two houses could barely be seen for the clouds of sand. The eucalyptus and palm trees were shaking about like crazy under the ghibli's intensity.

'I'll put the van under the Hunts' car port,' Nico said.

'Yes,' said Alberto approvingly. 'We'll find it under a sand dune if we don't.'

Nico parked in front of William's Land Rover and Marlene's Ferrari. Then they quickly took shelter in the Balistreris' living room, with its shutters closed, the lights on and the air conditioning working all out.

The hot wind whipped Nadia's back as it pushed her along the path she knew like the back of her hand. Beside the wind, it was now filled with the deafening noise of cicadas.

Flies continually landed on her face, but she let them be. She would have had to lift her hands to brush them off, which would have made her sweat more, and force even more flies to land on her. All around her, the *ghibli* had raised a yellowish cloud of dust that rendered outlines a blur and anything beyond thirty metres invisible.

She focused on the pleasant thought of Mikey Balistreri and wondered if she would see him that day. Mikey was guarded with her, and she knew why. Ahmed and Karim. They would certainly have begged him not to look at their sister. If he so much as touched her and it became known, she would be ruined; no Libyan boy would ever marry her. But a part of her hoped that Mikey would not listen to her brothers. She could not understand what she liked so much about him. He was certainly not handsome; there were many better-looking boys. It had to do with something inside him, not his outward appearance. He was different from all the other Italian boys, who were so cocksure of themselves. And there was something she knew for a fact: Michele Balistreri looked calm, but he could flatten every one of them if he wanted to.

The *ghibli* was blowing burning sand in her face, making breathing difficult. She held the veil tightly over her half-closed eyes in order to avoid the red-hot grains and berserk flies as she walked down the dirt path on automatic pilot. She went down it every morning, and her bare feet knew every single stone.

In the howling wind, she heard the frogs croaking and knew she was almost there. She was on the large curve near the small pond, the last one before the Balistreri villa.

All of a sudden, she felt his presence more than saw him. About thirty metres from her, there was a hazy figure, motionless below a eucalyptus in the dusty sand cloud. There was no reason for him to be there and, for a moment, Nadia was confused. Then she smiled at him and shyly took another step forward. In the thick mist of sand blocking out the sunlight, she missed the gleam of his knife.

Jamaal the goatherd was a little addle-pated and confused as to his whereabouts. He had seen one of Mohammed's younger sons go past, either Ahmed or Karim. They looked so alike, and he had this damned glaucoma. And with all that sand swirling in the wind you could barely see a thing.

I'm lost. I need help.

Trusting his nose more than his eyes, he found the cesspit and walked slowly back towards the olive grove. He hated the *ghibli*, even more so now that he was over seventy. He could hear his three goats bleating frantically and, behind him, could feel the panting of the little mongrel that was supposed to be guarding them. He had no idea where he was.

Then, all of a sudden, he saw her. There was only one olive tree between him and the young girl. His eyes were poor and the *ghibli* was buffeting sand in his face, as if blown by a propeller. But he recognized her by the midnight-blue barracan.

That's Nadia, Mohammed's young daughter, the one who works for the wealthy Italians.

She was coming closer. His mongrel dog growled at that moment and Jamaal turned round, startled, because that dog never growled without a reason, even less in the heat. The mongrel was pointing at the girl in the yellow whirl of sand while Jamaal tried to get to the old olive-pressing shed.

It seemed to him the girl was making signs for him to come over, perhaps to ask him for help because she was lost as well. Jamaal brushed a hand over his eyes, trying to drive off the swarms of flies. Then the dog barked and he turned round to calm it down. When he turned back to Nadia, she had disappeared.

It was impossible: five seconds earlier the girl was there.

And round about him there was only empty space, nowhere where anyone could hide.

'Allah, my great Allah . . . The desert's swallowed her up! Or have I gone mad?'

The dog was growling again. Frightened, Jamaal took from his knapsack the long, serrated knife he used for filleting frogs before boiling them.

In the distance the muezzin called out his sorrowful prayer. It was nine o'clock.

I went into the living room. The muezzin's cry from the mosque had stopped. Alberto was having breakfast with Nico.

'What terrible weather to go fishing in,' I said as I flopped down in a chair.

Nico was eating toast and jam, dunking it in his caffè latte.

'Sorry, Mikey. Did the van wake you?'

'It's nine twenty – we need to get a move on,' Alberto cut in.

'Don't worry. Have Ahmed and Karim been to the Esso station for the cylinders?' I asked, while I poured myself some coffee. I drank it black with no sugar.

'They weren't there at eight fifteen, so we left the cylinders there for them,' Nico replied.

At that moment, my mother appeared in her dressing gown, her face full of sleep. She turned to the older housemaid.

'Isn't Nadia here?'

'I'm sorry, Signora, Nadia's not come in. She's probably not well. I'll make you some coffee.'

My mother looked at the tempest of sand swirling outside the windows.

'And you're going fishing in this?' she asked.

'Yeah . . .' I grumbled, sipping my black coffee.

'It'll certainly be better out on the water than in here,' Alberto explained, trying, as ever, to justify my father's demanding nature.

Breakfast over, Nico, Alberto and I went out on to the forecourt. The heat was dreadful and the sand engulfed us. You could not even see the front gate on to the main road. There was no sound now from the doves, frogs or cicadas. Even these creatures had to keep their beaks and mouths closed to avoid the sand.

Damned ghibli. *But perhaps Papa's right. It'll be better out on the water.*

Blown about by the red-hot wind, we reached the van under the Hunts' car port, in front of William's Land Rover and Marlene's Ferrari. On the seat was the tube of sunblock I had spread on her back.

Don't think about that any more, Mikey. That's enough now!

Alberto got in front beside Nico; I stretched out on the back seat. Behind my back, the metal sheet dividing off the back of the van was scorching hot. I had to watch out not to burn myself.

You've already burned your hands, Mike, on Marlene Hunt's back.

Nico drove carefully in the middle of the mist of sand, but the road was empty. After a few minutes we were at the Esso station. Ahmed was waiting for us on the tiny sand-swept forecourt.

'Put the cylinders on the seat. Let's get a move on or we won't get through,' Nico said.

Ahmed seemed upset about something. I helped him load the cylinders on to the back seat between the two of us, and off we went.

Behind us, we heard the noise of a vehicle coming from Sidi El Masri, but it was impossible to see it in that sand and I had no interest at all in knowing who it was.

'Isn't Karim coming?' Nico asked Ahmed.

'He says he's got stomach ache. I think he didn't want to come fishing,' replied Ahmed, a look of disgust on his face.

'Isn't Nadia feeling well either?' Alberto asked.

Ahmed looked confused for a moment.

'Nadia? No, she went out at the same time as our father to come to the villa. Isn't she there?'

'No,' I said. 'I think, with the *ghibli*, she must have turned round and gone back home.'

We entered Tripoli down Shara Ben Ashur at five to ten, a few minutes before the police blocked the road. Behind us, I could still hear the rumbling of the other vehicle's motor. Then, in the city, the visibility was decidedly better; it was further away from the sand and more sheltered by its houses and apartment blocks.

Over by the cathedral square, Corso Vittorio, leading into Piazza Castello, was already blocked for the Bedouin's camel parade by the edge of the crowd and the RAI's outside-broadcast vans. So we took Via Roma, Shara 24 December, then turned on to Shara Mizran. Outside the market entrance there was also a large crowd, and Nico had to stop to allow the pedestrians across and to let donkeys, bicycles and carts go by. Then he managed to park between a donkey cart and a horse carriage.

'I'll go,' I said.

I got out and ventured in among the market stalls. A mass of people stood in front of Farid and Salim's stall, buying fish. While Farid was serving the customers, Salim handed me the bucket of bait for the inshore trolling.

'Absolutely fresh garfish, Mikey. The amberjack should love them.'

I thanked him and went back to the van.

We turned down Corso Sicilia – Shara Omar Al Mukhtar – and set off towards the shore. We passed by the International Fair Grounds, the Lido, the Bagni Sulfurei and the Beach Club. We got to the Underwater Club at half past ten.

As usual, Papa was right. You felt the heat and the sand far less. Out on the water, it would probably be fine.

My father, Emilio Busi and Don Eugenio arrived ten minutes later. Busi looked a sight, as usual, ridiculously and totally inappropriately dressed for the fishing.

'My fault, boys,' he said, excusing himself. 'I was late.'

In a few minutes we had unloaded the cylinders and rucksacks from the MANK van and stowed them on the motorboat, then we set off with Papa at the wheel. The further we put out to sea, the less heat and sand there were.

La Moneta lay a kilometre off the coast, a little beyond the Giorgimpopoli suburb and twenty from the Underwater Club. It had the shape of a jagged coin and was about three kilometres across. The side of the island facing the coast was low-lying and covered in sand, then the land rose slowly over to the opposite side, looking out to Sicily and the open sea, reaching its highest point in a rocky cliff rising vertically from the sea where my mother went to read and paint. Twenty metres below the cliff were jagged spikes of rock that could not be seen from above because of an overhang of a couple of metres and, depending on the tide, were either underwater or totally uncovered. Crossing the island was a single sandy track that ran from behind the large villa and provided a brisk thirty minutes' walk up to the top of the cliff.

At eleven, we reached the sandy shoreline. Papa had built a small jetty and created a beach with little gazebos in front of the large white villa, built in the Moorish style.

Then we drew round to the rocky side, the one looking on to the open sea, where there were more fish. We were more comfortable there, sheltered from the wind and sand, and came to the shallows Salim had recommended.

While the others prepared the rods and bait for trolling, we boys put on wet suits and got the spear guns ready. Alberto and I had two new pneumatic Medisten guns, while Ahmed and Nico would use our two old spring-powered Cernias.

Don Eugenio took hold of a Medisten. 'New guns, boys?'

Seven years had passed since the business of the photographs and, since then, Don Eugenio's behaviour had been above reproach. To all appearances, at least. I really had the impression that he might have recovered from that *illness*. Perhaps it was by force of will, or perhaps he had received help. Nevertheless, for me, he remained a dangerous man.

And, despite continuing to show the placid and humble air of a country priest, Don Eugenio had become an important man. Alberto told me he was the bridge between Tripoli's influential Italians and the Christian Democrat Party in Italy. And Don Eugenio had added a degree in economics to the one in theology and celebrated Mass less and less in favour of managing a large number of funds, the proceeds of which he used to help Africa's sub-Saharan poor. At least, that is what my father maintained, and everyone else in Tripoli confirmed it.

A saint, a protector of the desperately poor. But also a priest with wandering hands.

We had not spoken of the photographs again. But my mother still had them. I was not concerned whether Don Eugenio knew or not. But Nico's lisp came back every time he saw the priest, and Ahmed and myself had certainly not forgotten.

In fact, it was only Alberto who spoke to him.

'Mikey chose the guns, easier to handle.'

Don Eugenio looked at me. No, he had not forgotten either.

'To get in where the fish hide, Mikey? You like sneaking into their abodes, then?'

As a boy, when I still went to him for confession, I had told him that I had sinned in thought about Laura's mother. I had dreamed of her in a bikini. And Don Eugenio had seen me coming out of Marlene Hunt's house the day I had put the sunblock on her. Had he picked up on anything?

I made no reply. I had nothing to say to him. I would happily have done away with him, like the three soldiers in Cairo. But I couldn't.

We put on our Cressi masks and flippers. We chucked in the float with its homemade line made of corks, and Alberto, Nico, Ahmed and myself dived in and spread out so as not to get in each other's way.

The water was warm. I went down to a depth of twelve metres, but had no desire to fish. All I could think of was Marlene Hunt's naked back when she undid the hooks and eyes of the bikini top, which my trembling hands had been unable to grip. And about the bikini bottom's line of elastic which my fingers had brushed against. And my voice hoarse with desire and the stupid things I said.

It had been more humiliating than arousing.

It was by instinct that I saw the grouper as it swam about the algae on the bottom. It must have weighed between six and eight kilos. I calmly took aim and fired. The spear pierced it exactly where I wanted, right in the eye. Then I swam silently up to the motorboat's poop to hand over the catch. On board, they did not hear me emerge, but I could hear their voices.

'Everything's OK in Rome. The President's been informed of the possibility,' said Don Eugenio.

'My connections have been kept up to date as well,' Busi added.

'Mohammed's been to Sirte with them. They're almost ready.'

This was my father speaking.

For some reason, the epitaph for the Folgore parachute regiment at El Alamein came to mind.

They fell for an ideal . . . and mark a pathway of honour and glory for the Italian people . . .

Unfortunately, Alberto came up noisily beside me. Everyone on the motorboat suddenly fell silent.

Afternoon

At one thirty, we were eating some fruit under the canopy in the boat when we saw the Underwater Club's lifeguard approaching at high speed in his motorboat. I could see my mother in the prow with Karim. Despite the *ghibli*, she was wearing one of her usual long kaftans, a scarf and dark glasses to protect herself against the sun. As soon as the two motorboats were side by side, she called to my father.

'We can't find Nadia.'

Her eyes were hidden behind the dark glasses, but I could clearly see the lines were etched more deeply on her face.

My father said nothing. The boats were bobbing on the waves under the baking sun and I felt a pain spreading through my stomach and getting worse. And yet I never suffered from seasickness. I looked at Ahmed and Karim, but they were waiting without a word while my father decided what to do. Ahmed was coolly intent; Karim tense and worried.

'She's not ill?' Alberto asked.

'No. I wanted to see how she was and I went to visit her.'

My father was speechless. In his view, his wife was not the sort of person to go off and visit a wooden shack standing near a cesspit. He knew very little about certain aspects of my mother.

'I went there at midday. There was only Karim, and Mohammed's two wives. He was at work in town, and Farid and Salim were at the market. I tried to phone Mohammed in the office but he wasn't there, and I couldn't get here any earlier. Entry into Tripoli was closed because of the parade. They only opened it half an hour ago.'

There was a prolonged silence while the *ghibli*'s noise suddenly increased. I shut my eyes to protect them from the sand. I could hear everyone breathing around me. I had the feeling, rather than the perception, that there was one person who was having more difficulty breathing than the others.

'We have to go back and find Nadia,' my mother said. No one objected.

We boys went back with Mamma in the lifeguard's boat, following Papa's wake. She smoked in the prow in silence behind the impenetrable wall of her large sunglasses and scarf. I was thinking about Nadia. Only Alberto was sitting close to Mamma, speaking quietly to her, while she listened. But it was clear that she did not agree with what Alberto was saying.

When we came to the Underwater's pier we shared out the tasks and separated. Papa took Busi in the jeep back to his house behind the cathedral and Don Eugenio to his presbytery. Italia went in her Volkswagen to fetch Mohammed from the office. We went into town in the MANK van, Nico at the wheel. We went to pick up Farid and Salim, but the market on Shara Mizran had already closed.

Then, with the vehicles in Indian file, we all set off towards Sidi El Masri. *A funeral procession.*

The *ghibli*'s intensity increased gradually as we left the seaside. It was a gloomy, slow and silent journey: the jeep, the van, the Volkswagen, Mohammed's pick-up.

Enveloped by sand and that oppressive humidity, each person kept to their own thoughts.

We arrived at the villas just before three and all parked on the dirt forecourt. Farid and Salim's pickup was already there and they were talking agitatedly with William Hunt, Marlene and Laura.

'Have you found her?' my father asked.

William Hunt shook his head.

'No, we only came back an hour ago. We couldn't any earlier, because of the camel parade.'

Farid was very agitated and ran a hand through his frizzy hair.

'When we came home, our mother told us that Nadia was missing and that Signora Italia and Karim had gone to tell you.'

'We've looked a bit for her here, around the cabin, but found nothing,' Salim added.

Naturally, William Hunt and my father organized a search. The men and boys only. Italia took shelter in our villa, Marlene and Laura in theirs.

We began to sweep the countryside around the two-kilometre path between our villa and Mohammed's shack, the route that Nadia walked every morning.

The *ghibli* was raising sand devils and, at Sidi El Masri, the visibility was poor. We looked like a bunch of phantoms, with sweat in our eyes, flies on our faces and sand sticking to our lips. We searched under every bush, behind every tree and in every dip in the ground.

At five, after two hours searching, we reached the Al Bakris' wooden shack. Visibility there was even worse and the smell of dung was much stronger.

How can they live like this?

We found no trace of Nadia. William Hunt said that, at this point, we should call the police. We all went back to the Balistreri villa and my father phoned the head of the police in person, one General Jalloun, who arrived in record time with no fewer than ten policemen. This was not efficiency but the influence of the powerful Bruseghin–Balistreri family.

'Does Nadia have any friends in the city, Ingegnere?' the general asked, studiously ignoring Mohammed and addressing only my father, in an obsequious manner.

My mother cut in immediately. 'Shouldn't you ask her father or brothers, General Jalloun?'

But the general was a friend of my grandfather and held him in high esteem; they had known each other for twenty years and smoked a *shisha* together at one of the outside tables in a Piazza Castello bar. Grandad broke in, to conciliate.

'Let's hear Mohammed first, General, if you don't mind.'

Jalloun looked at Grandad and nodded. Giuseppe Bruseghin was his friend, but his daughter was an arrogant Fascist and married to this Salvatore Balistreri, the most important of the Italians in Tripoli.

'Very well,' the general conceded. 'Let's hear Mohammed.'

At that moment, Laura came in. I felt her eyes on me, but avoided them. Since I had put sunblock on her mother's back and shoulders, stopping at the edge of those bikini bottoms, I could no longer look her in the eye. My mind was only on that body. Even in that tense moment, all I could think of was Marlene Hunt alone in the villa next door.

Hoping not to be noticed, I slipped out into the garden. After three days of hell, the damned *ghibli* was finally calming down and the sun's rays were now filtering through the curtain of sand.

You're crazy, Mikey. At a time like this?

But I was drawn by an irresistible magnetic force. I went over to the Hunts' house and peered in through the half-open door. In silence, I crossed over the threshold and began to climb the stairs.

Marlene appeared at the top of them, walking to the terrace door, completely naked. She stopped to look at me, and it was like receiving a *tae* blow to the chest. I staggered and fell back, rolling down to the bottom of the stairs.

As I was laboriously getting up, bruised in body and pride, I heard her laugh and the terrace door closing.

A young boy filled with desire, scorned and shut out of the Paradise Garden.

I was in flames as I ran towards the back gate and then on towards Grandad's olive grove.

The *ghibli*'s last howls hit me in the face as I ran. My mouth and eyes were caked with sand and the sweat was pouring down my spine. I got to the Al Bakris' shack in less than twenty minutes. I went quickly past the cesspit and on towards the olives. The sun was starting to set but looked like a ball of fire on the horizon now that it was able to penetrate the *ghibli*. Every so often, along the path I could see the goatherds' tin sheds. I could hear the goats bleating, tended only by the dog that kept an eye on them.

But the dog was barking too much. It was agitated, sniffing at the door of the brick shed that used to house the old olive press. It was parallelepiped in shape and was where the olives had been pressed for years, thanks to a mule that trotted round, turning the two enormous millstones that crushed them. One day, it had caught fire, but the charred ruin had been left standing, although it had been shut up for years.

The dog was barking at the brick shed and flies were buzzing around it – too many to have been caught up in the wind that was still blowing. There was a small lock on the door that bore no sign of rust. I glanced through the window, its glass left opaque with years of dirt. The sunlight barely penetrated, and all I could see was the sinister outline of the two enormous millstones.

The goatherd's dog was still barking furiously at the door. In front of it, the ground had been disturbed, and caught in a bush was a paper handkerchief stained red.

Innocent blood.

I picked it up and put it in my pocket. I could not make up my mind. Both my mind and my body were paralysed. I refused even to think about it. I could have broken the glass and looked in. But it was as if some kind of fever was making my legs weak.

As I was rushing back to the villa, I already knew what was in the shed.

Nadia's body.

I stopped and heaved up everything I could.

Led by General Jalloun and the other grown-ups, the police raced round to the charred brick shed. Women and boys were forbidden to follow but, after a while, we heard the sirens. More police cars, and an ambulance.

By now, dusk had fallen and it promised to be a sleepless night. Ahmed, Karim and Nico stayed with us, sleeping in the guest room. This was my mother's decision. Naturally, no one was in any mood for supper.

Before going back to her house, Laura came up to me. She pointed to Karim, who was trembling silently in a corner.

'Please, Mikey, stay close to him.'

Stay close to him? Me? I couldn't even keep my own emotions in check.

I put the bloodstained paper handkerchief in my Latin book, the one I never opened. I wanted to hold on to it, but not have it in my sight all the time. I knew that Nadia Al Bakri's blood would change the course of our lives.

Monday, 4 August 1969

Islam asks its believers to accept death as the will of Allah. Therefore, its funerals are simple and humble. The afternoon after she was found, Nadia's body was washed and wrapped in a white sheet. Immediately after the mid-afternoon Asr prayer, the funeral began in the Arab cemetery behind Corso Sicilia, near the old station for the diesel train to Sabratha.

The ceremony was conducted without anyone kneeling. The body was placed between two stone slabs, the head pointing to Mecca, then covered with earth. Mohammed had chosen a head-stone without a name, simply the dates of birth and death according to the Muslim calendar. His four sons watched in silence at his side.

From the gossip in undertones, but still audible, between General Jalloun and Don Eugenio and Busi, I caught those terrible words: 'raped', 'sodomized'.

Laura and Marlene were away in a corner, separate, faces hidden by large sunglasses. They came forward only to offer condolences to Mohammed and his wife.

Before leaving, Laura came up close to me.

'My mom and I are leaving tomorrow. Dad has to go to Vietnam and Marlene doesn't want to stay here alone. It's impossible not to think of Nadia, but it's even worse for Mom here.'

I was surprised, but in some way happy, they were going. The sight of Marlene was unbearable, because it reminded of where I really was: all at sea and hopelessly adrift.

'Where will you go?'

'Marlene decided everything at the last minute this morning. We'll go on a trip around Europe. Rome, Paris and London.'

I said nothing, and she repeated her request.

'We'll only be away ten days, Mikey. Stay close to Karim.'

'Ahmed lost a sister as well. Or have you forgotten?'

'He doesn't need you, Mikey. It's you that needs him.'

That evening, Italia was sitting in the swing seat out on the veranda, smoking a cigarette and drinking whisky. The light was on, and she was reading. I was sitting beside her.

'Mamma, I have to ask you something.'

She turned to look at me. She was almost forty and the lines in her face were getting deeper. But her aging went beyond the lines and white strands in her hair; it was as if something or someone had taken away her will to live.

I instinctively thought of Marlene Hunt. She was only five years younger than my mother but still looked like a student, with her golden skin, her rigid diets, her swimming, daily jogging and beauty creams.

'Go ahead, Mikey.'

'It's about Nadia.'

She didn't seem surprised in the least. 'I know. I think I know you a little, wouldn't you say?'

I plucked up courage. I had to put the question to someone.

'I heard Don Eugenio and Emilio Busi at the funeral today. They were talking to the general and he was saying that Nadia had been raped before being killed . . .'

Italia's tired eyes stared at the large garden in the dark where the crickets and frogs were making their noise. Yes, Mamma was tired, very tired.

'And then the general said something else as well, Mamma, he said she'd been—'

She raised a hand to stop me at the word. A tear fell from her eyes. I got up and left her in peace.

Tuesday, 5 August 1969

Normally, the fishing boats came into port at six in the morning. At six thirty, the men went to the market to sell the catch to the fish-mongers at the stalls before the market opened at seven thirty.

Farid and Salim were privileged. They had both a fishing vessel and a stall at the market. So they had to arrive only twenty minutes or so before the market opened to set the catch out on the stall.

I got up at dawn and was ready in five minutes. I went out by the usual exit through the gate at the back of the villa. I got on my bicycle and went over the fields so that my father would not see me from the car as he went to the office.

Pedalling along the path that Nadia used to walk down and which Marlene Hunt jogged along, I hurried past the cesspit and came to the olive-pressing shed.

Had she been killed there? Not possible. There was no room there to do those terrible things: *raped*, *sodomized*. Not even inside the building, which – from dawn until ten o'clock – was surrounded by herdsmen, dogs and goats.

They must have seized her there and taken her into Tripoli, or God knows where. Then, after the traffic stoppage, they'd dragged her back to the olive-pressing shed.

Had she gone willingly into the car with her killer? Or was she forced? Did she know him?

At that hour, Shara Ben Ashur was almost deserted. Opposite the Royal Palace, I turned off towards Shara Mizran. A few donkey carts were transporting foodstuffs to the market. I got there in twenty minutes, arriving at six thirty.

The weighing counter had just opened for business. In a furious round of negotiations shouted in Arabic, the fishermen were selling their fish to the fishmongers.

At the weighing machine, I looked for old Mansur, one of Grandad's old hands, who had the fish stall next to Farid and Salim. When Mansur had become too old for work in the olive grove, Grandad had given him a lump sum to buy a market stall and then taken on his son in his place.

'Signor Michele, how good to see you!' said Mansur.

His eyes would light up with gratitude to Grandad whenever he saw me or Alberto.

'*Ciao*, Mansur, how's business?'

'All good, Allah willing. And what brings you here, Signor?'

I could trust him. I immediately told him the truth. I wanted to know at what time Farid and Salim had arrived the Sunday before. Mansur didn't follow me and looked bewildered.

'The day of the camel parade,' I specified.

His yellow teeth showed a smile. I was under no illusions that Mansur would remember exactly. Two days had passed, and he'd had no reason in all that hubbub to notice when Farid and Salim arrived. But this was my lucky day.

'They were here well before seven thirty,' he said, straightaway.

'How can you be so sure?'

'They came to the weighing counter very early. Usually, they don't come at all. But, on Sunday, they had to bring the pick-up close to it because Salim had caught an enormous greater amberjack. A monster it was, over fifty kilos. Too big for a single stall.

'And you bought it?'

'Farid and I haggled for quite a while. Then we fixed on a price and I bought half of it.'

'And you're sure it was this Sunday morning?'

'Yes, because it's only on a Sunday I would buy a monster that big. All the Italians come to buy fresh fish for Sunday lunch with their families.'

'And both of them were here, Mansur?'

'Yes, both of them. Farid and Salim. Farid was doing the negotiating; Salim was cutting the fish.'

'I saw them at ten, Mansur, when I came to pick up the bait. But, before and after, were they always here?'

The old man scratched the few white hairs on his head.

'I think so. They opened the stall at seven thirty; it's next to mine. And both of them were there. And straightaway there was the huge Sunday crowd. Towards eight o'clock, your grandfather, your brother and your friend Nico came by.'

'And they never closed the stall, they never went away?'

'I would have noticed if they'd closed the stall, Signor Michele. The pick-up was just outside. Every so often one of them would go to cut a piece off the amberjack, which was being kept there on ice. After ten, the Bedouin camel parade began and the market emptied. Farid and Salim were still here, both of them. We talked a lot about the amberjack and joked about how lucky they'd been. They stayed here right up to the market closing at one o'clock.

I looked at my watch. I had to get away before the two brothers arrived.

'Thanks, Mansur, it was just a thought. You mustn't say a word, understand?'

He gave me a complicit smile.

Wednesday, 6 August 1969

Papa went to Rome on business for a few days. Before leaving, he insisted I go with him to see the new house he'd bought in Piazza di Spagna.

More bait to get me to move.

But there was nothing to attract me in Italy. Or Europe. Even less after all I'd read in the past few months about the student protest movement in 1968. Middle-class students marching alongside the workers. Universities occupied, hammer and sickles daubed on every wall, the partisans' '*Bella Ciao*' chorused in the lecture theatres.

I'd declined the offer, citing the stress from Nadia's death as my excuse. And this wasn't really a lie. Strangely enough, Papa didn't seem too put out.

Perhaps he doesn't want me under his feet.

When I went into the living room for breakfast, there was only my brother there, his head buried in a textbook of mathematical analysis. As soon as he saw me, he shut the book.

'You don't want to go to Rome with Papa, Mikey?'

'Thanks, Alberto, but I'd rather stay here. I don't like Italy. How can you live in a country where the students occupy the universities and sing the praises of China's Red Guards? I'd like to see them try it in Moscow or Peking!'

'That's democracy for you, Mikey. It's what distinguishes us from both Fascist and Communist regimes. With us, everyone has the right to free speech.'

'Bollocks, Alberto! Do you know what the Italians really want? A new Fiat, cheaper petrol, a job for life and, if possible, a not-too-demanding one at that.'

My brother looked at me understandingly. Like my father, he wasn't absolutely in agreement with my ideas and choices. But, unlike my father, his dissent brought him closer to me rather than distancing him from me.

'OK, Mikey, nevertheless, I'm here at all times for advice, anything you want. But don't argue with Papa, and keep an eye on Mamma.'

The last words took me by surprise. I thought he meant her health.

'She's aged so much, Alberto. She seems worn out.'

He nodded thoughtfully.

'Mikey, Mamma listens to you more than anyone else. And she does things and says things that could seriously damage Papa's business concerns and the family.'

I didn't like this, especially coming from my brother.

'Alberto, don't you think they should just sort out whatever's between them?'

'No, Mikey, not if the final consequence means separation. There's no divorce under Italian law, even less in the Church.'

I was speechless and, for once, thought my highly intelligent brother was mistaken.

'Alberto, Mamma loves Papa, I'm sure of it. She doesn't always agree with his ideas, but she loves him.'

'Papa was born into poverty, Mikey. He wants to be sure that we don't experience the same as he's lived through.'

'If I'm not going with Papa, it's because I can't stand Rome, not because I don't want to be with him.'

My brother nodded.

'Very well. But let's stop Mamma from doing anything too compromising, anything that could seriously damage Papa.'

'Just what do you mean, Alberto? What could Mamma do?'

He looked uncertain, unable to make up his mind. Then he decided not to say any more, perhaps so it wouldn't weigh on me.

And Marlene Hunt came back into my mind. My hands on her golden skin. Her naked body at the top of the stairs. And, for the first time, I realized that perhaps I wasn't the only Balistreri to have the same feelings.

Saturday, 9 August 1969

Rome was veiled under a summer heat haze, its ochre walls and red roof tiles spreading out from the banks of the Tiber as the river lazily flowed through it.

Mariano Rumor's new premiership was yet another Christian Democrat government, the same as all the others since the Republic's founding in 1946.

The air conditioning kept the temperature pleasant, but the air inside the private lounge in the hotel next to the Parliament building was fouled by the cigarette smoke of Emilio Busi, who was wearing a horrendous short-sleeved grey check shirt. His white socks left a hand's breadth of hairy calf on show.

'So everything's ready?' Emilio Busi asked Salvatore Balistreri, who was sharply dressed in a made-to-measure pinstripe suit.

'Yes. Mohammed's friends in Sirte have given word back. All the junior officers in the Qadhadhfa tribe are united in agreement. And the same goes for those in the Warfalla tribe, who control the south and west. Cyrenaica will have to bow to the evidence and follow suit.'

'Aren't these men rather young?' Don Eugenio asked.

'A little young, perhaps, but all the more enthusiastic for it.'

'And easy to manipulate, I hope?' Don Eugenio added.

Emilio Busi was worried. 'Wouldn't it have been better to make contact with Omar and Abdulaziz Al Shalhi? They control the police and senior officers in the army.'

'I've spoken to them,' Balistreri replied, 'but I gather they're loyal to the Crown and closely tied to American and English interests – while the junior officers we're supporting are against the King and the Anglo-Americans.'

'Who's their leader?' Busi asked, inhaling his foul cigarette.

'They don't want to say. It's being kept secret,' Balistreri replied.

'A secret?' Busi laughed. 'Is this all a joke? We come up with a *coup d'état*, organize it and finance it and we don't know who'll be in charge afterwards?'

Busi sometimes went back to being a Carabinieri officer. Information, checks, sureties. Balistreri answered him with his calming smile.

'Mohammed knows his name; he's from a family close to his. They've asked to keep it a secret for security reasons. It's better that Mohammed doesn't tell even us, but you needn't worry. Let's call him X for the moment. Anyway, Mohammed and myself are the guarantors. We're backing the coup.'

Busi stubbed out his cigarette and lit another, then looked at Balistreri.

'Last year Italy imported over a 100,000 tons of petroleum, 30,000 of which came from Libya. Do you think they come from our ENI? No, it's almost all drilled by the Seven Sisters. The oilfields are in their hands, except the new A100 field. With that we can meet half of Italy's petroleum needs. Except that the concession's blocked for us.'

'All that will soon change,' Balistreri said calmly.

But Busi was not interested in possibilities. He dealt only in certainties.

'What assurances do we have that this X won't do the same with Italy? We Italians are the ex-Fascist colonialists, the sons of those who massacred their women and children. Perhaps X hates Italians?'

'Mohammed and myself are meeting the junior officers at Abano Terme here in Italy,' replied Balistreri, completely unruffled.

Busi looked at him, surprised.

'Isn't that unwise?'

Balistreri shrugged.

'The only people who know are we three, X himself and Mohammed, who's organized everything. I also want some guarantees from X, gentlemen.'

Balistreri was well aware that the meeting in Italy was a gamble. But his brothers in Sicily and their friends did not want to risk all that money on an unknown Bedouin.

'Obviously, here in Rome, we'll have good political support from Moro, now he's the new Foreign Minister,' Balistreri said, wanting to change the subject.

Busi smiled. This was his playing field.

'The Honourable Aldo Moro's a clever man who never takes an impulsive decision; he trusts to reason and to Intelligence. And that Intelligence is furnished to him by us, via the Secret Services, which I believe we now call the SID.'

'From elements close to the Prime Minister?' asked Balistreri.

Don Eugenio was quick to clarify. There were certain safeguards to observe. Salvatore Balistreri needed to understand that politicians always liked to have a safety net.

'The Prime Minister doesn't deal with such things directly. All he wants in Libya is a regime that's less favourable to the British and Americans. If it were possible to achieve this peacefully with King Idriss, he'd be just as happy.'

Salvatore Balistreri brushed a hand through his thick, black hair. His dark eyes were calm. He had to go along with these two partners and put up with their doubts and hypocrisy, even if it meant he had to do it for the next fifty years.

'Tell your connections their interests are in good hands. After all, I'm risking everything here, putting all my family's money in. We're selling the Bruseghin olive grove for it. My brothers and their friends are also backing it.'

Busi was immediately worried by Balistreri's frankness.

'My connections know only that we're working to bring about a political situation that will be more favourable to Italian interests.'

Don Eugenio also wanted to maintain a certain distance.

'Furthermore, my dear Salvatore, let's be clear that, as far as our connections are concerned, the financing is yours alone. With the greatest respect, your brothers and their friends will not be holding any shares in any Italian businesses in Libya.'

Salvatore Balistreri smiled. The hypocrisy of Italians was phenomenal, as was their Machiavellian ability in plotting. In the end, his eldest brother, Gaetano, was right about his compatriots on the mainland.

These guys will only understand two things: hard cash and high explosives.

But he preferred to work with these men rather than spurn them or even oppose them, as his wife or son Michele would have done.

In the silence beyond the hotel windows, a few cars were slowly scuttling between the corridors of power: the President's Quirinale Palace, the Premier's Chigi Palace and Parliament in Montecitorio. Salvatore Balistreri decided there and then that he would one day have an office in the last.

Sunday, 10 August 1969

It was one week after Nadia's death and silence still reigned in the two villas.

Papa was in Rome, William Hunt in Vietnam, Laura and Marlene touring Europe. Italia read, smoked and drank her whisky, lost in her own thoughts. My grandad, Giuseppe, was unusually distant and preoccupied, while Alberto spent his days shut in his room, studying.

Nico, on the other hand, had bought an airline ticket for New York.

There's this really cool festival in Woodstock, Mike. All the biggest rock stars together in one place. Really very cool. Then I'm going to tour the States for the rest of August.

It seemed a ridiculous thing to do after Nadia's death. Especially as, on that one trip, he'd be blowing all the money he'd made in the two years in Cairo, if not more. But perhaps there was a reason behind it. Nico wasn't happy with just me around. I was even gloomier than ever. And, after all, it was the States, a music festival, and singers were his passion. What's more, I thought he might find girls there he wouldn't have to pay for.

Ahmed and Karim were still in mourning, shut in at home with their mother. We hadn't managed to see each other after the funeral.

Nadia's death had upset everyone's balance. It was as if each one of us were locked inside ourselves, trying to make sense of what had happened.

I no longer went outside. I spent whole days in my room with the shutters and windows closed. It was stiflingly hot outside and very quiet. Even the flies were taking it easy, resting on the fly screen. All you could hear was the occasional frog croaking in the fountain's warm water.

I tried not to think of anything. Not about Nadia, Marlene nor Laura. But solitude was no help in emptying my mind and clearing my conscience. So I stole my mother's sleeping pills from her cupboard.

I was sleeping that afternoon when I heard the telephone ringing in the hall. After a few minutes, Grandad knocked and put his head round the door.

'Michele, run over to Mohammed's house, quickly.'

Behind him, I saw my mother's face drained of colour.

'Why, what's up?' I asked.

'They've arrested the killer. Go on, Mikey, please.'

I took my time, without really knowing what I was going to say. When I got to Mohammed's place, he, Ahmed and Karim were kneeling in prayer on the ground outside, facing the Qibla, Mecca.

'They've found the killer!' I blurted.

Ahmed jumped straight up.

'*Haya al salat!*★ his father ordered. 'Signor Michele, if you could be patient and wait, we will have finished the *ruku* in five minutes.'

After the fourth genuflection, Mohammed sat on his heels, followed by his sons, for the part of prayer known as the *Tashahhud*, then gave the ritual salutation: *Al-salamu alaykum.*

★ 'Come back and pray!' (author's note)

'Who was it?' Ahmed asked me.

Mohammed looked at him, and Ahmed lowered his gaze.

'Ahmed, you and Karim stay here and look after the women. I'll go with Signor Michele.'

'Can I come with you, Grandad?'

Mohammed and my grandfather were getting into the jeep.

If it had been my father, he would have packed me off into the house without even replying. But Grandad was a different man from my father.

'Very well, Mikey, get in. But when we're there, you're not to say a word.'

The city was semi-deserted. In that heat, everyone was waiting for sunset so as to be able to leave the house.

As soon as we arrived at the large barracks of Bab Azizia, we were greeted by General Jalloun, who looked at me with concern. My grandfather smiled at his old friend.

'Don't worry, General, Michele's very discreet.'

The general nodded uncomfortably. Then he explained succinctly that, thanks to days of tireless work, they had solved the case.

'It was the goatherd, Jamaal. We've arrested him. And after a little taste of prison, he'll confess to everything, you'll see.'

'Is there any proof, General?' my grandfather asked politely.

The general was beaming at us with satisfaction, his chest puffed up in conceit.

'Overwhelming proof.'

Grandad was taken aback and conveyed this with the greatest respect.

'But, General, I've known Jamaal for over thirty years. He's an odd and solitary old man who talks only to his goats. But he's never been violent.'

General Jalloun's eyes shone with pride.

'After careful investigation, I found a witness. One of the other goatherds saw him with Nadia near the pressing shed towards nine o'clock. The time fits; the place as well.'

'And this witness is sure of the time?'

The question slipped out without me realizing it. All three looked at me in surprise.

The general gave me a scornful smile, then continued addressing my grandad.

'The goatherd's sure of the time because he saw Nadia and Jamaal immediately after he'd heard the muezzin, who starts punctually at nine.'

The muezzin's cry. Just before I went down for breakfast with Alberto and Nico.

And the general had yet more proof.

'We also found a knife with a saw blade in the pressing shed. The other goatherds say it's Jamaal's knife. It was covered in blood. And it matches the wounds on Nadia's body.'

Nadia's blood. Those stains on the handkerchief.

I found this difficult to believe and couldn't hold back.

'Jamaal's seventy and half blind. How could he manage to drag Nadia all the way there?'

The general gave me a withering look and turned to my grandfather.

'Would your grandson like to take my place in this investigation?'

My grandfather smoothed things with his more conciliatory manner.

'I'm sure there's a perfectly good explanation, Mikey.'

The general glanced in embarrassment at Mohammed.

'The explanation's in the knife. I won't say what was done with it to Nadia, not in front of her father and this young man here, but it was an atrocity and it took some time. You could only perform such butchery inside, not out in the open, that's for sure.'

I was beside myself. This was all a pack of lies.

'In that pressing shed, under its lock and key? By a half-blind goatherd?'

General Jalloun was clearly upset.

'And how would you know, Signor Michele?'

'I saw the lock on the door. It was brand new and very small. Jamaal would have had neither the money to buy it nor the sight to lock and unlock it.'

The general wavered. His expression darkened and he muttered something in Arabic. I looked at Mohammed, who was standing silently in a corner. Here we were, talking about his daughter. About her presumed but unlikely killer. And yet he had nothing to say.

'Mohammed, Jamaal's known Nadia since she was born! He's known you and your family for years! Come on, you know this isn't true!' I burst out.

Mohammed hesitated. I saw the uncertainty in his eyes, the effort he was making in having to choose between humiliation and fear. The humiliation of having to accept an unlikely killer of his precious daughter and the fear that Nadia had been killed by a descendant of the Italians, who had massacred his family.

If he accepts Jamaal as guilty, the case is closed. If he protests, it could damage his boss. And he'd lose everything.

Finally, with his eyes to the floor, he chose humiliation.

'Signor Michele, Jamaal was a very odd man. Sometimes he would give Nadia some milk from his goats. Sometimes cheese. Too many times.'

During the journey back to Sidi El Masri in the jeep, no one spoke a word. As soon as we arrived, Mohammed and Grandad went into the house to report the news to my mother. I went out by the back gate. It took me less than half an hour to get down the dirt track to Ahmed and Karim's shack.

I want to tell them before Mohammed does. I want to know what they think.

Ahmed and Karim met me straightaway.

'They've arrested Jamaal for it,' I said.

Ahmed stared at me and said nothing, as if he were waiting for my view. But Karim immediately said what he thought.

'They could be right. Jamaal was a very odd man.'

'My grandad knows him and says he wouldn't hurt a fly,' I protested.

'And what do you think, Mikey?' Ahmed asked.

'Jamaal's seventy, and shows it. How could he manage to drag her to the pressing shed, right past your house? Nadia would have screamed out. You were here, Karim, you would have seen or heard something.'

Karim shook his head. He was embarrassed for some reason.

'I was in the toilet, Mikey. I didn't feel well, and the *ghibli* was howling a gale.'

I pointed to the thin white scar on my left wrist. Our blood brotherhood.

'You have to help me find the truth. For your sister's sake!'

Ahmed looked at me. 'What do we have to do?'

'Let's write down everything we know. And note what we don't know.'

Karim was totally against it.

'What should we write then?' Ahmed asked.

It must have been the influence of all those Agatha Christie books I'd read over the years. Or perhaps a deeper intuition. That breathing on the boat out at sea when Mamma told us that Nadia had disappeared.

Someone there was panting rather than breathing.

I fixed Ahmed and Karim with a look.

'Nadia knew her killer.'

'Of course,' Karim replied. 'She knew Jamaal.'

'No. He was too old. Even with a knife he couldn't have managed to take her to the pressing shed.'

Ahmed's eyes looked serious, lost in thought. Karim's were burning with rage.

'You think it was one of us?' Ahmed said at last.

I said nothing. My reply was silence. That was enough for Ahmed. In the shack he found a maths exercise book with large-squared paper, the kind he and Karim had used in infant school. He tore out the last page and handed it to me with a stub of pencil.

Karim made a last attempt to stop us.

'Ahmed, it's sacrilege. What about Nadia's memory . . .?'

'Shut it,' Ahmed ordered. It was the order of an older brother.

I started things off. After a moment, Ahmed picked up on the procedure and gave a hand. Karim kept quiet and listened. It was his way of expressing disapproval of what we were doing.

We took two hours and, in the end, what I had filled almost a whole side of the squared notepaper:

Salvatore Balistreri, Alberto and Grandad Giuseppe went out at six thirty, seen by Mike. They were at Don Eugenio's Mass in Tripoli by seven, and at seven forty-five Salvatore was at the barber's, Alberto and Grandad at the market with Farid and Salim, who had been there since dawn.

Nico was at the market just before eight and together with Alberto took the Giornale di Tripoli *to Salvatore Balistreri at the barber's. He then went to read the paper on the Waddan terrace (CHECK) until Don Eugenio arrived at ten, and then Busi, who was a little late (CHECK BOTH).*

Alberto and Nico came back with the van. At eight fifteen they left the gas cylinders at the Esso station to be filled and were back at the villas just before eight thirty. They parked the van in the Hunts' car port and were together in the villa having breakfast. Mike Balistreri joined them at nine twenty.

Nadia left at eight with Mohammed, and they immediately went their separate ways. She went on foot to the villa; he took the pick-up past the olive grove and off to the office, where he remained until Italia came by to pick him up at two. When Italia called him at noon he wasn't there (CHECK).

Farid and Salim went fishing at two in the morning, as always. They were in the boat until dawn, then at their market stall. They were both there at eight, seen by Grandad, Alberto and Nico. At ten, they gave Mike the bait for the trolling. Mansur is almost certain they never left the stall.

Mike saw the three Hunts as they left together to go to the baseball game at Wheelus, and they returned about two, after the road was open again (CHECK).

Mike woke up early. He hung around for a bit, then went down and had breakfast with Nico and Alberto at nine twenty. The three then went to pick up Ahmed at the Esso station and went into Tripoli just before the road was closed.

Ahmed went out after Nadia and her father and walked through the olive grove to the petrol station, where he arrived, a little late. Nico and Alberto had left him the cylinders and he waited there for them until a quarter to ten.

Karim felt ill and stayed in the toilet at home.

At nine, a goatherd saw old Jamaal with Nadia near the oil-pressing shed. The muezzin was calling. Mike heard him just before going down for breakfast with Nico and Alberto.

I was surprised, and Ahmed was even more surprised.

This was like Hercule Poirot and Miss Marple.

The thought served to make another point clear.

'We have to include ourselves in the investigation,' I said to Ahmed and Karim.

Karim was strongly opposed.

'Our religion says that the dead should be left in peace, Mikey. And we're Nadia's brothers.'

Ahmed, on the other hand, agreed with me.

'There's no one above suspicion in an investigation, Karim.'

Karim was scornful and incredulous.

'Except this isn't a serious investigation. You aren't the police and they've already arrested the guilty man. And there are witnesses. You'll have Nadia's name on everyone's lips.'

I looked at Ahmed. He was gloomy and silently chewing something over.

'All right, Mikey,' he said finally. 'I can check your alibi and you can check mine and Karim's. But how can we check the alibis of the grown-ups?'

I had a ready answer. I folded the squared page and put it in my pocket.

'I'll check up on Farid and Salim. As for the grown-ups, I'll speak to my mother.'

Ahmed signalled his approval. Karim ruled himself out.

'I'm not going to help in this. So don't count on me.'

I stared at him coldly. 'Then we'll do without you. But don't say anything to Laura.'

I said it in the tone of an order, not a request.

'Laura's away touring Europe anyway,' he answered rudely.

Ahmed intervened.

'Mikey's right, Karim. When Laura comes back, you mustn't breathe a word of our investigation.'

And this was a peremptory order from an older brother. One who had cut the throats of three soldiers in a back alley in Cairo.

In the late afternoon I joined my mother on the swing seat out on the veranda. She now spent most of her time either there or up on the solitary cliff on La Moneta. The sadness in her eyes couldn't have been caused by Nadia's death alone. It had already been there at the beginning of August, when we came back from Cairo. During the time I was away something must have been slowly eating away at this woman made of steel and soft butter.

Steel for everyone else. Soft butter for Alberto and me.

She was drinking whisky, smoking and reading Nietzsche's *Beyond Good and Evil*. I sat down next to her.

'How are you feeling, Mamma?'

She raised her eyes from the book and smiled. There may have been many lines around her eyes, but her smile was the same. The same one she had when I was two and she sang lullabies and recited nursery rhymes to help me get to sleep.

'I'm tired, Mikey. I can't get used to Nadia's death.'

I pulled the crumpled sheet of squared paper from my jeans and handed it to her without a word.

She contemplated the pencilled notes in silence. For a moment, I was afraid she might refuse to read it. I saw her expression turn into a frown while she weighed up the points.

'I need your help, Mamma. Where it says "CHECK".'

I need you to check the alibis of the adults, your husband included.

She did not say, as my father would have done, that I was still a kid and these were serious things, for grown-ups and the police.

I saw her smile sadly, torn between pride and concern. She went over the page with my notes several times. She then folded it and placed it in the Nietzsche book.

'Very well, Mikey, I'll check. But you're not to do a thing.'

It was as if she were following a train of thought, as if there was an obvious solution on that page that I could not see.

Monday, 11 August 1969

I was alone having breakfast in the living room when Ahmed rushed in.

'Radio Tripoli's announced that Jamaal slit his veins in his cell last night.'

'Does your father know?'

'I've no idea. He left early this morning to go and pick your father up from the airport.'

'Then let's go and pay them a visit in the office. The plane from Rome landed an hour ago.'

'I can't go, Mikey, I'm not allowed.'

'Please come along, Ahmed. We have to speak to our fathers.'

'I have to stay with my mother and Karim. I can't disobey my father.' He meant, *Like you do, Mikey*.

'Don't worry. I'll speak to him.'

So the two of us took the jeep and headed for Tripoli. Corso Vittorio was quiet. Carriages, donkey carts, a few cars and bicycles. The bars on the street were empty; it was too hot outside.

We parked outside the austere white Fascist-era building in Piazza Italia, or Maydan as Suhada, where Papa had his offices, and walked slowly up the three flights of stairs. My father's private secretary rose to his feet when we entered.

'Signor Michele,' he said respectfully, but with a disapproving glance at Ahmed.

He led us into a meeting room. After a while, my father entered the room, followed by Mohammed, who looked severely at his disobedient son.

'Go home, Ahmed,' he ordered immediately.

'Mohammed, I asked Ahmed to come here with me.'

I had the authority of his Italian boss's son, which counted for more than a Libyan father.

My father dragged a hand through his thick, black hair. His forehead was sweating slightly, the bags under his eyes darker than usual. His good looks were a little jaded. Perhaps he had drunk too much and slept too little in Rome.

'Mohammed's right, Mikey. What are you and Ahmed doing here?'

'Did you know about Jamaal's death?' I asked them.

'Of course,' my father replied. 'He committed suicide.'

'Committed suicide? And who says? The police? General Jalloun?'

My father was a prudent and patient man; if not by nature, then from experience.

'Michele, he killed himself using the shards of a broken bottle. There were five other detainees in his cell, who gave evidence. It was his sense of guilt.'

I had had about enough of my father's omniscience.

'Papa, you're an engineer, not a psychologist. Do you always think you know everything?'

I saw both Mohammed and Ahmed give a start. But my father gave an understanding smile. Perhaps he still had hopes for me. Certainly, he still had patience.

'Whatever you say, Michele. But he committed suicide, that much is certain. General Jalloun told me he's closing the case this very day.'

I looked at Mohammed, but he was avoiding my eyes.

'Mohammed, how can you go along with this?' I said.

Ahmed placed a hand on my shoulder, took me by the arm and pulled me gently outside.

'It's no use, Mikey. Let's go, please.'

My best friend was trying to protect me from myself. And those words 'It's no use' were the most that his Islamic education allowed him to say about his father.

They were also a clear message from Ahmed to Mohammed. He was sacrificing the truth about his daughter's death on the altar of economic interest and a quiet life.

But I know that you don't forgive, Ahmed. Not today, not ever. Your sister's killer will come to a worse end than the dog that bit Jet.

Papa came home for lunch, something he never did on workdays. He had important news to tell us, much more important than Nadia's death and the old goatherd's suicide.

'I think we'll soon be able to move forward on the business with Busi and Don Eugenio's friends in Italy,' he announced to Grandad and Alberto, while Mamma was reading in her armchair.

Grandad didn't seem particularly enthusiastic.

'Salvatore, I've already asked you this. Where are we going to find the money to go into this business with them? They want such a lot.'

My father had a ready reply.

'I paid my brothers a visit in Palermo. They and their friends will loan half the amount. But they want to be sure that we're putting in the other half.'

'You're not to sell Father's olive grove,' said Italia icily.

Grandad's olive grove up for sale!

It was unthinkable. My mother's anguish explained the lines and sadness in her face.

Or perhaps only partly.

My father ignored her. He fixed his eyes on Grandad, speaking directly to him.

'Papa, the olive grove's the only thing we have to sell in order to embark on an enterprise this big.'

I hated my father when he addressed Grandad Giuseppe as 'Papa'. Grandad's real son, Toni, had been killed in the war with his head held high, while my father, born in 1925, was too young and missed the wretched World War by the skin of his teeth.

And now he was asking my grandfather to hand over his lifetime's work.

'I agree with Mamma!' I said, on an impulse.

My father didn't so much as glance at me, but I carried on.

'And as far as your partners go, Papa, Don Eugenio's a revolting priest and Busi's only a wheeling and dealing Communist.'

'Michele,' warned my grandfather.

Naturally, my father took it all with a smile.

This man who could sell ice to the Eskimos can change tack immediately when things don't seem to be working out.

'In the end, it's Grandad's decision. After all, it's his olive grove,' he said in his accommodating tone.

He then changed the subject, as if the previous conversation had never taken place. He turned to Alberto and me.

'As for you boys, seeing your excellent academic results, I have a present for you.'

My excellent academic results! Could Papa now tell fortunes? The results weren't out yet.

'Alberto, I've booked a language course in Oxford in September, the one you were wanting to take.'

Alberto looked concerned.

'But Papa, that course costs an arm and a leg! You could have waited. Perhaps with my results I could get a grant.'

'Please don't worry, Alberto. The money spent on your education is an investment.'

My father then looked at me.

And for me, Papa? Perhaps a holiday with the Foreign Legion?

'For you, it's a surprise. And we leave today.'

I was more incredulous than angry. I pressed the point again.

'I am *not* going to Rome!'

He slipped a brochure over to me. Three days on a lion hunt in a Tanzanian game reserve. A night flight that very evening. It was a childhood dream. I'd devoured books, films and photos on the subject.

He's able to engineer everything. He can read your soul and buy it, without giving you any time to think.

It was a shameless attempt to seduce me by his usual methods: a mouth-watering surprise with no time for me to consider the matter.

I was about to tell him to go to hell when a thought crossed my mind. Was it a thought, or simply a regret from a lost childhood?

Perhaps it's a last opportunity to understand one another, Papa.

I forced myself to smile, trying to be something of the son he wanted me to be. Not the one who, after peppering sparrows, lizards and frogs with pellets, had turned to killing human beings.

'Thanks, Papa. That's great. I'll go and get ready.'

I exchanged glances with my mother, just for a second. Then she looked at my father and asked him that damned question.

'Did you see Marlene and Laura in Rome, Salvo?'

The great salesman hesitated a second, made a vague gesture of assent and gave me a beaming smile.

'We'll have some great fun, Mikey! Go and get your bags ready.'

Tuesday, 12 August 1969

We took the night flight to Nairobi and then on to Dar es Salaam. From there, we went by light aircraft and were in Southern Tanzania's Selous region in less than two hours. It was both the best place and the best season for hunting lion. And for not thinking about Nadia, Marlene and Laura.

During the flight, Papa and I discussed rifles, calibres, tracking and bait. I wanted to use a 12-gauge smooth-bore shotgun, which is what I was used to, but Papa had already been on a few safaris and advised against it.

'You need a hunting rifle, Mikey, with .375 ammunition and a good telescopic sight for shooting at dusk or dawn. With the target lined up, you need rapid fire.'

'You don't need any rapid fire, Papa.'

'You're not used to a rifle, Mikey. Once we get to camp you'll have only a couple of days to learn how to use it. There's always the possibility of only wounding one, and a wounded lion is truly an ugly beast.'

'How could I not kill it with a .375 bullet that travels at almost seven hundred metres a second?'

'Believe me, Mikey, you need to hit in the chest between the ribs, and it's not that easy. Even a badly wounded lion can still run at you at fifteen metres a second, and for ten seconds. They can easily cover a hundred and fifty metres; the stronger ones even more.'

My father had little faith in my maths. But that hypothetical lion charging towards me and ready to claw my brains out held no fear for me.

What frightens me more is the life you want me to lead, Papa.

From the aeroplane window I could see the Africa I'd always dreamed about: first, a mass of vegetation, then the brick-red rough terrain with its low, dense bushes. As we flew over the Kilombero River, the pilot descended, and now I could see hippos flocking to drink there, along with buffalo, antelope and impala.

'Happy, Mikey?'

With this unexpected gift, was Papa trying to make me forget that everything wasn't right between him and me, and in my life? In part, he was succeeding. But it was only temporary. We both knew this. And yet neither of us wanted to face the fact.

I can never be the son you want me to be.

We arrived at the base camp on the Kilombero River in the afternoon. The temperature was agreeable, just over twenty degrees. In charge of the camp was Ian, a professional hunter from South Africa who Papa already knew. His French wife was in charge of the kitchen. The others were native Tanzanians, all smiling and extremely polite. We had only two and a half days' hunting and had to use the time well. So, for the rest of the afternoon, I practised with the hunting rifle.

Ian looked incredulously at my father.

'Your son's a real champion, sir.'

Yes, this son knows only how to shoot and land a punch.

We ate out in the open that evening, cocooned in large pullovers by the fire. It was under ten degrees and dead quiet, the African night illuminated by stars I had never seen before.

When Ian and his wife retired for the night, Papa and I were left alone. He had a whisky and was smoking a cigar. He offered the same to me.

'No, thanks, Papa. I don't like the smoke or the taste of alcohol. I'll never touch either.'

Papa laughed aloud, patting his thick locks of hair and showing his gleaming white teeth. It was true: he did look like Clark Gable.

'Always so cocksure of yourself and assertive! So you like it here? Would you like to live like Ian?'

I could have said that this wasn't the point. It wasn't a matter of starry skies, nature, hunting rifles, lions, Africa.

It's about freedom, Papa. Like the bird and the drunk in Leonard Cohen's song. The freedom to be as I am and not to be like you.

'Do you think a man's happiness depends on how wealthy he is, Papa?'

He took his time to ponder the question.

'That's not how it is, Mikey. Wealth doesn't bring happiness. But poverty's a sure-fire way of being unhappy, even if you and your mother can't see it.'

Because we didn't grow up in a family of five kids in a poky hole with no bathroom.

'Then why did you marry Mamma, if she doesn't understand you?'

There was only a moment's pause. But it was a pause too long.

Because she was rolling in it, Mikey. And I need that olive grove. What I'm doing is for you and your brother as well, you know.

Wednesday, 13 August 1969

I practised with the rifle all day. Calibration of the sights, magnification, position, target points. We shot buffalo, gnu and impala. But I wanted the king of the beasts. During supper around the fire, Ian gave us the good news.

'We've found the tracks of a lion of over two hundred kilos, an adult male. It's very, very big. We can have a go tomorrow before sundown.'

After supper, Papa took me to one side, away from the fire.

'The plane I've booked to take us to Nairobi can wait a couple of hours. What do you say, Mikey?'

'I'm all for it, Papa.'

'I know you're all for it. That's what worries me. You work on instinct, not by reason. That lion is very big.'

'Do you mean I'm not wise? Are you always so wise, Papa?'

'I try to be rational, which doesn't always mean wise. When you desire something that's dangerous, you have to weigh up if the risk is acceptable.'

Such as fucking Marlene in Rome, far away from Mamma and William Hunt?

'I'm not like you, Papa. If I really want something, then I go for it. No matter what the cost, and I'm ready to accept the consequences.'

Papa didn't agree.

'A lion isn't a dove or a hare, Mikey. You weigh up the possible benefits and make your decision, just as in business.'

'Business'. This word was the obstacle to any attempt to find a meeting point. I wanted to find that point. But in order to do so I had to be clear with him.

'I don't like business, Papa. And I don't like Italy. I'll never go and live there.'

My father immediately frowned.

'Why not?'

'Because it's a country where everyone's ready to go behind everyone else's back if they think there's some advantage to be gained.'

Clark Gable, the great salesman, gave me an understanding smile. He knew perfectly well when to let things drop.

'Very well, decision taken. We'll have the plane wait a couple of hours. Now, off to bed, it's going to be a tough day tomorrow.'

Thursday, 14 August 1969

It needed more than ten men to set the trap: a large piece of buffalo tied by a rope over a branch at a height other animals couldn't reach.

But not this beast. Not the king of the jungle.

Ian and my father looked on with satisfaction as the men hoisted
up the rope with its fifty kilos of carcass. They tied another thirty
kilos of blood-soaked meat to the Land Rover and dragged it from
the tree to where the lion tracks had been spotted.

We placed ourselves downwind on a mound two hundred metres
from the bait. The waiting lasted all afternoon and, as the sun was
beginning to set, I dozed off.

I dreamed of Marlene sunbathing naked on the terrace. I was
spreading sunblock on her shoulders, then lower down, towards her
buttocks.

'Mikey.'

I woke up suddenly, terrified. Had I been speaking in my sleep?
Papa's voice was soft as I roused myself.

'Quiet,' whispered Ian, ready with his rifle. 'Damn, it's so big!'

Ian's gun was much more wieldy than mine, with a single-point
sight which would allow him to keep both eyes open and fire a back-
up shot as quickly as possible.

In case I make an error and only wound it.

I looked at the bait in the tree. There was no lion. I let my eyes run between the trees and thorn bushes. And then I saw it. Huge, majestic and very close. Too close: about a hundred metres.

'Too close, Mikey. Too risky,' Ian hissed.

Yes, it really was too close.

If I only wound it, it'll be right on top of us, even if Ian fires a back-up shot.

I met my father's look. He was signalling no.

'Wait till it gets to the bait, Mikey.'

I had to get him to see what I'd said last night. He didn't want to understand this son who was so different from his ideal model. He didn't want to accept that I wasn't Salvatore Balistreri. Nor was I Alberto.

I started to set the rifle up. I fixed the lion in my sights. It only needed a six magnification. It was like having it there, two steps away from me.

'No, Mikey,' Ian warned. 'Don't shoot yet.'

I took the safety off and calculated.

At seven hundred metres per second a .375 projectile will hit the target in little over a tenth of a second. But it's not a question of velocity or power. It's precision that counts. I have to hit it in the centre of its chest and the shot has to penetrate between the ribs.

But the lion had its flank to us. I waited. I couldn't even feel my heartbeats. Then a slight noise. The lion turned round and, for a second, its eyes met mine in the sight.

The king of the jungle. Magnificent, strong, invincible.

The shot resounded like cannon fire in the wide open space, followed by a very long second when we all stopped breathing.

Then the lion dropped to the ground. Ian looked at me, speechless. My father was shaking his head.

There was no need for a back-up shot. The bullet had gone in between the ribs, passed through the heart and the entire length of its body and come to a stop in a back paw.

Everyone was full of praise. Everyone except my father.

He's looking beyond the lion. Now he knows who his son is.

Friday, 15 August 1969

Papa and I arrived back in Tripoli at dawn on the night flight from Nairobi. It was the day of my nineteenth birthday.

Outside the airport, it was already well over forty degrees. Mohammed was waiting for us in the jeep with Ahmed and Karim and took us to the Balistreri villa through a deserted city, in which everyone was holed up inside against the heat.

'Mr Hunt came back from Vietnam yesterday,' Mohammed announced. 'Signora Hunt and Laura are coming in from London late this afternoon.'

'Did you see Marlene and Laura in Rome, Salvo?'

Over a lunch of fish, Papa related the story of our Tanzanian trip in his own way to Grandad, Mamma and Alberto. He magnified the shot with which I killed the lion, skipping over the risk we ran, as if he and I had become the greatest of friends.

In the afternoon, I walked in the garden surrounding the villas. Although I didn't want to admit it, I was waiting for Laura and Marlene to arrive.

And which of the two, Mikey?

Consumed with anger, I went and shut myself in my room and

listened to Leonard Cohen until it was suppertime. And then the surprises began.

Papa had made a Sicilian dish of pasta and sardines, which he cooked very well on the rare occasions he ventured into the kitchen. Grandad had made *baccalà alla veneziana*, with help from Alberto. But the amazing thing was that Italia had made my favourite pudding, a Sicilian cassata, from an old recipe book. I hadn't seen my mother cook once in all those years.

But the surprises didn't end there. A few minutes before we sat down to eat, Laura arrived on her own, without William or Marlene Hunt.

'Laura's our guest tonight. Her parents have gone to a reception that'll end very late. She's dining with us and will stay the night here,' Italia announced.

I looked at my mother, who was so against plots of any kind. And yet she'd arranged all this, even down to inviting Laura. And all for me.

For this son of yours who has the same sour blood as you, who kills lions but still needs your affection.

But during supper the thought of Nadia still hung over us. We talked and smiled, but there was no real happiness. Laura explained the intricacies of the Rolleiflex, from which she was by now inseparable, and went on to the development of her art, from landscapes to portraits, and the contrasts seen in faces.

Good and evil.

In the end, Laura sang 'Happy Birthday' with my family and took snaps while I blew out the nineteen candles on my cake. It was Papa who asked me to make a speech, but I declined.

'Not even a few words, Mikey?'

I looked at him.

' "Better to be crazy on one's own account than be wise according to the wishes of others, Papa." '

They all looked at me, dumbfounded, but they were used to my strange behaviour, and the sentence wasn't offensive. I exchanged looks with Mamma. She knew very well what I meant; she recognized the quote from Nietzsche. But there was no smile. She was tired. Or frightened. Or both.

After supper, Laura and I strolled alone in the large garden around the villas.

'So you're going to be a photographer?'

'Yes, of real people, if I can. Like in the city of the living and the dead in Cairo, where Karim worked.'

'Ahmed helped the refugees as well.'

'No, Mikey, he doesn't care about the poor. Karim isn't anything like him. Nor are you, I hope.'

'How do you know what I'm like?'

The question was a little aggressive, and I knew it. But I was jealous and upset.

Laura didn't react. For her, arguing was pure folly.

'Do you remember Kirk Douglas, when he went to the gunfight with his pistol unloaded?'

'Yes, and so?'

'Winning isn't your thing, Mikey.'

'Don't start talking weird; I'm not Karim.'

'I know you're not Karim. You've got many things he hasn't, but he's got one advantage over you. He was born poor.'

'And Ahmed? He was born as poor as Karim!'

Laura paused for a moment, as if thinking about it.

'The poor have no middle way in life. For them, it's either ideas or strength.'

'Why do you hate Ahmed, Laura?'

Now she decided to be serious.

'I don't hate him, Mikey. But over ten years ago I met a young boy. I liked him a lot, and you know why?'

I said nothing. What was I expecting?

A declaration of love or a goodbye?

Laura pointed to the precise spot where Kirk Douglas fell all those years ago with his unloaded pistol.

'That boy didn't need to win. He preferred to be a loser, a beautiful one. And loved.'

And Ahmed takes me away from being that young boy.

Laura took a white envelope from the back pocket of her jeans.

'Two photos, Mikey. My birthday present for you.'

I took hold of the envelope gingerly, as if it held a bomb.

The first photograph was in colour and must have been taken by Marlene during the recent trip to Rome. Laura was wearing a low-cut black evening dress that went down to her ankles, with thin shoulder straps that left her arms bare. She was going down the Spanish Steps in Piazza di Spagna with the elegant, slow gait of an eighteen-year-old model. That was her age, but she had the knowing look of a woman of thirty.

'I look just like my mother, don't I?'

I was a little vacant, having no idea what to say. I didn't want to think that Laura resembled Marlene. Or perhaps I did, in part. I wanted both of them, but completely differently and separately.

One's an angel, the other's a devil.

'Your father invited us to an important party, in Rome, and Mom had to buy me a dress.'

'Did you see Marlene Hunt in Rome, Salvo?'

'So I asked Marlene to take a picture of me.'

'You look just like your mother.'

'What do you like about it?' she asked.

The usual too-direct question. Serious, but with no malice or irony. A question that took part of the reply as a given. It was that 'what' that made it impossible to give an answer.

I like that look that makes you feel like you're the only one in the world, but in two completely different ways.

She seemed to read my thoughts, as had happened since we were kids.

'It's the photo of how I'll never be, Mikey.'

And now you know, Mike. You can make your choice in life.

To change the subject, I slipped the second photo out of the envelope. It was in black and white, taken by surprise more than two years ago in this very garden: me, with the sun in my eyes, when I'd been expelled from school. A well-built boy just seventeen who had grown too quickly, muscular and awkward, with an insecure and belligerent manner, holding up an arm to protect himself from the setting sun.

Because of that arm, a sharp shadow cut almost diagonally across my face, leaving half in the sun and half in the shade.

Good and evil.

I was afraid that Laura could see into the depths of my soul, but I also wanted her to.

I drew close to her in the garden shadows.

'Give me what's missing, Laura. Please give it to me.'

She smiled at me and turned the photo over. There was an inscription.

To my beautiful loser.

She brought her face a few centimetres from mine.

'There's nothing to give, Mikey,' she whispered, 'because, for me, there's nothing missing.'

It was our first real kiss. A kiss between two faces divided in half.

Saturday, 30 August 1969

In the following two weeks no one spoke any more of Nadia's death. The only sign of that tragedy were the hours that Ahmed and Karim spent locked in their wooden shack on Mohammed's orders. Although Ahmed was nearly twenty and Karim nearly eighteen, their Muslim upbringing bound them to obligations that were incomprehensible to me. I saw nothing of them for two weeks.

Nico sent me several postcards from various American cities. After Woodstock he went to New York City, then Florida, then California, and yet all the postcards were the same. Bosomy blondes in bikinis.

Papa went to Italy again for several days with Mohammed. They came back on the evening of 28 August, two days before his forty-fourth birthday. All these trips meant that his activities now extended beyond the Mediterranean Sea, and his range of business even wider.

Mohammed had told my mother not to cancel my father's usual birthday party on account of Nadia. Probably because he knew how useful these social gatherings were to Salvatore Balistreri's business affairs. And therefore to himself as well.

Although my mother was against it at first, in the end she was persuaded to go ahead, but decided to cut down the celebrations by half.

There would simply be a dinner dance on La Moneta that Saturday night. The music would be light; no head-banging rock and no fireworks. Then most of the guests would go home.

I was glad the occasion meant that the four of us in the MANK organization could see each other again and decide what to do about our concern in Cairo. Nico had only been back two days, and there'd been no time to meet up.

After lunch that day, I was at the helm of the motorboat. We had the three Hunts on board. Italia had agreed to let them stay the night after the party. I knew she was doing it for Laura and me, for our hypothetical relationship, a relationship that would make her so happy.

While I was at the helm, Marlene decided she wanted to sunbathe.

'The sea's like glass. Can I stretch out on the prow?'

We were almost there; another ten minutes and Marlene could have sunned herself comfortably on the beach. But you couldn't say no to Marlene.

'Of course, Marlene,' my father said. 'Mikey, watch the sea, and careful with the waves.'

I shot a glance at my mother. As usual, she was wearing a long dress down to her ankles with long sleeves to protect her pale complexion from the burning sun. She had a scarf round her short hair, and large sunglasses. She was standing up astern with her back to us, smoking and contemplating the coastline. Her preference was to look at the sea from dry land. She actually disliked being at sea and even more being in it. And, that day, she seemed more distant than her usual self.

Observing her, I had the clear impression that something was wrong. There was a strange tension in the air, as if everyone knew something unpleasant about which no one knew what to say.

Laura was on my left, next to William Hunt, who was speaking in English to my brother, Alberto. They were talking about Vietnam and the war that was perhaps about to end.

'Would you really withdraw from Vietnam?' Alberto asked, incredulous.

'Unfortunately, our politicians haven't understood that you have to respond to barbarity with horror,' William Hunt replied.

Laura and I immediately exchanged glances.

We'll never be the same as our parents.

As we drew close to La Moneta, I saw the Libyan coast guard vessels patrolling an area particularly favoured by cigarette smugglers because it had lots of coves where you could dock and unload.

My father was standing behind me, like the true captain he was. I couldn't see him, but I was sure that, like me, he was looking at Marlene's splendid body as she lay flat on her stomach, sunbathing. I was studying the edges of the costume which ran over the curves of her hips and buttocks and down between her thighs.

What I felt for Laura couldn't sweep away that violent desire.

Instead of worrying about my parents' marriage, I was feeling impossible, unacceptable things. Jealousy, competition, anger.

What does Ingegner Balistreri have that I don't?

It was a stupid question. The jealousy of a nineteen-year-old facing two grown-ups who were perhaps lovers, one of whom was my father and the other the mother of my theoretical girlfriend.

'Watch out, Michele, there's the skin-divers' buoy!' my father warned.

I changed course sharply, the boat swerved and a wave caught the back of Marlene, who let out a yell. Then she began to laugh.

'Damn you, Mikey! *Mi hai schizzata!*'

The last three words she said in her Italian of sorts, learned in the years they were in Rome. Perhaps only I caught the possible double meaning: '*schizzata*' or '*scherzata*'? A splash, or a joke with a vague promise of something else?

My father ordered me to leave the wheel and hand it to my brother. Then he spoke in Sicilian dialect, as he did only rarely, and with a smile.

'Then you can give it a bit of a rest, eh?'

So he'd seen me looking at Marlene's backside, having been looking in the same direction himself.

It was two thirty when we got to La Moneta, and it was boiling hot. Preparations for the dinner had been followed to perfection by Mohammed, with the help of Ahmed, Karim and Nico.

It had been a good many days since we'd seen each other and we weren't used to it. And, on top of everything, there was Nadia's death. None of us had any wish to talk about the MANK organization and its business. We walked away to one side and Nico told us about his American trip.

Exciting stories: massive concerts, massive stars, Hollywood, its villas, drugs, long limousines.

'We should move the MANK organization over there,' he said in conclusion.

Karim pulled a face.

'I'd prefer to starve to death in Africa than live like an American. Islam will reduce it to ashes one day, anyway.'

Nico looked at him askance.

'You're wrong, Karim. It'll be America that'll reduce you to ashes, whenever it wants, because it's a civilized country and you're just a bunch of savages.'

It was pointless talk, and insulting to Ahmed and Karim. I fixed him with an ironic smile.

'The most you'll ever do, Nico, is open a knocking shop above our restaurant in Cairo. That's what you'll do.'

Perhaps I was too hard on him. But all that excitement, with Nadia only recently dead, was out of place. Except that Nico was hurt. I could see it in his eyes. But, at that moment, I couldn't deal with his insecurities.

I looked at my three friends in the MANK organization. And at

Laura, the girl I was in love with. I knew what was needed. 'Hey, let's go and dive off the cliff.'

'It's twenty metres down, Mikey. And from up there you can't tell if the water's deep enough,' objected Karim.

I checked the time. Almost three. Impossible to be sure. High tide was twice a day, but during the year the times changed.

'Oh, come on, let's go!'

We went over to Alberto and Laura, who were chatting on the beach, and explained the problem.

'The only solution is for someone to go with the motorboat and check, then give the signal to those on the cliff if the water's deep enough to dive into,' Alberto said.

'Laura could go,' Ahmed said. 'I don't think she'd jump off from up there anyway.'

She ignored him. 'If it's Alberto who's telling me it's OK, I'd be the first to go.'

As usual, my brother took on the most demanding and least pleasant job. While the MANK organization plus Laura took the path to the other side of the island, Alberto went round the coast in the motorboat.

It took us half an hour to walk the sandy track between the rocks and scrub before we were on the clear patch above the cliff. There was a single olive tree and seat, where my mother spent time with a book. The Mediterranean was a mirror of blue, twenty metres below us.

We went to the cliff edge. I lay flat on the ground and tried to lean my head out to see if there were rocks below. Impossible to see: the rock wall went in too steeply.

After a few minutes, Alberto arrived with the motorboat. He drew near to the shore and we saw him disappear below us. As usual, he was meticulous, cautious and prudent. He'd even brought a megaphone with him which my father kept in the house.

'The tide's going out,' he shouted to us. 'But if you jump straight-away it's still good.'

I looked at my friends.

'Ready?'

'How about all together?' Laura proposed.

We all joined hands. Laura was in the middle, myself and Ahmed on one side, Karim and Nico on the other. It was a fantastic sensation, unique. We gazed out into the empty space in front of us, without looking down.

'I'm counting to three!' Laura exclaimed.

One. I felt Ahmed squeezing my hand. Two. I squeezed Laura's hand. Three.

We set off at a run and leaped out, letting ourselves fall into the blueness of that welcoming sea.

Alberto took us on board and back to the villa's beach. The guests were starting to arrive.

Little Arab boys in waiter's uniform were keeping the flies off the food with fans. Arab women were preparing *pasta alla Norma* and a fish couscous. A Sicilian classic of pasta and aubergine and a native Arabic dish, just as my father wanted. They stood for union and reciprocal respect.

The guests were arriving in groups in the two motorboats: one piloted by Farid, the other by Salim; both hired specially for the occasion and both handsomely rewarded. They had expanded a great deal in the past two years. Their business had become a small industry: a much larger fishing boat, ten employees, a twelve-metre Zodiac rubber dinghy with two 200hp outboard motors. They had bought the motorboats to take the best fish in the shortest time to Malta's lucrative restaurant market. But, that afternoon, they were ferrying several ambassadors, dignitaries from King Idriss's court, two of his ministers and the directors of major companies out to La Moneta.

And, naturally, Emilio Busi and Don Eugenio.

Papa was looking his best. His hair was still naturally black, combed straight back, his slim moustache well trimmed, and he was sporting a tan from the Tanzanian trip. Wearing a spotless white linen suit, dark-blue shirt and a sky-blue tie, he looked relaxed, and evidently pleased with himself.

He was aware of the appeal of his good looks and power. He had succeeded in ridding himself of Palermo's unwholesome taint of poverty and was keeping well under control the slight trickle of saliva he felt as he looked at the world. Everyone – Italians and Libyans, the dignitaries from court and the ministers – had come to greet him and pay their respects.

The men then went on to pay their respects to William Hunt and, above all, to his extremely beautiful wife, as if she were the guest of honour. Marlene was wearing a light low-cut dress bought on Rome's Via Condotti. The cleft between her suntanned breasts and the curve of the dress over her buttocks attracted me as much as they did the court dignitaries, ministers, diplomats and company directors. William Hunt was clearly aware of the lustful glances directed at his wife, and yet he seemed neither concerned nor upset.

He's a man of integrity with a blind faith in his wife. He'd never think that she would cheat on him.

The only men not looking at Marlene were Don Eugenio and Emilio Busi. The first came as no surprise. But why not Busi? He was sitting on his own, smoking in the shade of one of the beach gazebos. While I was watching him I realized with a certain disquiet that the eyes behind those dreadful square hornrims were not on Marlene but on another woman, my mother.

She was seeing to the guests with a cordial formality equal to the look of regal disdain in her eyes. She did not approve of this party, less than a month after Nadia's murder. But it was something beyond that. I could feel her deep sadness and imagined I knew the cause.

It was my father and Marlene Hunt.

I met her gaze.

I hate to see you suffer, Mamma.

Italia went off to the rear of the villa, where the sandy track that led to the other side of the island began. Without thinking about it, I followed her, keeping enough distance so that she wouldn't see me. It was the same path I had taken that afternoon with Laura and my three MANK organization friends.

Back then, my spirits had been up. But now I felt oppressed, without really knowing why.

When I got to the open patch on the cliff top, Italia was looking across to Sicily. The sun had turned red and was beginning to set.

I settled myself behind a rock. A quarter of an hour later, William Hunt appeared along the path. Small drops of sweat dotted his forehead and square jaw. His short blond hair was turning grey at the temples. I hid myself better and waited.

Italia skipped the preliminaries and handed him a white envelope.

'Everything's in there. There's no room for any doubt.'

William Hunt took the envelope and put it in his pocket without opening it.

'How much time do I have?'

Italia thought for a moment.

'Two days, no more.'

It was certainly no friendly chat between two close neighbours. It seemed more of a business transaction.

Or an exchange of information between two people who have discovered they've been betrayed.

Italia turned away from him and started to walk. She stopped less than a metre from the cliff edge. William Hunt studied her for a long moment with those metallic blue eyes, his look more serious and concerned than usual. Then he turned the other way and started to walk down the path back to the villa. To the west, the sun's red ball was half in the sky and half under the sea.

Just like my face in Laura's snapshot. Divided between good and evil.

When I got back to the villa, all the guests had arrived. Papa was chatting to William Hunt and Marlene by the telephone in the large kitchen.

'You'll have to excuse me, Salvatore, I've just heard from Wheelus Field. Urgent business. I have to go.'

My father seemed strangely concerned, far too much so.

'But William, it's late. Can't you go tomorrow?'

'I'm sorry, Salvo. Marlene will have to sing "Happy Birthday" to you for me as well.'

Was there any irony in the words?

Or a subtle threat? A last warning both to him and to Marlene?

My father had to give in.

'Very well. I'll tell Farid to take you back to the Underwater Club.'

William thanked him, then turned to Marlene.

'I need to talk to you for a minute, dear. Would you excuse us, Salvo?'

'Of course, of course. I'll go and tell Farid.'

William Hunt and Marlene went off to one side, deep in conversation. I imagined there were difficult questions between them, evasive answers, the first accusations, perhaps even a threat. I saw my father giving instructions to Farid. Busi entered the house to make a phone call, and Don Eugenio looked worriedly at my father.

At the bottom of the lawn, with a scarf round her head and wearing those huge sunglasses despite the fact the sun had set, stood my mother. She was on her own in front of the villa, smoking in silence, observing the conversation between William and Marlene Hunt.

Whatever you decide, Mamma, I'll be standing right beside you.

★　　★　　★

When Italia went back into the house, I waited a moment and then followed her in.

She had poured herself a whisky and was talking to Emilio Busi, who had finished a phone call.

The tone of the conversation was calm and polite, the voices steady.

'If you think the same as I do about the Americans, Signora Italia, then please don't offer to help them.'

I looked closely at my mother. Her pale face was now whiter than ever.

'I have to go to the kitchen and see that Salvatore's birthday cake has all its forty-four candles. Enjoy the party.'

So I was left alone with him. Despite my feelings, Busi wasn't totally unlikeable.

He's prepared to fight for his beliefs, even if I don't share them. And he doesn't do it to line his own pockets.

'What do you think of the Americans, Mikey?' Busi asked me, through the smoke from his putrid plain-tipped Nazionale.

There was no sarcasm in the question. In some way, he respected me, even in the face of my continual sniping comments about Ingegnere Balistreri. Perhaps it was because I wasn't greedy for money and power like my father and Mohammed.

'Like you, I think that the world's had a raw deal from the Americans, Signor Busi. But it's you Communists who welcomed them in, you and the Sicilian Mafia. A very holy alliance indeed.'

Busi smiled. I had the impression he was listening to me, much more than my father did, and that partly – but only partly – he shared my feelings.

'I was still a boy under Fascism, Mikey. Do you know what it means to see your father taken from home and not know if he'll ever come back? And just for letting a word drop against a local party official after a few glasses of wine in the local inn.'

Busi took off his glasses and massaged his eyelids. He pulled a wry face.

'Do you know why I left the Carabinieri force and joined the Communist Party?'

'So you could make a load of money?' I said, straightaway.

He shook his head and gave me a condescending smile.

'If I'd wanted money, I'd have sided with my father. No, Mikey, I'm thirty-four; I have experience and determination. I want to fight Catholicism's backwardness and also change Communism from the inside.'

'And, in the meantime, engage in a little business.'

'Not a single lira goes in my pocket. The money all goes to the Party and they use it to buy votes. We need cars, petrol and the industrialists who make them, Mikey. They're the ones who create jobs and a better life. Otherwise, people would be starving to death.'

'Sure they would. And you'll all make us the gift of a world where we know the price of everything and the value of nothing.'

Busi thought seriously, and nodded.

'It could be. But, in war, there's always a price to pay, Mikey.'

True. There was a war going on. This was very clear to me. We were agreed about that.

The dance floor was full of couples. My father was dancing with Marlene Hunt. They weren't holding each other too close, being careful to observe the proprieties – but their smiles, good looks and extraordinary attractiveness said everything. And was seen by everyone looking at them.

Or perhaps not. Perhaps I was imagining it. You know, Mikey, the enemy of truth is a strongly held conviction.

Laura took my hand and led me on to the floor. She knew very well I hated dancing, and she had no liking for it herself. So why did she do it?

Procul Harum's Hammond organ was playing the final part of 'A Whiter Shade of Pale'.

Her light eyes were covered by those rebellious black curls.

'What's up, Mikey?'

'I have to talk to my father. And you must talk to your mother, Laura.'

She hugged me a little closer.

'Trust them, Mikey.'

'I can't,' I said brusquely, letting go of her.

I can't and I don't want to.

I left the dance floor and swiftly entered the house. I'd taken the decision on an impulse, but I knew it was the right one.

William Hunt's a hero and a man with loyalty. He'll know what to do.

I got to the telephone. I knew the Wheelus Field switchboard number off by heart. A telephonist answered.

'I'm sorry, sir. Mr Hunt's aircraft has just taken off.'

'Taken off? Where for?'

There was a moment's silence. Then the telephonist's polite voice.

'I can't tell you that, sir. It's a military flight.'

There was another path available, in the form of one influential person who could still be afraid of me.

Because of those nice photographs with Nico Gerace.

Don Eugenio was discussing finance with the managers of the Banco di Roma and Banco di Sicilia. Like Busi, he was only thirty-four, but was talking away as if he ran the Banca d'Italia.

'I need to talk to you,' I said, rudely interrupting a discussion on interest rates.

His light-blue eyes looked at me quizzically. With his cassock, sandals and delicate manners, he really seemed the benefactor he claimed to be.

'Do you need to confess, Mikey?'

'Not to you.'

My answer convinced him of the need to detach himself from the bankers. We went over to the beach, along the pathway of Positano tiles laid into the sand. Frank Sinatra's warm tones could be heard singing his latest hit, 'My Way'.

'Good song, isn't it, Mikey? And that's what you've wanted to be since you were a boy: the fearless knight in shining armour. Like when you wanted to save Nico by reading that sentence in his place.'

By freely referring to the event, Don Eugenio was letting me know he felt quite safe. Seven years earlier, I could have destroyed him with those photographs. But I was a child then, and it had been Mamma who had resolved matters in some way and saved me from becoming an altar boy.

No other unpleasant episode had emerged in those seven years. It was as if the priest who couldn't keep his hands to himself had found a way to cure his illness. Perhaps precisely because of those photographs.

'Don't you feel ashamed about that business? You were our teacher. You should have been looking after us, rather than . . .'

Don Eugenio stared at me. He appeared to be sincere.

'It was a grave error, never again committed. I have confessed and God has forgiven me.'

'And Nico Gerace? Don't you need his forgiveness as well?'

He looked far away, towards the sea between La Moneta and Giorgimpopoli, where two Libyan Coast Guard cutters were patrolling the waters, looking out for landings by cigarette smugglers.

'Nico's grown up, he's happy. Thanks also to you, Mikey. You've given him the self-esteem he needed. My apologies would be no use to him; they'd only bring back bad memories. But you've not come to seek me out for that old business, I take it.'

No, I'm here to make my father come to his senses.

'You must speak to my father. This business with Marlene Hunt . . .'

Don Eugenio sighed, as if he knew I was right.

'No one's perfect, Mikey. Not even us priests, as you've just reminded me. As to Marlene Hunt, not even you . . .'

He saw you, Mike. He saw you leaving the villa in a state after spreading sunblock on her back.

'You have to tell my father . . .'

Don Eugenio interrupted me, politely but firmly.

'I am his confessor, Mikey. I know what I should and shouldn't say to him. You, on the other hand, don't go to confession any more. Perhaps it's time you did.'

I would have been happy to land him in the water with a well-aimed *tae*. But that wasn't the way. I knew there was only one way to get to his soul. Fear. Not of me; he certainly had no fear of me.

'My mother still has those photographs, Don Eugenio. If you don't get my father to mend his ways . . .'

But he made no reply to the threat. I left him on the shore by the silence of that sea.

Night of Saturday and Sunday 30 to 31 August, 1969

From midnight onwards, Farid and Salim ferried the guests back in the two motorboats, then the serving staff, once they had finished cleaning up. After that, they came back to sleep at La Moneta.

My mother made it clear that guests staying the night would help themselves to breakfast the next morning and, for lunch, would go to the Underwater Club. With Nadia only recently dead, my father's party had gone on a little too long.

On the island that night were the Balistreri family, with Grandad, Marlene and Laura Hunt, Busi and Don Eugenio. Mohammed, his four sons and Nico would sleep in the servants' quarters.

Salvatore Balistreri, Don Eugenio, Emilio Busi and Mohammed were sitting in the dark under one of the beach gazebos set up for the party. Now that the guests had departed and the others were asleep, they could talk in the silence of the humid night.

'Is everything ready?' Balistreri asked Mohammed.

'Yes. The Al Aqsa Mosque in Jerusalem was set fire to recently by a Christian extremist and the Libyan police have been mobilized round the clock to stop any protest demonstrations by Islamic extremists here. The alert will end tomorrow in the early afternoon and, after three sleepless nights, General Jalloun will send them all home to rest. Tomorrow night, Tripoli will be without a police force.'

'Is General Jalloun on our side?' Busi asked.

'No,' Mohammed replied. 'He's loyal to the Senussi royals. But he's scared, won't do a thing and wants to ingratiate himself with the new regime.'

'This sudden trip of attaché Hunt worries me. Are we agreed nevertheless for tomorrow night?' Don Eugenio asked.

Busi interjected straightaway.

'I've already checked with Rome. The few in the know there assure me that all information about us is absolutely secure. Unless something leaks out here in Tripoli . . .'

Mohammed was more than ready with an answer. His role had now changed. He was no longer Balistreri's general dogsbody, but his accomplice in a *coup d'état* who was representing his interests for the new regime.

'It won't. These junior officers risk being hanged for high treason. And we still haven't given the go-ahead, therefore no one officially knows a thing. William Hunt will have been called away because of the worsening situation in Vietnam.'

'Are we sure about the new leader?' Busi asked in a last moment of doubt.

'We met him a few days ago in Italy. Everything's in order, isn't it, Mohammed?' Balistreri said.

Mohammed agreed.

'He's a young man with backbone who grew up in my very own tribe. I know his family and we're very good friends.'

'We're not concerned with your family's friendships here, Mohammed, but this X's future relationship with Italy.'

Balistreri looked at Busi. He really was a difficult man. He gave him an ironic smile.

'Did you know that X is actually a Juventus fan? He's said that, one day, when he's in power, he'll buy some stock in it. Doesn't that set your mind at rest?'

But Busi was in no mood for jokes.

'Great, we can all go together and watch matches with him. But, for the moment, I think we should stick very close to him.'

Mohammed replied in his serious manner.

'Of course. I'm leaving for Benghazi tomorrow, and tomorrow night will be right at his side.'

Don Eugenio turned to speak to Mohammed.

'It's essential to avoid any bloodshed.'

'Yes, that way the West will confine itself to working out who the leader is and what he's thinking,' Busi explained. 'I know my fellow Party members. They'll be sceptical to begin with, but they'll support the change if there's no violence.'

Mohammed smiled. By now, he was inured to these Italians and their base hypocrisy.

'There'll be no deaths, gentlemen. Perhaps several old men might die of fright and a few of the powerful from a broken heart, but no Libyan would give his life for this pro-Israeli and pro-American King.'

Salvatore Balistreri looked with pride at this ex-dogsbody of his, who was about to become their key man on the new Libyan power scene.

At the same moment, in Benghazi, William Hunt was sitting in a bare room in the airport's military zone. From the window he could see the aeroplane that had brought him from Wheelus Field.

He was ready for the fight. Just as in Korea, when those damned Chinese had crossed the bridge over the frozen Yalu River.

No, he was more than ready. He allowed himself to smile at a memory.

How many Chinese temples placed next to each other can a Colt 45 penetrate?

Unfortunately, President Truman was a politician and a coward. He had no balls to do what his chief of staff, General MacArthur, suggested.

Those Chinese need to remember what we did to the Japanese in Hiroshima and Nagasaki.

But MacArthur had been reinstated. And Hunt, taking advantage of his wounds, had returned to the United States. Except, American politicians still hadn't got it.

Horror can only be fought with horror.

Vietnam was proving this. You don't win wars by discussions with the media and with the pacifists. And you don't win them by political means.

He made his first call. It was afternoon in the United States. The person in Washington who replied listened to him carefully.

'Stay in Benghazi, Mr Hunt. We'll give you further instructions tomorrow morning.'

Tomorrow morning, fine. As if the hours didn't count at all.

He knew very well that, in certain cases, every minute was precious.

His mind turned to Italia Balistreri, who was, without doubt, an extraordinary woman. Regal, rock solid and pure as ice. And she had given him proof of the orders and the ultimatum. And, to him, a Marine, a war hero, one of the victors.

Forty-eight hours at most. You were optimistic, Italia. Everything will be decided a lot sooner than that.

Sunday, 31 August 1969

Morning

Dawn. I was already awake. I heard the mosquitoes buzzing around Alberto, who was fast asleep on the bed next to mine. Outside, I could see the dark becoming light on the horizon and could smell the sea as I heard the engines of the first fishing boats returning.

I got up. It must have been six o'clock. Mamma was alone on the veranda, sitting on the swing seat with an almost empty bottle of whisky and an ashtray full of cigarette ends. She must have spent the whole night out there. I sat close by her.

We were silent for a while. The only sound was that of the tide in the early dawn, still lit by the stars. On the jetty was moored Farid and Salim's fleet of two motorboats and the Zodiac rubber dinghy.

Nietzsche's *Beyond Good and Evil* was lying next to Mamma, a sheet of squared paper sticking out of the last pages.

'Are those my notes on Nadia's death?'

Italia nodded. She had promised to look at them, but the sheet was nestling there in the back of the Nietzsche book, unread. Her silence confirmed it. It was strange she hadn't kept her promise.

'Did you manage to check the alibis of the grown-ups for that morning?'

A shadow crossed her face. I couldn't interpret it. Too much sadness, too many other possible reasons.

Too much past, too little future.

'The matter was closed after Jamaal's suicide, Mikey.'

'So you think Jamaal was guilty as well? Just because he committed suicide?'

Incredibly, she smiled.

'No, not because of that. If someone takes their own life, then people think they're either mad or guilty.'

'Jamaal didn't kill Nadia, Mamma.'

She gazed out to sea. 'Of course he didn't. He was only mad.'

'Or else, he was neither mad nor guilty.'

'Michele, you must promise me something.'

She used my full name, not the diminutive. I already knew what she was going to ask.

'Do I have to make you a promise to show you I love you, Mamma?'

She gave me a sweet smile, her hand tracing out the movement of a caress in the air, but she stopped halfway, as if she had met an invisible obstacle that separated her for ever from the son for whom she had the greater love.

'No, I know you love me. But you must show more love for yourself, Michele. You're not the loser your father says you are, nor are you the crazy hero that your Uncle Toni was. And now you have Laura, and I know that you're perfect together.'

'Mamma, Nadia will never get any justice . . .'

She smiled at me again. The very sweet smile she gave me when she sang me that mournful song to get me to sleep when I was tiny. I wanted to go back to sleep like that, on the swing seat with my head resting on Italia's shoulders, as I did when I was a child. But I was no longer a child, and the sun was rising on my last day as an adolescent.

Around eight, Marlene joined us on the veranda. She was in a running vest, shorts and gym shoes, ready for her jog. Her tanned complexion, and her black hair, swept back in a long ponytail, contrasted with my mother's pale colours. Italia received her with unaccustomed civility.

'May I give William a call?'

'Of course. Mikey, show Marlene to Papa's study, where she won't be disturbed.'

I showed her the way. As we entered the study, I felt her breast brush against my arm. Had she done it on purpose? She smiled at me.

'Thanks, Mikey. Now, a moment of privacy, please. You know, things between man and wife . . .'

I left her in the study and went back to the veranda. My head was in a state; I could still feel the tip of her nipple on my arm.

You're just an oversexed little boy. She can do whatever she wants with you.

Italia was smoking in silence, her eyes already hidden behind her large sunglasses, her body covered by a long kaftan. Her exposed arms were very thin and white, her veins showing through. Next to her cup was the bottle of anisette with which she had laced her coffee.

'What are you going to do today?' I asked. I had to distract myself from thinking about Marlene.

'I'll go up to the cliff to read for a while.'

'Aren't you coming with us to lunch at the Underwater Club?'

'No, Mikey. I'd rather stay here.'

Laura came out soon after. Her tired eyes said she had slept badly, and with evil forebodings. She kissed Italia first, then me, and poured a coffee without saying a word. Marlene came back from the study. Her face was unusually tense, as if she had taken an important decision.

'Italia, I need to talk to you.'

I held my breath. It was the most surprising request I could imagine. And yet my mother seemed unsurprised. She replied in the most friendly manner I'd ever seen her use with Marlene.

'You can come with me to the cliff top, if you like.'

Marlene looked at Laura, who was staring at her in silence.

'I'm going to do my hour of jogging and then I promised I'd spend the morning with Laura on the beach.'

'Well, then we can speak when you've come back from lunch at the Underwater Club,' my mother offered.

'William's expecting me at Wheelus at two thirty, when he's back in Tripoli.'

I could see Marlene wanted to talk to my mother before she talked to William.

My mother was incredibly well disposed to this.

An urgent matter needs clearing up.

'Then let's do this, Marlene. I'm going up to the cliff top now, but I'll be back by half past twelve. I've already asked Farid to stay and grill some fish for me. If you like, we could eat together while the others are at the Club and, when they come back, you can go and meet your husband.'

'Thank you, Italia. I really appreciate it.' Marlene, too, was unusually accommodating.

They're sharpening swords for the duel. But this isn't a film, young Mikey.

The sea was beautifully calm. Farid and Salim's motorboats and dinghy were almost motionless. Marlene went off for her jog and Laura went to the beach on her own. I went back to my father's study and saw the notepad by the phone. There was nothing written on the top sheet, but I checked the waste-paper basket. There was a single ball of paper inside. I took it out and opened it up. A line of figures was scribbled on it. I dialled the number. A voice in English answered from the switchboard of Benghazi's military airport.

William Hunt's in Benghazi. What's he gone to do there?

I replaced the receiver and went back to the veranda. Shortly afterwards, Italia went off behind the villa, where the path across the island began. Her pale skin was protected by a hat, the glasses and the long costume down to her ankles that left only her thin white arms uncovered. She was the complete opposite of Marlene Hunt, the woman now taking her place in my father's affections.

A respectable woman well covered up to read without getting herself sunburnt. And a suntanned whore who goes about half naked for a run.

Over the next hour, everyone came out together in little groups. First Alberto, Nico, Ahmed and Karim. Then Grandad, Papa, Mohammed, Don Eugenio and Emilio Busi. Farid and Salim appeared last, with tired red eyes that said they had only had a few hours' sleep.

The day before, they had transported the guests back and forth in the two motorboats until late, and now they had to dismantle the beach gazebos with us boys and take them to Grandad's warehouses.

As soon as breakfast was finished, the grown-ups set off for Tripoli in one of the motorboats. Grandad, Papa and Don Eugenio were going to Mass, Mohammed to the office and Busi to the Italian Embassy.

'Please be sure to be on time at the Underwater Club,' my father told Alberto.

Marlene returned from her jog immediately after they left, as if she wanted to avoid my father. I bumped into her in the kitchen while she was heading for the shower. There was only a glance between us, but it was enough.

This isn't going to be any ordinary day.

We began to take the gazebos down. There were seven of us, and we wanted to finish before the sun became too strong.

Laura and Marlene were taking a walk along the water's edge. It didn't look as if the conversation was an easy one. A storm also seemed to be brewing in the Hunt household.

You have to tell her, Laura. Tell her to leave my father alone.

By eleven, the gazebos were all dismantled and stored aboard Farid and Salim's large rubber dinghy. There was nothing more to do until lunchtime.

'Why don't we all go fishing?' Salim suggested. 'We'll show you a new place that me and Farid found.'

'I have to stay and cook for Signora Italia and Signora Marlene,' Farid demurred.

'I'm staying here on the beach. I have to study,' Alberto said.

We four in the MANK organization looked at one another. All of a sudden, I couldn't bear the atmosphere on La Moneta any longer. That interminable conversation between Marlene and Laura Hunt could only have one possible topic.

But you won't be able to do it, sweetheart. Your mother's a demon.

'OK, Salim, we're up for it,' I said. I was the head of the organization. Nico, Ahmed and Karim made no objection.

After ten minutes in the motorboat we came to the place that Salim had mentioned.

'There are shallows under here that are full of fish. It's only ten metres deep; you don't need scuba equipment.'

When we submerged, the heat and sunlight finally gave way to the cool and the dark. But even there in that blue water I couldn't find any peace. When we came to the bottom of the shallows, Salim was right. It was full of grouper.

But I didn't fire a single shot. If I killed any living thing that day, it wouldn't have been a grouper. My mind was full of the same series of images.

Marlene Hunt in Rome with my father. My hands spreading sunblock on her skin. My mother's sad, tired eyes. Laura watching and listening.

We were a little late getting back to La Moneta, just after twelve thirty. Laura and Alberto were already waiting on the jetty, Farid beside them. Salim brought the motorboat up next to the dinghy and Laura and Alberto stepped quickly on board.

'Has Mamma come back?' I asked Alberto.

'Yes, I saw her a few minutes ago, coming down the path to the villa.'

'And she's going to stay here?'

With that whore?

'I haven't spoken to her, Mikey. We were already out here waiting for you on the beach when she came back.'

I met Laura's look. She was decidedly upset, but she gave me a silent warning to keep quiet.

Let them have a talk between themselves. We can't do a thing.

Alberto loosened the moorings and called me into line.

'Come on, Mikey, we're late. It's better if we don't get Papa angry.'

Of course. We don't want to get Papa angry.

Instead, I got out of the boat and took hold of Laura's hand. 'Can you make do with a bit of fruit?'

Laura got out of the boat as well. Perhaps she was doing it for me. Alberto gave me a resigned look while Salim got the motor running and he, Nico, Ahmed and Karim left to meet the grown-ups at the Underwater Club.

We went into the kitchen. I pointed to the hall that led to the lounge where Marlene Hunt was telling my mother how everything was about to change.

Your husband doesn't love you any more, Italia. He wants to live with me. You'd better get used to it.

'Do you want to go and eat with Signora Italia and Signora Marlene?' Farid asked, looking concerned.

Laura beat me to it. Her answer was also directed at me.

'No, thanks, Farid. Mikey and I'll eat some fruit on the beach.'

We should leave them in peace. We can't interfere. It's pointless.

Laura and I went back to the beach and lay down in the sun while Farid went to sit on the veranda in the shade.

It was nearly one o'clock and there was a slight breeze that made the air more breathable, but the sun was hellishly hot. Laura was wrestling with her arms behind her back to put on sunblock by herself. It was the same cream I had put on her mother's back.

The American gahba.*

'Do you want me to do it, Laura?'

She smiled. There was no evil in it, only gratitude for an unexpected kindness.

'Thanks, Mikey, just a little.'

My hands and fingers repeated the same movements they had over her mother's body but, if their two bodies were similar, everything else was different. She didn't undo the bikini top and I didn't think for a minute of going anywhere near the bikini bottom.

I looked over to the villa where the decisive battle was taking place between the woman I worshipped and who had brought me into this world and the one who was about to wreck my life.

Either you stop what you're doing or I'll make you stop.

Afternoon

Laura and I got into the water. The struggle between anger and calm, between desire and love, between Marlene and Laura Hunt was eating me up.

What I wanted to destroy was what I also wanted to have.

'What did you and Marlene talk about all morning?' I asked her.

'A lot of things, Mikey. About things that unite us and things that separate us.'

'What separates you two, then?'

---

* 'Whore' (author's note)

She took my hand as we began to walk in the water, Farid watching us as he sat on the veranda a hundred metres or so away.

'Several things, Mikey. One of them being you.'

I looked at her in surprise and took my hand from hers.

'Me? You talked about me?'

'She talked about a lot of things, including you.'

'And I'm one of the things that separates you?'

'Mikey, it's anger that separates us.'

'Could I know what Marlene has to say about me?'

That I dream of her body every night? That I spread sunblock on her? That I saw her naked?

Laura stopped to fix me with a stare, there in the water, her back to the beach, the villa and the sun, which was directly in my eyes. I instinctively raised an arm for shade so I could see her better.

'I think the shadow part, the part that looks at Marlene, is only a mask.'

But Marlene knows the opposite's true, Laura, from direct experience. And she's right. That part of me does exist. And it's inside me.

At that moment Farid got up and went into the house. He came out again after a few seconds.

'That was Salim on the phone. They're coming back,' he shouted, at the top of his voice so as to make himself heard.

'Already?' I asked, surprised.

Farid shrugged and sat down again.

They'll be here shortly. My mother will confront my father. And I'll confront Marlene Hunt.

In the following half an hour I said nothing. I watched the coming and going of the two Libyan coast guard cutters and thought things over. Farid was on the veranda having a smoke, Laura was in a deckchair beneath an umbrella and I was a few metres away under the sun on the burning sand. Each one of us with our own thoughts, a few metres away from the other; silent prisoners of our emotions, waiting for what fate had in store for us.

It had just gone half past one when the motorboat with the grown-ups from the Underwater Club was in sight of La Moneta. Even in the water, the heat was unbearable; it turned the surrounding view into a kind of gleaming mirage. Salim was at the helm and from the beach I could see Ahmed going to the bows to help with mooring. About a hundred metres from the jetty, the motorboat slowed down further. A breeze was stirring.

'Should I go?' Farid asked us. He was on the veranda, about fifty metres from the jetty.

Laura and I were much closer.

'We'll see to it.' We got up on to the jetty to get ready to receive the mooring ropes.

While the motorboat was coming close, travelling at less than two knots, I saw my father deep in conversation with Busi and Don Eugenio. He was looking drawn, and at a certain point I saw his worried face looking towards the villa.

I turned as well, shading my face with an arm. The villa door was open; Farid was talking to my mother with a cigarette between his lips.

I wondered if my mother could see my divided face. Half light and half shade. The light and dark of my soul.

She looked at us briefly from behind her dark glasses, her hair in the usual scarf, her body enveloped by the long linen kaftan that left only her thin white arms bare. A book was sticking out of her pocket, probably Nietzsche.

Without a smile, she raised an arm in a kind of greeting and stopped halfway, as if that was all she could do, and left the gesture unfinished. Then she turned and went quickly towards the villa.

There we were, about fifty metres away, left wondering. In those two or three seconds on that jetty open to the sea, wind and sun, I distinctly picked up on the general feeling of fear washing in. Not the fear of one individual, but of everyone around.

Mamma doesn't want to talk to Papa, not with all his minions around.

We moored the boat next to Farid and Salim's rubber dinghy and everyone began to disembark, unloading the water and food. I gave a hand for a couple of minutes, but in that half-hour of silence on the burning sand I had made my mind up. And that melancholy gesture from my mother had removed any lingering doubts.

I'll take care of the American gahba.

I set off slowly towards the villa. Laura saw me, but said nothing.

Don't do it, Mikey.

But I couldn't trust her blindly like that. I knew she loved me and also that anything I said to Marlene would be useless. But what was driving me was stronger than either reason or love. I turned and went towards the villa. Farid was still on the veranda next to the door through which my mother had just come out, a habitual cigarette hanging from the corner of his thick lips.

'Where's Marlene?' I asked him brusquely.

His coarse features were suddenly worried. He blocked my path.

He can see that I'm crazy as well.

'I think she's in the bathroom taking a shower before she goes.'

'I have to speak to her. You stay here,' I ordered him, physically pushing him aside and going into the villa.

I had no more than two minutes before the others arrived. The door to the guests' bathroom was closed. From outside, I could hear the noise of the shower. I gave three loud knocks.

'Yes?' came Marlene's voice.

'It's me.'

The son of your lover and the woman whose heart you're breaking.

The key turned in the lock and the door opened a hand's breadth. Marlene's wet face stared at me, while her body was hidden by the door jamb, and I was hit by the scents of shampoo and body lotion. Immediately, desire mingled with the anger. It was an unbearable animal desire, made even more unacceptable by the hate I felt for her in that moment.

Her naked body was only twenty centimetres away. The scent of her body lotion.

'I have to speak to you, right now.'

I wanted my voice to have menace, but it came out wavering and weak and this increased my anger.

She looked at me with that mocking half-smile she had.

'I'll be home at three. Now go and take a cold shower – you're far too hot.'

Full of lustful hormones, that's what she means.

She shut the door in my face and I made it down just in time to be back on the veranda before they all arrived to eat the now-cold hamburgers. My grandfather was not with them.

'Where's Grandad?' I asked Alberto.

My brother was uncharacteristically subdued.

'He preferred to stay at the Club. He's waiting for Farid and Salim to come with the dismantled gazebos to take to the warehouse.'

I went up to my father.

'I have to talk to you.'

He didn't even glance at me.

'Not today, Mikey. Tomorrow.'

But tomorrow will be too late, Papa.

I looked for Laura, but she wasn't there. She had gone into the villa to look for her mother.

Five minutes later, suntanned in a short white skirt and pink T-shirt, looking as beautiful as a goddess, with her black hair loose, Marlene Hunt came out on to the veranda, followed by Laura and Farid, who was carrying her luggage, a large black leather bag with Marilyn Monroe's face on it.

She gestured to my father.

Here, Salvo. Just like a little puppy.

For a moment I had the impression that Papa was about to resist the gesture, but he looked afraid and went over, while I followed behind.

I was prepared for anything, but not the exchange I heard.

I told her everything, Salvo.

You're crazy, Marlene.

Did I hear them right? Or did I imagine it? I wasn't sure.

Marlene then kissed Laura and went off to the jetty, where Farid was stowing her bag on the boat. Salim was ready in the rubber dinghy with the dismantled gazebos to take to Grandad's warehouses.

Farid helped Marlene to get on board. There was no more time; I had to decide. I could go to my mother on the other side of the island and try to comfort her, or I could go and face my father and threaten to cause a scandal. Or I could stay behind on the beach with Laura, my only hope for the future.

Or I could follow Marlene Hunt, the real guilty party.

'Give me a lift,' I said to Salim, all of a sudden, getting into the dinghy.

His thin lips curled into a mocking smile.

He knows I'm crazy as well.

Many pairs of eyes were following me. But Laura was no longer on the beach. While Farid piloted the motorboat, with Marlene settled in the bows, Salim and I started the dinghy's motor. During the short trip he went over the plan again: that Grandad was waiting at the Club to go together with them to the olive grove in Sidi El Masri, and that we were to leave the gazebos in the warehouse there.

'You want to give us a hand, Mikey?'

I made no reply. I had something completely different in mind.

★   ★   ★

Half an hour later we were at the Underwater Club. It was ten past two. While Farid was taking her bag to the Ferrari California in the car park, Marlene and I walked on the jetty in silence.

I could not see her eyes, but I heard the words whispered from the mouth I had so often dreamed about.

'Today's the day, Mikey, now or never.'

Grandad came up to us. Marlene said hello to him and went off to her Ferrari.

'Are you coming with us to the olive grove, Mikey?' Grandad asked me.

I shook my head.

'I've got a headache, Grandad. I'm going home.'

A moment later, I was in the jeep.

I followed the Ferrari at a distance of a hundred metres. Perhaps Marlene could see me in the rear-view mirror, but it made no difference.

At two fifteen, the aeroplane from Benghazi changed course over the sea and made for Tripoli. William Hunt was thinking what cowards politicians were. All the same, they were: fence sitters, opportunists and manipulators. *Let's not meddle here. We'll wait and see what happens.*

He knew he would find Marlene waiting for him, as arranged. And would learn whether he could truly count on his extraordinarily beautiful wife.

Today's the day, now or never.

The red Ferrari was travelling slowly along the Adrian Pelt seafront road across the empty city. The palm trees were motionless and everyone was hidden away in the cool and shade of their houses.

Marlene was at the Wheelus Field entrance a little before two thirty. I parked the jeep at a suitable distance from the air base. While

Marlene was showing her ID papers, a military aircraft was landing on the runway.

There was a pair of binoculars in the jeep that we used when we were hunting. Through the perimeter fence, I saw William Hunt exiting the plane. Marlene was waiting for him with the Ferrari directly below the air stairs. There was no hug, not even a kiss. They were immediately in deep conversation in the aeroplane's shade. In fact, it was Marlene who was speaking, while William listened.

As I watched them through the binoculars, I tried to read Marlene's lips and imagine what she was saying.

It's over, William. Salvo told his wife yesterday and I said the same today.

William Hunt was a dangerous man, an ex-Marine with ice-cold eyes who, I had heard, worked for the CIA. A man who had always commanded and had never been betrayed or humiliated. A man certainly capable of killing for such a grievous wrong. He listened intently, impassively, like a soldier getting ready to act.

After nearly half an hour's conversation, William said something to his wife that I imagined he would.

I'd rather kill you, Marlene, than let you go off with that Italian fancy man.

Then he got into the Ferrari with her and they drove to the office blocks on the other side of the base. After less than five minutes, the car appeared at the entry bar, with Marlene alone at the wheel.

She waved to the guards and took off towards Tripoli at high speed, the Ferrari's tyres squealing. I followed in the jeep, but the distance between us was growing. Marlene was driving along the coast at nearly one hundred and twenty miles an hour. I knew she had seen me in the rear-view mirror. It was a challenge.

Frightened, Michelino?

At the crossroads before the city, the Ferrari turned off towards the Garden City and Sidi El Masri at sixty miles an hour, and I let her go; otherwise, the jeep would have overturned. She was only going home anyway. And there we would settle matters.

It was half past three when I got to the iron gates with my parents' linked initials. The Ferrari was parked in front of the Hunt home. The pair of villas was wrapped in the most total silence, as if the torrid heat of that last day of August had made even the sparrows, the cicadas and the frogs mute.

I tried to consider matters, thinking of my mother's sad eyes, the humiliation, the loneliness, alone on that cliff edge, thinking about the end of her marriage.

I saw that half-raised hand again, that gesture she had made just before the motorboat was docking. Suddenly, I had a presentiment.

She wasn't waving at us, or anyone. She was saying goodbye. Goodbye to life.

Anger and anguish churned uncontrollably in my blood. I got out of the jeep and strode in the direction of the villa.

As usual, the door to the Hunt villa wasn't locked. No one locked doors in Tripoli then. I knew that by opening that door I would close many others. I stood there motionless, like a compass needle caught between two opposing forces.

My photograph. The sunlit side and the side in shadow. Good and evil.

I swore to myself that I wouldn't touch her, only speak to her. I would persuade her to leave my father alone.

When I entered the villa it was enveloped in shadow, but a thin strip of light was coming from under a door at the end of the hall where the bedrooms were. Our villa and theirs were exactly the same, so that door had to be that to William and Marlene's bedroom.

I went up slowly in silence. I had no idea what I was going to do. On the living-room carpet were scattered the few clothes Marlene had been wearing. I picked up the pink T-shirt and little white skirt and smelled her scent on them: her body lotion and her sweat.

When I opened the door Marlene was sitting on a chair, busily brushing her shiny wet hair. She was wrapped in a towelling dressing gown, tied at the waist.

What was she wearing underneath?

She looked at me in the mirror.

'What are you doing in my bedroom?'

Today's the day, now or never.

'You said I could find you here,' I almost stammered.

'And you come in without knocking – while I'm half naked?'

I was beside myself. More with myself than with her. On the one hand, I hated her. On the other, my eyes were fixed on the knot in the towelling belt that was keeping me from heaven.

'The front door was open,' I said, weakly trying to justify myself.

There was that sarcastic smile again.

'Perhaps I should call the police. But then you're not a dangerous thief, are you, Michelino? A thief that comes and looks, that's all, and takes nothing away. A thief that only wants to talk, talk, talk.'

I was on the divide between her provocation and derision.

She's a devil, Mikey. You'll throw away everything. Laura, your mother, yourself.

Marlene looked at me. Then she said it again, and this time I was sure of what I was hearing.

'Today's the day, it's now or never, Michelino. Either pluck up the courage or get lost.'

I grabbed her by the collar of the dressing gown. Her eyes opened wide with surprise. Then the green of her iris became dark as the winter sea.

'Are you upset, Michelino? Do you want to hit me? Is that what you want to do?'

'You'll be used to that with your marine of a husband.'

The anger and desire gave me away. I felt like a boat in a storm at sea, and she was the storm. She was in charge; she made the decisions.

'Michelino, you don't think for a minute that William is the kind of man who would hit me, do you? It's only you Italians who do such things to women. Ask your father.'

I ripped the dressing gown off her and threw it on the bed. She was wearing a bra and briefs underneath. I threw my eighty-five kilos of weight on top of her, while she kicked and screamed and hit me furiously in the face. She scratched at my shoulders and I felt blood trickling down my back.

But I was heavier and stronger. I gave her a slap and took hold of both her wrists in my left hand as she fought to free herself. Then, with my right hand, I ripped off her bra. The sound of the material tearing increased my strength and anger.

Marlene spat in my face. I grabbed the elastic of her briefs with my free hand and pulled hard, but they did not tear.

'You're not strong enough, Michelino. Too much jerking off, thinking about me.'

I could no longer see anything. I let go of her arms and tore off her briefs with both my hands while she tried to claw my face. But she was a prisoner under my weight. I got up on my knees, straddling her body so I could look at her.

She was underneath me, naked, sweating, her hair all over her face. She wrestled against me, screaming insults, her eyes now as green as a stormy sea. And I was there, tossing about on those waves, raging with hate and desire.

It's today, now or never, Michelino. No, I won't do it.

I paused for a minute to try to calm myself down. Then she stretched a hand out to my jeans and had them undone in three seconds.

I heard her speak, her voice hoarse with passion.

'Tie my wrists to the bed, Michelino. Then it won't be my fault. No one can blame me.'

I tied her up and pulled off my jeans and briefs. I wanted to devour her, destroy her, and do to her body everything that was the most ugly, vulgar and insulting that my lost adolescent's imagination could suggest.

She bit my lips and drew blood as I penetrated her, then she spat my own blood mingled with her saliva into my eyes. Now she wrestled even more, but in a different way, so that I could enter her more deeply, with the fury of desperation.

This was hell: blood, flesh and flames.

Marlene Hunt got up and put her dressing gown back on.

'Get dressed and hop it, Mikey. Now. It's already five fifteen,' she said, shutting herself in the bathroom.

I did as she said in silence, before she came out.

I arrived at the Underwater Club at a quarter to six, while Farid and Salim were getting out of one of the motorboats. They had gone to pick up Mohammed on La Moneta and were taking him to the airport.

'Can I take the boat?' I asked.

Mohammed stared at me, his lean features forming into a silent query.

Where have you been, Mike?

'Yes,' Farid replied eventually. 'We have the dinghy.'

It was a little less hot on the water; the wind from the land had died down and now a breeze was blowing from the sea. In the thirty minutes it took to reach La Moneta I could not get my thoughts together. I had a feeling of disaster. But it lay *ahead*, not behind me.

You've displaced the first boulder in the avalanche.

Evening

The sun was setting over the island when I moored the motorboat to the La Moneta jetty. There was a certain animation on the little beach: everyone was there, grown-ups and children.

Papa looked at me, rubbing a hand over his suntanned face. His dark eyes looked unaccustomedly worried.

'Where've you been, Mikey?'

Fucking your woman, Papa. Instead of going to look after my mother.

I made no effort to reply.

'Where's my mother?' I asked.

They all looked in each other's faces, as if I were talking about an extraterrestrial.

'She'll be in her room, won't she?' my father replied.

I turned my back on everyone, entered the villa and knocked on Italia's door. No reply. The door was unlocked, the room tidy and unoccupied, the windows were closed, and there was no smell of cigarettes. My mother still wasn't back.

I went back outside and said I couldn't find her. Then I shot off up the path to the other side of the island, despite knowing very well there was no reason to run. The difference of a few minutes would change nothing.

But I ran just the same. Alberto was struggling behind me and Ahmed was at my side. I was running and looking at the watch my mother had given me for my confirmation. I was saying to myself that, if I could beat my record, then I would find my mother contemplating the seas in the twilight's semi-darkness.

It was almost totally dark by the time we reached the cliff, but the always provident Alberto had brought an electric torch, and switched it on. The area underneath the large olive bent by the wind was deserted. There were only the folding chair and her copy of Nietzsche's

Ecce Homo. That book left open on the chair was a silent witness that something either out of the ordinary or untoward had happened.

I looked down over the steep crag into the impenetrable dark that ended on the rocks twenty metres below.

'I'm going down,' I announced.

It was a very steep and slippery descent, even by day. To go down in the dark was almost insane.

'No, Mikey,' Alberto said. 'Let's go back to the villa and call some-one from the police or the coast guard.'

'Leave me the torch, Alberto. You run back and call the others.'

It was the first time I had given an order to my elder brother. It was as if the exceptional circumstances had turned the roles round, the emergency we both saw unfolding now making me the elder brother. Alberto assented without a word and went running off to the villa.

'I'll come with you, Mikey,' Ahmed said.

Telling Ahmed that it was dangerous would have been offensive and useless.

I set off, torch in hand, and he came along behind me. You couldn't see more than a metre ahead. We went down slowly, one step at a time, first testing the ground cautiously. When we came to the steep-est part, I stopped.

'Watch out, there's loose gravel in this stretch,' I warned.

Too late. The foot I was standing on lost its grip. If I tried to resist I would have tumbled off into mid-air. So I let myself slump on my bottom and began to slide straight down until I grasped at a twisted root with my right hand and my legs traced an arc in the air and banged against the rock face.

Perhaps I had cracked something. The pain rose piercingly from my ankle, but that was the least of my worries. I had grabbed that root with my muscles all tense and could hold on only for a few seconds.

Lying flat on the ground, Ahmed came worming his way towards me, using both hands to stop himself from slipping down and falling on top of me; otherwise, we would both have ended up in mid-air. The pain in my ankle was now extending to my whole leg.

'Ahmed, stop, or you'll fall as well.'

He wouldn't even listen to me, he was so focused on trying to get to me. He slipped his right ankle under another root that was sticking out and pushed his heel through to the other side.

'It won't bear our weight, Ahmed.'

'It doesn't have to.'

He stretched horizontally against the descent and stretched his right arm out to me. Like this, only half his weight was pulling on the root.

I saw his right hand coming slowly towards mine. And saw his foot very slowly lifting up the root. Then his hand locked round my wrist like a vice.

'Leave me, Ahmed, it's impossible.'

'The left one, Mikey.'

With a huge effort, I lifted up my left arm and stretched out my hand. I still needed two or three centimetres to reach his arm. My foot felt as if it was being pulled off my leg.

'One last effort, Mikey. First breathe out entirely. Empty your lungs.'

I gathered my strength, breathed out and lunged upwards as my left hand grasped his right arm. The pain in my leg was now so strong I felt sick.

'Keep holding on to the root with your right hand and pull yourself up with your left.'

It was the right moment to thank my father for letting me have years of training in the gym, and for paying for Ahmed to do the same as well. Our honed muscles were as tense as violin strings. Now I could no longer fall, but we were stuck.

We stayed like that, in total silence. I saw the scar on Ahmed's right wrist, where we had made our blood brotherhood as kids. As a left-hander, he had saved my life with his weaker arm. And he held me firmly to be sure I would not fall.

If the root gives way, we'll go together.

When Alberto came back with the grown-ups, he had brought a rope with him. They lifted us up, one at a time. I tried to stand up, but my ankle gave way. I tried not to scream and to breathe.

As I was bent double being sick, I felt a cool hand holding my forehead. It was Laura. My vision began to cloud. Before I fainted, I had one last thought.

Damned woman.

The conspirators in the army ate a frugal supper together in a Benghazi barracks. Immediately afterwards, each one of them made their prescribed telephone calls to their colleagues in Tripoli, where the junior officers had dined at the Waddan Hotel, and to Sebba, Sirte, Misurata, Tobruk, Derna and El Beida.

They knew exactly what to do: disarm the police loyal to King Idris and the Al Shalhi brothers, take control of the ports, airports and borders, take over Radio Tripoli and Radio Benghazi, and persuade the Crown Prince to renounce his claim to the throne immediately, while King Idris was abroad.

All in one night, without killing a single soul, as they had promised their Western friends via Mohammed Al Bakri.

Sunday Night, 31 August to Monday, 1 September 1969

I woke up in the place where my mother had given birth to me, a bed in the Villa Igea hospital. I had no recollection of the motorboat taking me ashore, nor of the ambulance to the clinic. Evidently, they had pumped me full of tranquillizers and put my ankle in plaster.

The clock on the wall said it was midnight. My eyes came to focus on a figure collapsed in an armchair. It was Nico. Karim was staring at me from the sofa. Ahmed was walking up and down the room.

We made a blood brotherhood, the four of us. We're inseparable. For ever.

But the hand I was gripping was Laura's. I was gripping it as tightly as when I was holding on to that root so as not to fall headlong down the crag.

I've fallen right to the bottom of the abyss.

I woke up again during the night. In the dim light of the hospital's bedside lamp I glimpsed Laura sitting beside me, holding my hand. Ahmed, Karim and Nico were in the furthest corner, listening to a transistor radio with the volume turned right down. Nico was terrified, Karim excited, Ahmed tense.

I tried to fight against the sleeping tablets and painkillers they had given me and ask *What the hell's going on?*, but was unable to. I fell asleep again.

The radio station in the centre of Benghazi was a bare two-storey building faced with whitewash.

The twenty-six-year-old junior officer whom the Qadhadhfa tribe had placed at the head of the Libyan revolution arrived in a dusty jeep just before two in the morning with an armed escort and Mohammed Al Bakri by his side. The small number of armoured cars had been more than enough to convince any dissenter to stay at home out of the way.

In front of the microphone, Mohammed handed him a sheet with the speech he had prepared with Salvatore Balistreri. It was a very short speech, which Muammar Al Gaddafi read out, a little unsure of himself. There was to be no violence; cities and frontiers were secured; everyone was to stay at home; a curfew was in place. Gaddafi did not give his name. All part of the agreement.

At that time of night, there were few Libyans awake and listening to the radio. But the message was really for the leader's supporters – who had already occupied ministries, the radio station and airports in many parts of Libya without meeting any resistance. It was they who extended the news to the rest of the population, firing celebratory shots from their rifles and pistols during the night.

Salvatore Balistreri and his friends were in the living room in the villa on the island. On the telephone, General Jalloun was desperately trying to excuse himself. He had called his men out to start the search for Italia, but the police were being held in their quarters by the military and there were roadblocks everywhere. He was not even free to go out himself.

That night, Ingegnere Balistreri and his associates were among the few people listening to the short live broadcast in which Gaddafi announced the end of the Senussi monarchy and the birth of the Libyan Jamahiriya. They had waited so long for this moment, but not one of them dared to smile.

In a silver frame by the radio, Italia's photograph watched them mutely.

Monday, 1 September 1969

When I woke up, my room was empty, and so, it seemed, was the whole of Villa Igea, which was completely silent. Outside, there were a few sounds, including the noise of lorries. Then I heard isolated shots. I rang the bell and, after a while, a nursing sister came in, panting and out of breath.

'Have they found my mother?' I asked her.

She looked at me, dumbfounded.

'Your mother? I've no idea. Look, I think you should know that there's been a *coup d'état* during the night.'

I had no idea what the hell she was talking about, and began to shout.

'My mother, you bloody fool, my mother! Have they found her?'

The sister ran away. After a few minutes, Ahmed appeared, his bony features more sunken and morose than usual.

'Sorry, Mikey, we were on the floor below. The military's outside. No one can leave the building – there's a curfew in place.'

I started to shout like a madman again. A doctor came running in with a syringe. It took four of them to hold me down to give me the injection to make me sleep.

★　　★　　★

Still without revealing who he was, Muammar Al Gaddafi gave his second speech as the new head of the Libyan Jamahiriya Republic at noon from Radio Benghazi. It had been written for him by Mohammed.

Gaddafi was fairly trusting of Mohammed Al Bakri. Fairly, but not totally, as his infallible instinct kept telling him. Anyway, he knew that the man had the right contacts in the two countries that would be initially decisive for the success of the operation: Italy and Egypt.

Gaddafi was aware that, without his allies in Italy, the West would unite within hours in reaction against him and his fellow junior officers, and that the United Nations would follow immediately afterwards. After these declarations, American and British troops would patrol the streets, the Italian Navy would be there, bringing a swift end to his dream by means of the gallows.

In a hoarse voice showing no sign of enthusiasm, he read out his communiqué giving assurances that, under the new Libyan Jamahiriya, not a single drop of blood had been shed – nor would be – and that the new regime would respect all human rights and United Nations directives in every detail and for every single person. But, from his ever more confident tone, it was clear that things would be changing.

He knew that, sooner or later, he would be free to do things his way. But, for the moment, he had to show *the face of an innocent lamb*, as his mentor and adviser had suggested.

I woke up again in the late afternoon. There were no more sounds outside the clinic's windows. It was as if the whole of Tripoli had been abandoned. Then I heard distant shots and shouting. But the shots must have been fired into the air in celebration, because the shouting seemed to be full of joy.

The other members of the MANK organization were in the room.

'Have they found my mother?'

Again, silence. Then Ahmed spoke.

'They've given us permission to leave the clinic for an hour, but only to go home. Mr Hunt came a little while ago to pick up Laura.'

'Have they found my mother?'

'Mikey, there's been a *coup d'état* during the night. The monarchy's fallen; armed troops have taken over the city.'

I looked at him. Ahmed had never lied to me. He would have considered it a betrayal.

'Have they found my mother?'

'I don't know, Mikey. Your grandad called. They've been stuck on La Moneta all last night and this morning. They only managed to get back to Sidi El Masri a little while ago.'

I signed my hospital discharge. A young soldier said he would escort us home, given the curfew was still in place. We drove through the deserted city in the MANK van, followed by the escort jeep. There were more soldiers than passers-by, and more military jeeps than cars. Not one of us said a single word.

The young soldiers looked at us hostilely. Outside the royal palace with its two golden domes, various military vehicles were parked, as well as two armoured cars. But no one fired a shot. We passed quickly through the chic residential district of Garden City. Not a soul was about.

Then we set out through the eucalyptus trees towards Sidi El Masri. Nico's Esso petrol station was now a car park for military jeeps.

When we drew up to the gates of the villas, I took my crutches and got out of the van. The military jeep stopped behind us. There were no vehicles in front of Laura's house; the blinds were all down. The Hunts must have gone to Wheelus Field to wait for the situation to become clear.

As far as I was concerned, all I wanted was to look my father in the face.

'You go on home, guys. We'll be in touch later.'

As I was hobbling off on my crutches, Ahmed got out and caught up with me.

'I'll take Karim home and then come back, Mikey. I'll sleep outside this gate. I'll be here if anything happens.'

We looked at each other for a moment. 'You can sleep in the house – you have before.'

He shook his head. 'It won't happen again. I'll be out here. Now, off you go.'

In the Farnese Palace, the Foreign Minister, the Hon. Aldo Moro, was given a short note from his secretary. He was happy to read the translation of the speech by the unknown young man who was heading the new Libya and was even more interested to read the note from SID, the Italian intelligence agency, *Servizio Informazione Difesa*.

He is Muammar Al Gaddafi. A steady hand, not anti-Italian, nor a fanatical Muslim.

Moro let out a huge sigh of relief and shot a brief glance of gratitude at the crucifix on his desk. Italy was a peaceful nation undergoing development. The last thing she wanted was to be faced by an enemy across the sea from Sicily.

Later, he took a call from his English counterpart, who asked him if he would receive the British ambassador in Rome. He met him in his office at sunset.

'Omar Al Shelhi came to see us at the Foreign Office. He's saying that these junior officers led by Gaddafi are friends of Nasser and the Soviet Union. He's asking us and the Americans to use our Libyan and Sicilian bases to get them out and bring King Idriss back.'

In silence, Moro handed him the SID note.

'Are you sure, Foreign Minister?' the British ambassador asked in Italian.

It was not a very diplomatic question, but driven by British worries. Nevertheless, it gave rise to a small moment of concern in the Italian Foreign Minister. There were men he trusted more in SID, and those he trusted less. However, he reflected, no one could have any special interest in backing a young unknown Libyan. He decided that he could trust his information.

Moro gave the ambassador his habitual good-natured smile.

'Our SID is not at the same level as your MI6, but it works quite well.'

'I'm glad to hear it,' said the ambassador, taking his leave. 'After the Suez debacle it's better that we British keep a low profile in North Africa. Well, let's have faith in this Gaddafi, then. For a while, at least.'

Alberto came up to me. His eyes were red and sunken, underscored by dark rings of grief.

'Where's Papa?' I asked him, coming to a breathless stop on my crutches.

'He's in his study with Grandad and the others.'

'I'm going in to see him. I want to know what's happened to Mamma.'

Alberto tried to stop me.

'Mikey, let me make things clear. Leave him alone right now – he's in pieces. He really is.'

I made no reply, but limped on to the study. Resigned, Alberto opened the door for me.

My father was at his desk. Sitting opposite him in the armchairs were Grandad, Emilio Busi and Don Eugenio. They all looked terrible. But Grandad was the worst; he was deathly pale.

I studied Salvatore Balistreri. I think this must have been the first time since I was born that he had not shaved; the knot in his tie was twisted and one of his cuffs was lightly stained. All things you might see in another person, but unimaginable in my father. He did not wait for my question. His voice was sorrowful but calm, like an announcer on Italian state television when they broadcast a funeral.

'The Libyan coast guard found your mother's body out at sea this afternoon.'

'What kind of bullshit is this, Papa?'

He went on as if I had said nothing.

'The police couldn't look for her before. General Jalloun and his men were confined to their barracks during the curfew.'

'So?'

'Italia's body was taken out to sea by the current and the tide after sunset. She fell from the cliff near the old olive tree in the afternoon, when the water was at its lowest. There were traces of her on the rocks.'

Those were his exact words. 'Traces of her'.

'And who pushed her off?'

I could see my grandfather shoot me a look of alarm. Busi and Don Eugenio looked out of the window at the garden. I could hear Alberto draw his breath heavily behind me. Only my father remained unmoved.

'No one pushed her off, Michele. Your mother, sadly, decided she no longer wanted to live and threw herself off.'

If someone takes their own life, then people think they're either mad or guilty.

'Do you think Mamma was mad, Papa? Or that she had something unpalatable to hide?'

My father was highly intelligent but lacking in intuition. He never would have guessed those were words his wife had uttered only a few hours before she died.

And were they the words of a woman who was about to kill herself?

'I don't know what you're talking about, Mikey. Your mother committed suicide. Unfortunately, that's what it was.'

'And why would she have done it?'

'We'll talk about that another time, Mikey. Now, go and rest; you have a broken ankle.'

Because of you and that whore Marlene Hunt.

My grandfather and Alberto made a move, intuiting what I was about to do. In order to lash out, I would have to put my weight on my left crutch and try to hit my father with the other. Alberto was quicker and threw himself at me. The crutch caught him on his head and immediately drew blood.

My brother did not cry out, but held on to me tightly so I could do no more harm to myself or anyone else. The tears coursing down his face, mingling with the blood, took away my last reserves. As I crashed to the ground, I saw that last half-gesture from my mother.

Yes, she wasn't saying hello, but goodbye.

Friday, 5 September 1969

I remained standing at the back of the cathedral, leaning on my crutches throughout the funeral service, despite the pleas from Grandad and Alberto. I had no intention of shedding tears in front of my father.

Laura came on her own from Wheelus Field, without her parents, in a jeep driven by an American soldier. She held my hand in silence at the back of the cathedral. We exchanged no words.

It's enough that you're here.

At the end of the service, the coffin was carried away on the shoulders of Papa, Grandad, Alberto and the Italian ambassador. I waited until they placed her on the bier and moved away. Then I went hobbling up, supported by Laura.

I'll make them pay for this, Mamma, sooner or later.

Laura read my thoughts.

'She only wants you to be happy, Mikey. You must get rid of certain thoughts.'

There are too many, Laura. And some of them I can never get rid of. The three dead in a Cairo alleyway. Your mother writhing about underneath me.

★ ★ ★

After the funeral, General Jalloun handed my grandfather a letter of heartfelt condolences. My father wished to read it out to all of us that evening.

The Libyan coast guard continuously patrolled the stretch of coast facing La Moneta, where the smugglers slipped in and out, and they confirmed that no boat had been near the island on the afternoon of Sunday 31 August, when Italia had died.

Therefore, Jalloun concluded, this was the case of an accident: a chance fall caused by an attack of vertigo or fainting. The general avoided using the word 'suicide' out of regard for his old friend Giuseppe Bruseghin.

I knew it was true that the coast guard continuously patrolled that area because of its many hidden coves, which were indeed suitable for landing smuggled goods. I had seen the patrol boats myself that afternoon when I had gone to the Underwater Club with Salim. And also when I came back after the fiery encounter with Marlene Hunt.

There was only one possible berth on La Moneta, directly in front of the villa. Of course, a rubber dinghy could have anchored round by the rocks on the other side and someone could have reached the island by swimming, then climbed the rocks where they were only three or four metres high, run along the path, pushed my mother over the cliff, retraced their steps and swum back to the dinghy at anchor.

But it would have been risky and taken a lot of effort. An operation like that would have taken several hours. Three, at least. The coast guard would certainly have noticed a dinghy anchored for that length of time.

Someone like Marlene Hunt could have done it. She had the strength, the boldness, the cruelty and the motive. And, inside me, I would have been delighted to see her hang. But no one knew better than me that it was impossible. I was her alibi for that particular afternoon. She would have had no time, nor any way, to return to the island and kill my mother. But she was still guilty. She and my father.

If there was a killer, though, I wanted the real one, not the moral one. Given that Marlene could not have killed her, I examined the other possibilities.

William Hunt had the physique, boldness and intelligence to do it. But he was nowhere near; he was in Benghazi and then at Wheelus Field. And he had no motive.

Then there was Farid and Salim. But one of them had left with Marlene and the other with me. Afterwards, they had gone with my grandfather to Sidi El Masri and only later had they gone back to pick up Mohammed. I would check with Grandad.

There were the MANK guys, my brother and Laura Hunt. But that was absurd; I didn't even want to think about it.

That left the grown-ups who had stayed on the island that afternoon: Busi, Don Eugenio, Mohammed and my father. They were capable of anything and had a very good motive. Love and business for my father; business for the others.

It had to have been one of these four that crossed the island and threw her off.

Saturday, 6 September 1969

The day after the funeral my father left for Rome. He left me a letter, which Mohammed brought me. It was very short. It said that he understood my shock and was willing to excuse my behaviour, that he would always continue to provide for my education, and for me, if I wanted to start university in Rome. And that, for business reasons, he would have to undertake many journeys abroad.

He had put the two Sidi El Masri villas up for sale, not being able to live where he had been happy with my mother. The Hunts would be moving to Tripoli, to live in a town house on the seafront owned by the American Embassy. For Grandad and me, he had rented a two-storey maisonette in the Garden City. In conclusion, he was leaving me free to choose between staying in Tripoli or going to university in Rome.

Perhaps my mother's death had at least got him to accept leaving me free to make my own decisions. Or else he had simply decided that it wasn't worth taking any trouble over me.

Laura phoned me that evening. Now that we no longer lived next to each other, now that my mother was dead, now that I had slept with her mother, what was left for us?

Her voice betrayed regret.

'We're leaving tomorrow, Mikey. Dad has to go to Washington on business, and he doesn't want to leave Mom and me alone here with this new regime hostile to Westerners.'

'How long will you be away?'

There was a brief silence.

'I don't know, Mikey. I'll call you.'

Another silence. Neither of us knew what to say. We said goodbye without making any promises.

I was sad, but relieved. I had more time.

For what, Mikey? More time for what?

Monday, 15 September 1969

The traffic in and around Tripoli had returned to normal, foreigners had come back and half the world had officially recognized the new regime and sent ambassadors to meet the young Gaddafi. The only difference was in the streets themselves. The Italian names had disappeared. Corso Vittorio Emanuele was now Shara Istiklal; Piazza Italia now Maydan as Suhada; and so on.

The radio had announced the creation of an official organ of governance, the Revolutionary Command Council, composed entirely of the military and presided over by Colonel Gaddafi. There was only one external member of the Council to represent the civilian population, and he was excluded from meetings. He supported Gaddafi in secret, alone. His name was never disclosed.

In Rome, there was the cold drizzle with which the city said a final farewell to summer and went into autumn. The arcade and huge Bar Berardo opposite Parliament and Piazza Colonna were filled with crowds of people. The Roman population was out with umbrellas and raincoats, filling Via del Corso, the pavements and the shops. A great many went into La Rinascente department store.

Salvatore Balistreri, with Don Eugenio and Emilio Busi, entered Parliament through an entrance reserved only for the Senate, then were accompanied by an usher to the President's office.

The room was very large and plain, but warm. A secretary offered them coffee.

The President entered by a small side door several minutes later. Salvatore Balistreri had seen him only in the newspapers and on the television. He was a colourless, reserved man of few words. And yet this man counted for a lot more than the Prime Minister.

Balistreri stepped forward and introduced himself. He had chosen his clothes for the day with great care.

Don Eugenio and Busi had advised sobriety; no showiness.

Of course, that was easy to say for a priest in a threadbare cassock, and a Communist who made a thing of being poorly dressed. But he was different, he was Salvatore Balistreri, a man destined to become a highly successful entrepreneur, and a powerful one at that.

He had avoided designer clothes and limited himself to a dark-grey but well-cut suit, a white shirt and a midnight-blue tie. He had placed a black button of mourning in his lapel.

The President took hold of his hands.

'My sincere condolences, Ingegnere. I know your wife was an exceptional woman.'

It seemed to Balistreri there was a warning in those words.

'Thank you, Mr President,' he replied prudently.

'Do you believe in God, Balistreri?'

'Of course, Mr President.'

The President let go of his hands.

'Good, then we can understand one another more easily . . .'

He turned to Busi.

'It seems that everything in the Lower Chamber is going well.'

Busi nodded.

'Yes, very well. In today's session Moro said that Italy had to cooperate with Gaddafi's government. The intelligence he's received is totally reassuring.'

'And the Egyptians?' the President asked Balistreri.

Balistreri was feeling a little emotional and extremely proud. This all-powerful man was his ideal, the quintessence of all his thinking since he had been a boy.

'Everything's fine. The pro-Egyptian members on the Revolutionary Council are in the majority over the pro-Palestinian. Our man's in constant communication with them, and Gaddafi has their full support.'

The President took a sip of water.

'Nasser will want a great many things from Gaddafi in exchange for this. Do you have any thoughts on the matter, Ingegnere?'

Balistreri remembered very well what Mohammed had told him after a meeting with Nasser's emissaries.

We need houses and jobs. Right away. Not petrol for another war.

'It's possible,' he said slowly, 'that certain exchanges will be necessary.'

The President looked directly at him and, from the look, Balistreri understood why this colourless man could be so respected and feared. He suddenly felt naked in front of him.

'Exchanges that could be most harmful for the Italians still living in Libya?' the President went on.

'Only a matter of 20,000 ex-Fascist Italian colonists,' Busi broke in, 'who also happen to be blocking the interests of 50 million Italian anti-Fascists.'

The President did not even deign to glance in his direction. He knew very well that the 50 million Italian anti-Fascists were for the most part the very same people who had conveniently dumped Mussolini as soon as the war started to go badly. And, as a man who truly believed in the Lord, he had absolutely no liking for harming people. Atheists had no understanding of this kind of problem.

'I hope there are better alternative solutions,' the President said to Busi coldly. 'We Catholics don't like to cause anyone any harm, isn't that right, Balistreri?'

The Ingegnere hesitated. The President was also notoriously very slippery.

Is he really concerned about the 20,000 Italians in Libya? Or is he testing me?

Busi was not satisfied with all this hesitation. For him, it was the usual song and dance of Catholics who wanted a convenient solution to be found without compromising their consciences.

'Mr President, you know that we need an agreement for ENI to start working the huge A100 oilfield. We're not talking of personal advantage here, but the interest of the entire country.'

Even Don Eugenio felt moved to come to Salvatore's aid.

'Mr President, Italy has no other choice than Libya's gas and petroleum, and all the petroleum we do import from Libya is drilled by the Americans. If we can help Gaddafi, Italy can save thousands of millions of lira on its energy costs for manufacturing, transport and people's heating. It means development and jobs for millions. And plenty of money to fund charitable works for the world's poor.'

The President gave a small, disdainful smile.

'Are your friends very worried, Busi?'

But Emilio Busi was not to be intimidated.

'Many of them are your friends as well, Mr President. And all of them the captains of industry who support your party in the elections.'

'No, Busi, they support my party out of fear of you Communists. If, one day, the Communist Party grows any stronger, they will all find themselves on the Left. Anyway, you can reassure them all. We're not going to send in gunboats to bombard Gaddafi.'

Busi wanted to be sure that he had played all his cards right.

'Mr President, these contracts will also help management of the—'

The President stopped him with a gesture. He knew very well that a part of the petroleum money would become slush funds to finance the political parties and to oil the wheels of politics. But for an extremist like Busi to remind him of this was nothing but insolent. It was also rash and pointless to say it in front of Salvatore Balistreri.

The President looked out of the window. He had never forgotten the first rounds of the elections in an Italy devastated by the war. People without homes, food or work.

Now, from that window, he could see the Roman populace entering in their droves a shop like La Rinascente – the lights sparkling in its huge windows – or queuing in their Fiats along Via del Corso, or crowding into the bars along its pavements. This was progress, the economic boom to which the Christian Democrats had led the country, and it had to be sustained. Whatever the cost.

The President turned to Salvatore Balistreri.

'You have worked a great deal on this project. But you are also one of those 20,000 and have just lost your wife. You also believe in God. So you decide – you have more right to. I'll trust in your judgement.'

He got up and left the room without any gesture of goodbye.

In a flash Salvatore Balistreri thought of his days as a poverty-stricken child in Palermo: the single room, the five brothers, himself bent over his books, the others already out stealing. No, he really could not go back there and explain to his brothers and their friends that he had given up.

He looked at Busi and Don Eugenio, who were waiting anxiously for him to speak.

'I think it's right that we should continue,' he said in subdued tones.

For a moment, his son Michele crossed his mind.

My God, I beseech you that Mikey never comes to know what I've done.

Tuesday, 16 September 1969

With my foot encased in plaster, I couldn't use the bicycle, the car or my Triumph.

Forced into immobility, I stayed at home inside the new Garden City maisonette. A living room and three other rooms: one for Grandad, one for me and a storage room. For Papa or Alberto, when they came to Tripoli, there was the luxurious Waddan Hotel.

On the wall of my new room was Laura's photograph – with the bewitching look she had wearing that evening dress coming down the Spanish Steps in Piazza di Spagna.

The person I'll never be.

The Al Bakris had also moved when my father sold the two villas. They had a normal apartment, the same kind Italians had, rented by my father, near the office in Piazza Italia. It had running water, sanitation, electric light, a room each for the four boys and a large room for Mohammed and his two wives.

I spent the mornings playing cards with Grandad. He had lost about ten kilos in weight and knew this was not his house. We never spoke of my mother. In the afternoons, he would get into the old Fiat 600 and go back to the olive grove in Sidi El Masri, which he had never wanted to sell.

Ahmed, Karim and Nico came to my room every afternoon to keep me company.

Nico was terrified of Gaddafi and the new regime. He was afraid they would take his money and his life. Even his Guzzi motorbike and the MANK van.

'For him, we're Fascist torturers, not the ones who civilized his country. He'll have us all killed.'

Karim, on the other hand, was all for the new regime. He thought Gaddafi and his junior officers were honest, serious men. Above all, they were anti-American and pro-Egyptian. They would help Nasser destroy Israel.

As usual, Ahmed was the most pragmatic. There was our MANK organization, our business in Cairo. We decided to tackle the question at the end of September, when my plaster cast came off.

For my part, I was only interested in one thing: my mother's death.

Ahmed remained my eye on the outside world. The first day he came to see me on his own, I took advantage of this to question him closely.

'Tell me about that afternoon on La Moneta. Everything you saw and heard.'

He nodded. The lines in his cheeks had become deeper; at nearly twenty, his beard was darker, his eyes even more serious. We had both lost the people we loved most. Nadia and Italia. His faith in me prevented him from asking me the crucial question.

And where were you, Mikey, on the afternoon your mother died?

'After you went off with Farid, Salim and Signora Hunt, we boys stayed on the beach, and Laura was reading on the veranda. The grown-ups went into the living room. From the beach we could see them through the window. Then I think they all went off to their own rooms, because at half past two there was no longer anyone in the living room.'

'And the four of you?'

'We stayed on the beach. At least another hour, perhaps more. But it was too hot and, before four o' clock, we split up.'

'And what did you do?'

'Nico went off for a nap and Alberto had to study. I think Karim joined Laura. I swam for a long time. I was nervous, and only felt good in the water. I put on flippers and a mask and explored the rocks around the island.'

'Did you get as far as the cliff?'

'No, I stopped well before that. I was going slowly, trying to relax.'

'Did you see any boats at all?'

'No, Mikey, nothing.'

'And then?'

'I went back to the beach at about a quarter past five. After a few minutes, Farid and Salim arrived with the motorboat to take my father to the Underwater Club.'

'Yes, this tallies. I met them there half an hour later, towards a quarter to six. They were taking him to the airport and they left me the motorboat to go back to La Moneta. And then?'

'At some point we all found ourselves on the beach again. I can't remember in what order. The grown-ups came out one at a time, and then Laura as well. We were all there before six.'

I looked at him.

'And then I came back.'

'Yes.' He didn't ask me where I had been, or with whom. Perhaps he had an idea.

We exchanged looks. He was truthful; I wasn't. What should I have said?

It couldn't have been Marlene, Ahmed. I know very well why that was impossible.

Monday, 29 September 1969

Grandad took me to the clinic in the Fiat 600. Tripoli was calm and bathed in sunshine. There were fewer policemen and more soldiers, but the shops were open, carriages on the go, and the shoeshine boys were again polishing Italian men's moccasins under the arcades.

At Villa Igea they took off my cast, and now the crutches were enough.

'What do you want to do, Mikey, now you can walk?' Grandad asked me. I wanted to take my Triumph for a spin around Tripoli: Corso Vittorio, Piazza Italia, Via Lazio and on out to the Underwater Club. But I was still hobbling. And all those names had disappeared, as the street signs were now all in Arabic.

Grandad was pale and thin as a rake. In the last few months, his shoulders had stooped, and his calm and kindly eyes were now tired and red.

'Let's go out to the Sidi El Masri olive grove, like we did when you took me there as a boy.'

We went in the Fiat 600. Grandad drove slowly towards Shara Ben Ashur and Sidi El Masri, while the scents of eucalyptus and olives gradually took over from the smell of the sea. He parked in front of the two villas that were no longer ours. There were different cars, different people: the new proprietors Papa had sold them to.

We took the path that Nadia used in the mornings to come to the Balistreri villa. We walked slowly, in silence. I was limping on my crutches; he was tired.

We came to the old Al Bakri shack. Sheets of metal, cardboard and straw. An outside toilet built of old boards knocked together. A trickle of water that served as a sewer. The swing made out of a tyre. And that terrible stench in the heat haze.

All through my childhood and adolescence, I had no idea of the abyss that separated my life from Ahmed and Karim's. But could I – the kid who so despised his father's money – have survived a week under those conditions?

The cesspit smelled worse than ever, as it always did in the summer months. The hungry flies buzzed around it. It was here that the young woman and her baby had been found. Both coloured, black, as I had confided to Nadia in great secrecy.

We walked in silence past the goatherds' corrugated huts, including the one where Nadia's presumed killer, Jamaal, had lived, and on to the olive-pressing shed. It was here that the dog had barked, here that I had sensed death on the other side of the dirty windows, here that I had picked up a handkerchief stained with innocent blood and here that I had seen the lock that Jamaal would never have been able to buy, or even use.

Only two months had passed since that day at the beginning of August. And everything had changed. Nadia had been murdered, my mother was dead, I had been to bed with Marlene Hunt and Gaddafi had taken control of Libya.

After an hour's walking, Grandad was out of breath.

'Let's sit down for a moment, Michele. There, under that large olive tree.'

We rested against the wrinkled trunk, our shoulders touching, and

I realized how thin Giuseppe Bruseghin had become. I could feel his shoulder bones against my muscles, and could count the ribs showing through his white shirt.

'You've lost a lot of weight, Grandad.'

He smiled. 'I wouldn't know. I've never weighed myself in all my life.'

Then he glanced around and took a deep breath.

'You know, Michele, olive trees are like women. They give birth to fruit in October and, at this time of the year, I always feel like a father-to-be.'

'They're beautiful, Grandad. When I used to come here hunting with the shotgun, I always fired the first shot into the air – so as to raise the dove – and then caught it with the second barrel. It's fairer and doesn't damage the olives.'

He brushed a bony hand through my hair. It had the same light calmness as Italia's hand.

He let out a long sigh.

'Last week, I signed a power of attorney for your father and sent it to him in Rome so he can sell the grove, all of it.'

I looked at him, dumbstruck.

'It was necessary, Michele. Your father's right. He's got big business plans in mind and needs a lot of money to accomplish them. With the sale of the grove he's got the collateral; the main sum will come as a loan from his Palermo friends and the Banco di Sicilia.'

'But, Grandad, he's already had you sell the villas. These olives are your life's work.'

'They're not much use to me now, Michele. Your father knows what he's doing. Besides, this way, we can ensure a future for you and Alberto.'

I wanted to tell him that Alberto had a future anyway and that I had none at all. But that would only have hurt him. It was, however, the right moment to clarify another point.

'Grandad, when I left you at the Underwater Club with Farid and Salim that terrible afternoon, were they with you the whole time after that?'

He looked at me and shook his head. I didn't want to upset him, but I had to know for sure.

'Yes, Mikey. We left the Club in their pick-up and came to the warehouses here to deposit the dismantled gazebos. I let them leave at four thirty. They had to go to collect Mohammed from La Moneta.'

This excluded Farid and Salim from any suspicion. Fifteen minutes to get from the grove to the Underwater Club, thirty minutes by sea to La Moneta, where Ahmed saw them at five fifteen, another half an hour from La Moneta to the Underwater Club, where I met them with Mohammed at a quarter to six. It all tallied.

Grandad was looking at me.

'There's something else, Michele. It's about your relations with your father. And with yourself.'

I felt intuitively that he had placed a condition on my father, one that was non-negotiable, in exchange for his signature for the sale of the olive grove. And now he was going to place the same condition on me.

'I'm not going to say I'm sorry. And I'll never forgive him for—'

'There's no reason for you to say you're sorry to him. But he wasn't the cause of your mother's death. Get that out of your head, Michele.'

'Grandad, he and that woman—'

For a moment, his voice went back to the firm one of the soldier Giuseppe Bruseghin.

'That terrible afternoon, after Farid and Salim left at four thirty, I came back to the villa.'

I shut my eyes. 'Grandad . . .'

'In the forecourt were your jeep and Marlene's Ferrari, but there was no one at home in our house. A couple of hours later I saw you leave the Hunt's villa in a terrible state and get back into the jeep again . . .'

'Grandad . . .'

He placed a gnarled hand on mine.

'A father has the right to look after his son and the right to make mistakes in doing it. A son has the right to protect himself and a duty to understand his father, sooner or later.'

He made an enormous effort to complete the sentence, then his voice broke off. His eyes stared first at me, then at the trunk of the olive tree. It was the first tree he had planted. He then fell silent, his head on my shoulder. I thought he had dozed off. But he was dead.

Wednesday, 1 October 1969

It was the third funeral in two months: Nadia, Italia, then my grandfather.

Tripoli Cathedral was crammed with tearful Italians. After the service, when Papa, Alberto and I carried Grandad's coffin on our shoulders, along with the Italian ambassador, out on to the cathedral steps into the grounds, we could see a vast crowd stretching as far as Corso Vittorio, or Shara Istiklal – or whatever the hell Gaddafi wanted to call it.

There were huge numbers of Libyans as well. They clapped and wept more than the Italians for the good and honest man who had helped them build their country.

I was still hobbling too much. Mohammed came up to carry the coffin in my place down the steps.

Then there were the heartfelt condolences, so many of them, everyone having some tale or other to tell about Grandad. I was watching my father as I listened, his handsome suntanned Clark Gable face lost in grief. He was good at acting the part of the bereaved son-in-law.

Perhaps he really is overcome, Mikey. You promised Grandad. This hate will destroy both of you.

William Hunt came up among the last, with his forceful

handshake and square jaw. He gave his condolences to Alberto, then to me. He handed me an envelope from Laura.

'When is she coming back?' I asked, not daring to look him in the eye.

I screwed your wife that afternoon.

He looked at me without expression on his face, like a judge handing out a death sentence to the guilty party.

'Marlene and Laura are in San Francisco. They'll be back at the end of October. But Laura's off to school in Cairo to study photography and communication. There are no suitable colleges here in Tripoli.'

And you're not suitable for her, Michele Balistreri. So keep away.

Then he went over to my father. He shook his hand, offered his condolences and whispered a single sentence to him.

'Salvo, we must talk tomorrow.'

Among the things that were still functioning in me were my ears. And my imagination.

We must talk about you and my wife.

That evening, in my room in the Garden City, I placed Laura's envelope on the table and opened it. It was a cassette of *Songs from a Room*, the latest album from Leonard Cohen, which was still not available in Tripoli. I had heard one of the songs on the radio, 'Bird on a Wire'. And Laura knew how much I liked it.

There was no card. I put the cassette in the deck and sat on the bed looking at the photo on the wall. A gorgeous girl was looking at me as she came down the Spanish Steps in Piazza di Spagna. Cohen's voice was whispering the magical words about trying in his own way to be free.

I was the little bird holding on to the wire, the drunk in the midnight choir. And who was the girl in the photo? Was it Laura or Marlene? Was she in the light or in the dark?

If freedom is being able to choose between light and dark, then I was a prisoner in a dark cell.

Monday, 6 October 1969

The MANK organization was ready to leave for Cairo, but the Muslim period of mourning for Nadia and the Catholic one for my mother and grandfather demanded respect for certain formalities and a little more time. In the end, all four of us went for a few days, spoke with our associates and left Nico temporarily as our ambassador.

He was more than happy, seeing that the city was much more alive than Tripoli and that, two years after the war, they had reopened all the cinemas and bordellos.

On the day that Ahmed, Karim and I came back from Cairo, I happened to meet old Mansur. I was having my first ride on the Triumph after my cast had been removed and I was parked in Piazza Italia, which Gaddafi wanted to rename Green Square. Mansur saw me and came up. First of all, he remembered to offer his condolences.

'I'm terribly sorry, Signor Michele, both for your wonderful grandfather and your beautiful mother.'

'Thanks, Mansur. I didn't know you knew my mother – she never came to the market.'

Mansur smiled.

'I knew her since she was a little girl. But it's true, she never came to the market. It was a great surprise to see her in front of my fish stall at seven one morning.'

I was dumbfounded. Mansur was old. He was probably mistaken.

'Are you sure, Mansur? When was this?'

He didn't have to think for long. 'Quite sure. She came to see me a couple of weeks after you did.'

'A few days before she died, then? And what did she want?'

He hesitated a moment, as if he were worried about breaching a confidence.

'Well, the same thing you wanted to know, Signor Michele. What happened that morning two months ago when Nadia disappeared.'

So Italia hadn't forgotten that page of notes I gave her.

'What did my mother ask, Mansur?'

'She wanted to know about people's movements here on the market. Not just Farid and Salim, about everyone, more or less. I told her Farid and Salim had caught that huge amberjack, had come here early, had divided the fish with me and opened the stall to sell it.'

'Just as you said to me. Anything else?'

'Then your grandfather and Alberto came by, and Nico later. Then Nico and Alberto went off and you came, Signor Michele, to collect the bait from Farid. I'm not sure I can remember everything . . .'

'And Farid and Salim never moved from here, that's what you said.'

The old man scratched his head.

'When we opened, there was a great crowd of people. Their stall was open all the time, as I told your mother. I can't be exactly sure that they were *both* here all the time. But, after you came, Signor Michele, I'm sure they didn't move, because the camel parade had begun, there were only a few people and Farid and Salim were definitely here.'

There was something in his account that I found unconvincing. Perhaps it was the same thing that had excited my mother's curiosity – and it wasn't people's comings and goings. It was the fish, that enormous greater amberjack.

Saturday, 11 October 1969

I spoke to Ahmed immediately. That amberjack caught the night before Nadia's disappearance was really too large. It could only have been caught a long way off the coast, and not with Farid and Salim's equipment.

Then there was the new fishing boat, the motorboats, the rubber dinghy, the employees and the market stall. And too much cash around. Where did it come from?

Ahmed thought about it and came to a conclusion that he divulged to the rest of the MANK organization on the first weekend Nico was back from Cairo.

'Cigarette smuggling. An exchange on the borders of the territorial waters with a Maltese or Sicilian fishing boat. Farid and Salim load up with cigarettes and the giant amberjack is in payment and as an alibi in case the Libyan coast guard stops them and asks what they were doing that far out.'

We stared at him in admiration. I was proud of having a friend who could think like this.

'You're right. With the two motorboats and the excuse of taking fish to Malta, it's easy for them to leave Libyan waters.'

'You can make a pile of money from smuggling, Mikey,' said Nico excitably.

'A lot of beautiful sterling,' Karim agreed.

I, however, was not totally convinced.

'By smuggling cigarettes?'

Ahmed had already done a few calculations.

'If we got into it, we'd make triple what those two idiots do. And we could link the business up with what we already have in Cairo.'

I was sceptical. And had no wish to go into illegal trafficking again.

'That may be, guys. But that's their business, and their money.'

Ahmed looked directly at me. I had seen that look two years earlier, in a Cairo alleyway.

'And we can take over that business, Mikey, and the money, everything. Or do you want to go to university in Rome and become an employee of the Banco di Sicilia?'

He made the comment lightly, but it was the first time he had ever allowed himself the liberty.

A collateral effect of Colonel Gaddafi.

'We'd be rich, Mikey,' Nico added.

And yet they knew I cared nothing for money. I had never suffered hunger, never had to live under corrugated iron and cardboard with no running water, electric light or drainage.

'I don't know what to do with money.'

But Karim knew my real Achilles heel.

'Do you want to keep Laura with your father's money, Mikey?'

I should have ignored the challenge and understood that something was changing between us. But they were my only friends and we had our blood brotherhood. And I still wanted to prove something to my father.

I shrugged my shoulders. 'OK, guys, let's make some money.'

It was Ahmed's plan, therefore meticulously thought out. That same evening, he would go to the port to take down the mileages of Farid and Salim's motorboats. At that time of day they would be drinking *chai* and smoking *shisha* in one of the big open-air bars below the ancient castle near the *souk*. To be safe, Karim, Nico and I would keep an eye on them, so that Ahmed wouldn't run the risk of them catching him on the spot.

Then, the following morning, he would do the same while Farid and Salim were at the fish market. From the mileage, we could work out what route they had taken and it would give us an idea what they were up to.

If Ahmed's hypothesis was correct, we would follow them in my father's motorboat, which I was still allowed to use.

'And then?' Nico asked. 'We follow them, and what'll we do if it's all true?'

'Then,' Ahmed replied, 'we'll confront them. When we have the proof, they'll have to come to an agreement with us.'

'They'll carve us into little pieces,' Karim said.

I calmed him down.

'We can defend ourselves. Besides, I'm the son of Ingegner Balistreri, aren't I?'

Nico and Karim nodded, not at all convinced. Sure, I was the son of an Italian. And the most important Italian in Tripoli. But, with Gaddafi now on the scene, things were changing. And Farid and Salim had ten brawny fishermen to hand.

But I have my rifle and Ahmed his knife.

To be safe, I dug out my old Diana 50 and a box of pellets I had kept. In the afternoon, I went to the Underwater Club and hid it in the motorboat's locker. It was reassuringly there for any eventuality.

The colourful market of Souk Al Mushir had been crowded all day. When evening fell, the Italians went home or to the places that sold alcohol, like the Gazzella and Waddan hotels. The Libyans divided into two groups: women and children went home; the men to smoke *shisha* in the bars around the castle square.

Farid and Salim were drinking *chai*. Farid was smoking his usual cigarettes, Salim the *shisha*. Karim, Nico and I were hiding behind a car, crouching well down so as not to be seen. Ahmed was already at the port to note down the mileage of the motorboats before they went out for the night.

A bicycle stopped in front of Farid and Salim's table. It was one of their fishermen, who got off and said something to them in an agitated manner. The two jumped up immediately, got on their bicycles and headed off along the coast road in the direction of the port.

We looked at each other. 'They've seen him,' Karim said, already getting on his bicycle.

'Stay here, Karim. Nico and I'll go to the Underwater Club and take Papa's motorboat, so we can follow them.'

But Karim made no reply. He was already pedalling off to the port.

'Damn, Nico. Can you follow him and try to look after him? I'll go and get the motorboat.'

On the Triumph, I got to the Club in less than ten minutes. There was a dance in progress on the terrace with a vocalist singing 'Strangers in the Night' for an audience of wealthy Americans, Italians and Libyans.

I kept clear of the terrace, taking the path down to the beach and the jetty. A few minutes later, I was off in the motorboat towards the port with my lights off.

I had my night-vision binoculars with me. The sea was dark and flat. There were no fishing-boat lights on the open sea, so, evidently, they were still in port or at anchor. The October-evening air was hot and sticky.

I came in sight of the port just as Farid and Salim's boat was coming out. I slowed down immediately and let the motor run gently. Karim and Ahmed could not be seen on the quayside, only Nico, but I had no time to go into the port and bring him on board.

I followed the boat at a distance. I had to be sure that they neither saw nor heard me. After a short time, it was clear where they were heading: La Moneta. During the night trip the only lights visible were those of the boat in front of me and the coast-guard patrol boats.

They moored on the jetty in front of the villa. I put the engine in neutral, a hundred metres away. By the dim light of the lamps on the little quay, I saw them get down on to the beach.

Salim had a knife in his hand and was pushing Karim, who had his hands tied behind his back. Then came Ahmed, also with his hands tied. They bound them each to a lamp post with ropes they had on board.

There was no time to lose. Still trying not to make myself heard, I used the oars to bring the motorboat to seventy metres from the beach. I took my old Diana 50 from the locker in the bows, a lead pellet already loaded. The others were in the box, and I put a handful in my pocket.

I stationed myself in the bows with the binoculars and the rifle. Laughing, Farid was holding Karim's head still, while Salim held the point of the knife to his throat. A lit cigarette was dangling from Farid's thick lips while Salim's thin ones were stretched out into a sadistic line.

This was the vendetta they felt justified in pursuing against their younger brothers. Ahmed and Karim were better-looking, more studious, more intelligent than them. Karim had dared to throw Salim in the cesspit. Now, Ahmed was spying on their business.

There could be no surprise; there was no time.

'Let them go, right now!' I shouted.

There was a moment's silence on the beach, then Farid gave an oily laugh.

'Oh, well, well, Signorino Michele, as well, eh? Instead of hiding in the dark in the middle of the sea, why don't you come on out and enjoy the show right here?'

I saw Salim's grin through the binoculars. His thin face was a cruel mask. In the end, it was I, as the Italian boss's son, who had protected their brothers.

'Because he doesn't have the balls, that's why!' Salim shouted.

I saw the sharp knife cut off the end of Karim's right ear, while his cries could be heard above the coarse guffaws of his two torturers.

Then Salim turned triumphantly towards me, holding his bloody trophy between two fingers.

'And now,' Salim screamed, 'I'm going to cut off something more important from that nosy best friend of yours.'

Salim stepped forward, and I took aim, not giving him time to get anywhere near Ahmed. The Diana 50's pellet went cleanly through the hand that was holding the knife and he began to screech like an eagle.

After a moment's indecision, Farid ran towards Ahmed, while at the same time I reloaded and slipped the fisherman's knife in my belt. I put the engine in gear and set off for the jetty.

'If you shoot again, Mikey, I'll cut his throat.'

Farid's voice was less confident than Salim's as he pointed the knife at Ahmed. Karim and Salim, meanwhile, were groaning from their wounds.

The motorboat touched the jetty. Without bothering to moor it, I put the engine in neutral and jumped down, pointing the rifle at Farid.

'If you touch him, Farid, you won't leave here alive.'

Uncertain what to do, Farid lowered the knife. Ahmed's *tae* caught him in the testicles, making him bend at the knees and the knife fall to the ground.

Although hurt, Salim grabbed his own knife and tried to throw himself on Ahmed, who was still tied up. This time, the Diana 50 pellet pierced his cheek and tongue, coming out on the other side.

I felt neither fear nor remorse. In a certain sense, I knew that I had got to the point I was heading to sooner or later, anyway. I chucked the empty rifle down and took out the fisherman's knife with the saw-tooth blade. I freed Ahmed with it while Farid backed away towards the jetty.

Ahmed took the knife from my hands and went up to Salim, who was now lying on the ground, moaning. Farid watched him, terrified.

'Watch closely, Farid, so you'll remember this as long as you're alive.'

Our glances met. I knew what he was about to do.

For a moment, I thought about stopping him. Then Ahmed grabbed Salim's head by his sleek hair and pulled it back. I heard both Farid and Karim cry out as the knife sliced cleanly into Salim's carotid artery. There was a terrible sound, halfway between cardboard tearing and a sink being emptied.

Ahmed let Salim fall on to the sand. Then he went up to Farid, his knife dripping with blood.

'Ahmed, for the love of Allah,' Farid mumbled, terrified, dropping down on his knees.

'Do not blaspheme, my brother. Allah doesn't listen to worms.'

This was going too far, even for Mikey Balistreri.

'Ahmed, no. Not him.'

It was an order. I had given him hundreds, since we were little boys, and he always obeyed without a word. But things were changing between us.

'If we don't kill him tonight, Mikey, we'll come to regret it one day.'

I was still the boss. There was no argument about that. I turned to Farid.

'We won't kill you, because you can be useful to us. Tonight, you'll take us with you to whoever supplies you with the cigarettes, and you'll reassure them about us. From today, we're taking your business. Got it?'

Farid nodded repeatedly, his mouth gaping open and his eyes staring wide. I went on.

'Tomorrow, you will tell Mohammed that you had an accident at sea and Salim drowned.'

Farid signalled his assent like an automaton. He was aware that Ahmed was ready to kill him. But Ahmed wanted him to be in no doubt, and stuck the knife at his throat. Promises like that were not sufficient for him.

'Lastly, brother, I don't want to see you in Libya ever again. Tomorrow, you pack your bags, tell Mohammed you want to try your fortune elsewhere and leave. If I see you again, I'll cut your dick off and make you eat it. Have you got that, Farid?'

Farid was already nearly dead with fear. While we tied him up, his prominent lips still begged Ahmed to spare his life.

In the villa, we dressed Karim's ear as best we could with alcohol and gauze. The upper quarter had been sliced cleanly off. Fortunately, it was still early enough to meet the smugglers, but we would have to get a move on.

'I'll take Karim back to Nico in the port, and he can take him to hospital. I'll be back in forty minutes. You keep guard on Farid. And keep your hands off him, all right?'

Ahmed stared at me in silence. There was something in his eyes I had never seen before. Perhaps Laura was right.

He'll look after you if you're one of his gang. Otherwise, he'll annihilate you.

Ahmed relaxed and went back to his rational way of doing things.

'What should we say to the hospital about his ear? And to my father?'

'We say there's been an accident.'

'That's hardly believable, Mikey.'

'Karim and I can say we had a dare going with the knives. And that, without meaning to, I wounded him in the ear. Whether he believes it or not, Mohammed's not going to report me, is he? And Karim will back the story up.'

Karim was feeling a little better. 'All right, yes, I'll back the story up. Papa will have his doubts, but he'll never report Mikey.'

I pointed to Salim's body. 'We still have to get rid of that.'

But Ahmed had come back to being the cold and meticulous planner.

'You go off with Karim, while I clean up and put the body on their boat. I'll tie two stones to his ankles. When you get back, we'll dump him in the open sea, then we'll go with Farid to meet the smugglers. When we get back, we'll take the motorboat to the rocks and send it crashing into them. Farid will escape, Salim won't.'

It seemed absurd to be speaking like this. We were still not twenty and had already killed three Egyptian soldiers and, now, Ahmed and Karim's brother. And we were preparing to throw the body to the fishes and make money from smuggling.

For Karim, this was in order to stage a revolution. But I had no thoughts about any revolution; I wanted only to be with Laura and forget all the rest. I was still looking for peace. Without knowing it, I was marching to war instead.

Sunday, 12 October 1969

Fear can work miracles. The explanation Farid gave to Mohammed about the accident and Salim's drowning was faultless. Unlike Salim, who had never wanted to learn, he knew how to swim and so had been able to save himself. The fact that Salim's body had not been found was normal; the currents in that stretch carried anything far out to sea. And, anyway, there was no reason to suspect any friction between the two brothers.

The explanation he gave him about his decision to go and seek his fortune in Tunisia was also faultless. There were the tragedies to try to forget, first Nadia, now Salim and the loss of their boat; and his ability as a fishmonger would be much more appreciated in Tunisia, where fishing was big business.

The story about Karim's ear being cut and needing stitches was more complicated. Mohammed wasn't convinced for a minute that it was an accident which had happened while we were play-acting the duel in *Cavalleria Rusticana*. Although he could believe that we were crazy enough to do it, the cut was too clean to be the result of an accidental stabbing. And he also suspected a connection with Salim's death.

In the end, I had to have recourse to unscrupulous means.

'So you don't believe me, Mohammed?'

I saw him turn sullen. This was open blackmail. Whatever else, I was still the son of his boss. The outcast son, but the son nevertheless.

He turned to Ahmed and Karim.

'I've lost Nadia and Salim, and now Farid's leaving. You two try to keep well away from any trouble.'

He couldn't say so explicitly, but the worst of 'any trouble' was me.

Saturday, 15 November 1969

Ahmed was right. In one month, the four of us transformed that little cottage industry of smuggling into one of industrial proportions. The MANK organization did not exist on any business register, yet its profits were real and substantial.

I was the one behind the ideas and had impunity because I was the son of Ingegner Salvatore Balistreri.

Ahmed took care of arrangements with the Maltese traffickers and organized the fishermen we inherited from Farid and Salim. We went anywhere and everywhere in Papa's motorboat. Everyone knew who owned it – starting with the Libyan coast guard, which was still under the command of General Jalloun – and no one ever stopped us.

Nico and Karim spent most of their time in Cairo, where they looked after our Egyptian interests. Combining Nico's abilities with Karim's contacts and the money sent by Ahmed and me, they turned our old eating-house into the most talked-about place in town. It became well known for the quality both of its food and the whores available there, with the sole condition imposed by Karim that the girls were never Muslim.

The place could have no other name than 'The Mank'. Foreign visitors and a few wealthy Egyptians went there for lunch or dinner; as did

Karim's friends, leaders in the Muslim Brotherhood, who obviously paid for nothing but guaranteed a trouble-free life for us politically. Dressed in a white dinner jacket, his hair straightened and combed back, Nico Gerace received his illustrious guests. He also chose the prostitutes, after having first tested them for quality himself.

It was his complaints about Gaddafi that gave me the idea for a new business, which I proposed to my partners during one of the weekends they were both back from Cairo.

Gaddafi had drastically limited the export of capital, and the Italian and Jewish populations were desperate. When going abroad on holiday, the most that people could take was three hundred pounds sterling per adult and one hundred and fifty for each child. The Italians tried to entrust their money to diplomatic personnel, who were exempt from searches at departure. But the Libyans checked everything and searched anyone going in or out of an embassy or a consulate. If they found money, they confiscated it. So the Italians turned to the Jews, who had their own channels of communication with the Maltese, who ran the currency-smuggling operation and charged 30 per cent to act as intermediaries.

All this business, we were capable of doing. We had my father's motorboat, contacts within the Italian community, impunity derived from my father's name, and – last but not least – the necessary balls.

Currency smuggling was certainly dangerous, but much more profitable than smuggling cigarettes. Cash took up less space than cigarettes and was worth a thousand times more. All that was necessary was to get the money out of territorial waters, deposit it in the Banco di Sicilia on the Italian island of Lampedusa, west of Malta, then transfer it from our account to whoever had entrusted us with it, minus our 30 per cent.

Karim was against it initially. It was against Islamic religious principles to take a percentage. What is more, we were violating the laws of his beloved Gaddafi and robbing the Libyan people.

Nico exploded in rage.

'That money belongs to the Italians, Karim. Your Gaddafi's nothing but a common thief.'

I knew that, with Karim, a very different line of argument was needed.

'Karim, will you build houses for the poor and wage a new war against Israel with your wonderful Islamic principles?'

Karim thought for a moment, then nodded.

'All right, but the money we earn goes to the refugees.'

Every so often, since Gaddafi's arrival, they forgot that I was still the boss and, if I chose, the MANK organization would fold within five minutes. And that General Jalloun and the Libyan police turned a blind eye only because I was still the son of Ingegner Salvatore Balistreri.

I reminded them of this as brutally as I could.

'With your share, you can do what you want, Karim, and the same with us and our shares.'

'I'll still persuade you,' Karim persisted.

Nico looked at him scornfully.

'With my money, I'm going to buy a cinema with huge leather seats and then marry an actress.'

'Then it'll have to be an actress that's blind,' said Karim.

Ahmed had remained silent, as he often did before expressing his opinion.

'One of you two will have to come back to Tripoli to give us a hand,' he said to Karim and Nico.

'Nico can come back. I'm staying in Cairo,' Karim said immediately.

I had heard nothing from Laura Hunt since meeting her father at my grandad's funeral, when he handed me the Leonard Cohen cassette. More than a month had passed and I knew only that Marlene Hunt had come back a few days ago and that Laura was at college in Cairo.

Nico was against it. In Egypt, there were cinemas and prostitutes.

'Out of the question. I'm staying in Cairo.'

I looked him in the eye. Every so often, he also forgot who was boss.

'You're coming back here, Nico. Right away.'

'But Mikey . . .'

Despite the fact that he shaved every day, his beard was too dark and his deep black eyebrows were too bushy. Not even his smart clothes and straight hair could disguise the fact that he'd once been a petrol-pump attendant.

'This way, you'll be able to have more time with your mother.'

This was the key with Nico. The only real motive he could have for staying in Tripoli was his adored and venerated Santuzza, the one woman he didn't think of as a whore.

But there was more. I smiled at him.

'The Lux, the Mignon or the Odeon. Which one will you buy?'

His eyes opened wide, and it was Karim's turn to protest.

'With the MANK organization's money?'

'They will give us any cinema we want, Karim, if we help the owners to export their cash.'

Nico's eyes were gleaming with joy.

'I want the Alhambra, Mikey. The one with the sliding roof.'

'That one's not on offer,' Karim said. 'It belongs to Zanin, head of the Maltese clan. The same guys that control the currency smuggling.'

My eyes met those of Ahmed.

Couldn't be better. We kill two birds with one stone.

Sunday, 16 November 1969

Zanin was a practising Catholic. So we went to his house one Sunday after Mass dressed in our best and with some excellent Sicilian *cannoli* made by Nico's mother.

He had the best villa in Garden City. From the terrace, you could even see into the grounds of the King's palace. In the large garden were six Doberman Pinschers: one for Zanin, one for his wife and one each for his four children. Zanin's dog was called Killer, and it was almost like a fifth child; it ruled over the other dogs, ate with its master and was always at his side.

It was there when Zanin received the MANK organization in his living room, along with his two lieutenants: the manager of the Alhambra cinema and the head of his fishing fleet, the cover for his smuggling.

Zanin was a little over forty, with the face of a sailor, which he had been for twenty years, and the look of a criminal, his most recent activity. He had agreed to see us straightaway, out of respect for my surname, I thought initially.

The *mabrouka* served us *chai* and nuts and I outlined our proposal, which was in no way unreasonable or conflicted with his affairs.

'You've always been able to take Jewish money out of the country,' I began.

Zanin raised a brawny arm.

'We don't take out a thing. It's illegal.'

'All right,' I went on, 'then let's say that the four of us have received a lot of requests from the Italian population here. We wouldn't offer any of our services to Jews, Maltese or Libyans. They would remain your clients.'

Zanin stroked the head of his Doberman, which was looking at us in an unfriendly manner. He pointed to one of his lieutenants.

'Half of our fish is bought by Italians. We can't cede that market to you.'

The MANK organization had already discussed this and, in the end, we had all agreed. The opportunity to make money out of the illegal export of currency from Tripoli wouldn't last for ever and was worth a fortune. We had to go all out for it.

'In exchange, Signor Zanin, we can offer you The Mank in Cairo.'

'Which you have already visited on several business trips,' Nico Gerace added maliciously.

Zanin seemed surprised by the offer. It was difficult to weigh up the economic aspects there on the spot. But Ahmed came in with something to clinch the deal.

'What you have here could be over in a day, Signor Zanin. It all depends on the whim of Colonel Gaddafi.'

It was the first time I had heard him speak in that way: independently, decisive and very Libyan. Only his nationality allowed Ahmed to come out with an explicit threat like this, which affected not only the Maltese.

But it had the opposite effect. Zanin's mask of a face hardened.

'Your Gaddafi won't do a bloody thing. If he does, the Americans and Israelis will wipe him out, seeing as the Italians haven't got the bollocks to do it.'

I shot a warning glance at Karim, but he couldn't hold back.

'You're guests in this country only for a short while longer, Signor Zanin, and you've already robbed the Libyan people quite enough,' he said aggressively.

His manner upset the Doberman, which bared its teeth and growled. Zanin gave it a loving caress to calm it down.

'That's a good boy, Killer. These boys are just leaving.'

Then he got up.

'Your generous offer is refused, boys. That's my final answer.'

Friday, 21 November 1969

We couldn't give up the opportunity purely out of fear of Zanin and his gang. So we decided to start operations anyway.

From five Italian families among Nico's acquaintances and mine, we gathered over 30,000 Libyan pounds to take to Lampedusa.

We decided to take the first trip in my motorboat on a Friday night. It was the Muslim weekly holiday and the coast guard had other things on its mind. In order to avoid the port, we would leave from La Moneta. My father had left Mohammed in charge of the sale of the island but, for the moment, it was still our family property. Having Italian documents, it was Nico and I who would make the trip.

We arrived on the island at suppertime. Night in the middle of November was cool but not cold, and the sea was extremely calm. Karim and Nico had prepared some couscous and we were all sitting down to eat in the kitchen when we heard the sound of engines. Two huge inflatables were about a hundred metres from the jetty.

Nico immediately looked through the infra-red binoculars.

'It's Zanin and a lot of his men.'

Ahmed took his knife out.

'Put that away,' I told him. 'Karim, take the money bag. You and Nico go out the back way. Ahmed and I will wait for them here.'

'And then?'

'Then as soon as they come in, you get away in the motorboat. It's much faster than the inflatables. Here's the keys.'

'And you two?' Karim asked.

'We'll manage, brother. You two keep the money safe.'

Of course, it was possible that Zanin might leave a couple of his men on guard along the jetty. But if Nico and Karim took them by surprise they would be able to overcome them.

As soon as they left, Ahmed and I switched on all the upstairs lights in the house. They would lose a good deal of time in looking for us up there.

We went out by the back door, took the path to the cliff and started to run. We had a ten-minute start and the Maltese gang had no knowledge of the path. If Nico and Karim managed to escape, they would think there was no one else to look for.

At the highest point, a third of the way along, we stopped and climbed up on to a rock. You could see the villa lit up, the jetty with its two lamps and the two inflatables.

'There are ten of them,' said Ahmed, counting.

It wasn't the number that worried me.

'He's brought that damned Doberman.'

Zanin had left two men on guard on the jetty. They were sitting listlessly on its wooden planks, letting their legs dangle and having a cigarette.

Nico and Karim were already hidden on the beach. They were perfectly positioned and waiting for Zanin, his men and the dog to go into the villa. Then, in a flash, the two of them flung themselves at a run on the jetty. The two guards had no time even to get up and were hurled into the water.

We saw Nico jump into the motorboat and start the engine while Karim untied the moorings. Alerted by the men's cries, Zanin and the others ran out towards the jetty. But Nico and Karim were already on their way. Zanin then pulled out a pistol and aimed it at the motorboat.

Perhaps he would have hit it, perhaps not, but Ahmed had no wish to run the risk. His cry carried as far as the beach.

'*Ibn kalb almaltia!*'*

Zanin was distracted for a moment. But, in that time, Nico and Karim in the motorboat were already out of range. Immediately, however, Zanin and his men took to the path at a run. And that damned dog was in front of them.

We ran on in the dark; we knew the path like the back of our hands. We did have at least ten minutes' start on them, but there were problems: their torches, their number and their pistol. And that dog would sniff us out if we tried to hide.

We reached the edge of the cliff on other side of the island in record time, but behind us we could hear Killer's furious barking as the dog raced towards us, together with the cries of Zanin's minions.

The Doberman caught up with us, snarling. Ahmed took out his knife. But Killer was clever and in no hurry. It simply had to hold us there, penned in three metres from the cliff edge, and wait for its master to arrive with his men and his gun.

I looked at the sea and then at Ahmed. But he had already caught on.

'Think there'll be enough water, Mikey?'

This time, there was no Alberto down below to tell us. The tide had to be more or less at midway. We had a one in two chance. Better than being torn to pieces by Killer or shot by Zanin.

I smiled at Ahmed.

---

* 'Maltese son of a bitch!' (author's note)

'I'll go first and tell you. If you don't hear anything, best of luck with the dog.'

I took two steps to run up and leaped into the air. This time, I didn't have the courage to look down. I kept my eyes closed during the twenty metres my body was sailing through the air, waiting for water or rocks.

When my feet touched water and my body sank several metres, I hadn't even taken breath. I surfaced, panting and spluttering. It was a lucky chance I didn't drown there, after having escaped being smashed to bits.

'OK?' I heard Ahmed yelling above me. I had forgotten about him.

'Good luck with the dog!' I shouted back.

Three seconds later, I saw him leap and crash into the water a few metres away.

'Forgot about me, Mikey?' he said as soon as he surfaced, also gasping for air.

'No, I thought maybe you wanted to play with Killer for a while! Like you did with the dog that bit Jet.'

He started to laugh, and I joined in. Then a thought crossed his mind.

'Do you think that shit Zanin will start shooting at us from up there?'

'He won't be able to see with just a torch. Unless he has a searchlight . . .'

We swam towards the rocks and hauled ourselves out so that we were completely out of any line of fire and so as not to catch cold in the water.

Above us, the torches were lighting up the sea's surface. They shone for about ten minutes, then Zanin and his men realized they weren't going to find us and went away.

'What shall we do now?' Ahmed asked.

'Wait for dawn.'

We stayed there half an hour in silence.

'Are you thinking about that bastard Maltese?' Ahmed asked me.

No, my friend, I'm thinking about my mother, who wasn't as fortunate as we were in playing Russian roulette with the sea.

I made no reply. But he understood.

'Sorry, Mikey,' he said softly. 'Stupid question.'

In that moment, we heard the sound an engine drawing near.

'Damn,' Ahmed said, taking out his knife.

'It's OK, it's the motorboat.'

Karim was at the wheel. Nico threw out the ladder and gave us one of his wonderful smiles.

'Been having fun, you guys?'

Saturday, 29 November 1969

The following morning, the four of us went to find General Jalloun in his offices in Bab Azizia. The first thing we did was make him a gift of a rucksack containing ten cartons of Marlboro Reds and five bottles of Johnnie Walker Black Label.

Then I told him about our ideas for business, the difficulties with Zanin, the help we needed and how much we would cut him in. It was a generous but fair offer.

'I want twice that,' said Jalloun straightaway.

Sure, the poor general wanted to exploit his extensive powers to the maximum while he was still able to lick the new regime's boots.

I smiled at him. After all, he was an old friend of my grandad.

'It's already a generous offer, General.'

Jalloun spread his arms wide.

'I'm sorry, but I have three wives and ten children to support.'

Nico handed him an envelope.

'Then we can help you save in other areas, General.'

In the envelope was a card with the very personal greetings of the two Lebanese belly dancers he had got to know at our Cairo restaurant the weekend before. And also the very poetic photographic souvenirs that had been taken from behind a two-way mirror in the bedroom where the general had entertained the two ladies.

Jalloun burst out laughing. He looked again at the photographs Nico had brought him.

'Do you pick the girls yourself, Nico?'

'One by one, General. It's a very rigorous selection process. The next time you come to Cairo, I must introduce you to the two new Filipino girls. They can do extraordinary things with their feet.'

That evening the coast guard stopped all the fishing boats in Zanin's fleet. The police limited themselves to carrying out a search, discovering the money, taking 15 per cent and then letting them go on their way.

Before dawn broke, Ahmed and I entered the garden of Zanin's villa, after we had thrown in some poisoned meatballs. I was a little sorry to kill the dogs, but it was necessary.

Ahmed carved Killer's eyes out of their sockets and dropped them on the doormat in front of Zanin's front door.

Sunday, 30 November 1969

As on the previous occasion, we invited ourselves to Zanin's house after Mass. This time, without dressing up and minus the *cannoli*.

The meeting was very rapid. Our previous offer was no longer on the table and our request had changed.

We demanded absolute freedom to export Italian currency, without any kickback to him. In return, we would let Zanin and his Maltese associates have exclusive rights on all the other national currencies, but with a commission of 15 per cent to be given to us, which we would then pass on to General Jalloun.

'In order to protect your business from the Libyan police,' I explained.

'OK, offer accepted,' Zanin said quickly.

But I wasn't finished.

'One more thing. As it is, the Alhambra cinema isn't paying. So we should take it over. As from today, it'll be run by my friend Nico here. We'll give you 5 per cent of the takings.'

Zanin was in a hurry over one thing only. That we left as soon as possible.

'All right,' he said.

Ahmed stepped forward and pushed his face right into Zanin's.

'There's one last thing, Maltese. If I see you point a gun or even just a finger at any of the four of us, I'll carve your eyes out and put them in the couscous instead of the lamb's.'

Zanin bid us a courteous farewell. Killer's eyes and Ahmed's knife had persuaded him far more than the Libyan coast guard.

Sunday, 14 December 1969

Karim had come back to Tripoli after two consecutive weeks in Cairo. We were counting up the MANK organization's unbelievable takings in my Garden City maisonette. Each week, we earned a clear 10,000 Libyan pounds, which would soon rise to 20,000, given the Italians' growing fears.

Nico was over the moon, but also a little concerned.

'Perhaps we're overdoing it. The whole of the Libyan police could come down on us.'

'Not as long as there's Jalloun.'

'They'll replace him sooner or later, the royalist pig,' Karim said. 'I don't trust him anyway.'

'Easy, Karim. He's taking 15 per cent from us and 15 from Zanin. A hundred times his salary.'

Ahmed came up with another problem.

'We can't carry on putting our money in your cellar here, Mikey. Nor at the Banco di Sicilia in Lampedusa. It would attract too much attention — even a safety-deposit box would raise too many questions.'

Nico had his own solution.

'Why don't we just spend it all? There's a new motorbike I want and I've a whole string of whores waiting for me!'

'Don't even think about it,' I answered. 'Someone would get suspicious, and not even General Jalloun would be able to protect us.'

Karim came up with his own proposal.

'We could take them to Cairo and have the Muslim Brotherhood look after them.'

Nico was against this straightaway. And I wasn't for it either. Karim was really starting to get on my nerves.

I know you're seeing Laura Hunt in Cairo. Sooner or later, we're going to have a talk about this.

As usual, Ahmed had the right answer, complicated, but touched with genius. It was approved unanimously by all four members of the MANK organization.

Sunday, 21 December 1969

Ahmed had a blacksmith friend of his build four metal strongboxes similar to the safety-deposit boxes in banks. Sturdy, spacious and absolutely watertight, each of them had a ring welded on to them and a steel cable fitted with a lock threaded through them so they could not be separated.

The initials 'M A N K' were engraved on each box.

Ten kilometres out from La Moneta, a large rock surfaced from the water. No one went there, because, by a trick of the winds, the current was very strong and so it was rarely fished.

Several metres down, almost at the base of the rock, was a cave that went upwards to a point where it emerged out of the water.

It was here that we decided to put the money, once a week, already divided into four waterproof plastic sacks. There had to be at least three of us: two going down in scuba gear – which would be Ahmed and myself – while the third stayed on board as lookout.

The first time, all four of us went together on a Sunday a few days before Christmas. In the cave, we threaded the cable through the rings on the four boxes to link them, then passed it round a large rock and secured them all together with the huge lock.

It was a complex operation, but our treasure was worth protecting well.

We all had the keys to our own strongbox, where we could place our share. But, in order to take the boxes away, you needed the key to the lock that secured the steel cable round the rock.

And, without any discussion, as I was the boss and always would be, I would keep that key. And not even Colonel Gaddafi could change that.

On the motorboat, on a blue sea, as we returned to shore on that day of splendid sunshine in a blue sky, Karim reminded us of an evening many years earlier at the two villas.

He could sing in tune in a voice that was worthy of Modugno himself. Nico immediately joined in with him, as he also had a great voice. Ahmed and I were tone deaf, but in the end we joined in the chorus: '*Volare, oh, oh! Cantare, oh, oh, oh, oh!*'

When I got back to the Garden City from the port it was almost dark. I had taken the old Corso Vittorio on my Triumph. There was no one buying ice cream at Girus's parlour; a few passers-by were walking quickly past the cathedral.

I parked the bike and was opening the door when she touched my shoulder.

We hadn't seen each other since the day of my mother's funeral. In those one hundred days, Laura had matured a good deal. Not physically – at eighteen, her body was the same as Marlene's – but in her look and in her decision to start something with me.

There were a thousand things I wanted to tell her, but not one of them would come out.

I've always loved you. But it was your mother I screwed.

'Aren't you going to invite me into your new house, Mikey?'

We went into the maisonette in silence. She looked about a bit and saw the photo taken on the Spanish Steps in Piazza di Spagna that hung opposite my bed.

The photo of how I'll never be.

But she hadn't come to talk. She smiled at me, reached out her arms, placed them on my shoulders, then drew herself close to me.

She pointed to the photograph. 'Can you be happy with the reject version?'

We laughed together as we began to kiss. Then I switched off all the lights and closed the blinds so that not even the streetlights could shine in on us. I wanted the dark, because I knew that I was stealing and you steal better in the dark.

I put on the Cohen cassette she had given me.

She took off her clothes in silence and I followed suit. We got in naked under the sheets.

'Have you got some protection, Mikey?'

For a moment, I was perplexed by the unusual way she put it. I shook my head.

'I've got one. I got it two months ago, thinking of you at New York airport. I hope these things don't go out of date, like medicines.'

She put the condom on me. And she trusted me. She didn't see the darker side of me, which was clearly there in the snapshot she'd taken more than two years earlier. Or else she no longer wanted to think about it.

'There have been other girls, Laura.'

I said it like that, all in one breath, before it was too late. But she began to laugh.

'I never had any doubts, Casanova. An ugly moron like you, all muscle and no brain . . . I'm not surprised some poor girl might have found you interesting.'

It was true. I had had one or two adventures in those three months, nothing that amounted to anything, simply to distance myself from her. But I wasn't thinking about those adventures.

I was thinking about Marlene struggling beneath me after I had tied her wrists to the bed, spitting my blood back in my face while I was fucking her.

Your mother.

Laura got on top of me. Love and passion were united in her, inexperience mixed with desire, total trust united with the wish to grow together. And I clung on to her like a newborn at its mother's breast, knowing that, sooner or later, this would be over.

Afterwards, Laura told me all that was happening in her life.

William Hunt's job had lasted until the summer. He was head of the team negotiating the evacuation of Wheelus Field and the protection of American economic interests. Marlene had been with him in Tripoli.

'I'm taking a Communications and Photography course in Cairo and I'll stay there until the summer. Any objections you'd like to voice to this programme, Mikey?'

She was joking, but I was thinking about things I could not mention.

Do you see Karim in Cairo?

This was not the question I asked, but something else.

'Did your mother and my father have an affair?'

She suddenly became serious. Now, she was staring at me, her clear bright eyes focused on a memory that must have been very painful.

'That awful day on La Moneta, I thought my parents' marriage was over. I was ready to do anything to prevent it. But Marlene assured me that she and William would stay together. Then your mother died and things between them calmed down. Almost as if nothing had ever happened. In San Francisco, I never heard them argue or even talk about it.'

I was taken aback, incredulous.

'But you haven't answered my question. Did my father and your mother have an affair?'

'Why go on about it, Mikey? You'll only hurt yourself and others. Your mother . . .'

She never said *is dead*. Nor *killed herself*, or *was killed*. She said nothing more.

I held her close. We lay there, holding each other. She trusted me.

There was love, heat and peace in that embrace, but no future: that was already behind us.

That evening, Mohammed Al Bakri flew from Tripoli to Rome. He had mixed feelings for Italy. While the taxi was taking him in the rain from Leonardo da Vinci airport to the centre, the streets full of lights, shops and people buying Christmas presents made him feel happy and angry at the same time.

He could very well remember that September day in 1931 when he was only six years old. Marshal Graziani's soldiers took his father and his two elder brothers away, while his mother was shut in a room, from which came her screams and the sounds of her tears.

The rain was beating down on the taxi windows as the driver made slalom turns between the cars and pedestrians along the narrow streets of Rome's historic centre. Salvatore Balistreri was waiting for him in his top-floor flat in Piazza di Spagna.

His made-to-measure suit was a gift from Don Eugenio, and the black leather case on the seat a gift from Busi. Inside it were the restricted documents that the Italian ambassador in Tripoli had prepared for the Foreign Minister: the census of Italian properties in Libya and an analysis of the situation.

Twenty thousand hectares under cultivation – value 70,000 million lira; real estate – 100,000 million; savings – 15,000 million. With machinery and other possessions, a total of almost 200,000 million lira.

This was what Italy had to offer Gaddafi. And what Gaddafi had to offer to Nasser to gain his support. Before the end of the year, the Egyptian President would go to Tripoli and a pact would be sanctioned between them.

On the other hand, it was oilfields, car factories and contracts for weapons and radar that Gaddafi could offer Italy. They formed three sides of a quadrilateral. Then, Busi and Balistreri instigated secret negotiations with the Americans and did so, finally, from a position of strength. And that was the fourth side of the figure, the one that would seal the deal.

The Italian community was already going down day by day. Already, more than eight hundred families had left and another three thousand would leave between January and July in 1970.

And, at this point, the final push to have the rest out would meet with no resistance.

Thanks to Busi's contacts in the secret service, Aldo Moro had been ill informed. But then, he and the Christian Democrats also had a good deal of other things to think about. The laity's push for divorce, the Communist gains in the polls and, since 12 December, just over a week earlier, the bomb left in a bank in Milan that had killed seventeen people and injured eighty-eight. Whichever it was, Moro was sufficiently distracted. As for the rest, the few Italians who really counted, as Balistreri said, they were turning a blind eye, even if they weren't actually involved.

No one in this world either today, tomorrow or whenever would be able to accuse certain politicians and industrialists of having supported the end game that was about to be played out. They had *sympathized*, perhaps, but for political reasons, never out of convenience: Libya was changing from a corrupt and feudal monarchy to a true people's democracy! And as for Italy and its 50 million Italians, who could then pay a little less for petrol and heating, it was absolutely fine. And, besides, this Colonel Gaddafi was a moderate and could be controlled.

Yes, Mohammed thought, everything was going really smoothly, apart from the one grain of sand in the gears: Ingegner Balistreri's son, Mikey. He had seen him grow as rebellious and as Fascist as his mother, Italia. But it was a Fascism very different from that of the criminals who had hanged his father and brothers. Giuseppe Bruseghin and his daughter, Italia, were decent people, and Mikey had inherited their nature. And he had chosen his sons, Ahmed and Karim, as his best friends. Mikey Balistreri represented a minute grain of sand that could put all their workings at risk. His ridiculous insistence on investigating the deaths of Nadia and Italia could bring a lot of trouble.

He shivered and asked the taxi driver to turn up the heating. Mohammed Al Bakri closed his eyes and concentrated. His unfortunate little daughter, his beloved Nadia. He had a great deal to forget, otherwise he would go mad.

As the taxi was turning into a Piazza di Spagna soaked with rain and crowded with city dwellers and tourists, Mohammed recited a short prayer. He asked Allah and Nadia for forgiveness.

Wednesday, 24 December 1969

Papa and Alberto arrived in Tripoli from Rome on the afternoon of Christmas Eve. Papa still had this idea of the united family, even if Mamma and Grandad were no more. Perhaps he dreamed of going to midnight Mass with his two sons by his side. But this had not happened since we were kids. I had stopped going years ago and I only agreed to supper together so as not to offend my brother.

Alberto took a room and Papa a suite in the Waddan. We ate in the hotel on the terrace overlooking the seafront, as we had done so many times when we were children, but then, in those days, my grandfather and mother were there as well. So many things had changed. Only my father pretended that there was no split between memory and reality.

There were few Italians at the tables. There was no longer the atmosphere there had been at past festive events, when there had been an orchestra, dances and shows hosted by Pippo Baudo and Caterina Caselli. Now, it was quieter, with fewer civilians and more military.

Papa had changed. In these recent months after Italia's death, his hair had started to turn grey, along with his face and even his words.

His features were less affable, as if life had now taken him into a world where the struggle was more vicious.

He talked about his new deals with various Italian industrial groups: petrol, cars, foodstuffs. Every so often, he came out with terms such as 'joint venture', 'put and call options'. Perhaps he thought this rubbish would interest me. In actual fact, he was speaking only to Alberto, who seemed a little embarrassed.

My poor brother. What kind of a disgusting world has Papa dragged you into?

Then he began a running commentary on the situation in Tripoli and the Americans who had to give up Wheelus Field.

'But will the Americans leave Libya just like that?' Alberto asked him.

Clark Gable smiled.

'Americans are businessmen. They'll find a way to make a deal.'

I remembered William Hunt's words at my grandfather's funeral.

Salvo, we must talk tomorrow.

'What about you, Papa?' I cut in. 'Have you spoken with William Hunt? Have you made a deal with him?'

About Marlene Hunt.

Clark Gable turned slightly pale.

'I don't know what you're talking about, Mikey.'

But I had other things to ask him as well, things to do with Tripoli.

'You've sold all the family property, Papa. La Moneta, the Sidi El Masri villas, the olive grove, the town houses. And here we are renting in Garden City? Why?'

My question took him by surprise and was not welcome. He brushed a hand through his thick hair and smoothed his well-trimmed moustache. Here, as well, you could see the first white hairs, like those on his temples. The lines in the corners of his eyes were deeper, the shadows under his eyes darker. Yes, my father was starting to age.

'The situation could change here, Michele. The shares in foreign companies are one thing and property, land and commercial activity another.'

'What do you mean?' I asked him.

'That we Italians don't own Libya. One day, we invaded it and, one day, we'll have to leave.'

I looked out to the sea, dotted with the tiny lights of the fishing vessels. I looked at the carriages trotting along the seafront. I looked at the palms, stirring in the cool breeze of the end of December.

'Libya is our home, Papa. Thousands of good people like Grandad built it up without its oilfields, without "joint ventures" and "puts and calls". I don't ever want to leave Tripoli. Besides, the MANK organization's doing better here than in Egypt.'

Papa looked at me in silence. There was no hostility or irony in his look. Even his age-old disapproval, which I felt was a kind of scornfulness, had disappeared. Mamma's death had taken it away.

All that remained was concern for the crazy son who had shot at a lion from too close, and about his small-time trafficking, which could damage Salvatore's grandiose business schemes in Libya.

Remember that he always knows everything. He lets you do things to keep you happy.

Papa carefully wiped some froth from his beer from his mouth with his napkin. Then he stared at me with that look that I knew very well. It was the patient and good-natured look that hid his rage. But it was there, always lying in wait, even in the period of mourning when he wore the black button in his lapel. It was there in his words, spoken softly as a priest giving extreme unction.

'I'm happy for you, Michele. So long as your affairs don't damage our family's good name.'

There was no threat here. There was no need. He had all the weapons he required. He smiled at me, as usual. Paid the bill, as usual. And went off, as usual.

Alberto and I were left alone at the table.

'Alberto, I have to ask you something.'

His eyes were on the luminous dots along the coast at the end of the seafront beyond the castle, towards the old fortifications, the beaches and La Moneta.

'Do you really have to, Mikey?'

His tone was always that of a caring elder brother. But, this time, there was a hint of concern I had never picked up before. He already knew what the question was. But I could not spare him, I had no other choice.

'That afternoon . . .'

I left the question hanging in the air. In actual fact, I had no idea how to continue. My generous brother shook his head.

'You can't let yourself have any peace, can you, Mikey?'

It was more of a statement than a question.

'No, I can't, Alberto. Tell me about that afternoon.'

'I was on the beach for two hours with the other guys. Before four, we split up, and I went to my room to study for the rest of the afternoon. I saw Farid and Salim docking at the jetty about five fifteen. They'd come to pick up Mohammed and I went out on to the beach to say hello.'

'Was anyone else on the beach?'

He thought for a moment. 'Ahmed was there, perhaps Nico and Karim came along after a while. I don't remember.'

'And the grown-ups?'

He looked at me in desperation at my persistence, which he did not share.

'They came along later, in dribs and drabs. Mikey, you have to get used to it: Mother took her own life.'

Even I, who was not as rational as he was, could understand that his statement had little to do with reason and a lot to do with wishful thinking.

You can't know this, brother of mine. All the grown-ups were alone for enough time to go to the other end of the island and get back. Don Eugenio, Busi, Mohammed before he left. And, obviously, Papa, as well.

Suddenly, the night air was filled with the muezzin's cry coming from the mosque. *Allah akhbar.*

Sunday, 14 June 1970

Winter and spring passed into summer. Papa and Alberto had not been back to Tripoli, not even for Easter. Alberto often phoned, but Papa never.

The Italians continued to leave Tripoli in sporadic numbers, closing their shops and trying to sell their property, as well as taking their money out – something that was increasingly difficult to do via legitimate means. As a consequence, the MANK organization's business prospered and the Libyan pounds mounted each week in the four strongboxes in the cave under the sea.

Things were also going well in Egypt. Karim was now permanently settled there, dividing his time between our business affairs and the Muslim Brotherhood. I imagined that he and Laura saw each other in Cairo. But I preferred not to ask or think about it.

Laura often came for the weekend, and we would spend Sundays together. We went to the Underwater Club's beach on the Triumph or rode around Tripoli, then came back to my place in Garden City. An ordinary young couple, a normal life in front of them. A degree, perhaps, a job, marriage, a home and children. Or so it seemed.

I hadn't seen Marlene Hunt at all. I knew from Laura that she spent a good deal of time with her in Cairo, especially when William was in Vietnam. And when he was in Tripoli she stayed at home in their house near the Adrian Pelt coast road. No one saw her around any more, not in her Ferrari, not at the Underwater Club, nor at parties in the embassies or out on terraces overlooking the sea.

William Hunt was winding up negotiations with the new Libyan authorities for the American withdrawal from Wheelus Field. At the end of the summer, the Hunts would return to the United States. But what about Laura?

That Sunday, we were at my place in Garden City. We had just made love. She was lying on the bed, her head resting on my knees. The Rolleiflex was on the floor. It was always by her side. She was flicking through a series of black and white shots she had taken of 'the city of the living and the dead' in Cairo, the cemetery where refugees from Sinai in the 1967 war were still living. It was where Karim worked. I knew the destructive pattern of my thoughts started with me, not Laura, and from what had happened with her mother. But it was easier to start discussing our relationship than tell her the truth.

'You should have someone like Karim in your life. You can share all your cultural interests, like photography, with him . . .'

Laura became serious all of a sudden. Her sense of humour was never lacking, but my tone of voice worried her.

'Karim has some things I like that you don't have. But I love you for what you are, not for what you have or don't have.'

My beautiful loser. Her dedication on the back of the photo.

'Your parents will never agree to us as a couple, Laura.'

'I'm eighteen now, Mikey. Pretty well grown up. After this summer, we can go to Rome together, or wherever we like. It's all fine by me.'

I wanted to scream out, *Yes!*, but there was that memory, which wasn't only a memory. It was like an impending threat, and was always there.

'I've had other girls, Laura.'

'You've already told me that, Mikey. But that was before me, it's not important.'

'One was a married woman.'

She turned round to look at me. She was still calm, but a shadow of disquiet passed over her face.

'Was it an important relationship?'

I replied on an impulse.

'No, just sex. And it only happened once.'

Only once. Now it's over. Or is it?

Laura immediately started to play it down in that way she had.

'Well, thank goodness. A physical relationship is one that Plato puts on the lowest part of the scale. The least important.'

The least important point of the scale.

It was true. It was also a lie. I was running along the edge of an abyss.

Tuesday, 16 June 1970

I couldn't get to sleep that night. I had too many thoughts.

The most angry of these was that Marlene Hunt was the cause of my mother's suicide or murder. Now, not even a year had passed, and yet it seemed a hundred. Everyone had forgotten, including the police, who had never even investigated it.

Italia was an obstacle to the sale of Grandad's olive grove. And she was the obstacle to my father's life with Marlene. She had gone to see Mansur; perhaps she knew who had killed Nadia.

The last thought crossed my mind in a flash. I had been an idiot. Mamma had gone to see Mansur a few days before she was killed. She was checking on those alibis, as I had asked her to after the goatherd Jamaal had committed suicide. She believed he wasn't guilty and had told me so.

If someone takes their own life, then people think they're either mad or guilty.

I was suddenly wide awake and knew what I was looking for. Where had my mother's things been put after we moved from Sidi El Masri? Mohammed had been in charge, and he certainly wouldn't have thrown anything away.

I went down into the cellar. There were trunks, large boxes, bags and crutches and all the clothes in wardrobes. I rummaged through everything for two hours, sweating and overcome with heat while the mosquitoes hummed around me, unable to bite.

The book in which I had seen the sheet of notepaper wasn't there. It was Nietzsche's *Beyond Good and Evil*. A slim volume, I recalled. But that was not the one Mamma had taken to the cliffs that day. That was *Ecce Homo*.

I threw open a wardrobe and the kaftan was there.

The light kaftan Mamma was wearing that morning on the veranda.

It had a large side pocket and *Beyond Good and Evil* was inside it. And also the crumpled sheet of squared notepaper with my writing on it, the one I had handed to my mother, who had promised to investigate.

But on the other side of the page, in my mother's pointed writing, there now were two short sentences.

They knew each other. Check m.

It was an 'm' written in lower-case.

I still hadn't seen Mohammed Al Bakri's new house in Tripoli. I went on foot from Garden City, walking under the arcades along Shara Istiklal. Almost all the Italian shops had closed, the traffic was sparse, the Libyans on bicycles or in donkey carts. Arriving at the corner that the former Piazza Italia made with Shara 24 December, I went up the staircase and rang the bell beside a very middle-class door plate that said 'Al Bakri'. Finally, Mohammed's family was living in an apartment with rooms for everyone, with running water, electric light, sanitation and drains.

It was Karim who opened the door. I had thought he was in Cairo, not in Tripoli.

You're not in control any more, Mikey. It looks like the MANK organization is over.

Karim accompanied me to the living room, where Mohammed was drinking tea, before going to the office. Ahmed was sitting next to Mohammed, and there was an Egyptian housekeeper serving them toast.

The furniture was well made, the television set one of the latest models. I declined the offer of coffee and remained standing. I addressed Mohammed directly.

'Did Nadia know anyone whose name begins with "m"?'

The question took them all by surprise. They looked at me, visibly shaken.

'Apart from me and you?' Mohammed asked.

He had changed. Now he was well shaven, less stark in the face, better groomed. And more self-confident. And, for the first time since I was born, there was no 'Signor Michele'.

I showed him the sheet of squared notepaper.

'Whose notes are these?'

'Mine. I was making enquiries into Nadia's death.'

I saw Ahmed and Karim looking down at the floor. I absolutely had to keep quiet about them knowing anything about this, or Mohammed would punish them severely.

Then I showed him the other side.

They knew each other. Check m.

Mohammed recognized my mother's handwriting.

'Was Signora Italia also making enquiries into Nadia's death?'

He was indignant and could barely hide his anger.

'Mohammed, I'm asking you again. Who is this "m"? Is it one of Nadia's friends?'

I turned pale as he fought to keep himself under control.

'Nadia was still a child. She knew no one apart from her relatives and her schoolfriends. Her killer is in hell now. The case is closed, and you know it.'

★   ★   ★

The police barracks at Bab Azizia smelled of paint. The police themselves were giving the peeling walls a fresh coat, perhaps in anticipation of a visit from the supreme leader, Colonel Gaddafi.

General Jalloun didn't seem overly happy to see me. He received me in an office that was smaller and barer than the one he used to have. I quickly gave him the bottle of Johnnie Walker Black Label I had hidden under my jacket, and he put it in his briefcase.

I handed the sheet of paper to him. He read the part I had written, puffing out smoke. He knew he had to respond to me seriously, now we were giving him thousands of pounds each week.

'You wrote these notes yourself?'

'I did. Could you please look on the other side, General?'

They knew each other. Check m.

'Whose writing is this, Mikey?'

'My mother's.'

He was surprised for a moment, but not more than that. He probably thought Italia was mad, as I did. He drew on his Marlboro Red and exhaled the smoke through his nose. He liked a theatrical gesture. He must have seen John Wayne doing it in some Western where he's questioning a Sioux warrior.

'So? What do you want to know, Mikey?'

'Who "m" is.'

He blew out more smoke.

'I haven't the faintest idea. But what's all this got to do with Nadia?'

'She's referring to a person whose name starts with the letter "m", General. And, certainly, this isn't the goatherd Jamaal.'

'You watch too much Perry Mason on the television. Why don't you stick with your MANK organization.'

'Nadia was raped and sodomized. How could Jamaal have done that, General?'

He shook his head.

'There are certain things you should know nothing about. It was a long and painful business. Much more than you know. Perhaps this "m" was with Jamaal. Perhaps it was him who raped her. And then strangled her.'

I was taken aback.

'Strangled? But you mentioned Jamaal's knife with the saw-blade, and Nadia's blood. I thought she'd been killed with that.'

The general fumed in irritation. Despite the money, the whisky and the cigarettes, he was losing patience. But he had to give me some kind of an answer.

'The day before she died, my mother handed an envelope to William Hunt. She told him it was urgent, a matter that had to be resolved within forty-eight hours. Perhaps it was something to do with this "m".'

This information struck him more. Much more. Too much more.

'How do you know this, Mikey?'

'I was spying on them, General.'

'Seeing that you were spying, Mikey, can you remember what your mother said to William Hunt?'

I remembered very well.

'She handed it to him, saying that everything was there inside, no room for any doubt. Then he asked how much time they had and she said they had two days, no more.'

Jalloun lit another cigarette. He now seemed very interested, very much so.

'Could your mother have been party to some conversation between your father and his friends Emilio Busi and Don Eugenio? Or between him and Mohammed?'

I wondered where the question was coming from. Then my glance fell on the photo hanging on the wall behind Jalloun's desk. In the place of the aging King Idriss, there was the youthful Colonel Gaddafi.

The *coup d'état*. Forty-eight hours to foil it. Mamma had been too optimistic. Perhaps that envelope had nothing to do with either Marlene Hunt or the death of Nadia.

General Jalloun rose to see me out.

'Perhaps I may be able to offer you some business, Mikey, in the next few days. The biggest offer of your life.'

Wednesday, 17 June 1970

Piazza Navona in June was full of tourists as well as the locals. The Bar Tre Scalini had no free seats outside, but was quiet enough inside.

Emilio Busi was smoking a cigarette. You could see his vest under his checked shirt. Don Eugenio was reading the *Corriere della Sera*'s financial pages.

Salvatore Balistreri was filling them in on the situation in Tripoli.

'The reports from the new ambassador are reassuring. The Italian exodus is moving forward and the Americans should be leaving any day now.'

'I know that William Hunt is finalizing the agreements for evacuating Wheelus Field,' Busi said. 'Is he softening?'

'Yes, I spoke to him about things,' Balistreri said. 'The big American Seven and their little siblings are in agreement about the division.'

'They have to be,' said Busi. 'Their oilfields are going to be nationalized only in appearance. In reality, the sole difference with respect to the previous situation is that they'll have to share the pie out with us. Of course, it's not what Enrico Mattei wanted, but our present connections don't want too many problems with the Americans. The Yanks are attached to money and would have no problem bombing Tripoli to defend their interests.'

Balistreri knew that the former Carabiniere turned Communist was perfectly right. His brothers and their friends in Sicily had many contacts across the Atlantic and wanted no trouble with the Americans.

'The only ones left outside will be the old imperialist British and those bigheads, the French,' Busi concluded.

'Right,' Balistreri said. 'The only remaining problem is how Aldo Moro will react when Gaddafi makes his announcement.'

Busi shot him a fleeting glance. It was true: the death of his wife and his fights with Mikey had aged Balistreri. He was always too worried about things. But they had to move quickly.

Don Eugenio spoke a few calming words.

'The Honourable Aldo Moro will certainly not be happy, but he and the Christian Democrats will have other things on their minds when things explode in Libya.'

'Can we be sure?' Balistreri asked.

'We're secretly helping the divorce movement. *Very* secretly, I should add, seeing as I'm using Vatican funds. But they don't appear in any official accounts and I happen to be directly in charge of them. Anyway, it's all for a good cause. Don't you think that divorce is a sign of a civilized society?'

Balistreri could not fathom if it was just irony or if there was some other hint in the question. But perhaps Don Eugenio was being sincere, given that he was a *progressive* priest. Besides, he had always known. His elder brothers had said so repeatedly since he was a boy and had lent a hand in the barbershop to help support his education.

Don't trust those bastard Communists or the priests, Salvo. Making a deal is fine, but never make friends.

'So we can plan for July?' Balistreri asked.

'Yes,' said Don Eugenio. 'I'll drop a word to the President. He's not happy about this solution, but he trusts us. Unfortunately, we have to sacrifice one or two – just a few – for the benefit of the majority.'

He trusts us!

The President knew very well there was no alternative, thought Balistreri bitterly.

'Is everything ready in Tripoli?' Busi asked.

Balistreri hesitated. He could keep quiet, but Busi had the secret service behind him and Don Eugenio had the President. And therefore the secret service again. Perhaps they knew everything already. It would be too risky to lie.

'Mikey's gone to see General Jalloun. He wants him to reopen investigations into the deaths of Nadia and Italia. Mohammed has his spies in the police, obviously. We're keeping a watch on him.'

A shadow flitted across Don Eugenio's light-blue eyes.

'He's a problem, that boy. Always has been.'

Busi blew out a mouthful of smoke. He did not seem entirely calm himself.

'Fundamentally, your son's like me, an idealist. But we can't risk any trouble because of a young kid.'

Balistreri looked both of them in the eye. It was necessary to remind these two who he was, where he came from and who he had behind him.

'I have already given up a great deal, gentlemen.' He touched his mourning button. 'I will take care of my son, if you don't mind.'

Busi and Don Eugenio fell silent. The message was very clear. But Balistreri decided to set their minds at rest.

'Mohammed will get Jalloun removed very shortly, so Mikey'll no longer have anyone to turn to for support. The MANK organization will lose its protection. And, at that point, I really hope he'll leave Libya and come and finish his education in Italy.'

Salvatore Balistreri looked out at the splendour of Piazza Navona. A long summer was approaching for the Italians. Economic boom, cars, motorways, low-cost petrol. And, around the fountains and open-air cafés, hundreds of carefree young people.

Italy's growing. Our future has no limits.

'Fine,' said Busi. 'So, tonight, we can enjoy the match.'

Italy was playing Germany in the FIFA World Cup semi-final in Mexico.

Salvatore Balistreri hated football. It was a stupid and ridiculous sport that got people far too excited.

It'll end with the Italians thinking they really have a great country.

It was almost night. The President was watching what was happening on Rome's streets. The party outside was going crazy. The Italy–Germany game had ended minutes ago, after extra time and a total of seven goals that had almost given heart attacks to many Italians.

The President had followed the game with the sound off, barely paying it any attention, listening instead to a beautiful concert of symphonic music while he worked on his papers. But, now, the spectacle outside was interesting. He had even turned up the volume to follow the festivities live in the country's various piazzas.

The Italians were celebrating in their millions. This was the good life. Millions out on the streets, millions of Fiats, Vespas, Lambrettas. Millions of litres of petrol and champagne consumed over a game of football. It was also thanks to himself and the Christian Democrats that the Italians could allow themselves to celebrate a victory over the Germans who had once invaded their country.

Well, the President knew that was not exactly how it was, but history is written by the victors.

Italy's post-war political class had been composed of people like himself, who had fought for a just cause, for goodness' sake! Liberating themselves from Mussolini, who had gone insane, and that coward of a monarch Victor Emmanuel III. But, nevertheless, they had betrayed the government of their country and its wartime allies. This had not happened in Germany, or in Japan.

This is why in Italy, and for Italians today, personal convenience counts for more than a sense of honour, because we taught them that you win and take power by betrayal.

Now, there were these 20,000 poor souls in Libya. When you added it all up, a much *smaller* betrayal. And simple. They only had to be wary of Salvatore Balistreri and his friends and relatives in Sicily. And that hothead son of his, Michele.

He switched the sound off again and went back to his papers. There was a note from his trusted source in the Foreign Ministry, a request for the authorization of a mission to Tripoli.

'Michele Achilli, Socialist; Giorgio Granzotto, Socialist of Proletarian Unity; Michele Pistillo, Communist.'

If Moro had known, he would not have given them authorization. He asked his personal secretary to get Ingegner Balistreri on the phone.

'Did you watch the game, Ingegnere?'

'Of course,' Balistreri lied. 'A terrific victory.'

The President smiled. He was used to recognizing falsehoods. This Ingegner Balistreri cared nothing at all for Italy, except its money.

He explained to him that three Leftist MPs were about to go on a mission to Tripoli.

'Let them go, if you can. I'll tell Mohammed to arrange it so they meet some pro-Palestinian members of the Revolutionary Council. And that Gaddafi comes to know of it.'

'The colonel will be very angry with the Italians, Balistreri.'

'Precisely. So he'll bring an end to things.'

The President ended the call. There it was. Salvatore Balistreri was the perfect example of an Italian born of that great betrayal.

Shifty, no ideals, willing to make any compromise.

Saturday, 20 June 1970

Only a few days had passed since we had last met. General Jalloun called me at seven in the morning. He wanted to see me. Not in the barracks, but at my house in Garden City.

I called Ahmed, telling him to come over. Jalloun arrived punctually at lunchtime, when everyone in Tripoli shut themselves indoors to escape the heat. He was in civilian clothes, without his driver, his face hidden by his keffiyeh.

A secret visit.

Ahmed and I immediately sensed that the general was extremely tense. I gave him the usual envelope with his money. In addition, a carton of Marlboro Reds and a bottle of Johnnie Walker. Small tokens. A sign of respect.

For the first time ever, he didn't open the envelope and count the money.

'Shut the windows, please,' he told us.

He then lit a cigarette, sank into an armchair and asked for a whisky instead of tea. He had never drunk alcohol in our company. Let alone at lunchtime.

I had a very uncomfortable feeling about this. In fact, the news was very bad.

'Boys, they're transferring me to Ghadames. Ghadames – you understand? An oasis in the middle of the desert, more camels than human beings!'

We were done for. Without Jalloun, our business would be ruined.

'I'm sorry, General. How can we help you?'

He reacted to this question in a positive way. He was expecting recriminations, not the offer of help. But I saw him as much more than a source of revenue.

He knew things about Nadia and my mother.

'I want to speak to you alone, Mikey.' He pointed to Ahmed. 'Without him.'

Ahmed looked at me. Serious, impassive. And ready to leave if I gave the sign.

'Ahmed is more than a brother to me, General. What I feel, he feels. What I do, he does. There are no secrets between us.'

Jalloun must have thought a long time about what he was going to tell me. He swallowed a sip of whisky and addressed Ahmed.

'Word is that your father's close to Gaddafi.'

The statement packed a punch, but Ahmed didn't bat an eyelid.

'I think my father looks up to him, General. But he's never spoken to me about him. It's his business, anyway.'

I was a little surprised by his reply. Perhaps this was the first time Ahmed had kept anything from me. Certainly, it was only a matter of hearsay. But the fact that Ahmed had never even mentioned anything upset me.

Jalloun glanced nervously through the closed windows.

'A few days ago, I said I had an offer to make you, Mikey.'

I remembered very well.

The biggest offer of your life.

'I have some powerful friends, boys,' Jalloun went on. 'Friends who are not at all happy with Gaddafi.'

Ahmed rose up immediately.

'I'm leaving,' he said to me. But I was still the head of the MANK organization.

'Sit down, Ahmed. Let's hear what General Jalloun has to say first.'

It was an order, in the old style.

I'm your boss's son. I give the orders. Nothing's changed.

Ahmed remained standing a moment. It was a moment of resistance, to make me understand that things were changing between us. Then he slowly sat down.

'What do you want from us, General?' I asked.

He studied us at length. It was highly risky for him but, evidently, his powerful friends must have exercised a lot of pressure. And we really must have been indispensable to him, if he was being so open.

'In a couple of months, it will be a year since Gaddafi took office. And the more time that elapses, the more difficult it will be to kick him out.'

He said it all in one breath, looking Ahmed and myself directly in the face. Another minute's conversation with General Jalloun would mean we were conspirators and liable to be condemned to death for high treason.

Jalloun continued.

'With my transfer, the MANK business is finished, boys. But, for this job, my friends are offering a recompense of more than you could have earned in ten years.'

We kept silent, and Jalloun went on.

'One million pounds sterling, 2, 400 million Italian lira. To be divided among you. Enough for your entire lives and three generations to come.'

It was an enormous sum, unimaginable. But small compared with what was at stake.

Underneath the sand and the blood. Petroleum. Damned petroleum.

And what do we have to do for this figure, General?'

I already knew the answer. But I needed Jalloun to compromise himself, once and for all, in order to tell him my real price.

The general lit another Marlboro and poured himself a generous shot of whisky.

'Before the end of August, you have to assassinate that bastard Gaddafi.'

Ahmed was up in a shot. 'I'm leaving, Mikey. I'll pretend I've not heard a thing.'

Jalloun smiled, sipping his whisky.

'You'll not even get out of Garden City, Ahmed Al Bakri. Or do you somehow think we'd let you live?'

Jalloun already had his pistol in his hand. I had no doubt that he would shoot us, nor that he had killers waiting outside. I turned to Ahmed.

'Let's listen to all that the general has to say, Ahmed. Then we can decide freely.'

'Decide freely, Mikey?' Ahmed replied, gesturing harshly to the pointed gun.

'Put the pistol away, General, it's not going to help. We have a tape recorder hidden in the room. We use it all the time and give the tapes over to someone we trust who will send them to the police should anything happen to me or my friends. And I mean the Egyptian police, not the Libyan.'

The veins in the general's neck were standing out dangerously. And it was all true. The idea of the tape recorder had been Ahmed's, and it was proving to be a good one.

'I don't believe you!' Jalloun said.

I got up. The last tape, from the month before, was still in a desk drawer. I showed it to him.

He pointed the gun at me again. 'Where's the tape recorder?'

'I don't know, General. Nico installed it and, for security, we never asked where it was. He sees to all that; he gives us the tapes and we give them to Karim, who takes them to Cairo. Now that's all clear, can we get back to business?'

The general looked at me, and I caught a glimpse of respect and satisfaction in his eyes. Certainly, if we were to be killers for him we had passed a pretty close test.

Jalloun placed the gun on his knees.

'Gaddafi is making agreements with foreign countries, such as East Germany. He's going to pay a huge sum for a select group of bodyguards who have seen service in Communist Special Forces. They'll be here in time for the celebrations of the revolution's first anniversary, 1 September. From then on, he'll be beyond anyone's reach.'

'And right now?' I asked.

'Right now, his personal security is guaranteed by members of his tribe, the Qadhadhfa. He can trust them, but they've no experience.'

'So it has to be in August,' I said, 'but will there be a suitable occasion?'

'Yes, although Gaddafi's limiting his public appearances for fear of an attempt on his life. But, in August, several tribes, persuaded by my friends, will ask for a public audience, which the colonel can't refuse. We won't know the date until the last minute, but we do know where and how the meeting will take place.'

'It's a suicidal mission,' Ahmed said.

For the first time, he showed he could have an open mind. He was opposed, but at least open to the possibility. The colossal fee must have made him think twice.

'If they capture you alive, you'll be forced to talk, and I'd be caught in the middle as well.'

'So, how do we go about it?' asked Ahmed.

'The audience will mean that Gaddafi has to come out into the open. We'll see to that. You'll be dressed as policemen; we'll supply the uniforms and weapons. Mikey is so tanned and dark-haired he can pass for a Libyan. Nico as well, with his bushy hair and eyebrows. You can mingle in with the officers charged with crowd control.

There was no mention of Karim. For obvious reasons.

'And where?' Ahmed asked.

'Piazza Castello. It's a symbolic place. Gaddafi wants to address the crowd from the top of the castle wall in order to stay out of danger. However . . .'

I caught on.

'We'll need a precision sniper rifle, General. Preferably, a short-barrelled carbine. And a window at the same height, less than a hundred metres away.'

'We'll give you the rifle you want, Mikey, and a safe and secure apartment from which to fire, and at a lot less than a hundred metres. We can buy anything and anyone. And everyone knows about that lion in Tanzania.'

'I'll have to practise with the rifle, General. It's not that simple.'

'We'll let you have the rifle very soon, in Ghadames. Whichever one you choose. You can stay with me and practise out in the desert for as long as you need.'

'And what should Nico and I do?' Ahmed said.

Jalloun stubbed out his cigarette and picked up his pistol.

'Watch his back. You'll be dressed as policemen as well and will guard the main door down on to the street and the landing outside the apartment while Mikey does the job.'

Jalloun blew out smoke from his nose.

'I'll advance you 25 per cent. You'll receive 250,000 pounds sterling in American dollars before the end of July. The rest when it's done.'

'And who's to guarantee you'll pay?' Ahmed asked.

'My intelligence, Ahmed. This money, which may seem such a great deal to you, is nothing but spare change to these friends of mine. Once Gaddafi's dead, the country'll be in their hands, and they'll certainly want no trouble with you. And you have the tapes, haven't you?'

Ahmed got up, this time without asking my permission. I followed him into the kitchen and we shut the door.

'This is insane, Mikey. Not only do you need a good aim; you'll need nerves of steel. I'm out of this.'

'Ahmed, I killed a lion which, had I missed, would have made mincemeat of me. I shot right through your brother's cheeks with a Diana 50 pellet. Before you cut his throat.'

He stared back at me with those eyes, which I now understood.

A killer's eyes.

'If Karim knew what we were discussing . . .'

I looked at the thin white scar on Ahmed's right wrist and the one on my left. There was no doubt that Karim would have to be kept out of this. Money or no money, he worshipped Gaddafi and would report us.

'Are you frightened of our fathers, Ahmed? Do you think they're on the other side as well?'

He shook his head violently.

'You've gone crazy from sleeping with that girl!'

I lashed out before I could think. Ahmed staggered under the slap. He looked at me, surprised. A trickle of blood was running from his split lip. He fell silent, massaging his cheek. I could not fathom his thoughts at that moment. Then he relaxed and smiled at me.

'I'm sorry, Mikey, you're right. I won't say anything about Laura again. But I can't agree on the other business. It's madness, and I don't want to go behind Karim's back.'

'And you don't care anything about Nadia, Ahmed?'

The question threw him. 'What the hell's Nadia got to do with it?'

'It's the additional thing we're going to ask Jalloun for. The truth about Nadia and Italia's death.'

Ahmed looked at me for a long time.

There're only the two of us, as always, my friend. We're inseparable. As we were as kids. As we were in Cairo. On La Moneta against Farid and Salim. Against the Maltese and his dogs. Two killers.

'Let's hear what Jalloun has to say, OK, Ahmed? I'm not keen on being an assassin either, but I want the information and only he can give it to us.'

We went back into the living room, which was now full of clouds of smoke from Jalloun's cigarettes.

'We have a counterproposal, General,' I announced.

'What, a million sterling's not enough for you, boys? You really are quite greedy, aren't you!'

'No, the money's fine. But we want information about Nadia and my mother, which I'm certain you have. And if what you tell us doesn't ring true and prove useful, then not even 10 million could persuade us.'

Jalloun showed no surprise. Perhaps he had been expecting this.

'We already have a truth about the deaths of Nadia and your mother. Isn't that enough? What more do you want to know?'

'Then you had better find someone else for the job.'

'Mikey, even supposing your mother was killed – which I don't believe – it could have been anyone.'

'No, General, only someone who was already on the island. You said yourself that the coast guard didn't see any boats there that afternoon.'

Perhaps he was feeling desperate about his transfer to Ghadames, besides having drunk a good deal of whisky. And he had a desperate need of us for the job.

'The coast guard spotted an inflatable.'

He poured another whisky and lit another Marlboro. Outside, you could hear the muezzin's cry: *Allah akhbar*. Ahmed and I were speechless.

Jalloun went on.

'The coast guard saw it near the cliffs on the island's rocky side, at about a quarter to four. The information's secret, boys.'

'Did it put in anywhere?' I asked.

The general was about to blow smoke from his nose, but it went the wrong way and he started to cough and splutter.

'They're always on the move, Mikey; they don't know. Anyway, a little after four, they passed by again and the inflatable wasn't there any more.'

'Are you absolutely certain, General?'

'The only absolute certainty is death, Mikey. But the coast guard's report was clear. The inflatable drew up to La Moneta under the cliffs towards a quarter to four. Just after four, when they went past that way again, it wasn't there. Is that enough for our agreement?'

Not for Ahmed. 'No, not at all. What can you tell us about Nadia?'

Jalloun pulled a face.

'What do you want to know, Ahmed? Aren't you satisfied that Jamaal the goatherd was your killer?'

I turned to my friend. There was the look I knew. Cold and sharp as a knife. I shot him a warning glance.

'Ahmed wants the truth, General. Just like me. If you want to do business with us—'

Jalloun spat on the carpet and got up. He stared right in Ahmed's face.

'Do you want to know what they did to your sister for one whole hour, Ahmed? Do you really want to know? I don't think so. It's better you forget the matter.'

Threatened with a knife. Raped. 'Sodomized'. The word that had made my mother cry. I'd never told Ahmed. And, in the end, she was strangled.

Jalloun was about to leave. I stopped him at the door.

'One last thing, General. If that inflatable wasn't important, why is the information secret?'

'I admired your grandfather, Mikey. He loved you, and you already have trouble enough.'

'Why was it kept a secret, General?'

'If I tell you, will you shoot Gaddafi?'

No, I won't. I'll leave this country in peace with Laura Hunt.

I made no answer. Jalloun sighed and opened the door.

'It was a US air force inflatable, Mikey. It came from Wheelus Field.'

Ahmed tried to make me see reason.

'Think about it, Mikey. Tackling William Hunt about it's as dangerous as killing Gaddafi.'

And he's Laura's father.

But that inflatable had to be linked to the envelope my mother had handed over to William Hunt the day before she died, giving him forty-eight hours to sort out the situation with Marlene and my father. Or to stop the *coup d'état*. Or both.

'Go home, Ahmed. We'll talk about Gaddafi when I get back.'

I set off on the Triumph. All the shops were all closed; the city was deserted at the hottest time of the day. As I rode along the Adrian Pelt coast road to Wheelus Field, rain clouds were gathering to my left and the sea was looking choppy, the waves topped with small white crests.

They've tricked you, Mikey. Her first of all, the gahba. *She drew you away to leave the ground free for her husband. And he killed Italia.*

I approached the entrance to Wheelus Field and explained to the sentry that I was a friend of the Hunts. They made a call and, after a few minutes, the bar was raised. I left the motorbike there, and two soldiers took me in a jeep.

We drove past the hangars which once held the F100 fighter planes. There was no trace of them now.

The Americans are leaving.

William Hunt's office was in a low wood-and-metal building. His secretary showed me to a seat. After twenty minutes or so, she led me to a small meeting room with the air conditioning on maximum. I could hear thunder rumbling in the distance.

William Hunt came in and sat opposite me, without saying a word. His short blond hair was now lightly speckled with white and his intelligent blue eyes surrounded by small lines. What with Vietnam and Libya, his life was not short of worries. To say nothing of Marlene.

He had been my neighbour for twelve years, I had had sex with his wife and made love to his daughter, but I really knew little about the man. Only that he had met Marlene when she was sixteen and taking acting lessons in Hollywood, that he had been decorated for valour in the Korean War where he had saved the lives of many American soldiers, and afterwards had taken a course at Langley Air Base in Virginia.

And certainly you must have killed many yellow enemies, William Hunt. You're a very good assassin.

'So you want to speak to me about something, Michele?'

He spoke in English, with no opening pleasantries, but using my full Italian name, to maintain a certain distance.

I decided to adopt his own direct method and spoke in English, which I had learned from Laura while I was teaching her Italian.

'What did you talk to my mother about on La Moneta?'

He looked at me and sighed.

'The day before she died, on the rocky side of the island.'

'I don't recall, Michele. Certainly nothing that has anything to do with you.'

I couldn't care less if he was Laura's father, a decorated war hero and a secret agent. He was in that inflatable near La Moneta at a quarter to four that afternoon.

He dropped anchor where the cliffs are lowest. He climbed up the rockface. He threw Mamma off before I went to look for her. Then he retraced his steps. Three hours in all, with his body of steel and his nerve.

'My mother gave you an envelope. She said it was necessary to act within forty-eight hours.'

A frown appeared on his forehead. He weighed up his answer for some time. His intelligent eyes were focused as he concentrated.

'How do you know about this, Michele?'

'I was there. I saw you and heard her.'

'Who else knows about this?'

If he had killed my mother, he could also kill me, right there in that room. I could have said that Ahmed and Karim knew. But then he would kill them too. I was sure of it. William Hunt would show no mercy if he thought what he was doing was necessary.

At the cost of him shooting me. At least I'll know the truth.

'No one else, only me.'

'Not even your father?'

So that's what really worries him. My father.

'No, not him or anyone else. Only me.'

He took a moment to consider.

'Your mother discovered a secret, Michele. She furnished me with the proof. She gave me forty-eight hours to try to find a solution to the situation. Her only mistake was that we didn't have all that time.'

His eyes were steady and held my gaze. I knew he wasn't lying to me but, nevertheless, he was holding something back.

Everything is true in the words. Everything except the truth.

'It was the plans for a *coup d'état*. Except that Italia thought there was more time. And you did nothing to stop them.'

I saw him relax. Perhaps the fact that I knew everything made it easier. Or more difficult.

'You're a very intelligent young man, Michele. One day, you'll have a better understanding of politics. It's an ugly business, and I have no liking for it at all; it's full of cowards and wheeler-dealers. People who prefer compromises to questions of principle.'

'On Sunday afternoon, the coast guard spotted an inflatable near La Moneta. An inflatable from Wheelus Field. Was it you, Mr Hunt?'

I had entered dangerous territory. The proof was in William Hunt's icy look. But I had no fear either of him or his power.

'It wasn't me, Mikey. My plane landed at two thirty, and Marlene was waiting for me. I spent some time with her, as we had things to discuss.'

'Yes, you were with her until three and, at that time, Marlene went home and you stayed at Wheelus Field. So, what did you do then?'

I had committed a huge error. I could tell from his face. I had seen him with my mother when she handed him the envelope. I had seen him as he said goodbye to Marlene at Wheelus Field.

How do you know, Mikey? Are you a spy as well? And a killer?

I couldn't care less what he thought of me. William Hunt had killed my mother that afternoon between three and six thirty. He had the brains, the balls and the physical strength. And now I knew he had the motive as well: the CIA, his real employer, didn't want that crazy idealist to block Gaddafi's *coup d'état*.

Only you could have done it. A war hero, a spy and a killer.

'You Americans were happy with Gaddafi. And she was getting in the way.'

'You watch too many Bond movies, Michele. That afternoon, I went in my Land Rover to join Marlene at home.'

And this was certainly not true.

'That's not true, Mr Hunt. You're lying.'

You didn't go home to Marlene. How do I know? Because your wife was having sex with me.

I got up and quickly took off. I knew who to ask. Except that I had to do it immediately, before he tipped her off.

★   ★   ★

When I went out, I was hit by torrential rain. A genuine summer storm had broken.

I set off on the Triumph at top speed. I couldn't give him any time to agree on a story with his wife. In less than ten minutes, I arrived, soaking wet, in the residential zone off the seafront, next to Mehari. The Hunt family's home was there. William was in his office, Laura in Cairo, therefore I should have found Marlene alone at home.

The blood was pounding furiously in my temples. I was very close to the truth about my mother's death, because I was absolutely sure of one thing: William Hunt was not with Marlene that afternoon. She was with me.

Several months had passed since that day, and I hadn't seen her since. I knew from Laura that Marlene no longer went out when she was in Tripoli.

It was because of that American gahba *that Signora Italia was killed, the people were saying on the street, in the shops, on the market, in the cathedral yard, in the clubs on the seafront. And she had disappeared as well.*

I rang the bell, not even knowing what I was doing any more. I could hear footsteps on the stairs. There was still time for me to get away and save myself.

But perhaps I wasn't looking only for the truth about my mother. Without being able to admit it, I was looking for the truth about myself, and about the Hunt women, Laura and Marlene.

She's worse than those deaths in Cairo, the death of Salim and the smuggling. Laura could have understood those, perhaps, but not this.

As soon as Marlene opened the door, all my intentions crumbled. She was wearing only a petticoat. Her beautiful face had no make-up, the curves of her body under the transparent material were more sensual than ever. She stared at me coldly, while I stood there soaking and silent in the rain.

'What do you want, Michele?' Her tone was sharp.

'I want the truth about that day. That afternoon at your house.'

I saw her turn pale, then her eyes filled with rage.

'Please leave, Michele, before I call the police.'

'Where was your husband while you were letting me fuck you tied to the bed?'

The hate in her eyes was as intense as the seduction once was.

'Please leave now, Michele, while you still have time.'

'No, I'm not leaving. First you must tell me what time William came home.'

She gave a scornful smile.

'I called him at five fifteen, as soon as you left. He was in a meeting at Wheelus.'

So it couldn't be true. Two hours weren't enough to go and kill my mother and come back.

Filthy liar.

'I don't believe you.'

She shrugged.

'Too bad for you. William was still at Wheelus Field. I told him to come home. And, as you know, when I call, the men come running, Michelino.'

Had I been seduced or had I violated her? I never knew. But there was no doubt now. I was nothing more than a snotty-nosed intruder she didn't want around her or her daughter.

'You're a whore and he's a murderer.'

She gave me another scornful smile.

'At five fifteen, William was at Wheelus, in a meeting with the American ambassador. It's common knowledge. Half an hour later, he arrived at Sidi El Masri with the ambassador and other guests for dinner. And he never left; there are at least eight witnesses. They were all our guests for a barbecue that evening.'

With witnesses of that calibre, William Hunt was absolutely in the clear. Not even Superman could have been at Wheelus at three, where I saw him myself, and then again at five fifteen, having in the meantime killed my mother on La Moneta. It would have taken at least three hours to go there, kill her and come back.

I couldn't accept the disappointment and her scorn. I grabbed her by the wrist and dragged her outside under the pelting rain. The rain stuck the petticoat to her breasts; below it, she was wearing only her briefs.

I was a desperate child, hurt, screaming.

'He went there to La Moneta with an inflatable! It was him who killed her!'

She looked at me contemptuously while she tried to free her wrist from my grip.

'It's finished with, Michelino. And you're finished, too.'

I could barely see for rage and dragged her into the middle of the garden.

'Liar!' I screamed, flinging her on to the muddy ground.

The glint of fear and joy in her eyes warned me.

'Mom! Mikey!'

Laura was on the doorstep, wrapped in a heavy dressing gown, her eyes bright with fever. She looked at us, refusing to accept what the scene was screaming out to her.

It's all over, Mikey. That's an end to your films about heroes who marry the beautiful heroine and live happily ever after. You'll never be one of those.

Sunday, 21 June 1970

Salvatore Balistreri took the first flight from Rome to Tripoli as soon as Mohammed Al Bakri notified him of the latest stunts pulled by his son Mikey.

Having him tailed had been a good idea. Everything stemmed from that question he had asked at Christmas.

Have you spoken with William Hunt, Papa?

How could Michele have known about the deal with the Americans? It was still a mystery.

But at least they knew about General Jalloun's visit to Mikey, Mikey's visit to William Hunt and the furious row with Marlene Hunt, during which he'd flung her into the mud in her garden.

The poor boy's gone mad.

Of course, they had no knowledge of what had been said. Salvatore Balistreri wondered if Mikey's three encounters with Jalloun, Hunt and Marlene were linked to a single thread. A line of worry creased his brow. The most dangerous of them was General Jalloun, without a doubt. Here, they had to be sure they had the whole picture.

With William Hunt, they would reach an agreement. They were both pragmatic men of the world. The interests at stake were truly colossal and, in Italy, the Americans had many friends happy to be free of any obstacles created by the late Enrico Mattei.

Salvatore watched the thin line of traffic along the Adrian Pelt coast road from the large windows of his top-floor suite in the Waddan Hotel. The Italians were leaving in dribs and drabs, selling their property to the Libyans. It was almost time for the last thrust.

A nasty job, but – for the good of the majority – inevitable.

He was not going back to the dirty alleyways of Palermo he had left behind.

There was only a short time to wait, very short indeed. Then he would have his just reward for the huge sacrifices he had made. It had been a hard-fought battle, in which he had lost his wife and, now, it looked like, his son as well, but it was almost over.

The following morning, he would close the complex deals with Hunt. Then he would give Mohammed instructions on how to deal with General Jalloun and the MANK organization, especially Mikey.

But he was not going to leave him to die here in Libya.

He saw Mexico's Aztec Stadium appear on the television screen. Italy and Brazil were about take to the field for the World Cup final. He knew none of the Italian players, only the one Brazilian, Pelé.

Let's hope he scores a goal. Excitement's one thing, but let's not get carried away. I'd hate us to think we were a great power when Gaddafi slaps us in the face.

He switched to the American channel, which was showing that fabulous series from the early sixties, *The Untouchables*, about the struggle between federal agent Eliot Ness and Al Capone. Now, that really was good entertainment.

Monday, 22 June 1970

After the furious row with Marlene, I was staying at home with only Nietzsche and Leonard Cohen for company, besides my own thoughts. I hadn't answered the phone or watched the World Cup final in Mexico the night before.

Then, early that morning, Ahmed and Nico came knocking on the door.

'We have to talk about the MANK organization, Mikey,' Ahmed said.

'Otherwise, it's all going to go to the dogs,' Nico added.

I couldn't have cared less about MANK at that moment.

'Where's Karim?' I asked.

Ahmed hesitated slightly.

'He's gone back to Cairo to see to business, Mikey.'

'Is that his business or ours, Ahmed?'

'What do you mean?'

Ahmed's tone was harsh in a way it had never been before.

'Where's Laura?' I asked him.

'She's gone off to Cairo as well. Mikey, let's not confuse business with things that don't have anything to do with it.'

'I'm the one who decides what concerns the business or not, Ahmed.'

Nico had been silent, unable to intervene, but then he spoke.

'Listen, guys,' he offered. 'Today they close the American base. It seems that three bastard Communist MPs from Italy have arrived to celebrate the fact. Let's go and see what's happening out there. Then we can discuss MANK.'

I agreed to this because Ahmed and I would have otherwise come to blows. And I didn't want that happening.

We went on our motorbikes to Wheelus Field. As we crossed the city, there was no sign of any Italians. Below the arcades of Shara Istiklal and on the walls along the Adrian Pelt coast road, the graffiti said 'Fuck off, America!' and 'Brazil 4 – Italy 1'.

I had put aside Jalloun's proposal, but it came back to me. Looking at the graffiti, I became convinced. Jalloun was right.

I have to assassinate Colonel Gaddafi. Before it gets out of hand.

The crowd of Arabs thronging the Wheelus Field entrance had two reasons to celebrate that day: the Americans were being ousted, and Brazil had thrashed Italy the night before.

Nico was sitting gloomily on his bike, spitting date stones on to the ground. There were dark rings under his eyes and he hadn't shaved. He was starting to be affected as well.

'Somewhere in there are those three Communist fuckers. Italians who've come to lick the Arabs' arses,' he said, pointing to the crowd.

He spoke as if Ahmed weren't there, or weren't a Libyan, as we'd always done, since we were kids. But I knew that things were changing every day, and perhaps already had.

'You Arabs and Communists are nothing but cocksuckers!' Nico screamed at the crowd.

Many young Libyans knew Italian. Several of them turned round, and one shouted back at us, 'Yeah, you fucking Italian Fascists!'

'*An din gahba!*'* Nico hurled back.

A first stone whistled over our heads as we kick-started our engines, shooting off to pick up the Adrian Pelt highway to Piazza Castello, as Nico and I still insisted on calling it. From there, we took Shara Omar Al Mukhtar towards the Fairgrounds and the deserted beaches. No Italians went there any more, despite the sweltering heat, and the Libyans had never gone at all.

We stopped beside the public beach at Bagni Sulfurei, covered in sweat. It was the middle of the day and incredibly hot. Along the wooden pier out to sea, there wasn't a single fisherman, only the whiff of sulphur from Wadi Megenin and the braying of a donkey getting too much sun in a courtyard.

I had heard the sound of stones whizzing past us, heard the chanted slogans and read the graffiti celebrating Italy's defeat by Brazil. And I had lost Laura.

This country's all I have left. My grandfather's and my mother's country.

'Ahmed, let's say yes to General Jalloun, before Gaddafi kicks the Italians out, just like they have the Americans.'

'What horseshit are you on about, Mikey?'

Nico still hadn't been told about the general's idea.

Ahmed said nothing. The time of blind obedience was over. But I wasn't inclined to any kind of compromise. It was really nothing to do with Gaddafi. He could have been right in his own way and better than the corrupt old monarchy. This was about something else.

'You're either with me or against me, Ahmed.'

He was still silent. That deep, strong and serious face had been beside me for the first twenty years of my life. I looked at the scar on my left wrist, the same as the one on Nico's and Ahmed's wrists. Ahmed looked at it as well.

---

* 'Son of a bitch!' (author's note)

The blood brotherhood looked like breaking up for certain. Karim was out. Ahmed knew it was an emotional decision I was taking, based on the Libyan insults against the Italians and on Laura leaving. And he didn't like anything emotional.

But his cut is the deepest. The one that will last the longest. He's still with me.

Ahmed gunned his Ducati. He pointed to the pier that went out fifty or so metres into the sparkling sea and smiled at me.

'Want to play chicken, Mikey?'

I smiled back. Then I gunned the engine of my Marlon Brando Triumph Thunderbird.

'OK. First one to brake is chicken.'

'Are you two crazy?' Nico shouted after us, as Ahmed and I shot off side by side down the pier.

Then, when neither of us had braked and we both finished up in the sea, Nico mounted his Guzzi and, at top speed, whispering, 'Shit shit shit,' he joined us in the sea.

Wednesday, 1 July 1970

In the preceding days, locked inside my house in Garden City, Ahmed, Nico and I had gone through every detail of the plan with Jalloun before he left on his transfer to Ghadames.

That morning, Nico and Ahmed picked me up in the MANK van, the one with the Barbra Streisand poster. We had to transfer the organization's latest takings to the cave under the sea.

Nico drove calmly among the carriages and carts. Ahmed and I looked out of the windows at the half-deserted, sunlit city.

'I'm off in the jeep tomorrow. Jalloun's expecting me in Ghadames. The rifle's come. I can practise with it for twenty days. They'll leave the police uniforms, pistols and ID cards at my house here.'

'So what shall Nico and I do while you're in Ghadames?' Ahmed asked.

'Stay here. Keep the MANK business going. Do the minimum possible, just enough so you can still be seen going about.'

'Your brother could call from Rome.'

'I'll call him from Ghadames. I'll say I'm in Tripoli.'

'What if your father or Mohammed asks for you?'

'Papa won't call me. If it's Mohammed, you can say I'm home or out fishing, whatever you like. But be careful not to say a word to Karim.'

'And the money?' Nico asked.

'The advance is in my cellar. Two hundred and fifty thousand pounds changed into 400,000 dollars. I'm taking it to Italy, Ahmed. No one there would offer to exchange Libyan pounds.'

Ahmed was surprised. 'Italy?'

'I don't care about being here any more. As soon as this business is over, I'm going to empty my box and take the money to Italy.'

'Me, too!' said Nico immediately.

At the port, we had to put the cash in waterproof bags before loading them on to the motorboat. The back of the van was boiling hot, plastered with nudes taken from *Playboy*. Nico's mattress for his prostitutes was rolled up in a corner.

'How are we going to divide Jalloun's money up?' Ahmed asked.

'In three, aren't we?' Nico replied.

Ahmed looked at me. 'What about Karim?'

'What the hell has Karim got to do with it?' Nico protested.

'My brother's in Cairo, taking care of our business there. The only business we have left, so it seems.'

Nico gave him a shove and sent him banging into the metal partition.

I was just in time to see the knife drawn from Ahmed's back pocket. The point embedded itself deeply between a Playmate's tits a few centimetres from Nico's terrified face. The throw had been lightning swift and accurately aimed.

No one said anything for a few seconds. I knew I had to be the one to speak.

I went over to the knife, pulled it out of the van wall and, holding it by the point, handed it back to Ahmed.

'If I see that knife out among us again, Ahmed, I'll kill you.'

I said it with absolute calm. We both knew I wasn't joking.

Then I addressed Nico.

'We divide it up four ways, as always.'

We went out to the rock. Nico stayed at the helm so that the strong current wouldn't carry the boat away, while Ahmed and I went down in scuba kit to put the money in the boxes underwater, scrupulously divided into four parts.

When we surfaced, Nico was still very upset over the knife and the division of the money.

But I was happy. Now that I had decided to assassinate Gaddafi, I felt optimistic and wanted harmony in MANK. Or at least among the three members present.

I suggested a bit of waterskiing. At first, both Ahmed and Nico were reluctant. Then they began to enjoy themselves. For a couple of hours, we took turns skimming the placid sea's surface, and the tension between us slowly began to evaporate.

Nico drove on the way back, Ahmed sitting beside him, while I was on the back seat.

'Hey, Ahmed, did you know your aim's really crap? You missed me by a mile there,' Nico said.

'I was distracted by the tits of that *gahba* pasted on the wall.'

We all burst out laughing.

The MANK's still viable. The blood brotherhood's still hanging together.

Monday, 20 July 1970

Mohammed Al Bakri was worried. He was sitting next to Ingegner Balistreri in his Excelsior suite, watching the flood of American and Japanese tourists walking along the Via Veneto in the sultry heat. He was leaving for Tripoli that evening. He had to make sure that, the following day, Gaddafi would proceed according to plan.

'It's good that Jalloun persuaded them, Ingegnere. Mikey's been in Ghadames about twenty days now, practising with his rifle.'

Balistreri gave a bitter smile.

'My son's best talent. Shooting. From doves to lions and now human beings. How much money did Jalloun offer him?'

Mohammed shook his head.

'It's not the money that affects Mikey's feelings.'

He's not taken after you, Ingegnere. Unfortunately, he's taken after that madwoman Italia.

Balistreri studied his trusted old factotum. He had grown up alongside him. Mohammed knew him better than anyone else in the world. In the end, they shared a common beginning.

Poverty, hunger, filth, feeling humiliated in front of the wealthy. We know all of this.

'You'll have to break the tie between Mikey and Ahmed, Moham-med. That's the decisive link. I'll see to the rest.'

Mohammed was deep in thought.

'I'll try, Ingegnere. Sons still obey their fathers in the families that follow the rules of our religion. I'll speak to Ahmed.'

Balistreri nodded. Emilio Busi and Don Eugenio, his brothers and their friends had to know nothing about this business.

If they did, he would lose all credibility. And Mikey would be dead.

Tuesday, 21 July 1970

I woke at dawn in a hut made of wood and palm leaves in the Ghadames oasis. The sun rose pale in the desert, but the temperature rapidly rose to over forty centigrade. There were only a few white houses, a well, a lot of palm trees, Bedouins and camels. The ideal place for target practice.

I had trained for twenty days. Running, gymnastics, shooting. The rifle was the one I had requested. The old Carcano short rifle, Model 91/38 that took 6.5x52mm round-nosed cartridges and had a 4x magnification scope. In a shot from high to low, and less than a hundred metres, this type of rifle had already shown it could function well: it was the weapon Lee Harvey Oswald had used to shoot John F. Kennedy from a distance of eighty-one metres. The sixth-floor apartment that Jalloun had found for me was closer than that: Gaddafi would be on the castle walls, no further than seventy metres away.

And, every day, I thought about Laura. I pictured her studying in Cairo. She was probably seeing Karim, who was always there.

Jalloun came to say hello. But he looked worried.

'Are you sure about Ahmed, Mikey?'

'Course, I am, General. Everything's fine. What's up?'

'Because Ahmed's a Muslim, like me, Mikey. Faithful to his family, much more than you Christians are. So watch out.'

'I will. Were you able to get me that number in Cairo?'

He held out a slip of paper.

'No distractions, Mikey. First Gaddafi, then the rest.'

I thanked him, and he left. I switched on the radio while I shaved in the bathroom. The only channel here was Radio Libya, and I listened absent-mindedly to the announcer's monotonous voice. He was reading out the text of one of Colonel Gaddafi's new decrees.

In Article 1: restitution of all Italian-owned property to the Libyan people and, given the damages of colonialism, without compensation, followed by the expulsion of the Italian community. Within thirty days, Italian nationals must present themselves to the Libyan authorities with a declaration of assets, which they will renounce in writing and then leave for Italy with no more than an exit visa. Their personal safety is guaranteed as part of these conditions.

The Bedouins started to come outdoors, getting together in small knots and then larger groups, crying out for joy and shouting in the air.

Mamma, Grandad, here we are. This is what it's come down to. But I'll shoot him down like a dog.

On the top floor over Piazza di Spagna, they listened to Gaddafi's decree in silence. Salvatore Balistreri was contemplating Rome from on high, as he liked to do, letting his gaze travel beyond those ample windows over the incomparable panorama.

Busi and Don Eugenio exchanged glances. It was certainly not appropriate to propose a toast less than a year since the death of the Ingegnere's wife. But that man who was so handsome, so greedy and grasping, this Sicilian who came from nowhere, was exultant.

But he was also paying the price for his enormous success.

Twenty thousand Italians expelled. The death of his wife. And about to lose a son.

Mohammed Al Bakri was at home, listening to the announcement of the Italians' expulsion from Libya. He had just returned from the cemetery, where he had prayed at Nadia's unmarked grave.

Then he had gone to visit the old wooden shack in Sidi El Masri, and the memories attached to that damned cesspit, its shit and flies, and the olive-pressing shed.

A very high price. Forgive me, daughter. Forgive me, Allah.

He had done it for Ahmed and Karim. Two brothers so identical in looks and so different in nature. They were good Muslims, both of them. Sons who were respectful of the ties of blood.

Now, he would need them for the last decisive battle. Ahmed in particular, Mikey Balistreri's bosom friend. It would not be easy to persuade him to betray Michele.

Friday, 14 August 1970

After Ghadames, I spent twenty more days at home in Garden City, alone with my thoughts and the air conditioning, waiting for the phone to ring. General Jalloun was to pass on the date of Gaddafi's speech in Piazza Castello.

Every day, I went over and over the assassination plan. I thought about Laura, my mother, Nadia. Alberto called me virtually every day, wanting to know how I was and when I would be coming to Rome. I told him that it took a good many days to get all the right documents together.

In actual fact, it was Mohammed who was taking care of our final departure from Tripoli, made easy because Papa had already sold all his property some time ago.

My only radar on the outside world was Ahmed and Nico, who came by every evening. Tripoli was both blazing in excitement and dazed and stupefied: the Libyans euphoric, the Italians depressed. The confiscation related to all personal property, real estate, financial and non-financial assets. It included household furniture, even down to the mattresses and sheets: everything these poor people had earned in a lifetime's work.

Nico told me his version of what was happening.

'These poor folk are beside themselves, Mikey. The women are sewing the family jewels into the kiddies' cuddly toys. The men go traipsing from office to office, having to show they've paid all their bills down to the smallest Libyan creditor, just to obtain a miserable certificate that attests to the sequestration of their property. They have to produce family photograph albums to the Libyan censor to get an official stamp that allows them to be taken to Italy. And then there's this Office of Alien Property, where you have to go to declare yourself a person with no property. If you don't, these fuckers won't let you leave.'

Ahmed made no comment on these observations. He listened in silence, smoking and drinking scalding-hot tea to quench his thirst.

Nico was the first to arrive that day, precisely at lunchtime. He was alone.

'I'm worried, Mikey.'

'You mean scared?'

Nico shook his head.

'We haven't seen Karim for a month. Ahmed comes here, but he never says a word. Do you still trust them?'

It was a worry I shared. But, in my mind, Ahmed and Karim were two separate things.

Ahmed looks after his friends, and would risk his life for them. As long as he considers them friends.

But, out of prudence, I had to check this out and I had something in mind. Meanwhile, in order to distract Nico from his dark thoughts, I agreed to go out with him.

Tripoli was a morgue. We drove around in the van with the MANK sign and the Barbra Streisand poster in a spectre of a city. The temperature was over forty-five degrees, and there were Italians out in the burning sun. I saw families with their cardboard suitcases and trunks at the port entrance waiting for their turn to depart, while they were jeered at and mocked by Arab teenagers.

In order to have permission to leave the country, the Italians had to camp down on the pavement at night outside the Office of Alien Property on Shara Omar Al Mukhtar near the Fairgrounds in order to declare themselves of no property and obtain an inventory of the property and possessions they were leaving behind, all in the hope of getting compensation in their Italian homeland.

Nico was really beside himself.

'My mother left three days ago. They even took away her sewing box with her needles and threads. And then, when the boat docked in Naples, it was shameful, Mikey. She told me in tears on the phone yesterday.'

They had been disembarked as if they were a flock of sheep, or people infected with the plague. The porters wouldn't help them, because they knew the poor souls had no money for tips. And Santuzza told Nico what the people had said.

There they are, the Fascists coming back to steal our jobs.

'Where did they send them, Nico?'

'They rounded them up on the quay and made them stand in the sun for two hours while they waited to know which refugee camp they'd be packed off to. So Santuzza went up to some official – Foreign Office or Customs, I don't know – to protest about the wait. You know what he said to her, Mikey? That no one was going to put out flags and a band for any Fascists and they should thank their lucky stars they weren't being left out on the street.'

That afternoon Aldo Moro, the Foreign Minister, was ready to take a long-awaited holiday. A few days in the old family home in Puglia, not a month in the Caribbean or in Miami, like some of his colleagues.

At this time of year, the whole of Italy was on holiday, Parliament included. He had dropped in at the office for a last look at those papers. He had no wish to leave with that thorn in his side.

Twenty thousand poor souls left to fend for themselves.

He called his secretary.

'Could you get me the SID, please?' he asked, with his usual courtesy.

After a few seconds, there was a reply: 'The General's office'; and then a click as the call was transferred.

Moro trusted only *his* general. Unfortunately, the minister had been caught up by too many problems and had not realized that some information on Libya had come from another SID office, one he trusted less. And the information had proved to be wrong.

He came straight to the point.

'These poor nationals of ours are undergoing a grave injustice, General. What can we do with Gaddafi?'

'It's too late, I'm afraid, Minister. There are now eight thousand Egyptians in Libya ready to fill the vacancies left by our people. Doctors, accountants, farmers, teachers.'

'So it's true that this was all Nasser's idea?'

There was a good deal of bitterness in Moro's voice. He had been tricked, or used, perhaps. He would certainly remember this. But it was too late for 20,000 Italians.

The general hesitated. He knew the line was absolutely secure, but that was not the point. To explain to Moro his suspicion that, in actual fact, the idea had been formulated in Rome, in circles not too far away, perhaps in this very SID building itself, perhaps even by a fellow general, was too dangerous. He confined himself to saying the most obvious and decisive thing.

'Have you read the restricted notice?'

Moro said nothing. He was well aware of the figures and its peremptory tone. The notice had been sent to him with a worried note from his very powerful fellow Party member, the President.

Italy is dependent on Libya for 28 per cent of its petroleum imports. Any reaction against Gaddafi or a ban on these imports would in the short term create a serious increase in petrol prices and a collapse in the car market, with incalculable damage to the Italian manufacturing industry in the longer term as a result of the rise in energy costs. Furthermore, we would immediately lose 100,000 million lira in the export of pharmaceuticals, foodstuffs and in the construction sector, with immediate negative effects on employment.

For the sake of Italian industry and the country's general interests, we must show tolerance to the new regime.

'I hope you have a pleasant vacation, General,' said Moro, ending the conversation sourly.

'I hope you do, too, Minister.'

When Ahmed came over after supper, we sat down in the living room, as we usually did. I had prepared a test of his loyalty.

'Can you come up with an escape plan for Nico and me, Ahmed? If anything goes wrong, we'll need to flee to Italy.'

Ahmed was smoking in silence.

'There's only two ways of escape if things go wrong, Mikey. Across the desert by car or over the sea by motorboat.'

'Well, can you see to it, Ahmed? Have a think and come up with a plan.'

'Of course,' Nico said, 'we have to get our money before any escape.'

At that moment, the telephone rang. It was Alberto.

'We've just arrived at the Waddan, Mikey. I didn't tell you before, but we wanted to surprise you for your birthday, and Papa had to put his signature on a few papers about what we still have in Tripoli.'

I was happy to see my brother. But not my father. Not when I had to be ready to assassinate Gaddafi at any moment. I knew from Jalloun that the colonel would be speaking after sunset. A birthday supper was completely out of the question.

'Can we see each other for lunch tomorrow, Alberto?'

'No, Mikey. Tomorrow we're all going off at dawn to see the tuna fishing at Misurata.'

This annual spectacle – the *tonnara* – had been a passion of mine since childhood, just like lions had. But this was hardly the right moment.

'But this is August, Alberto. It's too late for the tuna to be leaving and too early for them to be coming back.'

'The season's more staggered this year, Mikey. The nets are full. And you've always loved it.'

'But it's boiling hot, Alberto.'

'Papa's got Mohammed to arrange it all for your birthday. Don't disappoint him, Mikey, please.'

Don't disappoint your father, Mikey. Like you always have done.

I heard the receiver being taken from his hand, then my father was on the line.

'Mikey, the tuna have arrived a month late this year – the nets are full. We set off at dawn; bring your friends from MANK. We're going to celebrate your birthday!'

A lovely, happy family outing, just like the good old times.

Alberto was speaking in good faith. He had no inkling that my father might have done anything wrong. He wanted to bring us together and take me back to Rome. I didn't want to disappoint him. And, when all was said and done, it was a way of passing the time before I took Gaddafi out. And it was better to have something to do during the day rather than in the evening.

'All right, Papa. Will you come and pick us up?'

'Of course, Mikey. Tomorrow at four.'

I put the receiver down and spelled out the programme of events. Ahmed looked pale.

'What's wrong, Ahmed? Out with it.'

'Nothing, Mikey. It's just that it doesn't seem to me the right thing to . . .'

A few minutes later, the telephone rang again. This time, it was General Jalloun.

'The event is set for tomorrow evening at seven. You know the address. The tripod stand is already in place.'

The conversation was over. I switched on the radio. The announcer was broadcasting the news of an important public meeting on the following day, 15 August, in Piazza Castello, at seven in the evening. The Supreme Leader Colonel Muammar Gaddafi was going to address the people.

I made a quick calculation. The tuna cull would last until four in the afternoon. We would be back in Tripoli at six.

It was actually better like this. Keeping away from the city during the day, reducing the tension. And keeping Ahmed and Nico with me at all times, up to the hour of assassination. This way they could have no doubts, no second thoughts. It could work out well.

Ahmed and Nico always kept a change of clothes at my place, so they decided to stay over for the night. The atmosphere was calm. While I listened to Leonard Cohen in my room, Nico watched Perry Mason on the box and Ahmed made notes in the kitchen.

We don't really look like three killers ready to go into action.

After a while, Ahmed came to my door.

'I've been thinking about your escape plan, should anything go wrong.'

Nico and I went to join him in the kitchen. We could still hear Leonard Cohen in the background, mingled with one of Perry Mason's courtroom speeches.

'If things go badly, you need to escape immediately, tomorrow night, using the most powerful motorboat that MANK has.'

'Where should we leave from?' asked Nico.

'Let's go out now and get everything ready. Mikey and I'll go to the port, take the inflatable and the motorboat and anchor them near the Waddan. No one goes past there in the dark. You go to the Esso station and get some jerry cans of petrol, as much as you need to get to Lampedusa. And stow them on the boat.

'And then?' Nico asked.

'Immediately after you shoot him, whichever way it goes, we come back here. You'll have a bag with a pullover and trousers, but nothing that suggests any escape. We'll leave at two in the morning, when the fishing boats go out.'

'But we have to get our money,' Nico reminded us.

'Sure. We'll stop and pick up the money from the cave. Then I'll come back to the beach in the inflatable and you carry on to Lampedusa in the motorboat.'

It was an excellent plan, as it always was when Ahmed was involved. We went out and, in less than an hour, everything was arranged. We were back home before midnight.

But I had a very different plan. Kill Gaddafi, get my money and Jalloun's, confront my father and go and get my girl. Then celebrate my twentieth birthday in a Tripoli liberated from Gaddafi. I had no intention of fleeing to Italy.

As soon as Ahmed and Nico had gone to bed, I took out General Jalloun's slip of paper. On it was a Cairo telephone number.

Although it was night, Laura answered at the first ring.

'It's me, Mikey.'

Silence.

'Tomorrow night, I may have to leave for Italy. But, first, I want to see you.'

Another, longer silence. Then the calm voice I knew so well.

'I'll be on the afternoon flight, Mikey. We'll meet up at my house.'

'Your house?'

'My parents are in New York. At eight, OK?'

No, Laura, at that time I have another appointment.

'Too early. Would nine be okay?'

'Yes, see you then. *Ciao*.'

I gathered all my personal belongings together, including books and clothes, and threw everything in the bin. I kept only the Nietzsche book that Mamma had been reading on the morning she died, *Beyond Good and Evil*. I slipped a few things into its plastic cover: the handkerchief spotted with Nadia's blood, the black and white snapshot Laura had taken the day I was expelled from high school and the sheet of squared paper with my notes on Nadia's death and the two short phrases added by my mother on the back.

They knew each other. Check m.

I also took the Leonard Cohen cassette Laura had given me.

Finally, I lifted the lid off the tank over the toilet and took out the plastic box with the keys to the locks: mine, and the one for the chain that secured the four boxes to the rock.

I put the Nietzsche book, the Cohen cassette and the plastic box with the keys inside the bag I was taking with me if I was forced to do a runner. All that was left was the poster of Laura in Piazza di Spagna, still hanging on the wall.

The picture of how I'll never be.

I left it there. If Laura left with me, then I had no use for it. And, if she didn't leave with me, it wouldn't be any use either.

Saturday, 15 August 1970

Papa and Alberto came to pick us up in a Land Rover driven by Mohammed.

The greeting with Alberto was very affectionate. We had left each other in a bad mood last time. And it was all because of me. Yes, I could trust Alberto.

But not my father. He had changed; he was still handsome, but he looked older. His greying temples and moustache and pale complexion made him look more refined, perhaps more suited to his new social role in Italy.

'Many happy returns, Mikey.'

He made no move to put his arms round me or kiss me. At least he was sparing me that.

'Do we really have to go off on this trip to Misurata, Papa?'

'I believe it'll be the last one for many years, Mikey. Since you were a child, you always liked seeing the fish caught and killed.'

'Yes, well, I'm a big boy now. Seeing a tuna's blood doesn't give me a buzz any more, like it once did. And it's August now – it's far too late.'

'The tuna nets are full, Mikey. We'll have a splendid time. And we'll have a better memory of the country before we leave.'

Of course we will, Papa. Who cares if it's the country where Mamma died . . .

I slept for the whole journey as we drove through the deep silence of the night. I woke at dawn, two hours later, as we were coming into Misurata's harbour, where the fishing boats were returning. The city, with its white houses, was still asleep.

Everything was ready for the *tonnara*. Eight galleys of twenty metres in length with twenty or so people to each, then the boat of the *Rais*, the head of the *tonnara*. The line of boats set off.

I was in a boat with my father, Mohammed, Alberto, Ahmed, Nico and a score of Libyan fishermen. I fell asleep again on the slow voyage out to the nets, partly because I hadn't slept the night before, partly owing to the tension and partly because I had no wish to talk to anyone. Anyone at all.

We arrived at the nets at eight thirty. The boats dispersed around the so-called 'death chamber', the net where the fish were killed.

'Do you want to go into the *Rais*'s boat?' my father asked me.

It was a treat I had asked for so many times as a child, and he had always said no.

Too dangerous, Mikey. Too much blood.

Now, though, according to my father, I was ready for it.

The *Rais* was the oldest fisherman in Misurata, an imposing man of sixty with a huge beard. He took me aboard his vessel without any objection. Perhaps because I was the son of the man who owned everything.

The 'death chamber' net was the fullest I'd ever seen it. Papa was right again. At least three hundred tuna between two and three hundred kilos in weight were frantically swimming round and round, bouncing off the sides of the nets, blind with fear.

We took our boat into the centre while the other galleys closed up around us, one next to the other along the four sides of the net, each side about thirty metres long. Everything was now ready.

Then, at a sign from the *Rais*, the propitiatory songs began – the *salaams* – and the men began to haul up the nets. This was the moment that excited me most, and had done since I was a child. It was when the tuna understood their fate. Each one of those large brutes tried to stay far away from the boats and the surface by flipping their weaker brethren towards the butchery with a flick of their tail.

Then began the slow hauling up of the nets by arm and by hoist. The victims fought madly among themselves as they rose to their deaths, the water boiling from that fierce primordial struggle, while the first tuna, the ones which were most tired, were caught by the long-poled hooks, thrown on board, hooked again by hand, taken by their two fins and flung into the bottom of the boat in a pool of their own blood. And there the fish died, looking their murderers in the eye.

Below me, in the centre of the square, the strongest was fighting to keep a safe distance.

'*Kullu quais?*'* the *Rais* asked me, seeing my face suddenly turn white as a sheet. He thought that I was frightened of the beasts, these huge fish that twisted their tails, surfaced, jumped and sank down into the blood.

But that was not what had made me lose colour. It was the body I saw in the bloody water, tossed about by the fish.

When they finally managed to gaff the corpse and drag it on board the boat where my father and friends were, I already knew who it was. I knew it even before my eyes met my father's icy gaze and the troubled ones of Ahmed and Nico, before even seeing General Jalloun's swollen and tortured face.

Have you understood now, Mikey? You'll end up the same way.

Mohammed called the Misurata police and spoke to the young commander. He seemed very much at ease.

---

* 'Everything all right?' (author's note)

The police took Jalloun's body away and allowed us to set off back to Tripoli without asking a single question. As if the general were nothing more than another tuna fish.

The Land Rover was running along the asphalt ribbon in a heat that was more suffocating than that of the day before. We were sealed inside with the air conditioning on full. Mohammed was driving, my father sitting next to him. The four of us were sitting behind: Alberto, Ahmed, Nico and myself. We sat in absolute silence. There was no need for words. The message had been clear.

We know everything. This is your last chance to call a halt, Mikey. Otherwise, you see how we punish traitors.

But the real traitors were the ones I had around me in the vehicle. The two adults certainly were. I could trust Alberto and Nico implicitly, but then there was Ahmed. He was my oldest friend, the one who had twice saved my life, first in a putrid Cairo alleyway and then on La Moneta's cliffs.

But can I trust you still? Are we still blood brothers in the sand?

As the Land Rover was hurrying towards Tripoli, I made my decision. I knew it was crazy, but there was only one way to get to the truth about him and our friendship.

I'm not going to call a halt to the plan, Ahmed. You're coming with me to Piazza Castello to assassinate Gaddafi.

We arrived in Garden City at around six that evening and pulled up outside the maisonette.

'OK, boys,' my father said, 'let's not ruin Mikey's birthday. Have a good nap now and we'll see each other later at the Waddan for supper and a celebration.'

I looked at my father. He took it as read that I had given up on the assassination attempt.

'No, Papa, we're too tired. Can we have supper later, when it's less hot? Say, about ten?'

I looked at Ahmed and Nico. They both were keeping their eyes lowered.

Fear or betrayal?

My father stared at me for some time.

Well, so much the worse for you, my son.

Then he gave a shrug.

'As you like, Mikey. You're old enough now to know what you're doing and what you shouldn't be doing.'

We were now ready, having gone over the plan one last time. Nico had raised a mass of objections, all legitimate, because he was scared. The principal one was that, with Jalloun dead, there was no one to pay us.

'We're not doing it for the money, Nico. We're doing it for us, for your mother and my mother, for those 20,000 poor folk who were robbed of everything here and then humiliated in Italy.'

Ahmed kept silent. He raised no objection. Said not a word.

All three of us dressed in the uniforms Jalloun had provided. We left at seven and headed off among the crowd for Piazza Castello. Once we got to the address Jalloun had given us, we made our last arrangements.

'OK, Nico, you stay here in the piazza and, from now on, don't let anyone come into the building. For reasons of security, you can say. Ahmed, you come up with me and stay on the landing outside and keep watch on the stairs.'

They were both extremely pale, but made no objections.

Salvatore Balistreri was with Mohammed Al Bakri in the Hotel Waddan suite.

'Are you happy with it, Mohammed?'

The Libyan nodded. Others would perhaps have preferred to take the opportunity of this lunacy to put a definitive end to the problem of Mikey Balistreri, but he had seen the boy grow up day by day from the moment of his birth. And he was different from the other Italian boys, with his sense of honour and loyalty, which were quite unusual. Certainly, he was violent, dangerous and stubborn. But he was also generous and had taken his son Ahmed as his best friend when he could have chosen anyone in the whole of Tripoli. He did not like to break such a true and deep bond, even less to have the boy killed.

Of course, Michele Balistreri was a problem and a risk. But a manageable one. This solution was the right one. There had been enough deaths in their families.

Ahmed and I went up the stairs. I was watching him, looking for any sign of hesitation or nerves. Nothing. Ahmed was as ice cold as ever.

Using the keys Jalloun had given me, I went into the apartment while Ahmed stayed outside on the landing. I found the rifle and ammunition hidden in a leather bag under the sofa, as arranged. It was already fitted with the scope. The tripod rest I had asked for had been placed thirty centimetres from the chosen window, on a side table with a heavy marble top. Through the half-closed shutters I had a perfect view of the platform.

Gaddafi was to speak for ten minutes, starting at eight. The platform was lit by four huge floodlights and stood twenty metres lower than the window I was to shoot from and at a distance of seventy metres. Exactly what I had practised for during those twenty days at Ghadames.

I had to hit him with the first shot. There would be no time to reload. I set the rifle firmly on the rest and began to adjust the scope without opening the window.

I opened the shutters a little more and allowed the barrel to swivel on the rest. Then, I calmly set the sights for the point nearest the microphone, where Gaddafi's head would be, and had it in the cross hairs. I was ready.

Gaddafi appeared in his uniform, surrounded by his bodyguards. I put my eye to the telescopic sight, but had no time to focus. There was a whistling sound, then one of the floodlights behind Gaddafi exploded into fragments, leaving the platform in the dark.

The crowd let out an '*ohhh*' of disappointment, but I knew this was not a short circuit. It had been a shot. Gaddafi's bodyguards knew as well and immediately bundled him away to safety. And Ahmed knew, too. He was banging furiously on the door.

I left everything there, the rifle and the rest, and got out of the apartment. I locked the door and we raced off down the stairs. Nico Gerace was waiting for us outside the main entrance, pale and trembling among the terrified, fleeing crowd, his dark eyebrows knitted in fear.

Mohammed telephoned Balistreri immediately. He was in his suite in the Waddan.

'Everything's fine. It all went ahead as planned, Ingegnere.'

'And Mikey?'

Mohammed wondered if the concern in his ex-boss's voice as he uttered his son's name was more out of fear for the boy's safety or more for their business affairs. He knew Ingegnere Balistreri like the back of his hand but, on this particular point, could never fathom him.

'He's all right, Ingegnere. Safe and sound.'

'Well done, Mohammed, an excellent job. Thank you.'

They ended the call.

Salvatore Balistreri was happy. Gaddafi had welcomed Mohammed's idea of arranging a bogus assassination attempt which he could attribute to the opposition, discrediting them in the eyes of the West. Naturally, the colonel did not know that a real attempt had been planned and thwarted and that its perpetrator was called Michele Balistreri.

Now his *son gone wrong* had his back to the wall. All he could do now was escape.

We left Piazza Castello, quickly crossed Piazza Italia and turned into Shara Istiklal. We walked hastily but without running, mingling with the crowd up until the cathedral square and from there to Garden City. We reached my house at eight twenty without having encountered any problems.

Nico and Ahmed threw themselves on to the armchairs in the living room. Nico was exhausted and agitated; he started to ramble, his 's' sounds lisping once again.

'*Santa Madonna*, they'll find us. We must get away immediately.'

I looked at Ahmed. He was impassive, cold and rational as usual.

'I think we should keep to the original escape plan,' he said.

I knew there was little choice. What I was enjoying right then was a last breathing space which my enemies were allowing me.

A birthday supper, congratulations, and then either you get out or Gaddafi's police will come and arrest you.

'Yes, we'll go to Italy by motorboat tonight, Nico. After supper with my father. Now, get some rest, the two of you.'

I went to the bathroom upstairs. I took off the police uniform and the holster with its pistol and took a quick shower. Then I put on a sweater and jeans and went into the living room.

'I've some urgent business. We'll meet up with my father at the Waddan at ten.'

I gave no explanation. It was obvious I had no intention of giving one. Nico tried to ask where I was going and pointed out the risk I was running by going out, but Ahmed asked no questions and said nothing at all.

It was a warm evening, with a full moon shining in a sky full of stars. I passed by King Idris's old palace and took the Adrian Pelt coast road into the inner city rather than the cathedral square route. There were plenty of police about, but none showed any sign of frenetically searching for Gaddafi's would-be assassin.

Because Gaddafi knows there was no real attempt on his life.

I arrived at the Hunt family's villa a quarter of an hour early for the appointment. There was an old Fiat 124 in the driveway in front of the garden and a light on in the living room.

I stayed outside, hidden round a corner. Karim came out five minutes later, got into the Fiat 124 and drove off.

Good. Couldn't be better. Now I know what I have to do.

I went across the garden. I had flung Marlene Hunt into the mud there. And, there, Laura had understood who I really was.

She opened the door as soon as I rang the bell. The last time I had seen her in that doorway, she had stood there incredulous as I dragged her mother around in the rain.

'Come in, Mikey. The radio's just announced that there's been an attempt on Gaddafi's life.'

She seemed neither angry with me nor ill at ease. And it was that resolute calm that scared me. As if a definitive decision had already been taken, but without me.

'I want the truth, Laura.'

These were the first words I spoke. And there was a violence in them, more perhaps than in the ones she had heard me say to her mother as I pushed her into the mud. Laura said nothing. I saw only sadness and compassion in her eyes. It was that compassion, after I had seen Karim leaving the house, that had made me lose my head.

'You were there on La Moneta that afternoon. Tell me it was my father, Laura. Then I can kill him, and you and I can leave here and live happily together for the rest of our lives.'

I saw a tear trickle down her cheek. It was a tear for me, not for her. For that boy she had known many years ago and who had chosen to die, like Kirk Douglas, with an empty pistol.

'Your father's got nothing to do with it, Mikey, and your mother killed herself. Why don't you forgive yourself?'

All of a sudden, she hugged me. I was immediately aware that, in that unexpected gesture, an inevitable one for her, there was something different, because there was no longer any joy in the way that Laura was holding me.

There's still love. But there's no future any more.

Laura was grabbing on to the boy she had stupidly believed in and of whom she was still fond, but with whom she couldn't live.

The thought suddenly struck me hard: this was the last time in my life I would be seeing Laura Hunt.

These were our last minutes together. Our last encounter. It could become a beautiful memory. But there was too much anger in me not to destroy that as well.

'I don't believe you. You're a liar. I know you're sleeping with Karim.'

Her arms fell by her sides in a gesture of surrender and resignation. I could now read what was in her eyes and I knew she was saying goodbye against her own wishes. I moved towards her, and she instinctively stood back.

This is your film, Mikey, your real role, the one in the shade, the evil one.

I threw myself on her like I had done with her mother, except she hadn't provoked me. Nor did she bite me or spit as I lifted her skirt. She didn't incite me to tie her up as I ripped off her briefs. She didn't whisper to me to fuck her harder as I penetrated her.

Even in that moment, suffering that violent attack, Laura Hunt was still consciously with me, spread out on the floor under me, neither encouraging nor stopping me, her head buried in my shoulder so as not to look me in the eyes, her hands placed lightly on my arms without trying to scratch or push me away. She let me be, even as I was violating her.

And she remained on the floor, motionless, half naked and silent, as I got dressed. She made no complaint, nor did she curse me. Neither of us had anything to say. It had all been said.

I didn't turn to take a last look at her as I left.

★   ★   ★

The Hotel Waddan was only a few hundred metres from the Hunts' house.

They were waiting for me outside. Nico was nervous and fretting; Ahmed, absolutely calm.

'What do you want to do, Mikey?' Ahmed asked me.

'Let's go eat with my father, then we'll go back to my place and change for the trip. It looks as if we have all the time in the world. There don't seem to be any police about.'

Nico was unhappy.

'Who cares about eating, Mikey? Let's go right now. All we have to do is get our money from the cave and leave this country.'

Ahmed pointed to the sea.

'Everything's ready. The motorboat, the inflatable, the cans of petrol to get to Lampedusa. We can leave right now, if you like.'

No, Ahmed. That's your plan, not mine. I want to look you all in the face during this supper. Before dawn, I'll know which one of you's betrayed me.

'No, guys. My father could get angry and start suspecting things. Let's stick to the original plan. The fishing boats leave at two in the morning, and we'll slip out among them.'

Papa had ordered the usual table out on the terrace overlooking the sea. The one where, as kids, with my grandfather and mother, we used to eat *pizza napolitana* while the orchestra played 'Volare' and 'Magic Moments'.

They were all there, friends and enemies, to celebrate my birthday: Papa, Don Eugenio, Emilio Busi, Mohammed, Alberto. Then there were Ahmed and Nico. Perhaps I could count on these two. Perhaps not. Anyway, I knew how to settle that doubt.

There's plenty of time.

Only Karim was missing but, officially, he was in Cairo, looking after our affairs and the poor – except for the fact I had seen him leaving Laura Hunt's house an hour earlier.

Supper was uneventful, the atmosphere absolutely normal, relaxed. A family get-together with old friends; not too happy and noisy, because it was still less than a year since my mother's death. The black mourning button on Ingegner Balistreri's blue linen jacket was still there to remind us.

But in sixteen days' time, it would be a year, and Papa would calmly take it off.

And, once the mourning was over, I bet that Marlene Hunt'll go and live with him.

Papa, Busi and Don Eugenio monopolized the conversation. They talked about the Libyan situation, General Jalloun's tragic end and the attempt on Gaddafi's life.

'Probably the two incidents are connected,' said Busi, blowing out a cloud of smoke.

'I'm sure they are,' Don Eugenio agreed.

'They'll be looking for Jalloun's accomplices,' Mohammed added.

I looked at my father. He looked back at me.

'You know that someone tried to shoot Gaddafi, don't you?' he asked me.

He was provoking me. He wanted to be sure I was leaving.

'No,' I said, looking at Ahmed and Nico, who were studying the food on their plates.

'You've not heard? But the radio's been speaking of nothing else for at least three hours!'

'I know. But they didn't shoot at Gaddafi. They shot at one of the floodlights.'

The looks of my traitors were interesting.

This kid isn't that stupid, after all.

But it was only Ahmed and Nico who really interested me.

Sitting opposite me with his eyes lowered, Ahmed was staring at his plate as if those pieces of grouper were the most interesting things in the world, while Nico, on the other hand, was staring at me, terrified, his deep dark eyebrows knitted together and his beard as black as pitch.

Are you crazy, Mikey? Do you want to have us shot?

I winked at him to calm him down. He had kept faith with me, my classmate with the lisp, Don Eugenio's victim, the pariah of Tripoli with a passion for whores and screen goddesses. The MANK organization and myself had been the lifebelt that saved his life.

The cake with twenty candles was brought in at midnight. Alberto called over the photographer, who took a group shot of us with the seafront in the background, my father and Alberto by my side.

They all sang 'Happy Birthday' to me and I blew out the candles. Once the cake had been handed round, along with the spumante, everyone raised their glasses for the toast.

'Here's to you, Mikey,' Papa declared.

I looked at him. I raised my glass as well.

'To Italia and Nadia. May they find justice one day.'

There was a moment's hesitation, then everyone drank the toast in silence.

Now that midnight had passed, it was time to go. I shook hands with Mohammed, Busi and Don Eugenio. I put my arms round Alberto. My father was last.

There was no hug or kiss or handshake with him.

'See you, Mikey. Goodnight.'

'Of course, Papa. See you, too.'

We would settle accounts one day. Not here. But in that country of traitors you call our homeland.

Saturday Night–Sunday Morning, 15–16 August

We walked back to Garden City a little after midnight.

We had two hours before we had to make a move. I sent Ahmed and Nico upstairs to rest for a while.

I was in a state. I hadn't slept for twenty-four hours, and it hadn't been an easy day. But I had plenty to do other than sleep.

My swimming trunks, denim cut-offs, white T-shirt and boat shoes were already in a bag. They were the only clothes I was taking with me, the ones I was going to wear for my arrival in Italy.

Also in the bag were the Nietzsche book, the old sheet of squared paper with the alibis, the handkerchief with Nadia's blood on it, the photo of me and the Leonard Cohen cassette from Laura.

All your memories are here.

Then there were the keys in the plastic box. I checked they were still there, where I had left them before going to see Laura.

The three uniforms and the guns in holsters were on the sofa in the living room. They would be useful for making it from the house to the beach. No one would stop us if we were dressed as policemen.

One thing was still missing, and it was the most important. I decided to do it while looking myself in the face. I took Nico and Ahmed's pistols and went to the mirror in the bathroom.

Finally, I gave a last look at Laura's photo opposite my bed.

The photo of how I'll never be. Your mother killed herself. Forgive yourself.

But Karim had left her house. My mother didn't kill herself. And she was just as she appeared in the photo.

A whore. Just like her mother.

I left the photograph there on the wall, along with my dreams.

At ten to two, I called to Nico and Ahmed. They quickly put on the uniforms and the belts with the holsters and guns. Nico had his bag, with a few clothes for the night crossing.

We encountered no one on the streets. In ten minutes, we were at the beach.

Ahmed's inflatable was in the water, two metres from the shore. The motorboat was anchored further out.

'The petrol?' I asked Ahmed.

'The tank in the motorboat's full. There're extra cans in the inflatable. Nico can transfer them, while we dive down for the money.'

We took the inflatable to the motorboat anchored at the port exit. Nico and I climbed into the motorboat and waved to Ahmed.

'See you at the rock.'

I switched on the navigation lights while Nico raised the anchor and started the engine. I checked the water, the petrol, the wet suits and the compressed-air cylinders. Everything was there. We departed with an easy motion, the radio playing Arabic music. But I could see that Nico was visibly stressed and worried and was singing to himself in an effort to keep calm.

We got to the rock in half an hour. Ahmed was already there, and was taking off his uniform to put on the wet suit. When we drew alongside him, he tied a rope from the inflatable to the bollard on the motorboat's bows.

Despite the calm sea, the current at that point was always stronger and pulled out to sea. Nico let the anchor down and switched off the engine.

I got ready in silence. I took the uniform off, placed the gun and holster on top of it, put on the wet suit and the air cylinders.

Apart from the moon, the only light was the one on the bows. We all knew that these minutes would be the last ones we had together for a long time, perhaps for ever. But none of us had any wish to speak. We had already said everything that had to be said. What remained was what we did not want to reveal to each other.

The blood brotherhood in the sand hadn't lasted with time. The MANK organization was dead.

While Nico began to transfer the cans of petrol from the inflatable to the motorboat, Ahmed and I dived into the water. We descended evenly, following the heavy chain that Nico had fixed to a bollard and dropped to the sea floor.

It was as if neither of us wanted to reach the end of that chain.

All we have together is that money. Nothing else.

The fish near the large rock were watching us, motionless. I let them swim in front of me as we entered the cave.

The steel cable was lying loose, the lock open. The four boxes had disappeared.

We looked each other in the eye for a single second. We both knew.

One of us won't live to see this night out.

I swim as quickly as possible; Ahmed's a few metres behind me. I reach the chain and begin the ascent. There's no time to be lost; he mustn't catch up with me.

Karim had already taken the money. But that wasn't all. Nico and I were about to end up like Salim and the Egyptian soldiers.

I get to the surface next to the motorboat. I tear off my mask and mouthpiece and unhitch the cylinders, which sink to the bottom. I hurriedly climb the motorboat ladder.

Nico's on the inflatable, moving the last petrol can. He stares at me, stupefied.

'Get out, Nico! Get into the motorboat!' I scream.

'What going on?' he replies, looking at me stupidly.

Ahmed emerges from the water. It takes him a while to climb the inflatable's ladder, as he's still wearing the cylinders.

Nico looks at him, stunned. 'So where are the boxes with the money?'

I yell even louder at him.

'Get in the motorboat, Nico! Right now!'

With his scuba knife, Ahmed cuts the rope tying the two vessels together.

Nico stares at him. 'Where's my fucking money?'

The inflatable starts to veer away, pulled more quickly by the current.

Ahmed grips his knife but Nico draws his pistol and shoots at him. One, two, three shots. But nothing happens. I loaded their pistols with blanks earlier, not knowing which of the two had given me away.

Ahmed moves towards Nico, clutching the knife.

The motorboat's about twenty metres from the inflatable. I start the engine.

'Jump into the water, Nico!' I shout, as Ahmed draws close with the knife.

But Nico acts as if he's paralysed. He stares stupidly at his pistol, murmuring, '*Shit, shit,*' his lisp again apparent.

I halt the motorboat five metres from the inflatable. Ahmed has the pistol in his left hand, the knife in his right.

'Leave now, Mikey! Turn that boat round and get back to your own country. Libya doesn't want you any more.'

'Or you'll kill us, right?'

Ahmed stretches out his left arm towards me and points the gun at my chest.

'That's right, Mikey. First you, then Nico.'

I pick up my own gun. It's too late now for words. Too late for him and too late for me.

I meet his gaze as he starts to fire at me. One, two, three shots.

In the moon's feeble light, I see his eyes looking surprised, then scared, when he realizes the roles have been reversed. This time, he's the Kirk Douglas character with the unloaded gun. And I'm Rock Hudson with the loaded one . . .

Ahmed throws the gun away and lunges at Nico with the knife.

The duels fought in the sun in front of the villas. The slit throats of Salim and three Egyptian soldiers. His arm that saved me on La Moneta's cliff face. The gouged eyes of Killer, the Maltese trafficker's dog. And that slap when he said that I'd gone crazy because of my relationship with Laura.

Perhaps the end had begun with that slap. It was then that I was ejected from his circle of close friends, the ones he protected. And, with him, there were no half measures.

Either you were close friends or mortal enemies.

The first bullet makes him twist round on himself and fall to his knees. He grips on to the inflatable's rail, trying to draw himself up.

At last, Nico jumps in the water and starts swimming to the motorboat. As he climbs the ladder, Ahmed manages to get to his feet and, staggering about, starts the outboard motor.

I fire the second shot level with his heart. Ahmed puts his hands to his breast, collapses over the railing and drops into the water.

I put the engine in top gear and steer towards the inflatable at top speed. I sail straight over it, crushing it. Then I stop twenty metres away.

Nico and I watch Ahmed's body sinking down under the weight of the air cylinders. In a moment, he disappears.

I stay there a few minutes in silence – to contemplate the smooth, dark surface that's swallowed up my best friend and the line of lights along the Adrian Pelt coast road where I forced myself on Laura Hunt.

Then I turn my back on Africa and point the bows towards Italy.

INTERMEZZO

In Lampedusa, I put my arms affectionately around Nico Gerace, and said goodbye without leaving an address or telephone number. We had some pretty ugly memories to forget, and no future to share. I was the son of a bourgeois entrepreneur; he was a son of the working class. These differences would come into play once we were back in Italy. I would go to university, while he would become a petrol-pump attendant or something of the kind.

From Lampedusa, I took a boat to Naples, then a train to Rome, carrying my bloodstained T-shirt and swimming costume in a bag that had 'Tripoli' written on it in Arabic. People in the second-class carriage cast surreptitious glances at me. I could hear the scornful comments whispered under their breath.

Look how black and filthy he is! He must be an Arab.

This was how Italy and the Italians welcomed me. It didn't take long to get further confirmation of what I'd always thought. Newspaper photos of the Libyan refugees disembarking in Naples, their faces wretched, their few suitcases falling apart, were soon superseded by those of the faces of the politicians who reassured them there would be aid, compensation and a good life.

The refugees never received a thing.

Despite the poverty and disappointment of the repatriated, Rome was full of gleaming shop windows, good-looking women wearing not very much – though that little was designer label – small family cars, high-performance motors, Vespa and Lambretta scooters, bars and restaurants. And there was an infectious optimism in the air.

To keep Alberto happy, at the end of September I enrolled in the faculty of law and even managed to pass a few exams. But I would have nothing to do with sharing the penthouse over Piazza di Spagna with my father and his lovers, who I imagined were many, and all as beautiful as Marlene Hunt. I found a room in an apartment with other students, paying for it with the generous legacy that my grandfather, Giuseppe, had left me.

I also enrolled in the MSI, the Neo-Fascist Movimento sociale italiano. This was mostly out of memory for my mother than for any true belief in its ideals, but also to distance myself completely from my father. It was only in the following months and years that politics became a part of me, as I attended university and the stormy meetings there, sticking up posters at night and taking part in the clashes between the Far Right in my Faculty and the Leftists in all the others.

But then, the MSI was a political party with seats in Parliament and followed its rules, and I wanted more action. So I joined the far right Ordine nuovo, which had no parliamentary seats. Under its Fascist insignia of a two-headed axe and its SS motto 'My honour is loyalty', I enjoyed three years of intense activity, during which I still hoped to change the world.

At the end of 1973, a Christian Democrat minister ordered Ordine nuovo's dissolution and had its leaders arrested. This was an act of folly that left scores of young men without any direction, several of them too young and naïve to distinguish clearly between political struggle and the edge of an abyss.

Many of my friends went for armed struggle, where enemies were no longer beaten up but simply killed. I could shoot at a lion or at someone attempting to kill, but not at a defenceless target. And I really couldn't see myself putting explosive devices in the waste bins of railway stations and public squares. Thus I saw my friends turn into common criminals who betrayed our own ideals.

It was Alberto who was able to offer me advice and help through his connections in the Christian Democrats. They suggested that I work with the secret services as a mole, so that we could stop the criminal manoeuvres of my former comrades. So, for four years, I was embedded in the Far Right underground, no longer knowing who I really was, having little certainty of being on the side of the good that was trying the thwart the massacre of innocent people.

In 1978, I had my answer. The Red Brigades kidnapped Aldo Moro. I was asked to lend a hand to find him, given that our Far Right terrorists had close links with the criminal world that controlled Rome. But the intelligence I supplied was ignored and Aldo Moro was killed. I protested, and suddenly my cover was blown.

I was a dead man walking when my brother rescued me once again. The Interior Minister owed him a favour. I managed to get a degree, albeit in philosophy, and managed to pass the requisite exams to add to those I'd passed earlier in the decade. Apart from combat and shooting, there was one other quality I had shown since I was a child, and that was for investigation. So, thanks to his connections, Alberto had me join the police and take the exam for the rank of *commissario*, which I duly won. In 1980, I had my first posting in Vigna Clara, one of the quietest spots in the whole of Rome.

As for relations with my father, at first they dwindled and then finally broke off well before 1973, when he transferred his head offices to Milan and his residence to a kind of fortress on the Isola delle Femmine, near Palermo. On the few occasions we did see each other, mainly at Christmas and through Alberto, who had never given up hope of reuniting us, the Hunts were never mentioned. Contrary to my expectations, my father didn't marry Marlene after his year of mourning, and I never knew if they ever saw each other again.

Although our contact became less frequent, I never lost touch with Alberto. And we, too, had an implicit understanding never to talk about Libya.

I didn't hear a thing from Nico Gerace. I never looked him up, and he never looked me up. Rather than unite us, our desperate flight had completely split us apart. As for the other friends I had of my age in Tripoli, they were now spreading across the globe – and if I happened to come across one in Rome, I simply looked the other way.

Emilio Busi I saw only in the newspaper photographs that charted his political rise: first, a Communist Party MP, then a board member of leading Italian companies with state involvement, then one of Italy's most influential senators. Although not yet fifty, he had become chief critic of Enrico Berlinguer's leadership of the orthodox Communist Party.

Don Eugenio Pizza, on the other hand, disappeared from my life completely. Fortunately, I neither saw nor heard anything of him at all.

As to Libya, a total silence. I could not go back and had not the slightest intention of doing so. And, slowly, one day at a time, Laura Hunt, Ahmed, Karim and all the others slipped into the margins of memory, though without ever disappearing completely. I had thought I could forget those who had betrayed me. But I found that time helps to wipe out the joys of suffering. Those forced on you and the ones you cause.

PART III

January–June 1982

The posting at Vigna Clara was ideal for a couple of years' break, while I decided what I really wanted to do with my life. In that tranquil residential quarter, I lived as if I were in retirement, among its beautiful housing blocks and luxurious condominiums, a park and swimming pool, villas, roads without potholes, little traffic and Filipino or Polish au pairs out strolling with other people's babies.

Its inhabitants had all succeeded in the race for the good life on which the Italians had launched themselves after the end of the Second World War, using any means possible, legal or otherwise: tax evasion, bribery and corruption, carefully controlled contracts. And so I found myself looking after the security of the capital's upper middle class; they were so incapable of being discreet about their wealth they could not help attracting the inevitable bag-snatching, theft or burglary.

In order to keep a certain distance from all this, I had taken a studio flat in Garbatella, well away from the centre and closer to the sea. It was a working-class district built by Mussolini where real people did real work, from schoolteachers to fruit vendors, manual labourers to postmen.

Beyond work, I mainly gave myself over to women, the only real passion I had in those days. And, after Laura, it was only a woman's body I was after – the rest was of no interest to me. I would get straight to the point: skipping the niceties of courtship, the opening gambits, all that fuss and nonsense that people use to justify and ornament a simple given end.

I extended the opinion I had of Marlene Hunt to the whole of the female gender: they were all potential cheats and part-time whores. Having said this, I also had to admit that they were otherwise excellent people and infinitely better than me.

My very good reason for this attitude was not to hurt anyone: I asked nothing of them other than to consider me a brief interlude in their lives. Words such as 'friendship', 'reciprocal understanding' or 'significant other' were never under consideration. Besides, women immediately know how to distinguish between a fling and a future husband. And I had no aspiration to play either the part of fiancé or eligible spouse.

If anyone suffered, I wasn't around to know. In the end, I gave them that moment of freedom they looked for in literature and films, and which they imagined – although they would never admit it – was only and exclusively for them. I offered them true freedom: that of going beyond the limits, yet being able to put the blame entirely on me. The freedom to do things they would never do with a boyfriend or spouse. And then forget all about it.

And it was easy to have so many of them. Although young and good-looking, I was helped by the desire for freedom that was growing in women during those years, not to mention their fascination with my role as a ranking officer in the police.

Yes, this was the life. In many ways, it was a privileged one, obtained for me by my brother to help distance me from the seventies and the wreckage of my past. It was a couple of years in which to rest up. A simple job, good food, plenty of sex, poker, thinking of nothing at all. A delicate balance between a full life and an empty one.

Yet, every day, I said to myself that I would go back to Africa as soon as possible and go hunting lions. I would not become a senior policeman, an old bureaucrat shut up in some office at the service of a cowardly and corrupt state. I wanted to get back to sand, blood and a real life, far away from the falsity and bigotry of middle-class Italy.

Then, one January evening in 1982, I met Angelo Dioguardi at the house of his wealthy girlfriend, Paola, having been invited there by a friend of hers Camilla. Angelo was there playing poker with other rich friends of hers. He immediately seemed to me both too stupid and too good-natured to win against such wealthy and experienced players. I soon had to change my mind about his poker playing, but not about his being too good-natured.

From that evening – during which Angelo gave me a hand in getting into bed with Camilla, we became inseparable. At night, it was poker, going to clubs, trips to Ostia for a winter dip in the sea, conversations on the meaning of life that went on into the dawn. During the day, it was work: I was at the police station; he was in a Vatican office, given to him to run because he was a good Catholic and the future husband of Paola, who happened to be the niece of a certain Cardinal Alessandrini. Unlike me, Angelo put passion and energy into his work.

He was also the exact opposite of me with women. He had plenty of opportunities, but never took advantage of them because of his unshakable loyalty to Paola. In many ways, he was the ideal friend for me. He drew them in with his sunny good looks, and I finished them off with my darkly fascinating ones.

Saturday, 26–Monday, 28 June 1982

The FIFA World Cup in Spain upset the ordered lives of every Italian, even more so in the case of Angelo Dioguardi and myself. After the Italian team had scraped through the first round by the skin of its teeth, the prospects were terrifying. The next round meant meeting the current title holders, Argentina, and the tournament favourites, Brazil.

Angelo called me at the office on 26 June.

'Michele, you got many killers to hunt these days?'

This was his usual witticism. The very height of excitement in the last few months had been the armed robbery of a perfume shop. It was subsequently discovered that the weapon was a toy gun and the robber a teenager from a very good family looking for a stronger buzz. The kids of Rome's wealthy bourgeoisie were forced to come up with something a little different to get away from their everyday lives of casual sex and marijuana.

Angelo had sourced a couple of tickets for Italy's games against Argentina and Brazil. So I took a week's leave and we left for Barcelona in my Alfa Romeo Duetto. After twelve hours' driving, fried by the sun and with our backs in pieces, we got to Barcelona on the 28th, the evening before Italy's game with Argentina.

'Apparently, you can put up tents by the stadium, so let's sleep there,' Angelo said.

We were speechless: all around the stadium, tents had shot up, a vast sea of them, thousands of youngsters camping out as best they could. T-shirts of all the national colours were mixing together: Brazil's gold and green, Argentina's white and light blue, and Italy's darker blue. Italian men were also mixing with the stunning South American women. There were hundreds of cars and motorbikes from every corner of Italy. The smell of cannabis hung heavily on the air and a carpet of beer cans littered the tarmac, which was half melted by the baking sun even at sunset.

We found space for our two ridge tents in a perfect spot, right next to Sonia and Susanne, two very attractive Brazilian students at Lisbon University.

'Angelo, I've died and gone to heaven.'

I immediately set about the business of being a good neighbour, while my friend went about in search of some unlicensed betting venues. He soon came back in high spirits to find me sitting on the ground outside Sonia and Susanne's tent, drinking beer and smoking a joint with them.

'Michele, they're giving Italy's progression to the next round at twelve to one!'

'Are you crazy? Only one of the three's going through. Italy will ship four goals to each of them.'

'We bet a thousand pesetas on Brazil, so it'll pay the petrol for getting back to Lisbon,' Sonia said, brazenly giving Angelo the eye.

'So, if you lose, you'll have to walk back then?' he teased.

'If Brazil are knocked out, we'll jump off a cliff,' said Susanne.

I looked ostentatiously at the tits beckoning from her figure-hugging top.

'Well, perhaps we can have a bit of fun, before you do that,' I said.

'Nevertheless,' said Angelo, 'the odds for Italy are a real temptation. The other night, I won more than a million at poker. I brought it all with me and intend staking it all.'

'*Tu es loco*, Angelo,' Sonia shouted after him as he went to place a bet. '*Tambien es muy guapo.*'

At midnight, we all went for a drive around the local boulevards, moving forward at walking pace among the dense mass of cars, mopeds and pedestrians, with Sonia and Susanne sitting half on and half off the car boot. There was an incredible atmosphere. Thousands of Brazilians were marching around, dancing the samba to the sound of trumpets and drums. We left the car on the pavement. Sonia and Susanne dragged us off to dance among the gold and green tide. The Brazilians were quite friendly to the Italians, much less to the Argentinians.

'That's because they're afraid of them,' I told Angelo. 'They have no fear of Italy, and you're an idiot for having chucked away that million.'

After a sea of beer and as many joints as you could want, Angelo confessed his unshakable loyalty to Paola, almost shamefacedly. In the face of Sonia and Susanne's obvious disappointment, he added the stupid lie he often used: 'I'm a practising Catholic.'

But it left the field clear for me. I winked at the two of them.

'Whereas I have no girlfriend, and am not a practising anything.'

We wound our way back, drunk and high, to the car and found three ugly-looking guys leaning casually against a black Jaguar that was blocking our exit. I noted the Italian number plate. It was from Palermo.

Sonia went up to them, tits wiggling out of her Brazilian top, her tiny shorts showing off her incomparable legs. She was clearly high as a kite. 'Excuse,' she said, mixing her languages with a polite bow, 'would you mind shifting your arses?'

She was clearly joking, but one of the three grabbed her by the arm.

'Suck my dick, you Brazilian slut.'

'Hey,' Angelo protested, 'what the hell are you doing?'

As the other two moved towards him, a first fist flew and caught Angelo on the shoulder.

I jumped in without a moment's thought.

'Hold it, you guys. I'm a policeman.'

'Bollocks you are!' replied the one who had landed the punch. He aimed one at me, too.

Perfect. Just what I wanted.

All through the past twelve years, I had kept myself in training. Judo, karate, Taekwondo, Thai boxing. And certain things you never forget how to do. A not too forceful kick in the chest was enough to floor him.

Then I pulled out my Italian police ID card showing the rank of *commissario*. The calmest of the three came up to look. He turned to the other two.

'Let's leave it out, boys. He really is a cop.'

Perhaps it was the ID card, perhaps the fear of more aggressive tactics that stopped them, but they left without even looking back.

We went back to the Duetto. The two girls were excited.

'Mike's just like James Bond!' Susanne said.

'With girls as well?' Sonia asked.

'Oh, worse, much worse than James Bond,' laughed Angelo, who was always willing to give me a good write-up.

We arrived back at the sea of tents around the stadium. Angelo retired to his own. Sonia and Susanne went into theirs for a confab. I have no idea what they agreed, but one of the two – I have no memory which one – came out of the tent soon afterwards, and followed me into mine.

Monday, 5 July 1982

After Argentina's departure from the Cup, defeated by both Italy and Brazil, came the great day of Italy's blue shirts against Brazil's green and gold. Thanks to the aggregate goal difference, the Latin American *seleçao* had only to draw to knock us out. All the Italian fans were almost certain this would happen. All except Dioguardi, who was lovingly cradling his betting stub as if it were a baby.

I was with Angelo, Sonia and Susanne outside a wine bar near the stadium when I noticed him approaching me. I almost didn't recognize him.

Nico Gerace had certainly changed a great deal. His unruly curls had given way to well-cut waves of hair that were swept back, leaving a clear forehead. His eyebrows had been thinned and given shape, the hair on his arms was almost non-existent. Naturally, he was wearing the latest fashion, with a white Lacoste polo shirt, tight-fitting designer jeans and Timberland shoes. But there were still rough edges around Nico Gerace, which was inevitable, given the genes inherited from his father Vito, the petrol-pump attendant.

He came up with his arms open wide. 'Mike! Mike Balistreri!'

He enveloped me in a hug. The reasons why we had neither seen nor heard from each other in all those years were very good ones. But the sympathy and affection were still there, as they were when we sat together in class and Nico's lisp was the object of ridicule to everyone except me.

I introduced him to Angelo Dioguardi and the two Brazilians.

'Where are you living now, Nico?' I asked him.

'In Rome. Been there ten years.'

'With your mother?'

He turned serious and shook his head.

'Santuzza died, broken-hearted, a few months after they kicked us out of Libya.'

I gave him my sincere condolences. She was a good woman, and Nico had worshipped her.

But Italy seemed to have done well for her son. It was not only a question of looks; Nico seemed much more self-confident.

'Always lucky with the ladies, our friend Mike!' he said laughingly to Sonia and Susanne. 'Watch out, he's dangerous!'

'What are you doing here?' I asked him.

He pointed to the crowds and the stadium. 'Isn't it obvious? I've come to see Italy win the World Cup!'

It was his innate joviality, inextinguishable optimism and this last remark that endeared him to Angelo. Nico had also bet on Italy winning. They were both soft in the head.

'All right, we'll celebrate together after the victory!' Angelo suggested.

Nico smiled. 'Not tonight. I'll have to dry the tears of several young South American ladies. Like you will, I imagine.' And he gave a big wink to Sonia and Susanne, who pulled their tongues out at him in reply.

I'm very happy for you, old friend. Now you know that you can have women without paying for them.

He handed out business cards. I slipped mine into the pocket of my shorts; Angelo put his in his wallet. We put our arms round each other and said goodbye. I never mentioned the work I did, nor did I promise him that we would see each other again. This was not because of him. I had always liked him, and liked him even more in his half-spruced-up fashion.

It's the memories you bring, Nico. The MANK organization, Ahmed, Karim, Laura Hunt.

That sweltering afternoon, we went with Sonia and Susanne into a stadium that was forty degrees even in the shade. Angelo was wearing a Paolo Rossi shirt; the girls each had one with the name of Brazil midfielder Zico. Looking at them wiggling in their shorts, I thought ruefully that this would be the last evening we had together, and so we had to end it in style. One of the two would be able to dry my tears after Italy's defeat.

Inside, there was standing room only. The crowd was blazing with colour. As the teams entered the field, they were greeted by the deafening clamour of Brazilian drums and Italian air horns. Squashed in the crowd and sweating like a pig, I was already in a state before the game began.

'Michele, you know, we'll have to give Sonia and Susanne the petrol money home,' Angelo whispered to me on the opening whistle.

'Don't be crazy. Look, if Italy wins, I'll do a streak round the avenues here, OK?' I had to shout it loud so the girls could hear.

And so it was that, in Barcelona on 5 July 1982, several things took place. Paolo Rossi scored three goals which drove the whole of Italy into ecstasy and left the whole of Brazil in tears. Angelo Dioguardi made 12 million lira on a bet and, of course, wanted to share it with me and give a million to the two Brazilians. Tens of thousands of blue soccer shirts, Italian tricolour flags, cars and motorbikes poured out on to the avenues, the tarantella taking the place of the samba. And I was arrested by the Spanish police for acts of obscenity while dancing naked among the crowd, and only released because of my Italian police ID. And Sonia and Susanne decided that the only way to console them was that I spend the night with the two of them.

Although I was on my last legs, I did Italy proud, just like Paolo Rossi.

Sunday, 25 July 1982

The phone was drilling into my brain. I felt the weight of Vanessa's head on my thigh, and caught the damp smell of sex from Cristiana where my cheek was resting. My eyelids were heavy roller blinds shut down on my studio flat's stale smoke; my tongue was stuck fast to my teeth, palate and gums. It had been one of those magical nights when my wildest fantasies had finally come true.

I didn't want to answer – I only wanted to sleep. But the ringing wouldn't stop. One eye managed to open. The digital clock said seven twenty.

'Oh, fuck off, will you?' I groaned, and shut the eye again.

Several minutes passed. The phone continued to ring. It was like drops of water eroding my brain, going ever deeper, up to the point where I began to wonder what was reality and what was dream.

Cristiana stared at me while I listened to the funereal tones of my boss, Commissario Teodori, who was calling me about the investigation on Elisa Sordi: a young girl murdered two Sundays earlier, the night Italy had beaten Germany and won the FIFA World Cup in Spain.

'Come down to Via della Camilluccia right away, Balistreri.'

'Sod it, now what's up?' I asked, suddenly awake.

★   ★   ★

It was only one of the greatest disasters that could be imagined in a police investigation. I had committed a colossal error during my first murder inquiry, an error that caused an innocent woman to commit suicide. It was an error that would probably remain as an indelible black mark in Italian police history, and for which I should quite rightly be demoted to traffic duty.

But, although I despised Teodori for his servile attitude towards the powerful, I had done him a great favour. I had saved his beloved only daughter, Claudia, from the slammer, and he, a widower, already ill and about to retire, had expressed his eternal gratitude.

And, in the face of that disaster, which we had to explain to the Chief of Police and the media – who would have torn us to pieces – I was ready to take all the blame. I had led the investigation and had arrested the wrong man.

Before speaking to the Chief of Police, however, Teodori and I sat in the Duetto, with the hood down, under the pelting rain at the end of that July. Teodori took out his pipe and lit it. He seemed calm, absorbed in his thoughts, whatever they were.

'I'll tell the Chief of Police you didn't agree with me,' I told him.

He looked at me with his yellow eyes and smiled. He was a humble bureaucrat: not very intelligent, and with big troubles. But I had solved the most important problem in his life for him. And he was a good man.

'You can't save me, Balistreri. Hierarchies are all-important. I demanded Manfredi's arrest – you weren't even there.'

'But I was the one—'

He interrupted me with a gesture. 'I took all the credit for the investigation. I was the one who explained everything to the Public Prosecutor, the Chief of Police and the undersecretary. I never mentioned your name; I took all the credit that was yours. So you don't come into it – you haven't done a thing.'

I stared at him in amazement. Now, I understood that he had

wanted to protect me. 'You weren't a hundred per cent sure and so you kept me out of it?'

He avoided my eyes. 'That was my mistake. I shouldn't have arrested Manfredi. An innocent woman would still be alive.'

'You had some doubts . . .' I muttered, bewildered.

'I have a daughter, Balistreri. I know things you couldn't know.'

'But you can't assume responsibility for my mistakes, Dottor Teodori.'

He now looked at me more firmly. 'I'll say it was all my idea, that it was you who were against it. I'm old, and I have hepatitis that's turned into cirrhosis. In exchange, you can do me another favour, the biggest one I can ask of you.'

'Claudia?'

'Exactly. My daughter. I'll be dead before too long; you must be a guardian and a friend to Claudia. I think you'll be able to protect her until she's more certain of herself. And you can do it far better if you remain a policeman.'

'You trust me to do all that?'

He forced himself to smile. 'Not entirely. You have to swear to me that you'll never touch her. Look, you would be an excellent guardian, but a very poor boyfriend.'

I was at that point in my life where I was fully convinced of what my father had said and that was that I'd never amount to anything because I had no talent and no will, nor the application to make up for it. And I didn't really care at all – whatever happened to me from that day on was inconsequential to me.

You might at least be able to protect a stupid adolescent with her hormones running wild?

It was for this reason I accepted Teodori's offer, not to save my own backside, but because I was worn out. All I wanted was to say yes, and then float away and fall asleep for ever.

And forget about my victims, those past and those present.

Sunday, 1 August 1982

Rome was boiling hot and practically deserted. The Vigna Clara police station was like a school without pupils. It wasn't a tourist area, so there were no Americans or Germans who had let their wallets get pinched while they were gawping ecstatically at the Coliseum, or had left a camera out on a bar table in Via Veneto . . . *It was only for a moment, sir* . . . which had miraculously vanished.

Therefore, I had a month ahead of me of what was effectively a holiday at work, with an enviable timetable to boot. One month in which to get myself back together after July's disaster, which Teodori really had managed to keep me out of, taking all the blame himself in such a convincing manner that, in the eyes of our superiors and the public, I was taken as a conscientious subordinate to whom he had stupidly refused to listen.

I arrived at the station at eight a.m., signed some papers for a couple of hours, and at ten was off in the Duetto to the most fashionable beach in Fregene, where you could find the bored wives of top directors and entrepreneurs who were still chained to their desks in Rome. The poor dupes wouldn't leave their wives on their own in villas in Portofino or Capri for fear of being cheated on, so they had them stay at home. The poor women reacted badly. Or well, depending on your point of view. There were delicious lunches with many servings: antipasto, first course, second course and ice cream.

In the evening, there were always the tourists. But only if, because of some mishap, I had missed lunch. If I had already had my fill, it was poker with Angelo and friends.

Saturday, 7 August 1982

The first Saturday in August signalled the great exodus from Italy's cities. Millions of Italians crammed into their Fiats, which were loaded up with bags, rubber dinghies and rubber ducks, and set off along our magnificent *autostrada del Sole*, the motorway south that took them to their well-deserved holidays, which the great majority would spend under umbrellas on crowded beaches. But the clever ones, and obviously the wealthiest, already had the boats they registered in Panama waiting at anchor for them in the picturesque ports of Porto Cervo on Sardinia's Costa Smeralda, or Portofino on the Italian Riviera.

In order to ensure a peaceful holiday, the current Spadolini government, the country's first non-Christian Democrat government in forty years, had hit on the bright idea of resigning that very Saturday, given a vote of no confidence for having presented too drastic a cut in the budget by a Parliament ready with its swimming costumes.

This country likes big spenders. The face of austerity only brings sadness and throws people into depression.

But I had to start looking after the man who had saved my career and my reputation as a policeman. Teodori had gone to the spa in

Chiancino near Siena to have his liver treated, and reminded me of my promise to keep an eye on his daughter, who had now left home.

I really couldn't see myself in the role of minder, even less for an eighteen-year-old girl whose photos showed she was a bit on the heavy side and with too deep a look to be a Little Goodie Two Shoes.

Claudia Teodori was now sharing a two-room flat with another girl on the fourth floor of a block near the central Termini railway station. When I called her, she agreed to meet up with me, but only for one reason. Her father had clearly explained that it was I who had kept her out of trouble when she had been arrested for driving without a licence under the influence of alcohol and drugs, along with a friend who had lost her life when the car ended up against a tree.

That evening, she was taking part in a show at the Altromodo in Testaccio, one of the most 'alternative' of the venues which had mushroomed in that period of liberalization in public tastes.

And Claudia had laid down conditions. We met in the Altromodo, or not at all. The trouble was that, in the case of the Altromodo, the word 'alternative' simply meant 'gay'. I knew only a few homosexuals directly and, although I would never have admitted it, found them likable. But dancing a slow foxtrot with them was something else. And I didn't want to venture there alone, so I asked Dioguardi to come with me. Better to be taken for a gay than to have to weave and dodge unwelcome advances.

A little bit of an escape would be good for Angelo, though. After Barcelona, he had broken it off with Paola. He never said why, nor did I ask, but it must have been eating away at him, because, all of a sudden, that sunny disposition of his had evaporated.

He accepted the invitation with an alacrity that worried me a little. Was it that his reluctance to cheat on Paola hid a latent homosexuality? Was that the reason for him ending their relationship?

I calculated our time of arrival to coincide with the end of the show. Then I went to pick up Angelo. Fortunately, he was dressed exactly as usual, no body piercings or make-up. My fears were groundless, thank God.

Testaccio was packed with youth of every kind and social extraction. I parked the Duetto on the pavement right outside the club, with the 'Police On Duty' sign clearly visible. Instead of bouncers, on the door there were two old guys who looked more like over-the-hill rock musicians: all long hair, huge sideburns and totally off their heads.

They looked down their noses at the Duetto. A bourgeois car for a young trendy from a well-heeled district. They were right about the car, but I had fallen in love with it watching Dustin Hoffman swanning around in *The Graduate*, and the feeling had never left me.

It was almost dark inside the club, which was full of sickly-sweet-smelling smoke.

Marijuana, hashish, crack. No one was smoking an ordinary cigarette.

As I imagined, the place was of full of people I disliked intensely. Long hair on the men, short on the women. Shiny leather costumes. Rings, earrings, studs and tattoos.

And the final catastrophe was that the show was still on. It was set in a concentration camp. Women in SS uniforms with naked men as their prisoners. The SS girls were bandying their whips around, the stronger prisoners pushing the weaker ones towards them.

Unlike me, Angelo was completely at ease and enjoying the show.

'How can you like this stuff, Angelo? And you, a Catholic! The Pope doesn't approve of homosexuals, you know.'

'I believe in God. And I believe God doesn't make any distinctions. I don't know about the Pope.'

'But do you know what this particular representation of hell means?'

He smiled and put a hand on my shoulder. I brushed it off immediately. This wasn't the place to do anything that might give the wrong impression.

'You know very well what it means, Mike. You remember one day you told me you went to the *tonnara* in Libya?'

The sight of General Jalloun's face bobbing about among the tuna on that last day in Tripoli rose up out of a remote corner of my memory, like a reflux. I pushed it to one side and tried to concentrate on the particular circle of hell in front of me.

I'd only seen Claudia Teodori in a photo on her father's desk. A baby-faced young girl with too much black make-up round her eyes. It must have been taken a few years before, because I almost didn't recognize her.

The version I now saw was a beautiful eighteen-year-old with huge, deep eyes, her black hair cropped in a pageboy. She was like Audrey Hepburn in *Breakfast at Tiffany's*, only without the chignon and with a bit more flesh. But her face was just as intense and expressive. She wasn't tall, but her curves were good. And her latex SS costume gave her an ambiguous air that in my prejudiced mind had only one connotation: *lesbian slut*.

If she lost some weight, she'd be really tasty.

I had to drink a couple of Lagavulins and suffer another twenty minutes of whipping, cries and incomprehensible dialogue.

When the show finally ended, Claudia came over to our table and sat down without asking. She had recognized me without ever having seen me before.

'You're the only one in here with the face of a cop.'

She gave Angelo a beautiful smile.

'That's a lovely name, Angelo. I saw you were following the show very closely.'

The usual situation. Angelo pulls them in, I make off with them. But not this one. Oh no. I made a promise to a father with sick yellow eyes.

'It was wonderful. The relationship between the prisoners, the SS and the kapos . . .' Angelo began.

'Leave off, Angelo,' I broke in. 'I'm in a hurry here.'

Claudia rolled a joint, but didn't light it. Her look towards me was not a friendly one.

'OK, so you're a tough guy, Papa says. What did you do with that shit Fratini? Papa said he didn't know. Or didn't want to tell me.'

So she'd agreed to meet me not in order to thank me for having got her out of deep trouble, but because she was curious to know how I'd done it. The shit referred to was Marco Fratini, the son of a bitch from the respectable Roman middle classes who had slipped amphetamines into her glass to soften her up before fucking her. Instead, Claudia had driven off and caused a deadly accident.

The only trouble was that there was no proof that the shit had done anything of the kind, and the only facts that could be checked were simply that she'd been high as a kite and drunk when she drove off without a licence. The crash killed her friend Deborah Reggiani, a young woman the same age as Claudia who was already making a career for herself as a television presenter. This was serious trouble which could have led straight to prison.

She lit the joint and took a drag. 'Do you two smoke?'

I wafted the smoke away.

'Not that rubbish. Why do you want to know what I did with Fratini?'

She shot me a hostile look.

'Papa's dying, and his mind's set on you protecting me. So I want to know a bit more how you go about things.'

Some shitty teenage girl looking for some excitement. A real pain in the arse.

But I'd promised her father I would help her. And, in order to help her, I had to get over the barrier of her antagonism. By getting some admiration.

For her, I'm just a bourgeois policeman to look down her nose at, like her father.

I decided to rattle off the part of the truth that made the best listening.

'I had help from an excellent accomplice. A most suitable young lady friend who offered herself for the job.'

'A lady friend you sleep with?' Claudia asked.

She had no interest in the story. She only wanted to know more about this policeman with whom her father had lumbered her. I made no reply. And I obviously made no mention that the lady friend was her father's secretary, Vanessa.

'My lady friend hooked up with Fratini in the disco and he put the usual little yellow pills in her glass, as he'd done with you. However, I warned her beforehand and she only pretended to drink.'

Claudia now showed a little interest.

'Not bad! And then what?'

I was hesitant. But I decided to tell her the truth. At least some of it.

'Then my lady friend went out with this piece of shit into the car park. And did a quick little service for him in his BMW.'

She raised her eyebrows, her curiosity really roused.

'What kind of service?'

'My lady friend has very delicate fingers. Like you.'

Angelo shot me a disapproving look.

'You mean, she wanked him off?' Claudia asked, in all seriousness.

I cut it short. This game of admitting things was making me nervous.

'As soon as he'd ejaculated, she pretended to feel sick and vomited all over him and his beautiful leather seats. Then along I come, with another three heavies in support. We dragged him out of the car, half naked and shaking. We told him that the girl he'd just drugged and tried to rape was the daughter of a boss in the Roman underworld. And that we were the guys who now had to cut his balls off before burying him under a metre of earth.'

She looked at me with those deep eyes of hers. She seemed interested, but not excited.

'Not bad again! So how did it end up?'

The look of disapproval from Angelo Dioguardi was a clear message.

But I was a policeman, formerly with the secret service. Claudia Teodori was not hanging on my every word in fascination. She was only trying to weigh up her future protector.

'Go on,' she urged, taking another drag from the sweetish-smelling joint.

'Fratini shits himself. He prefers a good few years in the slammer by confessing what he did to you. We took him to the police station ourselves. He even thanked me when he got out of the car.'

Claudia ordered a gin and tonic. She turned to Angelo.

'Your friend's a real ace, isn't he? Papa said he was.'

And what else did he say about me?

She read my thoughts.

'He told me to keep well away from you, because you'd fuck anything that moves.'

'Not exactly anything. Only the ones I find attractive.'

'Good. So Papa can rest easy, I hope.'

So this is your daughter, Teodori. A little lesbian slut.

Somehow, I had to wriggle out of this promise to help. Teodori would be back from the health spa, where he'd gone for his liver, after the middle of August. I would have to sort this out before then.

A stocky guy with a long ponytail came up to the table.

'You dancing?' he asked me, politely.

I heard Angelo Dioguardi's muffled guffaw and caught Claudia Teodori's look.

'Get your arse out of here, before I kick it out,' I growled. The stocky type did a hasty about-turn.

I regretted it immediately. Both the choice of words and their mode of delivery. But it was too late. Claudia gave me a look of disgust. She got up, said goodbye to Angelo with a handshake and a smile. But nothing for me.

'Thank you for saving me, Commissario Balistreri. But please don't worry about me. If you really do have to protect me, you can always send your friend Angelo here.'

Saturday, 14 August 1982

Life was pretty good for another week. Completely suited to the oblivion I was looking for.

A policeman by accident, not by choice. Little competence and little motivation.

I devoted myself to an entirely different field. And the bored, wealthy wives I serviced in a discreet little *pensione* near the beach resort could all bear me out.

I'd changed since the years in Tripoli. I hated summer, detested both sand and heat. I planted myself on the terrace bar in the shade and waited till they came to order a drink.

In the afternoon, I shut myself up in my office with the air conditioning on full blast, trying to avoid paperwork. When that was done, I listened to Leonard Cohen or read through some Nietzsche again. Old, innocent habits. I carried on like this until sunset.

This was the ideal moment to go out in the open Duetto and cruise the historic centre's roads, which were closed to the traffic of ordinary mortals.

I gave lifts to young foreign girls who were dehydrated and tired after a day of museums and monuments. There was one condition, one that turned an otherwise worthy action into wickedness: they had to be good-looking and clearly available. If not, then they could hobble off to the first available fountain.

Besides, I needed some alternative to my usual poker. My fellow players were all away from Rome. My brother, Alberto, was with his girlfriend, Ingrid, in Germany. Angelo was on a poker tour in America. So I had to amuse myself somehow.

But then, right in the middle of the best of it, the weekend when everyone was away, fate reared its ugly head. It was a day I'd set up brilliantly for my usual seaside lunch. A real work of art.

The attractive, mature wife of the proprietor of the luxurious beach resort in Fregene had noticed my mischief with her clients. But, instead of banning or reporting me, she had offered a deal: a free lunch for every visit with her to the *pensione* opposite. I was about to leave the station at noon for the first of these encounters when the damned call came through.

Some idiot who went out walking with his dog in this heat had found the body of a girl. And the best of this bad news was that it was on my patch.

I shot off in the Duetto, the traffic on that blistering weekend being almost zero.

Capuzzo, my deputy, was already on the spot. He was a fifty-year-old, born and bred in Rome, who had started with the police at eighteen. In all that time, he had only had to deal with one serious crime, the disastrous case of Elisa Sordi. But Capuzzo had friends everywhere and knew how to get around police bureaucracy. He was the man who lifted all the fines I incurred from the free and easy – and imaginative – use I made of the Duetto.

I found him rubbing away at his bald pate, which was gleaming with sweat.

'Always in the middle of August these terrible things. It's the heat, Dottore. This damned scirocco makes folk lose their minds.'

The idiot out walking his dog had come across the body in the middle of the greenery at the beginning of the Via Cassia, which leads north out of Rome towards Tuscany. It was lying half a kilometre from the road along a country lane, dumped there like a sack of potatoes.

The area had been cordoned off by the forensic team, but there were no curious onlookers. Capuzzo was looking green and I thought he was about to throw up.

'Capuzzo, go and look for tyre tracks between here and the metalled road. And watch where you put your feet.'

There was no need. Forensics would see to it all. But I wanted to let him go off to one side and puke without humiliating him. And, besides, I trusted his eye for detail.

The forensic pathologist was a very young medic who examined the corpse from half a metre away.

Some poor unfortunate on call who's never seen a murder victim before.

The victim was about twenty-five. She was short, dark, olive-skinned and naked, with numerous bruises and cuts all over her body. The bruises suggested there was a facial fracture, as well as one of the chest. The cuts were slashes and stabs. Her neck was swollen and black. It was a butchery that had required plenty of time. And a much more secluded place than this one.

And they had to dump her here. Right on my patch.

I turned to the pathologist. 'She's either Argentinian or Spanish.'

He barely looked up from the corpse. Through his thick lenses, you could see the irritated face of someone left behind in Rome dreaming of a quiet August holiday weekend. Just like me.

'I'm a medical man, not a travel agent. And who are you?'

'Commissario Michele Balistreri. And I meant that.'

I pointed to the tattoo on the girl's left shoulder. A heart with the number 10 inside and a name, Diego.

'So what?' the medic asked rudely.

'There's an Argentinian football player called Diego Maradona. Barcelona have just signed him.'

The man wiped the sweat from his face. I didn't like the look he was giving me.

'I appreciate your cultural knowledge, Balistreri. Now, how about leaving me to . . .'

'You could look at her teeth.'

'What?'

'Her teeth. I know about this, because I have some friends from Argentina. Dentists there do their fillings in a different way.'

The pathologist got up. He was ten centimetres shorter than me, but found a little knoll to stand on so as to look me in the face.'

'Do you watch much crime on television?'

I ignored him. I had latex gloves with me. I looked into the girl's mouth. Two fillings. Just the way they did them in Argentina.

The medic was speechless and furious. I turned my back on him and went over to Capuzzo. There was no time to lose. Not for the dead girl. For her, there was all the time in the world and I couldn't have cared less. The problem was lunch with the resort owner's wife.

'There are some tyre marks, Dottore.'

Of course there are, Capuzzo. You think he carried her here in his arms?

'One make or two makes?'

Vain hope. 'Lots,' Capuzzo admitted.

'OK. Go back to the station, inform the examining magistrate and Homicide and see what they want to do. And call Immigration: you need a visa to enter Italy from Argentina.'

He stared at me. 'From Argentina?'

'Yes, the girl's from Argentina. Ask for all the visas for women between twenty and thirty.'

'From when?'

'What do you think?'

'No idea . . .'

'Let's do it for as long as a visa lasts, OK?'

He took down notes for everything. I knew he'd be able to get the information in record time. In contrast to me, Capuzzo was perfectly at ease in the Italian bureaucratic jungle. Only someone born to it could negotiate their way through that labyrinth.

'Dottore, do you want to question the gentleman who was out with his dog?'

'Who?'

He gave me an understanding look. He was a humble, patient and highly respectful subordinate. Even with a boss like me.

'The man who found the body.'

'They didn't kill her here, Capuzzo.'

'But they dumped her here, Dottore. Perhaps this guy with the dog saw something.'

Perhaps. But I have a little bit of questioning to do to a lady at the beach. Much more important than the gentleman with the dog.

'You question him. And thoroughly.'

I couldn't make out if he was incredulous, terrified or gratified. His expression never gave anything away. I went off and left him there.

I was late. I launched the Duetto at full speed towards the beach with the hot southern scirocco wind blowing in my face. I pulled out the flashing light and the siren.

Was I on duty? Damn right I was. All in the call of duty.

When I arrived, my table in the shade was already laid out. Chilled white wine. Then *spaghetti alle vongole* with fresh clams, deep-fried squid and prawns in batter, a lemon sorbet and coffee. A delicious lunch.

The afternoon in the *pensione* opposite was just as exquisite.

I drove calmly to the Vigna Clara police station, back along a completely deserted Via del Mare, Mussolini's new road to the sea, with the wind in my face and in my ears the ridiculous words of the hit by Al Bano and Romina Power that was tormenting us that summer: '. . . *Felicità* . . . *Felicità* . . .' Of course, there was happiness around. And I had no wish to break my happy mood over the body of a dead Argentinian girl.

Capuzzo, on the other hand, was jumpy. In contrast to me, he was very respectful to his superiors.

'Did you check the visas, Capuzzo?'

He smiled. The smile of an aged subordinate who was convinced his boss was a roué but not a total prick. Despite the disasters I'd managed to create over Elisa Sordi, Capuzzo had stayed by my side, without so much as a hint of criticism or a question. Timid, but loyal.

'You were right. She's Argentinian, and we already have a name for her. Anita Messi. Twenty-four years old, from Salta in the north. It's near the border with Bolivia. She only flew in yesterday evening.'

'And what was she doing coming here to Rome? Apart from getting herself killed.'

Capuzzo pulled a slight face, suppressing his feelings. He'd no liking for my cynicism. But I'd no liking for this business either.

A brief interlude to let the wounds heal, to learn to forget and then return to Africa to hunt lions.

'She had a six-month student visa. Requested by the university college of the Sisters of the Virgin.'

I had already heard that name. Rome was full of universities and colleges attached to the Vatican, and I knew that most of the students lodged with them were from South America and Central Africa.

'I believe that even in August the students of the Lord take a break, Capuzzo. So what was Anita Messi doing here?'

He looked perplexed.

'I don't know. Perhaps she liked Rome, perhaps she had a boyfriend here. Can you give me more time for this?'

'It doesn't matter. Can you find out where she slept last night?'

Capuzzo gave a satisfied smile. Where imagination fails, then efficiency can take over. 'Already done. In one of the Vatican halls of residence, just near here. The kind your friend Angelo Dioguardi manages.'

So that's why she was found in this area . . . another five kilometres and . . .

This was a real nuisance. I called the Flying Squad, already fearing the worst, which was punctually delivered.

This is right in the middle of annual holidays. Homicide is below strength and has too many cases caused by the heat. Please carry on, Commissario Balistreri, and keep us informed, if that helps, but only if necessary.

I called the examining magistrate on duty. In the background, I could hear pop music, waves and a dog barking.

'I'll send you the necessary authority, Commissario. You can update me when you've identified a possible suspect. And only then, please.'

I really have to get away from this country of layabouts.

We went to the hall of residence in the open Duetto, the scirocco belching out hot gusts in our faces. Capuzzo was white as a sheet and begged me to pull the hood down and drive more slowly. There was another thing about me that got on his nerves, apart from my cynicism – and that was my rash behaviour.

'What's wrong, are you worried I'll mess your hair up, Capuzzo?'

He looked wounded, not because I was referring to his hair loss, but the fact that I was shooting my mouth off. But his worrying amused me.

At the hall of residence, the reception was manned round the clock. Even in the middle of August.

In the room Anita had occupied for the one night there were two single beds. One unused, without sheets, as her roommate hadn't yet arrived. The other was Anita's. There was a half-unpacked suitcase, personal belongings. But no books, no photos of family or saints. Yet already hanging over the bed was a poster of Diego Armando Maradona in his Argentine strip.

Odd for a theology student. Not a single book, and a picture of a football player over the bed instead of a crucifix or a picture of the Virgin Mary.

Capuzzo was about to open a window.

'No, don't do that. Leave it closed.'

'But it stinks of piss, Dottore.'

'It's not piss. It's ammonia.'

'Did she use it to clean the bathroom?'

Little imagination, yet again.

I had to know more about this Anita Messi. I looked in the waste-paper basket. An empty bottle of mineral water and a straw.

Capuzzo disappeared into the bathroom. I popped my head in and found him washing his hands.

'The bathroom's all clean. But there's no smell of ammonia. Look at this.'

He showed me the small bar of soap he had just used, round and black.

'Capuzzo, would you mind telling me what you're doing? You're not supposed to touch a thing.'

He stared at me, mortified. Of course, this was what the book said. But the book followed the FBI, and we weren't even distant relatives of the FBI. We were still at the *Starsky and Hutch* level.

Monday, 16 August 1982

At nine a.m., I was at the university college of the Sisters of the Virgin where Anita Messi was to have studied theology. From its location and its architecture, it could easily have been an exclusive hotel.

It was halfway up the Palatine hill, directly above the Roman Forum. From the windows of the magnificent hall into which I was shown, you could see what Julius Caesar had begun two thousand years earlier and Augustus Caesar and later emperors had continued: the Basilicas of Aemilia and Julia on the far side, the Temples of Caesar, Concord and Castor and Pollux from 7BC, down to the more recent Arch of Septimus Severus, built at the beginning of the third century along the Via Sacra. It was clear the Roman Catholic Church had survived the Roman empire, and this panorama was there to remind me.

Despite the holiday period and the half-deserted city, the domestic bursar responsible for administration, Sister Domitilla – who had been called at eight that morning – was ready to receive me. She was troubled by the death of a girl she hadn't even had time to meet.

She offered me an excellent cup of coffee and explained that only the Apostolic See can establish pontifical universities or else approve them in order for them to confer valid academic degrees with canonical authority. At the head of each university was the chancellor, then the Rector Magnificus, the deans, the presidents, the lecturers and officials, among them the chief librarian and a bursar, and the staff of the administrative and secretarial offices dealing with the students.

She handed me a glossy brochure for the university college of the Sisters of the Virgin.

Perhaps she thinks I have a daughter. If I had, this would be the last place I would put her.

I moved on to the questions.

'How many years would Anita Messi have been here?'

'Only six months. We have international exchanges with various universities all over the world which study theology. Mostly in South America. They send us students for several courses of study for a period ranging from three to six months.'

'Did you send anyone to pick her up at the airport?'

'No. She wrote to us that it wouldn't be necessary. Perhaps someone else was meeting her.'

'Did she come here in the morning?'

'No, we didn't see anything of her here.'

'I don't follow, Sister. She arrived at your hall of residence. She didn't have to come here to – I don't know – sign herself in or something?'

Sister Domitilla gave me a radiant smile.

'No, we try not to accumulate signatures. She would have come here at the start of her courses in the middle of September.'

'Exactly. She came a month early. Isn't that rather too soon?'

'The girls do sometimes come early. They visit Rome, Florence, Venice.'

'Did Anita Messi come to see Rome and Italy?'

'Perhaps Rome, Commissario Balistreri. But, to tell you the truth, I don't really know.'

'Do only the best students come to study with you here?'

Now Sister Domitilla looked a little embarrassed. 'Usually, yes.'

'And was Anita one of them?'

Sister Domitilla fixed me with her eyes. 'I don't see what that has to do with you, Commissario.'

I smiled at her. Instinctively, I followed her. I knew the difference between reserve and reticence. Sister Domitilla had no wish to speak ill of a dead girl.

'Sister, this is a murder inquiry. Unfortunately, everything has to do with me. I can't say if it'll help me or not. My job is to see that the guilty person is arrested.'

While I saw her reflecting on this, I remembered the exchange of views with Cardinal Alessandrini during the disastrous investigation into Elisa Sordi's death.

Earthly justice can sometimes make mistakes, Balistreri, but divine justice will get there sooner or later.

'Yes, Anita Messi was a problematic student. She was an orphan who came from a town on the border with Bolivia and wasn't well educated. Her marks from university in Argentina were low. Actually, she was behind with her exams.'

'So why did you accept her here?'

Sister Domitilla shook her head.

'I don't know. We give out guidelines to the home universities, but it's up to them to select the students.'

A complete balls-up. Carrying on this investigation in Argentina would be very complicated.

'How would she maintain herself here? I mean, apart from living in the hall of residence.'

'She had a grant from her home university.'

A not very studious student getting a grant.

As I left Sister Domitilla, I had the clear feeling of having set foot on a long and tortuous road. One most probably with no end in sight. And one about which I cared absolutely nothing.

Tuesday, 17 August 1982

Commissario Teodori came back from the health spa with his eyes more yellow and sunken than ever. But I had to talk to him about Claudia and what she was doing in those libertine clubs. I was hoping he'd release me from my unwelcome task.

And we were here for that very reason, sitting out on the terrace of a bar on the Janiculum: Teodori, Angelo Dioguardi and myself. It was lunchtime, and there was not even a hint of a breeze. And yet, as long as he could, Teodori wanted to stay out in the open. The day before, he had travelled the seventy kilometres from Chianciano Terme to Siena to see the traditional Palio horse race as the guest of a rich friend who had a balcony over the Piazza del Campo, where the race took place. He told us about it like an excited child: the horses, the jockeys, the flags of the competing districts, the wonderful square crammed with people. Perhaps he knew that, soon, he'd no longer be able to leave the confines of a hospital room. So he had wanted to climb the Janiculum and look out from the hill over Rome's rooftops, its ochre-coloured buildings, its hundred churches, the Tiber. I would have much preferred the inside of a bar with the air conditioning on full, but Angelo obliged me to agree to his wishes.

Below us, the Tiber seemed motionless, just like the people below the bar awnings and the pigeons on church cornices. A few tourists had collapsed at the tables around us. We three were the only Italians. In order to entertain Teodori a little, I told him about Anita Messi, the visit to her room and the Sisters of the Virgin university college.

He gave a feeble laugh. 'You always did have difficulties with priests and nuns, Balistreri.'

Quite, from the time I was little.

I moved on to the meeting with his daughter at the Altromodo and spared him nothing. He listened in silence.

'So Claudia's into drugs.' He said it like that, staring at me with those yellow eyes, the unlit pipe between his lips. And yet the illness gave Teodori a dignity it took away from most people.

Because he knew that soon his daughter would be left with only his memory.

'Unfortunately, yes,' I replied coldly.

'But only joints, Dottor Teodori. Nothing serious. And your daughter's a great actress,' Angelo hurriedly added.

Teodori smiled at him. 'Claudia phoned me after your visit to the Altromodo to tell me that she didn't want any guardian. But she spoke highly of you, Signor Dioguardi.'

Of course. Angelo's an angel and I'm the devil incarnate.

Hearing us talk about joints, the waiter was staring at us, disconcerted. The rattling of his tray with Teodori's glass of almond milk and my dry martini upset me.

'We're three dealers here,' I snapped at him, 'and would like a little privacy.'

The waiter quickly placed the drinks on the table and disappeared. Angelo gave a resigned gesture. Teodori shook his head. But, in contrast to all the other times he'd witnessed me mouthing off, this time, he smiled.

'You'll never change, will you, Balistreri? I don't know if it's a good idea putting Claudia in your care.'

Perfect. I couldn't ask for more.

'Very well. You look after her, then.'

Angelo shot me the usual disapproving look. Is this how I wanted to treat the man who'd saved me from getting fired? The man who had entrusted me with his daughter's care? Why?

You know very well, Mike.

Teodori reminded me why.

'Do you hate all fathers in the world, Balistreri? What the hell did yours do to you?'

I sank the dry martini and looked over to Quirinale Palace, seat of the presidency. The Italian flag was hanging from its yardarm. It was towards that magnificent palace that my father was directing his efforts. And certainly not as an employee. At worst, he would buy his way in.

'You think you're a perfect father, Teodori?'

He tried to light the pipe, but his hands were trembling too much. Angelo held his right hand to help him.

'There are no perfect fathers, Balistreri. There are fathers who do less damage than others. I was a boring father for Claudia. At one time, there was my wife to keep her company. Too much company.'

'When did your wife die?'

'Six years ago, when Claudia was twelve. It was my wife who passed on her passion for the theatre to her. She did a bit of acting when she was young, you know. Then she tried to get into television, which was her great love. But she never got further than a screen test with the RAI.'

'So where does Claudia fit into this?'

'When you become a father, you'll understand better. Parents want their children to succeed where they failed.'

Who knows where my incomparable father failed? In what field could I do better than he did?

But we were talking about Claudia Teodori. And I wanted rid of her.

'It was my wife who sent Claudia to acting lessons, when she was ten. Then elocution, singing and dancing. Only, Claudia didn't put much effort into it; she's never been slim enough and never wanted to go on a diet, as my wife wanted her to.'

I remembered the photo on Teodori's desk. A girl with the naïve make-up of an insecure adolescent.

Teodori fixed us with those tired yellow eyes. 'What can we do to help her?'

I made one last desperate attempt to free myself from this moribund man and his whore of a daughter.

'I've a lot on right now, including the misfortune of finding a dead body right near my own police station. And Homicide have kindly hung a notice out: "Closed for the holidays". I'm on my own with it.'

I knew he was a veteran policeman and didn't approve of my arrogant tone of voice. I saw him cough, and a shadow of doubt flickered across his yellow eyes. Perhaps he was mistaken in putting his trust in me.

But there was no question. I owed it to him and had made a promise.

'If it goes on like this, it'll be necessary to put a tail on your daughter, Teodori. But I can't see to it or use my own men from Vigna Clara.'

He nodded. He looked downwards at the stationary river in the shimmering August heat. Perhaps towards the house where he and his wife had brought little Claudia up.

'There are two trusted former colleagues of mine who have just retired. They're going absolutely crazy with nothing to do all day other than feed the pigeons in the Borghese gardens. They'll take it on willingly. And will report back to you and you alone, Balistreri.'

I could not hide my scepticism, or a hint of sarcasm.

'Two guys on their pension?'

'Two extremely effective former colleagues who retired only a year ago. Pietro Marchini's the one who invited me to Siena yesterday – he has remarkable intuition and can make the dead talk. Paolo Federico's from Capri – he can analyse anything and is a wizard when it comes to data processing.'

Perfect. Peter and Paul. Two retired apostles. Just right for the job.

'I've no idea what data processing is, Teodori. Or what use it is.'

'Have you never heard of computers, Balistreri? You'll see how useful they'll become in the long life ahead of you. Paolo's got a brand-new one, a desktop job, from IBM.'

'Listen, Teodori, I don't give a damn about sniffer dogs or calculating machines. I just need two men who know how to tail your daughter discreetly.'

A city policeman had come up to my Duetto, which was parked at an angle in the middle of the road, and taken out his ticket book. I'd forgotten to display my police permit.

'Off you go, or you'll get a ticket,' Teodori told me.

I took it calmly. I waited until the city cop had filled the form out. He slipped the ticket under the windshield wiper and went off under the shade of a tree. At that point, Angelo and I said goodbye to Teodori.

'I'll expect a report from those two pensioners, then,' I said, while Angelo was warmly shaking his hand.

'Their names are Pietro and Paolo. Pietro's the senior of the two.'

Perfect. My two apostles. And what does that make me – Jesus Christ?

I got to the Duetto, snatched off the parking ticket, ostentatiously rolled it into a ball and chucked it on the ground.

'Hop in, or I'll leave you there,' I growled at Dioguardi, who was staring at me, shaking his head.

The city cop's eyes came out on stalks, and he started to come towards us as I started the engine. I put the flashing light out and the siren on maximum. I left with a screech of tyres and just missed him as I passed by, leaving him trembling in the middle of the square.

In the rear-view mirror I saw Teodori's tired face break out into a smile.

Wednesday, 18 August 1982

Capuzzo called as I was staring out of my office in Vigna Clara at a couple of Filipino domestics who were taking their employer's poodle for a walk. The owners were probably in some holiday paradise far away from the hot, sticky and deserted Rome of August.

'There are two CID officers for you, Commissario.'

'CID officers?' I had no idea what the hell he was talking about.

'The two gentlemen are Pietro Marchini and Paolo Federico. On behalf of Chief Commissario Teodori.'

CID officers, Chief Commissario. Capuzzo was so respectful about ranks.

'They're *former* detectives, Capuzzo. In retirement. And leave this "CID officers" to the crime shows.'

As they entered my office, they seemed neither apostles nor detectives, more like a superannuated Laurel and Hardy. I silently cursed them, Chief Commissario Teodori and his daughter.

The two men didn't seem particularly impressed by either my office or me. Of course, for them I was only a young local commissario in a very placid district, while they were two sixty-year-olds with years of experience in the homicide squad behind them. I saw them more as experts in shuffling paper and following procedure rather than investigating crime.

I gestured for them to take a seat on the two wooden chairs in front of my desk, but offered no water or coffee. I wanted my contact with these two old pen-pushers to be brief and to the point.

'Now then, your role is to tail Claudia as closely as possible and have a written report for me every morning here in the station.'

'Couldn't we simply give you a verbal report, Balistreri?' asked Pietro.

Pietro Marchini was the Tuscan from Siena: a large man with an unruly shock of white hair who actually did look like St Peter, and who was probably filthy rich, seeing as he had a house on Siena's central Piazza del Campo. He wasn't entirely keen on my suggestion and, like a good Tuscan, had no reservations about letting me know.

I pretended not to notice the absence of the word 'Commissario' before my surname. My first conversation with Teodori had begun in exactly the same way.

'I don't see the reason for it,' I replied stiffly.

'Verbally, it's possible to communicate intuitions and feelings,' Peter the Apostle went on.

'Whereas I'm only interested in the facts, gentlemen. We're talking simply of tailing this girl, not investigating a crime.'

'It makes no difference,' Paolo Federico said, in his marked southern accent. He was the thin and bony one, dark and with short grey hair.

I gave him a curious stare. 'There's no difference between putting a tail on someone and a crime?'

'No difference at all. You need intuition as well as the facts. Paolo and I have agreed about this for years.'

This wasn't the moment to initiate a debate about investigative methodology.

'OK, let's do this. We'll keep to a written report each morning, but we can meet once a week to take stock of the situation.'

I let them go. As they were leaving, Apostle Peter muttered something in Tuscan dialect, and the other replied in his equally heavy language from Campania. The few words I could pick up weren't complimentary.

Monday, 23 August 1982

After a fortnight's holiday, the first Italian citizens were making their unwilling way back to the city. Among them were the ministers forced to break off their holidays to swear loyalty to the Republic in the sweltering Roman heat as Giovanni Spadolini made a second attempt to form a government.

On Claudia Teodori, there was nothing new. The two apostles took turns with the reports: one day Pietro, in his forceful and fanciful style; the next Paolo, with his crushingly boring attention to detail. But the essence was that, by day, Claudia Teodori took her singing, dancing and acting lessons and, at night, she went to the Altromodo to take part in that disgusting show. Then she came back to the modest rented apartment she shared, with a girl who worked at the cash register of a bar near Rome's central Termini station. No sex and no drugs.

I suspected that the two apostles were covering up for her, so as not to upset their old friend Teodori.

As for Anita Messi, in over a week, Capuzzo had not discovered a great deal. As I'd expected. It was one thing to seek out facts long-buried in the archives by bureaucratic procedure but another to investigate a homicide. Nevertheless, Capuzzo was mortified. He had no idea that his not finding any trace of Anita Messi was in itself a valuable piece of information.

Her days were already numbered when she stepped off that aeroplane.

Anita Messi hadn't used cash or a credit card during the few hours between arriving in Rome and the moment she was killed. Besides, she wasn't a privileged girl, and probably had neither cash nor a credit card. No one had seen her when she flew into Fiumicino airport or during the morning on which she was killed.

Only the duty porter at the hall of residence's reception had seen her. On the night she arrived, she had presented herself at reception at five minutes to midnight, a few minutes before any guests had to leave. He had spoken only a couple of words to her, to hand over the room. At seven thirty the following morning, the girl had confined herself to waving hello to him as she went out.

Anita had been wearing a T-shirt, jeans and tennis shoes and was carrying a small rucksack. The porter remembered the T-shirt easily, because it had 'Danger' printed on it in black letters on a purple background. From that moment on, no one had seen Anita. At midday, her body had turned up in a field with no trace of any of clothes.

In those four hours and thirty minutes, Anita Messi had been kidnapped, raped and killed.

I had begun to examine the various possibilities, as they had taught me on the course for the rank of commissario. First of all, was the violent episode perpetrated by a person unknown to the victim or by one known to them? It made a great deal of difference to the direction the investigation would take.

I had studied Anita Messi's photographs. She was short and dark, but with a good figure and the prominent cheekbones and facial characteristics of a South American Indian.

Not a girl to drive me wild if I came across her on the street.

And then there was the statistical evidence. Perpetrators unknown to the victim committed rape, not murder, but murder could follow during an attack if the victim exercised excessive resistance.

I took up the initial autopsy report, which had come in after a week. Capuzzo disappeared before I opened it. He didn't want to see it all again, even in a photograph.

Multiple bruising; fractures to two ribs, the nasal septum, right cheekbone and orbital bone; lesions consistent with blows from the fist rather than a blunt instrument in order to cause pain, not a fatality.

But then there were eighteen wounds inflicted by a sharp point – a pair of scissors, perhaps, or a paper knife – to the abdomen, the chest, the left eye, and several around the vagina. All were superficial.

The fatal wound was a single one to the neck. That uptight medic making the report explained that, judging from the bleeding, this blow had been struck last. This made a huge difference to the murderer's profile. It was one thing wounding to make a victim suffer, another to ravage a corpse.

The sexual violation was confirmed by traces of sperm in the vagina and anus.

Then there was the mutilation. The middle finger of the right hand had been cleanly cut off. Deliberately, not by chance. And with an axe or a butcher's knife. According to the pathologist, this, too, had been inflicted before death occurred.

When I told him this, Capuzzo pulled a face of disgust.

'Try not to capture him alive, Commissario.'

I looked at him in curiosity.

'Why's that, Capuzzo?'

'Because, in this country of ours, a clever lawyer will pay a clever psychiatrist to focus on that finger there and cite mental instability. The guy'll be out after a few years.'

I knew that Capuzzo was married, without kids. That is, without kids any more. At the age of sixteen, his son had been run over on a zebra crossing by a drunk driver who was now already out of prison.

That amputated finger was the most interesting detail about the murderer and his fixations. But it was also the most disturbing, because anyone who feels the need to do anything of this kind beyond the fact of murder possesses two characteristics: they are ice-cold and they will do it again.

I avoided telling Capuzzo this. He would have worried himself to death about it.

Anita Messi was a heap of trouble I had to get myself out of. As soon as possible. My intuition told me there were too many things that didn't add up.

The finger, Maradona, the ammonia, the maintenance grant.

I told Capuzzo to suspend the investigation and concentrate on other matters. He tried to object, but I didn't even reply. I then asked the examining magistrate to write a letter to Anita Messi's home university in Argentina. Essentially, he had to put a simple question to them, but in a considerate and polished manner.

Why had they picked such a poor student for an international exchange?

And, in this way, I bought some time. By the end of August, that damned homicide squad would be finished with its rubber dinghies and ducks, and they could take over the Anita Messi case.

Rossellini came to the Altromodo on Friday, Saturday and Sunday, and on three consecutive nights saw me acting out the part of a Nazi guard with a whip in my hand. After all, I'd gone to take part in the show on purpose. It was there that he'd spotted Deborah.

This evening, he waited for me outside the dressing room. Usually, no one does this. I didn't come out, so then, at a certain point, he opened the door without knocking and said, 'Hungry?' I was starving. So why not? Seeing as I had to get to know him, it was worth scrounging a meal off him into the bargain.

So I found out that, like all old men, he dribbled over his food, but at least he wasn't tight-fisted. He takes me to a smart place and chews my ear off, telling me who he is. I listen to him, keeping to myself a bit, as I always tend to with middle-aged men.

It's the breath of older people that's different from people my age. It's a mixture of poor digestion, stale smoke and neglected teeth. And the level of chat. Guys my age shoot off a string of more or less amusing idiocies and openly try to get me into bed with them. Older men don't do this. They say only a little about themselves, enough to convey how important they are, and then they pretend to be interested in me. Deborah explained all this to me.

I want to help, they say. You've got talent. How come you ended up here? What would you really like to be doing? If you put some effort into it, you could go anywhere you want. And you could really do it. For someone special like you, I could call on a few important contacts I have; you won't let me down; you're smart; you can be a smash hit. The only smash hit I want is to land one on their stupid, leering faces.

Of course, Rossellini says these things to all the girls he chooses to turn into stars. And what could a girl in an Altromodo show want more than to get on the magical box of television or the cinema screen? And, with the boom in new independent commercial channels, given good looks and a willingness to do anything at all, the doors are open to the less artistically talented.

Rossellini's known for his very young flames. Word is that he doesn't actually sleep with them, perhaps because he's impotent. What's important for him is to be seen with them, to show them off.

The mechanics of enticing me in are obviously tried and tested. First, praise my possibilities and then convince me of where I'm lacking or deficient, which only an expert such as he can help me overcome.

I have little experience, but a great deal of talent, he says. He goes on and on about the talent I have.

As if to say, I've picked you out, you know, from a thousand others like you, so don't waste my time; trust in me, body and soul.

And I'm not sure that all Rossellini really wants is a go on my tender young body.

Meanwhile, he wants to convince himself that I'll go for him, and the offer of my body will follow on from his command over my mind.

I have to listen to him, anyway. He's not really called Rossellini. It's a nickname they gave him at Extra TV after the success of his variety show.

And now he's telling me that in ten days Extra TV will be choosing new announcers. It's exactly the way Deborah began.

Wednesday, 1 September 1982

The sun was finally a little less intense. Unfortunately, along with the rain came the return of the good citizens of Rome and, with them, the traffic, the queues of mothers and children for the year's schoolbooks, the restaurants and cinemas full of people in the evening.

The race towards the good life was on again. Not even forty years had passed since the end of the Second World War, and already everyone was fed up with being a manual worker. Better to have a clerical job in the civil service, the post office or the state railways. A desk and a job for life. Half Christian Democrat, half Communist, the state of Italy offered this to everyone. And then everyone found a second job: moonlighting and, if possible, off the books.

Meanwhile my two apostles continued to hand in their report every morning. They took their task very seriously, as if following a dangerous Mafioso on the run, rather than their former boss's adolescent daughter.

In the past ten days, Claudia Teodori's life had been the same. She woke late in the two-room flat she shared with the other girl near the Termini station. Then her elocution and singing lessons, a pause for an undressed salad, then acting and dancing lessons. In the evening, the shows in the Testaccio clubs.

One thing surprised me deeply. There was no sign of a man. Not in the sense I meant, anyway. Nor of a woman. No lovers of any kind.

Thursday, 2 September 1982

Today's the big day. The alarm goes off at six. Three hours' sleep will do. It's dark outside and, four floors below, there's only a few lights from cars, and every so often you can hear a siren going by.

My flatmate's already in the kitchen. She has to be at work in the bar by seven. I sip a black coffee.

'Not eating anything?'

'No, thanks, I've got butterflies in my tummy.'

Then she leaves. I put on my make-up and choose what clothes to wear.

'Something simple. They won't choose you on your dress, but they can rule you out because of it.'

Drops of wisdom sprayed on to my face by Rossellini yesterday evening at the Altromodo. I'm doing what he says: not too much make-up, T-shirt not too tight-fitting, jeans that don't hug the hips too much. I mustn't show I'm a slut for all and sundry to have. Only at the right moment.

From the Rome Termini station, you take two buses to the northern outskirts and the start of Via Flaminia. The second bus is full of women, all heading in the same direction. Anxious mothers herding daughters plastered with make-up.

We all get off together and, just before eight, move on to the wide stretch of tarmac in front of the large industrial hangar housing the studios. A sign proclaims 'Extra TV'. The new face of Italy.

There are almost a thousand people in line on the tarmac. Just over half are girls my age. The rest are their mothers, looking as worked up as if the screen test were for them. Deep down, that's what it means: release from a disappointing life, a boring job, a husband who doesn't care and an ever more hurried missionary position in bed. Apprehensive and hopeful, they straighten their daughters' T-shirts and touch up their make-up almost unconsciously. They all have a little rucksack with water and sandwiches.

This crowded stretch of tarmac is the departure point for a journey whose end none of them knows, yet one they all think is worth having. The unrealized dreams of hundreds of mothers will all come true in the glittering lives of their adolescent daughters.

My mother isn't here; she died six years ago. But it's as if she were beside me. She'd be doing exactly what all the others are doing. Come on, honeybunch, put everything you've got into it. You know you can do it. And remember to smile – always keep smiling. Even at the security men.

Deborah had already passed this screen test before I killed her by crashing the car into that tree. She'd tell me to go home, enrol at university, find a boyfriend, a job, marry and have kids. Exactly what I'd have done if she hadn't died because of me. Or perhaps I wouldn't. Ever.

At eight o'clock, security men close the main gates with us inside, but leave us out in the sun. Outside, the poor latecomers are in tears as they cling to the gates, their mothers inveighing against Rome's buses, which are always late, and begging the man on duty to open the gates. But he doesn't even look at them. Get on back home, you stupid cows, with your idiot daughters plastered in make-up. There's no room here at Extra TV for women running late with the buses.

Many of the waiting girls aren't particularly good-looking. Some plainly aren't at all. Either they never look in the mirror or they're deluding themselves, or else they believe the Extra TV advert: 'Wanted: Radio and television presenters. If you're not good-looking, then you've a chance on the radio.'

It's a scam. They apply in their thousands and we get headlines in the newspapers.' Rossellini told me that they'd rather die than pick the ugly ones, but they help to make up the numbers and therefore get the newspaper coverage.

And so these ugly girls and their poor deluded mothers are prepared to stand for hour after hour on this desolate tarmac under the blazing sun at the end of summer. All for nothing. Sitting on the ground with their T-shirts pulled down under their backsides so as not to feel the heat, they'll slowly become aware of the fact that, in this man's world, their looks are an insuperable handicap. They can act, sing and dance. But, to Extra TV and its heads of programmes, it won't mean a damned thing. They won't be called for a screen test, they won't even let them set foot in that industrial hangar of promised paradise. And, from the experience, they'll learn that they'll have to resign themselves to the life of a shop assistant, employee or housewife.

Because the place you have in the queue means nothing; it's not given the least consideration. At eight o'clock, a pot-bellied bald guy whose sweat you can smell from ten metres away and who acts like one of the kapo guards in the show I act in every evening will call out: 'You, you, you, you and you, inside.' He doesn't even know the names of the girls he points out, only what he sees: face, tits, arse, legs.

I know I'll be one of the last they call – Rossellini told me so. 'It's better like that, when the others they're weighing up are tired. But then you'll have to get on with it by yourself, my little chick. Follow my advice, and you won't have any problems!'

And that's how it is the whole day. When the girls realize that the queue doesn't mean a thing, they camp down with their mothers, dehydrated mother–daughter couples who first had entertained hopes, then felt disappointment and finally had to accept the inadequacy of their looks. But they don't leave. They stay there, hoping there's been some slip-up, and drink the bitter cup of humiliation to the end.

The potbelly comes out for a last time at eight in the evening, when the sun's already set and the mosquitoes are eating us alive. 'You, you, you, you and you.' I'm the last one. We follow the guy's distinctive aroma into an entrance that seems like a cinema in the remote outskirts, then along a corridor full of doors leading off it. The last one gives on to the theatre, with the stage lit and the seats in the dark. They have us all sit in the first row of seats, where two mothers are already seated. The last two girls from the previous group have just taken the stage. A short distance away are three figures of men over fifty, almost bald or with long, untidy hair; all with a paunch, badly dressed and a bit flabby. These are the Extra TV directors who have to size us up. Ugly old men judging beautiful young girls who look upon them as if they were gods. And they are: gods of the wonderful new world of independent commercial channels. One of the three is Rossellini.

The tallest selector gives a hand mic to one of the two girls. 'You've just been raped, you go home and your mother's there and you talk.' The two girls are pretty, but are wearing too much make-up. The one with the mic in her hand starts to tremble. 'M-Mamma,' she stammers. The other one, who has to play the mother, starts to tremble more than the first girl. 'My baby daughter!' The tallest director is the head, Rossellini told me. He gestures to the two girls. 'Thanks, you can go now.' They'd lost it, in thirty seconds, after hours of waiting and perhaps years of lessons. I hear one of the mothers hiss 'Idiot!' at her daughter as she comes off the stage, keeping her eyes down. The other girl is crying, along with her mother.

I close my eyes when they call two of the girls in my group. I don't want to look any more. But I can hear. Same scenario. Same conclusion. Then another two. Now I cover my ears as well as close my eyes. A moment later, the sweaty potbelly taps me on the shoulder. 'Hey, wakey wakey, it's you now.'

I remember Rossellini's last words of advice: 'Look only at the tall one. Not at me or the other guy. Right in the eyes, and smile. He mustn't ever see that you're scared.'

'Name?' the chief selector asks me. 'Claudia Teodori.' He hands me the mic. 'Now, Claudia, you're a police inspector. There's been a crime. We three are the suspects. Now, improvise.'

I let only a moment go by. My eyes come to rest on him. But the smile becomes scornful. I step forward decisively, and he takes an involuntary step back. 'You're a dirty old impotent bastard. What did you rape her with, a stick? You make me sick, d'you hear?'

The director's taken aback, I can hear the panting breath of Rossellini and the other director. Then the tall one smiles. 'Good, Claudia, you can go now.'

When I leave, they've already announced to the hundreds of girls and mothers still sitting on the tarmac half melted with the heat that the selection process is over. I mingle in with the silent exodus. An army routed after defeat, consigned to a life of defeat. I go back home with them on a bus full of silent broken dreams.

Friday, 3 September 1982

In one of the daily reports from my two stalking apostles, I finally discovered the first real new detail about Claudia Teodori, which explained nearly everything: the strict diet, all those obsessive lessons, the role in the evening shows in Testaccio's clubs.

The day before, Claudia had left at seven in the morning and had taken a bus to an industrial hangar on the Via Flaminia on the northern edge of Rome. At eight, on the tarmac square beyond the gates off the road, there were already about a thousand people: all young girls aged between eighteen and twenty, many with their mothers. Outside the building hung a sign: 'Auditions for Extra TV's new faces. Italy's TV of the future.'

Pietro and Paolo had taken turns until evening; Claudia had been one of the last to go in and came out half an hour later.

The report ended with an invitation for an after-dinner coffee at Teodori's to discuss developments.

Three old men summoning me for this kind of crap.

The telephone rang just as I was about to call them and tell them where to stick their invitation. It was Angelo, who was inviting me for a coffee, and I explained the situation.

'Let's go together, Michele. The poor old guy's not well.'

I gave up. It was completely useless telling Angelo that this was a load of bollocks and that I had plenty of other things to do. Our friendship had already been through the mill because of my couldn't-care-less attitude, and I didn't care for a rerun.

I drove with Angelo to the house where Teodori lived, Claudia having left after the famous car crash, and noticed with pleasure the first real autumn raindrops starting to fall.

It was the large apostle, Pietro the Tuscan, who opened the door. Paolo was sitting at a desk in a corner of the living room, looking at a kind of screen.

Teodori was sitting in a comfortable armchair. He had a strange cough and the shadows under his eyes were very dark. He apologized for having made us come to his house, but the doctor didn't want him going out in the rain. Pietro and Paolo had already updated him on everything.

'Well then, Balistreri, what do you think of this new development?'

They certainly won't take her on. Unless she's fucked someone there who really counts.

'I'd say we wait. Of course, if they take her on at Extra TV, it'll be more difficult to keep an eye on her.'

Apostle Peter immediately broke in.

'We can follow her into the television studio, just the same.'

Teodori had a fit of coughing. He picked up a glass of water, but his hand trembled so much that he found it difficult to drink. Angelo got up and held it steady for him.

This farce has to end. I can't keep an eye on a sick old man and his idiot daughter.

'You'll have to give up your pipe, Teodori. It's not doing you any good.'

He swept a hand through his long and thinning grey hair.

'I don't touch it any more, Balistreri. The doctor's forbidden it.'

'And could we know what you find so interesting on that TV there?' I asked Apostle Paul in irritation. He hadn't taken his eyes off the screen for a second.

He glowered back at me. 'This is a PC, not a TV. It's a table-top computer.'

'A PC? And what the hell's that for?'

'I'm entering the details of all those who work at Extra TV, from the head of the board to the man on the front desk.'

I thought he was mad.

I went back to the subject of Claudia. 'Anyway, Extra TV'll never take her on, so we won't have to worry.'

Teodori smiled. 'I think Claudia'll surprise you, Balistreri.'

'I think so, too, Michele. Claudia's a great actress and a beautiful young woman,' Angelo said.

I gave a snort. Dioguardi had been shattered by his break-up with Paola. In order to soften his inner pain, he was probably imagining qualities in Claudia Teodori she simply didn't have.

'All right, so the girl's a star. But, look, I've got work to do, Teodori. I've got this Argentinian girl with the finger cut off.'

Teodori was coughing again. Longer and more harshly this time. He drank a little water, which Angelo had poured for him, then he fixed me with a look from those yellowish eyes.

'It's a great pity, you know, Balistreri. You have the brains and courage to be an excellent policeman. All you lack is a little compassion.'

'You're right, Teodori. Therefore . . .'

'Perhaps Anita Messi had parents, Balistreri. Like Elisa Sordi, like my daughter – like you, I imagine.'

'And so? I don't see what it's got to do with the investigation.'

'If you were able to feel the suffering of others a little, perhaps that missing finger you mentioned in such a tone of disgust might tell you something useful.'

They all looked at me without understanding where I was coming from. Elisa Sordi and Anita Messi were simply dead bodies I'd stumbled on by mistake. And I didn't give a damn about Claudia Teodori.

We said goodbye to Teodori. Angelo put his arms around him. I gave him a cool shake of the hand.

No clubs last night. Too tired after the audition.

The telephone rings without stopping. I look at the alarm clock: it's seven o'clock. There's no one in the flat. My flatmate leaves at six thirty in the morning and comes back late at night.

I lift the receiver, my voice thick with sleep. Rossellini's ecstatic. 'Welcome on board, my beauty!' What's he on about? Has he gone mad? He's calling at this hour, doesn't care if I'm asleep, or if someone's sleeping with me. 'They're taking you on, Claudia! You're in!'

So there we are: my life's now his; he can call me any time he likes. But, anyway, I knew what kind of an environment I was stepping into: Deborah told me about the world of the new private channels. All outward show, beaming smiles and great friends ready to stab you in the back. A mix of appearances and dreadful manners. Ignorance wrapped up in fake culture, an indispensable union for getting on in there.

When I get back into bed, there's a gnawing in my stomach. I haven't eaten for twenty-four hours. I feel sick, and I haven't even started.

I don't like this world. I don't like having to diet, and I don't like those ugly know-it-all men with their stinking breath. I remember Mamma, her eyes focused on me. 'Don't be an idiot, honeybunch, you won't get a second chance.' Who cares, and what chance!

Then I remember Deborah. I killed her just as she was becoming famous. It's for her that I have to do this.

My brother had left the top-floor flat in Piazza di Spagna after Papa decided to divide his time between Milan and Palermo ten years ago.

But my father still owned the place and used it as a base from time to time.

Alberto had taken a small rented apartment with a terrace in EUR, the modern district built according to Mussolini's wishes, construction of which had come to a stop in 1942 because of the war, though it was finished afterwards. It was one of the few things I'd always liked about Rome when I went there as I child. I loved its grid system and majestic rectangular buildings, most of them built of white marble or travertine to commemorate the buildings of Imperial Rome.

At night there, with the workforce gone and everything at a stop, this part of Rome was simply beautiful, and even more so under the soft rain that tokened the start of autumn.

Alberto wasn't living with his girlfriend, Ingrid. They were both of the same mind: you get married first and then you live together. I knew he'd passed up going out with her in order to invite me over that evening. But I also knew that my visits gave him great pleasure. Whenever I called, and he wasn't out of Rome on business, my brother always invited me to supper. There was only one word of caution that evening: he was only preparing a quick *carbonara*.

There were photos of Ingrid everywhere, showing the life they enjoyed together: travel, culture, sport. Everything I'd never been interested in. One black and white snapshot in a wooden frame showed the Balistreri family on the Tripoli seafront. Alberto and myself as children, in English-style shorts and long socks. Next to me, Italia was staring at the sky. Next to Alberto, my father was staring at the ground.

We never spoke of that time. Nor of our parents. It was as if both of them were dead. Italia was, of course. Her body had remained in Tripoli, as she always said it should. *When I die, bury me here, in my own ground.* On the other hand, my father was alive and kicking as he oscillated between Milan and Sicily.

The *pasta alla carbonara* was exquisite. The pig's cheek was crispy, you could just taste the egg and the pasta was cooked *al dente*. The chilled Frascati was the perfect accompaniment.

When I told him about Claudia Teodori, Alberto listened, as he always did, in his silent, concentrated and rational manner, making no comment. He served us a mozzarella and tomato salad and, to finish, ice cream. Only with the coffee did he ask a first question.

'What's this Commissario Teodori like, Mike?'

'Typical Italian middle-class, supposedly respectable. More worried about outward appearances than the reality, like everyone else in this country.'

He had a grappa in one hand, the other on my shoulder.

'All right, Michele. Let's just say that Teodori's simply a father who's worried about his daughter. And what's she like?'

'The worthy daughter of an Italian civil servant. Middle-class outwardly when it suits her, slut and social climber on the inside. She's now got it into her head to go for a career in one of these private TV channels.'

But Alberto wasn't listening any more. He was staring in disbelief at the television screen, which was switched on with the volume down. The expression on his face forced me to look at it, too.

We turned the sound up. The footage was from Palermo. A TV news extra. General Carlo Alberto Dalla Chiesa, the foremost driving force behind Italy's fight against the Mafia, had just been assassinated in Via Isidoro Carini, together with his second wife, Emanuela Setti Carraro, and one of his bodyguards, Domenico Russo.

It had been a military-style operation: four gunmen, two motorbikes and a car had come alongside the general's vehicle and opened fire with a Kalashnikov AK-47, a military assault weapon. Indeed, it was an out-and-out declaration of war: the Mafia against the Italian state.

Alberto and I watched the news without saying a word.

Our thoughts were travelling along different pathways, but arrived at the very same man.

This is Italy, Commissario Balistreri. The country your father dragged you to.

Monday, 13 September 1982

We're having supper, after my debut on Extra TV reading the children's bed-time story. Rossellini's staring at the television screen: RAI 1's evening news is on. The newscaster wears the usual serious face, assumes the usual gloomy tone of voice, saying they've arrested some guy called Gelli in Geneva.

'Better this man with his P2 masonic lodge than those Red Brigade pillocks with their P38s,' Rossellini groused as he devoured his tiramisu.

Then he took my portion away.

'Stick to your diet, Claudia, and make sure you go to the gym every day. You've got to lose ten kilos. As soon as you have, I'll introduce you to someone I have in mind.'

'But why have you got me into this, if I look fat to you? If I lose ten kilos, I'll be nothing but a skeleton.'

'Your face is very beautiful, and your eyes are wonderful. But the fat flattens you out, and the television screen accentuates it. Makes you have a pancake face. Instead, your eyes should shine out above your cheekbones and the dimples in your cheeks. Just like Audrey Hepburn. They should stand out from the screen and nail the viewer. Trust me.'

His breath and his manner are always the same. He's always trying to make me feel lacking: a woman without looks is like a car without wheels.

Incomplete and alone. But he's my safety anchor, my guide against the wolves of this world.

For the moment, he confines himself to breathing his stinking breath over me and holding my hand on the table. In order to make anyone who sees us together, and me as well, know that I'm already his.

Saturday, 18 September 1982

The report from the two apostles was tragically clear. Claudia Teodori had made her debut as a presenter on Extra TV. I couldn't believe it.

She must have slept with one of the directors on the selection board. Perhaps the producer as well.

I was again summoned to Teodori's home, as if I were a private investigator on his payroll. Teodori was in his armchair, sitting in front of the TV with the sound off. His cough was worse, and he was running a temperature. Pietro was sitting by his side, administering water and medicine. Paolo was sitting at the desk in front of his pointless computer, into which he entered everything.

I tried to keep it simple, but the business was becoming complicated. It was getting very difficult for these two retired men to keep following her. I couldn't see any dangers on the horizon, except for the one that Teodori feared the most. In that world, his daughter could sleep with a hundred guys, who would then simply chuck her away like a lemon squeezed dry.

Apostle Peter already had a clear idea.

'This Rossellini's a ridiculous figure, but he's inoffensive.'

'One of your intuitions, I imagine,' I replied forcefully.

'No,' Paolo interrupted from the desk. 'I've entered all the newspaper articles about him on the PC. I've checked all the reports. Nothing. He's a bit of a shit, but his record's clean.'

'Excellent,' I said. 'Then there's no problem.'

'The problem could be subsequent developments,' the Apostle from Capri went on, looking at the screen on his gadget as if it were the Oracle of Delphi.

Teodori coughed.

'What Paolo means is that, according to his analysis, the girls Rossellini takes an interest in then get passed along to others.'

'All right,' I promised, getting up, 'if anything happens, I'll see to it. But until then, we'll carry on as we have done.'

Tuesday, 21 September 1982

Rossellini still hasn't tried it on. It was the same with Deborah. Perhaps he wants me to think he's impotent so I'll lower my defences, I'll start to trust him and rely on him. Then I'll tell him about my weaknesses, recognize my imperfections.

I know I still need him for a while, but he can forget about the rest. After the first broadcasts, he showered me with advice, comments, criticisms. Do this, do that. Sometimes he's right, but mainly what he says is rubbish. He only wants to feed my insecurities and increase my dependence on him.

Now they're giving me 100,000 lira a day. A huge sum. All I do is read out the bedtime story and the news.

There's still no talk of me appearing in a variety show, even though I know how to speak and act, but I'm not so good at singing and dancing yet. Reminding me of what I'm not good at is all part of the game. Besides, the girls on those shows aren't there only because they know how to dance – they have to be good at another kind of dancing as well. But that's fine, Mamma. My turn'll come.

Wednesday, 22 September 1982

The sun was finally safely behind clouds and you could breathe again. And thank the heavens as well that the reports from the two apostles gave no cause for Teodori to worry and remind me of my duty.

I continued to dedicate more time and energy to poker and women than to Anita Messi. Besides, forty days after she was found, her university still hadn't deigned to reply to our questions.

There were no other clues to go on. Or perhaps there were, but I had no desire to find them. I had ordered Capuzzo to carry out no more investigations. Every so often, he would refer to 'that poor dead girl', and I made no reply. I knew that, sooner or later, Homicide would take the case over.

It was only that chopped-off finger and the smell of ammonia in the room that aroused any crumb of interest in me.

But I didn't want to exert myself. The case would soon be passed on to someone else, which is exactly what I wanted.

Thursday, 23 September 1982

The big moment comes. Rossellini creates a small role for me in a show as walk-on assistant to the presenter. He's not one of the very famous ones from the RAI, but not an unknown either.

I have to put up with Rossellini for supper every evening now, after the broadcast. Then he takes me home in the Lancia Beta coupé that makes him feel so young. Every time, he waits to see if I'll ask to go to his house, as he's too chicken to suggest it himself and too conceited to risk a scornful laugh of refusal. But I'm waiting for him to make the first move. Yesterday at supper came a turning point. Tomorrow, he says, there'll be a special guest on the show. You'll have your big opportunity, Claudia. Subtitle: thanks to me, your mentor.

Dino Forte's one of the top presenters on the RAI, along with Mike Bongiorno, Pippo Baudo and Corrado. He's Television with a capital 'T'. The television of the Sanremo Festival and Canzonissima, the variety show that attracts millions of viewers and publicity, the kind of broadcast that brings entertainment into the homes of millions of Italians with style and flair, but now finds it has to compete with the new aggressive and unscrupulous private channels.

Forte's handsome, elegant, impeccable and the secret heart throb of middle-aged women. But he's a confirmed Catholic, and a very serious one, too. His wife teaches catechism and he's apparently absolutely faithful to her. He arrives in the studio five minutes before we go on air, accompanied by his secretary, who's a short and fat but dignified lady, ten years his senior.

In the studio, he's received with applause, and there's an embarrassing climate of expectation behind the scenes.

He sits himself down in a corner of the production room to wait his turn, looking absently at the live broadcast and chatting to the fat lady. I know he's over there; perhaps he'll glance at me, perhaps say a word to me. Not that I really give a damn about him or the rest of them.

Halfway through the show, he comes down to us mere mortals while I do my brief sketch with the presenter. My mind's on Mamma and the cine film she would have made of me in the same studio as Dino Forte. Pure, unadulterated joy.

But the only reason I'm here is Debbie. She worked with Dino Forte. She spoke well of him, as a great pro and a true gentleman. Then nothing more. She had already been there and was a lot further on when I killed her.

I'm not sure how well the sketch comes across. By now, it's routine. Acting comes as naturally to me as lying. I can feel Dino Forte's eyes on me, and I don't force the part. He doesn't like to see people doing that, any over-the-top mannerisms. Debbie told me this as well.

When it's over, I don't turn to look at him. Nor do I go and pay my respects at the end of the show. I hide away in the dressing room I share with Extra TV's other announcers.

After a while, Rossellini comes in, all excited.

'You went down well, Claudia, they liked you. I knew they would.'

'Who liked me?'

'She did.'

'Who's she?'

'The fat one. The one that does the choosing for him.'

Then Dino Forte's secretary comes in and asks for my phone number. Just like she did with Debbie. All courteous and professional.

Friday, 24 September 1982

Bad news always has company. Pietro's report noted Dino Forte's presence in the studio the previous evening. He could see there might be developments. I prayed there wouldn't be.

Much more serious, on this grey, rain-filled morning, was the news from the examining magistrate. The Flying Squad's homicide section was still under strength, and so I had to continue dealing with the Anita Messi case.

Unwillingly, I called Capuzzo in and explained the situation to him in funereal tones.

'Oh, so we can get on with it, then? Aren't you glad, Dottore?'

'We'll just do a little bit, Capuzzo. First of all, check the files of the police and the Carabinieri to see if there are any similar cases of mutilation.'

He looked contrite.

'I already took the liberty, Dottore. You know, there's been little to do in the past few days. And it still pains me that this poor girl hasn't had any justice.'

He took no notice of my orders. Too high a sense of duty.

I let him describe the results of his investigative efforts. All useless, as I imagined. No other cases had emerged from the archives.

There was plenty of sexual mutilation, heads cut off, even whole arms and legs, and many hands, of course, so as not to leave any fingerprints, but no body with only a single finger or a toe removed. Of course, that was among the bodies that had been found.

I dismissed Capuzzo, asking him to take no more initiatives.

The clinical way in which this mutilation had been carried out suggested a person already experienced in killing in this way. But leaving the mutilated body out in the open in such a casual manner argued for the absence of any previous killings, otherwise the murderer would have tried to conceal the body.

He's already done things like this. And yet he wasn't worried about leaving Anita Messi's corpse out in a field. When two facts contradict each other, one of them is false. Or else there's a third element that can explain everything.

This contradiction pushed me into taking a risky decision.

In the afternoon, I called Gianni, a journalist friend who worked on the crime pages of Rome's biggest daily. In the bar below my office, I offered him a coffee, but he opted instead for a cappuccino and large cream bun.

'A cappuccino and a cream bun at this time of day?'

'And you with your martini and cigarettes? I'd rather be overweight than have lung cancer or cirrhosis of the liver.'

I let it drop, and told him about Anita Messi's amputated middle finger.

'That's disgusting, Michele. Now my bun won't go down very well.'

'But can you write something about it, this finger?'

A trickle of cream was running from the corner of his mouth and down his chin.

'OK, Michele, I get it. You want me to write something about it. But what d'you expect from it?'

I didn't exactly know. The killer wasn't worried about the missing finger. We'd kept the information secret, and nothing had come of it. Revealing it now wouldn't compromise the investigation.

'Just write the thing, Gianni. And go on a diet – it's disgusting the way you eat.'

Saturday, 25 September 1982

For once, the phone rings at an almost decent hour. It's eight in the morning. It's Dino Forte's secretary. The great man wants to see me this afternoon.

I pick the same clothes and the same make-up I wore at the start of the month for the first TV Extra audition. Plus an old raincoat, as it's raining.

I take the bus to his beautiful apartment overlooking Piazza Navona, right in front of Bernini's fountain. The square's full of tourists and people with nothing better to do trailing about among the bars, stalls and portraitists.

I take the stairs up to the top floor. The overweight secretary opens the door and takes me into the living room, where Dino Forte's at work, on his feet, watching the recording of an American variety show. He's well-dressed, with a light tan from a sunbed and his hair beautifully cut. He would be handsome, if he weren't such an old man. But the mammas all like him, and they're the ones who watch him.

He greets me warmly, then goes back to watching the show, while his secretary explains the situation.

Every year in June, the RAI holds auditions for new faces. But there's now an extra one at the end of October.

I know the one he means. Debbie told me about it. The legendary Fiera Milano! It was the supreme hurdle, and extremely difficult to get into, as it was by invitation only. And even more difficult to pass. Little smiles, winks at the bosses, and having a word put in for you didn't mean a thing. Either you were the best, or you didn't get in.

All the top presenters like Dino Forte create a small stable of candidates, which they take to Fiera Milano, and then later use the ones selected in their TV shows and the live shows they take around the clubs. I can be part of his team on the condition that, for a whole month up to the auditions, I prepare for it under his guidance. And no time off.

Forte says to me, 'Fiera Milano is a once-in-a-lifetime opportunity. Normally, you need months of lessons, Claudia. But you've already taken courses on your own. We have the time now to correct the errors, but you must put your whole life into it. Are you ready for that?'

Am I! This speeds up this whole disgusting business a great deal. I'm now well ahead of Debbie in time.

Gianni did a great job, with a well-placed piece among the crime pages.

'From privileged sources, we have learned that . . .'

The article focused on the fact that Anita Messi's middle finger had been cut off. There was also another supporting piece, which gave the opinions of various presumed experts: psychiatrists, crime writers, criminologists.

Next to the article was an unexpected and unwelcome photo of Commissario Michele Balistreri, 'who is conducting the investigation with meticulous care and patience'.

So I could enjoy a day of total relaxation. At one in the morning, I was in the Duetto, driving home along the Tiber after a Saturday night's poker. The day's rainfall that heralded autumn, combined with the reopening of the discos, was having its effect. The streets around Campo dei Fiori were flooded and the night traffic was going crazy, with horns at full blast, and with heated insults and finger gestures being exchanged from one car to another.

While I was stopped at a traffic light, trying to distance myself from the chaos, I saw a girl staggering along the side of the road. Behind me, two guys in a Porsche convertible came up alongside the pavement with Barry White's music blasting out so loud it must have been audible as far as the Coliseum.

'Hey, nice little tush there, wanna ride?'

The girl certainly did have a nice little tush. But she looked to be a minor, and as high as a kite. I got out of the Duetto and went up to the other car. The two guys didn't look ideal company for her. Long hair, three days' beard – hard men from the city slums. In recent years, Rome had become full of these characters. Born into poverty in Rome's Magliana, Val Melaina or Centocelle districts, they decided on the get-rich-quick life at the cost of killing each other off in order to gain a place and respect. Thanks to them, you could now even buy cocaine outside church after Mass.

'What you want, dickhead?' announced the guy at the Porsche's wheel.

'The young lady doesn't need any help, thank you kindly,' I said, with a decidedly insincere politeness. The language and my tone were just right to get me decked by these two.

Unsteady on her feet, the girl now stopped to watch us, hesitantly leaning up against a tree. When she turned round, I could not only confirm that she had a nice backside, but also that she was definitely on the young side.

The two men got out of the Porsche.

'And who's to say whether she needs help or not?'

'I'm her boyfriend,' I said, my voice full of concern. Then I made a gesture to the girl, pointing to the Duetto. 'Go on, get in the car.'

I realized too late that she wasn't Italian, and hadn't understood a word I'd said.

'*You what?*' mumbled the girl in English.

The two men stepped forward. One had the Fascist two-headed axe tattooed on his biceps. I'd given years of my life to that symbol,

first in support, then fighting against it. Seeing it displayed as a kind
of fashion accessory made my blood boil.

'Your "girlfriend" doesn't understand a word you say. Now fuck
off and be quick about it,' the guy with the tattooed biceps said.

I had only two things to take care of: one, make sure it was they
who let fly first and, two, that I left no permanent mark or damage.
Provoking them was simple. I pointed to the tattoo.

'You really believe in that bullshit?'

For a moment, they looked at each other in disbelief. I had to
be out of my mind. But even they had a limit, and I had gone way
past it.

I niftily dodged Tattooed Biceps' slow, heavy blow and, as he staggered forward after losing his balance, I performed a half-pirouette
and gave him a kick in the stomach that sent him reeling back into
the Porsche. While he was busy throwing up his beer, the other one
took out a knife.

You have to identify yourself, Mike.

It was important that the girl wouldn't be able to testify that I'd
had all the time in the world to say I was a *commissario di polizia*. But I
could benefit from the fact that she didn't know the language.

'Come on, let's see what you can do, then.'

But the guy suddenly stopped himself.

'You're a cop, aren't you?'

I was screwed. And beside myself.

*First Claudia Teodori, now this nobody from the slums. This damned
country's given me the face of a flat-footed cop.*

He put away his knife and got in the Porsche. He helped the guy
with the Fascist symbol into his seat, and they set off at top speed.

I went up to the girl. She looked at me with staring eyes and dilated
pupils. I had to make myself understood in a simple manner.

'German?'

'American. From Chicago,' she mumbled.

'Your hotel?'

She shook her head, confused. 'Can't remember . . .'

'ID?'

'In hotel.'

Wonderful, Balistreri, what now?

'Get in my car,' I said, holding her up so she wouldn't topple over.

I switched the siren on and crossed the whole of the pedestrian area, making my way through the young men with beer bottles and young women dressed as if they were dancers on an Extra TV show. Half an hour later, I was helping her into my apartment. I pushed her head under the kitchen tap and made her swallow a good deal of black coffee. Then I showed her my double bed.

She had come to herself a bit and was now frightened. 'Please, don't try to fuck me.'

It was then that I could smell her breath. Beer and ammonia. The same smell that had been hanging around Anita Messi's room. I let her stretch out on the bed and held her hand until she fell asleep. Then I threw myself fully dressed on to the sofa.

My last thought before collapsing into sleep was that smell of ammonia. It was becoming common in Rome. All too common, in fact.

The following morning, the young girl was still asleep when I went out. I left a note with my number: 'Call me if you can't remember your hotel.'

The apartment is silent. My flatmate still hasn't come home. Who can I tell about Dino Forte and the Fiera Milano? My father? I couldn't even mention it. It was only Debbie I'd been able to confide in.

That wretched smell of ammonia keeps coming back to me.

The first time I caught it on your lips, I didn't understand. And you said you'd eaten a yoghurt that was off. Today, while Dino Forte was speaking to me, I sniffed his breath, his house, his furniture. Nothing.

But I'll find him, Deborah. I'll find the ammonia man.

Saturday, 2 October 1982

Unfortunately, it wasn't raining any more and it was one of those October days when Rome fights back against the end of summer. When I got to the station, Capuzzo was typing out a report.

'There's a letter for you, Dottore. It's on your desk. Plus the usual report from Paolo.'

I entered the office, and the first thing I did was switch on the air conditioning and draw the blinds. Too much heat and light.

I read the report on Claudia Teodori straightaway. This time, Paolo was more succinct. Claudia had been to Dino Forte's home. Other people were there, of course. He didn't know what they'd spoken about, but would find out.

Then I picked up the letter. It was a normal brown envelope with my name typed on it:

Signor Commissario Michele Balistreri
Commissariato Vigna Clara
Roma

I immediately noticed the stamp with Colonel Gaddafi's image on it. I told Capuzzo that I didn't want to be disturbed. I slipped the

Leonard Cohen cassette Laura Hunt had given me years before into the tape deck and flopped down on to a chair. Then I poured a shot of Lagavulin and lit a cigarette. Now I was ready.

Are you really ready, Mike? Do you know what you're letting yourself in for by opening that envelope?

The letter was typewritten on cheap, unheaded notepaper, and in English. A neutral language.

Signor Commissario Balistreri,

We receive the Italian papers in Tripoli and have come to know of Anita Messi and the amputation of the middle finger of her right hand. We should like to inform you of a similar mutilation found on the body of a young girl murdered in Tripoli on 3 August, 1969. A photograph of the victim's hand is enclosed.

Yours faithfully,
PO Box 150870

There was no signature. And no name of the victim. But there was no need. I knew that date very well. I still had the bloodstained handkerchief so that I would never forget.

Nadia Al Bakri's blood.

I looked at the photo. A young girl's right hand. Nadia. The middle finger cut off at the base.

It could only be an incredible coincidence. And yet, inside the dusty angle of the attic where my conscience was stored, the ghosts I'd relegated there were beginning to stir. It wasn't enough to have a cigarette, or a Scotch in the morning, not enough to say that strange coincidences did occur.

I read those few lines over and again, and each time they seemed both clearer and more obscure.

Anita and Nadia. What linked them other than the missing finger? Who was it who was writing to me? And how did they know about Nadia's finger?

Too many questions, and not a single answer.

It's impossible . . . I don't want to go back there . . .

That letter changed everything. I didn't want dissatisfied wives any more, or tourists looking for an adventure, or even to play poker with Angelo.

I could tell myself that it was only a coincidence. But Anita Messi, an insignificant girl with a Maradona tattoo, suddenly became the most interesting corpse in the world.

It's Saturday, but it's work as usual. Dino Forte's paying for it all, but it's going to be really gruelling. They show me the programme. From today, and every day, morning and afternoon, there'll be lessons in elocution, singing, dancing and acting. But at a completely different level than I'm used to. In the RAI, it's something else. It's not enough to have someone else pulling the strings. Here, you really have to know what you're doing in order to perform in front of a television camera.

And they'll be personal lessons from true professionals. In my case, we'll work more on the dancing and singing, at which I'm pretty hopeless. But I have to get to a minimum level so I can pass through the Caudine Forks of the Fiera Milano. There, behind closed doors, I'll have to perform in all three disciplines alone onstage, with only the heads of the RAI for an audience.

Every day, I'll do two hours of singing and four of dancing, and practise one song and one dance routine, the ones I'll perform at the Fiera Milano. It's already clear that, if they take me, it'll be for the acting, as they'll never let me dance or sing. But I have to get by in those, at the very least.

In elocution and acting, I'm already doing very well, so I'm a good step ahead there. I'll work on a little sketch with Dino Forte. I'll make a real impression in it. He's a real pro, an outstanding person who you never stop learning from.

At the moment, all he seems interested in is that I get through the Fiera Milano audition. Total commitment. Then we'll see.

The letter from Tripoli had shaken me up. I tried to calm down by leaving the police station and going for a drive through Rome in the open Duetto.

After the rain had come one of those marvellous days in which this city that I detested became irresistible, like a woman I knew when I was still a kid.

The American gahba *with a filmstar's name.*

I knew that this memory was also a poisoned fruit coming from those few lines typed in English.

And by whom? Friend or foe?

I ruminated on the coincidences you could glimpse between those few lines. Anita Messi had been kidnapped as soon as she left the place where she'd slept. The same as Nadia Al Bakri in 1969. Anita had been raped and killed in the following few hours. Just like Nadia. And, finally, Anita had had her middle finger cut off her right hand. Just like Nadia.

Mere coincidences? Am I imagining things?

No, that amputated middle finger was too clear a symbol. And this explained the apparent contradiction between a crime already committed several times before, and the careless way in which Anita Messi's body had been unceremoniously dumped.

The killer wasn't worried, because he'd committed no more murders after Nadia. And, here in Italy, no one knew a thing about Nadia Al Bakri's death.

Nadia had been killed thirteen years earlier, on a different continent. According to the official records, her killer – Jamaal the goatherd – had committed suicide. Case closed; no further investigation. And obviously nothing at all recorded in the Italian police archives.

No one would have known a thing about Anita Messi's missing finger if I hadn't tipped Gianni off. It had been his article with my photo that had sparked the letter from Libya.

Except that, in 1969, nothing at all had been mentioned about the missing finger on Nadia Al Bakri's body.

So who knew about this, apart from the killer?

I didn't even want to run the slightest risk that the Flying Squad would relieve me of the Anita Messi investigation now. I went back to the station and immediately called Capuzzo into the office.

'We must try to trace all Anita Messi's movements from the moment she landed in Rome until the moment her body was dumped near the Via Cassia.'

Capuzzo's eyes came out on stalks. My sudden proactive manner shocked him.

'Must we? Who?'

This was a typical bureaucrat's attitude. But also the honest response of a man who was willing but also knew his limits. Certainly, the Italian state didn't have the resources to offer any justice to this girl, who had made so many mistakes: she'd come and got herself killed in the middle of the summer holidays in Rome, and wasn't even Italian.

Moreover, through my fault, we'd lost almost two months of investigation time. I should have started the investigation much earlier, the day after the body was found. Capuzzo knew this very well, but he would never have dared criticize a superior.

'Let's do it like this, Capuzzo. You concentrate on her movements, from the airport up to the morning she was killed.'

He looked at me, disheartened. 'Dottore, I'll try, but you'll see that—'

I banged my fist on the table. I'd never done this before, not even during the Elisa Sordi investigation. It was the first effect of the letter from Tripoli.

Remember, Michele. Anger and revenge are the enemies of the truth.

★   ★   ★

I come home exhausted after the first lessons. Everyone keeps telling me again and again: you have to put everything into it: the RAI isn't Extra TV, it's the top of the game.

The dance instructor was categorical. I absolutely have to lose more weight before the Fiera Milano. If not, then it's goodbye to the RAI.

From now on, everything's out except white meat. Small meals six times a day so that my glycaemia stays low and doesn't activate that damned insulin that blocks my metabolism.

Rossellini wants me slim. Dino Forte wants me slim. The target audience wants me slim. My mother wants me slim. Only Deborah liked me as I am.

OK, I'll become as thin as rake, just like Deborah. And without the aid of ammonia.

Monday, 18 October 1982

Both my investigations were in the doldrums.

The apostles' reports were clear. For three weeks now, after meeting Dino Forte, Claudia had changed instructors, was working more intensively and had gone on a diet. Someone must have made her a promise, but they didn't know what. But, in compensation, her life had calmed down even more. No more shows at the Altromodo; only a few suppers with Rossellini. Then early to bed, and always alone. This meant that at least Teodori was leaving me in peace.

On the Anita Messi front, after chasing around for two weeks in vain, Capuzzo had lost heart. Nothing had come at all from the taxi drivers or the company that ran the coach links between the airport and the city. Anita Messi had arrived at the hall of residence a few minutes before midnight, so there was a gap of several hours between her landing and her arrival there, but no one knew where she'd been. The same for the following morning. Anita had left the hall of residence, looking like a tourist, at seven thirty that day. And, until her body was found at midday in that field next to the Via Cassia, no one knew what she'd done.

The fault was all mine. This kind of research has to be done immediately, while people's visual memories are fresh.

Then, on that rainy Monday afternoon, the examining magistrate passed on a letter from Anita's home university in Argentina. He'd received it a week before but, with the bureaucracy, that was the time it took for documents to arrive from one office to another.

It was the answer to the question we'd put to them at the end of August.

Why had they picked such a poor student for an international exchange?

It read: 'Contrary to normal procedure, the name of Anita Messi had been suggested to us directly by the host university, the College of the Sisters of the Virgin in Rome.' It was signed by the rector of the University of Salta.

I remembered Sister Domitilla, her courtesy and her excellent coffee.

Had she lied shamelessly to me? No, she knew nothing about this. A recommendation like this could only matter if it came from a high level. A very high level.

In the Anita Messi folder, I'd stored the glossy brochure for the College of the Sisters of the Virgin that Sister Domitilla had given me. I hadn't even glanced at it. When I opened it, I found on the first page an introduction to the college written by its head, the chancellor, together with an excellent photograph of him.

Monsignor Eugenio Pizza, or Don Eugenio to his friends, the priest with the wandering hands, was beaming out at me in that gentle, friendly way of his from behind gold-rimmed glasses. I remembered that, only a few weeks before, I had found his name in an article in *Secolo d'Italia*, the only newspaper I read, because it supported the Neo-Fascist MSI party. He was mentioned among the entourage of Paul Marcinkus, President of the IOR, the Institute of Religious Works: investigated during the course of inquiries into the failure of the Banco Ambrosiano, whose president had been found hanging under Blackfriars Bridge in London.

I dismissed Capuzzo and stared at the photo for a long time, assailed by a series of memories, all of which were unpleasant.

Another coincidence? Or another link between Nadia and Anita after the missing finger?

If there was one person I never wanted to see again, it was that despicable man.

I reluctantly phoned the College of the Sisters of the Virgin. Sister Domitilla told me that Monsignor Pizza was abroad, but she would forward my request to him. She called back after less than ten minutes. The cardinal would be very happy to meet with me the day after he returned from South America, at the end of October.

Saturday, 30 October 1982

This is the big day. Yesterday, we took the train to Milan. After the really tough pre-selection inside the Dino Forte stable, only five of us were left from the original ten. We know that they'll see about thirty in all and, after the Fiera Milano audtions, no more than five will get into the RAI. Only the best of the best.

But this extra out-of-season selection has a special purpose. The state-run RAI needed to push back against the attack of the private channels. Channel 5 opened fire with its Premiatissima *show. So the national channel now needs new faces, but less common and flirtatious ones, fresh young ones like mine. The little Audrey Hepburn of Italy.*

We're staying in a modest hotel looking out on the luxurious Grand Hotel Fiera Milano. That's where all RAI's top managers eat and sleep, from the director general to the channel controllers, the heads of programmes and the most important scriptwriters and directors.

My companions have been spying from the windows until midnight, hoping to catch sight of some big fish or other. I've no interest at all.

There's security outside the Grand Hotel Fiera Milano to keep the curious away and us at a distance, just in case some candidate attempts to gain a private nocturnal audition.

From my window, I saw Dino Forte arrive in a chauffeur-driven limousine with his secretary. His thick hair was beautifully coiffured and his casual dress impeccable. Two middle-aged women who'd been waiting for hours ran up to him for an autograph while assistants and porters were taking his bags inside.

Morning comes quickly. I barricade myself in the bathroom before my room-mate's up. I look at myself in the mirror. We're there. One metre sixty-five; fifty kilos, well distributed. Together with a white protein diet, the three hun-dred ab crunches a day and two hours of swimming first thing have had an effect. And how! My stomach's now flat, the skin around my pelvis clings smoothly to the fine bones of my slender hips. There are one or two small stretch marks, but the costume will cover those today. Creams and massage can see to them later. If they can. But they have to. I have to make it.

When they lead us to the dressing rooms, we look like a herd of cattle heading for the abattoir.

While they do my make-up I clear my mind of everything, close my eyes and put on the headphones of my cassette player to listen to the music for my piece, 'The Girl from Ipanema'. I sing it silently and go over the anticipation and ritardando notes as the music teacher's taught me.

Only a few minutes to go. Other candidates, eaten up by the waiting, peep through the curtain. It's dark in the large theatre, but they know that fifty pairs of eyes are lying in wait to study them and decide if their lives are to be a success or a failure.

My last thought's for Deborah, my dearly loved Deborah. Then I shut my mind off and go onstage. I can see Dino Forte in the front row. He gives me a little sign of encouragement. But I don't need it. I'm not scared at all.

In the last two weeks of October, nothing new happens to Claudia Teodori. And now I don't even read the two apostles' reports. I pick them up and throw them in the bin right away. And nothing new had surfaced about Anita Messi either, but that day I had my appoint-ment with Monsignor Eugenio Pizza.

It wasn't easy to find information about him. There was no men-tion of him in any of the newspapers, except those two lines in *Secolo d'Italia.* Two lines that linked him to Marcinkus and the Vatican Bank.

Fortunately, I still had my old colleagues in the secret service. After I had pressed them a great deal, they told me that the position of chancellor of the College of the Sisters of the Virgin was a purely honorary one and that, in reality, Monsignor Pizza had been occupied solely with banking since 1977. And one bank in particular: the IOR, the Institute for Religious Works, otherwise known as the Vatican Bank. It was also known cuttingly by many as 'God's Bank'.

He had no official office, but was known as an *éminence gris* behind the Vatican's finances, which he used to fund aid projects for the poorest populations of Africa and South America.

All told, a financial wizard and a saint. But Monsignor Pizza was also a hidden general in the fight between the Vatican and Communism.

In fact, my contacts in the secret services had him as the head of a project that needed enormous sums of American dollars for financial aid to Solidarity to help bring down Communism and the Soviet empire. And, indeed, only a few days earlier, Poland had banned the new trade union that espoused freedom.

From Piazza Venezia, I walked through the light drizzle to the Palatine. It still wasn't that cold, but the number of cars and mopeds seemed to double each autumn as if, after the holiday period, the Italians came back richer and more optimistic than before. Perhaps I was wrong, and perhaps my brother, Alberto, was right.

Capitalist democracy reduces inequality and leads to peace and happiness.

Fundamentally, though, I didn't give a damn. I wouldn't be here to see how an Americanized Europe fell to pieces when its people discovered that the combination of democracy with capitalism and finance was a deadly recipe as far as the weakest were concerned, a dictatorship of secret powers.

Sister Domitilla was even more polite and friendly than during our first encounter. Someone must have let her know that the shabby and brusque Commissario Balistreri had once been a pupil of Monsignor Eugenio Pizza, the college chancellor. She took me directly to the top floor, where the important offices were. The view from the windows was sensational: Piazza Venezia, the Roman Forum, the Coliseum and Quirinale Palace.

Don Eugenio was no longer wearing clerical dress. No worn cassocks and dusty sandals. He was wearing a suit of sober elegance with a light-grey shirt that looked made to measure. Only the white clerical collar in place of a tie distinguished him from the managing director of a bank.

He was forty-seven now, but his light-blue eyes had not changed and his smooth blond hair showed no sign of grey. Time had not drawn any lines or dark shadows under his eyes. On the other hand, Don Eugenio had always been a moderate man and quite content with himself. He came up to me with a smile, his arms stretched out to take me by both hands, as if I were just one of his ex-pupils and the son of one of his great friends.

I confined myself to a handshake, without even a smile.

'Take a seat, Michelino. This is a real surprise.'

His familiarity annoyed me, especially the use of 'Michelino', as if we were still sitting at our desks in Tripoli or in St Anselm's parish church.

Put the hate to one side, Michele. It'll cloud the visit. You're here to get at the truth.

'Something of a surprise for me as well, Monsignor. You would be the last person in the world I'd want to meet if I hadn't been forced to by my job.'

He continued to smile away, not losing his composure in the least; just as he used to do with Michelino, the unruly child who happened to be the son of such an important father.

'Ah, yes, your job, Michele . . . I know that you've become a policeman. Italia was right: she once told me that you had all the makings of a detective.'

Hearing my mother's name on his lips made that age-old anger rise up in me.

I looked at him scornfully.

'My mother was right about many other things. If Italia was alive, perhaps you might not be here today.'

Even if it was only for those photos of Nico, which had gone missing.

'God will be the judge of that, Michele, not you.'

Careful now. Remember he's doing this on purpose; it's his way of controlling you.

'You betrayed God that day with Nico. If God really exists, you'll end up in the pit of hell.'

He shook his head, as if dealing with a pupil who was a bit slow.

'If God exists, Michele, and that remains to be seen, well, I'm sure he'll accept a little imperfection. We are mere mortals, while perfection is an attribute of the divine.'

OK, the time for hypocrisy's over. Now he's strong enough to say what he's always thought.

'I look after money, Michele, always have. I help finance poor countries and charitable works.'

Of course you do. And in your spare time you also help fund the enemies of Soviet Communism. It's nothing much, simply a hobby, like going trout fishing.

'Through the IOR bank?'

He was determined not to reply to this particular point.

'Michele, there are hundreds of millions of people living below the poverty line, suffering from drought, famine and disease, and whose children have no life expectation. It requires a vast quantity of money to intervene with aid.'

'Even at the cost of using the dirtiest money in the world?'

'The world is what it is. The kickbacks from petroleum companies to politicians are mixed in with Mafia drug money and the vast financial scams of the gentlemen in suits and ties who sit in sky-scrapers. In a bank, they all become indistinguishable. I take them to where they can at least be used for good works.'

'So you're a general in the ranks of the good, then?'

Monsignor Eugenio Pizza raised his eyes for a moment to the crucifix.

'Goodness doesn't consist in being perfect, Michele. If God wanted us perfect, I'm afraid he'd find himself alone in the kingdom of heaven.'

There was a photograph in a silver frame on the large mahogany desk. Monsignor Pizza in his cassock, next to Paul Marcinkus. Behind them, the Palace of Sixtus V, the Papal Palace, and next to them, clearly visible, the round tower of Niccolo V, headquarters of the IOR, the Vatican Bank.

Don Eugenio looked at his watch, as if to say that the preliminary chat was over.

'And so, Mike, you're here on official duty, about the business of Anita Messi.'

And of Nadia Al Bakri, Monsignor. But this I can't tell you, not straightaway.

I showed him the letter from the Argentinian university. He gave it a quick glance.

'Fine, Mike. You know that this is purely an informal chat between old friends. So, fire away. I'll answer you if I can and deem it proper to do so.'

'Monsignor, my investigation is into a homicide. If I'm not happy with your answers, then the examining magistrate will present the questions to you formally and it could be that several newspapers might be interested in writing a piece about it.'

He stared at me with those blue eyes and gave me his good-natured smile.

'Only Communist newspapers attack the Church in this country, Michele. Have you become an informer for the Communists? I thought your ideas were of another persuasion.'

I ignored this. I had no intention of discussing politics with this pretend cleric.

'Can you tell me who put forward Anita Messi's name for an exchange?'

Without hesitation, he said, 'Certainly, Michele, I did.'

'You did? And why was that? This wasn't the usual procedure, and Anita wasn't exactly a good student.'

He pointed to another photo on the desk. A smiling Monsignor Pizza in the middle of a group of South American Indians.

'I travel a lot to South America, Michele. It's an important continent for the Church, but it's going through a difficult time. Dictatorships, revolutions, wars. And terrible poverty, especially around the big cities.'

'You mean to tell me that you recommended Anita Messi on humanitarian grounds? Did you know her? Did you know her family?'

I could see him pause to consider, as he used to in Tripoli. Weighing up the pros and cons. The truth was of no importance, only its possible consequences. And those of his evasive replies.

'I didn't know her, but I had been told of her. She was an orphan; her parents had been extremely poor. She had only an aunt, who didn't even live in Argentina. Anita was a very devout believer.'

Oh yes, she was. In Diego Maradona, rather than any saint.

'And who told you all this about Anita Messi, Monsignor?'

'Michele, you have simply no idea how many people I meet on my trips and how many requests I receive. How can I possibly remember who spoke to me about Anita Messi?'

'I gather you have recommended many other girls besides Anita Messi?'

More silence. More weighing up of the pros and cons.

'Of course, several – I don't know, perhaps a few, perhaps many.'
Now came the delicate question.

'So Anita Messi was recommended by you. I imagine that she came to see you straightaway to thank you as soon as she arrived in Rome in mid-August.'

He thought about it, just for a moment.

'No, there was no reason to do so. I've never met Anita Messi.'

Are you sure? Were you in Rome on that 14 August, Don Eugenio? And whereabouts were you?

These were questions I couldn't ask him. Questions I couldn't ever ask him.

I was in a blind alley, as I always was with this man. To reopen the game, I'd have to tell him about Anita's and Nadia's missing middle fingers. But I knew I'd have to keep that card covered, at least for the moment.

Don Eugenio again looked at me as if I were a pupil at secondary school.

'I've followed your ups and downs in Italy, Michele.'

Of course you have – you people always know everything.

'I, on the other hand, had forgotten all about you, Monsignore.'

'How many years is it since you were in touch with your father?'

'Quite enough. And it'll never be enough. But I'll find out the truth one day.'

Don Eugenio got up. We were going no further than this point.

'I imagine you're not referring to Anita Messi, Michele. You haven't changed a bit. Not yet. But time will see to that.'

Yes, Monsignore. Time will see that the truth is told. And separate the traitors from those betrayed. And I'll be there to witness it.

I'm back in Rome. I slept a lot on the train. The greater the distance from Fiera Milano, the more I was convinced that it was too hard a selection process and they'd never take me. Ever.

And yet, between waking and sleep, it was my mother up in the heavens who told me. It went well, my lovely, my honeybunch, my everlasting joy. You've done it. Your life will now be a dream. Poor Mamma. Poor, deluded Mamma.

The phone's ringing as I open the door to the flat after going up four flights of stairs. I'm out of breath as I pick up the receiver.

Rossellini is beside himself, as if he'd passed the audition himself.

'A triumph. Only four of you got through: two girls and two boys. And you were the only one from Dino Forte's stable. You'll do the new Saturday-evening variety show with him. Two weeks of rehearsals beginning Monday, then broadcasts start the middle of November.'

I put the receiver down. It starts to ring again straightaway. I pull the connection out. I could eat a horse. I've got a terrible craving for a pizza, a beer and, more than anything, a joint.

Don't ruin everything, darling.

I can hear my mother's voice, reassuring and accusing at the same time. The voice she used when she caught me in the kitchen scavenging for biscuits.

Tuesday, 2 November 1982

The apostles gave me the news on the phone early in the morning, waking me up in fact. They must have known that I didn't read their reports any more.

Claudia Teodori passed the Fiera Milano audition and would be Dino Forte's assistant on the new Saturday-evening variety show starting in two weeks' time.

As soon as he knew the outcome of the Fiera Milano, Teodori summoned me via Pietro and Paolo to his home. I went straightaway, to put my mind at rest, Angelo Dioguardi offering to come with me.

Teodori had deteriorated. His hands were trembling more, his cough was almost continuous, the yellow tinge to his eyes more accentuated.

And yet he listened to the whole of Pietro and Paolo's report with great attention, because Claudia meant everything to him.

'Your daughter's obviously got bags of talent,' Dioguardi told him, meaning it kindly.

Of course she has. For giving the right people the right favours.

Teodori spoke after a fit of coughing. His voice was weak and slurred.

'You must take steps now, Balistreri. Try to get to know this Rossellini and find out what Dino Forte has in mind. He worries me, this Forte, no matter how respectable he seems.'

'Pietro and Paolo'll have to see to it. I'm in the middle of a murder investigation, Teodori.'

Angelo shot me a look and arranged a plaid rug over Teodori's legs, even though the room was well heated.

'Are you feeling cold?' he asked him.

'No, a bit of a temperature, but let's not lose any time over that. You must see to Rossellini personally, Balistreri. You promised me. Pietro and Paolo are too old to stick close to Claudia in those circumstances.'

'And who'll see to the Anita Messi case?'

He coughed a great deal, and then smiled.

'I see that you've finally decided to take it seriously. It does you credit, but how come?'

He was old, with one foot in the grave and deeply concerned about his daughter. At least the back-story might distract him for a while. I told him the events of August 1969 and about Nadia Al Bakri and the Tripoli letter, as if I'd known about Nadia's middle finger all along.

Teodori listened, totally absorbed, open-mouthed, like a child hearing a fairy tale. Angelo, Pietro and Paolo also listened closely while I related the part of my own history: from Nadia's death, up to the presumed suicide of Jamaal the goatherd and my mother's mysterious note.

They knew each other. Check m.

At the end, the first to speak was Apostle Peter. He was much less hostile than usual.

'You think the two cases of Nadia and Anita are linked, then?' he asked me.

'There's only the missing finger to connect them,' I replied. But that wasn't the only thing. There was another element, and that was Monsignor Eugenio Pizza.

Apostle Paul was entering everything on his PC.

'There are other analogies, Balistreri.'

I looked at him, surprised. 'Says who? Your little electronic gadget?'

'Same amputation, knife wounds, strangulation. Same way of capturing the victim along the road as soon as they left the house in the morning. Same way of dumping the corpse in a place where it would soon be found.'

Teodori suddenly seemed to come alive. His hands were trembling less, his yellow eyes less watery.

'Please, Balistreri, see to Claudia. Get closer to Rossellini, see what kind of a man he is. In exchange, Pietro, Paolo and myself will try to find out something about Nadia and Anita.'

Perfect. For help, I could now count on Capuzzo, two guys in retirement and a dying man.

Friday, 12 November 1982

It's been ten days of continuous, tiring rehearsals. As far as professionalism goes, there couldn't be a wider gulf between the RAI and Extra TV. But I've had no problems. Dino Forte's the kindest of men, but he always keeps himself aloof. He's the king of the stage, and I have to remember that. All the time. He encourages me, corrects me, but never lets his eyes dwell on me.

Tonight, though, Rossellini wants to show me off at the Jackie O, the evening before the new little star makes her debut on the RAI. His little Audrey Hepburn. If I go to this discotheque with him, people will think I sleep with him. And his reputation will grow. But that's fine with me.

The real nuisance is Michele Balistreri. He called me; he's dropping in on the disco to wish me luck, he says. As if I cared anything about that arrogant shit wishing me luck. No, he's coming to keep an eye on me, on orders from Papa.

I open the drawer to get the flat cardboard box and the photograph. Deborah and I on the pleasure beach in front of the big wheel.

I look at the other little box. Minnie's box. The death box. But I don't open that one.

The only way of getting to know Rossellini was to follow Claudia into her new social circle.

I parked the Duetto on the pavement and went into the Jackie O, jumping the queue by flashing my police ID.

The place was even worse than the dumps you found in Testaccio. There, you had the gays and the hip counter-culture smoking dope. Here, it was the Rome of the well-to-do, the young girls dressed up like sluts and vice versa, and small trays holding lines of cocaine.

Claudia was sitting with this Rossellini at a table in a private corner. He was a fifty-year-old with a spare tyre and long, scruffy hair, wearing a blue jacket ornamented by a sprinkle of dandruff. Beside him was his girlfriend, or something like that: a tall, slow-looking feline keeping her claws well in.

I sat down without being invited. Claudia looked at me askance but decided to smile and invent an introduction for me.

'Michele's my masseur at the gym.'

Nice fantasy, could well be true.

The tall creature's name was Tanya. Rossellini introduced himself by his real name. Then they went on with their conversation, as if I weren't there.

'It'll be a triumph for you tomorrow, Claudia. You'll see.'

The girl had lost an awful lot of weight. Dimples in her cheeks, slender hips, flat stomach. You couldn't say she wasn't attractive, but she was still a pathetic eighteen-year-old craving success.

'All down to you, Rossellini.'

He gave a royal gesture of assent, then turned to the tall girl. 'Now that Claudia's launched, I can see to you. We'll soon see to correcting all those defects.'

I saw Tanya turn her head away slightly to avoid his breath. 'Of course, with your help.'

Rossellini placed a hand on Tanya's thigh so as to let everyone know she was his property.

'If you'd like to go and dance, sweetheart, go ahead. I'll be watching you. At my age, I keep my movements to a necessary minimum, don't I, Claudia?'

Claudia made no reply, but she got up with him to greet a bunch of well-known faces. Actors, presenters, female assistants.

Tanya continued to stare at the dance floor, tapping to the beat with her long fingers. She spoke without looking at me.

'I did three hours of dancing lessons today. My legs are in pieces.'

She stretched one out under the table, then stuck an ankle on my knee.

'Perhaps you can show me how good a masseur you are. From the ankle to the knee, no more.'

Claudia and Rossellini came back and sat down. He was filling her up with advice for her debut while I was discreetly massaging his girlfriend's ankle and calf.

After a while, Rossellini decided it was time for him and the girl to leave. Tanya took her foot away and her bag fell, or rather, she let it fall. I crouched down to retrieve it and had time to get a clear idea of what was under the miniskirt. Something I could happily massage on another occasion.

When she shook my hand on leaving, she left a piece of chewing gum stuck to my palm with a piece of paper attached. On it was her telephone number. I hastily transferred it to my pocket, along with the gum.

'I'll join you at the Number One in half an hour,' Claudia said to them.

Then we were alone.

'So, well done, you. And all the best for your debut.'

'Well done you, as well, Commissario. You've made a good impression, I see. My father was right – you don't miss a trick, do you?'

Her tone was hostile, scornful.

'I don't know what you're talking about. And your father's condition's getting worse. Perhaps you should find the time to go and see him.'

'Perhaps I will, Commissario. But that's my business.'

'Your father's worried about the circles you're moving in.'

Her beautiful eyes glinted above her dimples.

'He should worry about having landed me with someone who screws every woman he comes into contact with.'

'Your father's got nothing to worry about. I prefer real women to wilful little tramps.'

She maintained her cool.

'You know, Balistreri, something awful must have happened to you as a child. Or else you wouldn't be such a shit.'

'Perhaps to you, as well. Or else you wouldn't hang around men like Rossellini in order to make yourself a little star. And you wouldn't happen to kill your friends out driving when you were over the limit.'

When she hates someone, her beautiful eyes grow crazy. She could kill me now.

I could have said something to open a bridge between us, make an effort to understand her. In the end, she was a lonely, mixed-up eighteen-year-old, and very soon to be an orphan.

No, she's just a little shit like all the others, ready to stab anyone in the back, even herself. Just like Laura Hunt.

Claudia rose to leave.

'You don't know a thing, Balistreri. Not a thing.' And she left.

I took out the piece of paper stuck to the gum. Yes, there it was, that faint smell of ammonia.

I called Teodori.

'I've just seen Claudia with Rossellini. I think your daughter's managing things really well. There's no need to worry.'

'Thanks, Balistreri. I'm also trying to help you with your investigation as well, remember?'

His voice was weak, long pauses between the words. I said nothing. Better to let him think he was still capable of something.

'I'll soon have something more to tell you about Anita Messi.'

I left him with the double illusion that his daughter was a respectable girl and that he was still a policeman.

Saturday, 13 November 1982

Via Teulada, just below Monte Mario, is a sacred site. It was in the studios here that Italian television was born and made such an important contribution to the spread of culture across the country. I've studied my script, been through the rehearsals and, without a murmur, accepted the hairstyle, make-up and costumes, which all seem unsuitable to me.

'You're extremely beautiful,' Rossellini tells me before we go live.

Don't disappoint me. *That's my mother.*

I love you so much. *That's Deborah, of course. Nothing from Papa. He'd never say a word.*

'He can't come to the show, Claudia, he's got a raging flu. But Angelo Dioguardi's taken him a small colour TV.' *That's what that arrogant Michele Balistreri told me last night at the Jackie O, making me feel like crap because I won't go and see my old papa.*

And yet I don't think Balistreri's a total idiot. If only he wanted, he could try to understand who I am. And perhaps he could try to understand why. And help me get it sorted.

Behind the scenes, I can see that smelly scuzz Rossellini hoping he can now get his just reward. Triumphant debut first, pay the bill later. A real gentleman. Nothing in advance. I wonder if that's the case with Tanya, the beanpole that played the idiot with Balistreri. Or will payment be demanded in advance with her? And I wonder if it was Rossellini who caused Deborah's ruin.

I feel a hand on my shoulder. It's Dino Forte. Groomed, made up, impeccable-looking in his calm assurance of being a star. He gives me a light caress, like an old uncle who's had you on his knee. Always caring and always professional.

'Just be yourself, Claudia, that's all you need to be.'

Fine words, already delivered to many others, including Debbie, and spoken with the mint in his mouth that he'll spit out before we go on air. Forte's a cautious and painstaking man. He knows how easily the acids of a fifty-year-old's stomach can create indigestion and halitosis. He protects himself, and he protects you. But these polite manners could be hiding the bastard that ruined Deborah.

'Nervous?' I ask him.

He looks at me, taken aback, and smiles. The debut girl asks him if he's nervous. I'm not, I'm as cool as a polar iceberg.

I'm just trying to find out if it was you.

Sunday, 14 November 1982

It was the start of another gloomy day, a grey sky full of driving rain. I woke up in a bad mood. And for several reasons.

Firstly, the amount of money I'd lost playing poker against Angelo Dioguardi, who, rather than concentrating on the play, was busy following Claudia Teodori's television debut, muttering enthusiastic eulogies of her as he won pot after pot.

Secondly, the Anita Messi investigation had stalled. Don Eugenio, alias Monsignor Eugenio Pizza, maintained that he hadn't seen her after she arrived in Rome. In over a month, Capuzzo had drawn nothing but a blank and, as a consequence, I was left in a blind alley.

Although I wasn't on duty that morning, I dropped into the station and found the letter to the examining magistrate from the rector of the Argentinian university. There was a telephone number included in the letterhead. On a hunch, I gave it a call.

Nothing doing. The great Italian state doesn't allow a police commissario to have a direct international line. I called in Capuzzo, who knew the bureaucracy's nitpicking procedures inside out.

'I must make a call to Anita Messi's university in Argentina.'

'You have to get the cost authorized, on the appropriate invoice, signed by the examining magistrate, and then call through the police switchboard.'

I looked at him aghast.

'And how much time do we need for the authorization?'

Capuzzo smiled at his own efficiency. This was his preferred ground.

'Following procedure, two weeks. Doing it my way, half that.'

The usual wretched Italian bureaucracy. Pitiless to those on the outside, but accommodating to those in the know inside.

'All right, Capuzzo. Do it your way.'

At that moment, there was a call and Capuzzo took it.

'It's a woman for you, Commissario, but I can't understand a word she says.'

I took the phone. 'Hello, Michele Balistreri.'

'I forgot hotel. By Tiber. Remember?' The young female voice was trying to speak in Italian.

That American girl. I'd completely forgotten.

I answered in English.

'Have you forgotten your hotel again?'

She gave a happy little laugh. 'No, that's OK, I'm in my room.'

She went on to say that she'd been struck by my courage in saving her from those two louts from the slums. And by my sense of propriety in not taking advantage of the situation that night.

She had been thinking about it for days and had finally plucked up the courage to give me a call. She wanted to repay me with a pizza.

It was Sunday, I'd had a bloody awful Saturday night, the TV had nothing other than the Spadolini's government resigning again over an argument between two ministers, it was raining cats and dogs and I had absolutely nothing on the cards. I accepted the offer.

Rossellini calls me at daybreak. In the newspapers, the reviews of the opening programme are enthusiastic, the critics praising Dino Forte's new discovery. Rome's own little Audrey Hepburn.

While I'm having breakfast, a huge bunch of roses arrives from Dino Forte. Then he calls me, full of congratulation. For the first time, he hints at an invitation to dinner. No rush, whenever he has an evening free. But I gather he wants to discuss work. Doesn't this obsessive workaholic have anything else in his head?

I drive the Fiat Panda to Verano cemetery, having finally got my licence, and take along the weekly TV guide Settegiorni di sorrisi e canzoni. *I rip off the cover with my photo on it and wrap the fresh roses in it, and place them on her grave.*

Well done, my lovely girl, well done. You'll become the most famous of them all.

I go over to the columbarium, where the niches for the cremated are. It was something that Deborah had told her parents on her eighteenth birthday.

'If I die, you have to cremate me.'

Her parents had laughed but, a few days later, she was dead. Through my fault.

I don't say a prayer. I only ask for forgiveness.

'Forget it, Claudia. Let it be. You won't change a thing.'

No, Debbie. If I've got this far, it's for him, and not for myself.

The girl's name was Kate, short for Kathryn. She came without any make-up, in a Harvard sweatshirt, jeans and trainers. She chose the pizzeria, obviously by now well acquainted with the city. It was one of those in Testaccio, where the *supplì* and the pizza are excellent and the tables always full of Romans rather than tourists. The conversation put my rusty English to the test, but I managed to get by.

'How did you find this place, Kate?'

'Two months in Rome, you make a lot of friends. I've been here since the middle of September. I'm studying the history of art and touring the whole of Italy.'

She'd already downed four beers, and I wasn't even sure she was old enough to drink legally.

'Friends who make you drink and smoke weed? Like that night along the Tiber?'

Give over, Michele. You're not her father.

Kate took another sip of beer. 'I can hold my liquor, Mike. And also take a joint. But, that night, they'd given me crack to smoke.'

The cocaine crystals you could smoke. Obtained by dissolving freebase cocaine in ammonia.

'Who gave it to you?'

So after playing the father, you're now the cop?

'Some guys in a piano bar. Look, OK, so you're a policeman, but you're not on duty, right? And a good-looking girl invites you out to supper. She's American and clearly available and yet, instead of courting her, you . . .'

We both burst out laughing.

'How old are you, Kate?'

'Twenty.' She was bluffing.

'Let me see your ID.'

'Oh no, not ID again. You know, you really are the cop tonight.'

She was a really likable girl, and pretty, too. But she wasn't my type. Too wild, too simple. And too young, still a baby.

It occurred to me that she might be the same age as Claudia Teodori. But Claudia was a different kettle of fish. Beside her, Kate seemed like a kid sister you took to the park.

'Anyway, I am of legal age,' Kate went on, 'and you Italians are so old-fashioned. At eighteen, we Americans are already very sharp.'

'I know. I've only known one eighteen-year-old American, and she was very sharp. Too much so.'

It struck her that I was suddenly serious. 'Too much so?'

'I don't know. Perhaps I was too young.'

'But you *are* young, Mike!'

Oh yes, a very old young man.

'It happened many years ago, Kate. I was twenty, she was eighteen. It was in Africa.'

She smiled at me. 'Is that why you're not interested in me?'

She was so likable: tender and really naïve. She had been running a terrible risk that night along the Tiber.

'Who gave you the crack to smoke, Kate?'

She looked at me, disappointed. She'd understood she wouldn't be having my scalp. Not that evening, anyway.

'I told you. Some guys in a piano bar where a lot of us go, American students, you know. They always hang out there, and they had a great stash of cocaine. I can take you if you like, seeing as you don't care to do anything more interesting.'

We took the Duetto and got there around eleven. It was behind Piazza di Spagna and, despite the clientele, had an Italian name, I Tre Peccati'; the 'three sins' were advertised by a neon sign featuring a stylized little red devil.

As we entered the smoke-filled bar, I realized it was the typical place for rich tourists out for adventures they could pay for. The three sins were obviously the traditional mix of ancient and modern: Bacchus, tobacco and Venus.

The place was already full, but I spotted them straightaway, sitting at a secluded table. The three delinquents from Barcelona who'd tried to lay hands on my two female friends and Angelo Dioguardi before the Italy–Brazil match.

Kate whispered in my ear. 'It's those three.' But I already knew. They weren't there to score, but to sell. And suddenly I remembered the Maradona tattoo on Anita Messi's shoulder. That was enough for me. We made a swift exit.

How boring the newspapers are! All the same, all saying the same things. So pretty, so clean, so normal.

It was that word 'normal' that annoyed me most. What was so normal about the middle-class values Mamma and Papa brought me up on? So that I would find a job and get a husband? They certainly hadn't hoped I'd have a friendship like the one I had with Deborah.

In fact, I did need a man. Not one for sex, of course. I don't want any of that. But I want to talk to one, someone who'll listen to me from the same point of view as the man who ruined Debbie. Someone who can help me understand who it was.

Certainly not an insensitive prick like Michele Balistreri. Although even he's better than the ignorant parasites you meet in this world based only on appearances; people who snort coke as easily as they clean their teeth.

You know who I want, Deborah? The friend of that shit. The one who came with him that first time to the Altromodo in August. The one with the beautiful name. Angelo. Angelo Dioguardi.

You should have seen how he watched the show, Debbie. You know, the one with the prisoners in the concentration camp and the kapo guards. Balistreri was smoking and yawning. But this Angelo was totally captivated. I even told Papa that he'd phoned to congratulate me. And he told me that he'd also met this friend of Michele Balistreri, who always helped him when his hands were trembling too much.

Poor Papa. He's got a dreadful cough. He told me it's only bronchitis.

Friday, 19 November 1982

Thanks to Capuzzo's extraordinary efficiency in dealing with Italian bureaucracy, I managed to speak to Anita Messi's university in Argentina less than a week on from the official request.

The dean of the theology faculty was as polite as he was brief and to the point.

Anita Messi had been enrolled at Salta University for two years. She was an orphan, her only living relative an aunt who lived in Colombia. She'd taken very few exams. A recommendation had arrived several months ago from the pontifical College of the Sisters of the Virgin, signed by the chancellor, Monsignor Eugenio Pizza.

In June, Anita had gone to Europe with two friends from university. They had made a tour of Europe, then she and her two friends had flown back to Argentina together. Anita had carried on to Colombia and, from there, to Italy. She had landed in Rome on 13 August, in the late afternoon . . .

. . . and was found dead there the following morning.

It was certainly strange that a girl without any obvious means could afford a trip to Europe, but it appeared she worked as a waitress and had put some money aside. As to the rest, she had her feet firmly on the ground and no dark secrets in her past.

The main point was this: why had Monsignor Eugenio Pizza recommended a student as academically poor as Anita Messi?

After rehearsals on the evening before the second transmission, we all went to eat in Prati, a district near the RAI headquarters.

Being under the watchful eyes of Rossellini and Dino Forte, I had nothing to drink.

I expected one of them to make advances on me. But nothing at all. Perhaps I had to make the move myself. Out of gratitude to Rossellini for his past help. Or to Dino Forte for my future career. But the difference between Rossellini and Forte is that one's a dreadful, boorish pig and the other a gentleman with cultivated manners.

I try to remember what Debbie told me. The little I knew of what she'd been through. I know where it started, I know who was around her and how it ended. All I need is the name of the ammonia man, the one Debbie simply referred to as 'Him'.

Sunday, 21 November 1982

I'd lost at poker again on Saturday night and woke up on Sunday morning feeling out of sorts. After reading the papers, my mood took another nosedive.

Claudia Teodori's photo was on the front pages of several dailies, alongside the ones of politicians. Italy couldn't come up with a new prime minister, but it had discovered a new star.

Teodori's call came at the end of the day, inviting me to come over after supper; it would be just the two of us.

I found him sitting in the armchair in a corner of the living room with a table lamp lit beside him and a plaid rug over his knees.

I was expecting to get a lecture from him.

'Look, I went to the Jackie O. Rossellini's a swine but, for the moment, Claudia's able to keep him at arm's length. I've found a contact to keep me up to date.'

A contact by the name of Tanya, whose long legs I massage from time to time and without the ban on going beyond the knees.

Teodori had a coughing fit. The table beside him was full of medicines. Pills, drops, creams. The smell of them filled the air of that respectable middle-class living room.

'This isn't about my daughter, Balistreri, but about Anita Messi. I promised you some help.'

Yes, help from an old bureaucrat on his deathbed. And what help could that be?

He handed me the brochure from the College of the Sisters of the Virgin. It was like the one that Sister Domitilla had given me.

'Turn to the last page, Balistreri, where it lists the institute's benefactors.'

And there was the first germ of a response to my question.

Why had Don Eugenio recommended Anita Messi?

The clue was staring at me, but I hadn't noticed it. Among the benefactors was the Nuova Banca del Sud. And who was chairman of this new Sicilian bank? None other than Ingegnere Salvatore Balistreri, now deemed a *cavaliere*, who had been knighted for his services to industry.

The man who was once my father. The man morally responsible, if not materially, for my mother's death. The man who betrayed 20,000 Italians by getting them kicked out of Libya.

It was for this reason that Teodori wanted to see me alone, to spare me the double humiliation of being both an incompetent policeman and the son of that man.

I could have told him about the ammonia smell, not only in Anita Messi's room but also on Tanya's chewing gum. But it would only have started him worrying. Rome was flooded with cocaine in all its possible forms, and this was surely just a coincidence.

I told him instead about the ammonia smell on the breath of Kate, and about the three Barcelona guys dealing at the Tre Peccati behind Piazza di Spagna.

Teodori listened for a while, then nodded off while I finished my story. At least, that's what it seemed to me.

I left the house and its medicinal smell as quietly as I could.

★　　★　　★

My flatmate's brought me the papers. The second transmission of the Dino Forte show's gone down very well.

I have ended up on the front pages, next to the politicians competing for the post of Prime Minister.

The television's new princess. Successor to the late, lamented Deborah Reggiani, her great friend. What an incredible story, guys!

I'm the daughter every parent wants to have and the girl all the young men want to marry. Yes, parents. Papa called me again to congratulate me. His cough's a lot worse. I think he's got more than bronchitis. Perhaps I'll go and see him.

Dino Forte's again mentioned having supper, without saying if it's to be alone or in company.

Perhaps something's beginning to move.

After visiting Teodori, I crossed the city in the Duetto to Garbatella. What with the rain and the end of the weekend, everything was quiet. Even the traffic alongside the Tiber was moving at a decent pace.

As soon as I was home, I lay down on the sofa with the windows open to the rain, accompanied by my cigarettes and whisky and Leonard Cohen playing on the stereo. I was faced with the gruelling task of again having to deal with the man who'd done away with my mother and caused me to flee the country of my birth.

Over the course of time, I had wiped away the memory of Ingegner Salvatore Balistreri, at least in his private role of being my father. The public role, I had tried to ignore as much as possible, which wasn't easy. Two years earlier, in 1980, the old Banca del Sud had, technically, become bankrupt. This would have left thousands of small savers destitute and thousands of employees without a job. And almost all of them in the poorest and most underdeveloped regions of the south, starting with Sicily itself.

But a group of southern businessmen had come up to save the

bank, led by one of the biggest names in Italian construction, Ingegner Salvatore Balistreri, who, in the seventies, had built up half of
Palermo, and all along the coast as far as Cefalù. The deal benefited
from generous funding from the state and included the remission of
thousands of millions in back taxes owed by the bank.

The favourable contacts Ingegner Balistreri enjoyed with politicians in Rome, in particular the Christian Democrat Party and one
of its most powerful members, the President of the Republic, did
nothing to harm the deal. Initially, the press on the side of the Communist opposition had gone up in arms, speaking of a sell-off and
favouritism, also alluding to 'possible infiltration' in the private part
of the capital raised for the investment.

No one ever used the word 'Mafia'. Many thought it, yet no one
dared to allege a connection with Ingegner Balistreri. His lawyers
were the most expensive and therefore the best in Italy. With a well-
constructed case for defamation, they would have made short work
of closing down a newspaper.

Only one small magazine, associated with the Far Left, mentioned
the fact that Ingegner Balistreri's four elder brothers were the owners
of hundreds of bars and state lottery concessions in Sicily and northern Italy. And that the eldest, Gaetano, nicknamed Tano, had been
on trial, accused of being the real brains behind the illegal betting
network that had taken over Italian football in 1980, using the thousands of outlets he had. This was in addition to the accusation of
Mafia-style criminal conspiracy, a cover for actual Mafia affiliation.
But excellent barristers had defended him and the accused was acquitted for lack of evidence.

At this point, an open letter from the Hon. Emilio Busi, rising MP
and star in Italy's Communist Party, was published on the front page
of Italy's most authoritative daily newspaper. Busi was the face of
'modern Communism', as its many supporters called it, or 'Communist capitalism', according to its detractors. The letter sang the

unconditional praises of Ingegner Balistreri, a man of huge capabilities and absolute integrity. It underlined his absolute non-involvement in any activity of his brother, who, in any case, had been acquitted of any wrongdoing. It was a harsh put-down of his comrades on the Left, who the same article defined as 'those who applauded the Soviet tanks in Budapest and Prague and the witch-hunting ideologues of a culture of eternal suspicion'.

And so the deal went ahead successfully. Papa and his friends bought the bank for very little and renamed it the Nuova Banca del Sud. And, that same year, Ingegner Balistreri received the highest decoration for services to industry from the President of the Republic and was named *Cavaliere di lavoro*.

Except that, when I was still working for the secret services, I discovered an internal SISMI memo containing the information that, in 1975, Emilio Busi had been a witness at the marriage of Tano Balistreri's daughter. No newspaper of whatever political stripe had ever mentioned this.

I now had several points of contact: a missing finger and three old friends in Tripoli, my father, Don Eugenio and Emilio Busi. Could they be purely coincidental? No, a single thread linked Nadia Al Bakri and Anita Messi.

And perhaps also my mother's death.

I knew that no evidence that could link Nadia Al Bakri to my mother had emerged from investigations, neither in 1969 nor today. And I knew as well that the irresistible desire to discover the truth about that death came not from a longing for justice but one for revenge.

Revenge creates a distance from the truth.

Indeed, I shouldn't start thinking about my mother's death again. That fixation could only distance me from the truth about Nadia and Anita. There were two things I could do about those deaths: follow the crack trail for Anita and write to Tripoli about Nadia. The first was a complex investigative procedure. The second attracted me more than it should. And it was this magnet in my conscience that frightened me.

You've done so much to make you forget, Michele. To put the memories and the pain to sleep. And no longer look over the edge of the abyss.

But I knew that only by looking at the bottom of that black hole would I find the truth. I had to have the courage and the strength to write to Tripoli.

Monday, 22 November 1982

The third man, the one I've been waiting for, presents himself even earlier than I'd expected. Dino Forte announces him during Monday's rehearsals after the second show in the series. His warm voice has a sarcastic edge to it.

'Giangiacomo Zingaretti wants to meet you. In a few days, when he has time.'

Then he adds several words without sarcasm, merely a slight note of anger. He's frightened of having his prize snatched away.

'Watch out for the red couch.'

I know very well who Giangiacomo Zingaretti is, as Debbie told me. He's the man who put the RAI where it is with variety shows.

Well-educated, from a good family and very powerful. Between him and the Director General it's difficult to say who counts the most. But, in the career of Claudia Teodori, it's certainly him. As it was for Debbie, too.

Almost two months had gone by. Every day since it had arrived, I'd thought of that letter from Tripoli and PO Box 150870 but had resisted writing.

But now there's the Nuova Banca del Sud in the picture and the man decorated for services to industry, Cavaliere Salvatore Balistreri.

That Monday in the police station, I thought about it all day and, still in my office, started to write at seven in the evening: by hand rather than typing it, and in the neutral language of English.

Dear Sir or Madam,

Thank you for your letter. Besides the missing middle finger, two other details have emerged that link Anita Messi's death here in Rome to that of Nadia Al Bakri in Tripoli in 1969.

The chancellor of the college where Anita Messi had come to study is Monsignor Eugenio Pizza, and it was he who recommended this student for the course in Rome. He says this was in answer to a request; he cannot remember by whom. Furthermore, among the benefactors of the college is the Nuova Banca del Sud, born of the old Banca del Sud, which was saved from bankruptcy several years ago by a consortium of public and private money put together by a group of southern businessmen. President of the Nuova Banca del Sud is Ingegner Salvatore Balistreri, who was decorated for his services to industry in saving the bank.

As a link between the two cases seems highly probable, finding the guilty party in one could mean finding the guilty party in the other. I will investigate the Anita Messi case in Rome. I hope you can do the same for Nadia Al Bakri in Tripoli. To that end, I am enclosing the notes I myself made a few days after Nadia Al Bakri's death. Although it has been a long time, you can perhaps complete them and fit them into the picture, or refute them.

With good wishes,
Michele Balistreri

I enclosed a photocopy of the old squared notepaper, but only the front, not the reverse with my mother's six words.

Salvatore Balistreri, Alberto and Grandad Giuseppe went out at six thirty, seen by Mike. They were at Don Eugenio's Mass in Tripoli by seven and at seven forty-five Salvatore was at the barber's, Alberto and Grandad at the market with Farid and Salim, who had been there since dawn.

Nico was at the market just before eight and together with Alberto took the Giornale di Tripoli to Salvatore Balistreri at the barber's. He then went to read the paper on the Waddan terrace (CHECK) until Don Eugenio arrived at ten and then Busi, who was a little late (CHECK BOTH).

Alberto and Nico came back with the van. At eight fifteen they left the gas cylinders at the Esso station to be filled and were back at the villas just before eight thirty. They parked the van in the Hunts' car port and were together in the villa having breakfast. Mike Balistreri joined them at nine twenty.

Nadia left at eight with Mohammed and they immediately went their separate ways. She went on foot to the villa; he took the pick-up past the olive grove and off to the office, where he remained until Italia came by to pick him up at two. When Italia called him at noon he wasn't there (CHECK).

Farid and Salim went fishing at two in the morning, as always. They were in the boat until dawn, then at their market stall. They were both there at eight, seen by Grandad, Alberto and Nico. At ten, they gave Mike the bait for the trolling. Mansur is almost certain they never left the stall.

Mike saw the three Hunts as they left together to go to the baseball game at Wheelus, and they returned about two, after the road was open again (CHECK).

Mike woke up early. He hung around for a bit, then went down and had breakfast with Nico and Alberto at nine twenty. The three then went to pick up Ahmed at the Esso station and went into Tripoli just before the road was closed.

Ahmed went out after Nadia and her father and walked through the olive grove to the petrol station, where he arrived, a little late. Nico and

Alberto had left him the cylinders and he waited there for them until a quarter to ten.

Karim felt ill and stayed in the toilet at home.

At nine a goatherd saw old Jamaal with Nadia near the oil-pressing shed. The muezzin was calling. Mike heard him just before going down for breakfast with Nico and Alberto.

I sealed the envelope containing my first letter to Tripoli. I wrote the address by hand: PO Box 150870.

Thursday, 25 November 1982

I leave the flat at six p.m., an hour before the appointment with Giangiacomo Zingaretti at the RAI HQ, my dress and make-up elegant, but sober.

Dino Forte keeps telling me the same thing, but without any malice.

'Remember, Claudia, you're a symbol for the whole family, with just a hint of sex appeal. If you become a sex symbol, we'll have to kill you off.'

November's at an end; it's raining and already dark. Tomorrow I've the last rehearsals, the day that the third show goes on the air.

For the first time in my life, I take a taxi. I'm now earning loads of useless money. I tell the driver to go to the RAI in Viale Mazzini. 'At the double,' he says to me.

When I get there, it's pouring down on the giant bronze statue of the Dying Horse, *a great sculptor's brilliant conception of art for a modern building. Four and a half metres high by five and half metres wide, it stands outside the RAI and became its TV symbol, an image I'd seen countless times while my mother whispered, 'That's where you want to be, Claudia.'*

On reception are two old porters in uniform, looking snooty behind the glass window. I whisper the name Giangiacomo Zingaretti. A quick glance, out of curiosity. They take my ID and in exchange give me a green striped card, as if it were a holy relic. On it is Giangiacomo Zingaretti's floor and room number.

The porters announce my arrival and point to the lift. I walk across the vast entrance with its small but beautiful garden of tropical plants and a fountain, just as Debbie described. A garden of Eden to remind you that here you're entering paradise.

No one accompanies me. I go up in the lift and find the office. In the small waiting room is Renata – the angular secretary who is quite obviously an old maid – with four other people, all actors of some importance that I've seen on the TV for years. They come there every day and wait. They're waiting for him, waiting to speak to him for a moment, only one moment, a couple of words with the great man who can decide if they'll have a new contract or have to rest for a little while, perhaps for a long while.

As soon as she sees me, the secretary leads me to the padded door of leather and mahogany.

'Do go in, Signorina Teodori, the director's waiting for you.'

As I cross the threshold, I feel the venomous looks of those waiting behind me. The office is large, the walls covered in wooden panelling. The furnishings are expensive, but are of the highest class. In contrast to Extra TV, the wealth here exudes culture rather than poor taste.

The large desk is overflowing with papers and photographs, including one of Zingaretti's wife and three children. In front of it are two brown leather arm-chairs. The far wall is all glass, the curtains in steel-grey vertical stripes, and gives on to Viale Mazzini.

Near the door are two banks of monitors set into the wall. What are all those doing there, when RAI has only three channels? Then I get it. They're linked to the television studios, also by sound. He's following a dance routine, his hand moving in time to the music. When the leading dancer comes to a stop, Giangiacomo Zingaretti presses a button.

'Dreadful. Scrub it.' His voice echoes in the studio and freezes some famous faces: director, choreographer, leading dancer.

'But Gian—' the director tries to protest. Zingaretti presses another button and cuts the audio link.

Now he looks at me, two grey eyes over an aristocratic nose, thin lips, wide forehead; his thinning black hair is combed straight back. His gaze automatically travels over to the red couch directly under the monitors.

'Watch out for the red couch,' Dino Forte had told me.

Zingaretti smiles at me. 'Pleased to meet you, Claudia.'

I know that smile from when I was a child. The smile of the big bad wolf disguised as the grandmother in 'Little Red Riding Hood'.

He presses the intercom button. The angular old maid on the other side of the wall replies straightaway.

'Send the pests away, Renata. I'm not here.'

Then he looks at me, studying me as if I were a statue. A fanatic for perfection.

'You still have a long way to go, Claudia. But I can help you.'

Was it him, Debbie? Am I alone with a demon in disguise?

Friday, 26 November 1982

On that rainy Friday late-afternoon, the heating was too high and the smell of medicines stronger in Teodori's gloomy living room. Less than a week had passed since my last visit there, when I came on my own. This time Angelo was with me. Teodori's condition was worse. He couldn't hold papers or a glass. His hands trembled incessantly and his cough and temperature were still pronounced.

Pietro and Paolo updated us on the unpleasant news of Claudia's visit to Giangiacomo Zingaretti.

Teodori coughed many times, his voice now more like a whisper.

'This Zingaretti has a dubious reputation, Balistreri. A great professional, a very cultured man, but he has a weakness for young girls. Try to get near to him, and tell him to keep well away from Claudia.'

Of course, with my refined ways, I'll do that, won't I, Teodori? The ways I've used once already to get your daughter out of trouble.

'And what can I do? Beat him to a pulp? You should advise your daughter to steer well clear of him.'

He managed a smile. The yellow of his eyes was slowly extending to his eye sockets.

'Do you think Claudia would listen to me, Balistreri?'

'All right. I'll think of something. But, remember, I'm busy with Anita Messi.'

He nodded.

'That business of the three young men with the black Jaguar, Balistreri. The ones from Barcelona . . .'

'By "the ones from Barcelona", do you mean those three delinquents?' Dioguardi asked.

'What of them?' I asked Teodori.

'Doesn't it seem strange to you, Balistreri?'

'What? What's strange about it?'

'Finding them in that piano bar behind Piazza di Spagna, I Tre Peccati.'

'I don't understand.'

Paolo, the IT Apostle, broke in.

'The world's a big place and full of dealers. And yet you meet the same ones twice in two different places. Statistically, that's almost impossible, Balistreri.'

Pietro felt the need to add a prediction of his own.

'And you'll meet them again.'

I stared at all three of them. Two retired policemen and one nearly in the grave. I couldn't contain myself any longer. It was time to put an end to this business.

'A load of shit,' I said angrily. 'And please don't trouble yourselves any more with Anita Messi. As to Claudia, there's nothing I can do. I'm busy with more serious matters.'

I left without saying goodbye to anyone, followed shortly afterwards by Angelo. As we were driving back through the centre in the Duetto with the rain beating down on the hood, he was deadly silent.

'What's up with you?'

'You're wrong, Mike. You should see to Claudia a little longer. For your own good, as well.'

I know, old friend, I should. But I'm washing my hands of it. Right now, I'm thinking only of those two missing fingers of Nadia Al Bakri and Anita Messi and waiting for another letter from Tripoli.

Sunday, 28 November 1982

The third show in the series was a real success. The reviews were enthusiastic, audience ratings sky-high and receipts from advertising at record levels.

And now everyone knows that Giangiacomo Zingaretti called me into his office. Rossellini knows; Dino Forte knows. I remember what Debbie said. At the RAI, Zingaretti is highly thought of, feared and hated. His passion for young actresses and presenters is known about, but tolerated, because he's a real genius, someone who – in the end – chooses what's best and has never caused a scandal. Otherwise, genius or not, in the Christian and democratic RAI, he would have been sidelined.

In the RAI, Zingaretti makes and ends careers, even those of the best directors and presenters.

Dino Forte among them. But they told me Dino always had his back well covered politically. In fact, I've never seen him having to sweat it out in Zingaretti's waiting room, like all his other colleagues.

Papa called me again. He's got a temperature and a cough and can't go out. More compliments. No criticism, no suggestion that I should go and visit him. Only the inevitable and annoying 'Be careful.'

It's because of that 'be careful' that I don't go and see him. He told me that the first time I went out dancing with Deborah, and I've never forgiven him.

Thursday, 2 December 1982

Teodori and his apostles had been out of my life for days.

Before going to the office, I'd flicked absent-mindedly through the papers as I drank a coffee in the bar below the flat in Garbatella. The ordinary folk there are always in a good mood. That day, they were discussing the new Christian Democrat government.

Their gossip took me away from my investigation, which was mired between the past and the present. I'd come to a stop, voluntarily, waiting for a reply to the letter I'd sent to Tripoli ten days earlier.

Since I'd sent it, I went into the office every day, hoping to find a new envelope bearing a Libyan stamp on the centre of my desk.

And now that it was there sitting on my office desk I almost couldn't believe it. As with the first, it was an ordinary brown envelope with my name and address typed on it.

Signor Commissario Michele Balistreri
Commissariato Vigna Clara
Roma

The stamp bore Colonel Gaddafi's image. It served to remind me that I couldn't go back there again.

As before, the letter was formal, typewritten, in English and without a signature. Only the same PO Box: 150870.

I read it all in one go.

Signor Commissario Balistreri,

We have examined the facts described in your letter, including the ones given in your old notes on the circumstances of Nadia Al Bakri's death.

We can tell you that after he said goodbye to his daughter, Nadia, Mohammed Al Bakri went to his office by car.

He stayed there until just after ten, when he went to the Waddan Hotel to meet Ingegner Balistreri, who was there with Don Eugenio. Busi arrived a quarter of an hour later, apologizing for his lateness. He said he had been to the market to buy fish and fruit and been home to put the fish in the refrigerator.

We hope you can verify some of these movements. We realize it is difficult, in that these people now enjoy very privileged positions in Italy, but the links between the deaths of Nadia Al Bakri here in Tripoli and Anita Messi in Rome a few months ago are very significant, and we are ready to help you find the culprit, who is presumably the same for both.

Yours faithfully,
PO Box 150870

It was time to see another old enemy, Senator Emilio Busi.

It's raining again on the huge bronze statue of the Dying Horse, *as I look down on it through the grey stripes of the curtains, my nose pressed against a window of Giangiacomo Zingaretti's office. My breath condenses in a mist on the cold window.*

'What do you think of Fanfani, Claudia?' I can feel his mouth close to my ear.

'A senile old bigot. My father always votes for him.'

With his courteous tone of voice, like an old uncle, Gian spells out where I need to improve: tone of voice, stepping to one side. Truly, it's valuable advice.

As he talks, his hands don't touch or grope me but brush lightly over me, no more. My shoulders, my back, down to my hips. Lightly, innocently. Hands that don't want to be accused of anything.

'You're improving, Claudia. In the fourth show, you'll have a bigger role to play.'

'Is Dino Forte OK with that?'

'Of course. Everyone agrees with me, sweetheart.'

I see the red couch reflected in the window.

Is it on that red leather couch that you fucked Deborah, while your hatchet-faced secretary kept back the actresses, presenters and those seeking favours in your waiting room?

Friday, 10 December 1982

—

Arranging a meeting with the Hon. Emilio Busi was a lot more difficult than arranging one with Monsignor Eugenio Pizza. Pressing political business, the new Fanfani government, parliamentary undersecretaries, parliamentary commissions: Emilio Busi was an important man, and he knew it.

From 1970 onwards, his career had taken off. He'd been placed on the board of directors of Italy's largest nationalized companies. By 1972, he was a member of parliament and, in 1976, he became the youngest member elected to the Senate during the elections when the Communist Party gained more votes than the Christian Democrats.

Nevertheless, poisonous whispers emanating from some orthodox Communists, rather than his political adversaries, had linked him to a series of shadowy events: the death of Enrico Mattei, the disappearance of a Sicilian journalist investigating the case, contacts with the secret intelligence agencies of the SID and SIOS, and later the SISDE; also with the IOR, the Vatican Bank and with the Masonic P2 lodge. And, once only, with the Mafia clans that ran Palermo, when he acted as witness at the wedding of the young daughter of the Sicilian businessman Gaetano Balistreri, the eldest of the five brothers, though Tano's record was, and still is, unblemished.

None of these whispers ever got to the newspapers. Many of those who had fed the rumours later apologized, maintaining that they had been mistaken, and then withdrew from political life.

After a week of waiting, once the voting for the Senate ended that Friday afternoon, his assistant finally called me. I should be at the PCI headquarters in Via delle Botteghe Oscure at six o'clock.

I only knew the famous PCI building from the outside. It wasn't far from the balcony in Piazza Venezia from which, forty years earlier, Mussolini had addressed the Fascist masses. I was familiar with the walls, of course. At the beginning of the seventies, I used to go there at night with two other crazy friends and spray Ordine nuovo's Fascist axe sign on them, along with the words the Reds hated the most: '*Sieg Heil*'.

A long time had passed since then. Both within me and outside. But it hadn't been enough to fill the gap or build a bridge over the chasm that separated me from the occupants of that building. Certainly, those years had served to get me to understand that neither bombs nor bullets against innocent people were *my way* towards justice. But nothing had changed the old convictions that my grandfather and my mother, Italia, had instilled in me since I was a child, more by the way they behaved than by what they said.

The Hon. Busi's office was on the second floor, where the important leaders were not too far away from the office of the Party Secretary, the one with the balcony over the main entrance.

After I'd signed in, I passed the bust of Antonio Gramsci, the Party's founder, and a middle-aged secretary came to the bottom of the staircase to meet me.

Busi's office reflected his origins. It was a large, bare room. Sober furniture; sober pictures; a large, austere desk; the armchairs a little worn. A photograph of his wife and ten-year-old son in a frame that was most certainly not of silver.

But this manifest sobriety couldn't hide the fact of what Emilio Busi had become and, above all, was preparing himself to become. He was now a well-established political figure. The humble origins he vaunted and used so publicly in the past were now betrayed by small details. Things that anyone who hadn't known him many years before wouldn't have noticed. But I did.

I had the means of comparison. His hair wasn't long and dishevelled any more, but well cut and smoothly layered at the back and the front. Those dreadful square hornrim frames had gone and been replaced by slender titanium ones. The clothes that carelessly mixed stripes and checks together with short white socks and never matched had also gone, in favour of an iron-grey pinstripe suit; not from a high-class tailor, because that would have exposed him to criticism from his colleagues, but too well made not to have been made to measure. And, obviously, no more dusty brown moccasins, but polished black lace-ups. Lastly, the cigarettes. The quintessentially elegant Italian Muratti in place of those foul-smelling plain-tipped Nazionali.

In contrast to Don Eugenio, he didn't welcome me with open arms and a smile. In this, he hadn't changed at all.

When I entered, he was sitting at his desk, speaking on the telephone. He gave me a brief glance and pointed to the two chairs facing one another in a corner of the room. He ended the conversation and came and sat down opposite me. He had a note in his hand from his secretary.

'Now, Balistreri. They tell me here that you've requested to speak to me informally. Which is quite out of the ordinary for you, in that I don't think you're here to pay me a courtesy visit. Nor to ask me a favour. You haven't changed that much. At least, so they tell me.'

So you've kept up to date. You know that I daubed 'Sieg Heil' on the walls here. But do you know how many I've saved from terrorist bombings?

Busi went on with what he was saying.

'But now you're a commissario in the police and I'm a member of the Italian parliament. I imagine you know this country's laws.'

Your country, and certainly not mine. Where members of parliament have an immunity that renders them untouchable.

'I'm not here to ask a favour, Onorevole. Obviously, you're not in any way implicated in the investigations I'm pursuing.'

He looked at me, a little perplexed, through the cloud of smoke from his Muratti.

'Good. Then let's call this a conversation between two old acquaintances. I don't have much time, so can we get on with it?'

'I'm here because of Nadia Al Bakri,' I said simply.

Busi studied me with his sharp, intelligent eyes behind those thick lenses. He took a drag on his Muratti.

'A case you have no jurisdiction over and which was closed many years ago. Given that your salary is paid by the taxes from the citizens I represent, I'm wondering if this is professionally correct.'

I was ready for this objection.

'There could be a connection between that case and one I'm working on right now.'

'Oh, really? Sounds quite odd to me, Balistreri. Are you sure it's not one of the films you used to act out in the garden with your little friends?'

I made an effort to be polite with him. As became my new role. And his.

'I'm only asking for some cooperation, Onorevole.'

'What's the connection then?' Busi asked.

I allowed myself an evil smile.

'I'm afraid the laws of your country don't allow me to reveal it, Onorevole. Confidentiality of investigations. It applies to members of parliament as well. We're obliged to maintain secrecy in investigations before a trial.'

Busi stared at me for some time.

'Michele, you know what's keeping me from showing you the door, don't you?'

'Of course: your relationship with my father and my uncles. But, look, you can forget all about that, because my father's not cared anything about me for years.'

'No, Michele, because you've remained an immature young kid incapable of seeing the reality of the world. At the time, I couldn't understand why your father didn't let you end up in prison, or even the cemetery, which is where you deserved to end up.'

'And I don't suppose you've changed your mind, have you?'

'I'm now forty-seven. I've a son aged ten, and I can understand your father. You don't ever give up on your children. But you don't want to accept this very simple fact.'

You don't give up on them, but you can humiliate, betray and forget them.

'My father's Nuova Banca del Sud is benefactor to a pontifical college whose head is Monsignor Eugenio Pizza. A student of the college was murdered this summer.'

'Pure coincidence. We're all still in touch: your father, Don Eugenio and myself. And your father gives aid to many charities.'

'But the Nuova Banca del Sud doesn't help finance only that college, Onorevole. It has very different interests as well.'

For a moment, I thought he would physically kick me out of the office, but Emilio Busi was too intelligent to give in to anger. He wanted to know what I knew.

'And what are those, Michele? Just out of curiosity.'

'The Nuova Banca del Sud buys up enormous quantities of American dollars in the international financial markets. It also gets money from very dubious provenances in Italy, which needs to be laundered. A large part of this money is loaned to the IOR, which doesn't have access to those markets and yet needs dollars, lots of dollars.'

Busi raised his eyebrows.

'Really? And why? Surely not to pay the salaries of its priests.'

For yet another of your wretched plots. Like the one that brought me to this country.

'In order to finance Solidarity and bring down Communism. A common goal shared by the present Pope, the American President and the Mafia. A perfect threesome. And yet, despite being a Communist, you still watch out for my father?'

Busi gave one of his scornful little smiles. And yet there was a thin line of worry on his forehead.

I know. You should have had me captured by Gaddafi's hired thugs and shot. But my father couldn't do it; he would have lost Alberto as well.

He lit another Muratti and looked at his watch. He readopted the formal manner he had had at the start of the conversation.

'You should start writing political thrillers, Balistreri. You say things that make no sense and have no proof behind them. I know where you get this rubbish from, because I also know the secret services in this country.'

'I've no doubt you do, Onorevole. Since the days we were in Tripoli, no doubt. So perhaps you can tell me how things stand?'

Busi looked instinctively out of the large windows and down at the street. The impenetrable stream of cars and buses was running slowly towards Piazza Venezia in the winter darkness of the late afternoon.

'Can you see the affluence, Balistreri? Do you know how much crude petroleum this country needs for its cars, central heating and industrial energy? You have no idea of the state Fascism reduced this country to, simply because you weren't around. I fought for this, and will continue to fight for it, in order to build a country without poverty and the poor.'

Of course you will, with petrol at a good price from dictators like Gaddafi – on the backs of the entire Libyan population and 20,000 Italians.

And what now, Onorevole? Are you going to allow your good old friends to destroy your Communism?'

I was sure he'd deny everything. Instead, his reply surprised me.

'We're about to reach the end of a phase. Ten years, fifteen years at most. It's not a question of a Polish pope, Ronald Reagan or the Mafia. It's that *kind* of Communism that isn't useful any more.'

' "That *kind* of Communism," Onorevole? Which kind?'

'The kind with all the comrades waving the red flag and singing "*Bella Ciao*" with their fists raised. Or the kind that sends tanks into Budapest and Prague. It was useful at one time, but now it's over.'

'Over? I don't really think it is. Your party has a third of the seats in parliament.'

Busi pointed to the stream of traffic, the gleaming shop windows, the crowded bars.

'People in the Soviet empire and its satellites want the same things as people in the West do. And someone will give it to them. There's no need for the Nuova Banca del Sud, the IOR and Mafia dollars. Nor even for Solidarity. It's simply a natural process. And we Communists either move with the times, or we'll become extinct, like those dinosaurs that didn't know how to adapt.'

'But you'll not become extinct, will you?'

He smiled. 'I don't think so. I'm not a dinosaur.'

That's true. You're a cold-blooded reptile.

'Then why do you help my father? Why don't you stay out of it, if everything's going to happen naturally?'

'Because alliances will change. The Left will never govern by itself in Italy, at least not in the next two hundred years, even if my colleagues are convinced otherwise. But then they're the dinosaurs, you see.'

I knew what it was that I had hated most in Emilio Busi from that evening in Tripoli when he'd said to my grandfather there was no longer any future in his olives.

The wealth lies under the sand, not above it.

My father, Don Eugenio and the others had never been friends, only allies. I hated the total pragmatism and intellectual superiority that was taken to extreme lengths in order to protect a more general interest, which, according to Emilio Busi, was that of the world.

I'd had enough of this scholarly lecture.

'As I mentioned, I'm here because of Nadia Al Bakri,' I reminded him.

Busi looked at his watch.

'Then you've used the time you've had badly. You've got five minutes left.'

'That morning, you were to meet my father at the Waddan at ten. We were all going together to the Underwater Club and then fishing. But you, who were always so punctual, arrived late.'

He looked at me in silence, and I went on.

'My father tried to call you at nine thirty. You weren't at home. Mohammed came by to try and find you, and you still weren't there. When you did finally arrive at the Waddan, you were out of breath.'

He fiddled with the knot of his Marinella tie, one of his small concessions to success.

'And so what, Balistreri? You think I made a trip out to Sidi El Masri to get Nadia and shut her in a broom cupboard? And even if I had, do you think I'd tell you?'

'Don't you want to help me understand, Senator?'

Busi was lost in thought, and curious. Once again, all he wanted to hear was what I knew.

'What does Nadia Al Bakri have to do with Anita Messi?'

'I can't tell you that. But there could be a connection. Those who betray people are capable of repeating themselves.'

He shook his head.

'You're a policeman, Balistreri. You should be searching for a killer, not a traitor or a personal enemy.'

'It amounts to the same thing, Senator. Italy's governed by a ruling class that came into being by betraying its country during the war. And, from the example you set, every Italian's learned that personal convenience comes before loyalty.'

'Balistreri, I don't see what this has to do with the murder of these girls. We're simply dealing with a killer who uses a knife.'

'You're wrong. This killer uses his brain. And, for his personal convenience, as you and your people have taught him.'

He took another minute to think about this, perhaps to remember that fateful day. Or perhaps to forget it.'

'All right, let's try to remember. I went out about eight that morning and walked. I didn't want to drive because of the *ghibli*. I first went to buy a newspaper and then went to the market in Shara Mizran.'

'The market?'

'Naturally, Michele. I went to the market to do some shopping. I came across Nico Gerace and Alberto, who were taking the paper to Ingegner Balistreri at the barber's.'

'And you were there for that long?'

'Yes, I often went there on Sunday mornings. Wandering among the fruit and vegetable and fish stalls was a way of picking up on the mood between the Libyans and the West. It was both interesting and enjoyable.'

'To the point where you were late for a meeting with my father?'

'That happened because of Farid and Salim's amberjack. It was wonderful, but there was a huge queue at their stall. Everyone wanted to buy a piece, and Salim couldn't manage on his own.'

'Salim was on his own?'

'Yes,' Busi affirmed calmly. 'When I got to their stall at about nine thirty, there was only Salim there. I had to queue for about twenty minutes.'

'And Farid?' I asked, incredulous.

'He wasn't there. Salim was on his own. And when one chunk of amberjack had been sold, he went out to where their pick-up was parked and cut off another huge chunk and came back to the stall.'

Farid wasn't there, but the pick-up was. Mansur must have been mistaken.

'And yet Farid was there when I came to pick up the bait around ten. It was him who gave it to me,' I said.

Busi shrugged his shoulders.

'He must have just got there. When Salim finally wrapped up my fish, it was almost ten and Farid wasn't there. I went home and put the fish in the fridge and then went to the Waddan, this time in the car, driving slowly, because of the wretched *ghibli*. That's why I arrived late.'

Your father has no alibi, Farid has no alibi, Busi has no alibi, Mohammed has no alibi, Don Eugenio has no alibi. Do you really want to uncover all these tombs?

Busi had to go to the Senate.

'I'm a member of the new parliamentary anti-Mafia commission,' he told me.

Perfect. We're in great hands.

We went out together. In the inside courtyard, his driver was waiting with the blue Lancia Thema.

'Good luck, Balistreri,' he said, and waved goodbye.

Leaving the Italian Communist Party building, I went past Gramsci's bust again, and wondered if I was now closer to or further away from the truth.

We're rehearsing tomorrow night's show. The television studio's crowded. Dino Forte's still in the dressing room, with the make up-artist and the hairdresser.

We begin with the part I do solo. Halfway through the number, there's a voice over the loudspeaker.

'Put more life into it, Claudia.'

Everyone freezes. Everyone's silent. Dino Forte's just come in, and looks dumbfounded at the director, who himself is looking, ashen-faced, at the loudspeaker.

Everyone knows whose voice that is, and so they now know that I'm his protégée and that he's out to make me improve. And also that no one else can touch me.

'Have a good rehearsal,' says Zingaretti through the loudspeaker without waiting for a reply. We hear the click as he switches off. End of communication.

Dino Forte looks at me strangely. He'll be wondering if I've already been on the red couch. And yet I haven't even been to dinner with him.

'We must speak, Claudia,' he says to me.

Of course. Perhaps something's been set in motion. Perhaps 'He' will come out into the open.

I was in a really bad mood after the meeting with Emilio Busi.

There was my sense of guilt over the disastrous outcome of the investigation into the death of Elisa Sordi, for which Teodori had unjustly taken the blame. My complete disaffection with my job as commissario and with Italy in general – the land of betrayals, small and large, where everyone complained about others in public only to follow their example in private. Also, I was losing patience with having to feel guilty over my lack of interest in Claudia, whose success on television was turning her from a common little slut to a national hero.

Quite obviously, I was at a dead end. But the analogies and connections were everywhere. A missing finger linked Anita and Nadia.

I felt absolutely certain we were dealing with a careless moment, an uncontrollable habit or an irresistible temptation for a killer who was otherwise cold and implacable but who felt so safe that he could repeat the outrage at a distance of thirteen years.

What Emilio Busi had said made imperative another encounter with the past. I knew that I'd immediately thrown away Nico Gerace's business card after the chance meeting in Barcelona, but hoped Angelo Dioguardi had kept his.

Christmas and New Year were almost upon us. It was a matter of waiting two or three weeks. But I'd already waited thirteen years. And the festive season was the time for seeing old friends again.

Saturday, 25 December 1982

In the end, I waited until Christmas to go and see him. And then I learned that Papa would never ever leave that apartment, to which I'd sworn I'd never return.

How much the place has changed. It already seems dead, like Papa. Now I realize he's dreadfully ill. I've brought him a book as a present, the one with the wonderful title by Milan Kundera.

He holds it in his hands and reads the title. 'Life is Elsewhere,' he murmurs.

Hearing it on his lips, it seems more poetic and moving than usual.

And Papa seems precisely there, suspended in the empty space between life and elsewhere.

I kiss him. We haven't even spoken. I have to go; the RAI car's waiting for me down on the street.

Today is Christmas Day, but it's also Saturday evening.

The show must go on. Life is elsewhere.

He makes a sign to me as I leave. 'Be careful, sweetheart.' His usual warning.

The Night of Friday 31 December and Saturday 1 January 1983

It was really easy to see Nico Gerace again. Firstly, because Angelo Dioguardi had actually kept his card and, secondly, because it was New Year's Eve and he was happy to see an old friend.

Angelo and I didn't celebrate at all, because I was in a black mood and Angelo was still getting over his split with Paola. We took a turn through Garbatella, Angelo wrapped up in a quilt jacket and fur hat against the biting cold, myself in the only winter jacket I had. We walked in silence through that district – built so people could live in a humane manner in a city ever less humane – while everyone else was drinking toasts and letting off fireworks. Then, two hours after midnight, we reached Alberto's flat in EUR.

Nico Gerace arrived a few minutes later, by taxi. I had phoned to invite him. He was wearing a spotless dinner jacket, his hair was beautifully cut and too perfect not to have been tinted. His eyebrows had also been well trimmed. The awkward hairy adolescent had become a handsome, self-confident young man.

He first gave the traditional embrace to Alberto, the elder brother, as true Sicilians do, while Alberto looked at him – amazed at the transformation – trying to disguise his state of shock.

Then Nico shook hands with Angelo and, lastly, put his arms around me.

I didn't want his embrace. I didn't want it when we left each other twelve years earlier in Lampedusa, nor when we met by chance outside the wine bar before the game in Barcelona. And I didn't want it now. But it was part of the pathway to get at the truth.

The embrace that links two accomplices. Only we know it.

It was like accepting that part of me that I'd never wanted.

The night of 15 August 1970.

We sat down at the table with four glasses and a bottle in front of us.

'Sorry about the dinner jacket. Professional duty,' Nico said. 'I've done the rounds of all the most important nightclubs.'

'And what profession would that be?' Angelo asked him, with a smile.

'Guys, don't you read the entertainment pages in the papers?' Nico protested.

'I only read the politics and economics sections,' Alberto said.

'Sports section for me,' said Angelo.

'I should read the crime pages, but I haven't opened a newspaper for years,' I said.

'Why the crime pages, Mike?' Nico asked me.

I looked at him and smiled.

'Because I'm a *commissario di polizia*, Nico. And, from the look of you, I imagine you've become a pimp.'

We all burst into uproarious laughter.

Yes, it's good to be here again, among friends new and old, and forgetting about those no longer with us.

'In a way, it's true I look after girls, but not whores. I loved the world of entertainment, you remember? So I look after the interests of artistes, actors and musicians. I'm an agent for them.'

I remembered what was written on the card I'd thrown away: 'Artistic Management'.

'Any famous names?' Alberto asked him, curious.

He offered three or four: all stars of cinema, TV or the music scene.

'Are you pulling our legs, Nico?' I asked him.

The glance he gave me was one full of pride.

Nico related his past twelve years to us. Indeed, he had followed his true vocation and succeeded. He was full of energy, and proud of himself. Along the way, he'd had to change his appearance: massage, gym, sauna, hairdresser, manicure, hair removal.

'I've even had laser treatment to get rid of that damned hair!' he said, laughing.

'But no laser could do anything with that beard of yours!' I pointed out.

In effect, that was the one ineradicable sign of his previous appearance. That habitual very dark beard that became a shadow again two hours after shaving was what gave him that rough-about-the-edges look he'd been fighting since he was a child.

He took a small battery-powered razor out of his bag and ran it over his cheeks, laughing.

'There you are,' he said, all happy. 'I do it whenever I need, like having a drink of water.'

As the hours passed away with the cigarettes and whisky, the jokes and the memories around the table, an idea took shape in my mind.

Free me from Claudia, my father, the two apostles. And free me from my sense of guilt.

I waited until the first light of dawn, when we slumped down in the armchairs in the living room with a final whisky and a cigarette, in order to talk about it.

'Do you know Claudia Teodori,' I asked Nico.

He pulled a deliberately scornful face. How could I even think of asking?

'Of course. Not personally, but, in my business, I have to know all the upcoming names.'

'Is she any good?'

Nico thought for a moment; he seemed uncertain.

'Technically, she's good, Mike, really well trained. But there's no sacred fire burning in there.'

'What d'you mean?'

'Passion, overriding ambition. Call it what you like, Mike. You've got to be prepared to do anything; otherwise, you don't get to the top.'

I was surprised and sceptical.

'I'd say that Claudia Teodori was prepared to do anything.'

It was unusual for Angelo Dioguardi to interrupt, but he couldn't contain himself.

'You should stop looking only at arses, Michele, and try to listen to what women say as well. Nico's right.'

I burst out laughing.

'OK, Nico, given you used to go only with whores, what should I be listening to in women?'

Angelo broke in again.

'Give over, Mike. You're not being funny. And Claudia Teodori isn't the little slut you think she is.'

'Word gets round in our world,' Nico said. 'Dino Forte isn't screwing her. Not that he matters. As far as anyone knows, he's never had any extramarital affairs.'

'And Zingaretti?'

'He's losing his head over her, Gian is, the devil. But all the gossip says the same thing. Claudia's not given him anything yet.'

'And she never will,' said Angelo.

'I wouldn't like to swear to it,' Nico replied. 'Zingaretti's very powerful and doesn't have any scruples. He puts the actresses up on cloud nine in every possible way and, if they don't give him what he wants, then they're out.'

An idea came to me as we chatted and I looked at and listened to him. Nico Gerace had grown up with me, had had to put up with

Don Eugenio when we were still kids, had beaten our rivals to a pulp when it helped the MANK organization and had fucked thousands of whores. He knew the world, and he was now in the right position to relieve me of the unpleasant responsibility of looking after Claudia Teodori.

'Nico, you're right. Zingaretti'll get her, no doubt. Unless Claudia has an agent of your calibre who's there to protect her,' I suggested.

He gave a satisfied smile.

'I only look after the big names who've already made it. I don't have any time for bewitching little starlets who still need to mature.'

'And what if it's your old classmate who's asking? The one who stopped you from making the whole class fall about laughing?'

Nico blushed down to his roots.

'What are you two talking about?' asked Dioguardi, curious.

'Nothing, nothing,' Nico said hurriedly. 'It was a long time ago, when he was less of a shit than he is now. And what has Claudia Teodori got to do with you, Mike, I'd like to know?'

'She's the daughter of someone who did me a great favour, and I took on the job of looking after her. So, Nico, will you do it?'

He huffed and puffed, then he smiled and brushed a manicured hand through his hair.

'I'll have a go. But Claudia Teodori's a tough nut. It's not easy to make friends with her.'

I pointed to Angelo.

'He'll give you a hand. Angelo's every girl's friend. He talks to them and never tries to fuck them.'

We lit a last cigarette on the terrace; the vast city was now silent around us after the midnight fireworks.

I looked at Nico and my brother. Alberto was drinking mineral water; Nico was having a quiet smoke.

It was now time to bring up the real reason why I'd wanted to see him again.

In order to know if the Hon. Emilio Busi had been lying to me.

'Do you remember that day of the *ghibli* when Nadia was murdered in Tripoli?' I asked them, all of a sudden.

Alberto and Nico didn't even look at me. They knew very well what I was talking about but continued to stare out at the silent horizon of houses and parked cars, as if that day, that young girl and that place had only ever existed in our adolescent imaginations.

But I needed confirmation of what Senator Emilio Busi had said. I needed it before I wrote to Tripoli again.

'Did you see Busi at the fish market that day, after you'd taken the paper to my father?'

Nico flicked away his still-lit cigarette, which described a glowing arc into the night. Alberto answered me coldly.

'Yes, Mike, Busi was there at about eight.'

'What does it matter?' Nico asked me.

I can't tell either of you. I can't tell you about the letters from Tripoli. I can't tell you about the missing fingers of Anita Messi and Nadia Al Bakri. I can't tell you a single thing.

I said the only thing I could that I was sure about.

'It matters in that – because of it – we're here on this terrace in the middle of this sea of concrete, rather than on the seafront in Tripoli.'

We gave up on the truth about Nadia and allowed someone to sell our lives away.

Saturday, 1 January 1983

It's the New Year show this evening.

Last night, I toured the clubs a bit with Rossellini and his bunch of airheads. Only to see if he was going to come on to me, but no way was I going to let that happen. I used the upcoming show as an excuse to leave immediately after midnight.

Just after lunch, I spot Dioguardi in the Via Teulada canteen. It's one of the few places where I can eat in peace without being pestered for autographs.

Angelo's sitting with an elegant and not bad-looking young guy who I've seen several times in the canteen.

I go over to them. They're talking about Barcelona and the Italy–Brazil game.

'We were the only two who believed we'd win.'

Angelo got up and put his arms round me. 'Claudia, would you like to join us?'

'No, thanks. Lunch is a reduced-fat yoghurt for me, and I've already had it.'

But he's courteous, although insistent. 'A coffee, then?'

I smile. 'No coffee either. But I'll join you for a minute.'

I get a better look at the guy with Angelo. He really takes care with his appearance: gym, sunbeds, trendy, elegant clothes. He looks at me with cheeky self-confidence. 'Claudia Teodori. The most beautiful girl on Italian TV.'

His accent's strange. Perhaps it's Sicilian. Who does he think he is?

He holds out his hand to me. 'Nico Gerace. Pleased to meet you.'

I look at him and remember. Debbie once mentioned something about him.

Nico Gerace. An agent for the big names, and only the big names. He's very powerful, the one who can negotiate his clients' fees directly with Giangiacomo Zingaretti or the Director General. And always gets what he asks for.

I shake his hand.

'Pleased to meet you, too. I'm not the most beautiful. I'm just good at what I do.'

Just so we can get things clear.

While they have a coffee, a famous director and an old actor come up to the table to say hello.

'Ciao, Nico. Keep in touch, eh?'

'Were you two talking about football?' I ask.

They snigger.

'Football and women. A few months ago, we met by chance in Barcelona at the World Cup,' Angelo explained.

'And he and Michele were with two beautiful Brazilian girls,' Nico added.

Angelo smiles. 'I didn't have anything to do with them.'

Nico looks at me. 'And Michele? I'll bet he had something to do with them. Both of them, at the same time.'

They laugh, and I pretend to join in.

'Are you a friend of Michele Balistreri as well?' I ask Nico Gerace.

'Very old friend. Since we were in the same class in junior school.'

In fact, he has the same arrogant manner. Not as harsh or as scornful. He's softer and more polished, but there's something he has in common with that piece of shit.

'Nico's the best agent there is on the scene, Claudia,' Angelo tells me.

I smile at him. He's doing this to help me. 'I know. He only has the very biggest names on his books.'

'Well, now, for a friend of Balistreri, I could make an exception,' Gerace tells me.

'I'm not a friend of Michele Balistreri.'

Gerace continues regardless. 'Well, then, for a friend of Angelo Dioguardi.'

I get up. 'Yes, I'm a friend of Angelo Dioguardi. Can you give me some time to think about it?'

He smiles. 'Yeah, but don't think about it too long. I might just change my mind.'

I say goodbye and leave. I don't need an agent. I only want to find the man who ruined Debbie.

I spent the first day of 1983 at home in Garbatella. I felt lethargic, torn between waiting and doing something. My energies were totally absorbed by the letters from Tripoli.

Who are you writing to, Michele?

I had to concentrate on Anita Messi and Nadia Al Bakri. In order to do this, I had to free myself up from my less important task in the most absolute terms.

After supper, I gave Nico Gerace a call, and he told me to come and meet him at his house – a villa on the Via Appia Antica on the city outskirts. When I arrived, it was raining heavily. Nico was on his own, wearing a black cashmere sweater and white jeans. The living room was plastered with posters of his famous clients: actors and actresses, presenters, directors, singers.

Just like the Barbra Streisand poster in the MANK organization's van.

'All right, Nico. Have you managed to speak to the little shit?' I asked him, as soon as we sat down with a whisky in our hands.

'Yes, this afternoon. I was with Angelo. You'll have to be patient. If I press her, Claudia'll suspect something. It's not normal for Italy's top agent to go running after an absolute beginner. And, anyway, you don't have to worry. I know how to go about this. And no one's fucking her at the moment.'

'Not even Zingaretti?'

Nico pulled his typical scornful face.

'Now, that man really is a piece of shit. I know him all too well. He waits for them to get to the top and then it's payback time.'

'And does Claudia need him to get to the top?'

'Well, either that or a powerful saint in heaven. Someone like Giangiacomo Zingaretti or Dino Forte.'

'Or an agent like yourself?'

He made no reply. He stared at me with that half-smile of his. The one he always had whenever Ahmed and Karim started to speak of Italians and Libyans.

'And drugs?'

He raised his shoulders. 'I couldn't swear to it. But, from what I hear, Claudia's clean. She doesn't touch anything, not even weed.'

I can't believe this. No sex and no drugs. And yet she was rolling a joint at the Altromodo . . . I can't be that mistaken, can I?

'Listen, Nico, there's something else. It's to do with drugs, not Claudia Teodori.'

He smiled. 'And you're consulting me in what role: dealer, user or because I hang around with addicts?'

'Try to be serious a minute. You remember Barcelona?'

His face suddenly lit up. 'When Paolo Rossi flayed Brazil?'

'Yes, when we met up in that jungle of tents around Sarrià Stadium, there was all sorts of shit going round. I can still remember that sweetish smell.'

'Of course. I had a couple of joints myself. And you did as well, I imagine, with those two Brazilians!'

'Leave them out of it. Was there any cocaine going round?'

He was suddenly serious. 'Sorry, but really, how should I know?'

Because perhaps Anita Messi was there as well. How could such a huge Maradona fan travelling in Europe at that time miss out on her idol playing in the World Cup? And those three men, Sicilians like us, were also there, the same ones that gave some crack to the American girl Kate.

I decided to tell him all about Anita Messi and the three guys with the black Jaguar in Barcelona and how I came to see them again in I Tre Peccati. I told him about the connections to my father, Busi and Don Eugenio, and about the amputated finger. Anita Messi's. It had been in the papers already.

But I said nothing about Nadia or the letters from Tripoli. That was a door that would have led to somewhere I didn't want to go with Nico Gerace.

Back to 15 August 1970.

He listened in silence, paying close attention.

'This is something you could make a film about,' he said in the end.

'Nico, can you drop this crap about film and TV? This stuff is very real.'

'All right. But I didn't see either this Anita Messi or those three guys in Barcelona. There were thousands of people there.'

'I know that, Nico. But I know you know the drug scene, I'm sure of it.'

He looked at me, a little offended. 'Do you think I'm a crackhead?'

'No, but in the industry you're in, don't tell me you don't know who uses it in Rome and who they get it from. That's all the help I need.'

'Of course, Mike, in my world, almost everyone takes something. A little weed, a lot of cocaine, but no heroin – that's for those with a serious deathwish. And I can imagine where they get the goods from and who sells it to them. But, from there to the real bosses who supply it, there's a trail about as long as from here to paradise.'

'Or perhaps a little bit nearer, Nico. Let's say our own island of Sicily, perhaps?'

He shook his head. 'Is this because those three from Barcelona had Sicilian accents?'

'No, Nico. There are other reasons. But you can tell me what you know.'

The steady stream of money for laundering. The Nuova Banca del Sud. The IOR, Solidarity. And Communism as the common enemy of the industrialists, the priests and the Mafia.

'Rome's divided up into zones. It started with gangs from Marseilles, then the Camorra and the Mafia got in on it. The local gangs, such as the Magliana, are given the job of small-time dealing. People in the world of entertainment use a lot of discretion in procuring dope, so as not to get blackmailed. Let's say they get it from people in their own world: one-time actors, nightclub owners, journalists.'

'And agents – people like yourself.'

He looked at me askance and replied in that same distant and hurt manner he had had as a kid when I found him with a whore in the MANK van and told him that women had to be won over rather than paid for.

'Of course, the less important ones. I earn almost 500 million a year from my clients – I don't need to earn any extra.'

I smiled. I had offended him. And Nico had been a faithful friend, the hairy and insecure young boy who lisped his 's' sounds and was convinced the world considered him nothing but a pariah.

'I was only joking, Nico. You've given me some very valuable information.'

'And I can give you some more advice. Even though it's you who's the policeman.'

'Which is?'

'You told me that Anita Messi was taking a European holiday with two friends. So why don't you call them and get them to tell you if they were in Barcelona for the World Cup? It's simple, right?'

Extremely simple. Except that the wonderful policeman Michele Balistreri didn't move a muscle for two months and had to get permission to call Argentina.

'All right. Thanks for the advice. But hurry up with Claudia Teodori, will you? That way I can calm down that father of hers.'

Nico smiled sourly.

'I happen to be Italy's most important and powerful agent, Mike. Everyone wants to be with me, all except Claudia Teodori. And you know why, don't you?'

Of course I do, Nico. Because you're the friend of that shit Michele Balistreri.

'So tell her we've never been friends, Nico!'

He turned gloomy and looked me in the eyes. Then he shook off his thoughts and gave a lewd laugh.

'Come with me, Mike. I've got something to show you.'

We went outside on to the English lawn in front of the villa and walked more than three hundred metres in the pouring rain among the trees in the garden. Next to the outside wall behind the house was a large garage. The up-and-over door wasn't even locked, and Nico lifted it up.

Inside was Nico's Ferrari Mondial, and next to it was a red Fiat 850T van. Down one side was written 'MANK'. In the back was the Barbra Streisand poster.

I couldn't believe my eyes, and Nico was enjoying my total amazement.

'It's not possible,' I whispered. 'They wouldn't even let us take our mattresses out of Tripoli.'

He fell about laughing.

'To see your face, Mike! It's not the real one, only a copy. But sometimes the things that don't seem real are real. And the things that seem real are false.'

Monday, 3 January 1983

The show on New Year's Day was a real triumph. My photo is on the front pages of various newspapers today, next to Dino Forte's. The programme had more than 20 million viewers, all of them enthusiastic. Papa even called to congratulate me.

The final show will be on 8 January, the Saturday after Epiphany. They're anticipating 25 million viewers, an absolute record for this kind of show.

Rossellini's happy. We're having supper at his house. Not alone; there are other guests so that he can show me off. Showing off is his way of possessing. As for Dino Forte, perhaps he wants me to do the seducing.

He's not like Zingaretti, who only wants to gobble me up. He'll take me to the top first, then it'll payback time, or else 'bye bye' to dreams of glory. That's his method.

In contrast, Rossellini's happy just to show off the new young TV star, the one who supports the most famous presenter of Saturday night's variety show.

Now that I've been working a while with Dino Forte and I'm the new apple of Giangiacomo's eye, I could dump this inflated bag of wind with his bad breath.

But it's too soon. I'm still not sure if it wasn't him who ruined Deborah.

I have to wait, give him time, a little more rope.

I raise my glass flute with its thimbleful of Prosecco, the most alcohol I can allow myself.

'All thanks to you, Rossellini. I'll always be grateful to you.'

He wets his lips and speaks.

'Dino's forever thanking me for having discovered you, Claudia. And I know that Gian admires you a great deal.'

He says it like that, casually mentioning Dino and Gian, as if they were his oldest friends. But at Dino Forte and Giangiacomo Zingaretti's level, someone like Rossellini counts for nothing.

I have to be cautious. Frightening him a little, but not so he becomes of no use to me. I have to leave him free to make a move.

'Perhaps I need an agent. Some guy like Nico Gerace.'

Rossellini nearly chokes. He already sees himself dethroned, redundant.

'He won't take you on, Claudia. He wants his fish already big.'

I smile at him. 'You're right. I'm happy with you – that's enough for me.'

He smiles contentedly. So I still need him, at least for a little while. I'll wait and see if there's any crack cocaine among his proposals.

When I visit the guest bathroom with its black tiles and fittings, I have a good look for any sign of powder in the little cupboards and containers, even behind the lavatory. But there's no sign of anything strange. And yet the room gives me the creeps with all its black. It's not luxury. It's death.

Tuesday, 4 January 1983

Nico Gerace's idea was the right one. Follow the drugs trail, starting with South America. In Rome, I could put a tail on the three Sicilians from Barcelona. But, right now, there was nothing to link them with Anita Messi.

Except the smell of piss.

There was only the smell of ammonia with which cocaine is free-based to link the three from Barcelona to Anita Messi. Then I remembered the bottle with the straw in her room in the hall of residence.

Moreover, there was Anita's trip with her friends that summer. The rector of Salta University had said it was in Europe. Well, Spain – including Barcelona – happens to be in Europe.

As Nico had suggested, another phone call to Argentina would be helpful.

I found Capuzzo, the great manipulator of bureaucratic procedure.

'This is the second request to make a call, Dottore. This time, we're going to have to wait a bit.'

Damned Italian bureaucracy. How can anyone work like this?

'And analysis of the bottle?'

He gave me a proud wink.

'That's easier. I've got a friend, he's from my part of the country. We'll have it in two or three days.'

Giangiacomo Zingaretti's told me again: You're the most beautiful, but still not good enough. He tells me where I'm lacking. And he's right. The implicit message is clear. If I really do become a TV star, in spite of my faults, it'll be thanks to him. And, at that point, I'll have to sit on the red couch. Or 'goodbye, career'.

In the meantime, he advises me on the make-up and costumes for the grand finale on Saturday 8 January.

He has me come to the window overlooking Viale Mazzini, the one with the grey vertical-striped curtains. Five floors below are lines of cars under a leaden January sky. The people of Rome trapped in their good life.

'Do you see the horse?' I can see it down there, in the RAI forecourt, the huge bronze beast in its death throes. It's extremely beautiful.

'What do you think the sculptor meant to say, Claudia?'

You have to die a little in order to be reborn, I think, and tell him so. He smiles. I feel his arm around my hips. He goes no further; it's too soon. I'm still not at the top of the ladder.

'You'll make it, Claudia. You've got brains.'

'Thank you, Dottor Zingaretti.'

'Please, not so formal. My friends call me Gian. Would you like a cigarette?'

I take one. The match he lights it with has a dark-brown tip and is taken from a little red box.

I look at the horse, my nose resting on the window between the grey curtains. I remain there in silence, not moving, while Giangiacomo Zingaretti anticipates the prize he'll win.

I think about what my mother would say. 'Don't be difficult, dear. It'll be very quick, then a good scrub in the bidet.'

And I think about Deborah as well. I know she also passed through this office, but I still don't know if she was on the red couch and if Gian was the monster who destroyed her.

Friday, 7 January 1983

I'd seen the bottle of water and the straw in the waste-paper basket of Anita Messi's room on the day she died. But then, I was completely uninterested. It was now almost five months since the body had been found.

I'd asked for the analysis after Nico Gerace suggested it, and it came back in only three days, thanks to Capuzzo's hometown contact in Forensics.

We received confirmation that, on that single night spent in the women's hall of residence of the pontifical college of the Sisters of the Virgin, Anita Messi had used that bottle and that straw to smoke crack cocaine. This was something I could have discovered five months ago.

I called my deputy in. Speaking to the people in Argentina had now become very urgent.

'So, Capuzzo, who do I need to get in touch with about this call? The Pope? Or the President of the Republic?'

He spread his arms wide.

'You'll have to be patient, Dottore – I'm working on it. This is Rome.'

★   ★   ★

I've already been to Dino Forte's place overlooking Piazza Navona with a view of the Four Rivers fountain. We're coming back with the troupe for a drink after the last studio rehearsals for tomorrow's grand finale. They've been exhausting, each rehearsal as if it were the first.

Although I'm wiped out, I'm going along to see, watch and listen. To follow the ammonia trail.

Yesterday was Epiphany. Children are still on holiday, and Piazza Navona's a whirl of families and tourists mingling in between the shops, monuments, stalls and portrait artists.

Everyone recognizes Dino Forte as we push through the crowd, even the Japanese tourists, who ask for a photo instead of an autograph. He looks elegant dressed in his wool jacket and needle-thread cords. A youthful-looking fifty-year-old.

We come up to one of the portrait artists, a middle-aged woman with completely white hair. She gets up, takes his hand and almost kisses it, as if he were the Pope. She points to me, I shake my head to say no, but you don't go against Dino Forte.

'Charmene is my trusted portrait artist, Claudia. To my real friends, I make gifts of the portraits she draws.'

To my real friends. We'll become real friends, then.

I cast a glance at the portraits on show. In fact, they are very good. A little black boy with an ice-cream cone. An old Japanese tourist with a camera. A girl who looks like a South American Indian.

All right, I'll have my portrait done.

Thanks to the irreplaceable Capuzzo, the authorization for my second intercontinental call to Argentina came through. The university was closed, but they gave out a private number to call. And, that Saturday afternoon, I got down to business.

The line was perfect, apart from the second's delay it took the voices to cross the ocean.

'A great holiday,' said one of Anita's two friends, in Spanish an Italian could understand.

'Where did you visit?' I asked.

'Art galleries and beaches. Greece. Portugal. Spain. Not Italy, because Anita was going there on her own in August.'

'Art galleries and beaches. And for fun, boys, Ibiza?'

You're so basic, Balistreri. And old, so very old. Why don't you ask directly if they smoked crack? She might even tell you, seeing as you can't arrest her.

'No, no boys or nightlife. Only art galleries and beaches. And Maradona, of course. We went to Barcelona to see the World Cup. Except Argentina lost to you Italians, then to those damned Brazilians. Luckily, you eliminated them.'

I decided to chance it. 'Did you smoke anything in Spain?'

'Of course, those stinking Spanish Ducados!'

'I mean, marijuana, hashish, cocaine.'

'*Tu es loco, señor?* Are you crazy?'

'If not you two, what about Anita?'

Silence. Only for a moment, but a moment too long. A pause I'd learned to recognize.

'Who gave her the drug?'

'We didn't take any, *señor*. Anita made friends with three Italian guys, Sicilians.'

'With a smart black car?'

'Yes, *señor*. An *ingles* car. A Jaguar.'

I had an answer. Now I needed confirmation.

'When did you all leave?'

'The fifteenth of July.' She wasn't jovial any more, but terse and hostile.

'And Anita went to visit her aunt before leaving for Italy?' I asked.

'Yes, *señor*. She's a good *chica*.'

'And her aunt's in Colombia?' I asked. But I already knew the answer.

'Yes, *creo que si*. But I don't know her, *señor*.'

Anita Messi, a penniless orphan, gives herself an expensive European holiday with friends, returns to Argentina, makes a quick visit to Colombia and then comes to Rome to get herself killed.

Yes, everything was beginning to come clear. Everything.

When I get there for make-up in the early afternoon, Nico Gerace's in front of the dressing room's entrance. Beautifully coiffured, smart sports jacket, his cheeks are shaved but there's still a dark shadow. Everyone says hi to him; the director and he have a chat. Dino Forte shakes his hand.

Then he comes over to the corner where I'm sitting on my own, drinking mineral water.

He sits down and looks at me for a bit. 'You were right, Claudia.'

'Sorry?'

'You're not the most beautiful, but you know how to perform.'

He could be a handsome guy if he didn't have that manufactured air and underlying roughness. As if that showy self-confidence was only a shield to protect a man who was much less confident. Perhaps more real and likable.

'If you like, I'll put you on my books, Claudia.'

I look at him, perplexed. I know what the jargon means, but don't understand why. I'm still not famous enough to become part of his stable of clients.

He anticipates the question.

'I went into this game for money. And I'm still making it, lots of it, with big names like Dino Forte. But I'm missing the satisfaction of launching a star. And, from this evening, you'll be a star.'

'I'm not beautiful enough. You've just said.'

'I said you weren't the most beautiful. But you do have cucuzza and cabbasisi.'

I look at him wonderingly. He smiles.

'I'm sorry, it's what we say in Sicily. It's dialect for "brains" and "balls".'

The break's about to end. 'Thanks, Nico. I'm really honoured, but I can't accept the offer.'

He's disappointed. Who does this presumptuous little kid think she is? I give him the reason.

'I don't want an agent who's a friend of Michele Balistreri.'

He looks at me, taken aback. 'Why?'

'I'm sorry, but that's my business.'

He understands that I'm not going to say anything more.

'As you wish. Look, I was Michele's friend as a boy in Tripoli. We haven't seen each other for twelve years. We met by chance in Barcelona a few months ago. Angelo was also there. We haven't been friends for years really.'

'So you're no longer friends?'

He crosses his fingers in front of his mouth, a Sicilian gesture for telling the truth. 'I swear it on the dead body of my mother, Santuzza.'

At the end of the day, Nico Gerace could be helpful. Not for my career, but to find out who ruined Deborah. He knows everyone in this world. The break's over, and I get up. I hold out my hand.

'Then I accept.'

Nico told me the good news by phone just before the final show began. I was having supper at Alberto's with Ingrid and Angelo Dioguardi.

'She's accepted. I'm now her agent.'

While the images of Claudia Teodori's final coronation in the TV firmament were showing, I listened to the admiring comments of my brother, his fiancée and Angelo.

'She's a very good performer,' said Alberto.

'And she's a very good girl,' Angelo added.

Ingrid looked at me. She was very fond of me, because I was the *enfant terrible* brother Alberto worshipped.

'She'd be ideal for you, Michele,' she whispered softly, so the others couldn't hear.

But it was too late for that, and many other things.

I hadn't heard from the apostles with their intuitions and statistics, nor from Teodori. I hadn't even called him to wish him Merry Christmas and a Happy New Year. But I'd now delegated keeping an eye on Claudia to Nico Gerace, and so my conscience could rest easy.

However, it was to Teodori I owed the fact that I was still a policeman. And thus able to investigate the cases of Anita and Nadia. And when the television cameras panned first over Dino Forte's professionally constructed smile, then the grasping looks on Rossellini and that shark Zingaretti, I decided that perhaps Claudia Teodori merited a little more of my time.

Rossellini I'd met, while Dino Forte was a well-known face. Giangiacomo Zingaretti was the unknown quantity. So, after the show, I called Nico and asked him another favour. He said there was no problem at all; he'd already got the right opportunity set up. And I'd never been to Capri. Apostle Paul had once said that, in the winter, it was a real paradise.

Saturday, 15 January 1983

Capri's always so beautiful, and much more so in winter. The streets are less chaotic, the sky's a deeper colour and the sea seems even more transparent.

We're here for the prize of TV's Best Newcomer 1982.

I'm among the five finalists, thanks to the skill, success and influence of the magical union of Dino Forte and Giangiacomo Zingaretti. I'm sitting between the two of them, at the front. Behind me is my new agent, Nico Gerace. Further behind, I spotted Michele Balistreri.

When they're about to announce the winner, Nico taps me on the shoulder. I turn round and he whispers, 'It's you.' Now that he's with me, I really am everyone's favourite.

And it is me! Applause, flash photography, thanking everyone on stage. After the ceremony, we're out in the square for more photos, among the admiring looks of the Italians and a few curious tourists.

Then dinner at Punta Tragora. I can barely eat, while Giangiacomo Zingaretti's hand gently brushes against my knee, letting me know that payback time won't be far off. His beautiful forty-year-old wife stares at me from the other side of the table and every so often gives a passionate glance at Balistreri, who appears to have had an invitation, I'm not sure how. So I've found myself at the same table with him, while Nico's already left.

I go up to him on the terrace when everyone goes out for a smoke between dessert and coffee.

'Might I know what the hell you're doing here, Commissario?'

The view is breathtaking. Off the coast are the Faraglioni rocks, small points of light glittering on the fishing boats, the dark winter sea as cold and calm as the look of the shit who's now observing me through a cloud of cigarette smoke.

And yet there's something different in his stare. Yes, perhaps for the first time, Michele Balistreri's actually looking at the real me and not at my tits or my arse. And not looking at my eyes but into them, looking perhaps for the first time for my soul. He doesn't know that there's nothing he can do. My soul died with Deborah.

'Why are you here?' I insist.

'To protect you.'

'Who from, Zingaretti? He's only like you, but a better man, perhaps.'

But I can see he's concerned, different from usual, troubled.

'So, what are you doing here, Commissario?'

'Are you sleeping with him?' Balistreri asks me.

I didn't think I was capable of it. I could hold back angry tears, but not the resounding slap. I turn my back on him and go back inside.

All these beautiful people: the men in dinner jackets, the women in evening gowns. Jewellery, perfume, fine wines, silver cutlery. I was alone on the hotel terrace, enjoying the cool night, looking at the cold sea and feeling my cheek burning.

But it wasn't Claudia Teodori's slap that was making my skin burn, it was the awareness of my failure. On that other shore, the one full of sand and the *ghibli*, I hadn't left only Laura Hunt naked in body and crushed in spirit after forcing myself on her.

I had left myself and my will to live. And, with them, the ability to understand the feelings of others and feel the truth of them myself.

I had only a few feelings left, but they were a family unit: the sense of justice, anger, thirst for vengeance.

Settle accounts with the bad guys. With one in particular.

But, before anything else, there was Claudia Teodori, and not only because I'd promised her father. Not even because she perhaps wasn't the little slut I'd always thought she was.

It was for myself, because understanding Claudia Teodori – really and truly understanding her – was the last chance I had of coming back to the land of the living.

I was beginning to get a handle on the situation. *You can't protect her if you can't understand or believe her.*

I went back inside to the table. Claudia and Zingaretti weren't around, but his beautiful wife spotted me. A half-smile on her lips, she rose and came up to me.

'Is it cold outside?'

I glanced at her naked shoulders, tanned and beautiful. 'I think you'd get goose pimples.'

I saw her nipples grow hard and press against her silk designer gown.

'Would you accompany me to my room to get a shawl, Commissario Balistreri?'

I'm still thinking about that shit Balistreri when Gian takes me off to his suite.

'Are you sleeping with . . . ?' As if he gave a damn. He thinks I'm nothing but a little slut.

In the hall is his secretary, Renata, the person who won't let anyone in while her boss is having a quickie with me.

'What if your wife comes in?' I protested.

'We always have separate rooms in hotels. It's OK.'

He lights a cigarette with one of the matches with a dark-brown head, then takes me to look at the sea. He stands behind me, his favourite position. I stand

by the window as I do in his office with its grey curtains over the Dying
Horse. *I prefer to have my back to him and let him fondle my backside rather
than turn round and have to kiss him. I'll let him fuck me, if I have to, but I'll
never kiss him. I'd rather die first. I look at the rocks twenty metres down
below. It wouldn't be difficult, or even painful. But first I have to find out who
reduced Deborah to that state.*

He puts his hands on my hips.

'We have to be back down there in five minutes, Gian.'

*'That's right, Claudia. I have to make a speech for all those idiots. But my
wife's away next weekend, and we can finally have plenty of time to celebrate
your great success.'*

It was a silk shawl. Far too light for an evening walk in January, even
in Capri. And Signora Zingaretti didn't want to get her goose
pimples in that way. She had a much better way in mind. The
shawl served only to keep my tongue from her skin. For a moment,
that is.

Then the handsome face of her loving husband, Giangiacomo
Zingaretti, appeared on the CCTV screen in front of the large bed.

'I've got to listen to him,' she told me, lying flat on her stomach,
turning towards the screen. 'He likes to ask me afterwards what he's
said.'

'Well, you'd better pay attention, then.'

She picked up a little box and a tiny straw from the bedside
table.

'You're not going to arrest me, are you, Commissario?'

'Does your husband do a line?'

She laughed, pointing to Zingaretti's smiling face on the screen.

'Him? He's not the type. But he's understanding, and doesn't mind
if his women do.'

She did a line while I removed the shawl wrapped round her hips
and revealed her naked buttocks.

'Now there's nothing to distract me.'

It went on like this for twenty minutes or so, Giangiacomo Zingaretti making his senseless speech and his wife, who was much more stimulated, moaning and panting breathlessly.

In the end, she applauded. '*Bravo! Bravissimo!*'

I didn't ask who she was complimenting, Gian or me.

She lit a cigarette with a match from a red box. She handed me the packet, but I signalled no. Only one thing interested me.

'Does your husband sleep with these little starlets?'

She turned over on her back, resting her long legs on my shoulders.

'What do you care? You're not Claudia Teodori's boyfriend, by any chance, are you?'

'No, but I am a friend of her father.'

She snorted another line.

'Well, he hasn't. If he had, I'd certainly know about it.'

'How come?' I asked.

She looked at me defiantly.

'Because he likes to count me in. We have an agreement. After he's had his way with them, then it's my turn for a night of coke and sex. And it's not been my turn with Claudia Teodori yet.'

She was having fun, trying to shock me. But I was thinking about far worse things that they and their world did. And I was worried about what was to come.

'Claudia Teodori's father's a friend of mine,' I said again.

'Then you can tell him he has nothing to worry about. Claudia Teodori's under Nico Gerace's protective wing now. Gian'll think twice about laying a finger on her.'

I looked at her in amazement. 'How come?'

'Because this happened a few years ago as well. Gian messed up one of his clients. And Nico Gerace was very disagreeable. Is the questioning now over, Commissario?'

I licked her ankle. She softened immediately.

She arched herself so that I could do the same to the back of her knee.

'And Gian's very good. If he fucks them, he brings them to me and then never sees them again. He uses them once and then throws them away. Now use me, Commissario, then you can gently throw me away, too.'

Sunday, 16 January 1983

At six in the morning, I'm back from Capri, in time to have a brief chat with my flatmate, who gets up at that time. We're on the fourth floor in the kitchen, the French window open because she smokes. She has a coffee and I have a herbal tea, while we catch up on our two separate lives for ten minutes. And how I wish I could swap my life with hers, but I can't.

I tell her about the trendiest clubs in Rome and about Nico Gerace, who now comes to pick me up every night at eleven in his Ferrari Mondial, a four-seater, with one of the guys who works with him and one of his young flames of the moment. Then we're off: the Jackie O, Number One, Bella Blu, two hours in each place, in the private VIP lounges with the champagne that I'm not allowed to drink.

'Great!' she says.

'Really boring,' I tell her.

'So why d'you go?'

'It's in the contract. It's what my agent wants. I have to be seen around. Seen, but not touched.'

I don't tell her about Rossellini's bad breath, the portrait gift for Dino Forte's best friends or about Giangiacomo Zingaretti's wandering hands.

Nor about the private parties in Villa X or Villa Y: houses of the very famous in the entertainment world where powerful men and filthy-rich women mingle with young dancers, actors and actresses, assistants and presenters. Plus the court of bootlickers and lackeys.

Nor do I tell her about the trays with the mini pizzas, deep-fried delicacies, rum babas and white stripes and short straws: they never come to you full, those lines, to let you know that someone else has snorted first and that you can help yourself for free.

I'm suddenly tired, worn out. I've lost ten kilos, forced to stick to a rigid diet, hours and hours in the gym which is a real drag, then Turkish baths, massages, beauty treatment, hairdressers, make-up, trying on stage costumes and evening clothes.

I can't stand the nightlife that Nico forces on me, and already it'll start again tonight.

I hate Rossellini's bad breath, rehearsals with Dino Forte and Giangiacomo Zingaretti's wandering hands.

But I have to put up with it for Debbie. I have to know who it was. And then what will I do?

As soon as I get back from Capri, I call Angelo Dioguardi and tell him what I've found out about Claudia. And it was all good news.

'Let's go round and tell Teodori, Michele. It'll make him feel good.'

I hadn't seen or heard from Teodori for almost two months, since I'd told him and his apostles to go to hell for their stupid comments about the Anita Messi case. And I wouldn't have gone to his place if Angelo hadn't forced me to.

A Polish carer opened the door and said that Teodori could no longer get out of bed. He was now as yellow as a rotten lemon, but he could still breathe by himself, and gave us a weak smile when he saw us come in.

Angelo kissed him on the cheeks. I made the ridiculous gesture of trying to shake his hand, but he didn't even have the strength to raise it.

And he smiled at me. As if I'd never stormed off.

The old man still has some faith in me.

Angelo told him all the positive news, emphasizing my good points. I'd put Nico in charge of looking after Claudia and had made sure that Zingaretti hadn't taken her to bed or got her hooked on drugs.

'So everything's all right. Claudia's with Nico Gerace at the Jackie O right now. On nights out, he doesn't let her out of his sight.'

Teodori looked at me with gratitude. He even tried to smile at me from that sunken yellow face. But my face must have looked pretty sour.

'Problems with Anita Messi?' he asked, as if we'd never had those words about the case.

Something in his eyes finally touched me.

I told him *all* the latest developments, up to the call to Argentina.

'Bravo. Very good, Balistreri,' he said in the end. 'I knew you were a good policeman.'

This was possibly the last moment to tell him that he didn't really come into it. It was Italy and the Italians I detested, not him and his daughter. I found an indirect way to do it.

'I could do with Pietro and Paolo, seeing as Claudia's being looked after.'

Teodori thought about it a moment. I couldn't smell the medicine on his breath any more, but there was something bitterer and deeper.

Death.

Then he smiled.

'Agreed. Just one request.'

The usual aging father begging me to look after his daughter.

'I'd like my pipe,' he said. 'It's on the bedside table, along with a packet of Borkum Riff.'

I looked at him in shock. 'You must be crazy. It's out of the question.'

But Angelo Dioguardi had already fetched it and was filling it with tobacco. He helped Teodori rise a little, put the stem between his lips and held it for him. Then he lit the pipe and Teodori inhaled the smoke.

'Thanks, Angelo. And now, Michele, a drop of Chivas Regal. It's on the table in the living room.'

It was the first time he'd used my Christian name. I felt light on my feet, as I hadn't done for years. It was as if some magic had entered this house so full of death. I brought him a generous shot of the whisky.

For a while, helped by Angelo, Teodori sipped the whisky and puffed on the pipe, switching between the two, with the same contentment and pleasure of a baby sucking its mother's nipple.

Then he looked at me with that tired yellow smile.

'Where I am, you see things from a different perspective, Balistreri. I really care about your skin.'

He's delirious. He's dying. He doesn't know what he's saying.

He stopped for a fit of coughing. His voice was so weak I had to bend close to hear him.

'Some coincidences happen only in books and films. But not in reality, or else they're not coincidences.'

Then he leaned back on his pillow, exhausted. Two minutes later, he was asleep, his breathing more like a rattling sound.

Angelo Dioguardi decided to stay and keep him company. I left him to it.

I'm ready to go out. Nico's come up to collect me, looking smart in his gabardine overcoat with a fur collar. Always a little over the top.

The phone rings. It's Angelo Dioguardi. His speaks softly, the voice of a good man.

'I've just called an ambulance. They're taking him to San Giovanni. Can you get over there quickly?'

We rush there in the rainy night in Nico's Ferrari.

'Don't think about this,' he tells me.

'Great advice, Nico. Thanks.'

'Sorry, Claudia, I know. But it's too much for you.'

Even Nico Gerace understands me a little. Beneath his careless and super-ficial manner, he's a good guy. But he's not as truly and deeply good as Angelo Dioguardi. Angelo's something else.

Balistreri's the only one who doesn't understand. How can Angelo and Nico be friends with him? Because I do know that Nico is, even if he swore he wasn't.

'What was your great friend Michele like as a boy?' I ask him.

He thinks for a moment. He gives his scornful little smile and pats his hair back into place.

'All he knew was how to punch and shoot.'

And yet it was only that shit who could really help me. When I discover which of the three it was, I'll have need of something evil. And Balistreri is that evil.

Tanya was lying on my sofa, happily smoking after her massage. And the work-out. But I couldn't get those words out of my head.

Some coincidences happen only in books and films. But not in reality, or else they're not coincidences.

I shouldn't have been thinking about it. They were only words coming from a high temperature and delirium. And Tanya wanted another massage.

Angelo and Nico stay and wait for me in the hospital corridor. I enter the room alone. It's lit by a neon strip and filled with the beeps counting the time in the struggle between life and death.

Papa's got tubes everywhere. Up his nose, in his arms. He's got a catheter and an oxygen mask. No more medicines, only analgesics. The long war has reached the final battle.

That body on the bed is no longer his. His eyes are closed. I take a comb and scissors from the bedside cupboard. He cared a lot about his hair. I arrange it carefully for him and trim his moustache.

He opens his eyes. He looks at me from the door to another world. His lips are moving, there's no sound, but I can still understand.

'Claudia, my dear, sweet girl.'

The doctors had told me before I went in. His moments of consciousness are getting few and far between. Papa will die before tomorrow. I have a minute, perhaps my last.

What did my father want most for me? The simple things a good middle-class Catholic wants. A degree in law, a magistrate's job, a family.

'I've given up television. I'm going to enrol at university tomorrow.'

He looks at me. I'm not sure if he's taken it in. I need another lie, the most important one.

'I'm going to get married, Papa, I wanted it to be a surprise for you. I'm really very happy.'

That hollow yellow-mask smile; a finger moves to show he's pleased. Then Papa winks. Once, twice, three times, four times. It is a huge effort to ask me a question. It was an old game we had from when I was six and had had my tonsils out and, as a result, I couldn't speak. And I was a child who was always asking questions. So Papa taught me to ask by winking. Once: what? Twice: how? Three times: why? Four times: who?

I make up the answer I wish were true. The one he'd be pleased with, too.

'Angelo Dioguardi. He's waiting outside.'

He stares at me one last time.

'Please trust Balistreri,' he whispers. Then he shuts his eyes.

I rest my lips on his burning forehead and stay there, staring at the numbers on the heart monitor. As long as it takes. Up until the numbers say 'The End'.

Tuesday, 18 January 1983

Teodori's funeral took place in the Verano cemetery church at midday.

Angelo Dioguardi and Nico Gerace were in the front row, the Apostles Peter and Paul beside Claudia. Rossellini, Dino Forte and Zingaretti were in the first pews. I remained at the back of the church.

When my ex-boss's coffin was lowered into the ground, I saw the tears falling under his daughter's dark glasses.

Too late for crying now, sweetie. You should have shown him more affection when he was alive.

After the last spade of earth, she crossed herself. Then, gradually, everyone left, including Nico and Angelo. It seemed that she'd asked them to leave us alone together. I went up to offer my condolences, but she stopped me.

'Let's go over to the bar opposite, Balistreri. It's time to tell you a story.'

We sit down inside a scruffy bar that's almost empty, despite the fact that it's lunchtime. The room is damp, half in the dark and smells of frying. He orders a beer and a slice of pizza. He doesn't even ask me if I want anything.

'*Please trust Balistreri.*' *Those were Papa's last words. Please trust Balistreri, the evil man.*

He's right. Balistreri lured Marco Fratini into a trap, literally scared the shit out of him, sent him off to jail and saved me. He's capable of anything.

Who else could help me?

'*I want to tell you a story, Balistreri.*' *He makes a listless sign of agreement, drinks his beer and lights a cigarette.*

'*I met Deborah Reggiani at nursery school in San Giovanni. Her father worked on the building sites until he became disabled after falling off some scaffolding. Her mother was the concierge in the block of flats where I lived. After the accident in which she died, her parents left Rome and went to live out in the Castelli region. I was the idle girl from the bourgeoisie, she was the prole who was top of the class. I wanted to give her everything, but she didn't want anything; she was ashamed and indignant about it. I told my parents I lost things, and I gave them to her, anything from Barbie dolls to push-up bras. Deborah was good-hearted, intelligent and beautiful. She listened to me; we understood each other right away. Since she was a kid, she'd always had an unquenchable love of acting, dancing and singing. Her mother was dead set against it. It was me who secretly entered her at thirteen in a contest for an advertising agency. When they took her on, her mother was still against it. But, with my help, Deborah was able to set things up.*

And that's how it started. Advertising, then cabaret, then the theatre. And then the private channels came on the air, like Extra TV. And Deborah got to meet Rossellini, Dino Forte and Giangiacomo Zingaretti.

As soon as I tell him all this, Balistreri starts paying attention. Yes, he does have the instincts of a policeman.

For almost a year, she goes down the same road I have, except with more talent and drive. Then something happened that she kept hidden from me. I'm sure it was one of those three who gave her some crack to smoke. He took her to bed, then passed her on to his friends as well. I only came to know these things at the end, during those last terrible days with Deborah, when I went to visit her in the hole where she was living alone. I wanted to stay close to her. One day, I saw some marks on her arm, like cigarette burns. Some careless guy in a disco. That's what she said. But there were two burns, and far apart. He must have been a pretty clumsy guy.'

Balistreri lights another cigarette. He's following me closely now.

'In the days that followed, she began to get the shakes, nosebleeds and uncontrollable tears. Then moments of aggression alternating with depression, hostility and panic. Until I found a metal box in her bathroom with Minnie Mouse tape round it. There was white powder inside. She said she needed it to keep herself going through the ups and downs of the entertainment world. I took it away from her, that box, but it wasn't enough to account for her physical and mental decline. Then there was that dreadful afternoon when Deborah called me in a voice that seemed to come from beyond the grave, and she whispered, 'Goodbye, sweetheart.' I dashed over to her place in my father's car. I didn't have a licence, but I'd known how to drive for some time. Luckily, I had a set of keys to her one-room flat. The place was choking with gas coming from the rings, which she'd switched on full. Deborah was out of it on the bed, which was stained with blood, and there was a tube of sleeping pills that was almost empty. I opened the windows, dragged her into the bathroom, stuck her head under the cold tap and then two fingers down her throat to make her vomit. I poured black coffee into her mouth and made her walk up and down for two hours until she felt better. I asked her about it and sank into the deep, dark tunnel of horrors with her. At first, the same things happened to her as later happened to me: Rossellini, Dino Forte, Giangiacomo Zingaretti. The usual pathway that plenty go down. Then, at a party in one of the clubs, He had her try crack. Deborah was wiped out: exhausted through hunger and terrified. She never told me his name. She simply said "Him", as if he were the devil himself.'

'Would you like a cigarette?' Balistreri asks me.

He lights one and hands it to me. It's the first act of kindness he's shown me since I've known him. I carry on with the story.

'This Him has to be one of these three, the same three men I've come up *against: there's Rossellini, the rough one who breathes desire all over me and shows me off without ever coming on to me; then Forte, the handsome peacock who pays court to me with roses and kindness and once had my portrait made in Piazza Navona; and the powerful Zingaretti, who amuses himself by having me come to his office and who brushes against me between the grey curtains on his windows. It was one of those three who introduced her to crack and who fucked her. And that's where the nightmare started. After smoking that stuff and sleeping with Him, Deborah found herself with three men on the back seat of a white Rolls Royce. They abused her sexually, in every way, then offered her champagne. The same things began to be repeated every evening. This man sent her in the Rolls to elegant villas and yachts anchored off Ostia. Always different friends, to whom he offered a turn with the new little TV star. After a while, he said she was ready to start dealing among Rome's jet set at night. He pointed out the possible new clients, but never made the first move. Deborah had to do it. She refused, and so He showed her the photos he'd taken while those three men were fucking her brains out. But Deborah still refused, so He moved on to the use of burning cigarette ends. And so she began dealing coke and crack.'*

And here's the man Papa caught a glimpse of. I can see him myself now. The man who's offering me his glass of beer. But also the man whose eyes frighten me. Balistreri'll know what to do with that bastard. The man Debbie simply named as 'He' as she shook with fear.

'He turned my Debbie into a whore of a coke dealer. Two days before, he'd told her that, that night, she'd have to have sex with two gentlemen of a certain age, both important clients. She refused, and he tortured her again, doing something dreadful, and then he left. So Debbie shut the windows, turned the gas on and took the sleeping pills. Except she wanted to say goodbye to me on the phone. And I dashed over to save her. I promised I'd help her. My father was a police commissario. But Debbie was terrified and never told me his name. In the end, she told me only the name of the guy who gave her the stuff she had to deal.'

★   ★   ★

'Marco Fratini, the scum who put the amphetamines in your glass,' I said.

Claudia Teodori nodded. There was something in her eyes that hadn't been there before.

Or perhaps it had always been there, Michele. But you were too busy ogling her body to notice.

'I dragged her off to that club in Ostia. She pointed Fratini out to me there and I went over and tackled him. Deborah shut herself in the toilets so she wouldn't be seen, because she was already famous.'

'You should have reported him, Claudia, instead going in and acting the idiot.'

'I wanted to know who this Him was, the bastard that Fratini was working for. Rossellini, Forte or Zingaretti.'

'How?'

'As you say, by acting the idiot, the little slut ready to do anything to get an audition. Straightaway, Fratini said he would help me, if I'd be nice to him. I asked him who he knew at the RAI. I said he had to get me to meet the guy before he could have me.'

'But Fratini wasn't playing ball and he slipped those little yellow pills in your glass without you being aware of it.'

'I suppose so. But Fratini made a call from the phone in the club. Then he told me that he'd spoken to his boss in Rome, saying that I wanted to meet him. And he was about to come over.'

I looked at her, bewildered.

Something not quite right here, Balistreri. Something not right at all.

'I was terrified. One of those three was about to come over. He was about to come over there. He'd see Debbie and discover everything. I rushed into the toilets to get her and, although my head was spinning, I put her in the car and set off so as to get far away from there.'

'And you went off the road at that corner.'

Claudia was crying. Now she was nothing more than a young girl, her make-up dissolving under all those tears. First for her father, now for Deborah Reggiani.

'I saved her life that afternoon and then, that night, I killed her,' she whispered.

No, Claudia. That stuff about Fratini's phone call's ridiculous; he had no reason to want to please you and get Him over there. Or, rather, it was for a different reason.

I had to keep my anger, that old companion of mine, under control. I was no longer a kid, no longer in Tripoli, and Fratini wasn't someone like Salim who I could shoot with impunity.

I lit a cigarette while my mind raced. I ordered another beer and another slice of pizza with mozzarella.

Claudia was in floods of tears.

'I killed her, driving like crazy without any need.'

'No, Claudia, you didn't kill her. It was Fratini and this other man.'

She looked up and stared at me through her tears.

'What are you saying, Balistreri?'

'Fratini's phone call and him telling you that He was about to come over were a means to get you rushing to the car with Deborah to get away. And the amphetamines weren't so that he could take advantage of you, but to make sure you didn't get back to Rome alive.'

Claudia stared at me in disbelief. She dried her tears. I handed her a paper handkerchief and she blew her nose.

'So we'd die in a crash? Well, it's possible. But, equally, it could be that nothing happened at all.'

'They knew you'd try to get away at top speed.'

'All right, but that couldn't have been enough. Accidents always happen by chance.'

But, here, there's been nothing left to chance, nothing at all. Everything was planned.

'Claudia, I read the traffic police's accident report at the time, because I wanted to find a way to help you out.'

'And so?'

'You went off the road less than a kilometre out of Ostia, as soon as you'd taken the road for Rome. There was no fluid in the braking system and there was a good deal of it at the site of the accident.'

'True. Everything was broken in the crash, and the brake fluid escaped.'

'Perhaps. Given that no one had any suspicions about anything, the traffic police didn't investigate further.'

'What d'you think then?'

I think that, while you were in the club with Fratini, someone emptied the car's brake fluid and put a good amount of it on the tarmac just before that curve. He – Deborah's Him – was there. He was waiting for you.

'I'm not quite sure, Claudia. But I know that you have to go and rest.'

She looked me in the eyes. They had a deep, proud and clean look in them. I had been blind, arrogant, irresponsible and full of prejudice.

The poisoned fruit of Marlene and Laura Hunt. And my own anger.

She looked at the beer and the slice of still-warm pizza with its stringy mozzarella. I hadn't touched them. I pushed them towards her.

'I got them for you. Please eat.'

She smiled again. She took a nibble of pizza and a sip of beer.

But there was one last thing I had to ask her.

'Claudia, you said there were bloodstains on Debbie's bed when she tried to kill herself. Did she slit a vein?'

'No, the blood was from that dreadful thing that He did to her.'

I had an awful premonition, although a part of me didn't want to know any more.

'Which was?'

'She absolutely didn't want to have sex with the two men.'

'And so?'

'So he cut off the last joint of the middle finger on her right hand and told her that, if she made any more stupid fuss, he'd cut off the whole finger.'

Some coincidences happen only in books and films. But not in reality, or else they're not coincidences.

I stared at her in a daze, as if I couldn't even see her.

The ghibli. *The muezzin's cry. Jamaal the goatherd. The boat trip. My mother. The olive-pressing shed. The missing finger.*

Everything had begun there. Everything, in that sand and with that blood.

I went by bus to the police station and got off one stop before it. I walked in the rain to let my rage calm down and to regain lucidity.

As soon as I was in my office, I made a telephone call. Marco Fratini had been transferred a month before from the Roman prison of Regina Coeli to the Ucciardone in Palermo. He had been threatened by other inmates, and his counsel, a smart criminal lawyer for the rich, had got him the transfer.

I wasn't happy about this: neither the timing, nor the final destination.

Deborah Reggiani and Anita Messi. Two totally separate cases, and yet both lead to Sicily. Marco Fratini's transfer couldn't be ordered by just anyone, only by someone who had power. And that was Power with a capital 'P', Michele. Real power.

I needed an order signed by the examining magistrate, otherwise they wouldn't let me past the Ucciardone gates. And the examining magistrate wanted to know what Marco Fratini had to do with Anita Messi.

I told him what Claudia Teodori had told me about Deborah Reggiani. But the links were weak, hypothetical, and I had no proof. It was only the fingertip that persuaded him to authorize the request to question Fratini. Having the girl's body exhumed to see if the finger were missing its last joint was out of the question, though, and premature.

We immediately notified Fratini and his lawyer of the urgent need to interview him. I gave Capuzzo money and sent him off to buy me a ticket to Palermo for the following day. Better not to involve the police's own travel bureau.

I made ready to travel to my father's native land.

Wednesday, 19 January 1983

I left Rome in the rain and landed in Palermo at one in the afternoon in warm, almost spring-like sunshine.

We're almost in Africa.

As soon as I was out of the terminal, I saw a thickset man with a moustache and a cardboard sign: 'Michele Balistreri'. I tried to slip past him, but he must have known my face. He came up to me, all smiles.

'Commissario Balistreri, your Uncle Tano has a car for you while you're here in Palermo.'

My Uncle Gaetano. The eldest of the five Balistreri brothers. The only one who had been investigated on more than one occasion for Mafia-style criminal conspiracy. And regularly acquitted.

'Look, I never ordered any car, and I don't know how Signor Gaetano Balistreri knew I was coming to Palermo, seeing as I only decided on the flight yesterday.'

He gave me an understanding smile for my obtuseness.

'We're in Palermo, Commissario. And your Uncle Tano always knows everything that goes on. And before anyone else.'

'Right, well, do give my thanks to Uncle Tano, but I'll take a taxi.

And, seeing as he knows everything, you can tell him that I'm going to the Ucciardone prison.'

I turned in the direction of the taxi rank. The guy with the moustache looked politely offended.

'Your Uncle Tano knows where you want to go. But he has a better day in mind for you. A good lunch at a restaurant in Mondello near the airport here by the sea. They do wonderful *arancini* and a spectacular pasta with fresh sardines. So, have a good meal, enjoy some sunshine and then take the next flight back to Rome.'

I stared back at him. Then I got in a taxi. I had to control myself, keep personal matters out of the investigation, otherwise my anger would cloud things, like the *ghibli*. And I would miss the trail.

It was two when I walked into the Ucciardone. Marco Fratini was waiting for me in the interview room with his lawyer.

Fratini gave me a look full of hatred. I had tricked him that evening by pretending to be a thug and forcing him to make a full confession about how he had slipped amphetamines into Claudia Teodori's glass. They had given him four years. But, with a confession, there was nothing more he could do, except hate me. And, anyway, the hate was mutual, now I had discovered the trap they had set for Claudia and Deborah. He was still a criminal, whereas I had only been one once.

But that's the only way you can get to the bottom of this, Balistreri. Going back to what you once were: Mike the outlaw.

After the ritual courtesies, I moved quickly on to the questions.

'That evening in the disco, you were chatting to Claudia Teodori. Did you know that Deborah Reggiani was also there, hiding in the toilets?'

'Deborah who?'

All right, you son of a bitch. I'm going to take you to pieces anyway.

'Deborah Reggiani, the showgirl on television. The girl who died in the accident,' I explained calmly.

'Oh yeah. Hot piece of pussy. Shame.'

The lawyer whispered a word of advice in his ear.

'I'm sorry, Balistreri. My lawyer here says I should watch my language.'

'Just answer the question, Fratini. Did you know that Deborah Reggiani was there in the club?'

'No.'

'So when you made that call from the club, why did you mention Deborah's name?'

'That's not true – I didn't mention her on the phone.'

I gave him a nice smile. 'But you've just admitted that you did make a call.'

A worried crease appeared on Fratini's brow. The lawyer's face also grew dark.

'Dottor Balistreri, I'm not clear as to the reasons for this interview. My client—'

'Your client has only to reply honestly to the questions, as requested by the examining magistrate.'

I looked at Fratini.

'So, who did you call from the bar when you were talking to Claudia Teodori?'

He started to sweat.

'I don't remember.'

'Well, try. I want a first name and a surname. We've already asked for a record of the club's calls from the phone company. It's just a matter of time.'

Fratini gave a hopelessly lost look to his lawyer.

'May I have ten minutes alone with my client, Dottor Balistreri?' the lawyer asked.

I got up. 'Ten minutes.'

I went out into the courtyard to have a cigarette in the sunshine. Around about were the tumbledown houses of Palermo's old quarter, and from the harbour came the sound of a ship's horn as it was leaving. Yes, I was getting much closer to home.

And closer to Mike, the Balistreri brothers and Papa.

After precisely ten minutes, I went back to the interview room. I was ready to finish him off.

Fratini seemed calmer; his lawyer must have said something to reassure him. They were both having a cappuccino in a paper cup from the machine in the corridor. Fratini suddenly put his hands to his throat and began to shudder. He staggered to his feet, breathing in convulsions.

I dashed over to support him. He leaned against me with all his weight while his whole body was gripped by a spasm. Then his breathing stopped.

Everything exploded into pandemonium, but the damage had been done. I looked at Fratini's lawyer. It had certainly been him who gave the final order when he saw the way the questions were going.

And he would certainly inform the Balistreri brothers of the unfortunate episode. Teodori's spiritual testimony again came to mind.

Sometimes the truth is very simple, Balistreri. And dangerous.

I had pulled the rope too tight. And it had broken. I thought it could be simple. But they could kill much more easily than I could. They made their living by it.

They had taken him out before he could give me that name. It wasn't at all easy to kill someone like that. It must be a very important name. And those people must be very powerful.

And untouchable. And the next victim will be me.

I'm at home, alone. It's pouring down outside. At three in the afternoon, there's a phone call.

'It's Michele Balistreri. I'm calling from Palermo.'

He sounds upset. Incredible, I'd never have thought of that adjective with the iciest man I know. But Balistreri's all burning ice inside. There's a part of him hidden behind a locked door. And the only key to unlock it is anger.

'Fratini died while I was questioning him. Potassium cyanide in his cappuccino.'

I start to tremble. But it's not fear. It's the anger in me as well. 'Did he give you the name of this "He"?'

'No, but we'll have the phone records of that club in Ostia by tomorrow. So they can tell us the name.'

'Can you arrest him straightaway?'

I can feel what he's thinking. He'd like to lie to me, say something to reassure me, but he doesn't. Perhaps he's beginning to understand and respect me.

'Not for Deborah's death. The car in which you had the accident's been scrapped. There's no mention of any possible tampering in the traffic police's report, and Fratini's dead.'

'So he'll get away with it, this man who ruined Deborah? And who you now think killed her as well?'

'He can get away with Deborah's death. But I'll get something on him for pushing drugs.'

'He won't even go to prison, Balistreri.'

'Perhaps not, Claudia. But have faith and be patient. The coke and crack trail's the right one.'

'All right, Michele. We'll do what we can.'

I end the conversation and look out of the window. It's no longer raining and now the sun's out. And a rainbow over there behind the nice bourgeois district where I used to live as a girl with Mamma and Papa. Where Debbie's mother worked as concierge. And the courtyard where we played with our Barbie dolls. I used to give mine to her, and she taught them how to dance.

No, I can't do it by myself. I have to unlock that door, and the key is Balistreri's anger.

During the journey from the prison in Palermo to Punta Raisi airport, I realized that my thoughts went back a long way, to even before Nadia.

They began in 1962, with the young black woman and her baby found in the cesspit near the Al Bakris' wooden shack. I was twelve, like Nico and Ahmed; Karim and Laura were ten; Salim fourteen, and Farid sixteen.

They'd fallen in by themselves. Who'd said that? I remembered quite well. The same man who'd said that my mother had killed herself.

In 1969, Nadia Al Bakri's body had been found nearby in the olive-pressing shed with the middle finger of her right hand missing. Chopped off. The adults had no alibi, and Farid wasn't at the market.

Now there were Anita Messi and Deborah Reggiani. Two cases absolutely unconnected, except for the crack, Anita's finger and the tip of Deborah's. It was the way in which the killer terrorized his victims, or else disfigured them, as in Anita Messi's case.

And he hadn't counted on a letter from Tripoli.

Nadia Al Bakri's finger was buried under the sand and under Gaddafi's regime.

I don't know why, but I turned round to look through the taxi's rear window. I recognized the black Jaguar immediately. It was the one that had been in Barcelona for the Italy–Brazil game. The one owned by the three Sicilians who'd supplied cocaine to young Kate at I Tre Peccati.

It was moving calmly along thirty metres behind us on the Palermo–Punta Raisi motorway, clearly visible, just to let me know it was there.

They want to sort this matter out in their own way. Taking their time.

The final settlement had been only postponed. Now I knew for certain that the great Balistreri family was finally fed up with the Ingegnere's rebellious son.

Perhaps my father had protected me in the past. But now I was an adult, a policeman, who was getting too close to people who were untouchable.

I only need some proof to link you to Nadia. And to the killers who saw to Anita and Deborah.

During the flight from Palermo to Rome, the plane was buffeted about frighteningly in a storm. But I barely took any notice, so worn out was I by the tension. I expected there to be an explosion at any moment but, evidently, an attack of that nature wasn't in their interests. Too much fuss, too much attention, too great a disturbance to their businesses.

They'll wait until everything's calmed down and they can get you alone, isolated, and discredit you as a policeman and a man, which is what they always do.

When the plane landed in Fiumicino, I went to a phone box and called Pietro, the chubby Apostle. He responded morosely.

'Paolo and I were going to pay a visit to Teodori's grave.'

'No, you're not. I need the two of you. Let's meet in my office in an hour.'

At eight in the evening, I was in the Vigna Clara police station. I updated Capuzzo, Pietro and Paolo on the developments in the case, leaving out only the letters from Tripoli. I told them about Fratini's death in prison and the black Jaguar along the motorway to Punta Raisi.

'Is Claudia in danger?' Pietro asked me, looking alarmed.

I thought for a moment.

No, she's not in danger, she is the danger.

'No, but we don't want her doing anything stupid. If we find out who killed Anita Messi, we'll also find out who killed Deborah Reggiani. And that's what Claudia wants.'

'So what can Paolo and I do, Balistreri?'

'One thing, right away, tonight. There's a piano bar behind Piazza di Spagna, I Tre Peccati. Some time ago there, I saw the three that followed me today from Palermo, the same guys who were in Barcelona. Go over there and find out who they are and if people have anything to say about them.'

'All right. Anything else?'

'Anita Messi's movements from when she landed at six in the evening. She got to the hall of residence at midnight. How come? What had she been doing? With whom? And the same for the morning she died, after she went out.'

'That's a tough one, Balistreri. Couldn't you have done it in August?'

Capuzzo looked out of the window in silence.

I could have. I should have. But, at that time, I couldn't have cared less about Anita Messi.

I wasn't afraid that they'd do any harm to Claudia. I could discount that. There was no motive for it and they would only expose themselves even more by doing so. No, the fears I had for Claudia Teodori stemmed from that *We'll do what we can.*

As soon as Pietro and Paolo left, I gave Capuzzo his instructions. I needed to know who Fratini had called from that bar in the club. I asked him to contact the examining magistrate. This was a new branch in the Anita Messi investigation. The magistrate would raise all sorts of questions, but Capuzzo was very capable and diplomatic, unlike me.

I called in on the examining magistrate at nine that evening. He was still in his office and saw me straightaway.

'Your deputy called me, that nice man Capuzzo. I've signed the authorization for the telephone company.'

'Thank you, but it won't be enough, Signor Giudice.'

I explained to him that Fratini's death in prison, which he already knew about, supported my case that Deborah Reggiani had been murdered.

I made no mention of my Uncle Tano, Monsignor Eugenio Pizza, Senator Emilio Busi nor Cavaliere Salvatore Balistreri, recently decorated for services to industry. Nor did I mention Nadia Al Bakri and the letters from Tripoli.

'And so, Balistreri, you want to open an investigation into the death of Deborah Reggiani, which happened last year on 9 July? But there is no case. It was a road accident caused by Claudia Teodori because of the amphetamines that Marco Fratini put in her drink.'

'Yes, Dottore. But Marco Fratini's a lead that takes us a long way.'

'But this is beyond your area of responsibility, Dottor Balistreri. You have enough knots to untangle with the Anita Messi case.'

'It's all part of the same case, Signor Giudice. I've mentioned this, if you recall. On the day she died, Deborah Reggiani had a bandage on her right hand. The top joint of her middle finger had been cut off. I was informed of this by Claudia Teodori. The trouble was that in the wreckage of the accident no one noticed.'

The examining magistrate had taken a liking to me and trusted me, perhaps because I'd left him in peace in the middle of August when he wanted to enjoy the last of his holidays.

'So what do you plan to do, Balistreri?'

'Investigate Deborah Reggiani's death and also the three influential men who helped her rise to fame last year: Rossellini, Dino Forte and Giangiacomo Zingaretti.'

He was an unexpectedly courageous man. He smiled.

'A dog's breakfast. Well, best of luck, Balistreri. Try not to get yourself hurt, eh?'

After I'd said goodbye to the magistrate and returned to my office in Vigna Clara, it was a little after ten. The two apostles, Pietro and Paolo, were already back from their mission, and were waiting for me, along with Capuzzo.

'The request for the telephone records has gone off to SIP,' Capuzzo told me. 'I've a contact in the phone company, and it won't take long.'

It was as if I'd asked it as a favour. I had to get used to the fact we were on different planets. He was an earthling; I was the Martian.

'Thank you, Capuzzo. And you two gentlemen?'

They had already been to I Tre Peccati, and had some information. They'd said they were looking for three men with a black Jaguar and had been told that these men would be back later that night. Their names were given as Calogero and Luciano Nastasia, and Vito, a first cousin of theirs.

'Good. Now you can start looking into Anita Messi's few hours in Rome between 13 and 14 August, starting at Fiumicino airport. While you, Capuzzo, can check the alibis of Rossellini, Forte and Zingaretti for 9 July last year, when Deborah Reggiani died. And for the morning of 14 August, when Anita Messi died. And be discreet, no direct questions to them.'

'But how do I do that, Commissario?'

Paolo, the thin Apostle who looked like Stan Laurel, shot me a glance.

'I can help you there.'

Yes, he could. The two of them had years of experience in Homicide.

I took a cigarette out, but had no light.

Pietro took out a box of matches from his pocket and handed it to me. It was red, with a stylized black devil on it.

'Where do these come from?' I asked him.

'I got them there, at I Tre Peccati's piano bar.'

It was the same box I'd seen in a Capri hotel room as I was having sex with a woman while she was listening to her husband's idiotic words on CCTV.

Pietro and Paolo were no longer on-duty policemen and so I didn't want to risk them getting their fingers burnt. So Capuzzo and myself shot over to I Tre Peccati. I parked the Duetto in a no-parking zone in the middle of the piazza, which was still full of tourists, even on a cold January night.

The piano bar was already quite crowded. Some Americans, some Japanese. Several hostesses. Two tall, sinewy blondes, either Ukrainian or Polish, came over.

'Buy us a drink, boys?'

Capuzzo was visibly embarrassed.

'No,' I said. 'We're looking for Calogero, Luciano and Vito.'

One of the two looked instinctively at a small black door at the back of the club. We went over and tried to open it, but it was locked from the inside.

I turned to the barman – a cool character with affected manners – and pointed to the black door.

'I want to go in there,' I said.

He gave me a sugary smile. 'Are you a member, sir?'

I showed him my police ID. 'Yes, I am, and this here's my membership card.'

He tried to press a button, but I grabbed his wrist.

'If you attempt to warn them, I'll have you arrested you for aiding and abetting. And I'll make sure you're in a cell with a pair of thugs who've just beaten a queer like you to death.'

Capuzzo looked at me, horrified. The barman turned pale. He wasn't used to policemen of my kind in the democratic and libertine Italy of the eighties.

'You have to knock, Commissario. Twice, then pause, then once again.'

'I'll go. You keep an eye on the exit, Capuzzo.'

My deputy was also pale. 'Keep an eye how?'

I pointed to the pistol in his holster.

'With that. If one of the three tries to leave, make him stop. If he doesn't, shoot him in the legs.'

I knocked. Twice, a pause, then once more.

The door was opened after a while by one of those enormous steroid-fuelled guys typical of the time.

Calogero and Luciano Nastasia were sitting at a poker table in the smoke-filled room. They must have taken the flight after mine from Palermo. Vito was missing: he'd either stayed behind in Palermo, or was driving the Jaguar back to Rome.

Among the cards, stacks of cash and cigarettes, there was a pistol.

I showed my ID to the bouncer. But he didn't budge a millimetre.

'Got a warrant?' he asked me.

I ignored his question and tried walking past him, but he held me by the arm, which was what I wanted him to do. Instead of resisting, I let him drag me forward with all his weight. I then pretended to lose my balance and fell forcefully towards him, my forehead breaking his nasal septum. The blood started to flow from his nose, along with a stream of groans and curses.

Calogero and Luciano got up and calmed him down. Then they gave me an arrogant look.

'If it isn't Commissario Balistreri, all this time after Barcelona. What the fuck do you want?'

To kill you guys, if I could, just like those three Egyptian soldiers in the Cairo alley. And they were better men than you; they were only hungry.

Inside, I was boiling with rage but, on the outside, I was calm. Perhaps I was starting to learn something.

'I want to know if you sell coke to Giangiacomo Zingaretti.'

The elder brother, Calogero, gave me a mocking smile.

'Drugs? Us? Where on earth did you get that idea from? Listen, we're good honest citizens, us.'

I usually like to hear a Sicilian accent. But I hate it when one is purposefully drawn out, used to intimidate.

I pointed to the gun. 'Who has the licence for that?'

Luciano Nastasia, the one who put his hands on Sonia in Barcelona and received a good kicking for his troubles, came within ten centimetres of my face.

'I do, Commissario. And I really know how to use it, too.'

'All right, then, I'm closing this club for illicit gaming.'

Calogero Nastasia laughed in my face.

'In three days, we'll be open again.'

Oh, with your lawyers, I'm sure you will.

'We'll see. We could find something more interesting than gambling. Talcum powder, for instance.'

I walked towards the door. Calogero met me on the threshold.

'Zingaretti, I couldn't say, but perhaps that whore of a wife of his . . .'

Good. The message was clear.

I called the examining magistrate at home just before midnight from a phone box in Piazza di Spagna. I told him the news and explained to him what I wanted to do. He was very understanding.

'Very well, Balistreri. This is a can of worms you're opening. And, as you know, a custody warrant doesn't last for more than twenty-four hours, after which you'll have to hand Signora Zingaretti over to the judicial authorities on a charge or release her.'

'It'll be enough time, Signor Giudice.'

The Zingarettis' home was close by: a penthouse overlooking Piazza di Spagna with a view of the Spanish Steps and the church of Santa Trinità dei Monti. All the lights were on. A blue Lancia Thema was parked outside the main door to the building, the chauffeur leaning on the car and smoking a cigarette.

Enemies old and enemies new. There's no difference between the two. They're all in it together.

'Are you sure about this, Commissario?' Capuzzo asked me yet again as we went up in the antiquated lift. We were going to touch the untouchables, the ones who lived in places that Capuzzo and those like him could look at only from a distance.

'Calm down. We're the good guys. They're the bad ones.'

I was pretty calm myself, so he took courage from it. He swept a hand over his bald pate and followed me out of the lift.

It was Signora Zingaretti herself who opened the door. She was wearing the same evening dress that I had slipped off her in Capri. And the same silk shawl that had come between my lips and her skin for a moment. She stared at me, silent and incredulous. Giangiacomo Zingaretti appeared behind her.

'Aren't you the young commissario who was at our table in Capri? Claudia Teodori's friend? What on earth are you doing here?'

I looked directly into his eyes. Yes, he was the perfect product of this country.

Mixing with the right circles. Reciprocal favours. The power to do exactly what you want.

'I'm here to notify your wife that we have a custody warrant for her. She must come with us.'

His wife's eyes filled with fear; his with rage.

'What kind of bullshit is this!' Zingaretti exploded.

'I can have you accompany me as well, if you like, for insulting a public official.'

Capuzzo gave a start, as if I'd landed a punch on him. A crowd of people had emerged from the drawing room and gathered behind the Zingarettis, muttering that this was scandalous, the Italian police worse than Fascists.

'Capuzzo, please go with Signora Zingaretti. There's just time to prepare an overnight bag, Signora. No more.'

'An overnight bag?' she mumbled, looking at her husband, terrified.

Senator Emilio Busi came out of the drawing room and stood beside Zingaretti's wife. He shot a glance at me, the usual glance of old.

You're still just a child, Mike, who doesn't want to understand how the world works . . .

'Off you go, Lavinia, and don't worry. Commissario Balistreri's new to the job. He doesn't understand the difference between the homes of respectable people and a cell of terrorists. We'll send the lawyer over, and you'll be out in a couple of hours.'

It was the old tactic. Try to get the difficult kid to lose his temper.

My enemies of old. The ones who had my mother killed. But I'm not a kid any more. And we'll settle accounts. All of them.

The squad car we'd called was already waiting there when we came down: Lavinia Zingaretti, trembling with rage; Capuzzo with fear; and myself; followed by thirty or so people in dinner jackets and evening dress fuming against the forces of law and order.

I sent Capuzzo and Signora Zingaretti off in the Fiat 132 squad car, then went to the Duetto parked in the middle of the piazza, now with a parking ticket stuck on its windscreen.

Busi and Zingaretti were watching me as I left. Zingaretti's face was filled with hate; Busi had an ironic smile on his.

Night of Wednesday and Thursday, 19 to 20 January 1983

The Vigna Clara police station had a small meeting room sufficient in size to question Lavinia Zingaretti. We waited for her lawyer, who'd been summoned by Emilio Busi.

It was Morandi, an aggressively ambitious young criminal lawyer from Rome. He was my age, and a former adversary in the fights we had at university between right-wing blackshirts and Communist Reds in the early seventies, when I was in the Ordine nuovo and he was one of the student leaders on the Left. That was before he became a Leftist lawyer who defended only those who could pay very large fees.

The examining magistrate wasn't present. It wasn't necessary for the first twenty-four hours. Firstly, we completed the procedural questions. The warrant concerned the use and circulation of cocaine. Nothing more. Capuzzo took down the testimony without raising his eyes from the typewriter. The machine was his safety barrier.

'Signora Zingaretti, are you in the habit of using cocaine?'

She avoided my look. She remembered that evening in Capri very well, when she cut a generous line after offering me some.

Morandi whispered something in her ear.

'Only very occasionally,' she said.

'Have you ever offered it to others?'

Besides me, that is.

Another consultation with Morandi.

'I've never sold cocaine to anyone,' she said afterwards.

'That wasn't the question.'

She gave me a hateful look. She would have gouged my eyes out with her long, lacquered nails if she could.

'I don't remember, but I don't think so.'

'Did you ever offer cocaine to Deborah Reggiani?'

Immediately, I saw terror in her eyes.

Perhaps it wasn't fear of prison, but social disgrace. Bye bye to Gian, bye bye to the RAI and bye bye to the power, the parties and the life of luxury.

'I-I don't remember,' she stammered.

'Have you ever had sexual relations with Deborah Reggiani?'

'Commissario,' Morandi broke in, 'perhaps I need to explain criminal procedure to you.'

'Possibly, Avvocato. But if Signora Zingaretti doesn't want to sleep in a cell in Regina Coeli tonight, with five other detainees, it would be better for her to reply.'

Morandi had no time to react. The threat worked immediately. Lavinia Zingaretti sang like a little bird.

'You already know I had my turn with that little slut my husband fucked. And so what? Is it a crime?'

Morandi was livid.

'Are you acquainted with Signora Zingaretti, Balistreri?'

'It's *Commissario* Balistreri, Avvocato. So, Signora Zingaretti, do you want to spend the night in Regina Coeli?'

While I let them have a quiet consultation, I lit a cigarette and started to pace up and down the room. I was acting way over the top, and knew very well that I was.

A true policeman investigates suspects. He doesn't detest them. The important thing is to remain calm.

'Very well,' said Morandi in the end. 'My client admits to having had consensual relations, and I repeat "*consensual* relations", with Deborah Reggiani.'

I was ready for that answer, and also with my next question.

'And did you offer cocaine to Miss Reggiani on that occasion, Signora?'

It was then that Lavinia Zingaretti, the respectable lady of Roman high society, exploded.

'You already know that, you fucking son of a bitch!'

She tried to throw herself on me and scratch me with her nails, while Morandi made great efforts to hold her back.

'Commissario Balistreri,' he gasped, when he had managed to calm her down, 'I swear that I'll speak to the examining magistrate about this: I will cause you endless hassle.'

I got up and smiled at him. My special smile, which could be one of sympathy or derision – it was impossible to tell. I had learned it over the years from a great teacher, my father.

'Of course, Avvocato. But that's for tomorrow. Tonight, Signora Zingaretti will spend the night in Regina Coeli.'

Lavinia Zingaretti burst into tears.

They're not even tears of shame or remorse. Only from fear of the privileges she'll lose.

'It was Gian, damn him!' she hissed in between her sobs.

Morandi rushed to say something in her ear. She gave him a resounding slap.

'Stop it, you brown-nosing little shit!' she screamed at him. 'This son of a bitch is going to put me in jail. I'm not covering for that fucker any more!'

A truly respectable female member of Roman high society. Former member, that is.

'Where do you buy the cocaine, Signora Zingaretti?' I asked her calmly.

I already knew. But I needed to know that her defences had been completely broken down.

'There's a piano bar on the street near here. I Tre Peccati,' she replied, sobbing.

'From whom?'

She was at the end of her tether, in pieces.

'A big, tall guy, I don't know his name.'

Of course. Those three aren't fools. The customer's link is that enormous beefcake.

'How did you know about the club?'

Silence.

Here we are. Now she'll tell me, and Zingaretti's goose is cooked.

But instead she came out with something else. Something completely unexpected.

'From an acquaintance of my husband, that director with the foul breath. The one with the nickname of some famous director.'

I was dumbfounded. I looked her right in the eyes.

No, Michele. She's too scared to lie to you.

'Rossellini?' I asked.

'Yes, Rossellini,' affirmed Lavinia Zingaretti, whose face, like her future, was now in pieces.

With Morandi's agreement, we let her sleep in a room in the police station until I could find Rossellini. It was a guarantee against the risk of contaminating the evidence. I would let her go before the twenty-four hours were up.

Capuzzo had telephoned Extra TV and immediately obtained Rossellini's real surname and address. Driving through the cold, deserted Roman night, I got to his apartment block in San Giovanni in less than twenty minutes. I rang the entry phone, and it was Tanya who answered.

When I reached the hallway, the door was open. I shut the door behind me and went towards the room, which was filled with the sound of Barry White.

Tanya was lying naked in the bath, her nose white with powder and her legs resting on the side.

She pointed to her very shapely ankles.

'Would you start from there, Michele?'

I had other things to do.

'Not tonight. Where is he?'

'He left an hour ago,' Tanya told me.

'For where?'

'I don't know. But he packed a small suitcase and was off.'

'Had he planned to go, or did he leave suddenly?' I asked her.

She put on a sulky expression.

'He got a call about midnight and was gone within ten minutes. In the car. Could you soap my back at least?'

She handed me the soap. It was small, black and spherical. Just like the tiles and fittings of the bathroom. It was a bar of soap I'd already seen before in another bathroom, one much more simple and spare. One that smelled of piss.

Yes, this is where it all began. First Debbie, then Anita. It started with Rossellini.

The examining magistrate showed no surprise at receiving a call in the middle of the night. He was getting used to them. He authorized having Rossellini's mugshot sent immediately to borders, airports and railway stations. But it was Pietro who had the brilliant idea of including the motorways and ferries, as well as adding the detail of Rossellini's numberplate.

A message came into my office at ten minutes past six, after Capuzzo, Pietro and Paolo and I had drunk litres of coffee and smoked hundreds of cigarettes.

It came in precisely from where it had to come – the ferry line between Villa San Giovanni on the Italian mainland and Messina, across the straits in Sicily. Rossellini was on the first ferry that morning.

He's running to ask for help from his big boss in Palermo.

Thursday, 20 January 1983

I boarded another flight to Sicily at nine in the morning, less than twenty-four hours since my last trip.

On the flight, I was able to meditate on the fact that everything was fitting into place. Giangiacomo Zingaretti and Dino Forte were too rich and powerful to expose themselves by dealing directly to the Roman jet set. Zingaretti certainly used drugs to liven up his nights – about Dino Forte I'd no idea – but neither of them would be so stupid as to actually sell the stuff.

Whereas Rossellini was perfect. He wasn't powerful enough to have too much to lose, and he was well connected in jet-set circles. Perhaps Anita Messi had stopped by his house after she landed in Rome that very same evening. Perhaps taken there by Calogero, Luciano and Vito to deliver to Rossellini a quantity of the drugs she'd brought from Colombia: the allocation that he was to sell in the rich and gilded world of entertainment.

Probably Anita had used his bathroom and had simply pocketed one of those little bars of soap because she feared that none would be provided in the hall of residence.

Except that something had gone wrong, and the following morning they'd raped, tortured and killed her in Rossellini's apartment.

After he had cut off a finger, as he'd done with the tip of Deborah Reggiani's when she tried to create problems for him.

Perhaps. But something didn't add up.

What about Nadia Al Bakri? Where did she fit in? In 1969, Rossellini would have been about forty. He could have found himself in Tripoli for any kind of work in entertainment, especially for the many live stage shows which took place there.

Or else he'd simply copied Nadia's killer. His boss.

This was what drew all my thoughts in like a magnet. But I told myself not to be swayed by resentment, prejudice and hate. And, the more I said it, the more my thoughts came back to it. Or him.

The man who can do everything.

I landed in Palermo at ten o'clock. Once again, I was met by sunshine and a temperature ten degrees warmer than Rome, but not by Tano's driver. Instead, there was a police patrol which had followed Rossellini on his two-hour drive from Messina to Palermo, where he'd arrived an hour before.

'Where is he?' I asked the man commanding the patrol.

'On the coast in a block of self-catering holiday flats called Il Pescespada.'

'Where is it?' I asked. But I already knew the answer.

'In Isola delle Femmine, halfway between the airport and the city.

Exactly where Cavaliere Salvatore Balistreri has his fortified castle.

'And what's he doing?'

'Nothing. He's shut up in his bedroom, as if he's waiting for a call.'

It took us only ten minutes to get to Isola delle Femmine. The old alleyways, which were full of people during the summer and spring and the autumn weekends, were completely deserted in January. All the shops, restaurants and bars were closed. This was why my father spent the winter here and the summer in Milan.

Because he needs the empty space around him.

Il Pescespada was the only holiday place open. It was right on the seafront and it, too, seemed completely deserted. There was only one vehicle in the car park: Rossellini's. And a motorbike, probably belonging to the porter.

On reception was a friendly middle-aged man.

'How come you're open?' I asked him.

'For Signor Rossellini. He's been coming here at weekends for years. And he's very generous with his tips. He called me from Messina at seven o'clock and I got his usual suite ready for him.'

I wasn't happy with the explanation. I wasn't happy with the quiet. I took the stairs up two floors, followed by police officers. With our guns drawn, we knocked on Rossellini's door. No answer. We knocked again.

'Open it with the pass key,' I ordered the porter.

I went in, Beretta in hand. But I already knew this was unnecessary. I went straight to the bathroom. Rossellini was there, naked in the bath, as Tanya had been a few hours earlier, except the water in the bath and on the tiled floor was red with blood. At the foot of the bath was a bottle of whisky and a packet of sleeping tablets, both empty.

The toilet lid was down, and on it lay a pencil and a note: 'I killed Debbie and Anita. Forgive me.'

I went out on to the terrace overlooking the sea. Two chairs, a little table, no way of getting up from below.

'Has anyone else been in the room other than Rossellini?' I asked the porter.

'No one. I've been at reception the whole time. Of course, there's the fire escape, which goes straight up from there. But someone has to open the access door from inside.'

I had my answers. But none of them were any use, because, with the deaths of Fratini and Rossellini, the link with the Balistreri brothers was broken. Rosellini had come here to die beside his killers in one last act of accusation. And he had left that note confessing to the two murders.

But excluding the third. Otherwise, he'd have added Nadia's name to his victims'. Whoever made him write those names still doesn't know about the link I hold. The letters from Tripoli.

For the moment, there was nothing I could do. I was out of my area of jurisdiction, out of time and lacking positive proof against these untouchable men. I could only go back to Rome before Calogero, Luciano and Vito could finish their work. Or perhaps I wasn't a danger to them any more.

I knew I'd never find Anita Messi and Deborah Reggiani's killer. I could well imagine everything, but prove nothing. But I could surprise them with Nadia. If I could only find out who had killed Nadia Al Bakri over thirteen years ago, I could drive the lion into the open.

Outside, it's raining and cold. The telephone in the kitchen rings. It's Michele Balistreri.

'I'm in Palermo again, Claudia.'

I say nothing. I wait. And hope.

'Rossellini's committed suicide and left a note confessing that he killed Deborah.'

So the nightmare's over. Although I can feel that Balistreri doesn't think it is.

'Thanks, Balistreri. Is anything wrong?'

He tries to calm me down.

'No, Claudia. With regards to Debbie and Anita, everything's sorted out.'

I put the phone down. So this means it really is over now. There's nothing more to be done. Except for one last thing. As soon as I can, I must go and see Deborah's parents.

I made it in time for the one o'clock flight and got into Rome at two. At three, I was with the examining magistrate, who listened to my report of the latest events.

'So, it's all over, Commissario. My compliments.'

I said that the suicide was perhaps a put-up job, but was again simply complimented on my work. It was all over. He wanted to tell me that I was only chasing after phantoms here. That there was nothing else to find.

I set off to my office in the Vigna Clara police station, far from satisfied.

At four, I was at the station and in my office. Waiting for me were the apostles, and Capuzzo, who held the telephone records requisitioned – thanks to him – by the examining magistrate. We found Fratini's phone call on the evening of 9 July straightaway. The call he made to Him.

Capuzzo was exuding confidence. He was in his element: data, pieces of paper, figures.

'It was a call to Ostia. A large villa on the seafront. I've checked: there was a party there that night. Half the entertainment world was there, everyone who counted.'

'Rossellini?' I asked.

'He was certainly there. His girlfriend, Tanya, confirmed it.'

'Zingaretti and Dino Forte as well?'

'Oh, yes,' Capuzzo replied. 'The villa belongs to Dino Forte. Everyone was there.'

Apostle Paul cleared his throat and seemed almost reluctant to speak.

'There's another question mark about Dino Forte, Balistreri. You mentioned to us about that other case of a missing finger. Tripoli, 3 August 1969.'

I had a feeling about what was to come. Or confirmation of a fear that was lurking within me.

'I crunched all the data taken from the RAI's mainframe.'

'Mainframe?'

'The main computer,' Paolo said, cutting it short in the face of my ignorance.

'And how did you gain access?' I asked.

Capuzzo turned red. 'I have a cousin who works at the RAI, external relations . . .'

Thanks to some of the things I detested the most – special favours and modern technology – these two had succeeded in finding a link.

'Well, it's this,' Paolo explained. 'As a young man, Dino Forte presented a broadcast about some camel parade. I checked the dates on the worksheet. He arrived in Tripoli on the evening of 2 August and left on the evening of the 3rd.'

Teodori told you. Too many coincidences are no longer coincidences.

I shut myself in the office, lit a cigarette and poured myself a whisky, the windows open on the cold, dark afternoon outside.

Dino Forte, everyone's exemplary, untarnishable darling. Including the President in the sixties. I remembered that name, as well: 'The President', spoken in hushed tones and with great respect by my father, Busi and Don Eugenio. But, today, the President fulfilled only honorary duties. Forte must have other saints in paradise looking after him.

Don't let yourself become poisoned by resentment. Try to find out the evidence for what you're thinking.

I had Capuzzo call Il Pescespada in Palermo, the self-catering block where we had found Rossellini's body that morning.

'What can I do for you, Commissario?'

'When he was alone in his room, did Signor Rossellini make any calls out?'

'Just the one. You can't get an outside line from the rooms. You have to go through the switchboard.'

'And so you know the number he called?'

He read it out to me. I recognized it as I was writing it down. It was the number of Dino Forte's villa in Ostia.

Dino Forte, star of the RAI. Even in the sixties.

I had seen them, of course. In the crazy swirl of the *ghibli*, there they were, the RAI's outside-broadcast vans on that wretched day,

3 August 1969. I'd seen them with my own eyes, for that damned Bedouin camel parade.

I tried to keep myself under control as I called the RAI. There was something else I wanted to know. On encountering the first bureaucratic obstacle, I passed the phone to Capuzzo. He called his cousin and, in five minutes, he had the answer. Yes, coverage of the camel parade on 3 August 1969 in Tripoli had been presented by Dino Forte, at the request of several local persons of note, whose names the cousin obviously didn't know.

But I think I do.

There was one possibility left to me. I had to make use of PO Box 150870, Tripoli. The 15th of August 1970. I shut myself in the office and by hand wrote a letter in English.

Dear Sirs,

Another young woman, Deborah Reggiani, has been killed in the same way as Anita Messi. The last joint of the middle finger of her right hand was cut off.

There have been important developments. The main suspect for the deaths of these young women is a famous television presenter, Dino Forte. This man knew Deborah Reggiani. We have to link him to Nadia Al Bakri.

I have discovered that Dino Forte was in Tripoli on the day of Nadia's death. He was presenting a broadcast about the camel parade for Italian television.

But, before that, he could have gone out to Sidi El Masri.

This makes me think that the real time and place of Nadia's capture could be different to the one General Jalloun hypothesized at the time. She could have been taken at about eight thirty, rather than nine o'clock, and in the area of the Balistreri villa, rather than the area around the olive-pressing shed. In this scenario, Dino Forte could have had all the time in the world to act before the beginning of the broadcast.

This reconstruction goes against the witness statement of the goatherd who saw Nadia with Jamaal near the olive-pressing shed at nine. This statement could have been extorted from the goatherd by General Jalloun in order to protect people who were untouchable, and could therefore be false.

You have to check out the details of this.

Finally, I'm not sure if I'll be able to bring an end to this investigation myself. Two inconvenient witnesses have already been murdered in Palermo, one of them before my very eyes.

If I am unable to bring an end to it, I hand over the cause of justice to you.

Michele Balistreri

I left at six that evening and went to the central post office. There was no time for a letter. The telegram office was open around the clock. It cost me half my salary, but I wired the whole thing to PO Box 150870, Tripoli.

Friday, 21 January 1983

I didn't sleep a wink that night. I tried to imagine the face of whoever would read my letter.

Were they in fact enemies, and out to betray me? Or else people I had wronged or could do wrong to? Why should these people reply? Why should they give me any help at all?

At seven that morning, I went down to the bar on the street below.

Almost straightaway, the lady at the newsagent's came rushing in, out of breath.

'Commissario, there are some people for you!'

Parked outside the main door to my apartment building was a black Mercedes. It had a diplomatic-corps numberplate and carried the Libyan flag. Beside it was a middle-aged Arab gentleman who was waiting for me, an envelope in his hand.

'This is for you, Commissario. It came into the airport from Tripoli, along with the order to deliver it to you personally and straightaway.'

The envelope was the usual one, except for one detail: there were no stamps on it. I was taken aback. My correspondents in Libya had to be very important people who not only had access to old case records but could answer my questions within twelve hours using a diplomatic courier.

Either they really do want to help you, or they've found a way to trick you.

As well as the envelope, the man handed me a business card that bore only a single telephone number.

'If there's anything else urgent, you can call me. We can deliver it to Tripoli in twenty-four hours.'

I dashed back to my flat and opened the brown envelope. Inside it was the usual typewritten sheet and a smaller, sealed white envelope.

Signor Commissario Balistreri,

We greatly appreciate your efforts to find a solution to the murder of Nadia Al Bakri after all these years. We, too, are looking for the truth. A truth we have been waiting for these thirteen years. We will do anything we can to help you find whoever killed Nadia Al Bakri, if, as it seems, it is the same person who killed Anita Messi and Deborah Reggiani.

And we have some precise answers to your questions, taken from statements kept confidential at the time, but based on the few inquiries made by General Jalloun, perhaps to give himself a weapon of self-protection or even blackmail.

Dino Forte was sent to Tripoli at the express request of Don Eugenio Pizza to an influential Italian politician. He arrived on the evening of 2 August and left on the evening of 3 August. Forte had an aged aunt in Tripoli, Countess Colombo. He was her guest for the night. The Countess's villa was outside Tripoli, in Sidi El Masri, two kilometres from the Balistreri villa.

On the morning of 3 August, at about eight forty, Salvatore Balistreri and Don Eugenio went in the latter's car to the villa to pay Forte a visit. They had breakfast with him, and Don Eugenio heard the Countess's confession at home, as he often did. They went back to Tripoli at five to ten, just before the roads leading in were closed.

Balistreri and Don Eugenio went to the Waddan to wait for Emilio Busi, then they joined the boys at the Underwater Club to go fishing.

We know that you will find this news both interesting and disturbing. Nevertheless, unfortunately, the statement of the goatherd who saw Nadia Al Bakri with Jamaal near the olive-pressing shed half an hour before the presumed seizure of the girl is a truthful one.

Years later, a second witness confirmed the above. Karim Al Bakri was not feeling well that day. As he was going to the outside latrine, he heard the muezzin calling and, in the distance, saw his sister Nadia walking towards the olive-pressing shed with Jamaal.

Karim intended to ask Nadia to explain herself when she came home. Later, when the body was found, he remained silent out of shock, and so as not to pour shame on the memory of his sister, who had been seen walking with an older man.

It is for this reason that, when Jamaal was arrested, Karim Al Bakri was certain of his guilt. And he would be today if it were not for the missing finger on Anita Messi.

Our wish is that Nadia Al Bakri's murderer is identified and punished according to the rules of our justice system. Not the legal one, but the moral. We are sure you will understand and that only by working together can we bring this wish to realization.

We are also aware that you are in danger. Therefore we are enclosing a snapshot that will save your life.

Yours faithfully,
PO Box 150870

Moral justice. We are sure you will understand. A snapshot that will save your life.

As I opened the envelope, I knew that what I found inside would provide a definitive answer to part of my torments, something that went way beyond Nadia Al Bakri.

And it did.

That snapshot could save my life but damn my whole existence.

For days, the press had been speaking about the Nuova Banca del Sud's latest investment project with the support of foreign capital from America and several Arab states: a bridge over the Straits of Messina that would unite Sicily with the Italian mainland.

It didn't surprise me that my father could be behind such a project. It united a poor Sicilian's vengeful dreams with his actual interests of large entrepreneur, together with the interests of his Sicilian, Italo-American and Arab friends.

One newspaper gave notice of a much-awaited press conference given by Salvatore Balistreri on the afternoon of 22 January. It would be taking place immediately after a lunch and a folklore parade on his magnificent property in Isola delle Femmine, near Palermo, in the presence of important overseas guests and over one hundred Italian and foreign journalists. It was the perfect occasion for him to announce the new project and for me to be sure to find him at home.

But I had to take every precaution to avoid Tano and the Nastasia trio. Saying nothing to anyone, I took two days' leave and set off very early in the morning. No plane, no train, no motorway, no traces. I had to go by car and cross that stretch of sea between Calabria and Sicily which my father and his old friends wanted to bridge.

I had the bare essentials in my bag. No Beretta. It wouldn't have been of any use. So I set off in the Duetto and drove slowly for a while, checking to see if I was being followed.

After Naples and the Amalfi coast, I parked in the forecourt of a petrol station and pulled the Duetto's hood down. The January air here was already less cold than in Rome. I had a coffee in the bar and lit a cigarette.

Think like a policeman would think.

Anita Messi's corpse had been left on my patch on purpose. And my first meeting with Calogero, Luciano and Vito Nastasia in Barcelona had been deliberately set up. They had sought me out on purpose to get me into the game and to go to I Tre Peccati following the trail of that young American girl, Kate. A single thread linked my past enemies to the present ones. And that thread ran through Dino Forte.

And, in the end, I go to their home turf in Palermo, where they bump me off. The resulting investigation takes place there, and no one looks for any real motive. Not in the present, even less in the past. My past.

I was no longer the hunter. Here, I was the hunted lion. And all these events had been bait to draw me in. I had many enemies, and they all came from that time, the years spent among the sand and blood. And from the projects I had blocked, the ones I was blocking now and would render impossible.

The bridge across the Straits of Messina.

But why all this after so many years? What had I done to set off a plan of this kind?

The reply came like a bolt of lightning: Marco Fratini.

Fratini had been a drug pusher. His arrest had been a blow for these dangerous men for whom I had already created problems in the past.

Without knowing it, you've trodden on their toes again, Mike. Not they on yours. And, this time, they've decided to put a stop to it. But Fratini's not the explanation for everything. There must be something deeper behind it.

I could turn the Duetto round and go back home.

But there's no road back for you, Mike.

I set off in the direction of Palermo, to the final showdown with the hunter.

I've got Deborah's parents' new address. Good people, now living in Tivoli, a few kilometres outside of Rome. They knew how fond we were of each other.

But I was the person who killed their daughter. I hid behind a tree at her funeral. And I never got in touch.

In the afternoon, I go to the central train station, Roma Termini. The commuter carriage is freezing cold. I get to Tivoli at three.

When I ring the bell, Deborah's mother answers. She looks at me, smiles and gives me a hug. Then she shows me into the living room, which is very warm and full of Deborah's photographs. Her father's there in his wheelchair. I mustn't start crying, not now. Signora Reggiani offers me tea and some biscuits.

'Claudia, sweetheart, we've seen you on the telly. You're so beautiful and talented. Just like Deborah was.'

'Thank you, Signora. But Deborah was much more beautiful and much more talented. And it's because of her that I'm here.'

A slight pause. 'For her, Claudia?'

'It was that director, Rossellini.'

Debbie's mother turns pale.

'The radio said he was killed in Palermo. What's that got to do with Debbie?'

I spell everything out, avoiding the particularly bloody details.

In the following silence, we all look at the photos. I mustn't start crying, not now.

'I'd like to have a Mass said for Debbie, Signora. A Mass with everyone there who loved her. I don't want anyone to be left out.'

She smiles at me. 'Would the little address book with her friends' numbers in it be of any help?'

I'd completely forgotten about it. But I remembered it now: a very tiny address book, not much bigger than a business card, in which Deborah jotted down the numbers of her closest friends and acquaintances. Obviously, it had been returned to her parents along with her personal effects.

She brings it to me. I leaf through it distractedly in alphabetical order. I see there aren't many names.

I know several of them. My own name's there under 'C', but nothing for Forte, Rossellini or Zingaretti.

Under 'H' there's one entry: Him, with a capital 'H'. Next to it a number I don't recognize.

I get to the port of Villa San Giovanni in time to board the Duetto on the last ferry for Messina. The panorama was sensational; it's one of the most beautiful places in the world: the Calabrian mountains behind me, Etna's snow-covered peak and Messina's tiny houses in front and a stretch of blue sea in between. Italy behind me; Sicily in front of me.

What nature itself divided, my father wants to unite.

I was planning on spending the night in the car, just outside Messina's port. I didn't want there to be any trace of this trip.

Before getting some sleep, I found a phone box. I knew that, after her father's death, Claudia had asked Nico for a stop, for a few days, to the nights out. I hoped to find her in. She answered after the first ring.

'It's Michele Balistreri.'

'I tried to call you in the office. They told me you were on leave, and I tried to get you at home.'

Her voice was surprisingly calm.

'I'm not in Rome, Claudia.'

'Are you taking a holiday?'

'I'm in Sicily. I've come here to get Deborah's killer. And that of the girl whose death I'm investigating, Anita Messi. Also another girl, who was killed a long time ago in another country. We were mistaken, Claudia. It wasn't Rossellini.'

There was a long silence. The line started to crackle.

'Hello? Claudia, are you there?'

'Why do you think the killer's the same for all of them?'

It was a huge risk, but I owed it to her.

'The third girl had her middle finger cut off, just like Debbie and Anita. There's other proof as well.'

'So who was it?'

The Nastasia gang. Dino Forte. The men behind it. The hunter.

'It's not one person. I'll tell you tomorrow, Claudia.'

'Are you going to arrest them?'

I should have kept quiet. But I couldn't lie to her.

'Several of them, yes, but not all of them. But not for those crimes, however. I'll never get the proof for them. But I'll do them damage – serious damage – you'll see.'

Another silence. Then her voice came down the line again, as clear as a little girl's – not warm and theatrical, as she pitched it on TV.

'Will you call me tomorrow, Michele? Give me an exact time, so I can be at home and wait for it.'

'All right. I'll call you at three thirty. So, goodnight.'

'Goodnight, Michele.'

I went back to the car. I reclined the seat and lit a last cigarette of the day. Then I fell into a troubled sleep, where images of Elisa Sordi became mingled with those of Claudia Teodori. I soon woke, and spent the rest of the night smoking and thinking.

As soon as I got back to Rome, I went to the bar where my flatmate worked and asked her to call a number and try to find out whose it was. She used a phone-box in the Roma Termini station. She was very good at coming up with wonderful excuses; she was used to it from work. When she replaced the receiver, she had the name I wanted.

And now? Now I know who this Him is, but I can't do anything. There's not the slightest proof, apart from his number in Debbie's address book: final proof for me, but little use to a judge.

That left me Balistreri. But he sounded uncertain, confused. I have to hand Him over to him, but in such a way that there's no chance of escape. I can't do it directly – I need a go-between. I know how I can do it.

I give Nico Gerace a call.

Saturday, 22 January 1983

Morning

I set off in the first light of dawn.

The weather was magnificent, a real foretaste of spring: the sky was as blue as the sea and as warm as the landscape, whose colours looked so like Tripoli's.

I drove with the hood down and drew slowly closer to Palermo and my enemies.

I'm walking in the early-morning rain, and I'm invisible. No one can recognize the little star under her umbrella. Before I go up to the flat, I buy a piece of cooked ham and a bottle of whisky in the supermarket down on the street.

Then I go up.

Nico's coming for coffee after lunch at two thirty.

He was taken by surprise the previous night; I'd never invited him into the flat before. But he was worried by my funereal tone. I had just lost my father and Balistreri had told him to guard me against the wolves. So he couldn't refuse.

★　　★　　★

I got to the outskirts of Palermo at noon and took an hour to get through the chaotic traffic to the Favorita park and beach at Mondello. At one o'clock, I stopped in a bar along the seafront.

My stomach was tight as a knot.

I drank a double espresso and smoked a few cigarettes. Under that sun, facing the deserted beach and those scintillating waves carrying a few small boats, time seemed to come to a standstill.

At one o'clock, I open the bottle of whisky and down a couple of mouthfuls.

A little light-headed, I shut myself in the bathroom and look at myself in the mirror. How thin I am! My dark eyes look huge in my hollow face. Is this how you wanted your little star to be, Mamma?

As I prepare myself, I'm not crying from pain. I'm actually happy. I know that I can't turn back. I'll take this right through to the end.

Then I make up a parcel with pink paper. It's a colour I've always liked. And I do it meticulously while I take another sip of whisky.

At one thirty, I go out again and throw the rubbish out a long way from the block. As I walk through the cold, I see people having a quick lunch in the bars before they return to work. People who will go home to the ones they love this evening. I'm in no hurry. The ones I loved are all dead.

Near the Termini station is a Pony Express office, where I send the pink parcel off; delivery the next day is guaranteed. I pick up the receipt when I pay and throw it into the waste-paper bin there.

I'm back home by two, ready to receive Nico.

Afternoon

I turned off at the junction for Isola delle Femmine at two. By this time, they should have been on the dessert and watching the dancing, before my father's press conference at three.

Papa's villa was in the last bay looking towards Palermo. Access was via a private road, in which the only other villas were uninhabited. Papa had purchased them all: for reasons of security and to house his friends whenever necessary. There was an enormous car park at the turn-off. Two cars were parked there, with four athletic-looking young men and two elegant young women by them.

I drew up slowly in the Duetto. One of the young women smiled.

'Do you have an invitation?' she asked.

I showed her my national ID card. 'I have to see my father.'

She looked back at me a little uncertainly.

'There's a party going on. I'm not sure . . .'

I then showed her my police ID.

'I'm here on official duty, and it's urgent that I see my father.'

'Excuse me one moment, Commissario.'

She went up to the young men. After a few seconds, I was allowed to proceed.

'You can park the car here and continue on foot, Commissario. It's the last villa at the end of the road.'

I walked along, smelling the scents of the trees and the sea, and heard the music coming along the road from the grounds of the villa.

I came to a heavy metal gate set into a curtain wall almost three metres high. It was impossible to see a thing. There was no bell, but there were several security cameras. A wicket gate opened in the large metal frame. A smiling old man greeted me in Sicilian dialect.

'You must be little Michè, Salvo's son.'

Without another word, he let me inside. Everything there was different. The external wall separated two different worlds.

There were no security men. Only two villas surrounded by eucalyptus, and behind them a beach, a wooden pier and the sea.

A small path led to another gate set in a smaller wall. It was identical to the gate we had in Tripoli, with my parents' interwoven initials on it. The two villas were exact copies of the two where I grew up. For a moment, I imagined Marlene and Laura Hunt coming out and getting into the Ferrari California.

Behind them in the grounds was the buffet, an orchestra playing Sicilian melodies, waiters and tables with a hundred or so guests. A little beyond them was the beach, with an exact copy of the white villa on La Moneta. The one from which my mother came out that wretched day and said hello with half a wave.

Or was it goodbye?

'Surprised, Michele?'

He always managed to do that, approaching me from behind. I turned round to face my father. The old man disappeared with a respectful bow. A good many years had passed since the last time we met. And no letter or phone call between us since then.

He was as impeccably and elegantly dressed as ever. He still had a beautifully thick head of hair and his Clark Gable moustache, except that both were now grey. And there were dark shadows under his intensely black eyes, which were just like mine, and deep furrows in his cheeks and brow.

The signs of age. Or of guilt and remorse?

Neither of us dared to offer a tentative handshake or embrace. He, however, was happy with my astonishment at the incredible copy he had built of our past life.

'Even the interior of the houses is exactly same, Michele. There's your room and Alberto's. If you're not in a hurry, I'd like to offer a tour.'

Oh yes, everything's here, Papa. Except the people who loved you.

'I'm not here to talk about memories, Papa.'

I'm here to avenge my grandfather, used and pressed dry like his olives. I'm here to avenge my mother, deluded, betrayed and murdered. I'm here to avenge young Mike, the son you first considered useless and then a reprobate, driven out of his homeland.

'As you can see, I'm rather busy today. But I imagine you know that. Anyway, I'm listening, Mike. As I always do.'

You always listened to me with your ears, Papa, never your heart. You don't even have one.

'Are Busi and Don Eugenio here among the guests?'

He smiled.

'Of course. My old friends are always welcome. Only Mohammed's missing, but he hasn't left Tripoli in years.'

The letters from Tripoli.

'Are those three delinquents with the black Jaguar here, the Nastasia gang? Do they work for you and your brothers?'

My father shook his head in that denigrating gesture I'd hated since I was a child, the gesture that told me I was an idiot without actually saying it to my face.

'Here in Sicily, it's not like Rome. Everyone here keeps to themselves, Mike. My brothers mind their own business, and I mind mine. Actually, they're not among the guests. Perhaps these Nastasia men work for them, or perhaps for someone else, but I have no idea.'

Perhaps for someone else, such as Dino Forte.

'Naturally. You don't know a thing about their business, such as the traffic of cocaine from South America which Anita Messi got caught up in. Dino Forte's one of your friends. Do you know if he's a drug pusher for your brothers?'

My father showed patience, as he always did with his difficult son.

'I don't know how Dino Forte comes into this. I don't have anything to do with my brothers' business dealings, Michele. I have my own, which are always above board.'

'Such as gathering capital together from dubious sources to finance banks such as the Vatican's IOR, which in turn finances Solidarity and the P2 Lodge's other friends. Where does all that flood of money come from, Papa? Your brothers? From your old Sicilian friends?'

Oh, yes, he'd grown old. Ten years earlier, he wouldn't even have raised an eyebrow. Now, however, a single vein was throbbing in his temple.

'Michele, if you weren't my son—'

'Oh, I know, Papa. You'd have tossed me into those tuna nets along with General Jalloun. Or else you'd have had me captured and shot for the attempt on the life of that criminal Gaddafi you and your friends brought to power.'

'Michele, I have never killed anyone and never would.'

'Of course not, not with your own beautifully clean hands. So what about General Jalloun?'

He shrugged his shoulders. What did he care?

'Jalloun was an Israeli spy and a traitor to Libya's new regime. He was plotting to get rid of Gaddafi. Anyway, I didn't kill him.'

'Naturally, it was your man Mohammed Al Bakri who saw to that. But he didn't see to Nadia; he couldn't ever have done that. So who did see to her? Was it Dino Forte, Don Eugenio, you yourself? Or all three of you together?'

I'd raised my voice, and two bouncers were now making a move towards us. My father stopped them with a gesture.

'Mike, believe me, you don't know what you're talking about.'

But I clearly remembered the sound of that engine behind the MANK organization's van.

'You were behind our van while we were getting back to the city before they closed the road.'

He feigned the effort of trying to remember. Or it really was an effort, as if he were looking for some detail that time had buried.

'That's true. We'd gone to the countess's but, after a few minutes, Dino Forte told us that he had to go into Tripoli to prepare for the broadcast. He had one of those RAI outside-broadcast vans. Don Eugenio heard the countess's confession and as we came back he and I found ourselves behind your van. Up until the market, when you slowed down and Farid got out of the back of the van. We turned off for the Waddan. We were separated from Dino Forte for over an hour.'

I could no longer contain myself. I was tired of this pack of lies.

'Farid was at the market when I went to pick up the bait, Papa. Therefore, I'm afraid you're lying. You all killed her, like you did my mother.'

I had no time to dodge the slap. It was so sudden it took me by surprise. I had touched his one truly exposed nerve. My father then took a decision that he should have taken many years ago.

'I want you to leave this house immediately, Michele. I don't want to see or hear from you again. You're no longer any son of mine.'

'Then we're in complete agreement on that, Papa.'

A soft female voice rose above the sound of the orchestra. It was the famous Sicilian song 'Sciuri sciuri sciuri', about being given flowers all year and returning the love received:

> Sciuri sciuri sciuri di tuttu l'annu
> L'ammuri ca mi dasti ti lu tornu.*

The guests were clapping their hands in time.

I held a copy of the snapshot I'd received from Tripoli. My father took it between the tip of his thumb and forefinger, keeping it at some distance.

To keep his downfall at a distance.

It was a sharp photo, in black and white, taken outside the Grand Hotel in Abano Terme. Two men were smiling and shaking hands. One of them had the folded newspaper *Corriere della Sera* in his pocket, showing the date – 28 August, 1969 – three days before the *coup d'état* that would oust the Libyan monarchy.

The first man was my father. The other man was younger and, at the time, entirely unknown. Now he was known throughout the whole world as Colonel Muammar Gaddafi.

---

* 'Flowers, flowers, flowers all through the year. The love you gave me I will return.' (translator's note)

He stared for a long time at the photograph. In his eyes, where I had thought I finally caught a glimpse of fear, I felt there was only a hint of regret.

How much has that photo cost you, Papa? A wife, a son? Here, you've tried to reconstruct the past you lost, but bricks and mortar are no substitute for people.

He handed the photo back. He even seemed relieved. Perhaps he'd always imagined that settling accounts with his son would eventually come. And, in that moment, I would understand two things.

He ruined your life, Mike, but he's also saved it on many occasions.

'What do you want me to do?' he asked me.

'At the conference today, you'll say that the project for the bridge over the Straits has been premature and requires too many resources. Then you can tell Gaetano and your brothers that, if anything should happen to me, anything at all, this photo will end up in all the world's newspapers. And, in that case, someone will want to get a clear perspective on the history of the Nuova Banca del Sud's holdings.'

Silence. Only the music in the background and hands clapping to the song. I looked at the eucalyptus, the beach with its jetty, the two villas and the wrought-iron gate with my parents' interwoven initials.

We only had one thing in common, you and I, Papa. The inability to live under the same roof together.

'There's one last condition. This time, it's you who has to leave, Papa.'

I pointed to the grotesque twin villas, his ridiculous attempt at not being the loneliest man in the world.

'You are expelled definitively from this country in the name of my mother, my grandfather and those poor 20,000 souls that Gaddafi kicked out. Like Jesus, you can assume all the guilt of 50 million traitors on your shoulders. You've got two weeks from today.'

Then I looked at him one last time. Clark Gable, the man who could sell ice to the Eskimos.

'Such a shame, Papa,' I whispered in exhaustion.

Unexpectedly, he smiled. Over the years, I'd glimpsed many things in his eyes as he watched me grow: love, hope, surprise, concern, disillusion, anger. But I'd never seen the pain that I saw now.

'It's my fault, Michele. Don't give it another thought.'

I didn't turn back. I went back to the Duetto, switched on the engine and drove off, my grandfather's last words sounding in my ears.

A father has the right to look after his son and the right to make mistakes in doing it. A son has the right to protect himself and a duty to understand his father, sooner or later.

I hear the doorbell ring and look at the clock on the wall. Half past two.

Nico's on time, but lacking his usual air of optimism and slight arrogance. He's wearing a camel overcoat, a cashmere scarf and a Borsellino hat, which suit him very well.

He gives me a warm hug, then hangs up his outdoor clothes carefully on the hall stand.

He sees the plunging neckline of my top, my short skirt for dance routines, the almost empty bottle of whisky, and pulls a face, surprised. But he says nothing. Then he sees the bandage on my left hand.

'What have you done to yourself?'

'Nothing serious. I cut myself slicing some ham. Will you have a drink with me, Nico?'

He looks at me, bewildered. But my face is a mask of pain. I've only recently become an orphan.

'All right. Just a drop, though.'

He could have remonstrated with his client. It's even written in the contract I signed with him that I'm not to touch a drop of alcohol. Nico knows I'm suffering, so pretends not to notice anything.

I pour two glasses of whisky and hand him one. He sits down to my right on the sofa and drinks with me in silence.

He smokes one of his Marlboro cigarettes while I gulp half my glass down. He's worried.

'You shouldn't be drinking like this, Claudia. You should eat something, at least.'

'I wanted to, but then I cut myself. Could you slice me some ham?'

He gets up and goes towards the table. There's a long knife on the wooden chopping board next to the ham. He takes it in his hand and accurately cuts a slice, and then another.

'And some bread, Nico. Thanks.'

He patiently slices some bread, then brings everything over. I nibble a small piece of bread and immediately drink some whisky.

Then I take from my pocket Deborah's little box with the Minnie Mouse tape around it. I hand it to him.

'Could you open it for me, Nico, please? I can't do it with only one hand.'

He handles it as if it were an unexploded bomb. He opens it and stares at the white powder. He shakes his head. Now he's really taken aback.

I dip the tip of my index finger in the box and put it under his nose, just brushing it, and he moves away. I try to take the box back. Nico brusquely moves away again, spilling a little of the powder on himself.

'No, Claudia. Not this, it'll kill you.'

'Just today, Nico. Today, Claudia's not a star. She's simply a lonely girl.'

I put my right hand right there on the fly of his trousers. He looks at me, astounded. While he's staring, I try to grab the box, but I upset its balance and we're both covered in white powder.

He shakes his head in disbelief and embarrassment and draws away, shocked.

'Claudia, sweetheart, calm down, will you?'

All of a sudden, I kiss him. I really know how to kiss. Deborah taught me. My hand goes down to his fly. He's already hard. I lift the little skirt over my hips.

I'm the beautiful Claudia Teodori, the new star of television. The Italian male's latest dream. But that's not enough with Nico. I have to provoke him even more.

'Don't you know how to fuck, Nico?'

His face suddenly changes. He rips off my briefs and leaps on top of me. I tear off his shirt and with my one good hand scratch his back until it bleeds while my groin yields to his. I know how to do this so that it doesn't take long. In fact, with a grunt, everything's over within thirty seconds.

Now, Nico doesn't know what to say. He's embarrassed, lights a cigarette and goes to the bathroom to clean himself up. I stay on the sofa.

When he comes back, he gives me a caress. He's regretting his anger. Insecure men like Nico often do. Afterwards.

I finally manage to cry, thinking of my mother, who wanted so much for me to be an actress; and of Debbie, who was a true actress and who He killed; and of my father, who died happy a few days ago in that hospital bed.

I feel calmer. I stop crying. I have to remain clear-headed for the grand finale. I have to send Nico to Balistreri, and then Balistreri will nail Him.

'Are you all right, Claudia?'

'Yes, Nico. I'm all right.'

'Do you want me to stay with you?'

'No. But I want you to do something for me.'

He looks at me, worried.

'All right. I will, if I can.'

'When you leave here, you have to go to Michele Balistreri in the Vigna Clara police station and give him this envelope. It's very urgent.'

I hand him the sealed white envelope. He looks me up and down, confused.

'Nico, you have to go right away. The name of the man who killed Deborah Reggiani's in that envelope.'

Nico's eyes open wide.

'Killed? But it was an accident!'

I push him to the door, almost throwing him out.

'Go there now, Nico. I'll let Balistreri know that you're bringing him the envelope.'

He stays a moment in the doorway, uncertain. Then he leaves. It's a little after a quarter past three. I take off the bandage, cut it into pieces and throw it down the toilet, then flush it three times.

Now I'm ready for Balistreri's call.

It took me less than five minutes to reach Il Pescespada from the other side of Isola delle Femmine. It was three o'clock, and the porter was there to receive me, Capuzzo having called him and told him to be.

'Are you sure, Commissario?' he asked me, a little uncertain.

'Quite sure.'

He gave me the keys to the room on the second floor where Rossellini died. The cordons had already been removed, so I went in. I opened the French windows on to the terrace overlooking the sea. The sunshine was still strong but, in two hours, it would be dark.

I switched on the television, then sat down on the terrace to smoke.

What are you doing here, Michele? You know they've brought you here to kill you, don't you? Papa's most certainly had you followed. They know where you are.

I didn't give a damn. I was giving my father one last chance, but not to get us back to being a real family. No, that had died along with Italia.

But simply to be a father and a son.

The three-thirty regional news broadcast opened with Salvatore Balistreri's press conference, which had just recently concluded. In an unexpected turn, the financier had made a public announcement that he had given up on the plans for a bridge across the Straits of Messina. He mentioned the enormous difficulties with both bureaucracy and funding and complained that working in this country was impossible. He finished with the striking news that his group was withdrawing from the Italian market and that he himself was moving to the United States, where it was easier to run a serious business.

Bravo, Papa, you've found an excellent excuse, as usual.

But the question remained as to how Tano and the other brothers would take it. My life or my death depended on the orders my father would give out on the matter.

I called down to reception and gave Claudia Teodori's number to the porter. I'd promised to call her at three thirty, and was almost on time.

She answered straightaway. Her manner was the same as the day before. A young woman who was very calm, decisive and self-confident.

'So, Michele, what's the score?'

'It's a lot more complicated than I'd imagined, Claudia. I need more proof. But, in the meantime, I've scotched their most ambitious enterprise.'

I couldn't see her, but I was sure she was smiling; as if for some reason she had a blind faith that I would be arresting the killer.

'Nico dropped in for a coffee after lunch, Michele.'

'He's there with you now?'

'No, I sent him away a quarter of an hour ago with an envelope for you, saying it was terribly urgent. He'll be at the station by now.'

I had no idea what she was talking about, but I didn't like what I was hearing. She went on in the same level tones.

'Call him there right now; he can read it out to you. But you mustn't tell anyone about this phone call with me. Anyone at all.'

There was something in her voice that worried me.

'What's in the envelope you gave to Nico?'

A slight hesitation.

'The name of the murderer, Michele.'

'The murderer?' I felt terribly stupid and impotent.

'I knew since you sorted Fratini out and saved me from jail that you were the right man.'

'The right man for what?'

By now, I was babbling like an idiot. I could only repeat what she was saying.

'To obtain justice, real justice. I've sent you a gift as well. You'll get it at home tomorrow.'

I started to get really upset.

'Claudia, I will get him, please believe me, you just have to be patient.'

A pause. A sigh. Then she spoke, softly, without a trace of anger.

'And you have to believe me as well, Michele. Believe me, and believe in the impossible.'

I had no time to say a word. She hung up. I tried calling back straightaway, but the phone was out of its socket.

I suddenly felt old. Thirty-two years of resentment, anger, betrayals and killings.

You've fucked up, Mike. Just like with Elisa Sordi. You can fuck these women, but you don't see what they're like.

I called Capuzzo's direct line in the station. He answered on the first ring.

'Is Nico Gerace there?' I asked him.

'Yes, he came in a moment ago, Commissario. He's quite badly shaken.'

'Put him on, Capuzzo.'

Nico's voice sounded as if it were coming from beyond the grave.

'Hello?'

He was troubled, hesitant.

Just like my old classmate.

'What's going on, Nico? Claudia's just told me you've got an envelope for me.'

His voice was trembling, lisping his 's' sounds.

'Yes, Mike. Claudia's given me an envelope. She was strange today, out of her mind in a way. I don't know what's got into her . . .'

I looked at the time. I could get to the airport for four and be on the four-twenty flight for Rome. There wasn't a moment to lose.

I told Nico to stay in the police station and wait for me. Then I asked him to put Capuzzo back on.

'Capuzzo, I'm in Palermo. Nico seems quite upset. Keep him at the station until I get there. And call the examining magistrate. And also kindly ask Alitalia to hold the Rome flight in half an hour and let me get on it.'

'No problem. I'll see to it. I've got an uncle who works for Alitalia.'

I made it from Isola delle Femmine to Palermo's Punta Raisi airport in less than ten minutes. I left the Duetto with the local squad at the terminal. I would go back and get it one day. Then I dashed in for the flight.

I was on the flight to Rome. No one had tried to take me out in Isola delle Femmine, on the road or in the airport.

Papa had stopped the hand of Tano and the Nastasias. Or else I was simply mistaken.

The danger's not in Palermo, but in Rome. And you're not the one in danger.

I'd been an idiot. I should have told Capuzzo to go round to Claudia Teodori's, and spent the fifty minutes of the flight cursing myself for not doing so.

As soon as we landed, I ran to a phone and called Claudia. It was engaged. I called the station and had them put Capuzzo on.

'I'm back in Rome. Get in touch with Pietro and Paolo, Capuzzo. Send them round to Claudia's right away. That's right away, got it?'

'Of course, Commissario. A squad car's waiting for you outside the internal-flights exit.'

'Good. Is Nico still there?'

'Yes, he's not moved a muscle. But I had to give him a tranquillizer.'

'Wait for me, both of you. I'm on my way.'

The driver of the car caught my mood and the nature of the situation. He switched on the siren, and we were at the Vigna Clara police station in half an hour. For a place that was usually so quiet, it was now near pandemonium.

Capuzzo was stammering down the phone, Nico was white as a sheet and pretty out of it. He hadn't shaved in over two hours and his beard was a thick shadow. His hair was ruffled, his clothes were dishevelled and there was even a stain on his grey twill trousers.

I looked at the envelope he handed me.

'What's this?'

Nico was shaking.

'Name of Deborah Reggiani's killer.'

I tore it open at the edge. Together, we read what Claudia had written in the girlish hand I recognised. Just four words.

Do it for me.

In that same moment, Capuzzo put the receiver down. He was extremely pale himself.

'Pietro and Paolo are outside Claudia's door right now. She's not answering the bell.'

'She'll have gone out,' I said. But my voice sounded unconvincing, even to me.

'The phone line's always engaged,' Capuzzo said.

'Today, it was like she was out of her mind, Mike . . .' Nico whispered.

I looked at him and realized I hadn't seen him in such a state since we were at school and several of our crappy little classmates started ribbing him with the name of 'Whiffy'.

'Calm down, Nico. I'll get someone to go home with you.'

'Thanks, Mike. Appreciate it.'

Capuzzo and I leaped in the same squad car that had brought me from the airport. The police driver knew immediately that he had to go still more quickly than he had before. Even Capuzzo urged him to step on it.

We were outside Claudia Teodori's in less than twenty minutes. It was six thirty. I dashed up the flights of stairs to the right floor, where Pietro and Paolo were standing around, not knowing what to do. Capuzzo was breathing hard behind me. I didn't stop for a second, and broke the door down with several kicks.

But it was too late. It always was when I had to protect someone.

Too late for Claudia, for Elisa, for Nadia and Italia. And too late for me, too.

The flat had been turned upside down. She must have fought back against her killer. The knife I saw sticking in at an angle at the level of her stomach must have punctured her heart.

I stood there speechless, staring at Claudia Teodori's body lying in a sea of blood. And the missing middle finger, cut off so cleanly. And I saw the anger on the faces of Pietro and Paolo, and Capuzzo, too, as he ran off to throw up outside the door.

The pain I felt for Claudia came from a long way back. From a shady room in Sidi El Masri, where, thirty-two years before, Italia Balistreri, née Bruseghin, had cradled a newborn baby boy and hoped he would become as courageous and faithful as her brother, Toni, but not as crazy and disdainful.

Not a man who calls young women little sluts and allows them to get murdered under his very own nose.

As soon as he got himself together, Capuzzo notified Homicide, Forensics and the forensic pathologist. I called the examining magistrate, who arrived half an hour later ,with the head of Homicide.

It was a stormy meeting. I said that I had gone to Palermo to visit my father, because I knew he was going to leave Italy, and that I'd called Capuzzo and learned of the envelope Claudia Teodori had given Nico Gerace. I showed them Claudia's note.

Do it for me.

I explained my relationship with her, my promise to her father to look after her. I said nothing about the call I'd made to her from Palermo.

But you mustn't tell anyone about this phone call. Anyone at all, Michele.

I was suppressing an important fact. But I knew I could trust Claudia far more than I could trust myself.

Then I spoke about Dino Forte. Though not about his link with Tripoli, nor about his relationship with my father and Don Eugenio. It would only have complicated matters. I remembered that it was Dino Forte's seaside villa that Fratini had called the night of Debbie's death. But I mentioned Rossellini's last telephone call from the Pescespada block before he committed suicide or got killed.

Capuzzo and the two apostles confirmed everything and were allowed to leave. The Homicide chief immediately made some calls to try to establish Dino Forte's whereabouts.

Finally, holding back his indignation at my laissez-faire attitude towards the case, he told me that Claudia Teodori and her missing finger had changed the game. This was now a matter of the daughter of a highly esteemed homicide squad officer who had recently passed away. A daughter I should have protected. And this was the result.

The investigation was given over to Homicide. I was kindly asked to send in my report by the following morning, and then take some leave and much-needed rest. And keep away. Far away.

Evening

I arrived back at the station at ten. I wanted to write that damned report for the examining magistrate and Homicide and then to go home and sleep.

I described everything accurately, but kept out anything to do with Nadia Al Bakri, the Balistreri brothers and the letters from Tripoli. And the call to Claudia.

Capuzzo kept me up to date on developments. At that moment, they were questioning Nico Gerace about his afternoon visit to Claudia Teodori. Dino Forte was nowhere to be found since he'd left the RAI at lunchtime.

I thought about my father again and what he'd said in Palermo only a few hours earlier.

My brothers mind their own business, and I mind mine. Perhaps these Nastasia men work for them, or perhaps for someone else, but I have no idea.

I had taken it for granted that this 'someone else' referred to Dino Forte. But then, I'd taken far too many things for granted.

Too many coincidences mean no coincidences.

Like the meeting with the Nastasias in Barcelona. Was that by coincidence or not? But I'd also met up with someone else in Barcelona. Was that also just by chance?

I'd also taken it for granted that Anita and Debbie's killer was the same as Nadia's. For this reason, I'd always excluded Nico Gerace, because he certainly couldn't have killed Nadia. But Anita and Debbie were a very different matter.

Nico was in Barcelona, like Anita. He knew Deborah Reggiani. He'd become an unexpected but resounding success in his career and he had to have been helped by somebody important. And he had to have been there at Dino Forte's villa when Debbie and Claudia had the accident.

I called Apostle Paul. I knew that, on that green screen of his, he had everyone's alibis, including those for 14 August, the day Anita had died. He answered straightaway and gave me all the details. I was changing my mind about that wretched PC of his.

I asked Capuzzo if Gerace was still being questioned.

'No, Commissario. It's over.'

'What did he say about his visit to Claudia's today?'

Without a word, Capuzzo handed me a typewritten sheet. The witness statement, signed by Nico. Then the first results from the forensics report. I avoided wondering how he'd managed to get hold of them.

I tried to get Nico at his villa on the Via Appia. He wasn't there. I found him in his office in Piazza Navona.

It was nearly eleven when I got to him. Nico came to the door, visibly upset. He was wearing the same clothes he had during the afternoon, he was unshaven, his eyes were red and his hair was dishevelled.

He looked curiously at the bag I had with me, but said nothing. We sat down on two armchairs in the office.

I took out the folders with my notes in them. Nico watched me in silence, perplexed.

'Can I pour you a shot of whisky, Mike?'

'No, thanks. I'm on duty, Nico.'

He looked at me in shock. 'Are you joking? I've just spoken to the examining magistrate, he said you were——'

'Just an informal visit, Nico. Just the two of us.'

He gave a weak smile.

'Just like old times.'

'No, Nico, we're not little boys any more. Those days are over.'

'Aren't we friends any more?'

'Not for years, Nico. You said so yourself to Claudia Teodori.'

'That was a lie so she would let me be her agent.'

'You swore it in your mother's name. So you were telling the truth.'

He poured out a drink and made no reply.

'All right. Now, Nico, did you know Deborah Reggiani?'

He exhaled a cloud of smoke and nodded.

'OK, OK, Mike. Let's play a little game, if it amuses you. Of course I knew her. I saw her on television.'

'Do you mean to say that's the only place you saw her?'

'Obviously not. You know we mixed in the same circles. I'll have met her at the RAI.'

'Once or twice? Or more?'

'How do I know? I can't remember. I'm Italy's most important agent – I see lots of people.'

'Was Deborah Reggiani one of your clients?'

'Absolutely not. She had no contract with me.'

I looked at my notes on the information supplied by the two apostles.

'In the spring of 1982, you were seen with Deborah Reggiani in a variety of places. Nightclubs, villas, yachts . . .'

'All places we were both invited to. Perhaps, once or twice, I even took her myself—'

'You said before that you couldn't remember.'

'That's right, I don't remember. I said "perhaps". Who knows?'

'You never took her home with you?'

'Never.'

'What about here in Piazza Navona. Was she ever here?'

'Could have been. It's my office. I see actors, actresses, presenters. I don't remember this Reggiani girl being here. But I can't rule it out.'

'Who's the owner of this property?'

'I don't remember.'

'I'll tell you. It's an estate agency in Palermo. You know who runs it?'

For the first time, Nico gave me a look of agitation.

'I'm telling you, I really don't know. What's it got to do with anything?'

'Have you signed a contract for the premises?'

He looked at me incredulously.

'No, like everyone else in Rome, Mike. Are you going to arrest me just because I pay cash under the table?'

I took another sheet from the folder.

'Where were you on the night of 9 July 1982, around midnight?'

'How should I know? What's special about it?'

'It's the night Deborah Reggiani was killed.'

'Oh, the night Claudia Teodori was off her head on stuff and went and crashed into a tree?'

'Yes, that night. And where were you?'

'From what I can remember, there were no suspicions about Deborah Reggiani's death. Or am I mistaken?'

'There weren't any then. But there are now. So, Nico, where were you?'

'I've no idea. How could I possibly remember?'

'Then I'll tell you. You were at a party at Dino Forte's villa in Ostia, less than a kilometre from the site of the accident.'

'Oh, so it was that night? Then, yes, I was there, with about a hundred other people.'

'Did you know Marco Fratini, Nico?'

'Never heard of him. Who is he?'

'The man who slipped amphetamines into Claudia Teodori's drink. Then he said something to her that scared her to death and made her speed off in the car with Deborah Reggiani.'

'I see. Well, I've never heard of this Fratini.'

'He died a few days ago. He was in prison in the Ucciardone in Palermo.'

'Heart attack?'

'Yes. Cardiac arrest. Poisoned coffee.'

'Wow. Do you put a jinx on people, Mike?'

'Marco Fratini made a telephone call from the bar he was in with Claudia Teodori, just before Claudia took off with Deborah.'

'So? I mean, who cares?'

'He called Dino Forte's villa in Ostia. And, just before he died, he was about to tell me the name of the person he spoke to.'

'He'll have spoken to someone at the party. There were loads of people.'

I moved on to another item of information the apostles had discovered.

'Did you know Anita Messi, Nico?'

'The girl you're investigating? The one with the missing finger? I'd never heard of her.'

'She was a student from Argentina. She flew into Rome on the evening of 13 August and was killed on the morning of 14 August. Her body was found at the start of the Via Cassia. Where were you that morning?'

'How the hell should I know, Mike? Middle of August? I'll have been on holiday in Elba. I've got a boat there.'

'Precisely. We've spoken to the Porto Azzuro harbour office on Elba, and with the skipper of your boat. You were there from 1 August.'

'There you are, you see? And so?'

'But, on the afternoon of 13 August, you came back to Rome. Your boat is registered as having moored in Fiumicino that night. The skipper says you didn't sleep on board and that, the following day, you came back at ten in the morning and left for Elba.'

Nico gave himself a little slap on the forehead with the palm of his hand.

'Now I know. That's the day I got paranoid about not having set the alarm in the villa. I've got several important paintings there.'

'And so?'

'So, on the 13th, I came back by boat to Rome. I took a taxi from the port at Fiumicino, slept over at the villa and the next morning was back off to Elba.'

'And the alarm . . .?'

'The alarm what?'

'Was it on or off?'

He thought for a moment.

'It was switched on – I was mistaken. But at least I was able to relax for the rest of the holiday.'

I consulted my notes again.

'And where were you between 29 June and 5 July last year?'

'Why don't you tell me, Mike, seeing as you already know everything?'

'You were in Barcelona, apparently supporting Italy against Argentina and Brazil.'

Again, the palm went to his forehead. Such a cheap theatrical gesture, like an old ham in a variety act.

'Shit, that's right. We even met each other there. You were with Angelo and those two Brazilian goers.'

But it didn't happen by chance. You gave those business cards to Angelo and me because you hoped we'd get in touch.

'Anita Messi was also there, to see Argentina's games. And she was also there on business.'

'Oh yes? Quite a coincidence.'

'Did you meet her?'

'You're the one who knows all the women and gets to fuck them. And what business was she doing there? Walking the streets, I bet.'

'No. Anita Messi was a drug mule. She couriered cocaine from Colombia to Europe.'

He raised an eyebrow. Again, like they did on the screen.

'Damn. That's a risky business.'

'Do you know the two brothers Calogero and Luciano Nastasia and their cousin Vito?'

Nico stared at me and smiled.

You had me come up against Calogero, Luciano and Vito Nastasia in Barcelona on purpose, so that I'd remember their faces when I met them again in Rome in I Tre Peccati, where little Kate took me. Someone else who was working for you.

'I know an awful lot of people, Mike. Who the hell are these guys anyway?'

'Three young Sicilian men who were in Barcelona on those very same days. Three coke pushers.'

'The names don't mean anything to me. I'm sorry.'

'They work from a piano bar in the centre, I Tre Peccati. A box of matches from that piano bar was in the room of Zingaretti's wife on Capri.'

Where you arranged for her to be.

'And what's Zingaretti got to do with it?'

'You were very clever in ruining him, Nico. A personal vendetta, right? He was interfering with business, wasn't he?'

'You're off your head, Mike. Zingaretti's a pig. That's all.'

'And Rossellini . . .?'

'Rossellini what?'

'He had small black spherical bars of soap in his bathroom. We found one in Anita Messi's bathroom.'

'That girl from Argentina? Then it was him who—'

'No. And he didn't commit suicide, either. After they killed him, the Nastasias called Dino Forte's villa from his room. Another enemy of yours.'

'An enemy of mine? How come?'

Because he's protected by that damned priest who touched you up when you were a boy. And we Sicilians just can't forget certain things.

'Do you know my father's four elder brothers, Nico?'

'Course I know your uncles, Mike. Everyone knows them in Palermo. Festivals, town-hall dos, regional-government receptions, marriages. That kind of thing.'

'And through business?'

'No, not through business. I don't have any business dealings with them.'

'They happen to own the estate agency that lets you use these premises for free.'

'And I happen to pay rent for it. On the QT, but it's paid. In cash. And I don't do any business with them.'

'They say that your rapid rise as an agent was — should we say? — helped by the Balistreri brothers.'

Nico said nothing.

Helped by the methods they use.

But this was simply gossip picked up by Pietro and Paolo. A lot of gossip, yes, but no proof. Although there was no doubt in my mind. This was payment for the real work that Nico Gerace did for Tano and his brothers, which was introducing cocaine into the world of entertainment: a world full of people who had money and the appropriate desires.

I picked up another bundle of notes, the ones with the first results from Forensics, pushed through for us by Capuzzo.

'You went to Claudia Teodori's flat today?'

'You know very well I did. I told both you and the examining magistrate. Claudia called me. She was feeling overcome by her father's death and asked me to come over.'

'This has been confirmed. You left your Ferrari Mondial on the pavement next to the building's main door and the traffic police gave you notice of a fine at two thirty-five. And what did the two of you do?'

He was now clearly embarrassed.

'Claudia was at low ebb, I comforted her a little, we drank a bit of whisky and smoked a couple of cigarettes.'

I had all this information from Capuzzo.

'Yes. Your fingerprints are on the glass. You brought some cocaine over as well, didn't you?'

'What cocaine?'

'Forensics found traces of cocaine on the sofa. I bet they'll also find some on your clothes, which we'll take in for analysis.'

'Look, Claudia had some cocaine in the flat. I certainly didn't bring it!'

'Your fingerprints are on the little metal box that contained the stuff.'

'Yes, because I tried to take it out of her hands. I didn't want—'

'A great number of people in the entertainment world are ready to testify that Claudia Teodori always said no to cocaine. You told me so yourself.'

Nico was now clearly unsettled, just as he was back in school when he had to read out a sentence full of 's' sounds. As if he really had killed Claudia Teodori. But I knew he hadn't.

'It was as if she'd lost her mind, Mike. As if she was someone else . . . .'

'Did you have sex with Claudia Teodori this afternoon in her flat?'

'Sex?'

'I think you know the meaning of the word, Nico. You denied it with the magistrate, but the first results from the pathologist indicate that Claudia had had sexual relations before she was killed.'

'No, I didn't—'

'There are traces of sperm on the sofa. Claudia's flatmate swears they weren't there when she left that morning. And perhaps we'll find traces of sperm on the trousers you're still wearing now. There's even a stain at the appropriate place.'

He looked at it and laughed nervously.

'All right, we did, Mike. A quick fuck on the sofa.'

'And it was consensual?'

'Of course it was. She provoked me—'

'Claudia's briefs had been ripped off.'

He gave me a defiant look.

'Fuck me, Mike. You know how it is with certain things!'

I do know, Nico, of course I do. I learned it with Marlene Hunt. But I don't go on to commit murder.

'You're seriously telling me that Claudia Teodori provoked you into having sex with her? A young girl whose father died only a few days ago?'

'Mike, give over. I don't know what came over her either. Claudia was out of her mind. Perhaps I should have stopped her. Anyway, we had a quick snort each and a quick screw. That's it.'

'Did you handle a knife, Nico?'

'A knife? What knife?'

'The one you stuck in her heart.'

'I really don't think—'

'Your fingerprints are on the handle.'

Once more, he slapped his forehead.

'I cut the ham.'

'You cut the what?'

'The ham, Mike. Are you growing deaf? She asked me to. And the bread. She was hungry.'

'In the pathologist's preliminary report there's no mention at all of any ham or bread in Claudia Teodori's stomach.'

Nico gave a tremendous punch to the table.

'She never ate it, the crazy bitch! Anyway, I didn't kill her, and no one knows that better than you.'

We'd come to the crunch because, on this point, there was no doubt. I'd heard Claudia alive on the telephone when Nico was already at the police station with Capuzzo. And he had only ever left there in my company.

'You went away and the Nastasia boys killed her.'

This time, he couldn't contain himself. The words flew from his mouth before he could reflect on their implications.

'No, they were in Palermo!'

That was right. The apostles had already confirmed this. The three Nastasia boys had returned on the flight after mine in the evening.

They hadn't killed Claudia Teodori. It was Dino Forte who had seen to that.

Or someone else entirely.

A long silence fell. Nico got up and poured himself another whisky. Then he came back and sat down in front of me. He now looked much more like the insecure child I had grown up with throughout school.

'I didn't kill her, Mike. I swear it on my mother's name.'

Perhaps Nico had killed Debbie and Anita Messi. Perhaps. He certainly knew the Nastasias and was a drug pusher for my father's brothers. But he certainly hadn't killed Claudia Teodori.

'Nico, I don't give a shit if you push cocaine for these pathetic actors and actresses. Perhaps it's also my fault. I started you off with the MANK organization, and you haven't stopped since. But we didn't kill innocent girls.'

He looked me directly in the eyes and pointed to the white scar on his wrist. The blood brotherhood in the sand.

'I haven't killed anyone either. You can arrest me for dealing, if you like, but I'll be out within three days.'

Part of me believed him; part of me didn't. But Nico Gerace's shady business wasn't my most urgent problem right now.

'OK, then I'll be going, Nico. We'll discuss this again.'

He got up as well.

'Me, too, Mike. I'm off home as well. I'll come down with you: the Ferrari's in the garage just near here.'

Piazza Navona was still crowded as we went across it at midnight. I was following Nico through the people and the stalls when we came upon a white-haired middle-aged woman who did portrait sketches. I remembered what Claudia Teodori had said about a portrait she'd let Dino Forte have done.

I went up to her, Nico at my side.

The portraitist was free at that moment. She looked at my former friend and smiled. It was a sweet smile, despite the few broken yellow teeth. Then she looked at me.

'Do you want your portraits, gentlemen?'

I pointed to the one of Marcello Mastroianni, which was pinned up among the nameless tourists.

'Do famous people sometimes come here?'

Another toothless smile.

'Yes. But not Marcello Mastroianni. I just use that to attract the tourists.'

'But, every now and again, someone famous does come along, right?'

'Yes, every now and again.'

'Like who? Who was the last one to come?'

I was playing the part of a curious prick of a tourist. Nico listened in, a little bewildered by the conversation.

'That girl on TV. Don't remember her name. The one on Dino Forte's show.'

'Claudia Teodori?' I offered.

'That's the one, sir. You know, it's Dino Forte who always brings me the famous ones. He's a friend of mine, lives in the piazza here. I can show you Claudia Teodori's portrait, if you like.'

I looked surprised.

'Didn't you give it to him?'

'Yes, but I always do two when it's someone famous. I sell one and pin one up in the middle of all these ordinary folks. The ones who refuse. You see, with Charmene, it's like this. If you don't like the portrait, you don't pay and I keep it. Although I sleep rough in the arcades, I'm not interested in the money.'

She pointed out several portraits hanging up behind her.

Claudia was there, a beautiful and mysterious Audrey Hepburn in the middle of an anonymous crowd. Hanging nearby were a little black girl with an ice cream, and an elderly Japanese tourist with a camera. And, right next to Claudia, there was a girl with the features of a South American Indian.

I was lost for words.

'Are you feeling all right, Mike?' Nico asked me.

'Yeah, it's nothing,' I said. 'Look, Charmene, is that one of the portraits no one wanted?'

She raised her shoulders.

'I don't know, I don't remember. I've no idea who it is.'

But I knew who it was: I recognized the face and that T-shirt with the word 'Danger' on it. And I knew the girl's name. She was called Anita, Anita Messi. And that portrait was done only a few hours before she was killed and had her finger cut off. A portrait made by the portraitist who was a friend of Dino Forte.

Perhaps I was mistaken about Nico. And about the fact that there might be two different killers.

One man alone killed them all. And it all began in Tripoli.

I'd never be able to solve the cases of Anita Messi, Deborah Reggiani and Claudia Teodori from here. I had to go back to the real starting point: Nadia Al Bakri, 3 August 1969.

If I could find out who Nadia's killer was, then I would find out who killed all the others. I had to go back to the very point that I had tried in every way to forget.

To the roots of evil.

Sunday, 23 January 1983

I went home by taxi and, at one in the morning, passed the latest developments to Capuzzo and the two apostles and told them what I wanted them to do. Investigate the links and alibis of Dino Forte, Nico Gerace and the Nastasias. Call in Charmene the portraitist and question her about Anita Messi and Dino Forte. All this was breaking the implicit pact that had saved my life on that first day in Palermo. Once they felt hunted, the killers wouldn't give a damn about any orders from my father and would throw all caution to the wind.

They won't wait for you to go back to Palermo to kill you. They'll target you wherever you are.

At six the next morning, the news on the radio gave the clamorous announcement of Dino Forte's arrest in his villa in Tivoli.

At seven, I called Capuzzo. He told me that Dino Forte was still being grilled. I told him to notify the apostles. I wanted them to shadow him in turns after his release and never to let him out of their sight.

At eight, Capuzzo called me back. Dino Forte's questioning was over. He had no alibi for the afternoon of the day before, when Claudia Teodori was killed. He testified that he was alone in his villa in Tivoli. His big-shot lawyer had defended him well. There wasn't the slightest trace of him in Claudia's flat, and no one had seen him in the vicinity.

For the moment, his passport had been withdrawn and he was ordered not to leave the city. Forte had gone to his apartment in Piazza Navona, and Pietro was down on the street outside.

While Pietro was tailing Dino Forte, Paolo had looked again at his alibi for the day of Anita Messi's death. He was with some friends, again in his famous Tivoli villa in the hills around Rome. None of them was able to confirm that Forte never left the house. Not a solid alibi, like almost all of the alibis for a day in the middle of summer.

Pietro had looked into the Nastasia boys. They had landed in Rome on the last flight from Palermo – which Paolo had been able to confirm after being given access to Alitalia's computers – and had then gone straight to I Tre Peccati. They'd just left when Pietro called in for a quick chat with the barman and a few of the regulars. Dino Forte had never been to I Tre Peccati.

The worst news came from Capuzzo at nine. From central head-quarters, he learned that, at about two o'clock that night, three hooligans had attacked a poor vagrant woman who was sleeping in her bundle of rags in an alley behind Piazza Navona. She had been identified as the portraitist Charmene. She was the only link between Anita Messi and Dino Forte, and now she was dead. Killed by three hooligans.

The Nastasias. Drug trafficking. The Mafia. The P2 Lodge. Dino Forte. The Balistreri brothers.

I remembered her white hair, the broken teeth, her long, delicate fingers. And the sweet smile she'd given to Nico and me to try to persuade us to have our portraits sketched,

Enough's enough. We'll sort this out like the MANK used to do. Like Ahmed and I used to do.

We would never find any positive proof against anyone for the deaths of Anita, Debbie and Claudia. The forces pitted against our investigations in Italy were all-powerful.

But my enemies' weak point was Nadia Al Bakri. The homicide squad wasn't investigating that case. And they didn't know about the letters from Tripoli.

You must find Nadia's killer, because he killed all the others as well. And you must do it before your enemies kill you.

At nine thirty, Apostle Peter called. Dino Forte had gone out alone. He had taken a taxi and in a few minutes was at the parish church of Sant'Anselmo on the Aventine. He had then returned to his apartment in Piazza Navona. Pietro hadn't been able to follow him inside the church, so he didn't know what he'd done there or who he might have met.

But I knew very well who Dino Forte had gone to see. The name of Sant'Anselmo's parish church was one that brought back sinister memories.

It was time to make a move. I was getting ever nearer to my enemies of old.

Sant'Anselmo's church was in one of the most beautiful places in Rome, on the Aventine hill, not far from the College of the Sisters of the Virgin. And, besides, Monsignor Eugenio Pizza was an important man. It must have been his habit to pick a church with the same name as the one in Tripoli to celebrate Mass in from time to time.

When I got there in mid-morning, the Neo-Romantic church and monastery were standing out against a beautifully clear sky. Inside its three naves, there were only three or four old ladies and Don Eugenio, who was bringing the service to a close.

The Mass is ended. Go forth in peace.

Monsignor Pizza seemed neither surprised nor pleased to see me.

'Let's go outside, Michele. This is a place for prayer.'

We set off for the Orange Garden further up the hill. Below us stretched the city: Trastevere's rooftops, the Tiber's slow curves between ancient noble buildings, the Tiberina Island, the numerous church cupolas in the historic centre. Seen from a distance, it was the most beautiful city in the world but, from inside, it was nothing but a nest of vermin. Around us there wasn't a soul, only the orange trees and their scent on the air. And between us the overwhelming silence that went all the way back to one day in a classroom.

When he allowed Salvatore Balistreri's son to leave and kept behind that wretched kid Nico Gerace.

'I'm ready to listen, Michele.'

The tone of voice was no longer the superior one of teacher to pupil or Monsignore to young police officer. Don Eugenio was troubled. And there was no shortage of reasons why. The failure of the plan for a bridge over the Straits of Messina, my father leaving Italy and, obviously, the fate of everyone's favourite son, Dino Forte.

I came straight to the point.

'I know that Dino Forte was here not long ago. I want to know where he was yesterday afternoon. Otherwise, he'll be arrested for Claudia Teodori's murder.'

A further silence.

'If he doesn't have an alibi, Forte's in deep trouble, Monsignore. Only you can help him.'

'What makes you think that, Michele?'

'He's your friend, isn't he? You're also his confessor. No one knows him as well as you.'

'He made confession with me a little time ago. But confession is a sacrament, Michele.'

'It's a life sentence for murder, Monsignore. And I can't see Dino Forte happy about being in jail, not even for a night.'

There was a long silence. Monsignor Pizza looked over to the dome of St Peter's and his voice dropped to a whisper.

'Dino Forte has a secret, Michele. As we all do.'

Naturally. Like me. Like you.

It was my turn to remain silent.

'A secret that's a vice. And can only be confessed to a priest.'

'I can imagine. Otherwise, an alibi would haul him out of this mess. What is it, drugs? Or a lover?'

'Worse.'

'Worse?'

A long sigh.

'Every so often, he takes a trip around Tor di Quinto.'

I was dumbstruck. I couldn't believe it.

'With all the women he could have he goes chasing after whores?'

Another sigh.

'It's not only women at Tor di Quinto.'

It was then I understood. For Dino Forte to confess that he'd had a relationship with a transsexual would mean the end of his brilliant career in the staunchly Catholic Italian television industry and also him having to face public pillory.

'Do you know the name of this transsexual?'

'She's called Marybelle. But you're going to ruin him like this, Michele.'

'I'm saving him from jail. Where he would otherwise be going tonight.'

Don Eugenio nodded.

'I said the same thing to him. He has no choice. Destroy his career or end up in prison.'

A terrible decision for a man like Dino Forte. I had to notify Capuzzo to have him arrested forthwith.

But there was another question.

'There's one more thing I have to ask, Monsignore. It's to do with 3 August 1969.'

Don Eugenio remained silent. Perhaps he was beginning to realize that Dino Forte's problem was a small one compared to all the rest.

'That morning, you and my father went to Sidi El Masri, a little further beyond our villas. Was Emilio Busi with you?'

He replied straight off, without any embarrassment.

'Yes, your father and I met Dino Forte at the countess's in Sidi El Masri. But Busi wasn't with us.'

'And after that?'

'Forte was on his own for only a few minutes. I heard the countess's confession and we drove back into the city before ten o'clock, behind you boys in the MANK van. We continued behind you as far as the Shara Mizran market, where Farid got out. We turned off at the market and went to the Waddan to wait for Busi, who still hadn't arrived at that point.'

'And where was he?'

He gave me a frosty look and shook his head.

'But why is any of this important?'

It had an importance that was absolutely vital. But, at that moment, Apostle Paul came running into the garden.

'Dino Forte's just hanged himself.'

Monsignor Eugenio Pizza crossed himself, then set off in a hurry back to the church, waving me goodbye.

We will come to settle certain scores, sooner or later.

I asked Capuzzo and the two apostles to come over for a meeting at my place in Garbatella. By eleven, we were all gathered in my narrow little flat, now suffering the invasion of Capuzzo's papers, Pietro's elaborate nitpicking and even Paolo's damned computer, which he'd taken great efforts to bring over.

Faced with an impossible choice, Dino Forte had hanged himself in his elegant Piazza Navona apartment. Rather than save his mortal existence and face moral ruin, he'd chosen to lose the former. Capuzzo told me that Homicide had no doubts about either the suicide or Dino Forte's guilt in killing Cladia Teodori. And Apostle Paul told me that no one had entered Dino Forte's apartment after he came back from the church of Sant'Anselmo.

I could agree about the suicide, but not about the fact that Forte had killed Claudia Teodori. I gave Pietro the job of finding Marybelle. I wanted to verify the alibi for the time of Claudia's death. And I had no doubts that, *on this point at least*, Don Eugenio had told me the truth. Indeed, it was Forte's suicide that confirmed it. He hadn't been able to face the huge shame and inglorious end to his career and image, because this Marybelle really did exist.

Pressing on with the recent murders had led us nowhere. There were too many forces working against the truth. We decided to concentrate on the past alone. On the death of Nadia Al Bakri: a crime committed over thirteen years ago on another continent.

This time, I told the story in every detail, starting with when I told Nadia that the bodies found in the cesspit had been those of two black women, mother and child, right up to the point where Nico Gerace and I fled for our lives from Tripoli. I left out only Ahmed's death and my questions about Laura and Marlene Hunt, who didn't come into it. But, for the rest, I filled them in on everything, including my suspicions about my father and his friends plotting a *coup d'état* and the subsequent attempt on Gaddafi's life.

And I read them all the letters exchanged with Tripoli in the past few months.

They were captivated, as if they'd been transported into the world of *Treasure Island* or *Star Wars*. At the end, Apostle Peter made a single comment.

'Nadia's killer's the same one who killed the two black girls, Anita Messi, Deborah Reggiani and Claudia Teodori.'

By now, I wasn't as sceptical of him as I'd been at first. I now knew very well that his intuitions and analyses were often spot on.

'Why? Because of the finger?' Capuzzo asked Pietro.

'It's not only the planning behind each crime that's struck me,'. Pietro replied. 'It's as if we're dealing each time with an exact copy of a single very complex notion.'

'Except for the case of Claudia Teodori, which is different,' I observed.

Pietro nodded.

'Perhaps that's right, Balistreri. That murder entailed less planning. But there's the usual trademark, the missing finger.'

'Can you let me have the original of this, Balistreri?' Paolo asked me.

He was looking at a photocopy of the famous sheet of notes that I'd also sent to Tripoli. I went to get the Nietzsche book and took out the old piece of squared paper and Nadia's bloodstained handkerchief.

Paolo took the page and sat down at his computer, while Pietro told me to handle the handkerchief with care.

'Why?'

'Because science has make great strides, Balistreri. We know you don't like progress, but very soon the stains on that handkerchief could tell us something important. Keep it nice and dry in that book, just like you have done all these years.'

'Can you come here, Balistreri?'

I looked over at Paolo. He had turned the sheet of notes over.

'What's this?' he asked.'

They knew each other. Check m

'I told you, my mother made some inquiries. That's her note.'

Paolo looked at the sheet with one raised eyebrow. He was making a comparison with green letters on the computer screen.

'It's odd the way your mother's written this letter "m".'

I stared at him. I couldn't understand what either of them were going on about: Paolo with this 'm' and Pietro about the handkerchief. They were just wasting my time.

It was twelve thirty, and I sent them all away in a less than gracious manner. They had a good many things to check out and I had several I needed to think about.

★　　★　　★

It was days since I'd had a decent meal. What with all the whisky, coffee and cigarettes, I was risking a painful ulcer. I went out unwillingly, but I absolutely had to have something to eat. I couldn't allow myself to get ill. Besides, my usual *bar-rosticceria* was only a couple of strides away.

The owner was standing in the doorway with the butcher and the fruit seller. He was pointing to the opposite pavement and complaining loudly.

'Bloody Americans! Even here in Garbatella now. Mussolini would have sent them away with a kick up the arse!'

I looked across the road. For over a month, a crew of workmen had been refitting a large shop that had been empty for some time. One of the men at the top of a ladder was handing a symbol of the new owners to another man to put up over the entrance.

'Fucking McDonald's!' shouted the man from the bar, already seeing his business in ruins.

At that moment, a first thunder-clap jolted the workman, who was left with the sign dangling down at ninety degrees.

I looked at the sign and couldn't believe my eyes.

It's odd the way your mother's written this letter 'm'.

It certainly was odd. So odd it had taken me thirteen years and a barman's cursing to get me to see it. Mamma had kept her promise, she had made inquiries. But then, in jotting down a note, she'd been purposefully cryptic.

She did it to protect you, Mike, in case you ever read them. Only in doing so, and without wanting to, she'd also protected the killer for thirteen years and condemned Debbie, Anita and Claudia to their deaths.

The first raindrops came pelting down. I wasn't hungry any more. I was only beside myself with fury, the old rage and adrenalin circulating unstoppably through me.

My stomach was churning.

Now you know everything and can't do a thing. You haven't even a shred of evidence. That 'm' was an 'e' written 'e' . . . and I'd even asked Mohammed if there was anyone Nadia might know with a name beginning with 'm' . . .

Back inside the flat, the neighbourhood's sounds were now muffled by the rain's pitter-patter. Cars, mopeds, a loud greeting and still some distant thunder. Life went on despite the rain, despite everything. The life of normality of which all those women had been deprived.

The doorbell rang. A courier with an express parcel.

I've sent you a gift. You'll get it at home tomorrow.

I snatched the parcel from the courier's hand and scribbled my signature on a form, then growled thank you and shut the door in his face.

It was a simple parcel, wrapped in pink paper. As I was carefully opening it, my thoughts turned to Claudia Teodori. She hadn't been a spoiled girl, a little slut or a talentless social climber. This was only the way Michele Balistreri saw women: through the distorted spectacles given him by Marlene and Laura Hunt.

Once the wrapping was off, I found a small address book and a bag with a zip fastener.

In Deborah Reggiani's address book, the corner of the page for the letter 'H' was folded down, and there was circle around the word 'Him' and the corresponding telephone number that I knew very well.

Inside the bag was the gift that Claudia had promised.

It was the gift of a life. Her life. The lives of these innocent victims.

Claudia Teodori had been incredibly brave. Indeed, heroic, a martyr.

There was a note inside the bag written in her childish scrawl.

To Michele from Claudia. Believe in the impossible. Do it for me.

I was crying and laughing at the same time. Laughing and crying. Yes, the impossible was now possible.

I called my father in Isola delle Femmine. Only twenty-four hours earlier, I had been there with him and forced him to leave Italy. A kindly voice answered in Sicilian, the old man who had greeted me the day before.

'Your father's in Rome, Michè. He's at the Excelsior. He went off yesterday just after the press conference.'

'But there were no flights to Rome before mine,' I said.

'Salvo has his own private jet, Michè.'

Naturally. Cavaliere Salvatore Balistreri, decorated for services to industry, wouldn't dream of flying with ordinary mortals and having to wait for an Alitalia flight. So, Papa left for Rome straightaway in his private jet, perhaps getting in before me, if he used Ciampino airport, which is nearer to the city than Fiumicino.

I called the Excelsior. They put me through to a secretary, who put me through to my father.

'You gave me two weeks, Michele. I'm here in Rome to arrange things and then I leave. I have a flight already booked for 6 February.'

'I'm not calling to get you to hurry up. I know you'll keep to the agreement because I saw the press-conference report on the news.'

And because you let me come back alive from Palermo.

My father said nothing. He was waiting for my question. I could have asked him what he'd done as soon as he landed in Rome and if he'd ever met Claudia Teodori. But this wasn't the question. The question was about Nadia Al Bakri.

'Don Eugenio's confirmed your version of events for 3 August 1969. The two of you were alone together that morning, without Busi, at Dino Forte's aunt's. And he says he saw Farid get out of the MANK van, as you said.'

'That's right. We saw Farid get out of your van in that sandstorm and run off towards the market. Mike—'

I cut him off short. 'I asked you about the Nastasias yesterday. Did you tell any of your guests yesterday that I'd left? Busi and Don Eugenio came back with you in the jet, I suppose?'

'Yes, why do you ask?'

'Because the Nastasias had come to Palermo to kill me. But after I talked to you, they didn't carry it out.'

'I'm happy they didn't, Michele.'

Yes, I can believe you are. It was you who stopped them. But it won't be like that today.

'Except that someone's become deadly scared, Papa. The Nastasias are back in Rome and, last night, they set fire to a vagrant woman, who happened to be a key witness for the murders I'm investigating. Did you know about this?'

There was a brief but very deep silence.

He's taking a decision.

'Watch out for yourself, Mike.'

The conversation was over. I had my answer. There was nothing else to say.

The Nastasias had to have been told by now.

That's enough of Michele Balistreri. Enough of him.

By the evening, I'd either be dead or back in Garbatella still alive. Anything would be better than what I'd become. I was that bird on a wire in Leonard Cohen's song, neither a boy nor yet a man, balancing in limbo. It was time to put an end to it.

A few hours earlier, I'd accused Nico Gerace of having killed Deborah Reggiani, Anita Messi and Claudia Teodori, while knowing very well it was impossible for him to have done so. But it had been useful because, in the end, Nico had crumbled and admitted he knew the Nastasias and that he also dealt coke to the entertainment world.

But the question remained about Nadia Al Bakri. Now I knew who had killed her, I wanted the answer to another question. And there was only one person who could give it to me.

Who had thrown my mother off that cliff?

I called him at his office in Piazza Navona. He was in and replied in a hesitant voice.

'Nico, I have to see you.'

He was immediately worried.

'Why? Are you going to have me arrested for dealing, Mike?'

'No. I want some information that only you can give me.'

'I'm off to police headquarters for another interview. The examining magistrate wants to hear about Claudia's relationship with Dino Forte. After his suicide, everyone's convinced he was the murderer.'

I said nothing, and Nico became panicky.

'Mike, you know very well I didn't kill Claudia Teodori.'

'I know that, Nico. It wasn't you.'

Nico Gerace didn't kill her. But he has the key to discovering the mystery around that August in 1969.

I had put my motorbike in the underground garage, which was accessed via the cellars and gave on to the rear of the building. Even if the Nastasias were waiting for me outside and tried to follow me in the Jaguar, I'd be able to shake them off in the rush-hour traffic when the offices closed. In the dark and the rain, Rome would become one solid mass of traffic.

I went down to the bar on the street. It was important that the Nastasias saw me there. The usual old neighbourhood friends were in the bar, enjoying the lunchtime quiet, discussing the Rome and Lazio teams' players.

I chatted a bit with them, but couldn't touch a thing. I just smoked a cigarette as I drank a couple of coffees, each burning my throat and stomach as they went down. Then, towards three o'clock, I walked slowly back to the flat in the rain. The black Jaguar was ostentatiously parked on the pavement outside the apartment block's main entrance. It was empty.

All right, let's get this over with.

I made a move at five thirty, giving myself plenty of time. I slipped the loaded Beretta in the pocket of my leather jacket and went down to the garages underground. I placed Claudia Teodori's gift in one of the Triumph's side panniers, together with a folder containing a few documents. I put on my full-face helmet and set off.

Outside, it was already dark and pouring with rain. As soon as I came off the ramp into the garages and on to the street, a large Laverda 750 motorbike with two of the Nastasias on it started to follow me as I left the Garbatella neighbourhood and drove towards Via Cristoforo Colombo, then crossed over it on to the Appia Antica. So they'd fooled me, but they had had years of experience in this kind of activity. The Jaguar had been left clearly visible so as not to arouse my suspicions. In fact, they'd been ready to follow me by bike, dividing up the watch on the possible exits. The third man would certainly be waiting for me at the main door.

They had no intention of wasting time setting up a complicated scenario for an accident.

They'll shoot me and have done with it.

I changed direction sharply, turning left into Via Cristoforo Colombo and back up to the city centre. I ran the first traffic light on amber at 130 kilometres an hour with the Laverda hard on my heels. All the other traffic lights up to the Baths of Caracalla were green. I pushed the Triumph as hard as I could, zigzagging through the other cars, but continued to see the Laverda's headlight in my rear-view mirrors.

As the road curved round the Coliseum, I knew I'd find it jammed with cars and be forced to slow down. It was probably here that the killer in the pillion seat would try to shoot at me.

I started to slow down towards the Arch of Constantine and used this opportunity to take out my pistol. Ahead, I could see the rear lights of the bottleneck of stationary cars around the ancient stadium. The Nastasias' bike was drawing closer.

Then, right behind the Laverda, another bike's headlight appeared in my rear-view mirrors. I knew the shape and sound of the engine. It was a Kawasaki 900. Then I heard the burst of fire: sharp, brief, accurate.

Kawasaki and Kalashnikov. Together, they formed a well-known trademark.

The Nastasias dropped on to the wet tarmac, while the Laverda went out of control towards the line of cars and crashed into a bus. I pulled up fifty metres further on. The Kawasaki stopped dead beside the two lifeless bodies.

The one in the pillion seat holding the Kalashnikov fired another short burst at the Nastasias. The Kawasaki then did a sudden about-turn and shot off like a rocket back through the traffic towards the Caius Cestius Pyramid and Via Ostiense.

They'd killed the portraitist on the orders of their direct superior, the murderer, but against the wishes of the real bosses. And someone had not been pleased.

I also did an about-turn on the Triumph, but hadn't the slightest thought of following the Kawasaki. I also had no doubt in my mind that the third Nastasia had now, too, had a taste of the Kalashnikov.

I drove on towards the Appia Antica, and my appointment with Nico Gerace, and the MANK's brotherhood of blood and sand.

I made it to the Appia Antica and parked the bike a hundred metres from Nico's villa. Although the temperature wasn't below zero, the humidity from the rain made the air feel like it was.

I knew from my last visit there that the alarm system protected only the villa, not the garden or the garage.

The surrounding wall at the back of the house was easy to climb. There was nothing in the garden to steal and the Ferrari Mondial was insured anyway. As I imagined, the up-and-over garage door wasn't even locked.

Next to the Ferrari was the red Fiat 850T van with 'MANK' written on its side and the Barbra Streisand poster inside. I opened the rear doors, put on overshoes, gloves and cap, and dived into the past.

Everything was as it had been then. The nude Playmates pinned up, the mattress on which Nico saw to his whores behind the Esso station forecourt. And the poster pierced by Ahmed's knife.

It can't have been easy getting the van out of Tripoli. Gaddafi didn't let Italians take even their mattresses with them. But you had someone to protect you, Nico. A very important someone. And you always did have.

I had to be careful. Observe everything with the eyes and touch nothing with the hands. No anger rose in me, but an icy coldness descended. That same iciness with which Ahmed and I had killed three young soldiers in Cairo, with which I'd shot at Salim and the lion, and with which we'd cut the eyes out of the Maltese's Doberman.

I climbed back over the wall and returned to the motorbike. I took the folder out of the pannier, went round to the gate at the front of the house and rang the bell. Nico came out to open it. He was wearing only a shirt and jeans, as if he didn't feel the icy dampness at all. He had dark rings under his eyes but, in contrast to the day before, he had shaved and recovered his usual composure. He didn't seem intimidated or likely to be open to any more accusations.

We went to sit in the living room, taking two armchairs, from which you could see the garden and its leafless branches swept by the rain.

I took the photograph out of the folder I was holding.

A small, dark-skinned hand with broken fingernails and stained with earth,
but missing its middle finger.

I turned it round to let Nico see it. He gave it a glance.

'Is that Anita Messi's hand?'

'Take a closer look.'

He fixed his eyes on it in silence. And, in that silence, like a poison
flowing in his veins, a doubt slowly began to creep up inside him.
Nico stared in fascination at the photo of that hand.

'Is it Anita Messi's hand or not?' he asked, a first real sign of appre-
hension in his voice.

'No, Nico, it's Nadia Al Bakri's hand. The girl who was killed in
Tripoli, Libya, on 3 August 1969.'

The previous night, when I'd accused him of having killed Anita,
Debbie and Claudia, he hadn't shown any sign of fear. This time, a
shadow crossed his face that came from way back in the past.

You're not dealing with Commissario Balistreri anymore, but with your old
friend Mike. The one who kills his friends if they betray him.

Then he smiled. Behind it was the unabashed pride of a madman,
as if my discovery of the infernal plan in which he and Farid had
captured and killed Nadia were the definitive demonstration of how
greatly his former boss in the MANK organization had underappre-
ciated Nico Gerace. After all, from the legal point of view, he knew
he had little to fear. Nadia Al Bakri was beyond the jurisdiction of an
Italian court.

'Bravo, Mike, although it's taken you enough time to work it out.
So how did you?'

'My father and Don Eugenio saw Farid getting out of the van in
the sandstorm. Getting out of the back – but they never gave it any
importance, because the guilty man was the goatherd Jamaal.'

'But, sorry, Jamaal had been seen with Nadia near the olive-
pressing shed, hadn't he?'

'Yes, and I've thought about that a lot, you know. Even when I began to suspect that Farid hadn't been at the market, that damned witness upset all my hypotheses.

'So now you've got it?'

I pointed to the window. In the darkness under the pouring rain, visibility was reduced to zero.

'Back then, there was the sand, not the rain. Without that, Farid dressed up as Nadia wouldn't have taken in even a half-blind goatherd.'

Nico smiled with satisfaction, giving some faint applause.

'Excellent, Mike. A little slow to catch on, but better late than never.'

'Why, Nico? Why did you do it? And with those two bastards!'

'Farid and Salim had their reasons. Nadia had seen them years before with that black girl and her baby.'

'Whom they chucked in the cesspit.'

'Not immediately, Mike. Before that, they had been hanging up, one against the other. They were already dead when they were thrown in the cesspit.'

'And you, Nico? What had Nadia done to you?'

He raised his shoulders and patted his hair straight

'I tried it on with her and she told me to fuck off. That stinking little Arab even gave me the finger. If she'd ever told that psychopath Ahmed, he'd have slit my throat. So I agreed to help Farid and Salim.'

'But Nadia had said something to my mother, either about the black girls or you trying it on with her.'

He was stunned for a moment.

'And how the hell d'you know that?'

'Italia left some notes. *They knew each other* and *Check m.*'

'What is it, some kind of quiz?'

'Almost, Nico. Because my mother wrote those words cryptically, in case they fell into my hands.'

'All right, but where do I come in? "They knew each other" refers to the two black girls and to Farid and Salim, yeah?'

'Yes, Nico. But that "m" refers to you.'

'The "m"? What the bugger d'you mean?'

I took out the photocopy of the sheet of squared paper and showed it to him.

'Can you see how the "m" is written with the two humps? It's not the initial letter of someone's name. Look at it carefully. Turn it round.'

'So? It looks like the symbol for McDonald's.'

'That's right, Nico, that's exactly right.'

I rotated the page ninety degrees anticlockwise.

'What else does it look like?'

He thought for a moment.

'Oh God! It's the Esso sign's '∈'!'

'Exactly. Your Esso, Nico. You were the one she wanted to check out.'

'Sure, she came around asking a few questions . . .'

'Is that why you threw her off the cliff?'

The colour suddenly drained from Nico's face. It was the same as with my father. The accusation of having killed Italia was too disparaging even for someone like Nico Gerace, who had killed so many women.

He shook his head violently. He was terrified, afraid that I was going to kill him.

'No, Mike. I helped Farid by driving him around in the van, but I never laid a finger on your mother. I swear it on Santuzza's name.'

I looked him right in the eyes. He'd never sworn falsely on his mother's name. Italia's death had not been by his hand.

But there were all the other deaths.

Do it for me, Mike. And for Nadia, for Debbie, for Anita. And for yourself. If you want justice.

'Right, you're coming with me, Nico. You're under arrest.'

He gave a laugh. He'd realized that I wasn't going to kill him in cold blood and knew that I only had proof for Anita and Debbie. And that I'd never have anything more than that.

'You're not going to arrest me for the murder of a filthy Arab girl in that sandbox thirteen years ago, are you?'

'No, for the murder of Claudia Teodori.'

'You're talking nonsense, Mike. When I left the flat, she was alive, as you very well know. You said yourself you'd just spoken to Claudia when I was already with Capuzzo at the police station. And I never moved from there.'

'Really? I don't remember having telephoned Claudia, Nico.'

He stared at me incredulously.

'What the bugger do you mean?'

'I simply don't remember, just as you don't remember having killed Anita and Debbie.'

'You don't have any proof in Claudia's case. None.'

I showed him Debbie's little address book.

'Your home telephone number's in here under the letter "H" for "Him" with a capital letter.'

'Great proof. You've got nothing. Not for Claudia, nor for Debbie or Anita.'

'With Anita, you were exceptionally clever, Nico. You took her to Dino Forte's portraitist, poor old Charmene. You paid her handsomely to draw Anita's portrait and hang it up there. And, just by chance, you walked me past and had me see it and so place the blame on Dino Forte.'

'All nonsense. Let's go and ask Charmene. Come on!'

This is what Nico Gerace had become. Tripoli's little hooligan had turned into a merciless killer.

'It was your friends the Nastasias who actually killed her, Nico. But on your orders.'

Nico looked instinctively towards the villa gate.

'The Nastasias won't be coming, Nico. They're dead.'

He looked at me, shocked.

'What bullshit is this now?'

'They're dead, Nico. In killing that poor, homeless portraitist they disobeyed Tano.'

He went slowly over to the mobile bar. There he fiddled around with the ice and glasses and poured himself a whisky, and also slipped a pistol into his belt behind his back.

He had decided it was time to put me to the test.

'All right, I did kill Anita and Debbie. But you don't have any proof, nothing. And I had nothing to do with Claudia's death and you know it.'

'So who was it?'

'You know very well. That little whore set it all up, didn't she?'

'What did she set up, Nico?'

'Everything, Mike, everything. She got me to go over there and had me go through all that shit on purpose, the cocaine, the knife, the quick fuck; and then she sent me over to the police station with a note that didn't say a bloody thing.'

'No, Nico. It had the killer's name written on it.'

'The killer's name?! It only said that stupid "Do it for me"!'

Exactly. Do it for me.

It was time to bring things to a close with Nico Gerace.

'We do have proof to nail you. Decisive proof.'

He was shaken, but still quite sure of himself.

'OK, so let's see this famous proof of yours!'

I took a photograph from the folder. I turned it round to let him see. It was a photograph of Claudia's body and clearly visible was the left hand with its missing middle finger.

Nico stared at it incredulously, and you could see many things passing through his mind. First doubt and consternation, then anger and terror.

'Impossible,' he whispered, his old lisp coming back.

Believe in the impossible, Michele. Do it for me.

Claudia Teodori had handed me Debbie's killer and the killer of all the other the women. A young woman whom I'd always thought a little slut and yet who'd made heroic efforts and been ready to make the ultimate sacrifice so that justice would be served.

She'd asked only one thing of me. *Do it for me.*

'Oh, it's possible all right, Nico, believe me. That finger's going to have you.'

He looked at me in disbelief. He pointed to the white line on his left wrist and on mine.

'You can't arrest me for a crime I didn't commit. You're a policeman. And we swore a blood brotherhood all those years ago, remember?'

'Yes, I'm a policeman and I'm also Mike Balistreri. Still. And that oath of blood brotherhood was broken in Tripoli when you sold yourself to my enemies and stopped me from killing Gaddafi. Because it was you who betrayed me, Nico, not Ahmed Al Bakri.'

Nico Gerace's face was transformed into a mask of rage and hate.

'Oh yeah, Ahmed. Your favourite little pal. While I was just a nobody, right, Mike? But if Don Eugenio had singled you out that day instead of me—'

'Is it for that you engineered all this? From the moment you left your card with me in Barcelona and set the Nastasia boys on to me? All part of a plan to get your revenge on me? You wanted to unleash the anger of my uncles on me, isn't that right?'

He stared at me as if I should always have realized the reason for all that hatred. And he was right.

From the moment I left you in Don Eugenio's hands, that was the moment we were no longer friends.

We could hear the police sirens in the distance. Capuzzo was as punctual as ever.

I got to my feet. I had a couple of minutes, no more.

'The police are on their way. And that finger's here. I put it a little while ago in the MANK van, where Farid killed Nadia.

Nico stood up, and I saw his hand go swiftly behind his back. This time, his gun was loaded.

I let him fire the first shot, as I threw myself to one side. But he had no chance.

In this particular film, I was the good guy and he was the bad.

The examining magistrate and the head of Homicide weren't in a good mood when they arrived on the scene. And they still hadn't linked Nico Gerace with the shooting in the centre that had eliminated the Nastasias.

My explanation was simple. I had gone to see my old friend Nico Gerace to find out what Claudia Teodori had said to him. The discussion had taken a turn for the worse with my accusations. It was the pistol in Nico's hand and the shot he fired which grazed my shoulder that legitimized my shot as self-defence.

I claimed I didn't know a thing about the deaths of the three Nastasias shot and killed two hours earlier, which, in essence, was true. I said that they were working for Nico and that he'd confessed to me that they'd killed the homeless portraitist and had helped him kill Anita Messi and Deborah Reggiani, which was absolutely true.

The examining magistrate and the head of Homicide didn't seem very convinced, but things happily sorted themselves out during the very long night that followed. Marybelle the transsexual confirmed Dino Forte's alibi. The Nastasias had been seen by a witness as they were setting fire to Charmene. The barman at I Tre Peccati broke down and confessed that the Nastasias knew Nico Gerace.

Then, following a search, the forensic squad found traces of Anita Messi's blood in the MANK van, where they also found a cool bag containing Claudia Teodori's middle finger.

Albeit a little through his clenched teeth, by daybreak, the examining magistrate offered his compliments.

'All right, Balistreri, well done. You saved us from cutting a giant shitty figure with the media over Dino Forte.'

The head of Homicide gave me a look that was a mixture of amused annoyance and admiration.

'I don't know how you did it, Balistreri. You'll turn into a great policeman.'

Monday, 24 January 1983

When I got back to Garbatella on the Triumph, it was six in the morning. I decided to write a letter to Tripoli right away. I needed to reply to all the questions and formulate the one question to which even Nico Gerace hadn't been able to give an answer.

Dear Sirs,

Nico Gerace is dead. I shot him last night in an act of legitimate self-defence while arresting him for the murder of the three young women: Anita Messi, Deborah Reggiani and Claudia Teodori.

He confessed to the murder of Nadia Al Bakri in Tripoli on 3 August in 1969, along with Nadia's brothers Farid and Salim.

Years earlier, in 1962, although they were only sixteen and fourteen years old, Farid and Salim were already two dangerous criminals who hated the Italians, and their own two brothers out of jealousy. They were also violent sadists.

They met a native black girl from the Sudan or Fezzan, a desperate soul who turned up in Tripoli out of the desert with a tiny baby girl. Farid and Salim tortured the girl, then hanged her and the baby and threw the bodies in a cesspit. When the bodies were recovered, no word came out that they were dark-skinned. I only came to know this by chance.

In 1969, two days before she died, I let slip to Nadia that the corpses were those of two black females. Nadia must have remembered having seen the girl and her baby years earlier with Farid and Salim. In fact, she was certain the baby was a little girl. It's highly probable that she innocently mentioned something of this to Farid or Salim and, unfortunately, this sealed her fate.

But, in order to eliminate her, they needed an alibi and an accomplice. They knew that Nico hated their sister. He had made sexual advances to her and she had gestured to him with her middle finger. If it had been anyone else, then perhaps nothing would have come of it, but Nico had an inferiority complex from his fixation that women did not like him and he also despised the Arabs. So he agreed to help them kill Nadia. He asked Farid to give him the middle finger as a trophy.

This was his way of making a fool of both myself and Ahmed, and taking revenge on me for having left him in the hands of Don Eugenio when he was a boy.

On 3 August 1969, there was the ghibli. Visibility was extremely poor. At eight o'clock that morning, Nadia left their wooden shack with her father, Mohammed, just before her brother Ahmed, and they all immediately went their separate ways, Nadia on foot to the Balistreri villa, Mohammed by car into Tripoli and Ahmed on foot to the Esso petrol station.

Nico Gerace stopped by the market, where he parked the van and met my brother, Alberto. They went together to take the newspaper to Ingegner Balistreri at the barber's shop, then walked back to the market, where they greeted Farid and Salim and then chatted a while with my grandfather. It was during those few minutes that Farid climbed in the back of the MANK organization's van.

Nico and Alberto – who knew nothing about this – then drove the killer to the appointed place. When Nico parked the van in the Hunt's car port, and he and Alberto went to have breakfast in the villa, Farid got out, exited by the back gate, which he closed behind him, and went to meet Nadia, who had almost reached the Balistreri villa. He threatened her with his knife and forced her to follow him to the van. Nico had guaranteed him at least an hour of time, counting on my expressed intention that I would only leave for Tripoli at nine thirty.

I don't know what happened next with any certainty. I have thought about it many times and I have arrived at a plausible reconstruction confirmed in part by Nico Gerace. The first thing Farid did was get Nadia in the van, put a gag on her, undress her and tie her up. Then he put her clothes on, got out again, ran over to the olive grove, went up to Jamaal the goatherd and led him to the olive-pressing shed, allowing himself purposely to be seen by a witness. And by Karim Al Bakri. All helped a great deal by the ghibli and the low visibility.

Then Farid went back to the van, raped Nadia and killed her. He cut off her middle finger, I hope after her death. He put the body in the back of William Hunt's Land Rover, knowing the Americans were out. He would be able to come back to pick up the body before they came back.

Then he hid himself in the back of the van again and it was we who took him back to the market. Farid was there behind the metal partition. The three of us – myself, Nico and Alberto – picked up Ahmed at the Esso petrol station, put the scuba cylinders on the back seat and set off back into Tripoli, getting into the city a few minutes before the road was closed. Don Eugenio came back from visiting an old lady and followed us a few metres behind in the middle of the sandstorm.

In the market square, Nico was clever, slowing down so that Farid could slip out of the back of the van. It was only yesterday that Don Eugenio told me he had seen him jumping out of the back, without realizing that this was an important piece of evidence. It explains why Emilio Busi had not seen him a few minutes earlier and why I was able to see him five minutes later when I went to pick up the bait in the market and he was there with his brother Salim.

Nico came out fishing with us and stayed with us the whole time. It was Farid who came back with his pick-up at one o'clock, just after the road was open again, and moved Nadia's body from the Land Rover to the olive-pressing shed before the Hunt family came home.

A complicated plan and, it has to be admitted, well thought out and executed.

Probably Nadia had said something to my mother about Nico's advances and perhaps, too, about the black girl and her child. My mother had glimpsed the truth, had questioned Nico and had written down the two phrases on the back of the notes I made and which I sent you.

They knew each other. Check m.

The first sentence refers to Farid and Salim and the black girl and her child. The second was even more cryptic: the 'm' was the Esso sign's '∈' rotated through ninety degrees. She did this to avoid me doing anything if I found those notes.

Unfortunately, my mother was dealing with other serious personal problems, and more. She said nothing about her suspicions about Nadia's death. She did this so that I would not get involved, and she was probably counting on having more time in which to identify the guilty parties.

Nadia Al Bakri's murder falls under Libyan jurisdiction. Salim Al Bakri is dead, and I have no idea what happened to Farid. We could not arrest him for these crimes in this country anyway. I am sure that you will see to it in yours.

The one remaining question is that of my mother's death. Neither Farid nor Salim could have killed her. One went back to Tripoli with Marlene Hunt and the other with me. They were then with my grandfather and then took my father to the airport. Their alibi here is rock solid. As to Nico Gerace, he swore on his dead mother's name that he did not kill her, and I believe him. You will know that Nico would never swear falsely in his mother's name.

The person guilty of the crime in a moral sense will shortly go into self-exile from Italy, thanks to the photo you sent me. The hatred I feel for him is strong enough to ruin my life, but not strong enough for me to kill him without being sure that he was my mother's actual murderer.

Would you be able to help me resolve this question before Salvatore Balistreri leaves Italy on 6 February?

Michele Balistreri

At eight o'clock, I called the number on the card left by the Libyan who had delivered the last letter from Tripoli directly to my flat. I made a photocopy of what I had just written. In essence, it was my witness statement.

Half an hour later, I handed him the sealed envelope on which I'd written 'PO Box 150870, Tripoli'.

'It's very urgent,' I told him.

He gave me a friendly smile.

'The letter will be in Tripoli after lunch, Commissario.'

Saturday, 29 January 1983

Farid Al Bakri was dreaming. He had been living in a good hotel room on the island of Djerba off the Tunisian coast for over thirteen years, since the moment that Ahmed, his crazy, murdering brother, and that Fascist Mike Balistreri had killed Salim and forced him to leave Tripoli.

Farid was dreaming of fishing in his boat twenty kilometres out along the tuna run that also attracted the sharks. A huge tuna had surfaced and, harnessed in his seat, Farid was slowly trying to get alongside it and get it on board. It was a dream that was particularly vivid. He could even feel the cool January breeze, the saltwater spray in his face, the sound of the engine and the smell of the sea.

It seemed real, and yet he knew that he was dreaming. His tongue was furry, there was a bitter taste in his mouth and his head felt heavy, such as when he was drunk or had taken sleeping pills. Still half asleep, he decided to switch on the lamp on his bedside table. But something was stopping him, blocking both his arms, like a strait-jacket. Meanwhile, the cold splashes of water and the irritating noise of the engine were slowly bringing him from sleep to waking. A window must be broken. He would make a complaint to the management.

But the hotel belonged to him. He had bought it after leaving Tripoli with the money put by from smuggling and with help from his continual source of protection. Although his white hotel facing the sea was small, it was profitable; tourists came all the year round to Djerba.

He had his bachelor pad there as well, where he brought the foreign and local *gahba*, taking care not to cause any trouble. Because Farid Al Bakri was a man with both feet on the ground. He had twice got away with rape and murder, first with that beautiful black girl and her useless baby. Sometimes, he still masturbated, thinking about that Somali girl hanging there with her daughter. Ingenious idea, very enjoyable, even if it had not been his. And then that little piece Nadia: naked, her clothes torn off and begging him to let her go. And when he had cut off her finger to give to Nico . . . And when . . .

A bucket of water landed in his face, he opened his eyes and realized why he had been dreaming that dream. It was not a dream, but a nightmare. And it was real. He really was on his boat, strapped into the game-chair in the stern so he could not even move his arms. The game-chair had been tipped back ninety degrees on to the wooden deck and two life buoys attached to it.

Looking straight ahead of him, he could see the blue sky, and seagulls circling overhead. There were certainly tuna there. But the four men surrounding him were definitely not his crew. They were young men, thin and ugly-looking, armed with pistols stuck into their belts.

'Who the bloody hell are you? And what are you doing on my boat?' he said, in a sudden rush of his old arrogance.

The boat's engine was running at full speed and they had to be far from the shore by now, near the fishing grounds for tuna and also for the shark. No one answered him. The largest of the four men, who could have been around thirty, shouted in Arabic, 'The son of a bitch has woken up!'

Farid felt a tremor of fear descend from his brain to his heart, to his stomach, then right down to his bladder and anus. He heard footsteps from the bows coming towards his shoulders, but could not see who it was. The footsteps circled around him.

He lifted his head up and found himself looking at a face he had not seen for so many years, a face with part of an ear missing.

It was then that Farid Al Bakri was sure that his vile life would end. He felt the urine flowing unstoppably from his bladder and soaking his pyjama bottoms. The smell of that piss was a sign of his imminent death. He began to sob desperately.

While two of the men removed his pyjama bottoms, the man with part of his ear missing bent over him. With the point of his knife, he made long, vertical incisions on both his thighs, from the groin down to the knee. The cuts were fairly superficial, enough to make him bleed for hours, but without killing him.

Farid was whimpering.

'You can't kill me, you won't, you're not an animal like Ahmed. You're a good boy.'

'Who was it who raped her? You or Nico?' asked the man with part of his ear missing.

Farid hesitated a moment too long. He was trembling all over now.

'Nico. I-it was him. He did it,' he stammered desperately. But it was too late.

The man with part of his ear missing grabbed hold of his penis and sliced it off with one stroke of his knife. Farid screamed in pain, his mouth open wide. The other man stuck the sliced-off penis between Farid's thick lips, as if it were a last obscene cigarette for a condemned man.

Then the man with part of his ear missing turned to the other four.

'We'll drag him behind us slowly. I want to watch as the sharks eat him up.'

Saturday, 5 February 1983

The usual man from the Libyan embassy brought me the package that Saturday evening, the day before my father went off into exile. My correspondent in Tripoli was right on time.

To give me the time to kill him.

It was a large brown package. I thanked the Libyan driver, went back into the flat and stretched out on the sofa. The package contained two smaller envelopes and a short typewritten letter. This time it was in Italian. The language of a friend.

Signor Michele Balistreri,

Thank you very much for your last letter. It was extremely painful to read, but indispensable for meting out justice for Nadia Al Bakri. I was surprised that such a miserable creature as Nico Gerace could have thought up such an ingenious plan. However, I am sending you a photograph which will bring this case to a close.

Regarding that of your mother and the suspicions you have about your father, I am enclosing a letter from a close friend of yours from many years ago.

I believe this letter will make your suffering more bearable. Inshallah.

And finally, please forget Libya, the scar on your wrist, the remorse and the regrets. Our correspondence has been useful, but must end here.

Karim's right. The two of us must stay apart.

There was nothing left of the blood brotherhood. It had been shattered by Nico when he killed Nadia, by Karim and his brother when they stole our money and, lastly, by me, when I killed Ahmed.

I looked at the two envelopes. On the first was written 'Farid'. It contained a very recent colour photograph taken with a powerful telephoto lens from the stern of a boat well out to sea. Clearly visible in the sea were Farid Al Bakri's face, contorted in pain and terror, a stream of blood and the fins of two sharks encircling him.

Then there was the letter in the other envelope.

An old letter from a close friend of yours. It will make your suffering more bearable.

I recognized the writing on the envelope. 'To Mike'. But I wasn't ready yet.

I switched on the television and stretched out on the sofa again, with a whisky and a cigarette. I decided I wanted to be drunk and not think about anything. But there was a surprise for me. It was the final night of the Sanremo Song Festival.

I hadn't seen it for twenty-five years, since that night in 1958 when we were all together. And happy together, with our whole lives in front of us.

I remained glued to the screen like a child.

I decided to put on the Leonard Cohen tape that Laura Hunt had given me all those years ago. Then I poured myself a double whisky, made sure I had put my cigarettes in my winter jacket and went to sit out on my tiny terrace with the letter in my pocket. It was a clear, cold night, the neighbourhood was silent; only the usual bar opposite was still open at midnight.

Leonard Cohen's music filtered through the French windows I had closed behind me, while I smoked and contemplated the array of tiny lights still shining in the windows of people's homes. There was little sound from the street other than the odd car passing by. At this hour, almost everyone had retired to bed.

I looked at the sealed envelope. I remembered Laura's words that night in Tripoli – the words that made me lose my head.

Mike, your mother killed herself. Believe me and forgive yourself.

I'd never accepted this, and never would. I could burn that letter and go to the Excelsior to kill Salvatore Balistreri, the man guilty of my mother's death and the exodus of all those Italians from Tripoli.

But I had to find the strength to read that letter.

I opened the white envelope with great care and took out the single sheet.

20 April 1971

Mike,

I wanted to write to you straightaway after that night when you ran away from Tripoli. And I did write to you in my head every night without being able to put a word of it down on paper. You and I both know that you can be close every day, but still far apart – like our parents. Or else far apart, and yet close, like the two of us . . .

Today is the day that my thoughts need to be set down on paper, because life has mysterious and wonderful ways which in time help us to understand.

One thing always united us: the desire to be different. Me from my mother, you from your father. We loved them as children, but they were everything we didn't want to be. What united us was the certainty that there was no dark side dark enough to separate us.

We were wrong, Mike, and you've seen that yourself. You only had to lie to me once for me to stop believing you. If our judgements are absolute ones, then our mistakes are unpardonable. And life is impossible for us.

That afternoon on La Moneta when Italia went out to the cliff, we were both wrong. You should have gone to your father and I to my mother to ask them what was going on.

Instead, we did the opposite.

I stopped reading. There were only a few lines left at the bottom of that one and only page.

I could have stopped there and burned the letter. I could have gone to the Excelsior to kill my father before he left for the exile to which I'd condemned him. I could continue my eternal battle against terrible memories, continue to build those memories into a cathedral of resentment towards my father, towards Laura Hunt for betraying our love, towards Ahmed and Karim for the stolen money, towards Nico Gerace for his atrocities of revenge, towards Emilio Busi and Don Eugenio and the 50 million Italians who preferred betrayal to keeping faith.

Or else I could accept injustice and injury as a part of life and not as wrongs to be cleansed with blood.

I could stop dreaming of hunting lions and start saving the Elisa Sordis and Claudia Teodoris of this world.

I could stop calling the place where I was born 'my country' and start calling 'my country' the place I was actually living in.

I could read Laura Hunt's last lines and let the thoughts of so many wonderful days occupy at least a small part of my memory again.

And I didn't need to build replicas of villas like my father to pick up those thoughts again. All I had to do was read those last words as a liberation rather than a life sentence.

Anyway, I already knew what they said. Laura Hunt had told me thirteen years ago on that wretched afternoon. And she had been truthful about that.

I turned back to the page.

As soon as you and my mother left with Farid and Salim, I made a decision. I went into the villa and sat outside the office where your father had gone. When he realized I was there, he invited me in and we talked for an hour. I won't tell you what was said. But straight after that conversation I went up to the cliff to talk to Italia.

Her book was open on the chair. But your mother had already disappeared.

That was it, not even a goodbye. The letter was over, and Karim was forbidding a follow-up. He was right. From his point of view, I had no right to any. He'd only sent me this single page after a delay of many years because I'd presented him with Nadia's killer.

And, in exchange, he'd presented me with the possibility of making my suffering more bearable. He'd saved me from adding the killing of my father to the list of my regrets.

Even if you don't believe your mother committed suicide, it wasn't your father who killed her.

I had to be satisfied with that letter and with no goodbye. I was free to reject it or remember that one last moment of Italia and hold it inside me for ever.

Without a smile, she half raised an arm in a kind of greeting, then she stopped, as if she had done all she could.

The last wave to a son she loved very much from a mother who didn't want a solitary hero, only a son that was happy.

I had to accept a life without knowing the truth. Just like Elisa Sordi's parents, whose eighteen-year-old daughter had been brutally killed while I was watching the World Cup final between Italy and Germany. And like so many people in the world who suffer great tragedy without knowing why it happened to them.

I was no more important than those people. My tragedies were only the same as theirs.

A burst of laughter on street broke the night's magical silence. A group of drunks was leaving, singing at the top of their voices, not giving a damn how out of tune they were.

> *Penso che un sogno così non ritorni mai più*
> *Ma dipengevo le mani e la faccia di blu*
> *Volare oh oh*
> *Cantare oh oh oh oh*

On the Marelli television set's black and white screen, Domenico Modugno's singing the winning song of the Sanremo Song Festival. I'm sitting on the three-seat sofa between the two most important women in my life. My mother, Italia, and Laura Hunt.

ACKNOWLEDGEMENTS

My thanks to the team at Marsilio Editori, especially Marco di Marco and Jacopo De Michelis: if I am the father of Michele Balistreri, they are at least his brothers. Also to Chiara De Stefani and Fabio Ferlin for their great tenacity and patience in working with an author who has another profession.

Thanks to my friends in Tripoli and Cairo, who gave me extremely valuable help in remembering: Diego and Stella Balistreri for locations and atmosphere on land, Angelo Lugli and Ettore Celi for those at sea, and Salah Omar for Cairo after the Six Day War.

My thanks to the authors who have written about Libya in the sixties, in particular Augusto Varvelli, Luciana Capretti and Luisa Pachera: their books gave me many helpful suggestions.

Thanks to Maurizio Bellacosa, who helped me make the legal procedures a little more credible, and to Roberto Pessi and Isabella Goldmann, who gave me many interesting ideas about Italy in the early eighties.

And enormous thanks to my son, Fabrizio, not only for having lent a hand with the adolescent Michele Balistreri and his friends – thanks to his being eighteen years of age – but also for having undertaken the task of reading this novel at least five times and each time helping me to improve it.